Fireborn

Sean Fenian

Fenian House Publishing

DISCLAIMER:

All of the characters in this story are fictional. (Obviously.) Any coincidence of name with any actual living person is just that: A coincidence. There are only just so many possible distinct names.

Any mention in this book of any present-day established trademark is not a challenge to that trademark.

References? *Of course* there are references.

PUBLICATION HISTORY:

First Kindle Edition January 2024

Second Kindle Edition October 2024, with corrections and updated cover

Third Kindle Edition January 2025, fully re-edited

First Print Edition February 2025

ISBN 979-8-218-60846-0

Formatting Conventions and Pacing:

This novel is intended to be styled like a storyteller at the bar spinning a yarn that's so good nobody is willing to challenge its veracity.

Where you see a single line of vertical space, as is above this line, imagine the narrator taking a breath to pause—or the characters pausing for a moment in brief thought before speaking again.

A larger double-line space, such as here, is akin to the raconteur pausing to replenish with half a pint and some pretzels; or, within the story, for an extended break between the characters that does not necessarily involve a change of viewpoint or scene. Now might be an ideal time to make a cup of tea, if you're so inclined, or otherwise attend to life.

===========

Finally, a double horizontal bar like this one denotes a scene or perspective break within a chapter: the scene or the viewpoint has changed, but no lengthy narrative pause is *necessarily* implied (although there *usually* is one).

Of course, we at Fenian House strongly advise you to read how you want, on your own schedule. The above is our guide to how to read our *intended* pacing of the text; but our suggestions are just, only, that. You paid good money for this book; we are your humble bards.

Fireborn

Acknowledgments

Thanks go out to:

- **Sonic!** for proofreading, critique, and invaluable assistance with improving several awkward pieces of exposition that were very difficult to do well;

- **Mackey Chandler** for advice and guidance on self-publishing;

- **Pasi Kallinen** and others on the Nordic Nerds Discord for assistance with construction of some Saamen words;

- **Wendy S. Delmater** for teaching me a few things to look out for and avoid;

- The quoted excerpt from *Ulysses* is, of course, by **Alfred, Lord Tennyson**.

FOREWORD

An end can be a new beginning... sometimes.

I will be honest: This story started out as pure wish-fulfillment, never intended to be published. But it became something more.

It grew on its own, unplanned, and became a story about past trauma, of savage emotional abuse, of surviving emotional wounds, of crippling long-term pain, of intolerable life situations, and the scars on the mind and soul that they all leave behind. Mostly in memory and past discussion, and nowhere dwelt on in *terribly* great depth. But **it is there**. Consider this a trigger warning. But it is important to the story, so if you don't want to read about that, then you probably shouldn't read this book.

And from there, it evolved into a story that is about hope, new chances, growth, fulfillment, relationships, *overcoming* all of that trauma, and finding meaning in life, as much as it is about wonder and adventure. And, of course, it is about love.

======

Life is not kind to everyone. Some would say it is cruel to more than it is kind to. But sometimes, someone's life can become so empty, so miserable, so filled with pain, that they simply don't want to live it any more. Life has become an unbearable burden. Some people in such a position choose suicide... or perhaps find death rushing at them and simply make no effort to avoid it.

Very often, that person doesn't really want to *die*. They just can't bear to continue *living* that life any longer. What they *want* is an escape, *any* escape, from a life that has become intolerable.

But even if you are somehow granted that escape, you must still somehow heal the trauma of the life you escaped—and learn who you are NOW. And you may find that even your second chance comes at a cost. To have fulfillment in life, your life needs to have meaning. Sometimes you have to find or build your own meaning. Sometimes meaning and purpose are thrust upon you.

When that happens, you need to be ready and willing to accept them. **You may only get the one chance.** When it comes, take it, and don't look back.

A GUIDE TO SAAMEN PRONUNCIATION

Do not take this as a guide to pronouncing the Finnish language. Saamen is not precisely Finnish, although Finnish words are used in this book to *represent* Saamen; there has been significant cultural and linguistic drift in the course of well over a thousand years. It is a quick-reference guide to give you the basic rules and get you into the right ballpark when pronouncing Saamen words and names. If you already speak Finnish, then **by all means** just pronounce everything the way you normally would. That's *ideal*. If you don't, here are some *approximately* correct rules:

- Primary stress in Saamen words, like Finnish, is always on the first syllable
- Secondary stress falls on odd-numbered syllables (third, fifth, ...)
- Doubled vowels such as **uu** are double-length flat vowels
- Dissimilar vowel pairs such as **ai** are pronounced distinctly
- **j** is always like English y as in you (example: Senja = SEN-ya)
- **y** is a vowel, *almost* as in tune (but not quite; English doesn't really have this sound at all)
- **a** roughly as in car or far (example: Kata = KAH-tah)
- **ä** roughly as in flat, mat or pat
- **e** as in ten
- **i** as in tin or pin
- **ï** as in ring or wing
- **o** roughly as in hot
- **ö** roughly as in pope or poe
- **u** is somewhere in between fruit and put
- **aa** roughly as in far, but longer
- **ee** as in where or air, but longer (example: Eero, roughly like Aero)
- **ii** like English ee (example: Liisa = LEE-sah, or Saana's hawk Kii = KEE)
- **oo** roughly as in floor
- **uu** roughly as in moon or loon, never as in use or fuse
- **yy** again is like **y** as in tune, but longer. Again, English does not really have this sound at all. Example: Nyysönen = *roughly* NEW-sew-nen.

These are BY NO MEANS complete or linguistically rigorous. If you want to try to get it all as accurate as possible, try reading the Wikipedia pages on Finnish phonography and orthography. You will never go *badly* wrong in this book by pronouncing Saamen as though it were still Finnish.

Dragon speech as shown in this book is represented as a Saamen speaker might try to write down the sounds. Follow the rules of Saamen, speak from your diaphragm, pitch your voice as low as you *comfortably* can, and take your time. Roll every sound on your tongue and savor it. It should take you at least five seconds to say *jankankavoroullakko* (a gate or rift). If you are getting out more than about three syllables every two seconds, you are rushing it. Dragons are a patient people wont to deep and lengthy consideration, and their language reflects it.

Only a few Old Norse words appear in this book, and there is a lot of overlap between Old Norse and Saamen phonology. As a result, there are only a handful of rules you will need to know:

- 'r' is always rolled;
- a (short) is flatter than in Saamen, almost more as in 'wrath' or 'halt' than as in 'path';
- ð, the *eth* character, is a voiced 'th' or 'dh' such as the initial 'th' in 'then';
- i (short) is as in English heat;
- the long á and í are like the Saamen aa and ii;
- f is sounded like v, EXCEPT at the beginning of a word.

Otherwise, follow the Saamen rules, including stressing the first syllable. Thus Járnhandr becomes 'YAARN-handr', Fjandrhamár is 'FYANDR-hamaar', *níð* is 'NEEDH', and *níðing* is 'NEEDH-ing'.

DRAMATIS PERSONAE

The Healers:

Master Timo, one of the three Master Healers stationed at Highwatch, married to Jaana

Mistress Jaana, the second Master Healer at Highwatch, married to Timo

Mistress Sirkka, the third Master Healer at Highwatch

Healer Esko, a great bear of a man with surprisingly gentle hands, married to Marketta

High Healer Katariina, an expert in head injuries, fiercely protective of those in her care. Prefers to be called Kata. More the academic than Liisa.

Healer Liisa, who loves poetry and has boundless compassion

High Healer Marja, a no-nonsense Healer with astonishingly deep reserves of power, married to Vallaïnen

Healer Marketta, petite, with eyes of the clearest blue, sees things many others do not, married to Esko

High Healer Raimo, a half-Huldre Healer with deep knowledge and hidden abilities

High Healer Vallaïnen, a Healer for over seventy years, an academic of immense knowledge, married to Marja

Healer Varpu, who brightens every room she enters, like a personified spirit of joy and love

Healer Vilja, a healer in training

The Guard:

Knight-Commander Mikkinen, Commander of the Highwatch Guard

Master-at-Arms Toivo, overseer of all Guard training

Eero, a Guardsman and quarterstaff trainer

Teppo, a wall guard

The Rangers:

Knight-Commander Jaako, Commander of Rangers at Highwatch

Piia, a Ranger team leader

Ari, Paavo: Swordsmen in Piia's team

Eino, Ragne: Archers in Piia's team

Karel, the tracker/hunter in Piia's team

Simo, the mage/diviner in Piia's team

Arja, Jouko, Kirsi, Markku, Raili, Usko, Torsti: The other Ranger team leaders at Highwatch

Kauko, A swordsman in Kirsi's team

Helle, Ilona: Swordswomen in Kirsi's team

Päivi, a swordswoman in Markku's team

Kaija, a 'scarily good' axewoman in Torsti's team

Pertti, an archer in Usko's team

Highwatch Pages:

Rami, an enthusiastic young page in his mid-teens

Senja, a sometimes excitable page, in her late teens, energetic and athletic

Tommi, Irja, Osmo: Other Highwatch pages

Other Highwatch people:

Mistress Kerttu, She Who Must Be Obeyed in the Highwatch kitchens

Juuro, Castellan of Highwatch

Master Smith Matti, an artisan smith of surpassing skill, jovial and always seeking to improve his craft

Saana, a falconer, with her hawk Kii, comparable to a Northern Goshawk

Pertti and Riku, carpenters

Master Falconer Tuokkola

Master Mason Perttunen

Master Woodworker Tauno

Mill-Master Kustaa, a master artificer in charge of the operation and maintenance of Highwatch's grain mills

Olavi, a skilled cobbler

Sage Nyysönen, a sage of the Collegium

Dragons (mentioned by name):

The Shadow Cast By The Third Moon As It Rises, *aka* Moonshadow

The Glint Of First Sunlight Off Mountaintop Ice In The Morning, *aka* First Sunlight

The Sound Of Wind Blowing Across The Northern Ice, *aka* Northern Wind

The Light That Shimmers In The Northern Skies, *aka* Northern Light

Historical and mythical figures of the Sunlit Land

Ilmarinen, the forge god who hammered the bowl of the sky into being in Finnish mythology as told in the Kalevala, the Finnish national mythic epic poem

Väinämöinen, a wizard-demigod who quested for the Sampo alongside Lemminkäinen in the Kalevala

Lehtinen, a master woodworker who wrote many books on woods, their uses, and working them

Tumarïnen, a stonemaster and firebinder who long ago wrought the hot-water system for the Highwatch bath-house, and wrote a book on binding fire and stone together

Vehviläinen, a master firesinger who wrote five volumes on fire-working and fire-binding

GLOSSARY

Saamen words and concepts

Adept—A Talented with an exceptionally high level of skill, power, or both. Adepts are highly respected, but relatively rare among the Talented.

Auringon Valaista Maata—Literally, the Sunlit Land, the name by which those who live there refer to their world.

Gauru—A large and very dangerous venomous reptile similar to a monitor lizard.

Healer—Any Talented whose primary Talent expresses itself primarily as an ability to heal sickness and injuries in others, and to a limited extent, in themselves. Healers are universally honored and respected.

Helvetti—Broadly covers concepts such as hell, purgatory, the Inferno.

Highwatch—A fortress built to guard the plain below from two particular passes through the Spine of the World.

Huldrefolk—Mystical forest-dwelling humanoids of Scandinavian myth, described as beautiful, friendly, helpful, even sometimes seductive, but always possessed of some significantly inhuman feature. In the Sunlit Land they are very real, although still rare, and have formidable strength and often mystical abilities.

Imp fingers—A sweet, crunchy, brightly colored bean-like fruit harvested from a bush. They are strongly hallucinogenic if eaten raw, but cooking breaks down the hallucinogen, leaving them with curative and restorative properties.

Kalakeitto—A rich fish-and-potato chowder that is almost a stew, made with any fish to hand.

Kalsiumia—Calcium

Karjalanpaisti—Karelian hot-pot

Kirjoitekone—Literally a "writing device" or "writing machine"

Kusipää—An obnoxious person, an asshole.

Kuurii (koo-ree)—A plant with many uses that yields a soft yet strong cloth, strong fibers suitable for cordage, juice, and a tasty fruit with curative properties.

Leviataan—A leviathan of the Sunlit Land is NOT a whale, though both are large marine creatures.

Lihakeitto—Literally "meat soup".

Linnavouri (pl. linnavouret)—"Castle hill", a hill-fort.

Lohikeitto—A variant of *kalakeitto* made specifically with salmon (or with the Sunlit Land's equivalent).

Metallurgi—A metallurgist

Moukka—A boor, an oaf, an uncivilized person.

Níð (from Old Norse)—From Norse law, a person adjudged guilty of a heinous crime, or who has done wrong and refused to make restitution, or shows no remorse for their wrongdoing. Literally an outlaw, and no longer protected by the law.

Níðing (from Old Norse) act—Any crime or action sufficiently heinous that the offender is adjudged *níð*.

Nousuvesi—High Water, Paavo's soulbound *katana*.

Painakone—a printing press (or printer).

Rautakoivu—Iron birch, a Sunlit Land hardwood tree possessed of exceedingly tough and fine-grained wood that resists both fire and water well.

Piru—A humanoid demon or imp, usually malevolent.

Redbelly—A small, shy, mildly venomous lizard, considered mostly harmless.

Rieska—A traditional Finnish unleavened flatbread.

Saamen—The principal language spoken in the Sunlit Land. It is close to Finnish, but it is not Finnish, because while the people of the Sunlit Lands have Finnish-sounding names and share much of Finnish mythology, they are not Finns. (Though some of their ancestors *were*... once.)

Sade—A shower, as in rain.

Sielunjuoja (see-el-un-yu-o-ya)—Literally "soul drinker". A kind of psychic vampire.

Spine of the World—A high, jagged, snaking mountain range that divides the land in two.

Suihku—A shower as in 'take a shower', a Finnish word that Saamen does not have (yet).

Susimetalli—"Wolf metal", or tungsten.

Talented—A person able to bend *voima* to their will to accomplish things often not possible by mundane means. Talent takes many forms, including Healing.

Tuuli metsässä—Wind in the Forest, Piia's soulbound *katana*.

Voima (voy-ma)—The word used in the Sunlit Land to refer to the energy pool that powers all Talent, and to which all spirits are tied.

Japanese sword terms

Boshi—The short curved section of edge immediately behind the point

Fuchi—A ferrule around the forward end of the *tsuka*

Ha—The edge of a sword

Ha-machi—The notch in the *ha* where it meets the *habaki*

Habaki—the ferrule that holds the sword in its *saya*

Hamon—The temper line dividing *yakiba* from *ji*

Hineri maki—A plain style of *tsukamaki*

Ito—The cloth ribbon used for *tsukamaki*, hilt wrapping

Ji—The softer steel forming the body of the blade

Katana—The classic single-edged sword of the *samurai*, properly called *uchigatana*

Kashira—A cap on the end of the *tsuka*, often decorated

Ken—Literally just 'sword'

Kissaki—The sharp point of a sword

Koiguchi—The ring-shaped piece that holds the mouth of the *saya* tight

Kojiri—An end cap on the *saya*

Kurikata—A pierced knob that the *sageo* is tied through

Mei—The smith's signature on the tang

Mekugi—the wooden pin that holds the hilt in place on the tang

Mekugi-ana—the hole in the tang for the *mekugi*

Menuki—Small decorations bound to the hilt to aid in hand placement

Mune—The back of the blade

Mune-machi—the notch in the back of the blade for the *habaki*

Nakago—The tang of a sword blade

Nihonto—A vague term used to group all Japanese swords in general

Nioi—Tiny grains of martensite just behind the *hamon*

Sageo—A silk cord for tying the *saya* to the *obi*

Samé—Sharkskin or rayskin that provided a non-slip surface on the *tsuka*

Saya—A wooden scabbard, often highly decorated

Seppa—Metal or leather spacers between the *habaki, tsuba,* and *fuchi*

Shirasaya—an unornamented white wood *saya* used for blade storage

Shinogi—The ridge that runs along the side of the blade

Shinogi-ji—The flat section of the blade above the *shinogi*

Tachi—A two-handed Japanese sword with a blade as long as five to six feet

Tsuba—A metal handguard, usually roughly circular, often elaborately decorated

Tsuka—The hilt

Tsukamaki—The wrappings on the *tsuka*

Tsumami maki—A more elaborate style of *tsukamaki*

Yakiba—The hard steel along the edge of a sword

Yokote—the line of division between the *ha* and the *boshi*

Other Japanese words and terms mentioned

Bushidō—The Way of the Warrior, most of the Samurai code

IAI—An explosive, wordless shout to focus energy, such as when drawing the sword in iaido

Iaidō/Iaijutsu—The art of drawing the sword

Kata—A formalized, choreographed martial-arts exercise

Kendo/Kenjutsu—The art of fighting with the sword

Mu-shin—Short form of '*mushin no shin*', "mind without mind", a Zen concept describing a mental state of freedom from thought, emotion, or judgment, leaving the mind totally open to everything and free to react without restraint

Obi—A cloth sash worn around the waist

Seiza—A formalized kneeling posture

Sekai no Kattā—Cutter of Worlds, Alrekr's soulbound *katana, aka* Worldsbane

Shakudo—An alloy of gold and copper that can be treated to be almost black

Shōgun—The Japanese Emperor's supreme military warlord

Tameshigiri—Cutting practice

Zazen—Properly refers to a meditation form, but also used to describe the seated posture also known as lotus position or *padmasana*

Fireborn

1: A Sudden Arrival

Everything was hazy, and everything hurt. His head hurt. Hurt strangely. As though there was an unfamiliar pressure inside.

He vaguely half-remembered an argument, in the car, just one more of *so many*. The resignation, the despair, the heartfelt wish for it all to just END and be done with it. The bridge over the broad river. The shimmer in the air, above the bridge deck, higher than the side rail, before the suspension tower. The car drifting toward the rail, not responding to the steering any more. A black tear in the air and a stabbing pain behind his eyes. A violent lurch, the Toyota leaving the ground, nose high, starting to roll in the air, spinning sideways, a strange feeling of weightlessness. Grinding, tearing-metal sounds as the car came apart. Hanging in the seatbelt as the car flew upside-down toward the tower. No airbags. The airbags hadn't fired.

Then a crushing multiple impact, and then nothing.

He wasn't in the car any more. He wasn't sure how that had happened. He hurt all over. And it was cold.

He opened his eyes. It was harder to do than he expected. He was sprawled on the ground in a narrow ravine. Low sunlight poured in from the open end. There was snow in the deeper shadows, in sheltered spots. There seemed to be something wrong with the shadows. Like they were out of focus, or perhaps double-exposed. Probably his vision was not right, he thought to himself. He must have hit his head. He was reasonably sure he'd never seen this place before. It certainly was not anywhere within easily a couple of hundred miles of where he thought he ought to be. These mountains should not, *could* not, be here. He thought he saw scattered pieces of painted metal and dark plastic. There were glittering shards on the ground in

1

front of his face. He couldn't feel his legs. That was... probably *really* bad. It probably meant his back was broken.

He was vaguely aware of vomiting.

Before his eyes closed again, he thought he saw movement some way off. It looked like riders on horseback, coming nearer. He thought they might be wearing some kind of armor.

He heard voices, coming closer. At first he could not make out what they were saying, then he made out words, although it was obvious that they were not speaking English. In fact, it sounded very like Finnish. There were several voices. At least one of them, he thought, seemed to—perhaps—be talking about him? Certainly the voice was nearby. He managed to partly open his eyes again.

One of the now-dismounted riders, a pretty woman with strong features and dark hair in a braid, knelt over him, gently felt him, touched his head. She was wearing leather light armor, and looked fit and strong.

Her fingers came away bloody. The woman spoke with concern, gesturing toward him.

He tried, but he could not keep his eyes open.

«He's in bad shape,» said the dark-haired woman, first. «But alive, for now.»

«I do not think he is any threat,» one rider stated, thin of face and build, with piercing blue eyes and nearly white hair. «Though there was a *lot* of power used here, and recently.»

«You're *sure* this is the location of that surge, Simo?» asked a second man, dark-haired and compact.

«Definitely,» Simo replied. «Here or very close. A rift, I think. But closed now. Perhaps just a transient tear. But *strong*.»

«You think maybe he came through it?» the dark-haired woman asked. «Or something that came through it attacked him?»

«I think... maybe he *opened* it,» said Simo. «But whatever happened, he's badly hurt. Dying, most likely, by the look of him, unless he gets Healing—and quickly.»

«Where do you think he came from?» asked a third, a tall, muscular man with dirty blond hair.

2

«I have no idea,» the other woman among them declared, flaming red hair cut above her shoulders, a bow across her strong back. «His clothes are unlike any I have seen before. And... what are these? Pieces of *something*, but... *what*? And what rent them apart this way?»

«Perhaps he opened it... from the other side?» the third man mused. «And came through? Perhaps *escaping* something?»

«Rig a stretcher,» the first woman ordered. «Scout the area. Pair up. See if there's anyone else. And someone toss me a cloak or a blanket to get over him before he freezes. It's cold up here. We'll hurry him back to Highwatch and deliver him to the Healers. Eino, ride ahead, have the Healers waiting... No, have them *meet* us. *Minutes* may make the difference here. We can send another party out later with a cart, to gather these pieces for study.»

He heard footsteps departing in several different directions, then someone came close. Something thick and heavy and warm settled over him. It was going to be alright, he told himself, his consciousness fading. It was going to be alright.

He was aware of being carefully rolled over and lifted, then laid down onto a yielding surface. Then there was just gentle, rocking movement and the sound of horses' hooves. After a little while, the darkness swallowed him again.

He was not awake to hear the woman softly say to him, «Please live.» But he would probably not have understood the words anyway.

———————

When next he woke, he was resting on something soft and padded, his head and shoulders raised, head resting on a pillow. There was warmth on his face, and there were soft voices nearby. Women's voices. Two different women, he thought.

With some effort, he opened his eyes. There was a fireplace nearby, with a steady fire of logs burning. That was the warmth he had felt. He ached, bone-deep aching all over, not just in the old injuries. Judging by the angle to the fireplace, whatever he was lying on did not seem particularly high.

He tried to move his head to look around, and the voices stopped. After a moment, one of the women said something again, but he could not understand the language. It still sounded *like* Finnish, and yet not. Footsteps came closer, then a petite dark-haired woman with vividly green eyes came into his field of vision. She leaned down, held out a

3

hand and touched his shoulder, speaking in a reassuring tone words that he could not understand.

He tried to speak, but his mouth was dry. He raised his right hand, intending to pantomime drinking, but it felt strangely numb. The woman took his hand and held it gently in hers, still speaking. He wished desperately that he could understand her. She sounded as though she might be asking a question. She paused, waited. Repeated the same again. He weakly shook his head.

"I'm sorry," he managed to croak out. "I don't understand."

The dark-haired woman looked at him for a long moment, then looked up.

«Do you recognize that language? I have never heard it before.»

«It is new to me as well.» The new speaker was another woman, across the room. «I have no idea where he is from.»

The first woman frowned.

«We have healed the *physical* head injuries,» she said pensively. «But we need to be able to talk to him. Find out what happened. In case there is a danger to Highwatch.»

A second woman stepped into his view. This one was taller, blonde, lissome, brown-eyed. She moved to stand beside the other woman, and they both looked at him, talking between themselves.

«Perhaps... do you suppose that Master Timo might be able to Impress Saamen *itself* upon him?"» the second woman asked.

«I... do not know. But it seems worth the try.»

The words seemed *almost* familiar. He strained to understand, but could not—although it still *sounded* almost like Finnish. Then the second woman walked to the door, opened it, and spoke briefly with someone outside. When she returned, the two women sat down, one on either side of him, within arm's reach, the blonde to his left, the dark-haired one to his right.

After a few minutes, the door opened and a heavy-set older man entered. His flowing hair and full beard were snow white, but he was clearly still spry and in good health. He nodded to the two women, and they spoke briefly, punctuated by nods of agreement.

The older man stood in front of him and looked down at him, then slowly reached out both hands and rested them on his head. The two

4

women reached out their hands and each took one of his hands, then rested her other hand upon his shoulder. Then all three began to whisper under their breaths, looking intently at him. After a minute he felt the odd sensation of pressure again. It seemed at first it came from outside him, then from inside. He felt bewildered, uncertain what was happening. The feeling of pressure grew stronger, and then suddenly they stopped and looked at each other. The white-haired man drew his hands back.

«He is blocking us,» the older man remarked. «He is definitely Talented. Strongly.»

«But... he is not blocking us *deliberately*, I believe,» the dark-haired woman replied hesitantly. «It is reflexive, I think. I'm not sure he even knows he is doing it, but... he is *strong*. Even in his condition. Strong enough that even an unconscious reflex is enough to keep us out. And yet, gently. But too much effort, even unconscious, might still break open the blood vessels again.»

«Again,» said the man. «Slowly. Carefully.»

The man put his hands back, and began whispering again, at a slower pace.

Once again, after a couple of minutes he became aware of the pressure, and then the answering pressure from within. He felt bewilderment, frustration, and yet also curiosity—and just a little fear. What were they trying to do?

After several minutes, they looked at each other again. The blonde shook her head and took her hand away.

The dark-haired woman leaned forward, grasped both of his hands in hers and spoke directly to him, low, but urgently.

«Please. Trust us. We are trying to *help you*. Don't fear us. We are Healers. We are *sworn* to do no harm. Master Timo is trying to give you knowledge of our language.»

She lowered her eyes for a moment and bit her lip, then looked directly into his eyes again.

«Please. Please, trust us, and let us *help* you.»

2: Awaken

I still could not understand the words she was saying, but as I looked back into those brilliant green eyes, her sincerity came through. I had a feeling that she was trying to tell me something. A feeling that they were trying to help.

She was still holding my hands. Unable to answer in words, I squeezed hers gently and nodded, and then released the pressure. She caught her breath quickly, then smiled and spoke a few words over her shoulder to the second woman.

They resumed their previous positions, and before they could begin, I took a deep breath, held it for a five-count, and let it out slowly. The blonde gave me a measuring look, then nodded approvingly. Then the three began whispering again, all looking directly at me. I could not help but notice that the blonde had lovely eyes, too, a deep, rich brown. The white-haired man's were piercing, as though he was somehow seeing right *into* me.

Once again, I began to feel the pressure. Instead of thinking about the pressure, I focused on breathing. Deep, slow breaths, in, hold, out, hold, only four breaths per minute. I was distantly aware of a warmth where their hands were touching me. I felt slightly dizzy, but did my best not to think about dizziness, not to think about pressure, just breathe, breathe...

—hän on reunalla—

A word. I was sure I'd caught a word. Though I knew the word I had heard was not actually 'edge', somehow I *felt* strongly that that is what it meant. Was it something to do with the pressure? Don't think of pressure, I reminded myself.

Focus. In. Hold. Out. Hold. In. Hold. Out. Hold. There is no self, no mind, only breath.

—haluamme antaa—

More words. I tried hard not to be distracted by them. I almost had it, I was sure. Had... SOMETHING. I just didn't know *what*, didn't understand what was happening. But the pressure, the humming in my

7

head, had something to do with it. And their voices, the words they were speaking now, taking turns, low and urgent, yet patient. The dark-haired woman was speaking to me directly. If I just knew what she was saying —

—*sinä avaat*—

Another word? I strained to understand. I thought she wanted me to... open... *something*. I tried to visualize opening everything I could, to let the warmth I was feeling flow in. I *wanted* that warmth so desperately. *Needed* it.

There was a sudden painless feeling like a bubble silently bursting. Something I could not explain pushed gently into me, like a warm wave. I... had the feeling that it was something good. I tried to relax, to let it flow in unimpeded, to float on it, to be the willow, not the oak. There was a rush of something, a sense *of* sense. It felt as though something soft and warm had just been wrapped around my head, on the *inside*.

«Ah!» The blonde's eyes widened, and she swayed back for a moment. The dark-haired woman glanced at her for a moment, looking concerned, then looked intently back at me. The blonde let out a long breath, then looked back into my eyes as she steadied herself. I felt dizzy for a long moment, as though I had just been violently shaken, but then it cleared. I blinked, several times.

The blonde woman spoke to me, but I still could not understand. Yet... as she spoke it was as though whatever had been placed into my head began to seep down into my mind. It felt strangely as though it *belonged* there.

The older man nodded approvingly, then spoke to the two women. They spoke in return, giving him deep nods of... respect? Gratitude? Both? Then he smiled deeply, said something else, directed a slow nod at me, then turned and left.

The women turned back to me. The dark-haired woman spoke, but the meaning was still tantalizingly out of reach. Yet the more she spoke, the more it seemed the... strange presence in my head settled onto me, shaped itself to me. I began to grasp shreds of meaning, connections. As though I was hearing echoes of a sound I could not make out, but becoming clearer. As it settled further into my mind, a realization started to grow—in a way that I cannot explain—that it was

8

as though the white-haired man had somehow placed a soft, folded map into my head, and now that map was settling onto my mind, unfolding and stretching as it went until it fit perfectly. And the more time passed, the more they spoke to me, the more areas it felt that it settled into place in.

There came a point when it felt as though it finished unfolding all in a rush, and then there was nothing left but for it to finish settling into place.

"—me?" I heard. A word! Coincidence? Just a misinterpreted familiar sound?

"Can..." —something— "... me?" I blinked and looked intently at her. She spoke again, more slowly. I was certain I was on the edge of understanding.

"Can you understand me?" she asked. It was as though I heard her twice, first in unfamiliar words, and then a split second later as what those words meant, as though I saw a feature on one of two maps and then immediately found it on a second.

I nodded, suddenly breathless and shaking. I felt a nervous need to laugh, but forced it down, because I didn't think I could stop if I started, and anyway, this did not seem something to laugh about. I didn't entirely succeed, but what escaped was closer to a sob than a laugh.

"Breathe slowly," the blonde woman said, placing her hands on my shoulders. "Just as you were. In... out... in... out... in... out." I followed her instructions, letting her pace me, trying to calm my racing heartbeat. Each word seemed easier to understand than the last. The repetition helped.

The dark-haired woman spoke again.

"That was..." and I missed a word. "We can tell there is much" — something— "within you, and also that you are—"... something else I lost... "— in its use."

It was a struggle to keep up. Unable yet to answer, I tried to gesture to her to speak more slowly. After a couple of tries, I think I got the point across. She restarted, speaking more slowly, and I thought using simpler words.

"There is much *voima* within you, but you do not know how to use it, you have no training. We can tell." I caught the word that time, but could not grasp its meaning yet.

9

"And yet, despite" —*something*— "guarding yourself, you were able to open your defenses and let us in to give you the knowledge of *Saamen*." It became easier to understand her as she spoke more.

"This is Liisa," she continued, "and I am Katariina. But call me Kata. We are healers, and also teachers. We have been with you for the past six days, since you were brought here to us, healing the injuries to your body, the most urgent first. This is the first time you have woken fully since you were found."

The strange double-echo effect was very noticeable at first, but it seemed that as they both spoke, the hearing of the sounds and of their meanings were becoming closer together, starting to merge together into a single thing. In my mind I could feel the—language map?—settling more securely into place.

"You were terribly hurt when our rangers found you," Liisa told me. "They brought you here to us to take care of you, and it is well that they did. You were bleeding inside your head. Had they not found you when they did, or had they not brought you directly to us, perhaps had they not sent a rider ahead to ask us to meet them part-way, you would have died."

"And that, I think," Kata said slowly, "would have been a great loss. Did you know that you are strongly Talented?"

"Ta—... Talented?" I looked blankly at her, my tongue stumbling over unfamiliar words in a language that *somehow* I was beginning to know how to haltingly speak, but which was increasingly becoming easier to understand.

"It is one word for what you have, what you are. We prefer it because it is a neutral, un-freighted word. The ability to use *voima* to impose your will upon reality and bend it to your wishes. Other words have been used in the past—kenning, magic. But these are misleading terms and carry bad associations for some people, so we no longer use them."

"Magic?" I repeated. A memory stirred. "The will and the word?"

Kata blinked.

"Is... that a Path known to you?" she replied.

"A path?"

"A way of using your Talent. There is more than one Path, more than one Way. It may be yours. It may not. Time will tell. Though almost without exception, Adepts here chant or sing our workings."

"I... I don't know," I managed. "Talent—magic—is not... real in my world."

Kata gave me a puzzled look.

"... That would explain why you are untrained," she nodded. "But we can talk about that later."

"Once we felt your defenses stir," Liisa said, "we were prepared to shield if you lost control of your resistance or lashed out. But you did not, although there was some... backlash when you finally lowered your defenses. Some of it, I think, is simply that your latent Talent enabled you to take hold of the impression much more quickly and easily than we expected. As though we were attempting to force a stuck door open, and then you unexpectedly opened it from the other side."

"Some who are strong in Talents use power as though it were a battering ram," Kata continued. "They simply hurl power at whatever is in front of them, smashing everything in their path heedless of what they destroy around them. But you instinctively hold yours in check. This is good.

"You seem to be very strong. But you also show signs of being an apt student. It is apparent we will be spending a lot of time teaching you, as well as continuing to heal you."

"And there is much still to heal," Liisa interjected. "Both your body and your mind."

"We have not touched more than the surface of your mind," Kata went on. "It would be a violation of our oaths as Healers to do so without your consent. But it is clear that great harm has been done to you, for a long time, and we would like to try to heal as much as we can of that, as well."

"If you will permit it, of course," Liisa added.

"Now?" I croaked.

"Not now," Liisa said. "First you need proper rest. And food. Food would be a good idea now. Not too much. Wait and rest here for the moment."

Kata stood and walked to the double doors leading out of the room. When she got up I was able to see that she had been sitting on a short, comfortably padded stool. She partly opened one door and spoke for a moment to someone outside, then closed the door and returned.

"I have sent for food," she told me. "Simple food, broth and bread, easy on your stomach. Then we will take you to a proper recovery room where you can rest, now that you are finally awake and out of danger. For too long, it was uncertain whether you would recover. We were terribly afraid you might never wake." The strange echoing effect was almost entirely gone now. Now, I just understood as she spoke, hearing her voice without the slightly delayed echo. She had a very pleasant voice.

"Thank you," I said. "For... everything." I paused. "Where *is* this place?"

"You are in the infirmary in Highwatch," Kata replied, "in the Western Marches, below the Spine of the World."

I looked back at her blankly.

"Spine of the World?" I asked. She looked back at me.

"If you do not know them by that name, no matter," she reassured me. "We will focus on healing you first. There will be time later to talk about where you are, and where you came here from.

"The Rangers who brought you in said they found you near what they thought might have been a transient rift. Do you know anything about that?"

I shook my head.

"A rift? I'm not even sure what that is. In this context. It has... multiple meanings in... in my language." I stumbled, tongue-tied, tripped by a centipede problem. I knew that I was speaking their language almost naturally, but I didn't know *how*. I didn't even know what it was called, let alone how I seemed to know it; I thought what I intended to say, and the right words just formed themselves. Until I started thinking about it and wondering how I was doing it. Then I tripped over my tongue.

Liisa smiled at me.

"Relax," she told me. "This difficulty is not unexpected. It takes time for knowledge given by Impression to properly settle in. Your mind needs to absorb the new information. Master Timo usually uses it to give knowledge of advanced healing techniques. Using it to give you our language was an experiment that we were not fully certain would work. You will doubtless speak much more easily in a day or two. Even a few hours should make your grasp of the basics a lot better, and a good night's proper sleep should help greatly. You should be close to fluent by the time you wake tomorrow morning.

12

"Making Impressed knowledge second nature depends upon actively *using* what has been given, as much and as soon as possible... but I do not expect that to be difficult in this case, of course. It is hard to avoid speaking."

I smiled, and nodded embarrassed agreement.

As she spoke, there was a knock on the door. Kata went to open it, and a boy perhaps twelve years old walked in carrying a bowl. Under his arm was a cloth-wrapped bundle. He walked by out of my line of vision, and I heard him put the bowl down on a table I hadn't seen. A moment later, he left.

Kata came back, and she and Liisa helped me to stand, one on either side of me. Oddly, it was not until then that I really became aware I was not wearing my own clothes any more. Instead I was dressed in a sort of long nightshirt of soft, silky cloth in a pale blue. I had been lying on some kind of couch, raised at the head end. There was a second stool on the other side, I could see now.

They led me around the end of the couch towards a small square table with two straight-backed chairs next to it, where the bowl and the bundle now rested. After several steps my knee buckled under me and I swayed and nearly fell, but they caught me and steadied me.

"I'm sorry," I mumbled, reflexively apologetic, "I'm sorry—"

"Do not be sorry," Kata said gently. "There is nothing to apologize for. You were *badly* injured. You are doing well. We will be able to do more now that you have woken. We could not fully heal you while you were unconscious. But we can speak of that later."

They led me to the table, then Kata pulled out a chair for me and they helped me to sit down, then Kata sat down next to me, while Liisa stood nearby. The bowl was full of a rich-looking brown broth in which meat and vegetables were visible.

On my left, Liisa unwrapped the bundle, which proved to contain a small loaf of dark brown bread and a carved spoon with a deep bowl. Kata handed me the spoon, and I looked at it closely. It appeared to be of some very fine-grained, nearly white wood. While I examined the spoon, Liisa tore the loaf in half, then pushed it over to me on the red cloth that had wrapped it. I guessed it as probably some kind of black rye bread, or something very similar. I realized that I was very hungry. I didn't know whether to go for the soup first, or the bread, so I settled for picking up the half-loaf, tearing a chunk off, and dipping it in the soup.

As I began to raise it, Kata put a hand gently on my wrist. I looked at her, and she lifted her hand.

"Take it slowly," she advised me. "You have had no food in six days. Give your body time. Be gentle to it."

Very good advice, I realized. I nodded thanks, then took a careful bite of the bread. It was dense and tangy, and the broth on it was flavorful but not greasy. It tasted strongly of unfamiliar herbs. I dipped the bread again and took another bite, then put down the bread, picked up the spoon, and began taking slow, careful spoonfuls of soup, pacing myself, not bolting it as hunger urged me to do. The soup eased my thirst as well. I could not recognize the meat, though I was pretty sure there was carrot and potato in the soup, and something—like a radish? —but yellow, and it did not burn. It tasted almost like a roasted chestnut. Every few spoonfuls of soup, I took another piece of bread.

I finished the soup, but ate only half of the bread. I felt I could easily have finished it, but didn't want to risk overdoing it. Instead I reached for the cloth it had come in and re-wrapped it.

"I will save this for later," I said, "if I might."

"A wise idea," Liisa agreed gravely. "We will wait a little while to see how this sits with you, and then we will take you to a more private room. One is being prepared for you, now that you are ready for it."

I sat back and thought. Mostly I found myself thinking that the chair was very hard and not very comfortable.

"Could we return to that couch?" I asked. "This chair is hard."

"Of course," Kata replied. "If you are ready to walk again."

"I think so," I said.

Kata and Liisa stood, and once again stepped to either side of me, helping me stand as Liisa pulled the chair back, then they guided me back over to the couch.

It was more of a chaise-longue than a couch really, backless and designed more for lying on than sitting on, but it was at least padded. I scooted as far as I could to the raised end where I could sit mostly upright and have something to partly lean on. Kata sat down next to me, but Liisa walked around and stood behind me. She reached out her hands and held them just above my shoulders.

14

"I wish to give you some energy, some strength," she said. "May I?"

I wasn't sure what she meant, but I was certain by now that it wasn't going to be anything to hurt me, so I nodded.

"Of course."

She rested her hands on my shoulders, then slid them inwards to the base of my neck, her fingers resting on my collarbones. She began a soft chant, which faded in a moment to a nearly-inaudible whisper. I began to feel a warmth emanating from her hands that was above and beyond the warmth of her skin. It soaked into me like the warmth of the nearby fire, and it felt good. I relaxed and leaned back a little more into her hands, gazed into the fire, and drifted away.

The light in the room was the first sign that it had been several hours. The shadows cast from the window had moved quite a way around the room, and the light was redder. I realized it must be nearing sundown. I could hear Kata and Liisa talking in low voices nearby. I realized that they must have laid me back down at some point. I began to look around, and Kata's voice broke off.

"Ah, you're awake again," she said. "Welcome back to us. A recovery room is ready for you. Do you feel up to a short walk?"

"I think so?" I replied uncertainly. "...Maybe?" I felt noticeably less achy than I had earlier, particularly in my upper back and shoulders.

I went to stand, and by the time I had my weight on my feet, Kata and Liisa were on either side of me ready to support me if I needed it. I gratefully took the offered hands and levered myself up. I felt a little light-headed for a moment, but it passed quickly. The two of them braced me and did not let me fall. Kata, on my right, lifted my right hand with her left and rested her right hand on my forearm, and a moment later Liisa on my left did the same. We crossed the few steps to the doors, and paused a moment there as they opened both doors, then we set off slowly down the hallway revealed beyond them, leaving them open behind us.

Narrow windows across the hall opened over what seemed to be a large court, mostly in shadow. I didn't stop to look closely. The sky was red in that direction, too.

We turned right and set off, passing several rooms similar to the one we had just left. My left foot and ankle seemed partly numb, but at least they didn't hurt. It did mean I had to take even more than usual care not to stumble, though. After a short time, I became aware of a trickle of warmth from the two women's hands where they rested on my forearms.

"If I might ask," I said curiously, "are you... doing something? It seems as though I can feel—something—from your hands. Are you... feeding me energy again?"

"You can feel that?" Liisa asked from my left. "Very good. Yes, we are giving you energy. Just a trickle, to keep you from exhaustion as you walk. Your body reserves are very low at the moment. A Talentless person would not be able to feel this. At this slight level, neither would most untrained Talents."

"We have been as much as possible using our own energy to heal you," Kata interjected. "But when used on the Talented, the healing arts *always* draw upon the energy of the one being healed as well as the healer. It cannot be avoided. It is simply how *voima* works. Still, we have tried to draw as little as we could manage, and to replenish afterward what we could not avoid taking."

"This is in part why there are two of us assigned to you," Liisa added. "If two Healers work together on you, then more of the energy comes from us, and less from you. You have so little to spare at present."

"The other reason," Kata added, "is because your injuries were so severe." But she did not go into detail.

I thought about that for a moment.

"Surely giving that energy comes at a cost to you, doesn't it?" I felt a little guilty.

"It does," Kata agreed. "But we can spare it more than you can. You are injured, and we are not; and we are Healers, and you are not. We will regain the energy more quickly than you would. And in any case... it is what we do."

I had to accept that, I guess.

We reached an archway. To the left, a broad flight of shallow stairs spiraled up and down around a central well walled off by floor-to-ceiling fretwork of dark wood. We headed towards the stairs going up.

"Just one turn up the stair," Kata said. "Can you manage?"

"I can most certainly *try*," I replied. "They don't look too steep."

16

We set off up the stairs. I thought I felt the trickle of warmth grow a little stronger.

"You are giving me more energy now, aren't you?"

"We are," Liisa agreed with a smile. "It is good that you noticed. It seems you *are* a quick learner, indeed."

My thoughts whirled internally, and I could not keep back a heavy sigh.

"Sometimes," I mumbled, almost to myself. "Sometimes so terribly *slow*." From my right, Kata shot me a searching look, but did not say anything.

We reached the top of the stairs fairly quickly and without incident, stepped back out into the hallway, and continued on around the building back in the direction we had originally come from. The doorways were to the right now, the windows to the the left. The visible sky was mostly dark now. The second door was open, and shortly before we reached it, a youth somewhere in his mid-teens came out. He turned in our direction and nodded a perfunctory bow.

"The room is all ready, Honoreds," he declared. "Is there anything more?"

Kata returned his nod.

"Thank you, Rami," she replied. "If you could perhaps see to having soup and bread for three brought up from the kitchen?"

"At once, Honored," the youth said, and headed for the stairs, as Kata and Liisa guided me into the room. It wasn't particularly large. To the left there was a fire burning in the hearth, with two comfortable-looking chairs in front of it, with rounded medium-height backs. Beyond them a small sofa stood against the wall, next to drawn curtains of dark green brocade. Beyond them on the right side of the room was a small wooden table with a plain wooden chair, and then, glory be, a proper bed. Narrower than I preferred, but a bed was a bed.

Kata was also looking around the room.

"Food will be here shortly," she said, eyeing the table. "We'll need two more chairs."

"Why?" I asked. I pointed at the two chairs in front of the fire. "Why don't we turn these two chairs away from the fire a little, move that table over between them, and then bring the third chair over next to it?"

Kata pursed her lips and inclined her head.

17

"That would certainly work," she agreed. "I'll see to the table."

I stepped toward the fireplace, took hold of the back of the nearest chair, and tipped it back toward me. I had planned to pivot it on one leg, but my head spun, and I had to stop, let the chair drop forward again, and lean on it for support, gasping.

"No," Liisa told me, placing her hand on my arm. "Do not exert yourself yet. You need rest. We will move the chairs."

She pivoted the second chair around, then helped me to it, went back and turned the first chair. Kata had meanwhile brought the table over. She set it down between the two chairs, then went back for the wooden chair. She was halfway back with it when there was a knock at the door. Liisa went to open the door, letting in the boy—Rami?—and a girl about the same age. Rami was carrying a tureen, while the girl had a basket covered with a cloth. They brought both over and set them on the table. Rami uncovered the tureen to reveal what appeared to be more of the same soup as earlier, while the girl unpacked the basket, which held three wooden bowls and spoons, a small ladle, and a dozen or so small crusty white bread rolls this time. They finished their chore, sketched quick half-bows, and left without a word, closing the door behind them.

Liisa laid out the bowls and started ladling soup into them. I grabbed one of the rolls, tore it in half, and bit into it. It was tangy, reminiscent of sourdough, but with an unfamiliar flavor that I couldn't place. Kata handed me a filled bowl, and I set to, remembering to pace myself and not eat too quickly despite how hungry I felt. Liisa and Kata were eating slowly as well, but I had the impression that it was mostly because they were watching me closely as they ate.

I got through not quite three of the rolls before my bowl was empty. I looked into the tureen, and there was still soup left. I hesitated for a moment, aware of Kata watching me. I did not feel full, and my stomach did not seem to be raising any protests, so I reached for the ladle and dished myself a little more soup. I offered the ladle around, but both women declined, so I laid it back into the tureen. I finished the rest of the roll I still had, and that and my soup refill left me feeling well-fed, but not overfull. I sat back, feeling somewhat better.

"How do you feel?" Kata asked me.

"Comfortable," I replied. "No longer hungry. But tired. So *very* tired."

Kata nodded. "A great deal of your own energy has been

expended in healing your injuries," she told me. "Much still remains to do just to heal your body. And then... we have sensed that there are terrible injuries within your spirit and your mind, as well. That is harder. We will do what we can to heal those, too. If you begin exploring your talent while you have unhealed wounds within your mind, you could do yourself serious harm, and damage your Talent forever.

"For now, you should rest. Sit a bit longer in front of the fire, and then we shall help you to bed."

She moved the table out of the way, then moved to stand behind me, while Liisa knelt in front of me and took my hands. This time it was Kata who placed her hands upon my shoulders. Once more, as Kata this time whispered, I felt warmth flowing into me, and from Liisa as well.

"When you are stronger," Liisa said to me, "there is a thing about you we have not seen before... there are pieces of metal in your knees. Large pieces. And something else, some substance that we do not know. It seems like a terrible injury, and yet it also seems that these... objects... were intentionally placed there, by someone. Please, what is this?"

I took a deep breath.

"It is an old injury," I explained slowly. "My knees were shattered beyond my ability to fully heal on my own. Repairs had to be made. Where I come from, healing care is done very... differently, it seems, than here.

"The repair was imperfect, rough, and the cartilage in my knees gradually wore away. After years, it became too painful to even walk. So the—moving parts—of my knees, the broken and worn-out parts, were cut out and replaced with... these parts."

Liisa shuddered.

"That is no true healing," she replied, a tremor in her voice. "That is scarcely better than leaving a broken leg splinted forever without mending the bone. Did it not *HURT?*"

"It did," I answered. "It hurt terribly. I wore... bags of ice-water around my knees for weeks to keep the swelling down. I had to learn to walk again. For the third time." Liisa drew in her breath slightly at that. "But sometimes when all that you have is what is possible, you have to settle for what is possible, even when it is less than ideal. Our

19

—"

I realized 'doctor' was not a word in this language.

"Our healers are studying the problem of regrowing lost or damaged body parts, but have not cracked the secret yet."

Liisa looked at me, moisture glistening in her eyes. Kata's voice came from behind me, low and a little shaken.

"Now we know why some of your injuries seemed so old," she said. "It is because they ARE that old. We are used to seeing scars from old, healed injuries, but not old, never-properly-healed injuries such as this, except in cases of grave misfortune where the injured person could not get to a healer.

"Did your injuries at least stop hurting once your healers were done?"

"No," I replied truthfully. "They hurt every single day. I could count on my fingers the days that I was not in pain."

Liisa looked up above my head. I suspected she was exchanging a look with Kata. Then she looked back at me.

"How long?" she asked quietly.

"More than twenty years," I said. Kata gasped behind me, and her hands tightened for a moment. Liisa silently bit her lip.

"Unending pain over a long period scars the soul," Liisa told me.

"Yes," I replied, the words heartfelt. "Yes, it *does*."

"But yet you—learned how to walk again," Liisa continued. "Three times, you said. That speaks well for the strength of your spirit. For refusal to submit and yield."

"We will make you whole," Kata said after a long moment. "I swear it. No-one should have to endure that." The sincerity and depth of feeling in her voice was unmistakable. My voice caught in my throat when I tried to answer.

"Thank you," I got out at last. "It's been so long." I realized that I was shaking.

"You should rest now," Liisa said. "And we... need time to think on this."

Liisa got up, and they moved to stand on either side of me. They helped me stand, then steadied me as I walked over to the bed with their help. Part way there, I realized that something else felt different. When I got to the bed, I turned and sat down on the edge, and I lifted my slightly numb left foot and looked at it. My ankle... my ankle *moved*. It was still stiff, my foot still rigid, but I could flex and extend my foot. Neither was it reddened and swollen. I moved my foot in all the directions I could. I did not have full range of motion, and my foot itself was still mangled, but it moved more than it had in a long time, even though still stiffly.

I looked up to see both Kata and Liisa regarding me gravely.

"Your foot, another botched healing, then," Liisa observed. "We... wondered. But again, we were not sure what to do without asking you first."

"Yeah," I agreed, with feeling. "My foot is... a wreck. But I can see that it is already better than it was. My ankle has not moved half that much in years."

Liisa turned the covers back, and I scooted out of her way, then made to lie down. She stopped me before I could, though.

"You should not sleep in the shirt," she advised. "Kuurii cloth will keep you warm, dry and comfortable all day, but it needs a chance to dry. Look at yourself, you are drenched in sweat. This has not been an easy day for you."

I realized that she was right. I felt sticky. I had not noticed it through the exhaustion.

"Stand for a moment," she told me.

I did so, unsteadily. I swayed, putting my hands out for balance. She smiled, caught my hands, and guided them to her shoulders. When she was sure I was steady, she began to peel the long shirt off of me. I felt self-conscious for a moment, and it must have shown, because she smiled.

"We are Healers," she said wryly. "Do you think there is anything we have not seen before? Who do you think put you *into* this shirt?"

I could not help but laugh. In hindsight, it was a bit of a silly hesitation.

I heard the door open and close. By the time Liisa got the shirt off me, Kata had retrieved a basket and set it down next to the bed. She pulled out small folded towels from it, and handed me one. It was moist and steaming warm.

"For your face," she told me. I took it eagerly and wiped, then scrubbed my face with it, then just stopped with it over my face and breathed in the steam. It felt good. Then, while Liisa steadied me, Kata rubbed me down with hot, moist towels from the basket, starting at my neck and working her way all the way down to my feet. She didn't miss anything. But fortunately for my sense of embarrassment, I was too exhausted to, uh... react.

There was a large smooth stone beneath the towels, I saw. I guessed the stone had been heated to heat the towels in turn, or just to keep them hot.

Finally she unfolded a larger towel from the other side of the basket, also warmed by the stone, and toweled me dry. By the time she was done, I felt clean and fresh.

I sat down on the bed, rather more suddenly than I had planned, steadied myself again, then swung my legs up and tucked them under the covers.

I went to pull the covers up, but Liisa stopped me.

"Not just yet," she said. "It is difficult to work through so much cloth. Direct skin to skin contact is best. Lie down, please. We have work still to do tonight."

I laid back willingly, and Kata walked around the bed to stand to my left.

She and Liisa reached out, tracing their fingers across me, starting from my hands and working slowly up my arms. It was... stimulating.

"This shoulder," Kata said from my left. "Is there any remaining soreness?"

I flexed my arm experimentally, rotating my shoulder. It moved freely without pain, and only a little stiffness.

"None," I replied. "It feels good. Slightly stiff."

"The ligaments that hold your shoulder together were badly torn," Kata explained. "Your arm was barely attached. We reset and mended the shoulder. But treat it gently for now."

Liisa, meanwhile, was tracing her way down my chest.

"Five of your ribs were broken," she told me, somewhat distractedly as her fingers probed me. "They have mended well. The lung on this side was collapsed, punctured. And there was a tear in your liver. You were bleeding, inside." She looked seriously at me. "You would not have bled to death from this injury, but only because

22

the bleeding in your head would have killed you first." She reached a little lower and partly under me. "Your back was broken, too. A crushed bone, just above your hips. And other bones broken, as well.

"We healed all of these things. *Properly.*" There was some pride in that last word.

I shuddered. By all I knew, I *should* have been paralyzed from the waist down. Major spinal injuries did not heal. I knew that. Yet somehow, I could walk. A sudden half-sob unexpectedly burst out of me.

"You *really can do* this, can't you?" I said, suddenly feeling hope I had abandoned years before.

Both women nodded.

"We *can,*" Kata replied, "and we *will.*" Then she paused.

"I give you fair warning, it will not be at all easy. Removing the metal from your body and regrowing what belongs there will be terribly painful. But we *will* make you whole again."

Kata stopped with her right hand just above my hip, and her left just touching the hollow of my shoulder. Across from her, Liisa mirrored the position.

"Tomorrow," Kata said, we must talk more about your knees, and your foot, and your leg, and the pieces of metal in your body. They *must not* remain. And also... other things. But tonight, we will do only general work, to restore your strength and ease your body. Tonight, it is time for you to rest.

"Are you the only healers here," I asked, "or are there others?"

"We are two of around a dozen," Kata replied. "This is Highwatch." As though that explained everything.

"I am glad beyond words," I said slowly, after some careful thought about exactly what I wanted to say, "that it is to the two of you that I was brought for healing."

Kata shot me a brief, but radiant smile.

"We, too, are glad," she replied. Then she and Liisa nodded to each other and began a soft chant, in unison. As before, their voices quickly dropped to near-whispers. I felt a warmth begin to grow from where their hands lay upon me, spreading all through me. I could almost feel the aches melting away.

I was asleep before Liisa drew the covers up over me and they left the room.

3: To Sail Beyond the Sunset

When I woke, the curtains were drawn and the room was filled with bright sunlight. Kata and Liisa were back, along with another of the multitudinous pages, this time an olive-skinned girl who looked to be in her late teens. They were just in the process of setting up what appeared to be a light breakfast. I lay there and watched them for a few moments, then Liisa noticed that I was awake.

"Good morning," she called cheerily. "Did you sleep well?"

"It seems I did, thank you," I replied. "And I would guess the two of you had a lot to do with that."

"You would not be wrong," Liisa agreed, with a smile. "How are you feeling?"

I sat up and stretched. A lot of the aches and pains were gone. But it seemed my knees ached the more by comparison. Even my foot seemed to hurt a little less than I was used to.

"Better," I said after a moment. "Although my knees and my foot are not fond of me, as it ever is."

"Ah, yes," Liisa said. Her smile clouded for a moment. "We must talk about your knees. After you break your fast a little."

Kata, meanwhile, walked over to the bed and picked up another of the long shirts from the foot of the bed. It was the same slightly shimmering blue as the one I had worn yesterday, but seemed just a little darker.

"I do not think that you need us to dress you today," she said with a slight smile, offering me the shirt. "But I will help you if you wish it."

I wasn't sure how to answer that, so I swung my legs out of bed, tested my footing, and stood up. Swayed with sudden vertigo, and sat back down again, more suddenly than I had intended, as a look of concern shot across her face.

"I... think I will take that help, please," I said, trying to keep my voice controlled. Kata nodded, and shook out the shirt, then gathered it up. I raised my arms and held them out towards her, and she slipped the gathered shirt over my arms and head. Her fingers brushed my chest as she eased it down over me, just a gentle touch. I liked how that felt.

With the shirt down around my hips, she offered me a hand to help me stand. I was thankful for the support, after that disconcerting flash of dizziness. This shirt, I noticed, was slightly shorter than yesterday's, coming just below my elbow and just above my knees.

Kata led me to the table. Breakfast, it turned out, was several fruited pastries similar to Danish pastries, a couple of pieces of fresh fruit of which the closest to familiar looked like a purple apple or maybe a large and oddly-shaped plum, and a jug of... what I was fairly sure was some kind of fruit juice, but I could not guess at what. It had the solidity of color of orange juice, but was much paler, almost whitish. And finally there was a bowl of what looked very like oatmeal drizzled with honey.

Liisa had a chair ready for me by the time I reached the table, and I sat down gratefully. The floor was unyielding, and my left foot was not appreciative of the fact.

I looked for additional cups and plates, but found none. Liisa followed my gaze. "We have eaten already," she said. "You slept late, and we chose not to wake you." I nodded in understanding, and started with... well, it wasn't oatmeal. It tasted much nuttier than any oatmeal I had ever tasted. But it was definitely honey on it. It was very good. Liisa poured me a cup of the juice while I ate.

After the oatmeal, I tried one of the pastries. It was indeed a puff pastry, but not sweet like a Danish. The fruit in it was refreshingly tart, blood-red berries with an almost citrus-like tang to them. The juice tasted like some kind of melon.

"What are these berries?" I asked, unable to identify them.

"Those are the fruit of the kuurii," Kata said. "They have curative and restorative properties. It is of fibers from the leaves of the same plant that the cloth of the shirt you are wearing is made. It is a valuable crop and it is grown in great quantities. Even the stems are used, threshed for cordage."

"That sounds like a useful plant," I agreed. "And I've never heard of it before, by that name or any other. Though they almost remind me of salmonberries."

Kata nodded.

"You must be a long way from home indeed, not to know the kuurii," she mused. "Perhaps you truly did come here through the rift the Rangers mentioned. But... who opened it? And did you come through it by choice? Or were you thrown... or pushed?"

26

"I... don't know," I replied uncertainly. Fragments of visual memory flashed in my mind, too brief to grasp. Something... black, floating. Unsettled, I carefully got up and walked over to the wide window, now uncurtained. Kata followed me closely, a hand ready for support if I stumbled or swayed.

The window was actually glazed doors that opened onto a small balcony. I opened the doors and ventured a couple of careful steps out. The landscape spread below was forested hills rolling down to a plain also scattered with broken forest. It looked idyllic.

Then I looked up at the sky, and reeled back in shock. Kata caught me, her arms stronger than I expected.

"What is it?" she asked urgently. "What is wrong?" But I could not answer. Speech escaped me. I just stared mutely at the sky.

Up until this moment, everything had still seemed... unreal. I was dreaming, that was all. A very pleasant dream, but it couldn't be real. But now... this sky with its *two* suns was the straw that broke the camel's back. I could no longer pretend to myself that I was imagining this. Suddenly it all came crashing in on me. Reality hit me like a freight train, and my mind just stopped working. I felt like a cartoon character who has just looked down and realized that there is no ground beneath his feet.

I felt, but did not really register, a hand on my other shoulder. Then my vision was blocked, and that got through to me. I blinked, and realized I was looking at Liisa's hand. I turned my head slowly, following the line of her arm, to find her looking at me, concern plain on her face. I closed my eyes and shook my head to clear it, to bring myself back into the here-and-now. I felt her touch my cheek.

"Are you *alright*?" she asked, urgently.

I looked at her again, then I looked back at the binary star burning high overhead, raised my right hand and gestured shakily at the sky. The simple movement broke the log-jam in my mind. I found I could form words again.

"Two suns," I croaked out, my voice on the edge of breaking. "There are **two suns** here."

I did not know whether to laugh or weep. I closed my eyes again and dragged my gaze down, away from the impossible sky. When I opened them again, I found myself looking instead into Kata's brilliant green eyes, a much more comforting sight. As stunned as I was, I had not noticed her step around in front of me.

"Kata..." I said. I suddenly felt more lost than I had ever felt before. I could feel tears starting in the corners of my eyes.

"Oh, Kata, I am so very, *very*, *VERY*, *unimaginably* far from home. And I have not the *tiniest shred* of an idea how I got here. Or even where 'here' *is*."

Without a word, Kata shifted her grip on me and wrapped her arms around me, and a moment later, Liisa did the same from my side. I slipped my arms around them both and clung desperately to them, gratefully accepting the offered comfort, suddenly my only anchors in a world farther away than I had ever imagined outside of daydreams that I would ever be. After a few minutes, I managed to look back up at the twin suns and not freeze in disbelief. Really, it was—a revelation, an amazing sight, one I had never really even imagined ever seeing. But... how incredibly far away *WAS* this place?

"You came from somewhere that is *not* under these two suns?" Kata asked after a while. I nodded slowly.

"I... did not really believe that this was real," I admitted shakily. "I almost thought it a... a dream while dying, a last vision thrown up by my mind as a refuge. But it was such a pleasant one I did not want it to end. But then I saw that sky. And somehow... seeing that broke the illusion. The disbelief.

"But this is all real... isn't it?"

Kata nodded solemnly.

"As real as Liisa and I," she told me. "That is as much as I can say to you about it. As real as our hands upon you. As real as the injuries we healed. And the wounds of your soul we have *still* to heal."

I took a deep breath, then let it out slowly. Looking into her steady gaze calmed me as much as the breath did. Perhaps more.

"My world—the world I came from—circles only one sun," I explained. "It shares it with eight other worlds, all the others very different, and all of them lifeless. At least, we *think* them lifeless. It has a moon almost a quarter the size of the world, which is also lifeless."

"We have three moons," Kata said. "But they are all much smaller than that."

"We have looked far into the heavens," I continued. "We have

28

studied stars so far away that their light itself, that can circle the world seven times in a... heartbeat, takes thousands of thousands of years to reach us. We have instruments that can see the planets around the nearer of these stars. And never yet have we seen a green, livable planet that circles two suns. I cannot even *begin* to guess at how far this world must be from—from mine."

"I think that you are going to be here for a long time," Liisa told me softly from my left, after a moment. "I think perhaps it is past time that you told us your name."

The realization dawned slowly upon me that I had no ties at all to anything before I woke up here. Unless whatever means brought me here violated the laws of physics as I knew them, everyone and everything I had ever known must have been dead and dust for centuries at the very least. Probably thousands of years.

Everything I had known either did not exist any more, or was so far away it might as well have never existed. I fought to stay calm.

I started to speak, but my throat closed up. Something in me rebelled. I *did not want* to be known by the name I was born with. That name had too much misery tied to it. I didn't *want* to be that 'me' any more. Or *ever again*. That was... my deadname now, I realized. So *this* is what that felt like.

I took another deep breath to calm myself, and tried to think.

I didn't have to think for too long. The name almost spoke itself.

"Call me Alrekr," I said, with sudden confidence. "Alrekr Járnhandr."

"Alrekr," Kata mused. "That is a strong name. But not a Saamen one. *Old* words. From the earliest years of this land, I think. What does it mean?"

"It's all I have, now," I replied. "So best to start from a good place." I struggled, not very successfully, to keep my voice steady. "I'm not actually sure of the meaning of the first. Similar to... perhaps Erik?"

"Ah," she said. "Like Erkki, then. And the last?"

"It means 'iron hand,'" I said, "in the language of my world that I... took it from. But I am beginning to understand that *this*... wherever it is... is my world now."

"We call it Auringon Valaista Maata," Kata told me. "And it welcomes you, Alrekr. As do we."

I noted in the back of my mind that I had heard it as a distinct place-name, while simultaneously knowing the meaning of the words— the Sunlit Land. With two suns, it seemed an apt name.

After a long while, we went back inside and I sat down. Kata and Liisa moved the table out of the way and pulled the other two chairs closer.

"Alrekr, listen to me," Kata began. "We must talk. This is important.

"We still need to properly heal your knees and your foot. It is best that we do it soon, especially if they hurt you still. *All* of the foreign metal *must* come out."

"If we do not properly heal your foot and knees quickly," Liisa added, "then it may become impossible to *ever* properly heal them. You are lucky: You have just come to this world, by means beyond the ordinary. *To this world*, your injuries are not your 'normal' state of being—*yet*. We can *feel* that the world will let us change them—but we must do it soon. And that means we have a narrow window of opportunity to wipe the slate, to rewrite the page, before it becomes set."

"Today you will rest and we will help to build your reserves," Kata told me. "And then tomorrow, we will heal your knees and your foot, and repair the other damage to your legs. We will do it all at one time. It will be better that way, because you will only have to go through it once."

I nodded my understanding.

"You were stronger once, were you not?" she continued.

"I was," I agreed. "I lost a great deal when I was injured. I used to be able to run—"

I realized that I had no idea how to express distances in Saamen, and broke off. But Kata nodded.

"I can see from the marks left on your bones where the muscles attach," she said, "that once there was more and stronger muscle there. But you have lost muscle, and it has gone to your belly. Not normally a good thing for health; but the extra reserves will serve you well now.

You will burn all of that, and more, healing with our help. We will sing your knees and your foot back whole, and prime your body to rebuild muscle, bone, ligaments, cartilage. Your strength can be built back. You will not become *younger*, as such... but we can undo much of the effects of aging."

"When we healed your fresh injuries," Liisa broke in, "you were unconscious. And that was easier for you, and it was simple because the injuries were fresh. Your body knew how to heal them. We just needed to *help* it. But still it was a long and tiring session, because you had *so many* injuries. We could not heal them all at one time. Then we healed more of the smaller injuries since, while you slept.

"But now we go to repair these *old* injuries, and that is difficult, because your body has learned to live with these parts that are *not you*. We will need your conscious mind to help guide the healing."

Kata took my hands and held them tightly.

"And that means you will have to be *awake*," she said, "when all of this metal comes out of your body. We can make your body force out the metal and anything else that does not belong, and grow back as it should.

"But the pain will be *terrible*. It will be like tearing your legs off at the knee. And then we will need to help your body to grow back what was lost."

"We will need at least two more Healers to help," Liisa added. "Perhaps four. We ourselves cannot provide all of the energy that this Healing will need. But we will be in control of everything."

"I trust you," I told Liisa. Then I looked at Kata. "I trust you both." And I meant it.

She smiled.

"We will also be depending upon you," she told me. "Because you are new to this world, we have one opportunity to rewrite what your old world wrote in you. But *yours* must be the will that guides what we write."

I nodded slowly.

"I think I understand," I replied. "You are saying that I have control over how I come out of this healing, if... I can hold in my mind what I want?"

"Within limits," Kata cautioned me, seriously. "Even a drastic Healing such as this will be, cannot—for example—make you nine feet tall, or give you four arms, or the strength of a bull, or wings like an eagle, or scales like a dragon. You can come out of it only as what *you* know in your soul how to be. We *cannot* make you what you are not or have never been, or enable you to do things you have never been able to do. Such attempts by the unwise or the arrogant almost always end... badly.

"We can only restore you to the best of what you already are, what is *already* within you to be."

"Think on this, carefully," Liisa added urgently. "You must go into the Healing tomorrow certain and without doubt. If you lose focus, with such severe injuries, you are likely to come out... crippled. Or worse, twisted."

I thought hard.

"You know," I replied at length, "if I can get back from this," gesturing at myself, "to the best that I have been, that's not damn bad at all. I don't *need* miracles, I don't need to be Wolverine or The Mighty Thor." That earned me a couple of puzzled looks, but I didn't stop to explain.

"And keeping that image in my head is not going to be hard at all. Because that's how I still *am*, in my mind's eye. This—the mangled foot, the artificial knees, the limp, the blurred vision, the fog in my head —**this is not me**. The *me* in my head is still the me who was trained in five—" I fumbled for words— "five styles of unarmed combat, who knew how to use a dozen kinds of weapons, the me who could wrestle down a... an animal three times my weight, the me who could run... aagh! I don't *know* your measures of time and distance!"

Kata and Liisa both laughed. And after a moment, I joined in the laughter too.

"I can hardly believe this," I said shakily, after a minute. "A new start. A second chance."

"Well," Kata said, smiling, "we should start getting you ready for tomorrow."

I thought hard for a moment, then decided. If this was to be my world, there was no time like the present to begin getting used to it.

"I have one request," I said. "Whatever we need to do to prepare... can we do it out there?" I pointed at the small balcony. Liisa looked questioningly at me.

"You are sure?" she asked. "The two suns came as a great shock to you."

"And that is why I want to make myself used to it," I said. "It was a shock at first... but also it is *wonderful*. I have to accept that this world is real. I *want* to embrace it fully. And I would like to begin that now."

"Well, why not, then?" she agreed. "If you are sure, we can at least begin there. There is enough room, just. And we can move inside if it gets cold."

I stood, and together we moved the chairs out onto the balcony. There was just room, with a little to spare, enough room to stand and move around. I looked up at the clear sky with the twin suns burning in it. The shock had passed, and now it was only... magical, wonderful, *amazing*. I could feel a smile growing on my face. I wanted to shout, but I didn't know what. So I just spread my arms wide and drank in the double sunlight, and wordlessly welcomed my new world.

Then suddenly I knew what to say.

"Thank you for giving me a home!" I called out joyfully to the world at large. "Thank you... for giving me a place to stand."

Then I sat down in the middle chair, and Kata and Liisa sat down on either side of me. They each took one of my hands as they had when we had walked up to this room, but this time instead of resting their other hands upon my forearms, they instead laid them across the front of my shoulders. I was coming to enjoy their touch a lot. I found it... thrilling. Stirring. Calming. All at once.

I sat back and relaxed, gazing at the landscape with its subtly different shifts of light from having two sets of shadows, and they began chanting. This time their voices did not trail off into whispers and then silence as before; instead they maintained a strong, rhythmic chant in words I did not recognize. Once again I felt the warmth of energy flowing from them into me, but this time it was not a trickle, it was a steady stream. I could feel it suffusing me, a pleasant, comfortable, tingling warmth, relaxing and at the same time re-invigorating. Once again my aches and pains faded into the background. Even my foot and knees hurt less.

"To strive, to seek, to find, and not to yield," I said to myself, trying and failing to control my emotions.

Then I let go of the world and simply basked in the dual sunlight and the warmth of... whatever it was that these two beautiful women were feeding into me.

Some time later, I came to. Several hours, I judged, going by how far the suns had moved in the sky. (*Suns*. I was really going to have to get used to that.) My two companions were standing by the parapet looking out across the hills. I stood up, and took the couple of steps to join them. They both looked... tired.

"How much is this taking out of you?" I asked quietly, concerned.

Kata turned and smiled at me.

"Do not worry," she said. "Your concern for us does not go unnoticed, and it is appreciated more than you know. But we are trained for this, and we are Healers to begin with. As we told you before, it is a part of our Talent to recover life-energy quickly. Tomorrow, you will need all of the energy that we can give you today. Tomorrow will be hard on us, on all of us; but it is what we do. And we will have additional help for tomorrow.

"But how are *you* feeling?"

"Much... less tired," I replied. "It is as though weight and weariness has been lifted from me."

"We will do this several times more before you sleep tonight," she told me.

"Shortly after we began," Liisa ventured, "it seemed you went into a kind of trance. But before that, you... said something? In your own language, I think."

Interesting. I had not realized I had spoken in English. But, I mused, it made sense that I had, since I had been quoting.

"It was the final line of a poem from my world," I replied. "Written by the poet Alfred, Lord Tennyson. About a heroic figure, Ulysses, from an epic poem thousands of years older, and his company of companions. A sort of postscript to the older poem, the Odyssey. I have always found it inspiring." I suddenly found myself reflecting that Lord Tennyson was probably thousands of years dead now himself.

"Do you know the entire poem?" Liisa asked in an interested tone. "Or do you remember only that line?"

"I *think* I can remember... perhaps the last third of it," I replied slowly. "The part that resonates most with me. The *best* part. The *hopeful* part. Not the bitter, angry beginning where Ulysses is

34

complaining about the failings of his family and his kingdom. I never memorized that part of it. There was enough bitterness without memorizing more.

"Would you like to hear what I can recall?"

"Oh! Yes! A poem from *another world*? Yes, *please!*" Liisa actually clapped her hands softly in excitement, and Kata nodded eagerly.

"Then I shall try," I said. "For you. For both of you. It's all I have to thank you with."

I stepped forward to the parapet rail, gazed out across the hills, taking several deep breaths as I gathered my thoughts. I would have to translate this as I went. I hoped it wouldn't lose too much in the translation. It was blank verse in the first place, so it wouldn't matter too terribly that it wouldn't rhyme in Saamen. The meter wouldn't transfer properly, but... well. I would just have to do the best I could.

"I'm not sure how well I can preserve the... rhythm on this on such short notice," I apologized. I took one more deep breath, then pointed dramatically out and down, as though pointing out a landmark below us on the plain.

"There lies the port; the vessel puffs her sail," I declaimed.
"There gloom the dark, broad seas. My mariners,
Souls that have toiled, and wrought, and thought with me,
That ever with a frolic welcome took
The thunder and sunshine, and opposed
Free hearts, free foreheads – you and I are old;
Old age has yet his honour and his toil;
Death closes all: but something ere the end
Some work of noble note may yet be done
Not unbecoming men that strove with gods."

I paused to steady my breath, turned slightly to face them fully, and continued, fighting to keep my voice under control as the sheer *power* of Tennyson's poem cascaded over me. It was hard, especially as it suddenly dawned on me how truly, *perfectly* fitting to the moment *Ulysses* was.

"The lights begin to twinkle from the rocks;
The long day wanes: the slow moon climbs: the deep
Moans round with many voices. Come, my friends,

35

'Tis not too late to seek a newer world.
Push off, and sitting well in order, smite
The sounding furrows; for my purpose holds
To sail beyond the sunset, and the baths
Of all the western stars until I die.
It may be that gulfs will wash us down:
It may be that we shall touch the Happy Isles
And see the great Achilles, whom we knew."

I had to pause for one more steadying deep breath before the final stanza.

"Though much is taken, much abides, and though
We are not now that strength which in old days
Moved earth and heaven; that which we are, we are;
One equal temper of heroic hearts
Made weak by time and fate, but strong in will
To strive, to seek, to find, and not to yield."

When I finished, Kata and Liisa were both watching me, entranced. My eyes were stinging slightly. I bowed my head and stood in silence for a long moment, trying to regain my composure, almost overcome. I was very aware that I had just spoken Tennyson's words for the first time ever on this world, and I found I was barely in control of the emotions it had stirred up in me.

I closed my eyes, waited for a moment longer until my breathing steadied, and took a couple more slow breaths. Finally I felt ready to speak again.

"My dear, new-found friends," I said slowly, as I opened my eyes, aware now that the corners of my eyes were wet, and raised my head. "I do not even *begin* to understand how it happened, but I... I do believe that I have indeed sailed beyond the sunset. Just as Tennyson wrote."

There was a long silence.

"To strive, to seek, to find, and not to yield," Liisa repeated softly. "That... is *powerful*."

"That's part of why I like it," I agreed. "Determination, resolve, defiance, in the face of everything, even time and age. Even the

36

legendary Ulysses could not defeat old age, but he was still ready and willing to give it a good fight."

Liisa laughed, and Kata smiled.

"Do you know others like that one?" Liisa asked.

"I might be able to remember some," I allowed. "Possibly recall a few of my own. Perhaps even write some new ones... That would probably be better, actually."

"You are a poet as well?" she asked, perking up.

"Not in Tennyson's league, by any measure," I demurred. "But I like to think I have a little talent. Or *used* to, at least. I've... not written any poetry of consequence in years. My mind has been too— too dulled, too fogged, by pain and... sadness."

"Well," Kata remarked thoughtfully, "let us see what happens when we are done healing you. You have more than physical injuries, that much is already plain beyond argument."

I just nodded slowly. I didn't know how to answer.

"For now," she continued, "food has been brought. We should eat, and then we should begin another session."

She went into the room and fetched a basket covered with a cloth, which proved to contain soft bread rolls, soft unsalted butter, and hard white cheese with a slightly nutty flavor. There was also a crock of peach-colored juice that tasted like a mixture of canteloupe and lime. We ate our luncheon straight from the basket, then as Kata had said, we began a second preparation session much like the first.

The feeling of well-being I got from having Liisa's and Kata's hands linked with mine was not entirely due to all the energy they were pouring into me. I was coming to deeply appreciate their simple presence.

By the time we finished that second session, the sun was low in the sky behind the tower containing my room, and there was a chill in the air.

"We should move back inside now," Kata advised. "The nights are still cold here, this early in the year. Up in the peaks where you were found, had you not been found before night fell, you would likely have quickly frozen to death. Had you not bled to death before you froze. It would have been a race between the cold and the bleeding, as to

37

which killed you first."

So we picked up the chairs and moved back inside—or rather, Kata sent me inside, while she and Liisa moved the chairs. We put them back in front of the fire, which had been set again and lit by a page while we were outside. A third comfortable chair had also been brought into the room while we were outside. I had not even heard it being brought in. Supper, Liisa told me, had already been arranged for, and would be brought when it was ready. In the meantime, we sat and rested in front of the fire, myself in the middle chair with Liisa on my right and Kata on my left. I had to admit, I could get used to this lack of apparent urgency, but I suspected it wouldn't last. As long as it did, I thought I should make the best of it.

"So, you like poetry," I commented to Liisa, while we waited and bided our time.

She smiled and nodded.

"There is something about the way it flows," she said. "It can be like a warm breeze, or gentle rain, or a relentless wind, or thunder. What kind do you prefer?"

"All of them," I replied. "As long as it has form and structure, and says something that matters."

Liisa looked puzzled.

"How can you have poetry that does not have form and structure?" she asked. "Is that not what poetry *is?*"

"It is to me," I agreed. "But in... the world I came from, a lot of people seem to think that they can just say some vague, rambling thing, however deeply they feel it, or even a prosaic factual description of... the process of how ice melts, say, and sort of break it up into random bits and pieces, and it somehow magically *becomes* poetry. I think it comes from the participation-trophy mindset—the idea that you shouldn't deny someone the right to declare they're a poet, merely because they're no good whatsoever at it. That the runner who takes three times as long to finish a foot-race as the second slowest runner, who has to stop and walk, is still just as much an athlete as the fastest. Not that I mean in any way to diminish the *attempt*—or for someone who struggles against great handicaps to finish *anyway*—but..."

"That seems... very strange," Liisa said. "As if someone who cannot hit anything with a bow were to call himself an archer."

"I can't wholly disagree," I said. "The... difficult part is that sometimes they do have something very real to say. And I'm not saying they could not *become* truly a poet, in time, with work and practice. Or an archer. And I cannot help but admire the person who is disabled, but enters the, uh, the endurance race *anyway*— and *finishes*. In its way, that is perhaps a greater accomplishment than the athlete who wins. To enter the race *with no legs*—and yet *still* finish?

"But... *just* having something to say does not mean you are a poet, if you are not actually using poetry to say it. It just means you have opinions. Which is a separate thing from being a poet. And I do not for a moment mean to suggest that simply having something important to say, and the courage to say it, means any *less* if you don't say it in poetry... it just doesn't suddenly *become* poetry because you broke up the lines."

"You think poetry should always have something important to say, then?" Kata asked.

I shrugged slightly.

"Something *worth the speaking*, at least," I agreed. "A story, an idea, an elegy, a remembrance, even a feeling or a hope. Even humor. There were styles of verse that were *always* humorous. Even some that, as part of the form, *always* contained lines of pure nonsense. But something in it of substance. Even if it's just to make someone smile. If something is not worth saying, then why say it?"

Kata thought about that for a moment, then smiled mischievously.

"Tell me one thing, right this moment, that is worth saying here and now," she told me.

I looked at her, absolutely seriously, fully intending to find something profound to say about putting the past behind me instead of being bound to it. But that wasn't what happened, as I found myself gazing into her eyes again.

"You have amazingly beautiful eyes," I said. It just... came out, unplanned. Then my mouth dried up.

Kata looked me straight in the eyes for a long, searching moment, as I hoped desperately that I hadn't just made a terrible blunder. Then she smiled softly.

I started breathing again. Maybe I *hadn't* just put my foot in my mouth after all.

I was saved from further awkwardness at that moment by a tap at the door.

"That should be our supper," Liisa declared. "I will get it." I looked over at her as she stood to go to the door. It did not escape my notice that she was smiling at Kata and at me.

"You seem suddenly a little anxious," Kata told me softly. My mouth went dry again.

"That wasn't actually what I intended to say," I admitted, embarrassed. Kata raised her eyebrows.

"Do you want to take it back, then?" she asked, in what seemed a slightly teasing tone.

"No," I said fervently. "Not *ever*. It is *absolutely* true, and I stand by it."

"Then I am flattered that you considered it worthy of saying aloud," she replied, with that same slight smile again. I wished desperately that I was more sure what it meant.

"In the world I came from," I explained carefully, "for me to say so uninvited could be considered intrusive, or..." I floundered, trying to find a Saamen word that fit. I could not find a word for harassment. "Uh... baiting, taunting, making repeated minor attacks to annoy someone, to create trouble? You, uh, don't seem to have a word for it."

"Baiting?" Kata looked at me for a long moment, frowning in obvious puzzlement. "To honestly compliment a woman is *baiting* her?"

I sighed. This was going to be difficult to explain... but I thought it was important that I did. The absence of a Saamen word spoke volumes about how different this culture was. How much *healthier*, I thought. I had to try to explain this without completely stuffing my foot down my own throat.

By now, the pages had deposited our supper on the table and left, and Liisa had returned and was now listening as well.

"Where I am from," I began, "many men treat women very poorly, especially in the workplace. Some cultures, more so than others... Don't even get me *started* about, uh... Never mind. Not now. You don't have words for those cultures. It would take too long to explain. Some cultures actually regard women more as property than as people in their own right."

40

A thought occurred to me, and I made a quick mental search and found no single Saamen word that meant 'slave' or 'slavery', either. It took multiple words to state it. The concept simply did not exist in this language as a word. That probably meant it was not common, not normalized. I found I was starting to really like these people.

"Many people, both men and women, myself among them, feel that this is **deeply wrong**"—a fair bit of anger might have slipped through, there—"and do all we can to treat women—well, *everyone*, really—respectfully, as equals in every way. Simply because they are." Kata nodded.

"But a lot of people *don't*, and they act like obnoxious, uh, *moukkat*, mistreating people they have power over because it makes them feel big, including forcing unwanted attention on people. Usually, but not always, on women, but... anyone less powerful than themselves. Even when they *know* it is unwanted. Some people act like complete *kusipäät*, deliberately *forcing* unwanted attention on people—*mostly* on women, though the opposite is not unknown— whom they *know* full well don't want it, but who... are *denied* any power to tell them to stop, without consequences they cannot afford. So that they can *flaunt* how much power they have, show off that nobody can tell them 'No.'" Both women were starting to look appalled, but I gritted my teeth and soldiered on. Now that I'd started into this, I needed to finish the explanation.

"And it only makes it worse that some people become so sensitive about being treated in... belittling or offensive ways, that it makes it difficult to even just... be polite or friendly. You can unwittingly offend someone just by holding a door open for them. As though you were implying, simply by offering the courtesy, that they could not do it for themselves. Even though you would do the same for anyone." Liisa shook her head in puzzlement.

"It reached a point where a person can be dismissed from their job for an innocently-intended compliment. You have to be so *careful* that... some people, especially the more private and... less bold ones, simply never risk saying anything. Because they are afraid to speak, lest their words be taken in the wrong way. There are so many different ways that people find to look down on others, that... sometimes it feels one must bend over backwards to avoid even the appearance of doing so, no matter what one's intent. And some people seem to *look for* ways to interpret badly what is meant well. Sometimes because of raw nerves from being treated badly again and again.

"It is... *difficult* when you see the world through a veil of scars built up by enduring the contempt or cruelty of others. You become so used to unkind intent that you start to see it in everything. It becomes self-preservation to assume the worst of everyone. I can well understand where it comes from, make no mistake about that. Many people of my world treat others horribly. But to navigate it is still hard. Especially... when you don't really understand people well in the first place, but are trying to be kind and fair to those you meet anyway, as best you know how."

Kata stared at me, perplexed, then looked at Liisa. They exchanged glances.

"You come from a very confusing place, Alrekr," Liisa said to me.

"Yes," I agreed, emphatically. "Yes, I most certainly do."

"And I think," she continued, "that perhaps... you were one of those who did not really understand people well, who was sometimes afraid to speak?"

I hesitated, then nodded sheepishly.

"Yes," I admitted. "I was. I still am, I suppose, really."

Liisa smiled gently.

"Here," Kata replied, turning back to me, "you should never be afraid to *sincerely* compliment an unattached woman, as long as you do not press the matter if she rebuffs you. The worst that is likely to happen is that she is uninterested, unless you choose—very unwisely." She was looking very directly into my eyes, smiling slightly. After a moment, I realized that if I was not mistaken, she had just subtly told me that she was unattached. Unsure of what to say, I nodded gravely.

"Thank you for your guidance," I managed after a moment, nervous but not wanting to let the opportunity pass. "I shall endeavor to choose wisely. I hope I have made a good start in that regard." She smiled deeply, and I relaxed.

"Sometimes," she replied, "the deepest truths are those you did not intend to speak."

We moved the chairs around the table again, and sat down to eat. Supper was thin slices of tender meat in a spicy cream sauce, something rather like roasted yams, and a mixture of lightly cooked vegetables not too unlike string beans, their colors shading from dark red through bright yellow. At first sight I thought they were hot peppers, but they turned out to be sweet and crunchy, almost reminding me of water chestnuts, but with more flavor. There was a flagon of something fruity and fermented, and a basket of sweet dessert rolls almost bursting with fruit and honey.

"What are these?" I asked, holding one of the yellow ones. "They look like one thing I know, but taste like another, and have the texture of yet a third."

"We call them imp fingers," Liisa said. "They are harvested from a bush, in the late springtime, and they have healing and purifying properties."

"They're good," I said. "Really good. I like them."

"They can be eaten raw," Kata added with a smile, "but it is not recommended. Uncooked, they are tough, and will cause you to see strange things that are not there."

I looked at the... pod? between my fingers.

"A..." Blast it, no word for 'hallucinogenic'. "A bean that brings waking dreams," I mused. "I have a lot to learn."

"There will be time," Liisa told me in reply. "There will be lots of time."

When we finished eating, the suns were setting. It was my first ever double sunset, and I insisted upon going out onto the balcony to watch it. Unfortunately we were too far—east?—around the tower to be able to see anything but fiery sky. Disappointed, I came back inside after only a few minutes. There was a bite in the wind that had sprung up.

"We should channel to you one more time before you sleep," Liisa told me. "Let us help you get ready for bed now, and then you need not rouse yourself afterward, you can go straight to sleep. You will need to be well rested."

This sounded like a good idea to me. She sent for hot towels again, and she and Kata sponge-bathed me exactly as they had the previous night. This time I did not feel at all self-conscious about being naked in front of them. Then they helped me into bed. I lay down and relaxed as they probed my body again, then they placed their hands on me and began to chant energy into me for the third time this day. I lay there and watched them, listening to the harmony of their voices, looking back and forth from one to the other. Both were looking steadily at me as they chanted. As the energy washed into me, I felt calm, energized yet relaxed, drowsy yet not tired. I had a memory of finding my eyes locked with Liisa's for a while, and I heard my voice tell her without any conscious intention on my part, "You are beautiful too." She smiled softly and continued chanting, but her hand squeezed my shoulder for a moment.

Eventually I drifted off to sleep.

4: We Can Rebuild Him

I awoke the next morning to unfamiliar voices in the room. I could see when I opened my eyes that it must be late in the morning, from the angle of the light.

Kata was standing nearby; she turned to look at me when I lifted my head. Liisa was over by the balcony doors, and there were four other people in the room, two sitting on the small couch, two in the chairs.

"You are awake," Kata said to me. "We thought we should let you sleep until you woke on your own, to be as rested as possible.

"Today, we will take on the Healing of your knees and foot. We brought in, well, most of the other senior Healers to help." She beckoned to the strangers, and after a moment, they stood and filed over, as I sat up.

"This is Raimo," Kata said, gesturing to a tall man with dark skin, the closest-cropped hair I had ever seen, and... long, pointed ears? They had *tufts*, too. He placed his hands together and nodded solemnly, and I returned the nod and the gesture as closely as I could.

"And Vallaïnen," a weatherworn-looking older man with tousled, greying hair and smiling eyes. "Marja," a small, motherly woman with nut-brown hair and piercing blue eyes, "and Varpu." The last was a pretty, cheerful-looking blonde woman who looked to be in perhaps her thirties, with an infectious smile.

"Liisa and I will be directing your Healing today, with Raimo and Varpu assisting us. Marja and Vallaïnen will be standing by in case there are difficulties or additional power is needed. This is half the healers in Highwatch."

"I feel honored," I said, and meant it. I turned toward Raimo.

"I hope I do not offend," I said hesitantly. "I am new to this world, as I am sure Kata has told you. I could not help but notice the shape of your ears...?"

Raimo inclined his head again.

"No offense given nor taken," he said. "I am half Huldre."

My jaw dropped open. I knew that word. Now that he was closer to me, as well, I thought I could see an almost bark-like texture to the skin on the backs of his hands. And perhaps elsewhere. Not deeply rough like oak, but perhaps birch.

"*Huldre?*" I exclaimed, amazed. "There are huldrefolk here? In my... the world I left, they are no more than legend. How many MORE wonders does this world hold?" I shook my head in wonder. "I count myself doubly honored to meet you, sir."

Raimo smiled warmly.

"The honor is as much mine," he answered me. "Today you have met one whom you previously thought only legend, and I have met a man who travelled here from another world. One unimaginably far away, from what I hear."

"You are not wrong, my friend," I replied with feeling. "You are not wrong."

I looked around the circle of healers gathered around me.

"I do not know how to thank you all for coming to lend your aid," I said.

"Then don't try," Varpu replied. "It is what we do, how we repay the precious gift the world gave us. All will be well. You will see." She flashed that smile again, and I nodded. It was hard to be anything but positive in the face of her smile.

"We should prepare for the working," Liisa told me. "We must remake your bed. You can sit in a chair while we prepare it."

She offered me another of the long, silky shirts. I smiled, raised my arms, and she slipped it onto me. I almost shivered as her fingertips traced down my sides. Then she helped me stand and guided me to the nearest chair. By the time I turned and sat, the bedding was already stripped off my bed. Raimo was unfolding a sheet of a stiff-looking, flat-textured cloth, which he spread over the bed. I looked curiously at it.

"It is a kind of sailcloth," Liisa explained, catching my expression. "As well as making good sails, it is very waterproof. And proof also against other fluids."

I nodded in understanding. I could not help feel a sense of foreboding. I was pretty sure I knew what fluid she was talking about.

Three regular sheets went on top of the sailcloth, out of a large hamper that I had not seen was in the room. It must have been brought in while I was still asleep. Then they spread two layers of thick towels over the sheets.

"Now," Liisa declared, "it is time." She helped me up and I walked

46

over to the bed. I looked at it for a moment, then took a deep breath, turned around, and sat down. Liisa reached for the shirt and I let her take it off me, her eyes calm and steady looking into mine. Then she had me lie down, guiding me with feather-light fingertips, as Kata arranged the pillows so that my head and shoulders were slightly raised. Varpu draped a folded sheet across my middle and hips, then patted my stomach and grinned at me. I laughed. How could I not? (I admit the laugh was perhaps slightly nervous.)

Kata took my hand, looked into my eyes, and squeezed. I squeezed back.

"Let us take places," she said. She moved to stand next to my left leg, while Liisa stood next to my right. Raimo stepped up to my right shoulder, while Varpu took Kata's place at my left. Marja and Vallaïnen took places near the foot of the bed, waiting. Raimo placed one hand on my right shoulder, and one at my wrist, as Varpu placed her right hand on my left shoulder and took my left hand in hers, smiling down at me as she intertwined her fingers with mine. Kata and Liisa each placed one hand on the middle of my thigh, and one just below my knees. Then Kata looked at me.

"Remember," she instructed me again, "you play a crucial part here. Once we begin, *no matter how much it hurts*, you **must** hold the image in your mind of what your healed body should look like, how it should function, how it should *feel*. The image of what you should *be*."

I looked back at her, and nodded, my mouth dry.

"I'm as ready as I will ever be," I replied.

Kata nodded, and raised her head.

"Begin," she said.

As though with a single voice, all four began a low chant. It seemed similar at first to the one they had used to feed me energy, but lower in pitch, and slower. But I rapidly realized there was a lot more power in it. I felt an almost electric tingle in the air, and then after a little bit I could feel an energy begin to build. My hair stood on end. There was a steady, driving rhythm to the chant. I found myself inescapably reminded of the rhythmic beat of the Kalevala, and nodding along to the rhythm of the chanting.

I started forming an image in my mind of how I saw myself, how my body should feel to me. The room seemed to be thrumming.

It took me completely by surprise when, between the end of one measure and the start of the next, Kata and Liisa burst seamlessly into full-throated song. I *felt*, almost **saw** the wave of power that billowed out from them. Eight measures later, Varpu and Raimo did the same and the power redoubled. I could hear that they were singing something slightly different from Kata and Liisa, and that all four were singing distinct melodies, but the four separate parts fit together perfectly. The harmonies were totally unlike anything I had heard before, almost alien, and yet somehow at the same time, they felt more **right** than possibly anything I'd ever heard. I was distinctly aware of each of the four voices, while at the same time they blended together into something that was more than their simple sum. I was surprised at the strength of my own emotional reaction.

For a minute or two I forgot to think of anything but the singing. But then I remembered I had a job to do as well.

I did not try to picture what my knees should actually look like inside. I trusted my body—and my Healers—to know that. Instead I focused on the inner self that I knew was still there, somewhere. I remembered when my feet were *both* strong and whole, when there were no scars on my legs or body... or my hands. I imagined my knees not hurting, remembered when *nothing* in my body hurt, and I pinned that memory up as a background. Then on top of it, I pinned a memory of myself doing martial-arts *kata*. (*I'd love to do Kata*, came a stray thought, accompanied by an imagined vision of her naked in my arms. I pushed it away... but not very hard. It was a *beautiful* image, but right now I couldn't afford the distraction.)

I grabbed a memory of myself sprinting like the wind, running on my toes, myself running back-to-back five-minute miles, myself keeping pace alongside a cantering horse. The things I *KNEW* I *used* to be able to do. I merged them together and added that to the image. I remembered my eyes hawk-sharp, my mind alert and focused. In my head, Die Krupps sang, "Vision, 2020 vision!" (What would it be like if my eyes *really were* as sharp as a hawk's?) My own voice spoke in my memory, "The human eye is one of the strongest arguments *AGAINST* intelligent design, the goddamn retina is *INSIDE OUT*. That's why we have a blind spot."

I remembered restraining seals that outweighed me by three

hundred pounds. I remembered lifting a steel desk that weighed two hundred and fifty pounds, above my head. I remembered holding thousands of lines of code in my head, remembered recalling thirty digits of *pi* without error, remembered climbing cliffs and running down mountainsides. I remembered the feeling of boundless energy, and the feeling of inner peace and calm. I shaped all of these thoughts and memories into an inner *me*... and, okay, I will admit, I pictured my reflexes that little bit faster than they had ever been, imagined exercise coming more readily and *easily*, imagined myself a little bit more self-confident, imagined my body healing just that bit faster than it ever had.

...All right, a *lot* faster. More than his claws, I envied Wolverine his healing factor. I had wished for it so many times since I got hurt. But I heeded Kata's warning.

Not, then, anywhere near as fast as Wolverine; I had no illusions that I could wish myself a superpower. But faster than ever before.

I pushed all of these thoughts, memories and images together and shaped them into a coherent whole, an idealized internal concept of *me*, and I held it up and overlaid it on top of me, and I held onto it as the song washed over me. I painted myself with it in my mind, I hung it on the wall and filled it with me.

Then as the singing went on, my knees began to hurt. Not just a little bit, not just the way I was used to them hurting nearly all the time, not the way they had hurt before they were replaced. The pain built until it was like those long minutes lying broken in the road after the hit-and-run, wondering whether help would come. And then it got worse.

And then it got *worse*.

I hung on for dear life to that mental model of an unbroken me. And the pain got worse. I know I cried out, gasped in agony, trying to hold in a scream.

I know I failed.

And then, oh gods, ***it got worse***.

I could not see, my eyes were too blurred, my vision contracted to pinpoint tunnels. But suddenly I was aware that there was a FIFTH part to the song that Kata, and Liisa, and Raimo, and Varpu were singing. I still did not understand what any of the words meant, but somehow *I*

49

knew what sounds to sing, and I somehow *knew* that this fifth part would fit my voice.

So there was really only one thing I could possibly do.

I opened my mouth, and I sang with every fiber of my being.

I could not see Kata look at me, momentary alarm on her face, or see the dawning surprise that replaced it, could not see the urgent look she shot at Vallaïnen, could not see him and Marja step forward, did not notice when they pulled the folded sheet away and placed their hands on my sides just above and below my hips. But I heard when their voices joined the song. Now there were *seven* parts, *seven* sets of interwoven harmonies, *and it was* **GLORIOUS** beyond words. I held my vision of myself in my mind's eye, sublimated the agony into passion, poured everything I had inside me into the song, and just let the words come out as they would.

Together we sang, and sang, and sang, and sang.

After a timeless period I could not possibly estimate, the song seemed to come to an end of its own. My throat was dry, almost raw. I could almost still hear the echoes. I honestly could not have told you who stopped singing first, or whether we all stopped together.

After a little, I became aware that Varpu was still holding my left hand, but her grip had weakened.

With some effort, I opened my eyes. It seemed to take a long time. Raimo was looking down at me from my right. He looked... weary, even actually a little pale, but *exultant*. There was no other word. To my left, Varpu looked ready to drop, but then she shook her head, blinked, and gave me a huge, triumphant grin. Just seeing that grin made me feel better.

I looked further down towards the foot of the bed. Marja had already stepped back, drooping. Vallaïnen was heading for one of the chairs. He dropped into it like a sack of potatoes. Kata's head was bowed, she looked ready to pass out. Liisa, who looked worn and weary herself, had a hand extended to steady Kata. My heart caught in my throat. Marja seemed the only one not on the edge of exhaustion.

"Is she *alright?*" I gasped out, afraid for Kata, my voice a near-croak. Liisa looked at me, then nodded.

"She will be fine," she said to me. I could hear the tiredness in her voice. "This was an exceptionally... draining healing. We are *all* exhausted. You also, I think...?"

I nodded weakly. I was shaking, and soaked with sweat. On my left, Varpu touched her right hand to my cheek for a long moment.

"Seven parts," she said unsteadily, but she was smiling. "*Seven parts.*" Then she let go my left hand and stumbled back a step, before heading for the nearest chair.

Kata had straightened up a little.

"Forgive us, Alrekr," she said, tiredly. "We *all* need to rest for a moment before we clean you up."

I looked down further. The towels beneath my legs were *drenched* with blood.

I suppose, I thought to myself, *that's part of why I feel a bit shaky.*

Kata went to sit down, while Liisa took my right hand and squeezed it. Raimo threw an arm around her shoulders for a moment and gave her a quick hug, before excusing himself and heading across the room and out onto the balcony. I thought again that he looked a little pale.

Liisa looked down at me, then she sat down next to me on the edge of the bed and held my hand.

"It went *well*," she told me. "*VERY* well."

I heaved a deep, ragged sigh. She looked at me again, traced her hand down my cheek. It wasn't until she wiped a tear from my cheek that I realized I was weeping in relief.

After five or ten minutes, Liisa stood up and went to the door. I heard a ringing from the bell outside the door. A few minutes later, she spoke briefly to someone, then came back to wait. Shortly there was a tap at the door, then a page girl brought in a large basket of clean towels. She put them down hear the foot of the bed. Marja and Varpu got up, then Kata, then Liisa. Varpu lifted my feet—they were both WHOLE!—and Marja pulled most of the sodden towels from under my legs, then she and Kata together spread a new clean towel beneath me. Then Liisa, Kata and Varpu began washing me, from the shoulders down, washing off first the sweat, then, when they got to my legs, the blood. They rolled me onto my right side to wash the backs of my legs, then laid down another clean towel.

When they were done, Liisa stepped closer again.

"Do you think you can stand?" she asked me.

I thought for a moment.

"I'm willing to try," I said. "If someone is standing by for support."

She called out to Raimo, who immediately returned from the balcony. His color seemed to have returned, and his step was firmer. I swung my legs off the bed, and with Liisa on my left and Raimo on my right, went to stand up. I almost managed it, but a moment later I swayed dizzily. Raimo caught me instantly before I could fall, startlingly strong, then Liisa supported me from my other side.

Between them, they helped me to a chair. Liisa draped a towel over my lap, and I took it thankfully. Then, working together, the healers stripped the bed for the second time today. I was appalled by how much blood was on the towels and the bedding, and very aware that all of it was mine. How much blood had I lost? No wonder I was dizzy. Marja bundled all of the soiled linens up in the sailcloth, then Raimo helped her stuff the bundle into the hamper and wheeled it outside.

Kata came and sat down opposite me. She looked tired. I felt guilty.

Then she looked at me and smiled.

"You know," she said, "*we're* supposed to be the healers around here." Behind her, Varpu laughed.

She paused for a moment.

"Joking aside," she continued, "we almost lost the Healing when you joined in. Not because you did any part of it *wrong*, simply because it was so unexpected. I have not the very least idea where you got that seventh part. It was completely new to us. But *powerful*. That is why I immediately called in Marja and Vallaïnen. To be sure we had enough power.

"With you joining in as well, that made it a *seven*-part Heal, which is... almost unheard of. It was... *much* more powerful than a four-part or even a six, the most we normally ever try to do, but also more *demanding* than we had prepared for. Even with the extra energy from Marja and Vallaïnen.

52

"I do not know all that you sang. You even look more youthful in some ways, more hearty, *already*. Not that we did not expect that to happen—but not this soon.

"But there is an obvious question I cannot keep from asking." Everyone else had gathered around and was paying attention now. Her expression and her tone were intent.

"We all *know* that you are untrained, Alrekr. *How did you know what to sing?*"

I looked at her, trying to formulate an answer.

"The part you sang was not even one I have ever heard," she went on. "It was as though you made up your own part. But *how*, with no Healer training?"

"I don't really know," I answered slowly. "I—oh gods, it *hurt*, it **hurt so much**, Kata." I could feel my eyes were wet again. "Worse than anything I can remember." I saw her bite her lip. She reached out and took my right hand in both of hers. Standing beside me, Liisa put her hand on my shoulder, and I took hold of it thankfully with my other hand.

"I *tried*, but I didn't think I could keep from screaming any longer. In fact... I think I did."

"You did, Alrekr," Liisa agreed, quietly. There was no judgment in her tone. Kata nodded agreement. "There is a reason we try not to do Healings this drastic with the patient awake and aware. When we can, we sing our patients to sleep before we begin. Sleep is so much kinder."

A line from a Renaissance song popped unbidden into my mind. But I tried not to let it distract me.

"I didn't think I could hold the image any longer if I didn't do *something*," I continued. "But... there was... music. Song. *Wonderful* singing." I looked around the circle of Healers. "Your voices are amazing together. Incredible. I've never heard anything like it. Even if I couldn't understand a word.

"But it felt as though there was a harmony, a counterpoint, missi... well, no, not *missing*— not in the sense that there was a *gap*— but, I could feel there was *room* for another part that nobody was singing. A place for another part that was *waiting* to be sung." I fumbled for a way to explain what I meant.

53

"A famous sculptor of my world was once asked how he produced such flawless sculptures. 'To sculpt a horse,' he said, 'I simply start with the stone, and then I chisel away everything that does not look like a horse.'"

Raimo nodded thoughtfully.

"So," I went on, "I was surrounded by song, that had an... empty space in it that *wanted* to be filled. And—I had to do *something*, or lose my focus and lose it all. I could... *feel*... that extra part pushing at me. It *wanted* to get out, *wanted* to be sung. And the only way I could think of to keep from screaming, from losing my image of myself, was to sing it. So I *sang*. There was nothing else I could do."

"Do you understand the words you were singing?" Varpu asked.

"No," I said. "But somehow, I don't know *how*, I... knew what they needed to *sound like* to fit in."

There was a long silence as the six Healers all exchanged looks.

"There is no further doubt in my mind," Kata declared, releasing my hand for the moment and sitting back. "You are *at the very least* of Adept-level strength, and most likely more. You *must* be properly trained, as soon as it can be done.

"But that is for another day. How do you feel? Now?"

"Utterly exhausted," I admitted honestly. "Wrung out like a dish towel. But..."

I looked down.

"My feet are whole, and they do not hurt. And my knees do not hurt." I straightened my legs out in front of me. "Even the scars are gone." I felt the top of my right thigh, under the towel. "The scar where they took the vein graft—that is gone, as well. My *lower back* does not hurt. And..."

Something more felt different, but I could not put my finger on it. I looked around the room, noticing little details I had not before.

"My vision seems sharper," I said. "Maybe better than it's ever been."

That still wasn't it. There was still something else. My belly was flatter, I realized. I didn't have the beginnings of a paunch any more. But that wasn't it either. For the moment, I gave up trying to identify it.

"I feel **good**," I concluded. "Better than I've felt in a long time. But tired. *So very* tired."

"That comes as no surprise," Raimo replied. "There was power in your song such as I have rarely heard. You used a great deal of power this day."

"You should try not to do that too often, yet," Liisa advised me gently. "You could damage yourself."

For some reason I could not put into words, that struck me as funny. I could not help myself. I chuckled, then I giggled, then I burst out laughing. Then Varpu joined in, and next Raimo failed to suppress a grin, then Kata and Liisa joined in, and suddenly we were all laughing uproariously, and happily. On an impulse, I reached out my left arm and slipped it around Liisa's slender waist. She inched a little closer. Kata saw, and smiled.

After a little while, we ran down.

"Today," Raimo declared, "I have seen a wonder. An untrained Healer whose song holds as much power as any of ours, singing new words that none of us even knows, to heal *himself*."

Vallaïnen nodded.

"I am very glad it went so well," he said. "It could have gone so terribly badly."

I felt kind of sheepish.

"It wasn't anything I intended to do," I said apologetically. "I... I just... *couldn't **NOT** do it*."

"It does raise many questions," Vallaïnen replied, nodding solemnly. "I have been a Healer for many years. You say you did not understand the words that you were singing. But you were singing in the language of healing—admittedly, your pronunciation needs work—and you used a number of words that even *I* do not know. *And yet,* I know that they *were* actual words, with true meaning."

"How is that even possible?" I wondered aloud. "I mean, I'm having enough trouble with the idea of singing in a language I don't know in the first place, let alone introducing *new words* in it without knowing what they are."

"The languages of power are as they are and must be, because they are just that," Raimo interjected. "They are power shaped into voice. The word and its meaning are the same. The meaning *is* the word."

I suddenly found Moorcock's *Chant of the Black Sword* running through my head, but did not interrupt. I had the strangest feeling that it might be unwise, here, to casually speak it aloud. Or *any* words supposed to hold power, if song and chanting and the like held power here. And *certainly* not anything about Rings of Power.

"All of the words of all of the languages of power had to be found, once," Raimo continued. "Our oldest legends say that Ilmarinen sang the bowl of the sky into being. Did the words he sang mean anything before there was a sky? Did the words exist until he sang them? Was there such a thing as *sky* before he sang it into being?

"It is a deep question, how you knew to sing the words that you sang, in a language that you do not know. But I am equally interested to know what the words that are new to us *mean*.

"This is of course a question which you cannot yet answer, because you do not yet know what *any* of them mean."

There were nods all around.

"But I can say this much," he continued, his tone suddenly strange, looking piercingly at me. "The words that you sang shaped you into what you are meant to be."

There came a tap at the door. Marja went to answer it. It turned out to be fresh, clean bed-linen. There was also a fresh basket of wash towels, and a fresh shirt for me. Marja and Raimo saw to the bed, while Liisa helped me stand, then stood by for support while Kata and Varpu washed me down *again*. It didn't escape me that there was a little red on the towels, but it was not bright fresh blood, it was clearly spots that had gotten missed earlier. When they were done, Kata slipped the shirt over my head. This one was dark green. It only took a few minutes, but I was glad to sit back down again.

"I don't know about anyone else," I ventured, "but I am hungry. Perhaps we could send for food...?"

Vallaïnen looked around the room.

"I too am in need of food," he agreed, "but there are seven of us, and I see only at most places for five to sit, without resorting to awkward measures, and in any case seven will not fit around that table. Perhaps it is time for the rest of us to take our leave for now." Marja nodded agreement.

"Indeed," Raimo said to me. "You need peace and rest now, as much as food."

Varpu turned for a moment to me as the other healers began to file out.

"Do you happen to know the other person who was brought in at the same time as you were?" she asked.

I hesitated. A sudden chill shot through me. I didn't see the sharp look Kata shot her way.

"I have no idea," I said, after a long moment. "I was unconscious when I was brought in. I don't know who else might have arrived at the same time. And I remember... almost nothing of how I even came here."

She paused, then flashed that smile again.

"No matter," she replied. "It was a chance thought, no more." Then she turned to go. But now there was an uneasy feeling of foreboding in my mind, that came from I knew not where.

5: Revelations

We sent for food, but in truth I paid little attention to what it was, except that I recall it included more of the brightly colored pods. I was... distracted. We ate quietly, all three of us nearly exhausted, and me with doubts and fears haunting my thoughts and stilling my tongue.

"There is something on your mind, Alrekr," Kata said, eventually.

"Yes," I admitted slowly. "But I don't really want to think about it."

"Is it something we can help with?" Liisa asked.

I hesitated for a long time.

"I don't know," I said at last. "It's... something Varpu said. Someone else brought in the same time as me."

"Yes," Kata replied, somewhat guardedly. "There was another. Brought in at the same time, found in the same place. She was not as badly injured as you were. We *presume* she arrived here in the same manner you did."

I swallowed. No, no, **no**, I begged in my head. ***Please, no.***

"Someone... who might have come from the same place I did?" I asked, afraid of the answer.

"It seems... possible," Kata agreed. "But she has shown no trace of Talent. Though there is... *something* there. Some... power—or *potential* for power—that we have not yet identified."

My tongue dried up in my mouth.

"I can think of only one person who—*might have* come here from the same place, at the same time, in the same way," I said. *"And **I DO NOT WANT HER TO BE HERE!!!**"*

I hadn't meant to say that part. The intensity of the feeling caught me unaware. I had spoken more vehemently than I had meant to. It just ran away with me.

Kata and Liisa looked at each other. I realized my hands were shaking. Liisa stood up, took two steps towards me, and put her hands on my shoulders, as Kata reached out, took my hands and held them tightly.

"There are reasons we have said nothing until now," Kata told me softly. "Reasons why we have kept the two of you apart. We... were uncertain when to raise the subject. There is something that is—*not right* about her. Something... twisted. She is not a pleasant person— rude, demanding, self-absorbed. But there is something *beyond* that. Something that none of us have been able to pin down. Something that I feel I *should* recognize, but cannot.

"Varpu should not have said what she did, but she is not to blame. I had not shared my reservations with her. Please do not hold it against her."

I shook my head.

"I wouldn't think of it," I promised. "I cannot find it in me to believe Varpu could have meant any harm. She is too nice, too kind, a person."

Kata smiled.

"You judge her well," she replied.

"We will not be able to keep you and... the other apart forever," Liisa said from behind me. "Unless we send one or the other of you away from here, and we do not wish to do that. Yet. Not until we know—or before you are fully recovered. But do not worry about it now, or tonight. Rest and recover your strength."

She moved her hands and began to gently rub my temples, humming a low, wordless, almost tuneless... I didn't know what it was. But it eased me. I felt a sense of deep calm settle upon me.

"That feels good," I heard myself say. "Don't stop."

Kata smiled.

"I think we are done healing your body," she told me. "I confess I did not *expect* we would do all that remained, today. There may be minor things that can still be done, as the moment suggests, but all of the major remaining things—*all*—in *one working*. It was completely unexpected. There will be much talk about this... as there will about a healing of seven parts. *Seven.*

"Now the healing of your mind remains, after we build up your strength and your energy. We had hoped to heal it before burdening it again.

"Which reminds me that there is one more thing we must trouble you with."

She stood, and fetched a bowl. Pieces of metal and... plastic, I

60

remembered the word, lay in it, a strange mixture of smooth curves and sharp angles. They were bloody, and blood had drained off them and congealed in the bottom of the bowl. I drew in my breath sharply.

"What do you wish done with these?" she asked gently.

I shuddered.

"Please dest— No. Wait," I said, biting back my initial impulse to be rid of them forever. I thought for a moment.

"Is there anyone who might wish to study the materials of which they are made? This kind of steel resists rusting. A careful blend of other metals added to the iron in precise amounts. And the other material has... many uses, if used with caution and discretion. My world used it unwisely and to excess, even when it was inferior, simply because it was cheap."

Kata nodded.

"I will see that they are sent to the Collegium," she said. "They need no longer be a concern of yours. They can go on the first caravan after the spring rains, when the roads have dried."

"Thank you *so much*, Kata," I said fervently.

She placed the bowl outside the door and rang for a page. One must have been nearby, for I heard footsteps almost before the tinkling echoes of the bell had faded.

"Have these items sent to the Collegium on the next caravan," I heard Kata tell the page. "Mark them as a gift from the Newfound, Járnhandr, for study."

"At once, Healer," the page replied. It was a girl this time, one whose voice I did not know. Kata closed the door and returned.

I hadn't really noticed that Liisa's humming had stopped.

"Are you feeling better?" she asked me.

"I believe I am, somewhat," I replied. I let out a long, slow breath. "Thank you, Liisa."

"Always," Liisa replied. The single word felt freighted with meaning... but I wasn't sure exactly *what* that additional meaning was.

Outside, the sky was darkening. Not merely sunset, but clouds were rushing in. Kata went to the balcony and made certain that the

61

doors were tightly closed and latched.

"There will be a storm tonight," she remarked.

"Are you ready to return to your bed?" Liisa asked. "We will sit with you for a time, I think."

"I would enjoy that very much," I replied.

Liisa helped me stand, and followed beside me as I walked over to the bed. I felt more steady already. I pulled the shirt up so that I did not sit on it, then sat down on the freshly made bed. I went to take the shirt off, but Liisa reached for it at the same time. We both hesitated, then I raised my arms and let her take it off me. My shoulders seemed to move more freely. Her hands brushed my chest more than simple chance would suggest as she lifted the shirt off. I looked up into her eyes, but aside from a slight smile, her expression revealed little. There were depths of meaning in her eyes, but I could not read what it was. Her gaze lingered, though.

Kata, meanwhile, had brought a chair over and set it on the other side of the bed. I swung my legs up onto the bed, as Liisa went to fetch one for herself.

Then I just stopped for a moment, looking at my own legs. There were not even any scars. My knees looked smoother, more even. I looked at them again and drew in a deep, shaking breath.

Kata leaned forward, concerned, as Liisa returned with a chair and sat down.

"Is something wrong?" she asked.

"No," I said. "I just... When I was building my mental image of myself as I should be, a part of it was, 'The scars will be gone.' I suppose I didn't really specify WHAT scars. But somehow I did not *expect* to find the burn scars gone as well." I raised my hands and looked at the backs of my hands. There, too, the skin was clean and new. A sudden thought occurred to me, and I lifted my hands to my head, felt my scalp through the hair. My scalp felt... smooth, and I could feel no flaking, no scarring.

"You were burned, as well?" Liisa asked.

"When I was a very small child, before I could walk," I replied. "The fire started in my bedroom. My elder sister once said that she remembered me crawling out of a wall of flames. But she would have been scarcely three years old herself, and has denied it since, so I... do not know whether that part is true or not."

Kata and Liisa exchanged looks.

"Simply because she was young, does not mean the memory is not true," Kata said softly.

"I know," I replied. I paused, then added hesitantly, "Other children tormented me because of the scars."

"I am sorry," Kata said sincerely. "I can tell that it hurt you. But it did not break you."

"No," I replied. "That takes more. A man of my world named Nietzsche once said, 'That which does not destroy us makes us stronger.'"

She looked soberly at me.

"That is a cruel way to make someone strong," she replied quietly, "to try to break them." I could not disagree.

"I have become so used to the scars," I said. "It may be... it may take some time to adjust."

"You will have all the time you need," Liisa told me.

She leaned close and rested her hands on my knee, then traced her fingers where the scar at the top of my right thigh had been. I no longer felt at all self-conscious about having them touch and examine my body. She slid her hand up onto my belly, and I was surprised how much the skin moved.

"You used a lot of reserves this day," she commented. "Just as we told you that you would. Perhaps more even than we expected. The skin is loose now, but it will tighten and firm. Particularly with a little help from us." Her hand moved down a little lower. "The scars here are also gone, and, I think, the scarring inside. That is good. Being all knotted up there must have been... painful at times."

I nodded silent agreement, trying to ignore the stirring I felt as she touched me there.

Kata, meanwhile was examining my left leg. She lifted my leg slightly, feeling my shin and calf, which looked unfamiliarly normal.

"There is already more strength here," she stated. I looked at my feet, then I pointed both feet down as far as I could, then pulled them up, then rotated them in circles. I flexed my toes, and all ten flexed, then I spread them, and all ten spread. I realized I was weeping about the same time Liisa did.

"Alrekr?" she asked, concerned, and placed her hand on my chest. "Are you alright?" Kata was looking at me too.

"I am HAPPY, Liisa," I answered, tears running down my face. "I feel whole again. Whole as I have not felt in... far too many years. Far too many years of *being* **broken**. So much life I missed. It is... a lot to take in. This is going to take time to get used to."

I took hold of her hand and squeezed it, and she squeezed back. Her smile lit up her face. I reached out my other hand towards Kata, and she put hers in it. She, too, was smiling at me.

We sat like that for a while. Then I reluctantly let go of their hands, adjusted my position and lay back. Liisa pulled the bedding up, as Kata moved her chair a few feet towards the head of the bed. Then we all joined hands again.

After a little while, Kata opened her mouth just slightly, and began the same wordless... crooning?... that Liisa had done earlier. A moment later, Liisa joined in, not at the same pitch, but harmonizing with it. I could now see that it was not the humming I had thought it, but a low note sung softly in their throats.

Their voices seemed to merge. I did not feel the rush of power that I had when they had chanted energy into me, I sensed only the faintest trickle of power in it, but it was restful and calming, and filled me with a sense of peace and safety. It felt as though it was soothing something beyond my physical body. I could easily meditate to this, I thought. I wondered whether I could learn it myself.

We rested there, for a long, timeless time. I just kept looking back and forth between the two of them, even after they stopped the throatsong. That was a good word for it, I decided. Throatsong.

Something must have showed in my face.

"What are you thinking, Alrekr?" Kata asked me softly.

I hesitated a moment, gathering my thoughts.

"I am thinking," I replied, looking first at Kata, then at Liisa, then at Kata again, "about how impossibly fortunate I am, here in this place of wonders, to have two such wonderful and beautiful women taking care of me. Even above and beyond having old injuries I had learned to live with... *undone* in ways I never thought possible."

Neither of them said anything in reply, but their smiles both deepened, and Kata lowered her eyes for a moment, then looked steadily straight back in my eyes.

Outside, the storm had begun, rain drumming on the windows. Occasionally a flash of lightning lit the night, followed by rolling cascades of thunder.

Some time after that, I fell asleep, our hands still linked.

6: Confronting The Past

In the middle of the night, I woke up, tense and sweating, my heart pounding. In my head, memories I didn't want were replaying. That voice. Belittling, blaming, accusing, changing attacks faster than I could respond, deliberately keeping me off balance, taking away my voice, tormenting me, twisting anything I said into a weapon to attack me with.

"No, no, no, no, no, no," I found myself repeating, like a mantra. "*STOP* it. Get out of my head. *Leave me alone.*"

I got out of bed, pacing up and down trying to calm myself. Tried to steady my breathing. It wasn't working. I was shaking, damp with cold sweat, my heart pounding. I opened the doors and went out onto the balcony in the rain. I looked down at the forests rolling down to the plain, looked up at where one of the three moons was dimly visible through a break in the clouds, trying to distract myself, trying to break away from the unwanted memories.

"*In mercy's name,*" I cried out under the unhearing sky, "*LEAVE ME ALONE!*" But the sky, of course, did not answer. I had never expected it to. But I couldn't hold the words in. Even if nobody heard, somehow I needed to make the plea. It was *myself* I was begging, more than it was the sky or the world. I knew that, at some level. Yet that knowledge didn't help.

I stood there shaking for long minutes in the rain, before I went back inside. This was a new *world*. Surely this anxiety, this dread, wasn't supposed to follow me here. I thought I had escaped this. Adrenaline prickled on my skin.

There came a quiet knock at the door. After a moment, I went to answer it.

"Járnhandr. Is all well?" It was Raimo. "I was passing by and heard... something." He looked hard at me. "You appear—unsettled."

I took a deep breath.

"I'm sorry," I apologized. "Was I disturbing people?"

Raimo shook his head.

"Not at all," he replied. "The rooms on either side of yours are empty, and the walls and floors are thick. I simply chanced to be passing. But you sounded distressed. And you clearly *look* distressed."

I gestured him in, and collapsed into a chair, still shaking.

"I woke from a nightmare," I told him. "Memories that I cannot free myself from. Miseries that I thought I had put behind me. Thought myself free of."

Raimo looked at me gravely.

"Do you wish me to wake your Healers?" he asked. "It seems you are in need of their help."

"No," I said, shaking my head. "Not in the middle of the night. Let them sleep. They need to rest as well. Their sleep should not be disturbed because mine is."

Raimo nodded.

"Would it help to talk about the memories?" he asked.

"I don't know," I said hesitantly. "I... I thought..."

I couldn't frame what I wanted to say.

"If you cannot," he continued, "then perhaps I shall just sit with you a while, if you wish it. You do not have to face whatever haunts you this night alone."

I nodded gratefully.

"Thank you, Raimo," I nodded. I took several deep, slow breaths, trying to steady my breathing. Gradually the shaking faded. I rested my head in my hands.

"What sort of memories are these that trouble you?" Raimo asked after a little while. "If I do not intrude by asking."

I sighed.

"Past... cruelties," I replied. "Things I... never seemed able to find a way to defend myself against. Someone from my... past world. My past life."

Raimo nodded understandingly.

"That world is your *past*," he said. "This one is your **now**. Do not forget that. Live in your *now*. Not in your past."

I nodded understanding. I knew it was easier to say than to do, but... hearing it from a source outside myself helped.

I felt wrung out... but I was starting to calm down a little as the immediacy of the flashback faded. All of that was over, I kept telling myself. Over and past and done with. This was a new life. I fought to push away the memories.

"I think I should try to sleep again," I said after a while, when I felt a little calmer. "Thank you for sitting with me. I think the company helped, a little."

"You are of course welcome," Raimo assured me. "I will go now, and leave you to sleep. But in the morning, you should tell your healers what happened. They cannot help you, if they do not know that you are troubled."

I nodded understanding and agreement.

"I will, Raimo," I agreed. "I promise." My voice was still unsteady.

"Sleep well, Járnhandr," he told me. "Rest." And then he left, and I went back to bed.

It took me a long time to fall asleep, and I slept fitfully.

I was still tired when Liisa returned the next morning, accompanied by an assistant bringing breakfast.

"Kata will be along a little later," she told me. So we sat and ate breakfast together.

"Raimo mentioned that you might want to talk to me," she said, after a little while.

"Yes," I agreed. "I promised him I would." But I ate another piece of fruit, and another soft, warm bread roll first, and had a few more swallows of juice.

I was stalling, I realized. I took a deep breath.

"I woke up in the middle of the night from a nightmare," I said at last. "A... memory come back to haunt me."

Liisa looked at me and nodded slowly.

"Kata and I have both seen that you have many memories that wound you," she said. "Memories tied into scars in your soul. But we did not pry into them. We did not have your permission to look deeply into your mind. Though some of your memories color even your surface thoughts, and we could not help but notice them.

"Is this memory... something that you wish to talk about now?"

69

"It's... a little too fresh, a little too raw, at this moment," I said. Anxiety swelled, my chest tightened, my voice shook.

Liisa put her hand gently on my arm.

"You do understand that sometimes that is the best time, yes?" she said. I nodded.

"Yes," I answered, trying to keep my voice steady. " I'm... not sure I *can* right now, though."

"Then at least," she offered, "allow me to do something to ease your mind, to settle you, to put you in better balance to deal with your memories."

I nodded grateful assent.

The 'settling' technique consisted of me sitting with my eyes closed while Liisa sat facing me, close in front of me, her fingers lightly resting on my temples, chanting softly under her breath. It felt... odd, but restful, as though choppy water was calming and becoming smooth. We did it for what I estimated between fifteen and twenty minutes, then we took a break, and roughly at the next hour we repeated it again. I could feel that it was helping.

Kata came in during the second session, and she took the third. In between, Liisa briefed Kata quickly about my flashback.

"Do you have to do this for many people?" I asked Liisa. "It must take a great deal of time, surely."

"Only occasionally," Liisa told me. "From time to time others need it, but we try never to let anyone get—so far out of balance. When so much harm has been done it takes a lot of work to return the mind and spirit to what they should be.

"And there is... something deep within you that is fighting us, or resisting, as though it is unwilling to be healed. I do not yet understand what. Though..."

She stopped and shook her head.

"Is there...?" I began. But she lifted a hand to stop me.

"No. Please, do not concern yourself at the moment. It... is a question for another time. Let us restore your core as much as we can to its proper balance first." She paused. "Would you willingly begin a fight while off-balance?"

I wanted to ask more, but I pushed the question back. I could see the sense in that.

"I… trust your judgment, Liisa," I told her, after a moment.

"Thank you, Alrekr," she replied, with a smile.

"But the two of you are spending so much time on me. Does it not take away from your other responsibilities? Are you not needed elsewhere? Not that I mean to sound ungrateful, it just… seems unfair."

"There is nothing unfair about it," Liisa replied. "There are between six and seven hundred people at Highwatch, and a dozen Healers. A normal settlement this size would have one or two Healers, perhaps three—and yes, they would be kept busy. We have this many here for several reasons, all of which come down to why Highwatch is here in the first place. We will *all* be elbows deep in work, should something come out of the passes through the Spine. If there is a major incursion, all the dozen of us may not be enough.

"But in the meantime… we can easily spare the time. There are more than enough of us to handle the ordinary work load. And you *need* this healing."

She paused, and looked directly at me.

"And the honest truth is," she continued, "we both enjoy spending our time on you. *With* you. You are different, new to us. We see glimpses in you of what we think you may be able to become. And… we both like what we see."

Then she hesitated.

"Your past life was—not happy, was it?"

I thought for a long moment before answering.

"No, it was not," I replied at last. "But… if you don't mind, I would prefer not to talk too much about it at the moment. To talk about it, I have to think about it. And *thinking* about it sends me into dark moods. There are too many bad memories. I am… trying to move on from it. Put it behind me."

Liisa looked at me for a long moment, her eyes serious.

"I can understand that, Alrekr," she said. "Moving on from a hurtful life experience is good. But do not make the mistake of hiding from it. Sooner or later, you will have to address it and deal with it, before you can truly be free of it. Your nightmares are the proof of this. I *feel* how much you hurt inside. Sooner or later, that pain will have to come out. You cannot release it, become free of it, without first letting it loose."

I nodded. I understood. I knew she was right, and I told her so. But still... I wasn't looking forward to it. Not at all. I knew it was going to be hard. But there would be time. There would be lots of time.

As the next days passed, we worked on restoring my strength and building my reserves back. Between the healing working, and unexpectedly pouring so much into it myself, I had utterly exhausted myself, and the nightmares weren't helping. Talking about the nightmares helped, and it inevitably meant talking about my past, too. I gradually came to accept that I *could* talk to Kata and Liisa about my past, and they would hear what I actually *said*, without preconceptions, and not judge me for what I felt were my shortcomings, my failures. I could talk to them about what kind of person I wanted to be, tried to be, without any fear of being criticized for what I was *not* and could not be. It was... refreshing. Freeing.

It was five or six days later that we adjudged me physically recovered enough from the healing to get out and about again. As my recuperation continued, I had by now been given some additional clothes, a couple of pairs of loose-fitting breeches, a few more extra shirts, a hip-length sleeveless tunic of dark blue, a slightly longer one in green with tied-on sleeves, a pair of short boots that more or less fit, and a pair of tall sandals that fit somewhat better. Kata had promised me that when I was more recovered and my body had finished adjusting, we would see to having some clothes tailored to fit me properly, and have a cobbler make me some properly fitting footwear. We had already once had to swap out the shirts I had been given for broader ones as my shoulders began to fill out again. It was strange to be able to *feel* my body changing literally from day to day, returning to what I had once been... and more.

We started out by going out onto the upper wall and walking all the way around Highwatch atop the wall. The view to the northwest was a complete contrast to the view from the window of my room. An arc of towering mountains climbed toward the sky beyond the forest that surrounded the keep, filling nearly half the horizon.

"This is why it is called Highwatch," Kata told me. "It watches over the two passes, there, and there," pointing with her entire hand. Then she pointed in a slightly different direction amidst the jagged peaks. "And you were found somewhere in that area."

I looked where she pointed. I was struck suddenly by how sharply the mountains seemed to leap out at me. Interesting. My vision had been good, once, but it had never been *THIS* good. I could see a narrow, jagged cleft above the tree line. Above even that, I caught motion in the sky. Wings?

"Are there birds up in those mountains?" I asked. "*Big* ones?"

"There are lammergeiers in the nearer mountains," Liisa replied. "Their wings span twice the reach of a tall man's arms. Further in, among the higher peaks, there are wyverns, and even dragons."

"Dragons?" I replied, startled. "There are **dragons** here?"

"Are there none on your world?" Liisa asked.

"Oh, there are lots and lots of *myths and legends*," I replied. "Almost every culture on... my world, including ones that have been isolated for—as best we know—as much as thirty thousand years, has *myths* of dragons or dragon-like creatures. We have entire *bestiaries* of fanciful mythical beasts, some spawned from half-understood descriptions, others entirely made up. But nobody living has ever seen a dragon or found any fossil remains that could plausibly be one. Our scholars generally believe the legends of dragons to spring from misunderstood fossilized remains of giant extinct predators. They were once thought to be reptiles, but we have more recently learned that they were warm-blooded and may have had plumage like birds. In fact, it is currently believed that birds are their distant descendants."

"Well," Liisa told me, looking very serious, "I can assure you that our dragons are very much not mythical. We live in an uneasy peace with them, negotiated more than six hundred years ago."

"Will wonders never cease," I mused to myself. Then, aloud, "Truly your Auringon Valaista Maata is a place of wonders. I hope I *never* find an end to them."

Liisa looked back at me with a slight frown.

"You may find that not all of the differences between our world and yours are wonders," she told me seriously. "The dragons were terrors for a time, until we reached a settlement of our differences with them. And there are other creatures with whom no form of accommodation has ever been possible. Trolls are an ongoing problem, for instance, near to the mountains. And there are darker, fouler things. Gaunts. There are *horrors* in the dark places of the world. Some of them are why Highwatch guards these passes. And

73

part of why we do not venture into the Spine of the World."

After our circuit of the wall, we descended by a different route and went back inside through one of the great halls, and thence by a circuitous route back to my room. By then I was ready to rest, so we sat for the remainder of the afternoon out on the balcony while my Healers helped to build me up, and eased pains I was no longer consciously aware that I had.

And yes... we kept talking about my past. Not too much at one time. Not trying to unravel the whole excruciating tapestry at one go. Just seeking, little by little, to untie a single knot, or two. More than that was too painful to handle at one sitting. We took slow step, by slow, careful step, as my trust in my Healers grew. We talked about the mind games, the belittling, the slurs, the traps, the spite, about becoming afraid to speak lest my words be weaponized against me or reveal a hitherto unexploited weakness. Sometimes with Kata, sometimes with Liisa, more often both at once. They listened, and they guided me to see how I had been manipulated into doubting myself. I spoke haltingly, hesitantly, about the times I resorted to self-harm because the physical pain was easier to comprehend and deal with than the mental torment.

We made our walks a daily routine, too, as strength returned to me and my stamina began to recover. Sometimes we went up atop the wall, when the weather was good. Sometimes, when it was bad, we stayed to the hallways within the walls. And then when we came back, we talked. Physical therapy, followed by emotional therapy. A little at a time. A little each day, day by day, week by week. Whittling away at the pain. Cleaning out and closing the old, buried, festered wounds, one by one. They were without a doubt the best therapists I had ever had, because unlike any previous therapy I had ever had, they were not limited to teaching me ways to try to live with or shut away painful memories. The healing Talents of the Sunlit Land gave them the ability to actually *take away* the pain from the memories, once I was in touch with them. Even sometimes pain that I was not consciously aware of.

We kept on working at those wounds day after day, week after week, making sure we fit in sessions every day. With all three of us, when their schedules permitted. Sometimes that meant going late into the evening. But we persisted. Kata and Liisa were kind and patient with me. Kata was gentle, but firm, about pointing out where I had fallen into self-destructive patterns of thinking, while Liisa had an amazing ability to find and softly tease loose my tangled feedback-loops of pain and self-doubt.

As time went by I found myself growing increasingly close to, attached to, these two lovely Healers, *my* Healers, and while I was eager to be fully whole and myself, I found myself reluctant to think about being declared healed—because I feared it would mean losing their company. Sometimes food was brought to my room, and sometimes we walked to the main dining hall and ate at a table there. I wasn't sure which I preferred. It was good to go to the hall and see other people. But at the same time, it was good to have their company to myself, in a safe place of peace and restful quiet.

I wasn't really keeping track of the passage of weeks. Or was it months? But one day, as we were on our way to that very hall, everything suddenly went completely to hell. As we passed through a side ante-room of the hall, I glimpsed motion out of the corner of my eye. There was a cluster of people in the corner of the room, and one stood up as we crossed the back of the room headed for the far door.

"So that's why they've been keeping us apart," said a voice I knew far too well, in acid, cutting tones. "To hide that you're cheating on me again."

I turned to look, and there she was. Her voice dripped venom. I could feel my heart suddenly racing.

"How did you set all this up?" she accused. "I *know* it's somehow all *your* doing."

"What...? I haven't done..." I began to protest. "Do you think *all this* is something I *even could* do?" But she talked over me. It was the usual tirade. Everything was my fault, it was all to spite her, and so on.

"I **DIDN'T**—"

"Don't *lie to me*. Of *course* you did." A barrage of accusation after accusation. My head spun. My vision narrowed. The bottom fell out of the world. I remembered what Varpu had said. The other person found with me. It *was* her. Somehow she had been drawn here with me.

Liisa was looking at me, concerned. Kata was looking at the thin-faced blonde woman, her brow furrowing. The young Healer accompanying the woman was staring at her in sudden shock. The air in the room seemed suddenly close, almost thick. The Highwatch guard had taken her arm and was holding her back from crossing the room. She struggled to pull free, her face cold, still accusing, still...

Memories of past tirades and attacks flooded into my mind... and something else, something *new*, something cold, something filled now with hate and *hunger*. My head spun. I stumbled against the wall, found myself against a stone column, shaking. Please, not this. She CAN'T be here. She **CAN'T**. I *escaped* this!

I stifled a sob. My vision went dark. An intention that was not consciously mine drew my head back, went to slam it forward against the stone, to drive sense away, anything to make that voice GO AWAY —

"BE SILENT!!!"

Kata's voice rang like a lash, almost crackling with raw power. There was an electric feeling in the air for a moment. The cutting voice was suddenly stilled, silenced in mid-tirade. The... *depth* of the blackness assailing me seemed to diminish slightly... but something still had savage teeth in my soul. At the same time, I felt gentle hands against my head, holding me firmly back from the stone. I fought my eyes open, almost overcome by vertigo. Liisa had slipped into the small space between me and the column and was cupping my face in her hands.

"*No*, Alrekr, *no*," she told me urgently. "Do *not* let yourself be driven to harm yourself in this way. *Please.*"

Kata took my arm, and she and Liisa urged me quickly into a nearby chair.

"**Sit**," Kata said urgently. I was torn between compliance and the desperate need to escape whatever was tearing at me. She urged me again.

"Alrekr. **Sit**. I am sorry. I **must** look, see, things in your mind, your soul that we have not intruded into when we have talked before now. It is *important. Now.*"

I fell into the chair, dizzy from the assault in my head, raised my hands to my face, then reached blindly for... anything. Any comfort. After a moment I felt hands take mine. I thought they were Liisa's. Then Kata's hands, I thought, enfolded my face.

I forced my eyes open. Kata was looking at me from less than a foot away. I could not see her clearly. It was as though I looked at her from underwater.

"I am sorry," she said again, urgently, her voice seeming to come from a distance. "I **KNEW** there was something *wrong* about her. I *must* see for myself. I *know* she is hurting you—but there is more than that. I must know what she is doing to you. There are signs, things I must see— Look into my eyes and *let me in*. Please, Alrekr. **QUICKLY.**"

Looking into her eyes was not hard at all, even though she was obviously angry. I tried my best, through the... the dread, the echoes, the sudden hopelessness, to let her in. Something was still tearing at me, ripping at me, inside. Something cold and relentless and... *hungry*. Something new to me, something terrible that I had never felt before. I felt utterly helpless.

Kata looked hard into my eyes, and I somehow *felt* her presence in my mind. It was a warm, gentle, but firm presence, even though I sensed that she was prioritizing urgency over delicacy. I felt... a little stronger, somehow, just for having her there, as though her mere presence deflected a little of the black despair. I could feel her looking into memories I did not want to even *have* but could not free myself from, memories that were wrapped around in wounds that had never healed. But I could feel myself fading, falling. I couldn't breathe. I felt as though I was suffocating. I think I felt my heart stumble.

For a long moment, she looked through my mind, skimming past secret memories, including the ones even I tried to hide from because I could not bear them. But I didn't think the *memories* were what she was actually looking for. I *felt* her attention find and *settle on* the tearing, the rending inside me.

There was a moment of stillness. Then Kata released my head, straightened up, her fists clenched, her face white with fury. She spun around, staring at the other woman for a moment, before she raised her head and screamed in unbridled rage.

"SIELUNJUOJA!!!" she shouted as she stalked across the room. "Why did I not **see** it? *ABOMINATION!*"

Moments later, Kata was standing directly in front of the blonde woman. Through blurred eyes, I could see the other woman's face working as she tried to speak, but she was unable to break through Kata's command. The woman's eyes were filled with spite and cold hate and... relentless hunger. I thought I could see a strange light growing in her eyes. She was struggling against the guard, but his grip

77

on her arms was as firm as iron, and she could not break away—yet it seemed he was having a harder time holding onto her. As though she gained strength as I weakened.

"*Abomination*," Kata spat again, angrily, as she reached out with her right hand and drew the long dagger from the Highwatch guard's belt. The guard was holding both of the woman's arms now, trying to hang onto her. "You **WILL NOT TAKE HIM.**"

Then in a single motion, she drove the dagger up under the blonde woman's ribs and straight into her heart. The woman's eyes widened in shock, her mouth worked one last time in a silent gasp. For a long moment she struggled, clung on to life as the gleam in her eyes slowly dimmed—I felt one last, clawing **RIP** within me, as though something slashed at my soul—and then she sagged limply. The guard held onto her for a moment longer, then dropped her in a huddled pile and stepped back. Kata handed him back his dagger. He bent down to clean it on the dead woman's clothing before putting it away.

I did not really understand what had just happened—I had just seen gentle, kind Kata kill someone, right in front of me—but suddenly a crushing weight was gone from my mind, and the *tearing* feeling inside me stopped. I doubled over, gasping, retching until it felt I would turn myself inside out, then forced myself back upright enough to draw in a deep, shuddering breath. My vision started to slowly clear, but spots still swam in front of my eyes. It felt as though strength was pouring out of me. But I... felt my heartbeat start to steady.

For a long moment there was silence. Then the other healer spoke, nervously.

"I am *so sorry*, Honored," she said. "I did not know she was—"

"Of *course* you didn't, Vilja," Kata replied, her voice still tense. "Don't blame yourself. *None* of us knew. But I **should** have. You have never seen a sielunjuoja before—you *could not* have known—and we were not *expecting* one. It is no fault of yours that you were assigned to... this duty. I did not see it *myself* until she attacked him. And even **then** I still was not certain, until I saw the proof in his mind, his soul."

She turned and walked back over to Liisa and I, and knelt in front of me where I sat.

78

"I am **so *sorry***, Alrekr," she said gently, sincerely. "We... several of us *felt* that there was something deeply wrong with her, but we did not know what it was. Not until she attacked you." She paused and took a deep breath.

"You knew her, didn't you." It was a statement, not a question. "This is the one who tormented—abused—you in your past."

"Yes," I replied hesitantly, distantly, through what felt like a boulder in my throat. Kata sighed and nodded slowly.

"We... *suspected* this was the case," she admitted. "But we were not sure, and did not want to chance bringing the two of you together to confirm it. We thought that unwise."

"She was..." I couldn't bring myself to say the word. I choked on it. I tried again.

"I was... married to her," I managed.

"Gods above," Kata muttered, aghast. Liisa gasped and clapped a hand to her mouth.

"Did you *know* she was a souldrinker?" Kata asked. The meaning of the unfamiliar word percolated through, this time. Then she paused, frowned.

"...No, of course you didn't," she continued. "How *could* you have? You have said often that there was no *voima* in your world. I do not understand how this can be. Her... *ability*... the *perversion* perhaps did not manifest until she arrived here along with you. Perhaps not until this very day.

"This... the *chance of* something like this... is *why* we were keeping the two of you apart. Until we could learn what was wrong in her. Because you were so deeply hurt, and because... *several* of us could feel there was something... wrong, *twisted*, in her. We suspected there was a connection between you, and feared that letting you meet before you were fully healed and your core properly stable would risk harm to you. This meeting was unplanned, accidental. It was not supposed to happen. But we did not expect her to actually *attack* you. Much less this way. We did not anticipate... *this*.

"Are you **alright**, Alrekr?" There was great concern in her voice. It seemed to come from an immense distance.

"I—"

I did not have the energy to speak. Words died in my throat. There was a roaring in my ears, and my vision was going dark.

Liisa's arms enfolded me. Then she flinched.

"The marriage bond—of course," I heard her say urgently. "He is *dying*. His soul is unraveling." She began a rapid chant, and I felt her begin to pour energy into me. After a moment Kata placed her hands on me as well. She paused for a moment, her face intent, as Liisa raised her chant into song.

"Vilja," she called, "join and help us. *Hurry*. Learn to recognize this." The younger Healer scurried across the room and placed her hands on me as well. After a moment, she gasped, and then she began pouring energy into me too.

"This is how you close the soul wounds, Vilja," Kata told her, after a few moments. "How you knit a torn soul back together. See it, hear it, learn it, and *join*. All three of us is not too many here. We were almost too slow. More would be better... but we three will have to be enough."

Then she echoed a measure or two of Liisa's starting chant and joined the song. I could see Vilja nodding along with it, repeating it under her breath, and then after another repetition aloud, she joined her clear voice to the other two in soft song. The three-way harmony was beautiful. *This* song sounded almost ethereal, as though I was hearing it more with my soul than my ears.

I could feel the blackness starting to recede, the terrible chill and emptiness slowly fading. After a little while, I started to feel a bit more steady, a little less as though my life was running out down a drain. It no longer felt as though it was a race for the three Healers to pour life-energy into me faster than it could drain out. It felt like being woven back together after being ripped apart like an old rag.

After some time I could not measure, I could see more or less clearly again, although I was still dizzy. I felt ragged, but at least mostly whole, and no longer as though I was draining out of myself. A little longer, and then Kata broke off at the end of a measure.

"Enough, for the moment," she said. "The worst is staunched. We will do more later." First Vilja, then Liisa also stopped the song.

"Vilja, you will remember this?" Kata asked. Vilja nodded.

"I think so, Honored," she agreed. "I am fairly sure I have it."

"Good. Let us hope you do not need to use it again. But if you should, now you will know." Vilja nodded again.

"Had she done this to you before?" Liisa asked me gently. I could hear more clearly, now.

"Not—not like—*this*," I choked out. "The... the *abuse*... yes. But it never felt this... this *bad*. Oh **gods**." My head was still spinning. Or the room. I wasn't sure. Perhaps both. I still felt as though I was going to vomit at any moment.

"Like... tripping off a stair, before. When you—miscount the steps. But this was... like falling off a cliff. As though it ripped the bottom out of my soul."

"She *did*, Alrekr," Liisa replied intensely. "It feels like that **because she did**. She came within moments of killing you."

"Kata, you said... soul-drinker?" I asked, still struggling to speak. "Did I understand that right?"

Kata nodded solemnly.

"Sielunjuojat are... well, *used to be* people... who are broken on the inside," she explained. "Their souls are broken in ways that cannot be healed, because they *like* being that way. It is all they know. They enjoy their power, they *feed* on the despair of others. They drain the soul, the will, the hope, from others, to feed on. Especially from the Talented. A Talented is a rich feast to a sielunjuoja. If one can gain a strong personal bond to a person, that person cannot defend themselves. Sielunjuojat can sometimes pretend otherwise, but in the end, they care *only* about themselves.

"And you... you were *married* to her. There *is* no stronger bond. You were *completely* defenseless against her, as long as that bond remained. It is no wonder she was able to take so much from you, so fast. And you, I think, are not the kind to break such a bond lightly.

"Now that her power was fully awakened, the only way to break that link, to stop her from draining *everything* from you, *killing* you, was to kill *her* instead. Quickly."

She looked down. Looked up again, biting her lip. Her eyes were wet.

"I am **so sorry**, Alrekr. Can you *ever* forgive me?"

I fought to regain my voice. Not just to buy time, I reached out weakly and took Kata's hands.

"Kata," I fought out through the huge knot in my throat. "If I understand what you are telling me, you just *saved* me—*again*—in the only way there was."

81

I took a deep, shuddering breath. Then another. Eventually I found my voice again.

"I... When I learned that *she* might somehow be here too, it filled me with dread. I hoped desperately that it wasn't her. If I was the praying type, I would have *prayed* it wasn't her. I thought that somehow, however it happened, I had escaped. I thought myself free of her in this new world, one bright part of... losing everything. I thought I had lost the bad along with the good. I had mostly buried the thought that she might be here. I... when we talked about the abuse... I was thinking about it in the past tense.

"Now I *am* free of her, Kata. I don't know how it is that she followed me here...I don't even know how it is that *I* am here. Did I somehow **bring** her here? Did *I* cause this? Is this *my* fault?" I was shaking from more than just sudden exhaustion. I was terribly afraid that somehow, I had caused this... this *horror*.

"No, Alrekr," Kata assured me. "This is no fault of yours. No blame rests upon you for this. No will of yours brought the sielunjuoja here. But we should have *seen* it. We should have *recognized*."

"Forgiving is not even a question," I went on. "There was a dark stain upon my heart. And *here*... in this room... somehow it became *so much worse*, a cloud of blackness filling my entire world. Drowning me. But you banished it.

"*Thank you*, Kata. From the bottom of my heart. I have a chance... again. To *live*. Without that hidden fear gnawing at me. Without living my life waiting for the next shoe to drop."

Liisa looked at me curiously.

"The next shoe?"

"A metaphor of my... past," I explained. "A man had a neighbor who lived in the room above him in a boarding-house. His neighbor would come home late at night, take his shoes off, and toss them into the corner, against the wall. *Bang, bang.* And then one night he came home and threw only one shoe. And the man downstairs lay there, waiting for the other shoe, and there was no second *bang*. And he was unable to rest, waiting for the *bang* that he knew was coming.

"And eventually he got up, and went upstairs, and knocked on the door and begged, 'Please, throw the second shoe, so that I can sleep.'"

Liisa nodded slowly.

"The learned expectation that something unpleasant is going to come," she said.

"Yes," I agreed. "There was *ALWAYS* another shoe. Sooner or later. *Always.* I lived in dread of the next shoe."

She nodded again, understanding.

"That is no way to live, Alrekr."

Kata still looked uncertain and guilty. I could think of only one way to make it more clear how I felt about the matter. If I dared take the chance. Was I about to offend her?

I freed my hands from hers, gently cupped her beautiful face in my hands instead, leaned forwards a little, and kissed her. The truth was, I'd been wanting to do it for weeks now. Perhaps since that first day on the balcony. Her lips were so soft and sweet.

She did not pull away, and after a moment, she responded, kissed me back. It felt more than just comforting. We held the kiss for a long moment, then I let her go.

"Truly, Kata, *thank you.* I mean it."

Kata smiled, still doubtful, but looking less troubled now. She still did not pull away. I felt immense relief. I had been hoping it would be alright.

"I **mean** it, Kata," I repeated. I lowered my hands.

"Honored?" Vilja asked uncertainly. "What should I do now?"

Kata thought a moment, then stood and stepped back. She gave me a long look before she turned. I could not read what was in her eyes. I desperately hoped I hadn't made a mistake.

"Take a little time for yourself, Vilja," she instructed. "Take a break to get over this. Then return to Mistress Sirkka, when you are ready, and ask for a new assignment."

"Thank you, Honored," the young Healer replied. Then she nodded, and left.

"Liisa," Kata began. Then she looked at me.

"Alrekr, if you would permit it, Liisa needs to see for herself what I have seen in you this day. Will you permit it?"

I looked at Liisa.

83

"I trust both you and Kata with my life," I told her, with feeling, "and now I see my trust was more than justified. *Please*. Come in. Look at anything you need to."

Liisa knelt down before me as Kata had, to put herself on my level. She, too, gazed deeply into my eyes, taking my hands, and I looked into hers. Such lovely brown eyes, I thought. Eyes I could drown in and die happy.

I felt her slip into my mind. I tried to think about opening myself fully to her. I wanted no secrets to be barriers in between me and either her or Kata.

She looked into my eyes for a long time. Her hands tightened. She bit her lip, but did not draw away. I felt her shudder. I could not tell at what. I felt guilt claw at me, and my heart pounded in anxiety. What darkness had she just stumbled across?

Eventually she drew away and stood up. I released her hands reluctantly. She turned toward Kata, looked directly at her, her face tight, and nodded slowly.

"Sielunjuoja," she agreed. "Now that we *know*, the signs are obvious. I... don't know how I didn't see it in the wounds. It is no *wonder* they go so deep. There is so much to heal, *so much damage* to undo. So much, for so *long*. How *DARE* she!"

She turned to me again.

"There is no longer any mystery to me behind your nightmares, Alrekr. Now finally we *know* for certain what—*who*—caused them."

"This is a terrible thing, Alrekr," Kata apologized. "I am sorry that we did not recognize sooner what she had become. I am even more sorry that it all ended this way."

"It was *always* terrible," I said, fighting to keep my voice under control. "I'd sooner have had it end almost any other way. But at least now it's over. I hope." I didn't know what else to say. I felt numb. It was a feeling I was far too used to.

Kata nodded slowly, then walked back across the room to the guard and spoke to him briefly. He nodded agreement. And then we left.

I was weak and unsteady on my feet. Kata and Liisa had to help me stand from the chair and support me from either side, feeding me energy again to help me walk. I felt like a wrung-out dish rag, like a bucket with a hole in the bottom. I could feel the amount of energy my caregivers were feeding into me, and I could feel how fast it was leaking back *out*, and it was scaring me.

"Is there anything that can be done to... *cure* a—a sielunjuoja?" I asked.

"Yes, and no," Kata answered after a few moments. "The... weakness, the harm, the damage, that opens one up to *becoming* one... that, if it is recognized early, before it has manifested, can be healed, if it is found before the person actually surrenders to it and fully becomes a sielunjuoja. Sometimes, if they harm a person by accident, and *reject* it, and seek help, it is not too late. It can still be prevented from blossoming, the damage repaired, the soul made whole again.

"But once a person begins to willingly feed upon others, once they begin to *ENJOY* it, once the person fully *becomes and accepts being* a sielunjuoja—No. Their soul is *broken, twisted,* beyond any possible healing. It has been tried, and failed each time. To willingly embrace it is to become... abomination. They are the **opposite** of Healers. We swear an oath to heal, to save life. Sielunjuojat *harm*, and *steal* life. It is what they **do**. It is what they **are**."

"I *told* you that this world holds horrors as well as wonders, Alrekr," Liisa interjected quietly.

"Once that boundary is crossed—" Kata continued, then broke off suddenly.

"**No**, Alrekr. It is incurable, untreatable. There is no turning back. And it is an automatic death sentence. One of the few we have. Because a sielunjuoja will kill, and kill, and kill, *until* it is killed. *Because it **can**.* Because it *feels* good to them. Because it is how they feed, and their hunger is endless once awakened.

"I am sorry, Alrekr. When we find such an abomination, we **kill** it. There is no other way. It is... the worst, the *foulest* of *níðing* acts imaginable."

She paused.

"Could you... not *tell* what was happening?"

I stopped walking and buried my face in my hands.

85

"I could feel what she was doing to me," I managed to get out. "But..."

"Why did you **stay?**" Liisa broke in.

"Because I promised," I said helplessly. "I gave my word."

"You are bound by it no longer," Kata declared flatly.

"I promised I would stand by her and raise our children," I went on.

"She was *devouring your spirit* one bite at a time!" Liisa retorted angrily. "You owe her *nothing!*"

"And yet, my word bound me," I insisted. "I could *survive* her."

"You *could*," said Kata. "Before. If you call that surviving. But not *now*. Not with her power fully awakened. She would have *killed* you. She **WAS** killing you. She almost *did*. Had we not been there, you would be dead now, your soul consumed."

"Our children needed me there, also," I said.

There was a long, uncomfortable silence.

"Your children are beyond your help now, Alrekr," Kata said quietly. "I am more deeply sorry about that than I can say. But at least they no longer have *this* danger to contend with.

"Do you think that they will be alright?"

"I don't know," I said doubtfully. "I truly don't know. I HOPE so. But she... wounded, damaged them, too. She would throw anyone..." I realized I didn't know how to say that. "She would sacrifice anyone for the sake of vanity." I let out a shuddering breath, almost more a sob.

"I failed them, Kata. I *failed* them."

Kata nodded slowly.

"And that *tears* at you, does it not?" she said gently. Once again, it wasn't really a question at all. "Did you... fully understand what was happening?"

"No," I replied. "Only that it was terrible and unendurable, but my children needed me to protect them. After a time... I didn't have any hope left. Nor the strength to protect them any longer."

"She was already draining you *then*," Liisa said angrily. "Even with only a fraction of her power available to her. Because you *could not*

86

defend yourself against her, and she knew it, whether consciously or not. We have both seen the wounds where she deliberately twisted the knife just to see you bleed. She **wanted to hurt you**, Alrekr. She **chose** to hurt you. Because she *could*."

"I know," I said, miserably, defensively. "But... there comes a time when you feel that you have made so many mistakes, that there is no *point* in trying to escape them, because you will only make another, perhaps worse."

I raised my head and looked at Liisa. I could hear the concern and the anger fighting in her voice. I saw it in her face. I knew the terrible mistakes I had made, knew how contemptibly weak I had been.

"And we *failed to protect you* from her, Alrekr," Liisa said quietly. "From what we *should have seen*."

Now, at last, I heard the guilt in her voice, underlying the anger. And suddenly, in a flash of realization, I understood. They were not angry *at me*. I turned to look at Kata, and now finally understood the emotions I saw on her face as well. They were angry, I realized, *not* because I had—somehow—apparently—inadvertently brought a sielunjuoja here, *not* because a sielunjuoja had followed me here and attacked someone in their presence, but because she had attacked *ME*. Their patient. *That* was why Kata had been *so* furious. It was *personal*. And they were angry at *themselves*, because they had not recognized the danger before it struck.

"No," I said, trying to reassure her. "You *didn't* fail. You didn't *predict* her attack. But when it came, you reacted in time."

I reached out my arms slowly, and in a moment the three of us were in a tight huddle, our arms wrapped around each other.

"Thank you, thank you both so very much," I whispered fervently, trying hard not to break into tears.

"Alrekr," Kata declared firmly, holding me tightly, "*listen* to me. This is our *law*. No person may be bound against their will to the *evil* of another.

"I know that in your world, you married her and promised to stay by her side despite all. But **here** in the Sunlit Land, the moment she took the willing step into abomination, that marriage is *as though it never was*. A *níð* forfeits all rights and all status under the law. A *níð* is no different than any other dangerous beast. In this world, *you were*

87

never married. We do not recognize any such marriage.

"You *are not bound* to what she *chose* to be. You are *FREE*, Alrekr. *FREE*. Do you understand me? You are *FREE*. Free to do as you will." She gazed deeply into my eyes, unflinching.

It ... took a few moments for me to really internalize what she was telling me. But finally it sunk in... and the *feeling* was... I couldn't decide whether my heart had burst, or sprouted wings. Perhaps both at once.

I had already kissed Kata once today. So I did it again, because I did not know what else to do... and because I desperately *wanted* to. I wanted, *needed*, that reassurance of life. This time she pulled me closer to her and kissed me back, fiercely. When we pulled apart, I turned to look at Liisa and saw the expression on her face, anxiety mixed with hope, so I threw all caution to the winds and pulled her close and kissed her as well, and she responded as fervently as Kata had. There was a sudden huge flood of warmth through my heart that diminished the terrible, aching, tearing pain.

"I *treasure both* of you," I said unsteadily. "You realize that this is twice now that the two of you have saved me?"

"And we will do it again if we must, Alrekr," Liisa replied. "As many times as we must."

A realization came to me. I looked at Kata.

"Kata," I said, "you are a Healer. And I can *feel* how much that means to you. It must have been... hard on you. To be forced to kill instead of heal."

I felt her shiver.

"It... was not easy," she agreed slowly. "Perhaps that is part of why I hesitated. I did not *want* to be sure. Because if I was *sure*, then I would have to kill her. I have... this is... the second sielunjuoja I have seen first-hand, but the first time that it fell to me to strike the killing blow." The corners of her eyes were wet, and her voice trembled. This had cost her dearly. I held her tight.

"I *almost* hesitated too long, Alrekr."

"But you did not," I reassured her. "You acted in time. You *had* to be sure, because what you had to do *could not* be undone."

She nodded, and snuggled herself tighter to me, but I could feel in the tension of her body what that moment of decision—and the knowledge that she had hesitated—had cost her. I held her and Liisa tightly, clinging to them both.

Over the past two months—or was it three? I wasn't sure—a powerful bond had formed between the three of us. I could feel that, even as I wondered at it and how it had happened. And this... those terrifying moments of unexpected horror had, somehow, strengthened it. It had pushed out into the open, into plain sight, how deeply we had come to care for each other in just this short time.

7: Karlajanpaisti

After a while, we disentangled ourselves and walked on. I didn't really *want* to... gods, that had been so *nice*, holding them both—and being held by them, as well. It filled a place that had long felt empty. But I was half out on my feet, and desperately needed to sit down, somewhere safe, and rest. So I walked, sometimes stumbling, while the two of them supported me. Before very long we were back at my room. I was only too ready to collapse into a chair. They pulled the other chairs closer and fed more energy into me. No chanting this time, as they had before the seven-part healing; just a slow, gentle stream. That left us free to talk.

"Alrekr," Kata began. "We caught nothing of what she was saying to you. That language—your birth language, I think?—is strange to us both. What was it all? If it is not too much an intrusion to ask?"

"Accusations," I answered wearily. "Twisted accusations. Her usual stock in trade. That I somehow did all this. Which... *did* I? I don't *know*. That I was cheating on her, that I did this to hurt her, that I had abandoned her... So many things. I can't retain it all. It numbs my mind. It... is like being beaten in the brain with dull lead hammers."

"The things... she accused you of," Liisa said to me. "Were *any* of them true?"

"Every one of them, in her head," I replied, flinching inwardly from memories. "I always tried to do the very best I could and still remain... myself. Not just a shadow of her. But that was not what she wanted. There was room for one person in her life, and that person was her. Everyone else was just there to fill supporting roles in her play. There was never really any 'us'... Only her. Except where other people might see. It took me far too long to realize that.

"Do not misunderstand, I knew I was not perfect. I *know* I made mistakes. So *many* mistakes. But I tried the very best that I knew how to. Always."

"And it was never enough, was it?" Liisa asked knowingly.

I shook my head.

"No," I agreed. "Never enough, never good enough, always too little, or too late, or the wrong thing, or at the wrong moment. There was always some reason. I felt I could do no right."

They looked at each other.

"You do *understand* why it was, do you not," Kata said, "that it felt as though nothing you could do was ever good enough?"

I looked back at her, not sure what she meant.

"I... failed so many times," I answered wearily.

"You failed because it was a *trick*," Kata told me. "Each time you reached a gate that she had placed, she moved the gateposts. She was not *allowing* you to succeed. You were *meant* to fail. That was the *point*. As long as you kept failing, you *deserved* punishment... or so you were meant to believe. So she ensured that you failed.

"When someone deliberately sets up another to fail, Alrekr, it is the fault of the person who sets the trap. Not the fault of the one who is tricked into stepping into it.

"She was *broken*, Alrekr. And she broke you in turn. *Deliberately*. Relying upon your nature not to strike back. It was a way of gaining power, and it did not matter to her that she was gaining that power by harming you."

I'd never thought about it that way before. It was a small revelation... but at the same time, just thinking about it was exhausting. Thinking much about *any* of this was exhausting, draining, numbing.

"Why did she accuse you of cheating on her?" Liisa asked.

I laughed bitterly. They both looked puzzled.

"I walked into a room in the company of two women she did not know and could not control," I said. "Worse yet, both prettier than her. What else **could** it possibly mean?"

Kata snorted in disdain at this.

"And *did* you?" Liisa asked.

"No," I replied. "Though I will admit that once she almost *drove* me to it. And at times it seemed that she was deliberately *trying* to. So that she could blame and attack me for it. As though you were to hit someone in the face, then blame them for having been in a fight. I *know* that she spent half our marriage trying to push me away so that she could blame me for leaving. She even *admitted* that. Without the slightest hint of shame. Of course, later, she denied having ever made the admission."

Kata looked at me, nodding understanding.

"In what we saw of your memories, we glimpsed the fights," she

92

said, her tone serious.

I nodded my head in agreement.

"She would... continue her tirades, her accusations, until I was utterly drained," I said. "And then she would go to sleep *peaceful and recharged*. I thought it just a cruel and selfish streak. That she was only happy when she *won*, and defined winning as making somebody else *lose*. I did not know there was—actual... I did not know such a thing as a souldrinker existed outside of stories. Although even then, sometimes I *wondered*."

"And yet you stayed," Liisa said quietly.

I nodded miserably.

"*Why?*" she asked me, again.

I hesitated. Long moments in which I did not know how to even begin to answer, thinking about how to explain. Then I took a deep breath and plunged in.

"Do you remember," I began slowly, "I once spoke of... not understanding other people well?"

They both nodded.

"The day of the poem, you spoke of this," Liisa agreed. I was struck by that being the thing she remembered that day by. It must have made a stronger impression than I had realized at the time.

"I don't know whether it is a thing that happens here or not. There is something in my head that is... physically different. It is not without its compensations, but... it makes it hard for me, and people like me, to understand at times what other people mean, when they do not say it with words, or why they do the things they do. It is... yet another thing that I can find no word for in Saamen. And... I don't know how to make one. It was not until—past halfway through my life that I actually *knew* that this was what was happening. What was different about me.

"Until then, all I knew was that *so many* things involving people made no sense to me—that it felt I was missing parts of every conversation, that there was some *other way* that people conveyed things to each other, that I couldn't hear. I thought it a ridiculous idea. I never guessed that it was actually *true*." They were both listening to me intently, Kata nodding slightly.

"So for so long, all I knew was that many, many things made no sense to me that other people clearly understood. And when you become accustomed enough to thinking that, it is easy to come to believe that everything people tell you about the things you do not understand must be true, because *they* understand it.

"Even when what they are telling you is that you are *broken*, defective, deficient, that you are wrong, and that everything that is wrong in your life is your own fault. And this is doubled when it comes from someone close to you. Because if you cannot trust *them*, then who *can* you trust?"

Kata and Liisa looked silently at each other, then back at me.

"And she exploited that," Liisa said softly. "To hurt you further."

I rested my head in my hands and nodded wordlessly.

"By the time I finally understood," I began. Then I trailed off. Liisa put a gentle hand on my shoulder while I struggled for words.

"To find the will to get out," I managed at last, "you have to believe that it will make things *better*. But emotional abuse... destroys hope. It kills you inside, little by little. Leaving you numb and helpless."

I didn't know what more to say. I shook my head mutely. I felt shattered, drained, exhausted after my attempt at explanation. Hurting, and yet numb, at the same time. This was an all too familiar feeling.

Yet this time there was light in the darkness. *Two* lights. Kata and Liisa. So much brighter than any candle in the night.

I raised my head and looked wearily back and forth between them. Hesitantly, I held out my hands toward them.

They both took my hands without hesitation. Liisa put her other hand on my shoulder. Kata gently cupped my cheek.

"You have been so terribly hurt," Kata said softly. "And we failed you." I opened my mouth to say No, started to shake my head, but she continued over my objection.

"We failed to protect you, Alrekr. From a danger we **should** have seen. We did not recognize the threat in time." Then she looked me directly in the eyes.

"It **will not happen again**, Alrekr. This I swear." The intensity in her voice, the fire in her eyes as she said it, reached all the way through me.

I needed to change the subject. This was... more intense than I

94

could entirely handle right now.

"You mentioned *níðing*, a couple of times, Kata," I said after a long moment. She nodded. "Saamen is very like the... the *Suomi* of my... my past life. I think it clearly developed from it—or they developed from a common root.

"But how do you come to have words of Norse? I am familiar with the concept, from old Norse law. But that's a different culture, and I should not make assumptions just because it sounds like the same word. What, really, is *níðing*, here?"

The two women looked at each other.

"Yes," Liisa said, "we should explain."

Kata nodded. "There are perhaps many things we have not explained enough," she agreed. "We had more urgent priorities. Healing you, first. There would be time later to teach you about this world."

"There is much we—*should* teach you that we have not, Alrekr," Liisa told me. "But I am unsure exactly where we should start. You have adapted to Highwatch, to the Sunlit Land, well so far. Well enough that it is easy to forget sometimes that there is much about this land and its people that you do not know yet. And we have not perhaps introduced you to as many people as we should have, to broaden your perspectives."

Kata nodded agreement.

"There is much you do not know about our world, our customs, our traditions, our laws," she told me. "You simply have not had opportunity to learn them. You have not been here long enough. Some of them will be simply unfamiliar to you. Others, you may find strange, even perhaps shocking—just as we find much that you have told us about your world baffling or shocking.

"In any case, for the moment, you should understand that our system of law is based upon restitution, on making whole a harm that was done. And where no-one has been wronged, nor is there any intent to, there can be no wrong. But great harms incur great penalties. The greater a harm you do someone, the more it takes to make them whole again.

"This works at many levels. If you accidentally broke something that belongs to someone else, you would seek to replace it, would you not?"

I nodded in agreement.

"Of course. With one just as good—if not better, by way of apology."

"And so it is with other things. If you take something *from* someone, you return it, you make it good. If you do someone harm, you make recompense, in some way. If you *refuse*... you reject the law. And the law, in turn, rejects you and no longer protects you. This we call a níðing offense."

I nodded.

"So far, this is familiar to me from what I know of the Old Norse," I agreed.

"A person who commits a níðing act has *chosen* to be outside the law," Kata went on, "and is not protected *by* the law. To kill someone declared níð is not a crime. Only the very *worst* of people willingly become *níð*."

She paused for a moment.

"Let us tell you two stories to help illustrate this. Both are true retellings from our own experience, not metaphor or allegory.

"There was an accident known to us some years ago, in which a man accidentally killed the wife of another man he knew. There was no malice nor intent involved; it was a terrible accident that he deeply regretted. While working on a high roof, he slipped, dropped a tool, and missed the catch. His shout of warning came too late. By sheer misfortune, she was passing below, and it struck her in the head and killed her instantly. He was among the first at her side, but she was already dead.

"It was pure accident, and none would have spoken a verdict against him for it. But he judged *himself* nonetheless, and swore oath that he owed wergild. Nobody had any doubt about his remorse; he wept in open grief over her body. But how can one *replace* a lost wife? How can one make restitution for that?

"He was not a wealthy man, just a craftsman of moderate means. To pay a fair and proper wergild would have ruined him. He had nothing of comparable value to offer in restitution. But he had an unmarried elder daughter, who suggested to him that perhaps one wife might be replaced with another.

"So *with her agreement* and at her suggesion, he offered his daughter to the man widowed by his mistake, to become his wife in her place. And after talking to the elder daughter at length, the new widower agreed.

"He treated her well and respectfully, and over time, he and his new wife came to love each other very deeply. They were inseparable for the rest of their lives. The two men became the best of friends, and nothing could stand between them. They became almost as brothers."

She paused.

"Even once *declared níð*, it is still possible to return, to regain normal standing, if you can find a way to make restitution without being killed first. But most people will do much, to keep their honor and avoid a níðing act. Even if only their own honor says they have done wrong.

"You are no different in this, I think."

She stopped, and Liisa took over.

"There is another case that it is important you understand, Alrekr. It is the other side of the same coin, and it bears closely upon this day. It happened quite near to here, in fact, and only a few years ago.

"A young man and a girl whom he loved had pledged their troth to each other, and were to be wed. But another girl who wanted him for herself, in whom he had no interest, was jealous. So she poisoned the bride-to-be, only days before the wedding."

My shocked reaction had to have shown on my face.

"They sent a rider to us to beg urgent help, Alrekr. Varpu and Raimo got to her in time and were able to save her. Raimo quickly identified the poison, and sang it out of her while Varpu healed the damage it had done." I sighed with relief.

"The poisoner made no secret of what she had done. She was *furious* that Raimo and Varpu had managed to save the girl. She swore that if she could not have that young man, then nobody would, even if she had to kill both of them. She showed no remorse, and laughed at the idea of restitution. She even threatened Varpu. Threatened a *Healer*." I could hear in the tone of her voice that this was... almost unthinkable.

"She was declared *níð*, Alrekr, and her name forgotten. She was imprisoned and held. The wedding had to be postponed until a later date, when the bride was recovered.

"And the young man, whose betrothed she had tried to murder before the wedding, struck her head from her body with his own hands.

"This is not forbidden by the law, Alrekr. We consider a níð no longer a person, and no different from any other dangerous animal such as a wild boar. In *any* way. Unless they show remorse and make fair and honest restitution."

"The sielunjuoja tried to *kill* you, Alrekr," Liisa continued. "But it did not seek to simply kill you. It tried to *consume your very soul*. There can be **no worse** níðing act against a single person. It is perhaps the only crime we hold *worse* than murder. And sielunjuojat are not even *capable* of remorse."

"An unrepentant *níð* has forfeited their humanity," Kata interjected. "And a sielunjuoja is the *very worst* of níðing, an abomination, its humanity lost even *before* it is killed. A spirit so terribly broken, so terribly *gone wrong*, has no capacity for remorse, no capacity for anything but hunger. The person who once was, good or not, is already lost. It is almost a mercy to kill them, and we know of no other course. Please understand this."

I nodded.

"I... do understand that, Kata," I agreed. "Now. I just wanted to be sure I understood the rest as well.

"So all in all, then, very much the same as in Norse law. That suggests contact with Norse culture in the past."

Liisa nodded. "Those who first arrived in the Sunlit Land, as our oldest records suggest, *were* a mixture of peoples," she said. "It is not too strange to suppose that some of them were what you call *Norse*."

"You say 'arrived'," I mused. "Arrived... how? From where?"

"The honest answer," Kata replied after a moment, "is that we do not truly know. It was a long time ago. No written records survive from the earliest years, that we know of. We must rely on people who wrote down stories told by their parents or grandparents, much later. So much was lost. They had to start over from almost nothing.

"The little we know is that it was a terrifying journey, taken in great hardship, by people fleeing some great danger—about which we know only the words 'fire and destruction'—who were able to bring with them little more than their loved ones and the clothes on their backs. It seems no more than a few hundred people actually reached the Sunlit Land. Some of the fragmentary accounts that have survived mention a tunnel of night. But it is unclear what that actually means."

"Tunnel of night?" I pondered, struck by the phrase. I thought for a moment. "Could that mean... a rift? Like the one I... seemingly fell through?"

Kata frowned.

"I have never *seen* a rift myself," she said. "But the descriptions I have read speak of a... hole in the air with a different place on the other side. None of the recorded descriptions of rifts suggest one looking like a tunnel of night."

"The one I came through did," I said with a shudder, remembering that much. "If that is what it was. A... a *curdling* in the air. And in the center of it, a knot of blackness, more black than night. No stars; no light in it at all. I... remember being pulled toward it, into it, in mid-air. Then a great, crushing impact, and... then nothing." Another shiver shook me.

Liisa moved her hand from my shoulder for a moment, where she was feeding energy into me still, to brush her fingers across my cheek.

"It is not easy for you to remember, is it?" she said softly.

"No," I agreed. "It is not. It was a painful time. I..." I swallowed. "I remember that I was wishing to *die*, Liisa, if that was my only way out. But even more... I wanted to *escape*. From what my life had been. But I didn't have any idea how."

Kata got a thoughtful look.

"The first in the Sunlit Land traveled through 'a tunnel of night' to escape something terrible," she mused. And then she looked directly at me. "And so did you, Alrekr."

She had a point, I realized. I thought about it.

"What if those first people here *did* come from... my old world's past?" I mused. "The same way that I did?"

Kata nodded.

"It is not impossible," she agreed. "But there is probably no way to ever find out now."

"It is a simpler explanation than there being *two* such places with human people, and with pasts so similar," I pointed out. "And Saamen is *so* similar to... even the name—*Suomi*—is similar. You even have some of the same *legends*. Ilmarinen singing the bowl of the sky into being. The saga of Väinämöinen and Lemminkäinen. Surely it *cannot* be coincidence."

She nodded slowly.

"That is not untrue, indeed," she agreed. "But let us study that question more another time. Let me see once more how you are doing, if I may."

I nodded unhesitating assent.

I saw Kata's brow furrow in concentration for a moment. Felt her delve into me again, probing. Then she looked at Liisa, her face troubled.

"The wounds are so *deep*," she said to Liisa. "She took much from him."

"I did nothing to defend myself," I mumbled guiltily.

"*No*, Alrekr," Kata told me. "*Stop*. You judge yourself too harshly. Far more harshly than you deserve. You did not know what you were trying to fight off, an attack against which you *had* no defense in any case. There was nothing you *could* do, there and then, to defend yourself. Because of the marriage bond. It was like a door standing open and unguarded through any defense you could have made. That is how and why she was able to wound you so deeply, so fast. Without that bond, you could have at least resisted her attack. Fought against her. With it? You were defenseless."

"*And* because she had been laying the groundwork for so long," Liisa added. "In hindsight, you did well to hold as long as you did." She looked at me. I saw no judgment in her face.

"May I look again, also?" she asked.

I hesitated.

"I... saw you flinch when you looked into my memories," I began.

"Alrekr," Liisa interrupted before I could finish, "yes, I did. But what I flinched from was not any thought of yours. It was the *intentional cruelty* I saw inflicted upon you by someone who claimed to love you. The betrayal of your trust.

"I can see in your eyes that you are afraid of what you fear we might have seen in your mind. But *do not* be afraid. *Please*. Believe me that we saw nothing in you that we would turn away from. We see the dark corners, but we see also the torment, the pain, the unfulfilled need that drove you into them. *No-one* walks though such dark places and *does not* come out with shadows in dark corners of their soul.

"But not everyone emerges from those dark places unbroken. Not everyone clings on and holds themselves whole. Not everyone chooses to walk away from the shadows and leave them behind."

"We can help you to forget the thoughts and memories that trouble you most, if you wish," Kata said. "But we know that there are things that have special meaning to you, events that have shaped you. We would never touch such without your consent. Even things that we can clearly see have hurt you."

I nodded, and after a moment I felt Liisa, too, gently look within me. At the scarred, the wounded places. Her touch was gentle, feather-light.

After a minute or two, she withdrew, looked directly at Kata, put a hand on her arm, nodded. They stood and stepped away, just a couple of polite steps, but not out of earshot. I could hear their conversation without straining. They weren't trying to hide it from me.

"I think... perhaps we should not put it off any longer," Kata said quietly. "Should we make our offerings? Is it too soon still?"

Liisa nodded solemnly.

"Offerings, yes," she agreed. "It is so soon, I know. But I think it is time. The events of this day have forced our hands. We can prepare them together. Mistress Kerttu will help us, I am sure."

"*Today*, then. I wanted to wait longer. To allow him more time to heal. To find himself. But now I think we should wait no more. It is *time*, indeed."

"It is nothing we have not already talked about doing," Liisa agreed. "And he *needs* the healing of the soul that it will bring."

They were not excluding me, I knew. It seemed they just wanted to talk about things that clearly involved me, without doing it right in front of me that might possibly have been taken as rude. But without hiding that they were talking about me.

Then they both turned back to me.

"Alrekr," Liisa asked, "will you be alright on your own here for a while? You are out of immediate danger, but... you need to recover as much as possible of what was taken from you this day, and quickly. There is something *very important*—not in a bad way, do not worry, important beyond simple healing—to all three of us, I think and hope— that we must do. And... we must *talk*. There are more explanations that you should have. When we return."

"I'll be alright," I agreed, nodding. "I think." It felt as though I had stopped bleeding energy. But I still *hurt*, a soul-deep ache. "I will just... rest here. For a while."

Liisa nodded.

"We will be back, Alrekr," Kata said. "It is a day of unplanned events and weighty decisions. If we have misjudged and you need help in our absence, ring for a page." Then I saw her reconsider.

"... No, never mind that. Let us not take the chance. We will send another healer... Varpu, I think, if we can find her, to keep watch over you. She will take care of you until we return. Skill counts less in this than the capacity for caring, the capacity to love, and hers is perhaps greater than anyone else's we know."

"Varpu seems to love *everyone*," I said.

"Exactly," Kata agreed. "That is simply who she is."

Then the two of them left together. I could not read what was in the long glance that passed between the three of them as she left.

They were gone a long time, two hours or more. Varpu came by a few minutes after they left, sent to watch over me and make sure that I was alright. She clearly knew about the attack. She sat across from me and held my hands, concern on her face, whispering something under her breath. I could feel her doing something, above and beyond the energy that I could feel her feeding into me, and knew that it made me feel a little better, steadier. I half wanted to talk to her, but I did not know what to say that would not be awkward—and it would have interrupted her in any case.

No words really seemed necessary, anyway.

She waited with me until Kata and Liisa returned. Then she squeezed my hands, flashed that smile, and left, a quick one-armed hug for Liisa as she passed her, a touch of a hand on Kata's shoulder.

They had brought with them one of the small wheeled carts the pages sometimes used. From the top of the cart they each took a bundle wrapped in bright cloth, which they set upon the table. Then they moved the two other chairs next to the table, helped me up and to one of the chairs, then moved the third chair. They sat across from me, the three of us spaced around the small table.

They looked at each other.

"Alrekr," Kata began, "there is one other thing that it is important that you know and understand about sielunjuojat." Then she paused a moment before continuing. I could see her expression changing as she sought the right words.

"A souldrinker wounds the *soul*, not the body. We—as Healers—can repair most, though not all, of the direct *injury* done, but we cannot restore what was taken from the soul. That must be regained in other ways. And the sooner, the better."

"One thing that helps to heal some of that loss, Alrekr," Liisa interjected, "is a gift of food that is prepared with love, and *given* in love. Any gift of love, really, but food especially. But it must be *truly* a gift of love. It is the *love* that heals. And there is no pretending it. The love *must* be true, for it to heal."

"And so there is one last tradition of ours that we must explain to you now," Kata continued. "We wanted this to be fresh in your mind. We wanted to be certain that you understand what it means."

"When one person seeks the favor of another," Liisa said, "there is a custom. It is not always followed, and need not be, but very often is anyway. Because both parties *enjoy* it as a part of courting. It can be initiated by either party."

"And there need not be only two parties involved," Kata interjected. "Sometimes two will court a third."

I nodded approvingly. It didn't occur to me, yet, *why* she had just pointed that out.

"And that is regarded as just normal, here?" I asked. Liisa gave me a strange look.

"Of course, Alrekr," she replied. Then she reconsidered.

"It is true," she continued, "it was not *always* so. Long ago, hundreds of years now, people used to think that a love bond could be only between one man and one woman. But then people came to understand that if all in a bond love each other, no matter who they are, it is nobody's place to try to tell them that it is wrong. As long as all are old enough, matured enough, to choose wisely for themselves. We came to see that true love between people who can, and do, give their consent is *never* wrong, Alrekr. It is the one who sees wrong in it, or the one who does harm or forces another into what they *call* love, or uses another without love, who must examine themselves."

I nodded in fervent agreement.

"My own past world is only now beginning to accept and understand this," I agreed. "After far too long, in my opinion."

Liisa smiled, and Kata took up the explanation.

"In our custom, the one who seeks the favor of the other shows their intent to provide for their intended, by cooking a special meal for them. Wherever possible, the meal is something that has special meaning between the courting parties, or at least to the one it is offered to; or failing that, is perhaps made from rare or special ingredients, or even if the meal *itself* is ordinary, it is prepared with exquisite, loving extra care, and often decorated, or wrapped with bright colors." My eyes strayed unbidden to the two brightly wrapped bundles.

"And then the meal is presented in a formal manner to the intended. We call this the offering of the love meal, or simply the love offering.

"If the one courting finds favor in the eyes of the one courted, she will accept the love offering. And if not, then she is free to reject it, without consequence. If the one courting seeks to *press* the matter after such a refusal, seeks to *insist* on her attention, then there will be trouble, and he will be on the wrong side of the law, and all hands will be raised against him. To force attentions where they are known unwanted is an offense among us. It is unmannerly, uncouth, at best.

"If the love offering is *accepted*, Alrekr, then it is taken as a pledge of troth."

The two women looked at each other, then back at me. I was... confused. I did not yet understand what was happening here or why they were explaining this custom to me. The penny had not dropped.

"We have chosen carefully, Alrekr," Liisa told me hesitantly. "In all respects. We hope in the depths of our hearts that we chose correctly. And that we have correctly understood the feelings that we see in you."

She took a deep breath, then they looked at each other again. Liisa reached and placed a small cloth-wrapped bundle in the table in front of me. I unfolded it, puzzled. Inside was tableware—a sharp knife, a three-tined fork, a broad spoon.

Then Kata reached for her wrapped bundle. With slow, formal movements, she carefully unwrapped the brightly patterned cloth that was wrapped around it. Inside the cloth was a small tureen with a lid.

She pushed it slowly toward me.

"For you, Alrekr Járnhandr," she said, "I have made *lihakeitto*." I did not recognize the name, but I knew enough of the word to know that it must be some kind of soup. A meat soup, I was fairly sure. "This

104

is my offering to you in token of my love, Alrekr. May it find favor with you."

Love. She'd said love. Kata, beautiful green-eyed Kata, had just told me that *she loved me*. That jolted me to my core. I froze for a moment, stunned.

With my heart suddenly in my mouth, I reached out and slowly, as though in a trance, slid the tureen a little closer to me.

After a long moment, I dragged my thoughts together and lifted the lid.

Inside was a thick, creamy soup. I was very familiar with *lohikeitto*, and it looked very similar. But in place of the potatoes I knew, it was made with what appeared to be the yellow yam-like tubers I'd previously encountered. And in place of the salmon, there were slices of some meat that looked to have been roasted first.

Still half in a trance, I reached for the spoon. I dipped out a spoonful of soup, and tasted it. It was good. It tasted much like lohikeitto, but without the flavor of salmon. Instead there was a different flavor, richer, meatier, creamier. And... it was somehow more *warming*, more comforting, more *soothing* than it seemed food alone should be. It soothed the hurt *inside* me.

Then I spooned out a slice of the meat. I looked at Kata. She was watching me, biting her lip.

I slipped it into my mouth. It was rich, a little fatty, but mildly flavored, and so tender. It was delicious... and there was a tingle. A feeling that the aching pain inside me dimmed, just the tiniest bit.

I chewed it slowly, then I took another spoonful of the soup.

"This... is wonderful," I managed to say, unsteadily. I looked at Kata, saw her slowly let her breath out.

She turned and looked at Liisa.

Liisa took a deep breath and reached for her own bundle. She unwrapped it slowly just as Kata had hers. It was a shallow dish with a cover over it.

Just as Kata had, she pushed it towards me.

"For you, Alrekr Járnhandr," she said, "I have made *karjalanpaisti*. This is my offering to you in token of my love, Alrekr. May it find favor with you."

I did not know that word at all, but the word itself almost slipped past me anyway. Kata's declaration of love had shaken me. To hear the same now from Liisa *as well* was almost too much to take in. How could this be? I *knew* we three had formed a bond, but... this?

When I was able, I drew the dish towards me and lifted the lid. It was filled with a rich-looking, meaty stew.

I looked at Liisa. She was holding her breath anxiously. My pulse pounded in my ears.

I picked up the knife and fork, then hesitated. My hands were shaking so much I almost dropped the fork. I took several deep breaths to calm myself, then selected a small piece of the meat. I looked at it for a long moment. And then I put it into my mouth. I let it rest on my tongue for a long moment. It was flavorful and lightly peppery.

It, too, was delicious. After a few moments I began to chew, finding it tender, with just a little crispness in places. I felt a sudden prickling electric thrill. And... something more. The deep ache from the recent attack... receded a little, again, it seemed.

I looked at Liisa. I was utterly lost for words. I looked down at the dish, then back at Liisa. Then I chose another piece. I saw her relax slightly.

I put the second piece in my mouth and ate it slowly, almost reverently. Then I went back to the bowl of soup and had some more soup. I was sure by now that I was not imagining it. Even just the soup alone eased the inner pain a little.

After that mouthful, I paused. I looked back and forth between Kata and Liisa. *Now* I understood at last why they had told me the things they had. They had told me in just so many words why they were doing what they were, and I still had not understood. "There is no pretending it," they had told me. "The love must be true." And I could *feel* the food healing the wounds within me. I *had* to believe that either this was real—or *everything* was false, a dream, an illusion.

I had already set that thought aside. And I could not deny to myself that I loved them also.

"Please," I asked, *begged*, through a throat suddenly dry even though my mouth was watering, "help me to fully understand your custom. I have questions I *must* have the answers to. I *do not want* to make a mistake here, through ignorance, that I am certain I would regret forever.

"How... *common*... is it that two—love offerings are made to the same person, at the same time?"

"Not every day, or every week, but more often than you might perhaps expect," Liisa replied quietly. "When two people *know* that they are competing for the affections of a third, it is common—and considered fair and polite—to arrange to present their offerings together. For one to *deliberately* seek to outrace another to making an offering is usually thought selfish and unfair, though sometimes forgivable if he or she would have no chance otherwise."

I looked back and forth between them.

"What if a person receiving two... offers... were to find himself unable to choose between them?" I asked hesitantly.

"A person who finds such a position difficult," Kata replied carefully, "has the option to reject either, or even to decline both, if he cannot decide between them and if that is his wish."

"And if he does not wish to reject **either**?" I asked, my heart in my mouth. "You told me that two may sometimes court a third. Is it... permitted... to accept *both*?"

There was a long pause. They exchanged glances. I thought I saw hope in their expressions. This time I saw Liisa bite her lip and hold her breath.

"It is not without precedent," Kata replied, still speaking in careful, measured tones. But I thought I caught a hint of excitement underneath. "He has that option, and if all involved agree, then none will judge it wrong."

I took a deep breath, trying to calm myself. It wasn't easy.

"One last question," I asked. "Is it, uh, expected that I finish the... love offering... by myself? Or is the custom to share with the—the person who offered it?"

"It *can* go either way," Liisa replied, after a moment. "But the usual custom is that if the recipient finds favor in the one offering, then the meal is shared. So doing returns the pledge. And to eat it entire, then *reject* the offer, is... very rude and cruel. A mistake someone will likely only ever make once, because he probably will not receive a second offer, *ever*, if it becomes known that he did so. To give false hope, and then take it away, is needlessly cruel and selfish."

I realized my hands had closed on their own into tight balls. I willed them to open, trying to relax. My chest was tight.

"Then please," I said, struggling to speak, understanding fully now what I was about to ask, and feeling my eyes welling with tears from the sheer intensity of emotion, "it would do me greater honor than I know how to express if you would please—*both* consent—to share this once-in-a-lifetime meal with me."

For a moment there was silence. Then I saw wide smiles spread across both of their faces. Kata's eyes were bright and as wet as mine. They looked quickly at each other.

"The honor is ours," Liisa almost whispered.

"Yes," Kata said fervently. "Yes, Alrekr. We will. *Gladly* we will."

She produced and unwrapped another bundle of tableware. Then they both slid their chairs closer, next to me on either side, and we ate our fill. We fed *each other* more than we each fed ourselves, though they ate relatively little, leaving the greater share to me.

When we were done, the hollowness within me much diminished, I sat back. I didn't know what to say or do. I was still half-paralyzed by fear that this was all some kind of trick or hallucination, that it could not possibly have just happened. The... *pain* was hugely reduced. It still ached... but the ache no longer tore at me.

Kata looked at me.

"I am so glad that we made the correct choice," she said, her voice unsteady. "We were *terribly afraid* that it might be horribly **wrong**, that we had misread the feelings we thought we saw, that we might be pushing you into something you were not ready for and might drive you apart from us forever... but we *hoped* that it would be the exact thing, the healing *release*, that we judged you needed. Over and above the healing itself. And... we *wanted* to offer to you, so much.

"I am sorry that we were so—careful, reticent, about answering your questions. We were trying not to force your choice in any way. We wanted your choice to be freely made."

"You endured so much pain," Liisa added, "you were so badly wronged, betrayed in so many ways. We hoped so much that you would be—*ready* to accept our offerings."

"Did you... *expect*... me to accept *both* of your offerings?" I asked, shaking slightly.

"We—we both desperately hoped that you *would*," Kata replied. "Even though it is so soon. We see within you that you are what we both have sought. We *both* desire no other here. We have talked about it much together when we were not with you."

"I still did not understand at first," I said. "I was confused as to why you were explaining this custom to me. Because I... didn't understand. I didn't see how it could apply. Not to me."

"It is alright, Alrekr," Liisa said. "I am sorry if we did not clearly—"

"No, no," I assured her. "In hindsight, you were... All of the pieces were there right in front of me. I just didn't put them together in my head. I should have understood sooner than I did, but I ... found it so hard to believe it possible. Until you both said it *out loud* in just so many words." I could feel tears forming in the corners of my eyes. "And... I could feel the pain receding with each bite—and you had already told me that it would only work if the love was real. And you have never lied to me. Not once. Surely it had to be true.

"I wanted *so much* to hope. Because I had already fallen in love with both of you. Yet until that moment I didn't dare to *believe* it. Much less speak it."

Kata excused herself for a brief moment, went to the door, and rang for a page. Then she returned, leaving the door open. Liisa, meanwhile, stood, pulled me to my feet, and led me to the small couch. She sat at one end and guided me to sit next to her. When Kata returned, she sat on the other side. There was just room for the three of us. I was lost for words and afraid to speak. So I put my arms around both their shoulders, and pulled them close, and just kept looking back and forth between the two of them. We huddled together and held each other.

It was only a few minutes before the page arrived. This time it was the olive-skinned girl from the... second day, I thought? And several times since.

"Senja," Kata said, "please tell Castellan Juuro that new permanent quarters will be needed as soon as possible, for Newfound Járnhandr, Liisa, and myself. Proper long-term quarters for three, Senja, not a recuperative guest room. And Senja. Make *certain* he understands that there is to be one bed, sufficient to hold three."

"At once, Honored," the girl, Senja, replied. "Permanent new quarters for three, with one bed *also* to hold three. And... you will wish

109

your things moved from your current rooms, Honoreds?"

"Yes, thank you, Senja," Liisa replied. Senja kept looking back and forth between Liisa and Kata. There was something in her face I could not read. Anticipation, perhaps. Or excitement. Perhaps both. She looked at the table and the two empty dishes sitting there, and the bright cloths.

Kata smiled.

"Yes, Senja," she said. "We are now troth-pledged."

Joy and excitement lit up Senja's face. She looked back and forth again.

"*Both* of you?" she asked.

"*All three* of us, Senja," Liisa corrected her. "Alrekr, Kata, and I are three together, now."

Senja let out a joyful whoop, and shot a dazzling smile my way.

"It will be done, Honoreds," she said excitedly. "It *will* be done." Then she raced off at a dead run.

It was real. It was *real*. This was *really happening*. In this new world, these two beautiful, wonderful women, these two highly skilled senior Healers, clearly respected here, who had spent uncounted time and energy to repair my damaged body, who had saved my life, *twice* now, had *chosen*... me. Flawed, broken, battered, damaged, scarred, *me*. No matter how much I felt I was shop-soiled goods. The leavings.

It was too much to take in all at once. I found myself starting to shake. I tried for a moment to hold it in. Then I broke down, completely. First a gasp that turned into a sob, and then the floodgates opened. The dam broke, *shattered*, and all of the secret pain hidden for so long came pouring out. Finally I knew it was SAFE to feel it, to stop hiding it. Finally I could acknowledge it, release it, instead of burying it to fester. I wept, uncontrolled, great shuddering sobs that wracked my entire body. From either side, Kata and Liisa wrapped their arms around me and held me, murmuring quiet words of comfort and support, as I cried my heart out.

After what felt like hours, I started to get myself back under control again. I wiped my eyes clear.

"I'm sorry," I started to say. But Kata interrupted.

"Stop. *Right. There,*" she told me sternly. "Alrekr, Liisa and I both *know* from your own memories that this is pain you have been locking away for *decades. **Do not*** apologize for finally letting it out."

I rested my head in my hands for a moment, and took a few deep, slow breaths.

"You tell yourself that you can deal with the pain," I said slowly, shakily, after a time. "You tell yourself that you will deal with it later. You tell yourself that you can just push it away. You tell yourself that if you ignore it, it will fade. You learn that nobody wants to hear. You learn that letting people *see* that they have the power to hurt you, exposes a weakness that will be used to hurt you further. You get told once too often that it's your own fault. You get told once too often to suck it up and deal with it. Eventually you begin to convince even yourself that you're alright.

"But deep inside, you know that you're *not.*"

Kata nodded gravely.

"We have only twice looked deep into your mind," Liisa said, "beyond what you have shared with us. And the second time we were in a great hurry. We did not go *looking around,* Alrekr, but some of your buried memories are so searing we could not *help* but see them. They begged, *screamed out* to be seen. Your despair when it felt everything you tried to do was wrong, your misery on occasions you accidentally hurt someone. When... the one you married flayed pieces off your soul to punish you for not being exactly what she wanted. The times she drove you to consider killing yourself. To drive someone to take their own life is willful *murder,* under our law. It is yet *another* níðing crime to her account.

"If you keep trying to chain up that pain, it will destroy you. Don't apologize for showing it. Let us *help.*"

"We have pledged ourselves to you, Alrekr," Kata said. "When you are weak and weary, we will be there to lend you strength."

"When you do not know the way," Liisa said, "we will be your guides."

"When you are cold, we will be there to warm you," said Kata.

"When you are lost, we will find you."

"When all is blackness and despair, we will be your light in the

111

darkness."

"When you scream out loud, we will be there to soothe your anguish."

"When you cry out in the night, we will be there to hold you."

"We are yours now, Alrekr, as you are ours."

"You are part of us, as we are part of you."

I could not speak to answer. I was overcome. So for the moment, I settled for putting my arms around them and pulling them both close. I was facing more towards Liisa at that moment, so I kissed her first. Then I turned and kissed Kata as well. Then we all kissed a few more times for good measure. And then for a while I just held them both as close as I could.

"Everything has changed," I managed to say at last. "I feel adrift, and yet I have the two of you as my anchors. For what is perhaps the first time in my life, I feel... *safe*. Not alone."

Liisa looked curiously at me.

"How can you be married to someone," she asked, "and yet feel alone? That sounds very strange."

"You'd really think so, wouldn't you?" I replied. "The realization comes..."

Then I stopped myself.

"No," I said, as much to myself as to anyone else. "I don't want to talk or think about that now. This is a time for happy thoughts. Not for brooding over past misery. I need to let it all *go*. But... well, remember that *you yourselves* told me that sielunjuojat cannot truly care for anyone but themselves."

Kata nodded solemn understanding. Liisa actually looked a little embarrassed.

"I... should have thought of that myself," she admitted. She snuggled a little closer to me. "As long as you remember that we are always here for you to talk to, when you need to. Especially now. It cannot have been *easy* being married to... an awakening sielunjuoja. There is no wonder it broke and scarred you. But we will make you whole. Whatever it takes."

About then, there came a tap at the door. Kata went to answer it.

It was Senja again.

"Honored," she said, "Castellan Juuro sent me to tell you that he has assigned you the quarters in the northwest tower last assigned to Knight-Commander Viljainen. They are being warmed and cleaned now. The bed in there should be adequate, and there are an abundance of shelves for your books. We will do everything possible to have the rooms ready for you tonight." Then she sketched a fast half-bow and departed again at a run.

Kata closed the door behind her and turned around, the smile still on her face. Her eyes twinkling.

"I hope you don't *mind* it being common knowledge, Alrekr," she said. "When two Healers, who for the past two months and more have been treating a mysteriously-appeared stranger from a far-distant *world*, take over a part of the main kitchen to *both* at *once* prepare love offerings, there is no such thing as a secret in a place this size. Especially in a fortress, where word travels fast."

"Secret?" I repeated. I could not help myself. I laughed out loud. The release felt wonderful, and it cleared my mind for now of things I didn't want to think about. Even the ache receded just a tiny bit more. "Kata, my love, it saves me the trouble of risking my neck to shout the news from every rooftop I can climb to!"

"Not yet, please, Alrekr," Liisa told me, smiling joyfully. "When you have recovered more of your strength, if you must."

"I... will try to find patience, beloved," I replied with a slightly fragile chuckle. If it were possible, I think her smile grew even wider.

"I am relieved that you want to tell the world, Alrekr," Kata said. "Because if anyone in Highwatch does not yet know that Liisa and I brought offerings to you this eve, and that you accepted both, I guarantee you they will have heard it by tomorrow noon at the latest."

"Kata, Liisa," I replied honestly, "in truth, I could not possibly be more proud that not even one, but *both* of you, chose... me. I am still struggling to believe that it is real. Of all the wonders I have yet seen since coming to this world, that is perhaps the greatest wonder of all."

We sat together on the couch again, just enjoying each other's presence with no pressure, for once not focused on healing.

"I have an admission myself," I said. Kata gave me a curious glance. "I think I began to fall in love with you—*both* of you—that day on the balcony. But I dared not say anything. Because—"

113

"Hush," Kata said, laying a finger gently across my lips. "*Why* does not matter at this moment. Do not dwell on past pains and fears. It is time to plan your—*our*—future."

I kissed her again. Because of course I did.

"You and Liisa are all the future I need," I told her. And then of course I kissed Liisa again as well. Because this is what you *do* when you find yourself with your arms around two beautiful women, both of whom you have finally admitted to yourself that you love, and whom you have discovered that you *do not have to choose between*. You kiss them both, and regret only that you cannot kiss them *both at once*.

"Your future holds more than just us," Kata replied. "We still need to heal your mind, your soul, the—not even scars, the *still-open wounds* on the inside as well as on the outside."

"And now," Liisa added with a shudder, "finally we understand **WHY** they were still open."

"And then when you are finally whole," Kata told me, "then we must begin to train you properly in how to use and control your Talent. And we shall see what you become."

8: New Accommodations

Senja was as good as her word. Late in the evening there came a sharp rap at the door. Liisa went to the door and opened it, and there was Senja. She was actually bouncing up and down with excitement.

"All is ready, Honoreds," she announced. "We are not quite finished moving the last of your things yet, but the rooms are ready for you.

"Will you let me be your guide, *please*?"

Liisa laughed happily.

"Of course, Senja," she said. "We would be honored to have you guide us. Let us be on our way."

I stood up, needing only a moment's anxious support from Kata as I swayed for a moment upon reaching my feet. But after a moment, the brief vertigo passed and my head cleared. Senja was hugging Liisa, I saw. We walked to the door, and she threw her arms around Kata as well, hugging her tightly, then she turned to me. I saw her begin to reach out, then hesitate.

I smiled and opened my arms, and she stepped in with a big smile and hugged me too. I wrapped my arms around her and hugged back. It was wonderful to me how generous the people of this land were with affection. It seemed a far healthier society than the one I had... left. I didn't know which of those was cause, and which was effect.

She looked up happily at me.

"You are truly one of us now, Adept Járnhandr," she said.

"I am not an Adept—at least, not yet," I replied.

"From all I hear, you *will* be," she said. Then she let go of me and almost skipped out the door to lead us on our way. I was fairly sure I was the only one present who didn't already know the way, but no-one was going to deny Senja her self-set task.

We could have gone up atop the wall and gone that way, but it was getting late and doubtless chilly. Instead we stayed to the second floor, following the wide, vaulted passages within the wall. We passed two or three people going the other way, to friendly smiles and waves. Then we were at another of the broad stairs. We climbed two floors before the stair ended at a large double door, one side already standing open. A handful of Highwatch staff were just coming out as we arrived.

Senja stood beside the door and waved us in with a half-bow and a huge smile. We stepped in through the door into a large room. It was *full* of people.

In the first moment, I recognized familiar faces—Vallaïnen, Raimo, Marja, and Varpu. We had scarcely entered the room before Varpu came over to us at a half-run and threw her arms around first Liisa, then Kata, then me. I hugged her back, and then she gathered all three of us into a hug. Her eyes were dancing. And very blue, I noticed.

"I am *SO* happy for you all!" she declared. Her joy was obvious and infectious. Then Raimo joined in as well. Vallaïnen and Marja were standing back a little, holding hands, big smiles on their faces, but they were the next in line to hug us.

When I got the chance to look around a little, I recognized Vilja, the junior Healer from the... encounter that morning. She was guiding a group of pages in shelving books from several small handcarts. She happened to look up, caught my glance, and gave a happy wave. I waved back. Nearly a quarter of the wall of the room was lined with bookcases, I saw. Several empty weapon racks also stood against the wall, near to the doors.

I did not know anyone else there but the various Healers, but soon there were introductions, too many for me to take in all of at once. There was a tall, rugged-looking man who was introduced as Knight-Commander Jaako. He was so normally proportioned that it took me a few moments to realize he had to be close to six and a half feet tall, a near-giant of a man. The Rangers who had brought me in were under his command. Several of those very Rangers were here tonight, too.

One of them, an athletic woman with dark hair, I suddenly recognized.

"You... were there, in the crags," I said. "You found me."

She smiled, obviously pleased.

"I am glad that you remember that," she said. "And I am *so* glad that you lived. I... have a feeling it will someday be important.

"But actually, it was Simo who found you." She introduced Simo, thin, almost white of hair, with piercing blue eyes.

"That name I remember, I think," I agreed. "But I never caught yours."

"Piia," she told me. "I am Piia."

"It is very good to meet you, Piia," I replied. "Thank you—and your team—for saving me." She smiled warmly.

Another I recognized was Master Healer Timo. I had already met him once, but hadn't been introduced. It was he, I recalled now, who had laid the Saamen language over my mind the day I had woken up.

"Adept-to-be Járnhandr, I am told," he greeted me, inclining his head slightly. "Winds of your own making already circle you, or so I hear from Healer Vallaïnen. This will be an interesting time, indeed."

I returned the nod.

"I have a great deal to learn," I replied. "But I hope I can contribute *something* to repay all that—" I looked around the room. "That *all* of you have done for me."

"We will have to be careful with you," Timo said. "We must not push you too far before you are fully recovered from the sielunjuoja attack. We owe you at the least an apology for not preventing that. I am still uncertain how it slipped past us."

A thought came to me. It must have showed on my face, for Master Timo looked curiously at me.

"You have some insight to offer?" he inquired.

It wasn't a subject I really wanted to talk about right now, but it would have been rude to decline to answer the question. I owed these people, my new friends, so much.

"I... think I *may*... be able to shed some light on that," I said hesitantly. "From what I have learned since I came here, and... this day. Though I admit it is mostly speculation."

Suddenly I had the attention of nearly every Healer in the room, as well as several of the Rangers.

"Tell us your thoughts, then," Master Timo told me.

I gathered my thoughts and took a deep breath. I would have preferred not to talk about this, not *now*, not so soon, but... very well.

"The... sielunjuoja came from the same world that I did," I began. "Understand, please, that I do not know *how* it was that I *myself* came here. I have only fragmentary memories, that I only partially understand. It is all a blur. But it is clear that... either she somehow followed me, or... somehow, I brought her here with me. Against my

117

will. ***Very much*** against my will."

Kata, standing next to me, took my hand and squeezed tightly.

"No few of you have told me that I am strongly talented," I went on. "Yet I come from a world where Talent, as you use the word, is... a superstition, a fantasy, a plot device in fiction, no more. Unknown in the real world. Many *claim* different forms of it, but all who make the claim turn out to be unable to prove the claim under close observation. It always turns out to be some form of trickery, flummery, intentional fakery to fool the gullible—and usually, to get them to part with their money. A well-known stage illusionist, a performer who fakes the *appearance* of magic in order to entertain audiences who pay for the privilege of being fooled in ways they cannot detect, offered a prize of a very large sum of money to anyone who could simply demonstrate to him any feat of—uh, *beyond normal* ability that he could not *prove* could have been done by mundane means. Nobody ever claimed the prize.

"Beyond any reasonable doubt, in... on Earth there is either no *voima*, or no-one who knows how to use it. Magic, Talent, call it what you will, does not exist there. At least not in any detectable way.

"So consider," I continued, figuring out as I went along how to explain my thoughts, "a room from which all the air has been removed. Into this room you place, oh, a wooden table, a tablecloth upon it, perhaps some books and papers. And you also place on this table a block of metal or stone that has been heated almost to the point that it glows.

"It scorches and chars the cloth and the table beneath it, underneath it, and perhaps for a little distance around it. But with no air, no oxygen, there can be no fire." Since Saamen had a word for oxygen, I considered it safe to assume the basic chemistry of fire was known.

Timo began to nod slowly.

"... Until you let air into the room," he said thoughtfully. "And then suddenly, all is aflame."

I nodded agreement.

Timo pondered.

"There are signs when someone is becoming a sielunjuoja," he mused. "But without air, there can be no fire; without *voima*, there can be no Talent. The clearest warning signs *cannot* show. And yet beneath, the table is still scorched and blackened."

"As were you, Alrekr," Liisa murmured, softly but intensely, from my right.

"Without *voima*, the... ability... cannot fully develop," Timo went on. "But the soul is perhaps already broken beyond any healing, already twisted.

"And then, by accident, we let the—*nascent* sielunjuoja, and you, her chosen prey, *already* wounded, into the same room, now in a place filled with *voima*."

"And suddenly all was aflame," Raimo concluded from behind me.

Timo nodded.

"It was an unimaginably rare set of conditions," he said. "I think you are probably right that this is how it came to pass. That this is why we did not see the signs, why we had no warning."

"Only... that something was *wrong* about her," Kata added quietly.

"Kata," I said after a moment, "I am curious. Just one more question, and then... please let us change the subject."

"Of course," Master Timo said. "Forgive me, please. I should not have mentioned it now. This should be a time of celebration."

"Kata, how *did* you... make her *stop?*"

Kata frowned at me for a moment, then she realized what I meant.

"Ah, I understand," she said, her expression clearing. "I am a Healer, as is Liisa. That is my primary Talent. But also I have a second manifested Talent, one that we call Command. I can power a single, simple command with *voima*, and *for a short time*, the one I direct it to is *compelled* to obey. Within strict limits. It must be clear and specific, it can take no more than a couple of words to express, it cannot be overly complex, it cannot be something that they *cannot* do or is strongly against their nature, it cannot be directed to more than two or three people, and I cannot command someone to knowingly do harm to themselves or another."

"I... see, I think," I said. "Such as 'Be silent.'"

"Exactly," she said. "Though I did not realize at that moment that she was attacking you with more than just her voice."

I nodded.

"And from what you have told me, telling her to stop attacking me entirely would not have worked anyway, because it would be strongly against her nature?"

Kata nodded silent agreement.

"The truth is," she admitted somewhat ruefully, "I seldom find it actually very useful."

I nodded understanding.

"It was a life-saver this time," I pointed out. Kata nodded again.

"Do all Adepts have such secondary Talents?"

"Not all," Kata replied. She gestured toward Master Timo. "Master Timo has a second Talent that we call Impression. He can take something that he *already knows*, and place the knowledge directly into another person's mind. Most commonly he uses it to teach advanced healing techniques. But on you, we tried to see if he could give you our language."

"And it worked," I said. "That is a powerful ability. It would have taken me months to learn it without that aid."

"Stronger Adepts are more *likely* to have more than one Talent," Liisa added. "But it is a matter of chance. Kata has a second Talent, but I do not. Or at least, none that I have yet discovered. And some people have several Talents, but all individually weak. Sometimes related, sometimes not. An unrelated Talent may go undiscovered for some time."

"Hmm." I pondered that. "A mead brewer whose mead never sours, I suppose, might also discover that he is never stung by his bees? As long as he sings to them while he works. But... a woodworker who can also... make crops ripen faster, perhaps? Or make dyes that never fade? Might never discover it. Something like that?"

Liisa nodded.

"That would be a good example," she agreed.

I had been going to change the subject, but I realized that we already had.

"So who else here has a secondary Talent?" I asked, curious.

"Who else in this room?" Kata asked. "Besides myself and Master Timo. Raimo has certain abilities that come with his Huldre blood, but that is not quite the same thing. And Marja... I am uncertain whether it should be considered a secondary Talent or not, but her reserves of energy are amazing. She has more capacity just in herself than Liisa and I put together. We try to use her on the most... *demanding* Healings."

"Like mine," I suggested.

"Indeed," she answered, her eyes serious. "Like yours."

"If I might have your attention a moment," Master Timo said, a few moments later. His voice was pitched to carry, and conversation paused.

"This day we have seen our newest, and two of our best and most loved, joined in marriage." He spread his hands wide, looking at the three of us. "A marriage of three Adepts. This is a day of joy and celebration for Highwatch.

"I congratulate the three of you, from the bottom of my heart," he said, smiling, "and I give you my best wishes for a long and happy future. May you find great joy in each other. The joy that all three of you deserve."

There was a chorus of enthusiastic agreement with that, and then everyone wanted to talk and congratulate us. Piia introduced me to Ari and Paavo, two more of her Rangers, and I had the chance to thank them in person as well. Paavo was compact, dark of hair and complexion, brooding and saturnine, while Ari was tall, blond, muscular, like an adventure-movie Viking warrior.

After a little longer, people began drifting out. It wasn't long before only the three of us, Varpu, Raimo, Vilja and a few pages were left. Then the last books were shelved to Vilja's satisfaction, and she chivvied the pages out, then came over and hugged all three of us. Senja gave us a happy wave as she left.

Raimo hugged us one more time and congratulated us again, then wished us all the future happiness we could find. Then he left, after promising to be available to help with my training in any way that he could, when I was ready. Varpu hugged—and kissed—each of us individually, all three of us, then gathered us all into one last hug before she left, flashing us one last brilliant smile before she closed the door. I found myself almost struggling to understand how a day that had begun with such a horrific morning had ended up so wonderfully.

And then we were alone in our new rooms. I took a few minutes to finally look around and explore, along with my lovely ladies.

This level, it turned out, was immediately below the top of the wall. A large rectangular table with a dozen chairs around it occupied the middle of the room, set up with what I inferred were reading stands. A second group of two chairs and a short sitting couch, with what looked almost a coffee table, was arranged in front of the fireplace. A medium-sized window with six tall vertical panes looked out across the inner bailey. About a quarter of the wall was taken up by a spiraling stair with a handrail. I followed it upstairs to find a small sitting area with a table and four chairs near to a small fireplace, already lit, set in the wall that crossed the room. Another weapon rack stood against one wall, next to a bolted door that apparently led outside.

Something smelled spicy. I traced the scent to a covered flagon on a tray on the table, with three silver goblets next to it. The flagon was hot to the touch. I lifted the lid and was rewarded with a gush of aroma. Mulled mead or wine, I wasn't quite certain which.

A wide door in the wall led to a third room. This room held a four-poster bed that certainly looked as though it would hold three in comfort, a sitting couch like the one in the old room, two wardrobes and a chest of some blond wood, and through an arch, an actual bathtub that appeared to be a single seamless piece of stone no more than an inch thick. I hardly knew which to look at first. A fireplace backed upon the one the other side of the wall, only a thick sheet of iron separating the two. Like the one downstairs, this one had been fueled and lit to take the chill off the rooms. A sizable window in one wall looked out generally eastward across the inner bailey of Highwatch, like the one on the floor below, while two smaller windows faced outward to the north and northwest. I found myself missing our little balcony, and said so.

"The entire top of the wall can be our balcony," Liisa pointed out. "And the tower roof is flat, also. We can go up there any time we wish."

The bath was tempting, but it was late, I had no idea how to fill it, and I was tired. I investigated the bed. The sheets smelled freshly changed. There were hard objects under the covers. Feeling under, I found a half dozen flat, heated stones, the size of dinner platters, evidently placed there to warm the bed. I realized that that was what the empty iron rack at one side of the fireplace was for—heating the warming stones.

"I don't know about you two," I said, "but I am tired, and ready to try out this bed."

"We have a treat first," Liisa reminded me. "Don't forget the wine."

I nodded agreement.

"Of course," I agreed. So we went back out onto the anteroom... no, morning room, really, that was a better word, and sat.

"Permit me," I said, taking the flagon. I poured the hot spiced wine, filling all three goblets, then handed one first to Kata, then Liisa before taking my own. I raised mine, held it out, and they both looked at me.

"Together," I said, at a loss for anything deeper to say. "We are together."

"We are together," both women echoed. Then Liisa added, "May it always remain so."

We clinked our goblets together, and drank. The wine was light and sweet, with flavors of both fruit and honey, and redolent of spices. I looked back and forth between the two of them as I sipped my wine.

"This is another of our customs," Kata told me. "Spiced honey-wine for the wedding night. Tradition says that it brings good fortune."

"Also," Liisa added with a laugh, "it is very good."

"It is indeed," I agreed. "But it would not be half as good, I think, were I not drinking it with the two of you."

After we finished our wine, we returned to the bedchamber, removed the warming stones and set them in their rack, and began to prepare for bed. Kata and Liisa began to unfasten their clothes, but I held up my hands.

"Wait, please," I asked. Kata shot me an inquiring look.

"The two of you have dressed and undressed me many times," I explained. "As a patient, it is true. But now that we are together... please, this time, let *me* be the one to undress *you*." I *ached* to touch them.

That earned me slow smiles from both women.

"If that is your wish, Alrekr," Liisa said softly. So I began with Liisa.

I reached for her waist and just rested my hands there, for the first time. Then I unfastened the sash around her, and slowly unwound it. I dropped it to the floor, then slid my hands under the dark blue sleeveless tunic that fell nearly to her knees and slipped it off her shoulders. Below it she wore a blousy-sleeved, ankle-length dress of silky *kuurii* cloth dyed deep red.

I knelt to unfasten her sandals and slip them off her feet, then stood again. She rested her hands on my shoulders, smiling. I untied the

123

ribbon that held the dress snug around her midriff and loosened it, then bent to catch the hem of the dress and began to slowly gather it upwards, exposing first her long legs, then her slim hips. I caught up the cloth in my hands and she raised her arms, then I slipped the dress off over her head. I drew in my breath and let it fall to the floor. Beneath it, she wore a sleeveless light shift that covered her to mid-thigh. I slowly lifted that off over her head too, letting my fingers slide across her skin as I did so, and then she was naked.

She put her hands back on my shoulders. I gazed up and down the length of her body, the curves of her hips, her pert breasts. I put my hands back on her hips, then slid them around to the small of her back, up towards her shoulder-blades, then pulled her towards me and kissed her. Her arms went around my neck and pulled tight.

We held the kiss for a long moment. When we broke it, I bent slightly, put my right arm behind her knees, picked her up, and carried her the few steps to the bed. Kata had been watching the whole time, with a growing, intense smile. Her face was slightly flushed.

I set Liisa carefully down upon the bed, and she sat on the edge and kissed me once more before she let go. Then it was Kata's turn.

I turned to Kata. Today she was wearing a broad red sash over a golden-yellow *kuurii* blouse with wide ruffles, black breeches, and boots that reached her knees.

I knelt in front of her, put my left hand behind her calf, and tugged gently. She let me raise her leg knee high, putting a hand on my shoulder, running the fingers of the other hand through my hair. I tugged the heel of the boot loose, worked it off her foot, and drew it off her leg. Then I put her foot down and took the other boot off her the same way.

As I stood, she pulled me close to her and into a fierce kiss. I held her tightly as we kissed, then freed a hand to loosen the sash and pull it away. I dropped it, put that hand on the small of her back, slid it down onto a lovely buttock and squeezed, pulling her against me, before I felt for the ties on her breeches. Her tongue probed my mouth. I pulled the ties loose and eased the breeches down over her hips, enjoying the feel of my fingers trailing over her skin with nothing but her blouse in between.

When I got them past mid-thigh, her breeches dropped to the floor. She took a half step forward out of them. Now just the blouse covered her, to the tops of her thighs.

I took hold of the bottom of the cloth and began to slowly lift it up, running my hands up her body. I didn't want to miss a single touch. As my hands passed her breasts she lifted her arms above her head and I slipped it off of her. She draped her arms around my neck as she lowered them.

I looked her up and down, seeing her too naked for the first time. She was *exquisite*. There was no other word. I dropped to one knee in front of her, pulled her closer with an arm around her waist, and kissed her breasts, one after the other, then her navel. She drew in her breath in a little gasp. Then I picked her up as well, carried her to the bed, and set her down next to Liisa. It was Liisa now who was looking a little flushed.

I kissed them both, Kata then Liisa, then stood and took a step back. I began to reach for the fastenings of my tunic, but Liisa caught my hand.

"No, Alrekr," she told me, with a wicked smile. "Now it is *OUR* turn."

"We have undressed you many times," Kata said to me, smiling, "as a *patient*. *Tonight*, we *all* undress each other as lovers."

Liisa stood (gods, she was beautiful) and reached for the fastenings herself. She undid them slowly, then she and Kata, on either side of me, slipped the tunic off me. I reached my arms backwards so that they could get it free, then rested a hand each on their shoulders as they began to peel my shirt off me. I lifted my arms to let them get the shirt off. Liisa was still pulling the shirt free of my arms when Kata began running her hands over my chest and down my sides.

She unfastened my breeches, then pulled them down off my hips as Liisa let me get my hands back. I cupped Liisa's face in my hands and leaned forward to kiss her, as Kata began kissing her way down my belly. Oh my. I shivered slightly with pleasure and had to take a breath. Liisa met me halfway and kissed me first. I dropped my hands to Liisa's shoulders, then down to her breasts, as her hands ran down my side and traced the line of my hipbones.

Kata had my breeches around my ankles now. I was aware enough to lift one foot, then the other. Then she stood and pressed herself against me. I pulled Liisa in on the other side, and we all three of us held each other, naked, for the first time. I could feel I already had a raging erection. And I was sure I somehow felt... *their* arousal as well, in some way I could not explain.

Then Liisa and Kata took a hand each and pulled me towards the bed. Having never been a *complete* fool, I did not resist. We climbed into bed, and they cuddled up on either side of me, and we kissed and cuddled and explored every inch of each other with our fingers, our lips, our tongues. I had been *wanting* this so badly. I kissed Kata's collarbones, worked my way down to her breast, took her nipple into my mouth, my hand between her shoulderblades, as the fingers of my other hand traced down Liisa's ribs and across the small of her back. I felt the smooth swell of Liisa's hip as she kissed her way down my chest, stroked her thigh as she continued across my belly, as I kissed my way in turn down Kata's side. We repositioned a little so that I could reach Kata's hip with my lips, and Liisa slid into the gap, and then Liisa's smooth belly was in front of me, so I kissed there instead as I cupped Kata's breast and teased the nipple, my other hand sliding over Liisa's butt, then I saw Kata's mouth on Liisa's breast and felt her tremble. We wanted to touch every inch of each other, and I had the strangest feeling as though I was touching with more fingers than I had, feeling touches that were not on my body. I found that if I could get into just the right position against both of them, I could hear both of their hearts at once. Theirs were beating as hard as mine. I would swear our hearts were all beating *together*, in time with each other.

After we had played and explored and licked and kissed and tickled for a while, Liisa turned me onto my back, and then Kata climbed on top of me, adjusted her position a little, and then lowered herself onto me and guided me inside her. I had my right hand on her left thigh, stroking the strong, smooth muscles, and my other arm wrapped tightly around Liisa, lying half across my chest, kissing me/us. I couldn't reach Kata's back, but I/we could and did raise **my/our** right hand to her chest, cupping **her/our** breast and teasing the nipple. Somehow I could... feel... **our** hand, on **our** breast, **our** nipple hardening, as **our** bodies joined. I could feel Liisa's/my kiss from both sides at once.

"This is—what it is—like, Alrekr," Kata managed to say between gasps, "when—when Adepts—make love." She stayed there for a long while, rocking **her/my** hips against **me/her** as *our* excitement built, before **she/I/we** let out a long, shuddering moan, then half-collapsed across both **me/us/all-of-us**.

After a long moment, she shifted herself over a little to my right, then half-rolled off me and pressed herself against **my/our** side. Then Liisa/we rolled onto *our* back and pulled *us* on top. Kata followed *us*, *our* hands and lips touching and probing. Liisa/we slowly spread *our* lovely thighs apart and *we* slipped between, then adjusted *our* position to align ourselves. *We* thrust carefully into Liisa, all the way in, and *we* gasped, then pulled *us* even tighter against *us* and kissed *us* again. Kata wrapped *our* arms around *us* and held *us*. I was very aware of *our* breasts pressed tightly against *us*. What can I say. I like a pretty pair of breasts. I felt Kata's inward smile at the thought, and heard Liisa silently agree. Liisa/I/we/all-of-us climaxed together—the first time—and it was... transcendent.

It felt as though the three of us made love for hours. It was not even that I felt everything that Kata or Liisa did. All three of us felt *all* of us, and we felt us feeling us feeling us. I felt Liisa feeling Kata feeling all of us, everything we did. It felt as though we were one joined soul occupying three bodies.

When finally we collapsed across each other, spent, sated, drenched in bliss, we just lay and enjoyed the contact with each other, exchanging occasional gentle kisses. And it did not escape my attention that often it was Kata and Liisa who kissed. Seeing that made me happy beyond words. My one fear had been whether we would make this work, but it was clear we were not two couples in an awkward triangle, we were truly *three*. A triad, not two intersecting with two. The same joy had filled me earlier when I had found myself looking up at the two of them kneeling across me, Liisa's/our head thrown back in ecstasy, Kata's/our mouth on her/our breast while I/we held the other, my/our other hand in the small of Kata's/our back, such a perfect and delightful curve.

"I love you with all my heart," I murmured sleepily. "Both of you."

"And I love you, Alrekr," Liisa replied equally drowsily, "and you, Kata." Kata just gave a contented half-sigh, almost a purr, and squeezed us both a little tighter.

Eventually, we drifted off to sleep, in a happy, contented tangle. I don't think I have ever felt happier in my life.

9: The Living and the Dead

When we awoke in the morning, we had shifted around a bit, but we were still cuddled together. My head was pillowed on Kata's chest just then, between her breasts. There was a breast right in front of my face, so *of course* I kissed it, then moved my head enough to take the nipple into my mouth. She stirred, then gave a contented sigh.

"Mmmmmm," she said. "Good morning, my love."

I released the nipple.

"Good morning, beloved," I replied.

We lay there a while longer, looking at each other, then I reached for Liisa and we both began to lick and nibble at her. After a few minutes, she woke up, giggling.

"Good morning, beautiful," I said.

"Good morning to you too," she replied, laughing.

I looked at them both.

"Last night was incredible," I said, still feeling awed. "I have—literally—never felt anything like it."

Kata smiled sleepily at me.

"That is because we were connected on more than a physical and emotional level," she told me. "When the Talented make love, they are connected also through *voima*, through their Talent. This is... something that all know, here. Your energy merges with mine and Liisa's, Alrekr. And the stronger the Talent, and the love, the stronger the merging. And... even between two... but *three* of us, Alrekr, and we are *all* strong. And that is why it was..." She trailed off.

"Transcendent," I finished.

"That is a good word," Liisa agreed contentedly. "It becomes... so much *more*." Then she yawned, and stretched like a cat. I gazed at her and enjoyed the view.

"So how are you feeling this morning, Alrekr?" she asked.

I thought about that one for a while.

"Refreshed," I said at last. "And... *refilled*, somehow. And very, *very* happy."

"Mmmm," Kata murmured, and leaned over closer, running her

hands over me. "Yes... actually, you look quite a bit better. Last night did you good in more ways than one. Your spirit is still... torn. But the wounds are closing well."

Eventually we resigned ourselves to climbing out of bed. I happily admired their bodies as we washed ourselves and each other, then dried each other off. We got dressed, went downstairs to the main room, and Liisa rang for a page.

"How do those work, anyway?" I asked, curious. "Surely nobody can hear that tiny bell all the way in the main keep."

"They don't have to," Kata explained. "Most of an entire wall in the pages' hall in the keep is covered in bells like this one. They are laid out as though on a map of the keep. There is a smaller page room on this side of the fortress, with fewer bells, to serve the towers furthest from the keep. The bell outside the door is linked to a bell in each of those halls. When Liisa rang it, the bell in the page room on this side rang. A page in that room will have looked at the bells, seen immediately where the call came from, and be..."

There came a tap at the door.

"... on the way here right now," she finished, laughing, as Liisa answered the door. I glanced that way and noticed that Rami was our page this morning. I gave him a friendly wave, and got a bow in return. Liisa asked him to fetch us breakfast, and he sped off.

"So why aren't the bells inside the room?" I asked.

"Because then they would be in a separate space from the page halls," Kata told me. "The page halls are completely open on one side, just columns floor to ceiling instead of a wall, so that they are a continuous space with the hallways."

I nodded, understanding the concept but not the reasons why it worked that way. That was alright. There would be time later to learn things like that.

"You said my spirit is still 'torn,'" I asked, while we waited for breakfast. "And you've told me that I should not try to... use, or presumably, train... my talent when my spirit is still damaged."

"Yes," Liisa agreed. "It would be dangerous for you."

"So... does that mean that I always need to be careful about using, uh, power while... injured?"

"No," Kata replied. "... Well, all right, yes. But the special danger at the moment is that you do not yet know how to *control* your power. You could do yourself terrible harm. Once you know how to control your power, you would need only not over-exert yourself."

"And what will heal those tears?" I asked.

"Time, mostly," Liisa said. "But there are things we can—and *will*—do to help it along."

"*Besides* the most utterly mind-blowing sex I've ever had?" I couldn't keep the grin off my face. Liisa laughed.

"Yes, Alrekr," she agreed. "*Besides* that. But I hope there is plenty of that too." Now it was my and Kata's turn to laugh—not that I disagreed for a second.

"Anyway," I went on after a moment, "what can I do in the meantime? I want to get... active. Be useful. I have *so much* to repay."

"I would truly encourage patience for a little while longer," Kata cautioned. "Another few days at least. Until you are fully recovered from..." She hesitated for a moment, and looked at me. "From the attack."

I swallowed, my mouth suddenly dry. I still didn't want to think about that any more than I had to.

Kata stepped closer, put her arms around me, and rested her head on my chest. My arms went reflexively around her.

"I'm sorry," she said quietly. "I should not have mentioned that. Not yet."

I hugged her tightly.

"It—it will be alright," I told her. "I have to deal with it. Come to grips with it. I may as well start now."

She looked up at me.

"Alrekr," she said, "you should know this. After you were attacked yesterday, I ordered that the body be... set aside. For you to decide what to do. You were in *no condition* to decide a proper disposition at the time. And it is your place to decide." She hesitated, biting her lip. "Was that correct, Alrekr?"

I squeezed her tighter and kissed her forehead.

"I have absolute trust in you to make the right decision, Kata," I told her. "Though I have to ask. What are the, uh ... options?"

"Burn it or bury it, really," she said. "That is the gist of it. And with a sielunjuoja we always burn the head in any case. It probably makes no difference, but... it is the custom that came to be."

131

I thought. About whether it mattered to me. About whether I even wanted to be involved in the decision at all. Or whether I just wanted to be *done* with the entire thing and put it behind me as soon as I could manage.

"You know," I said at length, "I think... that when it comes to... disposition... what I want most of all, at this moment, is to *never have to think about it again*. To put everything involved as far from my mind as I possibly can.

"Can you please see to that?"

Kata nodded.

"I will make arrangements on your behalf," she agreed. "You need not be involved any further if you do not wish to."

"*Thank you*, Kata," I said, with feeling. "It is a horrible chapter of my life that I just want to be *done* with. Once and for all."

Then I slipped a finger beneath her chin, tipped her face up a little further, and kissed her. She relaxed, pulled my head back down and kissed me back.

We were interrupted by the arrival of breakfast, which we took upstairs to the morning room. Breakfast was an unleavened flatbread, piping hot, rolled and stuffed with a delicious buttery cheese, boiled eggs in their shells with the yolks still slightly creamy, and fresh fruit. Something purple, segmented like an orange but with much more delicate membranes, sweet with just a hint of tartness.

"Tell me if you would, please," I asked, after a little while. "How *do* you generally handle your dead?"

"The sick are always burned," Liisa answered, "so not to spread disease. Those who fall in battle are usually burned upon a pyre, to honor them, but sometimes burial in the ground or the air is chosen."

"Burial in the air?" I asked.

"The body is cleaned and placed on a high platform," she said, "for birds to carry the soul away. Then after a year we bury the bones.

"Those who die of old age or accident may receive any of these also, in accordance with the preference and personal beliefs of any family who survive them, or any preference they may have declared during life. Criminals sentenced to death are almost always beheaded and buried.

132

"The stillborn are almost always given to the birds, as usually are—women who die in childbirth."

"Does that happen... often?" I asked, quietly. I sensed something wrong.

"Not if there is a Healer within reach," she replied. "Though—" She broke off. It was clear that something had deeply upset her. I stood, took a step closer, and put my arm around her shoulders.

"Liisa," I said, "something is wrong. Isn't it? Did I say something wrong?"

She took a deep breath. Now I *knew* I'd accidentally pushed a hot button. I felt terribly guilty. I hadn't intended to cause her pain.

"I attended a difficult birth last year," she explained, her voice unsteady. "There was... a crisis, a complication, at the last, and no time to send for a second healer. I could save the mother, *or* the child. Not both. No matter how I tried.

"The husband said, Save my wife, please, I have two other children. But the wife begged me, Please, Healer, let me go, save my child.

"I saved the child."

She was crying now. I knelt to her level, pulled her close as she sat, and held her, stroking her hair. Kata had left her chair, and laid her hands on Liisa's shoulders from the other side.

"It breaks your heart that you could not save both, doesn't it?" I said gently.

Liisa nodded silently, her face wet with tears.

"We know we can never save *everyone*," Kata said to me. "Though Healing is among the most common Talents, still there are not enough of us. Sometimes we simply cannot do enough. We can save many. Most, who are not too badly injured for us to reach in time. But we lose some, and some losses are harder to bear than others. This one hit her hard. Being forced to choose which of the mother and child would live."

I nodded in silent understanding.

"Liisa," I apologized, "I'm truly sorry I brought that up. I didn't know." She took my hand and squeezed it. "That depth of compassion is a part of why I love you, I think."

After a little, we resumed our breakfast. I held Liisa's hand as we ate.

"Kata," I said, "that is three methods of putting the dead to rest. And...?"

"And what of the fourth?" she replied. I nodded.

"There are three ways we *honor* the dead, Alrekr. A *níð* does not deserve any honor. They are just as any other animal. An unmarked grave, or burning."

I thought it through.

"I understand now," I said. "Thank you."

A little later, I found a moment while Liisa was out of earshot. I didn't want to risk further upsetting her.

"Kata," I asked, "about that birth. Was there... any trouble afterward?"

Kata looked at me seriously. It seemed she understood my concern.

"No, Alrekr," she told me. "Not in the least. Liisa was—distraught, and the father heartbroken, but he saw how hard Liisa had fought trying to save *both*, even risking herself in her effort to save his wife as well. He understood that she had done *everything* she possibly could, and that in the end, she had honored his wife's dying wish. That she had started by saving the one she *knew* she could save... and then tried to save the other, *as well*.

"He named his newborn daughter after her, Alrekr. To honor her."

After breakfast we went walking around Highwatch again. We started by climbing the outside stair to the top of our tower, for another look at the mountains. Then we came down again and walked the wall eastward until we came back to the keep, and went exploring parts of the keep I had not yet seen. There were a lot of those. For one thing, I was curious to see the page hall.

Almost as we reached the page hall, we ran into Rami coming the other direction—or more accurately, Rami almost ran into us. He changed course abruptly and came to a sudden stop right in front of us.

"Honored!" he said, sketching a half-bow before Kata. "I was just sent to seek you. You are called for, urgently. A Ranger thrown from a horse. Raimo is there already, he says he needs you as well."

Kata was instantly all business.

"Lead the way, Rami," she told him. "I will find you later, Alrekr." And with that, she was gone at Rami's heels.

"Should we go after her?" I asked.

"No, Alrekr," Liisa replied. "If she needs more help, she will send for it. And if *you* go, I *know* you will want to try to help her, and you will hurt yourself. If you are able to do anything at all, which you probably will not be."

I gave a brief, embarrassed chuckle.

"Guilty as charged," I said sheepishly. "We'd better find something else to do."

Liisa smiled and led me away.

Some time later, we found ourselves wandering through the main bailey. To one side, a group of young men were training with the quarterstaff, under the watchful eye of an older man.

"That is Master-at-Arms Toivo," Liisa told me. "They are new recruit candidates for the Guard. He will see how they do with the staff before deciding which will be admitted and receive further training."

She introduced me.

"Newfound Járnhandr," Master Toivo said, with a twinkle in his eye. "From another world, they say. I hear you have already stolen two of our best Healers from us."

"I assure you, sir," I said, "I have no intention of taking them away from here."

"Rumor has it you are our newest Adept."

"Rumor has been exaggerating," I replied. "As it often does. I cannot even begin training yet. Not until I am fully healed."

We stood and watched for a while as the inductees sparred.

"How often are new recruits accepted into the Guard?" I asked.

"Typically twice a year," Toivo replied. "No more than six to eight are accepted at one time. Those admitted, unless they come to us with skills already, will spend as much as a year training before they do any more than stand watches."

"You don't want to send anyone half-trained into harm's way?" I hazarded.

He snorted.

"I would keep them three years if Knight-Commander Mikkinen would let me," he said. "He is the Guard Commander in Highwatch. *His* opinion is that if a recruit is not ready for field assignments in a year, then they never will be. But either way, they will all continue training as long as they are assigned in Highwatch. Even the veterans spar at least every other day."

"That seems sound to me," I said. "Can't let soldiers lose the edge or they stop being soldiers. But they need some downtime too, so they don't become brittle."

"Spoken like a soldier yourself," he replied, eyeing me appraisingly. "You have experience?"

"Some," I hedged. "But not in a long time, and not here. I... know many weapons, but the staff is not one of them. I used to use a bow, and have some skill with the sword."

"The sword, hmm? And what style of sword do you prefer?"

I hesitated. I glanced at his hip. I was not greatly surprised that he wore a one-handed sword that from this superficial glance looked generally like a Frankish Ulfberht, though with a little more hilt and quillon to it.

"There are two types I prefer," I answered. "The one, similar to yours, but about two hands longer in the blade, and with a wider guard and a two-hand hilt.

"The other, I expect you have never seen. About a handspan longer than yours, with a two-hand hilt again and a small round guard, the blade slightly curved, single-edged, differentially tempered, sharp as a razor." I sketched the shape of the blade in the air.

His eyebrows rose at that.

"Intriguing," he said slowly. "A curved sword. I have never heard of such a thing. Do you think you know enough about it to tell our smith how to make one? I would like to see one."

Now it was *my* eyebrows that rose. I paused and thought about it.

"I know—in theory—much of the basic principles," I began carefully. "How the blade is constructed, how and why the steel is

136

folded, how and why it is tempered as it is. And I know how to build the box-bellows to obtain the necessary heat to smelt the steel. But I have never made one, nor seen one made first-hand." I hesitated.

"I could *TRY* to share what I know with your smith. But I make no promises."

"A man can do no more than try his best," Toivo answered.

I watched the trainees a little longer, and then a thought occurred to me.

"Liisa," I said, "you told me I must not try to exert my Talent until my spirit is fully healed. But will exerting my *body* do me harm?"

"No, not at all," she said. "As long as you do not overdo it, it should do you good. Exerting your body and exerting your spirit are two entirely different things—although both will tire you."

"Well, then," I said. "Master Toivo, I have a request. I need to do *something* to keep me occupied while I heal, and I cannot spend all my time keeping Liisa from her duties. I have never mastered the quarterstaff. Could you perhaps arrange for me to receive some training with it?"

Toivo looked me up and down measuringly.

"You have some height on you, and look to have good reach," he judged. "Good strong shoulders." He grasped one of my hands and looked at it. "Good hands. You're not afraid of a little hard work."

He nodded, and turned towards the training group.

"Eero!"

One of the sparring pairs broke off and looked our way. Toivo waved one of them over, a compact, dark-haired young man.

"Eero, this is Alrekr Járnhandr, the Newfound whom the Rangers brought in from the crags at winter's end. He would like to learn the staff. I wish you to begin teaching him the basics."

Eero gave him a half-bow.

"At once, Master Toivo." He turned to me.

"Take off your tunic, or you'll overheat."

I took it off and handed it to Liisa. He tossed me a padded sailcloth jack instead, then pointed to a rack of staves.

"Pick through those and find one you like. Then we'll judge your

137

choice."

I walked over to the rack and started sorting through them. I noticed Eero and Toivo were both watching me intently.

The first I pulled out was very slightly curved. No. Not that one. The next, straight, but... I bounced it on the ground, butt-first. No. I didn't like it. Too light. I shook my head again.

I put it back and tried a third. Good weight, but... it felt dead, dull. I looked more closely. It had the faintest green tinge.

"This one isn't fully seasoned," I said, putting it back. Toivo nodded approvingly.

The next felt... *off*. I didn't know how to explain it. I bounced it on the ground as I had the first. There was...

I *felt* it, somehow. There was a flaw inside. A shake in its core.

On impulse, I tossed it to Eero.

"This one will break," I said. "Two, maybe... three good blows left in it? I would guess little more than that."

Eero examined it closely.

"I see no flaw," he said. He passed it to Master Toivo, who also inspected it.

"I see nothing either," Toivo said. He bounced it experimentally, as I had, nodded, then handed it back to Eero. "But... yes, it feels off. Test it on the pell, and let us see."

Eero stepped up to the pell, took a good grasp on the staff, then whirled it around his head and struck at the pell. It hit with a flat THWACK, and he took the rebound and fed it into another blow, THWACK, THWACK, THWACK. The fourth strike sounded a little off. So did the fifth.

On the sixth strike, there was a sharp CRACK, and the staff split lengthwise and flew into three pieces.

Eero looked at the broken staff in his hand, then picked up the other two shards and examined them as well.

"Well, well," mused Master Toivo.

"How did you know?" Eero asked me.

"I'm... not sure," I replied. "I *felt* the flaw in its center. I don't

138

quite know how."

"Interesting indeed," said Toivo. "Continue."

The fifth, again, felt too light. The sixth—

"*This* one," I declared, almost as soon as I picked it up. It was a good weight. It *felt* right. I bounced it like the others, though I think I already knew I didn't need to. It struck with a solid THUD, and rebounded with no shivering. The sound was clear and sharp, not dull or flat.

Eero held out a hand, and I passed him the staff. He bounced it himself, twirled it a couple of times and whirled it around his head.

"Good choice," he said approvingly. "How did you choose?"

"I... started out just ruling out ones that felt *wrong*," I said. "But this one did not simply—not feel wrong. It felt *right*, the moment I picked it up."

Toivo nodded thoughtfully.

"Have you any previous staff training?" Eero asked.

"None of any consequence," I replied. "And the very little I have was in a completely different style that used a shorter, lighter staff called a *bo*."

"Let us begin, then," he said. He tossed the staff back to me, and I caught it. Liisa sat down on a bench to watch.

"This is the basic grip..."

By the time the sparring group broke up, I knew how to properly hold a quarterstaff, and the basics of how to block and guard myself against blows. I was also dripping with sweat, and had a fine collection of aches that would probably turn into bruises.

It felt surprisingly good. The staff I had picked out had been set aside as mine.

"I'd love a... Um. *Suihku*? Like... *sade*? No." I fumbled for a word as Liisa handed me back my tunic, but there was none. "You don't have a word for it."

"You... want it to rain?" she asked.

"No, I— Hmm." I thought a moment. "Sort of. Imagine a very small room, just large enough for one or two people to stand in. No larger than the span of your arms. And it has a drain in the floor for water, and a—like a sieve, or strainer, up above your head, that sprays heated water downward. You can adjust the warmth of the water as you prefer."

As Liisa thought about that, she began to smile.

"That sounds rather nice," she said. "But I have never seen such a thing."

"I suspected that, when I found no word," I said. "I suppose I shall have to 'invent' it. Which will mean indoor, uh, pipes for water.

"Which reminds me. How did Knight-Commander... Viljainen get that bath filled? I see no sign of running water in our rooms."

Liisa laughed. "I hear he had all the available pages and servants busy running pots of hot water up the tower for an hour at a time to fill it," she said.

"Well *that's* no good," I replied. "I won't make people wait on me like that."

"He wasn't popular for it," she agreed. "And he decided after a while that Highwatch was a bit too rustic of a posting to suit him. So he moved back to the capital, and he was replaced by Knight-Commander Mikkinen, who took rooms next to the guard barracks with his men.

"However," she went on, her smile growing, "Highwatch has a bath-house with a heated and a cold bath, and a sauna. Anyone can use it at any time."

"Well, what are we waiting for?" I said. She grinned. "Lead on, my love."

The bath-house was actually not far from our northwest tower, nestled nearly against the north wall, a mostly-timber building I had seen before but never asked about. We went in, and inside were two small pools, each about twelve by perhaps thirty feet, set in a flagstoned floor.

"The cold pool is fed directly from the same underground spring that feeds the cisterns," Liisa explained, pointing. "The other is the same water source, but heated by passing through a bed of hot stones." Behind the two pools was a further enclosed area within the building that was clearly the sauna. To one side was a small area with benches and baskets of wash cloths, clearly for washing off before entering the baths. To the other, a similar area had shelves piled with towels.

"What keeps the stones hot?" I asked.

"They are—bound—to hot stone deep underground, beneath the roots of the mountains," Liisa said. "An adept named Tumarïnen built it more than four hundred years ago. The hot stones never cool."

"Wow," I said. "Free hot water for life. He must have made a lot of people happy, over the centuries."

We had the place to ourselves at this time of day. I happily admired Liisa's beauty again as we undressed each other. Liisa reached out a finger and traced a few of the bruises on my arms and shoulders. We piled our clothes on a shelf, and washed off, me especially. Then I went directly to the hot pool and lowered myself in. It was perhaps four feet deep, stepped along three sides to make seating. Liisa slipped in next to me. I stretched, letting the heat soak in and soothe the aches where I had failed to block blows.

After a little while, Liisa gently laid her fingers on my arm and began softly singing. I felt a trickle of power and realized she was singing the bruises away. She worked her way down my right arm, then moved to my other side and began there. Then she stopped unexpectedly. She looked at my arm closely, running her fingers over the sore spots.

"Is something wrong?" I asked.

"Wrong?" she repeated. "No. But these bruises are healing on their own, much more quickly than is usual. Compared to when we washed, they have already visibly faded in the time I spent on your other arm."

"Huh," I said. I thought about that. "I have to admit I always envied Wolverine his healing factor."

She looked at me curiously.

"You have mentioned that name before," she told me.

"A fictional super-powered hero," I explained. "His superpower, really, is his healing factor, his ability to heal within seconds any injury that does not kill him outright. Though he is best *known* for his—uh..." I paused and reconsidered how to say it.

"His entire skeleton was replaced with an—*also* fictional—unbreakable metal called *adamantium* that has the special property that it can be worked only once. This included replacing his other... born superpower, retractable bony claws in his hands, with longer claws of the same *adamantium*. Only his incredible healing power enabled him

141

to even survive this process."

"These... super-powers that you speak of... like Talents?" she asked. It was a good insight, I thought.

"Yes," I agreed. "Although they were completely made up. Just stories. Not real, nor pretended to be."

"And when you re-wrought yourself, you wished for this healing factor?"

"No," I said immediately. "I would be afraid to try such a thing. I heeded your warnings. I don't know how it... *works*. Even were it not a tale of fiction."

She sighed in relief.

"*Good*," she said, fervently. "That would have been a *terrifying* risk. And would almost certainly have ended badly."

"But," I continued, "I might have envisioned myself... healing a bit faster than before. I have always healed all but the most severe injuries more quickly than most people. Minor cuts would close completely in days. After I was... injured, the—healers—told my family I would never walk again. I proved them wrong."

"I am very glad of that," Liisa told me earnestly.

"But even if I knew how it worked," I continued, "I would not actually ask for his healing factor. It came at too high a cost."

Liisa looked curiously at me.

"In what way?" she asked.

"Well," I replied, "Logan—that is his name, Wolverine was his nickname—was *utterly* alone. Every woman he had ever loved, died. He was forced to kill his own greatest love—because she had lost control of her own power, and it was turning her into something terrible, a force of pure uncontrolled destruction, and there was no other way to stop it. She *begged* him to kill her, to save her from becoming a monster."

Liisa looked down for a long moment, then back up at me.

"That is terribly sad," she agreed quietly. She snuggled up against me.

We still had the bathhouse to ourselves, so after a moment I lifted her into my lap. We sat and cuddled and soaked in the hot water. And, well, yes, there was some kissing too.

After we'd both had a good soak, we got out and dried each other off. Liisa looked at my left side again.

"Your bruises are almost gone," she said. "Already." I stretched and worked my arms and shoulders a little. I could feel a slight residual stiffness, but that was all.

We got dressed, still alone in the bath house, and left.

"So where now, Alrekr?" Liisa asked.

I thought.

"I don't know," I said slowly. "Just... show me around more of Highwatch, perhaps?" Liisa nodded.

"This way, then," she replied.

I followed her as she led me around, showing me what was where. Eventually our steps took us deep into the keep, and into a hallway where numerous staff were coming and going, some of them carrying covered dishes, and then past the hallway into the kitchen itself. There was a row of brick ovens along one wall, chimneys rising through the ceiling above them, and work tables stood in rows. There were nearly a dozen cooks at work, not to mention numerous assistants, most of them looking to be in their teens or not much older. A stern-faced woman with iron-grey hair intercepted us.

"Healer Liisa," she said. "Is this...?"

"Mistress Kerttu," Liisa replied, "this is the newfound, Alrekr Járnhandr."

"Well," Mistress Kerttu said, looking me up and down, "it is good to meet you. Don't get in the way of my cooks."

"I wouldn't dream of it, Mistress Kerttu," I said, giving her a half-bow. "I know better than to interfere in a working kitchen."

She nodded approvingly.

"Good," she replied. "That is a good start."

"I understand," I ventured slowly, glancing at Liisa, "that you, uh... gave some assistance to my two lovely ladies yesterday evening."

Mistress Kerttu smiled.

"I was pleased to be able to help," she replied. "It is a good and happy thing to see."

"I owe you thanks, then," I said, bowing my head slightly. "It was very good. All of it."

"Well, thank you for the words of kindness," she answered me. The smile grew.

Liisa looked at me, biting her lip slightly. I caught it.

"... Something troubles you?" I asked.

"Not troubles, exactly," she said. "It is more... I do not know whether I should say something that may trouble *you*."

"Perhaps you should explain, then," I told her.

She hesitated.

"I *know* you mean no harm by it," I reassured her. She nodded.

"I know that you said that you did not want to be involved," she told me. "But... well... until disposition was decided... Kata had the body sent to the kitchen cold store. To preserve it."

It was my turn to hesitate.

"I see," I nodded slowly. I didn't know what to think.

"I... don't really *want* to look," I said hesitantly, at last. "In truth. But I probably *should*."

Liisa nodded understanding.

"Mistress, might we visit the cold store?" Liisa asked.

"Ahh," said Mistress Kerttu. "Yes. The cold store." She gave me a searching look. "I understand." She looked back at Liisa. "Well, you know the way. Don't dawdle."

Liisa nodded and led me around the edge of the kitchen towards the back corner, where stone steps led down to a heavy door. I put my hand on the door. It was cold. Liisa opened the door, and we went in.

Inside, the cold was startling after the heat of the kitchen. I gauged it no more than about forty degrees just inside the door. Wooden racks held baskets of perishable vegetables and fruit, as well as large glass bottles holding what I presumed to be milk. Cured hams hung on hooks from the ceiling.

Liisa led me towards the back of the large room. It got colder as we went further in. I could see that the back wall was covered in thick frost. Butchered carcasses hung near the back wall. I could see what looked like boar, and what I guessed to be deer or antelope of some kind, as well as a few smaller animals and various sizes of plucked game birds. Tubs a little further from the wall held an assortment of

144

fish.

I looked at that back wall.

"Let me guess," I said. "This is more of Adept Tumarïnen's work?"

"Actually, no," Liisa said. "This was done by a different Adept, about—a century later, I think. But he was following Master Tumarïnen's ideas. I am told the copper plates that line the back wall are attached to bars that run into an ice-well, which is bonded to glaciers in the high mountain peaks."

"So you get free refrigeration... unless the glaciers ever melt," I said. "Clever. I think perhaps you have wrought wiser things with Talent here than my world wrought with our technology."

"Why would the glaciers in the mountains ever melt?" Liisa asked.

I looked at her, suddenly envious of the luxury of that naïvete. Then I sighed heavily.

"The people of my home world are wrecking—probably have long since wrecked, now—that world, Liisa. At first out of ignorance, then, even after they knew what was happening, they kept going, because they could not break the habit of pure, short-sighted greed." I sighed again. I imagine my bitterness was evident.

"Let that be a discussion for another time, please," I said. Liisa nodded.

What we had come for was about half-way back in the room, against a side wall. The body lay on a table, covered by a cloth. I stopped, looking that way, for a long, long minute. Then I slowly walked over and pulled the cloth back.

The head had been cut off and lay separated by a few inches from the body. I looked at that, and then I gave Liisa a questioning look. She nodded.

"It is a souldrinker, Alrekr," she told me. "An abomination, a terrible thing, that can consume someone's soul from a distance. On the rare occasions when we encounter one, we make *absolutely certain* that it is dead."

I nodded understanding. On Earth that I had left behind, vampires were only the stuff of legends, horror stories, but they were terrible things. Here... sielunjuojat were *real*. And perhaps even worse.

I stood there and looked at the body. I remembered that this had once been a woman I had known well. Even, once, been close to. For a while.

I *also* remembered that that woman had, only the previous day, tried to literally consume my soul while I still lived. On top of far too many years of past torment.

I could not repress a shudder. I realized that I was tense, trembling. I took a deep breath, and let it out slowly.

After a while, I nodded again.

"You know," I told Liisa slowly, "I wasn't *at all* sure how I would feel about this. But I think it was important to find out." I reached out a hand to touch the body. The flesh was cold and firm. "But this... isn't a person any more."

I turned to look at Liisa. My heart felt somehow lighter, though I was still tense.

"I won't deny," I said, "I still have—complex, conflicted feelings. But... I think I am done here."

"Have you seen what you need to, Alrekr?"

I thought for a moment.

"Yes," I said, with a nod, slightly uncertainly at first. Then, more confidently, "Yes, I believe I have."

"Then we should go," Liisa said. "It is cold in here."

"Of course," I said. And so we left.

When we had closed the door behind us and climbed the stone stairs, we waited for a few minutes while the heat of the kitchen took away the chill of the cold store. After a few minutes, Mistress Kerttu bustled by, calling out instructions.

"Mistress Kerttu," I said. "Thank you very much for indulging me. And I apologize for the, uh, for any disruption to your kitchen."

She gave me a long look, then nodded abruptly, approvingly.

"Some things are important to be dealt with," she replied. "It is only a minor inconvenience to my kitchen. And all is well that ends well."

And so we left.

When Liisa and I reached our rooms, Kata was already there, sitting in the middle of the couch in front of the fireplace. She looked weary.

I immediately went to her, sat down beside her, and put an arm around her. She snuggled contentedly into me.

"It was a difficult healing?" I asked.

"It was," she agreed tiredly. "A ranger's horse reared and threw him when a serpent struck at it, just south of the bridge. He hit his head on a stone when he fell. He is lucky to be alive."

"That would be why Raimo specifically sent for her," Liisa said to me. "There is no Healer in Highwatch more skilled when it comes to head injuries."

"Is that why you were assigned to me?" I asked. "Because I had a head injury?"

"In part," Kata replied. "You had *so many* injuries, Alrekr. Head injuries, spinal injuries, one shoulder half ripped apart, broken ribs, a collapsed lung, torn liver, internal bleeding... and more. You looked as though you had been trampled by a troll."

She looked up at me.

"That is why we worked on you for six days before you woke, Alrekr. There upon the trail, the two of us first stopped the bleeding inside your head, which would have killed you within hours. Then as soon as we got you back to Highwatch, Raimo and Vallaïnen joined us to work on you. We repaired the other internal bleeding, and then, we put you into a deeper sleep to buy more time to work on everything else, starting with your broken back.

"But then... for alarmingly long, we could not rouse you from it."

I nodded appreciatively.

"And... the other?"

"She was—much less injured—*physically*, Alrekr. Some of us wondered whether at least some of your injuries were actually received protecting her."

I gazed into the fireplace and let out a slow breath.

"I still don't *know* what happened, Kata. The little I remember of it is just... blurred fragments. Mostly pain, and things smashing, and a black void. But the honest truth is, even with everything I know now, **had** I needed to defend her so... I *would* have."

"I know, Alrekr," Kata told me seriously, turning to look into my eyes. "We have both seen it in your mind. And that is a part of why I love you. Because you are so driven to protect the lives of others,

147

when and where you can. Even if it comes at great cost to yourself. It is a thing healers understand well."

"And... part of it," I added after a little more thought, "is that... despite all, I think I do not want to believe that she *chose* to become what she did."

Kata gave me a long, measuring look, and then nodded slowly.

"I think I can understand that," she said. "There must have been something to see in her, once."

She sat up a little straighter and stretched.

"So what did you two get up to, while I was busy healing a shattered skull?" she asked.

"Mainly, we explored," I said. "And Liisa introduced me to Master-at-Arms Toivo and Mistress Kerttu."

"Mistress Kerttu, hmm?"

Kata gave me a thoughtful look, but I knew what the real question was.

"Yes," I said. "I looked. And... I'm *alright* with it, Kata. I feel... *better*... now. It feels as though a burden has been lifted from my soul."

"I see. That is good." Kata nodded approvingly. "Does that... change your mind in any way about the disposition?"

I hadn't thought about it further, to be honest. But now it seemed a little easier.

"Please just have it burned," I said, at last. Kata nodded.

"I will see to it," she agreed. "So what is this about Master Toivo?"

"Well," I replied, "he has assigned Eero to train me in the quarterstaff. For exercise, and to keep me occupied until I can begin training my Talent."

"I see," she said, smiling. "And you have a collection of new bruises to show for it, no doubt?"

"I took him to the bath house," Liisa interjected. She sat down in one of the side chairs and turned it to face us a little more directly. "I began to sing away the worst bruises. But they were healing nearly as fast as I could sing them away. They were almost gone before we left the baths."

Kata gave me a questioning look.

"I do not *think* that is normal for you, Alrekr... is it?"

"Well," I hedged, "I'm used to healing small injuries quickly. But not *that* quickly. But Liisa and I talked about this. I may have, uh, without intending to, sung a *further* healing boost into myself in the big seven-part Healing."

"Indeed?" Kata's slight smile turned into a broader one. "I think we have interesting times ahead of us, finding out what *else* you sang into your Healing that you do not know you did, Alrekr."

"Hmmmmmmm." I thought and counted things off on my fingers.

"One: I am now healing bruises, at least, ridiculously fast. Two: My vision is sharper than it has ever been." I paused. "I can't think of anything else that has shown up so far. Besides the obvious repairs of physical damage."

Kata looked thoughtful.

"Alrekr? May I look at your eyes?"

"Of course, Kata. It means I get to look into yours."

She smiled again, a big, sweet smile. I loved that smile.

"Please look at me and try to keep your eyes as still as you can."

Such a request. I gazed happily at her. She placed her spread fingertips across my temples, almost touching my eyes, then looked intently into my eyes. I could see minute changes in the direction and focus of her gaze. From her chair, Liisa was watching intently.

"Hold steady, Alrekr," she said. "Do not be startled. I am going to put light into your eyes to look at the insides of them." Then she whispered a few words, and soft white light filled my vision. I could scarcely see her through it, but I tried to keep my eyes still. I could feel her adjusting the positions of her fingertips as she whispered.

Then the light was gone. I blinked. My eyes were watering a little. I blinked again and my vision cleared. Kata was looking at me with a very thoughtful expression.

"How much do you know about human eyes, Alrekr?" she asked me.

I thought.

"Quite a bit," I replied. "I know that we aren't entirely sure of how they evolved, but think we know the broad picture. I know generally how they work, the two kinds of light-sensitive cells, the iris and the lens, the... uh, the two different fluids that fill the eye, how the lens hardens with age. I know about..."

Okay, more words that either I didn't know, or common Saamen had no words for.

"... Several different forms of eye disease," I continued. "I know that some people have claimed the human eye is proof that humans were created by some intelligent creator, because they argue that nothing so complex could have arisen by chance. But I argue that the human eye is proof that if humans were *created*, then the creator was an *IDIOT*, because he built the... back of the eye inside-out."

Both Liisa and Kata laughed at that. Then after a moment, Kata looked at me seriously again.

"Do you know that the human eye has a blind spot, Alrekr?"

"Yes," I replied. "It is the spot where the optic nerve comes *through* the back of the eye before spreading out across it."

"Exactly," Kata agreed. "Everyone has that blind spot in each eye, but we seldom notice it is there. We learn not to be aware of it." She paused.

"Have you noticed that you *don't have one* any more?"

"...What?"

"Look directly at my eyes, Alrekr. Yes, like that. Close your left eye. And now, without moving your gaze..." She held up her left hand, curled into a loose fist, moved it to an exact spot, then raised her thumb and crooked the top joint.

"Is the top joint of my left thumb bent or straight, Alrekr?"

"Bent," I replied without hesitation. She nodded.

"This is a vision test, Alrekr. You should not be able to *see* my left thumb at all in this spot. It should be in your blind spot. But you don't *have* one.

"In the spot where the visual nerve enters the eye, creating the blind spot, the back of your eye continues uninterrupted. There is no blind spot there. As far as I can tell, your visual nerve now connects to the back of your eye from *behind*, from the outside, instead of coming through it and connecting from within." She paused for a moment to let me absorb that.

"And there is something *else*. There are fewer blood vessels on the inside surface of your eye than is usual. And there is... an additional part in your eye that *was not there* when we repaired your head injuries. Like a tiny wall around the inside of your eye, that holds many

150

blood vessels."

I hesitated for a long moment, took a deep breath to calm my thoughts.

"Kata," I said carefully, "you seem to be describing something like what I know as a *pecten oculi*."

She looked at me quizzically.

"Those words are unknown to me," she said. "What is it?"

"It is a structure found in the eyes of hawks," I replied. "In my... on my past world, it is believed, *was* believed, to play a major part in their acute vision."

Kata looked at me for a long moment. Then she jumped up, strode swiftly to the door, and rang the page bell.

In a few minutes, we had a page.

"Tommi," Kata told him, "my compliments to the Master Falconer, and please have him send us one of his falconers with a hawk. A calm hawk, please, that does not mind too much being handled and examined."

"At once, Honored," Tommi replied.

"That trick with the light," I asked, while we waited. "Is that still another Talent?"

"Not really," Kata replied. "It is a very minor ability. Most people with any Talent at all can do it, or learn to. At some point, I will teach you."

She pointed at one of the glowstones on the wall that lit the room with a soft, pearly radiance. With so much new to adjust to, I hadn't really paid attention to them before she specifically pointed them out now.

"Those are another matter. It is the same light, but only a few Talents—principally crystal-wrights and some stone-singers—have the ability to bind it permanently into glass or crystal, to make glowstones."

I nodded understanding, reflecting upon how easily we gloss over and pay no regard to that which *appears* familiar.

Before very long there came another knock at the door. Liisa answered the door, letting in a solidly built woman I estimated to be in her early forties, carrying a large hawk hooded on her wrist. She introduced herself as Saana, and her hawk as Kii.

"May I ask what it is that you require, Healer?" she asked.

"If I might, please," Kata said, "I would like to examine his eyes closely. Would that be alright?"

"I do not think that would be a problem," Saana replied.

She picked a spot not too near to the fireplace and stopped, stroking her hawk on his chest and back with a finger.

"Good boy, good boy, Kii, Kii," she crooned, waiting for him to settle down. "Kii is a good boy." Then, when he seemed calm, she slipped his hood off. Kii blinked a few times, looking around the room.

"Do not move suddenly, Healer, please, he does not know you," Saana said. "Let him scent your hand first, and then stroke his chest, like this." She demonstrated, and Kata did as she was shown. Kii bobbed his head back and forth a little, dipped his head and rubbed his beak gently on her hand.

"He should accept your presence now, Healer. You can gently stroke the back of his head and neck if you wish."

"Will light in his eyes startle him?" Kata asked.

"Try not to make it sudden," Saana replied.

Kata took several minutes to closely examine the hawk. After a little while, she stepped back and pronounced herself satisfied.

"Thank you so much for indulging me, Saana," she said. "And of course Kii as well."

Saana left shortly after, and it was just the three of us again.

"Well?" Liisa asked.

"It is... very *nearly* the same structure," Kata said, her voice certain now. "Modified for a human eye instead of a hawk's, and I think to avoid creating a new blind spot, but... in base, the same structure. At the least, it serves the same purpose, I think."

She looked at me.

"You took a big chance, Alrekr." There was tension in her voice.

I took her hands.

"Kata," I said, "Liisa, I swear to you, *I didn't know I was doing it.* I

152

just… sang the only thing I *could* sing there and then."

Kata's expression softened.

"Alrekr," she replied, "did you think I was *angry* at you?" She took a step forward and wrapped her arms around me and hugged me tight. Then in the middle of the hug, she hesitated. She looked up at me.

"Oh, Alrekr," she said, softly, "you *were* afraid of that, weren't you? I can feel it in you." She rested her head on my chest. "You have been so *terribly* hurt. But I was concerned at the risk, that is all." Then her smile brightened again.

"But intended or not, you seem to have pulled it off. This is *fascinating*, Alrekr!"

I could not help but grin at her excitement. She was so good for me.

"Kata," I said, "I'm curious about something. You are acting as though this is something new and unknown. Has this—have things like this—truly never been done before?"

Kata thought for a moment.

"There is much you do not understand yet about how healing works, Alrekr," she began. Then she paused, still snuggled tightly against my chest, as she thought about how to explain it.

"We are Healers, Alrekr," she explained, "not creators. *Menders*, not *makers*. We set things back as they were, as they are *supposed to be*. We *mend* a broken arm; we do not make a new arm." I nodded.

"We can often re-attach and repair a severed limb, if it is not too badly damaged, and we get it promptly and mostly intact. But we cannot make the body grow a new arm if it is *missing*. We can only repair what is there. And if the damage is too great, there may be nothing we can do. We can repair an arm severed in a logging accident, if we have the arm in good condition and quickly, but not one pulverized in a mill-wheel. The Healing that regrew your knees and your foot took six Adept-level Healers—*and* you, somehow—and it still stretched us to our limits.

"I am certain you do not understand yet how remarkable *seven* healing parts is. There are good reasons why we stop at six. The more Healers we add, the more energy is needed, and the cost increases faster than the healing power gained. Three four-part Healings is—*under normal circumstances*—a better use of twelve Healers than two six-part. Finding a seventh *useful* part that benefits the overall healing by enough to justify the *voima* spent is... extremely difficult.

"There are some limited special cases. From time to time a baby is born—damaged, with something wrong. Or sometimes we find it even before the birth. A cleft lip. A hole in its heart. A club foot, a partly formed hand. These things are *not meant to be*. They are wrong, and the... world *knows* they are wrong, and it *lets us* repair them, set them back as they *should* be. But we can *only* set them back as they were supposed to be. And the greater the deformity, the harder to heal it. The—*most* damaged sometimes die anyway despite all we can do. All we can give them is mercy.

"And we can make the body make *more* of... blood, a few other things. We could regrow your foot and knees only because the world was willing to accept that they *should be* whole, and still it was as much as we could do. Even with seven parts.

"From time to time, some unwise Adept decides to try to change themselves, or another, into something they were **not** supposed to be. And this almost always goes **terribly wrong**, Alrekr. The world *fights back*. It does not wish to allow the change. With enough power and enough unconcern, enough cruelty, the change can sometimes be *forced*. And most of the time, the result is a twisted monster. The best that can be said is that the... victims... usually do not live long."

She pulled back just enough to lift her head a little. She tapped a finger on my chest for emphasis.

"You are a *very special case*, Alrekr. Possibly unique. Because you somehow traveled here from another world, *this* world... did not fully *know* you. It knew you as human, clearly, but because you were new to it and it was *unused to* you, the world was willing to a limited extent to let *you* shape its idea of what you are supposed to be.

"It would have fought strongly had you tried to make yourself something *not* human, Alrekr. But it seems it was willing to accept that you were, in some small ways, slightly *differently* human, or perhaps to let you make yourself slightly *more* than human. There is, I think, less difference between what you were then and what you are now, than between you and Raimo. Discounting your injuries, of course."

I thought about what she had said.

"Kata," I said, "you speak of this almost as though the... the *world itself* has volition and will."

Kata looked up at me.

"Oh *yes*, Alrekr," she agreed, her voice utterly certain. "Without

154

any question, it does. Whether the world itself, exactly, or something else. There are, there have been... things we can explain no other way. Not perhaps a will that we are able to understand, but... yes. It does. We are fully convinced of it."

I hesitated, thinking.

"You have another of your ideas, don't you, Alrekr?" That was Liisa.

"I... think I do," I said slowly. "I'm not sure I'm ready to *accept* it. But I know I don't know enough to rule it out." Both women looked at me, intent and curious.

"The fifth part in the big Healing working," I explained. "Singing in a language that I do not understand. Singing... *new* words, Vallaïnen said, that even *he* did not know. But he knew that they *were actual words*, with meaning."

I took a deep breath.

"Kata, stop me if this sounds stupid. But... *what if*... the world *showed* me the fifth part? Somehow read my intention from my mind, and **told me what words to sing?** Accepted *what* I wanted to do, and *told* my subconscious mind *how* to do it? What to sing to accomplish it?"

Kata's mouth dropped open. She blinked several times.

Just then there came a rap at the door, and Liisa got up to answer it. After a moment, Kata recovered her composure.

"Tomorrow," she said, "we will discuss this with Master Timo. But... I cannot say that you are wrong, and I *think* you may perhaps be right. It would raise new questions, but would also explain many things."

It turned out the knock at the door was the arrival of our supper, brought by a group of the kitchen assistants and led by a page I did not know. (Which, to be honest, was still most of them.) There were two covered dishes, a stoneware bottle, a set of clean goblets, a small basket of fruit, and a bundle wrapped in cloths.

We chose to eat at the big table downstairs. They set our food down and unwrapped the bundle, which contained silverware and warmed plates. Then they bade us enjoy our meal, and departed.

We opened the bottle first. It proved to be the fruited honey-wine again, not spiced this time. Liisa poured, while I lifted the lids from the dishes.

The first dish held imp fingers scattered over a bed of what looked like wild rice. The second contained thick slices of roasted meat, with what looked like the spiced cream sauce I had had once before generously poured over the whole. We shared it all out, and we sat down to eat, sitting next to each other, holding hands whenever we had a hand free.

"We can feel that you are more whole now," Liisa told me, after we finished our meal. "But do *you* feel a difference?"

After a moment I realized what she meant. I stopped and thought about the question, closing my eyes and focusing on how I felt *now* compared to how I felt before the meal they had made for me the day before.

"There was... a deep ache left inside, a hollow place," I said at last. "A freshly ripped hole. It... is not *gone*, but it is much reduced. I feel... somehow *lighter*. As though my heart is beating more easily."

"That is very good," Kata said with a smile. "We will have you fully healed in no time. We should impose again on Mistress Kerttu and cook a few more meals for you ourselves, to give you the greatest benefit that we can."

After we finished our supper, we all cuddled up together on the couch in front of the fireplace, just enjoying each other's presence as we slowly sipped the rest of the honey-wine. Then we went to bed.

It was, if anything, even more memorable than the previous night. It seemed we more quickly found that transcendent *I/we/us* state, our feelings mirroring each other forever. My last conscious thought before I fell asleep, after I/we returned to being just me again, was that I could *really* get used to this. It felt like being whole, for possibly the first time in my life. *More* than whole. More whole than I had ever felt. We became more than the sum of the three of us, when we joined like this.

10: Crouching Mystery, Hidden Knowledge

The next day both Liisa and Kata were called away on duties elsewhere, and I was left to my own devices. I made a point of finding my way back to the kitchens and personally thanking Mistress Kerttu for supper, which seemed to please her no end. One should always strive to be friends with the head chef. And besides, I liked her. She was clearly a good person—though if truth be told, I had yet to meet anyone here of whom I could not say that.

I explored some more on my own, before making my way back to the bailey for quarterstaff training. I learned some drills and exercises with the staff, intended to work the upper-body muscles most important for using it well. The sparring practice was still focused upon defense, though Eero showed me two basic strikes and had me practice them on a pell for a while as he watched and critiqued. I still came away from sparring with bruises, but it seemed as though he was having to work a little harder to land a blow. Even a little skill with a quarterstaff is better than none at all, I suppose. At least I could block some of the easier blows.

I treated myself again to a quick visit to the hot bath, then went back to our rooms and put a fresh shirt on. It was mid-afternoon by then. I realized I had missed luncheon, but there was some fruit left from yesterday's supper, so I had a little fruit for a snack. Then I started looking through the bookshelves, trying to see what titles I could puzzle out. Having been given a working command of the language was not the same thing as understanding the writing system.

I was still at that when Kata came back.

"Oh, that's probably too advanced for you," she said. "And we don't know yet whether your actual talent—Oh! We were going to talk to Master Timo! Come, let's go find him now." She took the book from my hand, put it back on the shelf, grabbed my hand instead, and pulled me after her.

"Actually," I said sheepishly, "I wasn't trying to read the books, I was just trying to puzzle out the writing system. I can't read any of your books yet."

She laughed happily.

"Well, we'll have to take care of *that*," she said. "But first, let's find Master Timo."

We found him, as it turned out, in the infirmary, the first place we looked. He was talking to Raimo about the head injury patient he and Kata had treated the day before, who was apparently doing guardedly well, but hadn't woken up yet.

"Kata," he said, "how are you? You were looking for me?"

"We were," Kata replied. "And it is good Raimo is here as well, since he was present at the healing."

"Ah," Timo mused, eyeing me. "This is perhaps about the fifth part, yes?"

"Yes," Kata agreed. "We have—actually, Alrekr has—a theory."

"Well, don't beat about the bush," Timo said, his eyes twinkling. "Share it!"

"All right," I said. "To first summarize what we know: Despite no training and not knowing the language of healing, I was somehow able to take an active part in my own healing, singing a part that contained words that even Vallaïnen said he did not know the meaning of. Somehow I just knew what sounds to sing, in a way that I have no explanation for."

Both Timo and Raimo nodded.

"Agreed. Go on," Timo said.

"Yesterday, Kata and I were talking about what is possible in healing, and what is not wise and should not be attempted. And some of the things Kata said implied to me that you view the world itself as having volition, and permitting or resisting certain things."

"This is true, yes." Timo nodded. "Whether the world is actually aware of what we do in a conscious sense is a matter best left to sages, who have studied it in far greater depth than I. But it is at least *useful* to regard the world as having volition and will."

"Kata has also explained to me," I went on, "that it was possible to heal my... *old* injuries... because being newly arrived in this world, the world was not sure yet *exactly* what I was supposed to be, and was—willing?—to accept *guidance* about what 'normal' *means* for me."

Timo nodded again. Raimo was listening attentively.

"We believed it to be so, based upon things learned in the past, yes," Timo agreed. "We hoped strongly that it would apply also to you. But we were not *fully* certain that it would work, until it did."

I felt a sudden shock of apprehension. What if it HADN'T worked? Would I be a cripple now? It must have showed upon my face, because Timo held up a hand.

"We do owe you an apology, Alrekr," he said gravely. "Yes, I had some doubts, and so did Vallaïnen. We were not *certain*. I prevailed upon Kata and Vallaïnen *not* to voice those doubts to you, because I believed it critically important that **you** had no doubts. If *you* doubted the healing would work, I felt it much more likely that it might fail."

I thought about that for a long, long, moment, fighting back horrible mental visions of how it could all have gone terribly wrong had I not had unshakable faith in what Kata and Liisa could do. Then I half-bowed to Timo.

"Master Timo," I said, "I believe that you did the right thing. Had I **known** there was any doubt... yes, it would probably have been very bad. Even now, at just that mention, I find myself struggling not to think about all of the ways in which it *could* have gone wrong." I tried and failed to suppress a shudder. Kata sidestepped closer to me and put an arm around me. I put my arm across her shoulders, took a deep breath, and tried to move on.

"Anyway, the thought that occurred to me yesterday—and I will admit, it is a thought I struggle with—is this: Is it *possible* that I was able to sing the fifth part in my healing because the world... accepted... my intention of what I felt I should be, and *told me*—subconsciously—how to... sing it into being?"

Raimo's eyebrows rose in surprise. Master Timo put a hand to his chin and gazed into the far distance, lost in thought.

Eventually, his gaze returned to us.

"I cannot say that it is *not* correct," he said slowly. "I also cannot say that it *is*. It is an intriguing theory, and a question for minds in the Collegium more learned than mine. It might answer other questions as well as this one. It might be beyond even the Collegium sages. But it would possibly explain how you were able to sing words new even to us, in a dialect unknown to you. And how it *worked*, despite you not otherwise showing signs of any actual healing Talent that we can determine.

"Do you have any insights yet as to what any of those new words might mean, by the way?"

Kata and I exchanged glances.

"There is... something, yes," I replied. "I have noticed that my vision is sharper than it has ever been. Last night we discovered that there is a new structure in my eyes. Several structural changes, in fact. It is similar to a structure in the eyes of hawks, which the... sages... of my past world call a *pecten oculi*, which is considered to play a major part in their acute vision.

"Some of those new words may have had something to do with that. Unfortunately I cannot tell you which words, since I did not understand them myself."

Timo nodded slowly.

"That definitely bears study," he said. Then he gave me an acute look. "If it is true that the world is willing to guide your singing, then it has... interesting implications for what you may learn to sing in your future, perhaps. We shall see, hmm? And I will send this question on to the Collegium and see whether they have anything to say on the matter. Please keep me informed of any new insights that come to you.

"Raimo, when next you see Vallaïnen, please ask him whether he believes any of the new words that he remembers might have anything to do with vision."

Raimo nodded.

We left Timo and Raimo to return to their discussion, and wandered off through the keep. Kata seemed distracted or preoccupied about something, but I was not sure what.

"Alrekr," she asked hesitantly after a little while, "does it trouble you that we hid our doubts from you?"

So *that* was what was on her mind. Now I understood her preoccupation.

I caught her arm, stopped, and gently turned her to face me. I took both of her hands in mine.

"Kata, my love," I told her softly, "look at me. Look into my eyes.

"*I trust you*, Kata. You hid your doubts with very good reason, *for my own good*, and I have *not the slightest doubt* that you were right to do so. I... don't want to think about how terribly things could have gone wrong, had I doubted for one moment that you could do it. So much has gone wrong in my life... had I been afraid you could not actually do it, that fear would very likely have run wild and filled my mind with thoughts of the myriad ways it could all go wrong.

"Think back to the moment when I realized that you *really could do* this. You *saw* how deeply it affected me.

"I have *absolute faith* in you, Kata. I *know* in my heart that neither you nor Liisa would do anything that you thought would harm me."

I didn't know what else to say to drive the point home, so I gathered her into my arms and kissed her, and then we just stood there for a long while and held each other.

"Still," she said, after a while, "what if it had *not* worked, Alrekr? What would you then have thought of me? Of us?"

I had to think about that for a long time.

"I can only guess, Kata, that you would have assured me you had tried your hardest, done all you could. And... I would have had no reason not to believe you. I think I know you well enough to know that the truth of it would have been evident.

"What we would have all done then... I do not know. But I *do* know that it is not productive to think about it now. So let it go. There is no point in dwelling now upon what *might* have gone wrong."

She thought about that, then nodded slowly. I could tell she still wasn't entirely comfortable with it, though.

I bent and kissed her again, and then we walked on.

Before we left the keep, we went by the kitchen and I asked for dinner to be sent to our rooms again.

"More of the same?" Mistress Kerttu asked me. "Or something different?"

"I leave it entirely to your judgment, Mistress," I said. She gave me a huge smile.

When we got back to our rooms, Liisa had beaten us there. She was sitting at the table reading a book. She did not seem to notice when Kata opened the door, but when I closed it behind us she looked up. A smile lit up her face, and she put her book down and came to greet and hug us. We held the hug for quite a while.

"What are you studying, Liisa?" I asked.

"Oh, the book?" she said. "It is a compendium of fungi. I treated a young boy who appears to have been poisoned—not badly, he is in no real danger—by something he ate. It bears the signs of a mushroom

161

poisoning, but I'm not quite certain which it was, to tell him what to avoid that he evidently does not know. But I'm thinking possibly a blue-cap, or possibly an unripe blackball, which could possibly be mistaken for a gray woods-hen."

"You know," I replied thoughtfully, "I wouldn't know either, here. In my past world I knew that the mushrooms most commonly eaten were, ironically, among the ones most easily confused with deadly poisonous ones. But here, I have no idea at all." That 'past world' thought was becoming easier each time I thought it.

"Well," Liisa told me with a smile, "here are your first two mushroom rules: First, avoid eating any mushroom that has spots. *All* of the spotted ones are poisonous. And second, avoid eating any mushroom with orange spores. None of them will kill you, but they will all make you violently ill. And don't eat anything that looks like a black ball."

"That seems like a good start," I agreed with a grin. "I'm not a big fan of being violently ill."

Suddenly I remembered the last time I had been violently ill. Vomiting as I lay on the ground somewhere in the fringes of the mountains. I could not repress a shiver.

Liisa's concern was immediate.

"Alrekr? Is something wrong?"

I reached for the nearest chair and sat down.

"A flash of memory," I said. I felt slightly dizzy. Liisa moved to stand next to me, her hand on my shoulder.

"Lying on the ground. Cold. So cold. Broken glass around me. I think I threw up. I couldn't feel my legs. Almost everything else hurt."

Kata, lovely Kata, slipped into my lap. I put an arm around her. Then I reached the other out to Liisa's waist.

"That must have been shortly before the Rangers found you," Liisa told me. "You were in luck that a patrol was passing not too far away."

"How *did* they find me?" I asked.

"They said that their mage detected a surge of *voima* nearby, a brief but powerful working. They searched for the source—lest it be the harbinger of some attack—and found you, and pieces of broken glass and metal scattered around. You were obviously badly hurt. They thought that you might have come through a rift. Perhaps fleeing something. Perhaps thrown by something."

"A rift?" I asked. "You've mentioned that before. So did Piia." I recalled now that Piia had told me that it was Simo who actually found me. "What exactly *is* a rift?"

"A—tear in the world, connecting one place to another," Liisa answered. "Usually deliberately opened. It takes a great deal of power, and the larger the rift, the more power is needed. Only in vanishingly rare cases are they natural. They close on their own if not held open."

I thought about that.

"I've heard of such things," I mused slowly, "but only in stories. Many, many stories. So what happened then?"

"They rigged a stretcher between two horses and transported you back to Highwatch as quickly as they could," Kata continued. "They sent a rider ahead to have us meet you part-way, so that we could sooner begin treating your most urgent injuries, which turned out to be stopping the bleeding inside your head. Meanwhile the rest of the patrol searched the area so see if there was..." She trailed off.

"Anyone else," I finished. "And they found... her."

"Yes, Alrekr," she said quietly. "And they brought... her here as well."

I thought for a long time about that.

"Would she have died of her injuries had they not found her?" I asked.

Kata shook her head uncertainly.

"Perhaps. Perhaps not. It is hard to say for sure. But probably not."

"And if not... then she would be loose in the world."

"Yes."

I had to think for a long time again.

"It is better this way, I think. All things considered."

Kata looked down, then looked into my eyes.

"Even though she nearly *killed* you, Alrekr?"

I looked steadily back at her.

"Better she *almost* kill me, than *actually* kill someone else," I said. "And once she started, she would never stop, would she?"

"No, Alrekr," Kata replied levelly. "She would not. A sielunjuoja *cannot* stop. Any more than a fish can stop swimming."

I thought some more.

"I've been wondering," I said slowly. "Why *did* you and Liisa decide that night to..."

"To bring love offerings to you?" Kata finished for me.

"Yes," I said.

She took a deep breath.

"When you were brought in," she said, "we sensed immediately that there was power about you. We could feel as we were healing your injuries that power was being drawn from you as well. Then when you woke up, we could feel that you were blocking us—even though it seemed you did not intend to—but yet, even though you seemed not to *know* that you were blocking us, you were able to lower your block.

"We could feel you were *strong*, Alrekr, even though untrained. Perhaps Adept level, or even higher. The Talented... are not common. Adept-level, rarer still.

"Talented and untalented... *should not* share their lives, Alrekr. It ends with both miserable, most of the time."

"That day on the balcony, Alrekr," Liisa broke in. "When you recited the poem from memory. The depth of *feeling* you put into it... I think we both started paying attention to you that day more than simply as a patient. That was the first day we glimpsed the depths of your soul." Kata nodded agreement.

"Truth to tell," I said, "I think it was on that day that I first really paid attention to the two of you, as well. Not that I'd had much chance before, of course, having been asleep for most of the time. But still— the first day I was awake, I was aware of you as my caregivers, my caretakers. It was that second day, on the balcony and afterward, that I began to really *enjoy* having you near me."

"And we enjoyed being near you," Kata agreed. "And... touching you." So I *hadn't* been imagining the intimacy in some of those touches, then.

"And then on the day of the healing," Liisa went on, slightly hesitantly, "the power that you revealed, the *determination* that you showed, the unexpected fifth part... it was clear you were beyond the ordinary. And Kata and I began... talking, that day. About you. That there was no-one else here for us, and you—*were* here.

"But we were worried it might be unfair to you if we pursued you.

164

You were new to our world, and did not know our ways. So we talked... but we did not *do* anything. We waited. We planned to wait until you knew our world better, until we felt it *fair* to you to declare our interest. Or until you showed open interest in us."

"But then the sielunjuoja attacked you, Alrekr," Kata broke in, her voice suddenly intense. "And we almost *lost* you. And only then, when we *looked* deeply into your mind for the first time, did we realize how terribly you had been hurt, what grief and loneliness lay buried within you. And yet despite all of that... you were still willing to love and trust.

"We saw *who you are*, Alrekr.

"I realized there and then that I was willing—no, *happy!*—to share you with Liisa, but I was *not willing to lose you* without at least trying. The thought of you dead, your soul consumed by that—abomination, made me realize how much I wanted you to be a part of my life. Forever."

"And I felt the same way," Liisa agreed. "We had *wanted* to allow you more time to heal, to recover. But the wounds left by the sielunjuoja forced our hands. Forced our decision. We dared wait no longer."

"So... had it not been for the attack?"

She nodded.

"We would have waited, Alrekr. Until you were further healed, until you knew more of this world, until we thought it... fair. But when we felt the time was right, we would still have offered to you."

"And so you both went to the kitchens, and had Mistress Kerttu help you cook love offerings that night," I said.

"Yes, Alrekr," Kata said. "We risked rushing it. And I confess we did have a dual purpose in mind. Your spirit had just been cruelly torn open. It was not *just* that we wished to... make you ours. It was that the offering is a powerful token of love, and that love *itself* would help to heal you. To some degree, even if you chose not to accept our offerings."

"And in truth, we *both* desperately hoped that you would choose both of us," Liisa added quietly. "Because... we have been the closest of friends for many years, and each of us knew the other's interest in you, and neither of us would choose to take you away from the other. But we could not steer you *to* that choice. It had to be *your* free choice."

"That is why we were... so careful about answering your questions that night, Alrekr. Your choice had to be freely made, without pressure. We had to try to avoid *influencing* your choice. We told you this much then, if you remember."

I looked back and forth between them.

"Let me repay your honesty with my own," I replied. "Please. By that time—uh... My heart was in my mouth when I asked what happens when two offerings are made at once. And whether a man could accept both." I swallowed. "I do not know what I would have done had you answered that I could not. I don't know how I could possibly have chosen between you. I don't think I could bear now to be without either one of you."

Kata and Liisa exchanged glances, then a slight nod.

"Had it come to that," Kata told me, "had it seemed that you... could not decide, we would I think have asked whether you *wanted* to accept our offerings."

"And had you said yes," Liisa added, "we would have made sure you understood that you did not have to *choose between* us."

I didn't know what to say. I slipped my other arm further around Liisa's waist and pulled her a little closer.

"The two of you... *complete* me," I told them both. "Before I had you, I was not whole. Had never *been* whole. Had never known what it *means* to be truly whole."

We moved to the couch so that we could all sit together. I pulled Kata back into my lap, where she fit so wonderfully; Liisa snuggled up against us, and we held onto each other while we waited for supper to arrive.

"There is another thing I am curious about," I said, slightly hesitantly. "When we first shared a bed, that night. It was... *transcendent*. I *still* cannot think of any other adequate word to describe it. As though the three of us became one person, feeling *everything*. Three times at once... and somehow *more*.

"You explained to me why this happens, how adepts... merge. That this is known among the talented, when two Talented share themselves. But..."

I ran out of words, unsure how to ask what I was curious about. But Liisa stepped in for me.

"You want to ask," she guessed, "did we know it would be... that... *intense* between three?"

I nodded.

"No," she began. "We both knew that it *would* be intense..."

"... But we were not prepared for *THAT* much," Kata finished, her face slightly flushed. "I do not know whether there has ever *been* a true romantic triad of Adept-level Talents before. Certainly not here at Highwatch. The capital, perhaps.

"Highwatch is an unusual place, Alrekr. There would be at most three or four Healers here, were this any normal place its size. But here there are nearly two-score Adepts, a dozen Healers *alone*, because the passes that Highwatch guards are so important. And that is why there are *always* Ranger patrols out, and that is why there was a patrol there to find you. It is sheer good fortune that the one Ranger team in Highwatch to have a diviner Adept attached was the one in the area when you... arrived.

"It was only in the last two centuries or so that more than two people in a committed relationship became truly accepted as normal. And Adepts are relatively rare. So this... may be new ground."

I nodded, and couldn't help a sigh.

Liisa looked at me.

"What memory troubles you now, Alrekr?" she asked.

I paused for a moment to choose my words. Both of them were coming to know me well.

"In my past world," I said, "there were three... schools of thought, let us say. Three kinds of attitudes.

"The first group believed that it did not matter who, or even how many people, you loved, as long as you could make the relationship work without hurting anyone. And it wasn't even a hard-and-fast rule that you had to identify as—uh, that is, *feel right* talking about yourself as and living as—either strictly male or strictly female." That got me a raised eyebrow from Kata, but I left it for now.

"The second group were *sort of* alright with a man loving a man or a woman loving a woman, as long as they didn't do it in front of them, but under no circumstances could there *ever* be more than two people in a romantic relationship.

"And to the *third*, a relationship, romantic or otherwise, meant exactly one man and exactly one woman, and preferably the woman always obeying the man in everything. And if you didn't fall into that model, then you should just go and die somewhere, because your very existence was an offense in the sight of the god whose laws they professed to follow when it suited them to, which was mostly the most hateful and self-serving parts, and utterly ignored when it didn't.

"Most people were probably in the second group. But there were a scary number of people in the third group, and they had historically written most of the laws. And they tended to write them in ways that made it lawful for them to hate and persecute anyone they wanted to."

Liisa shuddered.

"Our people once thought this way," she admitted. "Shameful, awful things were done. But we learned better, many hundreds of years ago."

"So what do *you* think, Alrekr?" Kata asked, with a twinkle in her eye. "*Should* a woman always obey her man?"

"Kata," I replied seriously, looking her straight in the eyes, "I have *always* sought a partner, a companion, a lover. Not a..." I had to search for a way to say it in Saamen, for which I was once again thankful. "Not a servant, nor a master. Someone to walk *at my side*, hand in hand, not in front of me or in my shadow."

I looked at Liisa, then at Kata again.

"And now somehow, I have the two of you on *either* side of me."

"At this moment," Kata pointed out mock-seriously, "I am in your lap, not at your side."

I laughed. I could not help it. That was exactly what I needed right then.

"And for the life of me," I continued after a moment, "I still cannot understand how I came to be so fortunate."

"Fortunate?" Liisa said. "You were ripped bodily from your world, and nearly died. *Twice.*"

"And having you two—and a chance at a fresh life, one with some meaning—is worth all of that," I replied, with feeling.

"And Kata, there is another thing. When you tell me to do something, like when you told me you needed me to allow you into my mind, my memories... I *trust* that you have a good reason for doing so. And I will not question you."

168

"Tell me something seriously though, Alrekr," Kata said. "You spoke of people who—I think you said identify?—neither as male nor as female. Can you explain that? I... am not sure I understand."

"Alright," I said after a moment. "That actually covers a huge amount of ground, and I have to start out by saying that I... don't understand enough of all of the issues myself to feel qualified to explain. But I will give it my best try.

"One aspect of it is that sometimes children are born whose development went wrong. Perhaps they have a mixture of male and female body parts. Or parts missing, or just not developed right. Have you ever seen such?"

"It happens, sometimes," Liisa replied. "Not very often."

"And when it does, what do you do?"

"We heal the child," Kata said, "as soon as possible after birth, to... *finish* what the body wants to be. And what of your world?"

"Not my world any longer," I corrected. "Please. My *past* world. It is no longer mine.

"The... healers would TRY to complete whichever set of organs seemed closest to completion, or at least as close as they could get to *looking* complete. They *tried* to figure out what the child was 'meant' to be and make it as 'normal' as they could, from what was there to work with. But..."

"But the tools they had for doing so were—primitive," Liisa guessed. I nodded.

"Exactly. The result was rarely fully functional, and such children often lived out their lives in misery. Many died young, for various reasons.

"But it goes beyond that. There was a term—'*gender dysphoria*'—that eventually came into use. It describes people who were born with a fully functioning body of one gender or the other—which, to their mind, their soul, is nevertheless *the wrong one*. A mind and soul that *desperately* wants and needs to be female, that cannot bear to live as a male, but is trapped in a male body. Or the other way around. Or sometimes, neither one nor the other. There was a phrase... uh..."

I trailed off, unable to figure out how to express 'non-binary' in Saamen. Kata and Liisa exchanged significant looks.

"The words you use for it are new to us," Kata said, "but this conflict of body and soul is known to us. We call it being cross-souled. It is terrible torment for those so afflicted, but we can do almost nothing

169

to help them. Because the *body* is not actually *broken* in any way that can be healed. It simply *does not match* the soul.

"The healers of your... past were equally helpless, I expect."

"I can understand that expectation," I began. "And it's true there was a long way still to go. But... a lot of progress was being made. Our healers were learning."

Instantly I had the attention of both women.

"You *had a way* to help them?" Liisa demanded. "***How?***"

"Well, it's complicated," I admitted, "and only a partial solution, and I'm nowhere near being any kind of expert. Keep that in mind, please. But I will tell you all I know.

"The scholars of my past world learned that whether the body grows to be male or female is controlled by—substances they called *'hormones'* that are made in the body as it develops and grows, almost from conception forward. And they discovered that if you give a person born as one gender *enough* of the right hormones that select bodily traits of the other gender, at the right times, the body will *change*, start developing traits of the other gender. Changes in voice, body fat distribution, hair changes, muscle development— even growing breasts. The organs already there were *set*, but enough of the right hormones could make the body largely—*change its mind* about what gender it was."

Liisa was staring at me open-mouthed. Kata was looking rapidly back and forth between the two of us.

"If we can make the body *change its mind about its gender*—" Kata began.

"Perhaps **THEN** we can guide it to **reshape** itself!" Liisa finished ecstatically. Then she grabbed hold of me and kissed me fiercely.

Kata jumped up, hurried to the door, and rang the page bell hard. Then she waited at the door for a page to arrive. This time it was Tommi again.

"Tommi," she told him, "summon the Masters and as many of the senior healers as you can find here, as soon as you can. Tell them Alrekr Járnhandr may have given us a way to heal the cross-souled."

I think Tommi brought *ALL* of the healers. Everyone I already knew came in, and I was newly introduced to Mistress Sirkka and Mistress Jaana, the other two Master Healers of Highwatch, and two other

Healers of Kata and Liisa's rank—Esko, a big red-haired bear of a man, and Marketta, a petite blonde with eyes as blue as the sky. Our supper actually arrived while people were filing in, and Liisa had the page who brought it take it up to our morning room.

"*Two* revelations in one day?" boomed Master Timo as he arrived. "I can hardly wait to hear this!"

As soon as introductions were completed and as many as possible seated—I found myself glad we had a lot of chairs—Kata spoke up.

"Alrekr has been telling us much, at different times, of life in the world of his past," she began. "I admit Liisa and I have given little thought to the healing knowledge of that world because... well, those of you who were part of the seven-part Healing *saw* his knees." There were nods of understanding from Raimo, Vallaïnen, and Varpu.

"But today we learned that even as their healing methods seem primitive to us, there are ways in which their knowledge of the body perhaps exceeds ours.

"Alrekr, please explain to everyone what you just told us."

So I explained about ontology, and hormones, and how they affect fetal development, and about gender dysphoria, and how hormone treatments could help.

"And then," I went on, before anyone could speak, "*Kata and Liisa had the insight that if hormone treatment can change the body's idea of what its gender *should* be, then your Healing can perhaps sing the body *fully* into its *new* 'right' shape.*" There was *no way* I was letting my lovely ladies make me steal their thunder. "The knowledge of what hormones do in the body, I brought with me from my past world, it is true. But it is Kata and Liisa, not I, who realized, together, that this knowledge could help the—cross-souled, I think you said?"

I was startled by a loud CRACK. Then another. I realized after a moment that Master Timo was clapping his hands, joined a moment later by Raimo, then Vallaïnen, then... well, pretty much everyone, in fact.

After a minute or so, the applause died down. Liisa was flushed of face and looked embarrassed, so I went and stood next to her and put an arm around her. Then I reached out and wrapped the other around Kata for good measure.

"Alrekr Járnhandr," Vallaïnen asked, "can you help us to identify these '*hormones*' of which you speak?"

"I will help all I can, of course," I agreed, "but I am no... scholar of the subject. I can tell you what my past world called the three principal sex hormones I know of, I can tell you that all are expressed both in males *and* in females in differing amounts, and I can tell you where in the body they are principally produced—which will probably surprise none of you. But I think that it will be up to you to learn to identify them and how to sing the body into producing them in the right amounts. And I do not think you should expect an overnight treatment. In my former world it took as much as a year for the body to show its new form, and the treatment had to be maintained or the body would try to revert. I hope that your Healing will have the edge, there, as I hope you will be able to bring about a more complete change than the healers of my world could manage."

About that point, everything broke into smaller discussions. I sat down to rest, and that was where Varpu found me a little later.

"How *are* your knees, Alrekr?" she asked. "Now that you have had time to recover?"

"Doing very well, thank you," I replied, standing to greet her. "I have been learning the quarterstaff, and I think I should try some running and see how they hold up."

"That is very good." She nodded, then hesitated. "And the... soul wounds?"

"I am feeling much better," I said. "Much closer to... whole. Thank you for asking." I had the feeling she was about to say more, but instead she just stepped in after a moment and gave me a long, tight full-body hug. I wasn't shy about returning it.

"Do you suppose that you could help me to pry Kata and Liisa loose?" I asked after a little while. "Our supper must be getting cold, but I don't want to break up the discussion if it leads to a new way to help people."

That won me one of her huge smiles.

"Wait here a moment," she told me. "I will see what I can do."

She walked away into the hubbub of discussion, and with a little deft nudging, managed to shepherd three groups into two, from which she emerged with Liisa in tow. Then she went back and managed to extricate Kata, and all four of us sneaked off upstairs.

Supper was a fair-sized roast redolent with herbs, accompanied by piles of roasted root vegetables, soft yellow beans, soft bread rolls, and a large flagon of mead.

"Varpu, would—uh... that is, if I'm not making any cultural blunders here," I said hesitantly, shooting Kata a quick glance, "would you care to join us? I'm pretty sure there is enough here for four."

There went that smile again, and the approving nods from Kata and Liisa were enough to convince me that I hadn't mis-stepped. Varpu accepted the invitation willingly.

I freely admit I wolfed mine down. I was *hungry*. The women ate more sparingly, though there was plenty to go around. I indulged myself more than a little. We talked among ourselves—which mostly meant the three of them talking among themselves, me having little to offer when it came to Healing—about the cross-souled; not a common problem here, but not unknown. I couldn't help but wonder whether it was as common as it had seemed... *back there*... simply because there were *so damned many* people, or because we'd so thoroughly poisoned our world, made it such an intolerant, intolerable, heartless place.

I wondered—not for the first time—how much time had passed, and whether the question even meant anything.

The thoughts running through my head saddened me. But it was Varpu, sitting directly across from me, who first noticed the tears trickling down my cheeks.

"Alrekr," she said, concern in her voice, "are you alright?"

It wasn't until she asked that I realized my eyes were stinging. Then Kata and Liisa turned to look at me too. I tried to say yes, but I knew it wasn't true. My eyes filling with tears, I *felt* more than saw Kata reach out for my hand.

"No," I managed to gasp out, "I'm not." Then I broke down again and wept. I heard movement to my right, then Liisa wrapped her arms around me.

Some combination of the three of them—I'm not even sure which two—helped me to my feet, and guided me through the door into the bedchamber, and to the couch, where they sat me down.

"I should leave you to yourselves," I heard Varpu say, uncertainly.

"Stay, if you would," Kata told her. "You are a friend, and I think he needs friends now. He has not truly found himself yet, and friends are all he has."

"Friends, and the two of you especially," Varpu replied.

I felt arms around me and bodies pressed against me from both sides. There came the sound of a chair being moved closer, and then

173

someone put a hand gently on my shoulder. Varpu, I realized dimly.

I entrusted myself entirely to them and wept my heart out.

"When your heart is breaking, Alrekr," I heard Kata say softly from my left, "we are here to make it whole again."

Eventually I ran down, and was able to see clearly enough again that there was any point in lifting my head and looking around me. Indeed, Varpu had pulled a chair right in front of the couch and was patiently sitting there holding my free hand.

"Thank you—all—for being here," I said unsteadily. I found I had an arm around Kata that I didn't remember putting there, so I turned to her, pulled her in a little tighter, and kissed her. Then I turned to Liisa and kissed her too.

I heaved a deep sigh and struggled to my feet, which triggered a general wave. No sooner was I on my feet than Varpu stepped in closer, slipped her arms around me, and gave me another tight hug. Then she gathered all three of us quickly into the hug for a moment, before stepping back.

"I am going to go and chase out anyone else who is still downstairs," she said, "so that the three of you can have some peace and time to yourselves." I nodded gratefully, and she gave us all another of her room-brightening smiles, then slipped away out the door and down the stairs.

"You need bed, I think," Liisa told me, and I found myself in no mood to argue. So we all went to bed and curled up together.

The next morning, Kata declared I was due an examination.

"Not of your physical condition," she said, "although your... progress there is visible. But I want to be sure about the wounds of your spirit."

It was true, I thought, as I considered myself. The skin had tightened across my belly, my thighs felt firmer, and it was plain muscle was returning to my arms and upper body.

"What do you need me to do?" I asked.

"Just sit, or lie down, as you prefer," Kata said, "and relax as much as you can."

"Lie down, then," I said.

"And Liisa and I will, if you will let us—"

"Silly question," I interjected, smiling. She and Liisa both laughed.

"Take this seriously, beloved, please," she said, her eyes twinkling. "We need to look at the state of your spirit and make sure that the wounds from the... attack are closed and healed.

"But also... We know you are impatient to begin to learn how to use your Talent, to learn how it manifests. But first—this is an intrusion, I know..."

She broke off awkwardly. I sensed where this was going, and I understood her discomfort. I took hold of her hand.

"You need to look into my mind," I guessed, "and make sure that there is no... unresolved trauma lurking that could ambush me at a critical moment."

Kata nodded.

"Yes, my love," she said, seriously. "That is exactly it." She seemed relieved that I knew what she was asking without her having to say it herself. "And there are things that we can do to help, if you wish it."

"Kata," I replied, "you and Liisa just *being* here helps. Knowing that after seeing into my mind, seeing all of my... flaws, my weaknesses, my failures, you both chose to live with me *anyway*, means more to me than anything else in my life that I can think of. And... and even aside from everything else, I am so *old* and worn. Neither one of you looks more than half my age."

Liisa laughed out loud, not unkindly, and after a moment, Kata joined in. I looked back and forth at them, bewildered.

"Alrekr," Liisa asked after a few moments, "how old are you?" She was smiling.

"I am in my mid-sixties," I answered. Her smile didn't falter. "Though I *feel* better than I have in years. Decades."

"And how old do you think I am?" she continued.

"I... would guess not more than your mid-thirties," I replied.

"Alrekr," Kata said, "do you remember that we told you we **expected** you to begin looking younger after the healing?"

"I... think I do," I agreed. "But I don't understand. Just... from undoing some of the wear and tear? Improving my overall fitness?"

"How old would you guess Master Timo is, Alrekr?" Liisa asked me.

I thought about that, picturing him in my mind, white-haired but still hearty, still sharp-eyed, recalling his voice booming as I had heard it when he had walked in here.

"Somewhere in his seventies?" I guessed.

Liisa smiled gently.

"Alrekr," she told me, "Master Timo is well over two hundred years old." My jaw dropped. I gaped at her, amazed and stunned. "Vallaïnen is nearly a hundred and fifty. I have been stationed here at Highwatch as a Healer for eighteen years, and I did not learn Healing here. And Kata has been here longer than I have."

"Being Talented extends lifespan and slows aging," Kata said. "And as you are beginning to see, can even turn some of its effects back. The stronger your Talent, the more closely you are linked to the world, and the more slowly you age, and the longer you live. Adepts live for centuries, barring accident or mischance.

"I am older than you are, Alrekr. And Liisa is no more than five years younger than you. You are in your sixties, you say. Another month from now, you will *feel*—and *look*—half that age. Had you not noticed—no, of course you hadn't. You cannot see yourself.

"The roots of your hair are coming in dark, Alrekr. I should ask for a mirror so that you can see it for yourself. Even now, you already look younger by fifteen years or more."

"This is part of why everyone was so happy about our betrothal, Alrekr," Liisa said. "All the time that we have been here at Highwatch... Vallaïnen and Marja are married. Master Timo and Mistress Jaana are married. Esko and Marketta are married. But for Kata, and Varpu, and I, for all of the time we have been here, there has been no-one."

"There are nearly seven hundred people here at Highwatch," Kata said. "You would probably think it easy for someone to find a partner here to love. But do you remember that we told you that talented and untalented should not share their lives? That it ends in misery?"

I nodded.

"For all of the hundreds of people you see about the keep and the bailey each day," she continued, "perhaps forty are strongly Talented, Adepts or above—and that is a higher proportion than is usual. Because this is Highwatch. Rather more than half of those are already paired off as couples. And several of those left are near to or in their second, or even third, century. There are far *fewer*... possible partners than it might at first seem."

"We have been so *lonely*," Liisa said quietly. "There were times we shared a bed simply not to sleep alone. But now at last that loneliness is over."

I thought about what she had said.

"But not for Varpu," I said.

"No," Kata agreed. "Not for Varpu. She and Raimo are *close*, as friends, but there is nothing beyond friendship between them. I know. She and I have talked. There is no-one here who is right for her."

I envisioned Varpu's brilliant smile. And then I thought about such loneliness hidden behind that lovely smile, and I felt achingly sad for her.

"We should invite her to spend time with us, when she can," I said hesitantly. "If it would help."

"It is a kind thought," Kata agreed thoughtfully. "But it is not friendship that she lacks. It is that special person to share her heart with."

"I'm no stranger to loneliness," I admitted. "For me, the loneliest place in the world was a room full of happy people where I was the lone misfit, the fifth wheel, the awkward stranger who did not, *could not* belong, and could not understand why."

"I... saw such memories," she said. "There are many such memories that still hurt you, are there not? And there is loss and grief that you have not fully come to grips with. That was plain last night."

I nodded, my throat suddenly tight.

"It is your past life, isn't it?" she said gently. "And those you left behind."

"... Yes," I admitted, unsteadily.

"Do you wish that you could go back, Alrekr?" she asked quietly.

"*No!*" I said, immediately, emphatically. "*No*, Kata. *Never* that. *Anything* but that. I'd sooner be dead than go back. I... I *think*... that at the moment whatever happened that brought me here, I was *wishing* for death. And yet, at the same time, not. I *hated* my past life. I was *done*. I was miserable beyond words. Reduced to utter despair. If I couldn't escape it, I'd sooner have died. But if I had the choice... I wanted to escape it, to try again.

"I feel... more *whole*, more *complete*, here than I have ever felt before. Especially since... because of the two of you. You fill a huge gaping void in my soul that has been there, empty, all my life. And...

and I feel that here, I might perhaps be able to make a *difference*."

"If what you told us yesterday enables us to find a way to help the cross-souled," Liisa broke in, "you *already have*, Alrekr." I looked at her and saw the honesty in her face as she looked back at me. I felt tears starting in the corners of my eyes again. But I knew that this time they were spurred by happiness, not grief and loss.

"I would not give the two of you up for an entire world," I told them both, and meant it absolutely.

"But...?" Kata prompted me.

"... But I wish I could find a way to bring my children here," I said. "I think they would like it here."

And that huge, aching loss center-punched me right in the heart again.

Kata nodded silently, stepped in and held me tightly. After a moment I felt Liisa wrap her arms around both of us as well.

"You feel terrible guilt that you do not know whether your children are safe," Kata said. It wasn't a question. I nodded, all I could do.

"If *anyone* can find a way to reach them," Liisa said quietly, "I expect that it will be you."

"And in the meantime," Kata said, "we will continue to work with you to ease that guilt, to heal the pain that you still feel. To heal the wounds left by what was done to you."

11: What Lies Within

The good news was that when we finally got to it, the examination showed that the rents torn in my soul were almost entirely healed. The bad news, of course, was that I still had, as Kata had said, a lot of unresolved pain and grief. And yes, trauma. It would take a long time for those scars to fully heal. At least now, though, they had a chance.

In the meantime, though, Kata and Liisa agreed that I was healed *enough* that I could begin training and learning how to use my Talent. And the first step in that was going to be finding out how it manifested.

Also, it was past time I learned to read Saamen. That would be important. There was a lot of knowledge within the books entrusted to the Adepts of Highwatch, my two lovely ladies among them. Liisa explained to me that most Adepts acquired a collection of books over the years—or the centuries. It was almost certain *some* of them would turn out to be important to me.

We began, in fact, with meditation exercises. Not quite like any I was used to; the basic exercise was not dissimilar, but instead of seeking to still my mind, to reach a state of *mu-shin*, I was to seek what Kata called my core.

"At first your goal will be to simply feel where it is," she told me, "and learn to recognize what its presence feels like. Then we will teach you how to see it with your inner eye, and then to touch it, and then how to draw from it and strengthen it.

"But first, we will just show you how to find it."

Liisa suggested that we place chairs in a circle where we could sit and hold hands. But any meditation is as much about mental preparedness and familiarity as it is anything else, so I had a different suggestion. We gathered up some cushions, because sitting on stone is hard and uncomfortable, and then we went outside and up onto the flat roof of the tower. There we arranged the cushions, and I picked a spot that had me facing towards the suns, then dropped to my knees and sat *seiza*. I wasn't quite ready to try *zazen* yet. I didn't want to be struggling just to maintain my posture. First Liisa on my right, then Kata on my left, followed suit.

As they had on several occasions before, they each took one of my hands. Then Liisa told me to close my eyes.

"I want you to focus on awareness of your body, Alrekr," she said. "Try to be aware of every part of your body, and then try to move your attention within, and see if you can find a warm place within you.

"Start by breathing slowly, in and out, as you did that first day, and being aware of every breath as it fills you and empties..."

I did as she told me, focusing on my breathing, the feeling of the air rushing in and filling my lungs, my lungs swelling within my chest, how the rest of my body moved in response, how the curve of my spine changed as I drew each breath in and let it out, how my shoulders moved, how that moved my arms. I was no longer consciously aware of her speaking, but at some level I was aware that she and Kata were gently directing my attention within, deeper within myself in a way I didn't know how to explain. As though one were to reach further into water in a basin than the depth of the basin.

I never felt anything that seemed to me to be warmth. But it did seem as though I was passing below the surface of a storm-tossed ocean, down to quiet depths where the waves above did not reach, where all was calm and still. I was aware of a whimsical thought crossing my mind that perhaps there ought to be whales down here.

I did in fact have a sense of something moving near me. Not a whale-like movement, though. Something quicker and stronger. And then after a while I realized that it was the presence of my two lovers that I could feel.

And somewhere below... something? I wasn't sure what.

Then I became aware that someone was calling my name, softly but urgently. I mentally shook myself and opened my eyes.

"Alrekr," Kata was saying. "Alrekr, come back now."

I shook my head to clear it.

"I'm here," I said. Then I noticed from the shadows that the suns had moved nearly to the zenith. It had been several hours.

"Alrekr, good," Kata said. "That was rather deeper than it is wise for you to go yet. The time for reaching that deep within will come, but it is not now."

"I'm sorry," I replied. "I... guess I don't know my way around in... here? Yet."

"That was very good," Liisa told me, "but not quite the right direction. We can try again tomorrow. Enough for today.

"Kata and I have duties. We must leave you to your own devices for a while. Then later today we can work on reading."

"That sounds good to me," I agreed. "I shall go and find Eero and get some more staff training in. And perhaps talk to the smith as Master Toivo asked me to."

We picked up our cushions and took them inside, then went our separate ways for a few hours. I went first and found Eero, and spent a couple of hours at staff training.

Eero was having a much harder time hitting me now, I noticed. I was also getting through his guard more often. But then as I went for an opening, he twirled his staff in a way I did not expect and hit me in the ribs.

"Ouch," I grunted. Then I grinned sheepishly. "... Can I see that again?"

Eero grinned broadly.

"Good," he said, "that's the right attitude. I think it's time to move on to some intermediate level techniques like that one I just used.

"Let's go through that last exchange again slowly, and I'll show you what I did."

This time he called my attention to the slight shift of his grip, and let me see how a twist of his wrists and a slight flex of his shoulders both rotated one end of his staff into a guard position, and at the same time swung the other end into position for a strike that my staff was out of position to block.

"There's a variety of different ways to use that," he told me, showing the movements slowly. "Like this... or this... or this... or even this.

"Now you try it. Slowly at first."

We practiced that technique for about an hour before he pronounced himself satisfied with my performance of it for the day, and directed me at one of the pells to practice the basic strikes on it again for a half hour. I worked hard at it, delivering the pell a sound thrashing while keeping on the move, working up a good sweat. My palms stung slightly from the pounding by the time I was done.

"Very good," Eero declared as I finished up. "We'll definitely make a staff-man out of you. A good one, too, if I'm not mistaken."

I racked my staff, asked a few directions, and then went to find the smith.

I found him without difficulty, of course. It's seldom hard to find the smithy once you're in the right general area. If the smoke from the forge doesn't draw you to the right spot, the sound of hammering will. As I arrived, he was forging horseshoes and passing them hot to the farrier, who was shoeing a... well, it wasn't *quite* a horse. Horses as I knew them didn't have *teeth* like that, nor those blade-like hooves. I didn't get too close. The shoulders were a little different, too. Heavier. It was muscled like a big cat. The farrier was singing softly to the not-quite-horse as he worked. I sidestepped past the farrier and 'horse', and went to wait for the smith.

"Can I help you?" he asked, in between hammer strokes.

"Master Toivo sent me to you," I told him.

"Toivo needs something made?" he asked, as he shaped another shoe.

"Not right now," I replied. "But he suggested I might be able to share some knowledge with you."

The smith shot me a sharp look.

"You'd be Newfound Járnhandr, then?"

"I would," I agreed.

"Well, my congratulations on your betrothal to two of the finest and most beautiful women in Highwatch!" he said, with a broad grin. "I'll be with you as soon as I finish this last shoe."

I grinned in reply and nodded, watching as he worked and glancing around the forge. I quickly realized that it was not at all what I had anticipated.

For one thing, the anvil was not the black iron I was expecting. It gleamed. And there was a *huge* rack of attachments nearby, and other forms, things I recognized as planishing irons, things I did not recognize at all. There were several balance scales, and bins filled with metal ores and chunks of metal. I quickly realized that this was a smithy unlike any I had ever seen. A water-wheel set off to one side of the forge proper was connected by what looked like a slip-clutch to a shaft that drove a bank of bellows.

182

It didn't take the smith long at all to finish up the last shoe and hand it off to the farrier. Then he set his hammer down and held out a hand.

"I am Matti," he said. "Pleased to meet you."

"Call me Alrekr," I replied, taking his hand. His grip was firm, but he had no need to prove anything.

"So Toivo mentioned something about a different kind of sword?" he asked.

"Yes," I agreed. "But... well, I'm looking around your forge and it is different from any I have ever seen before. I don't recognize even *half* of the tools here, and have never seen such an assortment of metal and ores. Before I make a complete fool of myself by making stupid assumptions, would you do me the favor of a quick explanation of how you work?"

Matti pondered that, eyeing me closely.

"It's a wise man who knows and admits what he does not know," he said at last. "Very well then. I'll assume you know the very basics of hammer and anvil." I nodded. "And I'm going to take a guess that your questions have to do with more than basic forging." I nodded again. "And specifically to do with weapons and armor?"

"Exactly," I agreed. I figured I'd narrow it down. "The type of sword that I mentioned to Master Toivo was made possible at the time it was invented, more than a thousand years before my time, by two things: The discovery of ways to make better steels, by the standards of the time, and the invention of then-completely-new methods of blade construction and tempering."

Matti nodded.

"So I should probably tell you about how I make my steels, then," he said. He made an expansive gesture across the bins of metal pieces and ores.

"A horseshoe like those you just watched me make is simple, soft wrought iron, soft tempered on the anvil. It has no need to be anything more. A harder steel would hurt the horse's foot. But tools and weapons must be made of better metal." I nodded. "I mix in other metals to obtain the qualities I need, sometimes by mixing carefully measured quantities of the ores, sometimes by mixing the metals themselves. I melt them together in the smelter, and then I sing out the impurities, and sing the metals together to mix them perfectly, so that they will be uniform throughout and have no hidden weaknesses. I cast the molten metal into a billet, and test it to see that it is right and has no voids or dross within. Only then can I transfer it to the forge."

I understood what he was saying, and I was impressed beyond words. He was not just a smith, he was a metallurgist. He was doing work in this forge and foundry, by hand and with his Talent, that would take industrial processes on so-far-distant Earth. His Talent took the place of a metallurgical laboratory.

"How do you know what metals to mix, and in what proportions?" I asked, curiously.

"Experience built upon what my master taught me in turn," he replied, "and listening to the metals as I work them. They have each an inner song of their own. A good smith must know to avoid combinations that are discordant, and seek harmony in the songs, and shape the song for what he wants the metal to be in the end. To a smith with a trained ear, the metals themselves will say which to use."

"A trained and supremely skilled ear," I said, awed. "You are saying that you craft alloys *by ear*. This is... almost unimaginable to me. Master Toivo did not mention to me that you were a master smith."

"Master, mister, moster," Matti replied with a snort. "I'm just a smith, with a hammer in my hand and my metals all around me. And that's how I like it."

"Either way," I said, "it seems your knowledge of—uh, metalcraft is far more advanced than I was expecting. I apologize."

"Rubbish," Matti snorted, again. "You have nothing to apologize for. You are new to this world, they all say. You have been here only a few months. You should spend less time apologizing for what you have not had time to learn about it yet, or you will spend the rest of your life apologizing, and have no time for learning.

"So tell me, how did the smiths who invented this sword type of yours improve their steels?"

So then I explained to him about repeatedly folding and hammer-welding iron back into a billet, and about coating the billet with straw ash and forging it that way to modify the carbon content of the steel, and about varying the number of folds and forging cycles to make steels with different properties, and how the folding forced impurities out of the metal and distributed the carbon through the steel, and how the double-acting box bellows enabled a hotter forge by creating a nearly continuous flow of air.

Matti nodded understandingly.

"A clever way to get the impurities out of the steel and control its hardness, if you cannot sing the properties you want into the steel," he said. "And then? They forged together billets of these different steels to make the blade?"

"Yes, exactly," I agreed. "Tough steel in the core that would not crack, springy steel on the sides to give it flex, very hard steel along the edge to take a razor edge. An intermediate steel in the back of the blade for parrying. And then they would wrap the blade in clay and scrape it away from the edge before returning it to the forge for the last time, to differentially temper the edge. Smithing schools, and even sometimes individual smiths, could be recognized by the shape of the visible temper line. They called the temper line the *hamon*, and the patterns shaped in it *gunome*."

"Very clever," he mused. "There might be something I can apply from that, though I would do it differently. Fold the steel to make the billets, yes, and keep the layering structure, then I would sing the billets together in the forge, as normal, but not mix them fully. Hmmm... yes. *Partly* mix them where they meet, so that the properties blend smoothly, instead of sharp changes between the parts. One solid piece with a smooth blend of properties, instead of separate pieces hammer-welded together.

"The clay to control the tempering is clever. I cannot do that kind of graduated tempering myself, I am not a firesinger and do not have that level of control over my fire. And the curvature of the blade... it is surprisingly difficult to forge a perfectly even curvature into a narrow blade."

"Oh, that's one of the more *interesting* parts," I explained. "You see, the blade is *forged* straight."

"Oho! And then shaped into the curve after forging?"

"Not exactly. It is the final quenching, in the clay coat, that gives it its curve."

"The final *quench*? With the clay... hmm..."

Matti paused, deep in thought. He paced up and down. "Forged straight. Different steels assembled together. Coat with clay, scrape the edge clear, and quench... What does the metal sing? How does its song... AHA!"

He stopped his pacing and spun around.

"A *single*-edged blade, like a knife, you said. The edge different from the back. Harder steel along the edge, softer in the core and the back. The edge is exposed, the core and back covered in clay, so the

185

edge cools fast in the quench bath, the core more slowly.

"The fast quenching sets the edge in fine dust-grain, but the slower cooling of the core and back allow the steel time to form pearl-grain, which is more compact... so the back and core contract, and THIS pulls the blade into its curve! Actually *during* the quenching! Is that the secret, Járnhandr?"

I grinned.

"That is it exactly, I believe. As best I understand it myself."

"Brilliant!" he half-shouted. "A magnificent inspiration! How did they come up with it, do you know?"

"Sadly," I said, "I cannot tell you. Amakuni Yasutsuna lived nearly thirteen hundred years before my time, and no original written records of his discovery survive. There is only a legend surrounding his invention of the curved single-edged sword. Before Amakuni, all swords from that nation were straight and double-edged. A sword called a *ken*... which word, in truth, means only 'sword' itself."

We talked a little about variations in blade internal construction, and I did my best to answer his questions. I mentioned the ways that master smiths would sign the tangs of their blades, and told him the story of Masamune, and mentioned the Seven Blades Under The Sun, considered to be the seven finest swords ever forged in Japan, and talked about fittings and the parts of the sword. Matti scribbled down copious notes as I talked.

It was late afternoon by the time we finished talking.

"I thank you for your time and the insights, Adept Járnhandr," Matti told me.

"I am no adept yet," I protested for the umpteenth time.

"I have no doubt you *will* be," he said. "And with a name like that, perhaps you should see whether smithing lies within your Talent.

"At any rate, I am pretty sure I can use some of these ideas, and I think I can improve upon them. Give me a while to experiment a little with differential alloying and folded steel, and see what I can do with them. When I think I am ready, I will send a message and we will talk about this sword of yours, and see what I can make for you."

I bowed. It was the only response that seemed fitting.

"Thank you for taking the time to listen to me, Smith Matti," I said. "I'm very happy that I was able to give you something of use."

"You'll be doing a lot more of that, I imagine," he replied with a chuckle. Then he went to attend to his next customer.

As for myself, I decided it was time for a bit of a run. So I made my way to the top of the wall, picked a direction, and set off running at an easy pace around the wall. On my first circuit, I made a few false turns and had to double back, but after that I had a route that would let me run a complete circuit of the wall top without stopping.

On the second lap I did not have to worry about route-finding, I only needed to follow my route, and I was able to look around and take in the view as I ran.

Running again felt *wonderful*. It had been far too many years. I deliberately tried not to push it; better not to overdo it. But when I had completed three laps, I felt so good I couldn't *not* run a fourth. It lifted my spirits, got my blood flowing... I felt *alive* again. I found myself laughing softly as I ran. I was *WHOLE*. Somehow.

I made a quick visit to the bath house to clean off and freshen up, noticing as I did that the remaining loose skin on my belly was tightening up nicely, and my belly flattening out. I also realized there was perceptibly more bulk in my thighs and in my shoulders than the last time I'd looked, and noticed as I got dressed that my shoulders were starting to strain my shirt. I'd be needing to trade out shirts again.

Then I headed back to our rooms to wait for my lovely ladies. I was looking forward to a reading lesson.

Again, I was first back to the rooms. As I arrived, a thought occurred to me.

There being a first time for everything, I rang the page bell myself.

A few minutes later, Senja appeared.

"Hello, Senja," I said.

"How can I help you, Newfound Járnhandr?" she asked with a smile.

"Senja, please," I said. "Call me Alrekr. I don't plan on being 'newfound' here forever."

She nodded. "As you wish, Honored Alrekr," she replied.

I chuckled wryly. I suppose I should have predicted something like that.

"Senja," I asked, "would you please do me a favor and drop the 'honored' as well? At least until I feel I've done something to earn it? Unless I'm missing something that would make that uncomfortable for you."

She nodded.

"If that is what you wish... Alrekr. Have I offended you?"

"Offended? Goodness, no," I reassured her hurriedly. "I just don't feel I've done anything to deserve any kind of honorific. I want to earn it honestly. I have *so much* to repay."

She nodded again.

"I think I understand," she said.

"Anyway, what I wanted to ask is—after the big Healing, the... parts that were removed from my knees were to be sent to the Collegium," I said. "Have they gone yet?"

Senja frowned in thought.

"I don't *think* so," she said. "There will be a caravan heading that way in a few more days, now that the roads have dried. It is all but certain they would be sent on that caravan. There was no urgency."

"Please do something for me, then," I asked. "I would like you to find who has charge of those pieces, and take one of the larger metal pieces instead to Master Smith Matti. Tell him that it comes from me, and that it is a gift in the hope that there is anything new in its songs that he can learn from."

She nodded.

"At once, H... Alrekr." I smiled.

"Thank you, Senja." And she scurried off.

Today, it turned out Liisa arrived back before Kata. So it was Liisa who was my first reading teacher.

We started out with the alphabet—the *aakoset*, in Saamen just as in Finnish—after a pause for welcome-home kisses. It looked as though once upon a time it might have been on speaking terms with Elder Futhark, but that had been a long time ago, and it had traveled a lot of hard roads since then, keeping many hard and angular features but also acquiring sweeping curves as adornments. There were thirty-three letters, seven more than I was used to.

Between us we worked out a conversion chart between Saamen and English orthography, helped out by my own very limited knowledge of Finnish. It took us a good two hours. Then it was time for me to start working on memorizing it. At least it had no diacritics, though several of the additional letters mapped to familiar letters *modified* by diacritics.

I'd been at that about an hour when Kata got back. Engrossed in trying to memorize orthography, I didn't hear her come in, and didn't know she was there until she leaned in and kissed me.

"Hello, Kata," I said, and caught her and pulled her into my lap. We kissed again.

"I hear you had one of the, ah... the *removed metal parts* sent over to Smith Matti," she said. I nodded. "That was a good thought. It will be interesting to see whether it holds anything new to him."

"That was my hope," I agreed.

We called a page—Rami came this time—and requested supper sent, chef's choice, and then we sat down together and talked about our days.

"Matti is a very good man," Liisa noted, "but not one for standing on formality."

"I'd noticed," I chuckled.

We talked until supper arrived, then sat down to eat. Mistress Kerttu had sent us lohikeitto, flatbread—*rieska*, I knew now—fresh butter for the bread, and honeyed fruit juice, tart and sweet at the same time. Over supper, we discussed some nuances of Saamen orthography and how it represented changes in pronunciation.

"Let us explore your soul a little further before we sleep," Kata said after supper. "I do not want you going in deep this time. I want you to practice just going in and out, and letting us guide you, so that we can steer you in the right direction, and away from any trouble."

So that's what we did. We sat cross-legged on the bed, actually, holding hands, and we worked on taking me in and out of light trance, and following their guidance until they could... just *nudge* me in a particular way without words, and I would feel it and know which way they wanted me to go. Kata explained, and *showed* me, that there was an important difference between *deep* and *inward*, and that I had gone

189

deep—*very* deep—when what I needed to do to access my core was to go *inward*.

"If you go too deep, before you know what you are doing," Liisa explained, "you could lose yourself entirely." I shuddered. I'd *been* there, once before, and it hadn't been fun at all.

We worked at it for a couple of hours, and then we went to bed, cuddling each other and making slow, languorous love until we fell asleep.

After breakfast the next day, we went atop the tower to meditate and seek my core again. This time I did not make the mistake of going deep. Kata and Liisa guided me gently inward instead. After some time, I began to become aware of what seemed like a circling wall of dark clouds, like the eyewall of a hurricane, but more felt than seen. I had the feeling I was supposed to go inside; I couldn't make any headway into it, though. I just found myself outside it again.

I had to explain to my loves what a hurricane was, after we came out, and about the eye and the eyewall. This time we were not in the trance nearly as long, as I did not get lost in the depths and it was easy for them to pull me out.

"That is not a bad analogy at all, it seems to me," Kata mused. "That 'eyewall' is your inmost defenses. And somewhere within, in the 'eye', you will find your core."

"Your—'eyewall'—is... very large," Liisa said seriously. "Whether because it is thick, or because the space inside it is large. Either one... speaks to the strength hidden within you. I—No. I should not say more now."

"Enough for today," Kata said. "Learning to get that far is a good step. Tomorrow, perhaps, we will get you further. But you must not fight the—the eyewall. If you try to fight your own defenses, you will only exhaust yourself losing. You need to acknowledge that defense as yours, learn to recognize yourself, and then you will be able to pass through. This will require you to accept, *truly* accept, who you are now... which may be difficult for you, because I do not think you truly *know* yet who you are."

I nodded ruefully, thoughtfully.

"I don't disagree," I said, "you're not wrong. I *am* still coming to grips with this, on some levels. Part of me still says this can't be real."

I reached out then, and took their hands.

"But most of me desperately, *desperately* wants it to be. Because... the two of you are my world. Truly."

Liisa smiled, and leaned in and kissed me.

"We must go for now," she said. "We have our duties."

"And I, my studies," I replied. I pulled Kata closer and kissed her as well.

"Until later."

Kata and Liisa went off to whatever calls there were today on their abilities, and I went for my daily staff lesson. We worked on the diversion move from the previous day, and Eero showed me another such technique, as well as starting me on spun blows. I practiced those for a while on the pell, the staff becoming more familiar to me with every strike.

This time, when I went to rack my staff, Eero stopped me.

"Take it with you," he said. "You have made it yours now. It is right for you. It will serve you until you find—or make—a better."

"You think I will make a better staff than this one?" I asked.

He gave me a searching look.

"Yes," he said. "I believe you will. Though I do not know what you will make it *from*, or what it will do."

He would not say more, only suggesting that I talk to Matti to have it shod—but only once I knew what it should be shod with.

I went to the bathhouse again, then dropped off the staff at our quarters and went atop the wall to run. As I ran, I found myself thinking about that circling wall, the eyewall at my center. I found myself visualizing the bands of cloud around a hurricane, and the clarity of the calm at its core, and I found myself mentally revisiting what that unseen wall had felt like, trying to recall its structure, recognize the currents within it, recall its rhythm. I could *solve* this. I *knew* I could. I *had* to.

I came to on all fours, half against the parapet, somewhere around the wall. I shook my head to clear it. There were hands upon me.

191

Hands I knew. I raised my head, and looked into Kata's beautiful eyes.

"Are you alright, Alrekr?" she asked, seriously.

"I... think so. Gods, I'm exhausted. What happened?"

"You ran until you dropped, Alrekr. Hours. After the guard in the southern watchtower saw you run past his position for the thirteenth time, without looking to either side, he decided he should send a message. That was nearly two hours ago. You have run past him twenty-three more times since. I have been watching you run for the past hour. I called out to you, but you did not seem to hear or see me."

She was gently feeding me energy, I realized. I pushed myself up and into a sitting position, leaning against the parapet.

"Now," she said, "perhaps *you* can tell *me* what happened?"

I closed my eyes, rested my head against my hand for a moment.

"I was thinking about hurricanes, and the comparison to the... barrier at my center," I explained. "I was trying to remember its patterns so that I could understand them."

Kata nodded slowly.

"And you slipped into trance as you ran," she said. "And ran, and ran, aware enough only to avoid obstacles. Until you collapsed.

"Come." She pulled me to my feet, supporting me. "You are drenched. Let me take you back to the bathhouse. It will do you good."

She led me to the nearest stair down, an arm around me. I tried not to lean too hard on her shoulders. She led me into the bathhouse, undressed me and herself, washed me off, and then led me into the sauna.

"Just sit and rest and relax," Kata told me. I did as she said.

After a while I became aware that I was gaining energy... but it was not coming from Kata. It was coming from the heated stones of the sauna... or perhaps, somehow, from beyond them. I looked at Kata and saw that she was watching me very intently.

"Did you know that you were drawing from the sauna stones?" she asked.

"No," I said slowly, "I didn't. Not until this moment. What does that mean?"

"Well," she said, "it shouldn't come as any surprise, I suppose.

What it *means* is that your power is awakening."

"That's good... right?"

"It is good that it is awakening. But it does mean we need to make sure you learn to control it as it wakes."

"I... see. I understand."

"Tomorrow we will work on reaching for your core again. You must learn to control it, to wield it, not let it wield you as it did today."

I nodded.

After a while, we moved from the sauna and took a dip in the cold pool. I swam from end to end of the pool, below the surface, before I came up again in front of Kata. She looked seriously at me, but her eyes were twinkling.

"You must teach me to do that, Alrekr."

"I'd be glad to."

Once we'd cooled off, we moved to the warm pool, and this time it was of course Kata whom I pulled into my lap. We sat in the warm water and relaxed, and snuggled, and I drank in the scent of her and nuzzled her neck.

After we got out and dried off, we went back to our rooms and I got a change of clothes. Then Kata insisted on taking me to the kitchens, where Mistress Kerttu looked at me and barked out an order. A minute later I was seated at one of the kitchen tables with a bowl of thick, meaty soup and a couple of crusty bread rolls that can't have come out of the oven more than five minutes earlier, split open and dripping with butter.

"Thank you, Mistress," I said. "You are a salvation as always." She gave me a stern glower with a smile hidden in the middle of it.

"You are *not* to run yourself to death on the wall, Adept-to-be Járnhandr, and that is final."

"Yes, Mistress," I replied meekly. She drew a tankard of mead and set it down in front of me.

"Now be sure you finish it all."

"Yes, Mistress."

When I was refreshed, we returned to our rooms, and I went back to my reading study. I was starting to get the grasp of the orthography, and I knew of course *how* to read... now it was a matter of putting them together and learning to read Saamen. Kata explained to me that once I had mastered that, then I would be able to move on to trying to read some of the special dialects used by specific schools of... no. Not schools of magic. I remembered Kata telling me that that word was disfavored. I resolved not to use it. Apparently different... disciplines within the realm of Talents *needed* to be written down in different ways, even to having their own languages and scripts.

Kata had me try a beginning book on rocks, minerals and gems, a book that was applicable to multiple disciplines and hence was written in plain, unadorned Saamen. It was slow going... but I could *read* it, and it was written in a language that I now knew well, and once I started reading for real, each new insight built on the last. I could almost feel words falling into place. By the time supper arrived, I was halfway through the book.

Liisa wasn't back yet.

"Where's Liisa?" I asked.

"She is attending a delivery," Kata told me. "She will likely be back late, if she is back today at all."

"I hope this one goes well," I said.

"Almost all of them do, Alrekr," Kata reassured me. "Do not worry."

Supper was more of the same soup Mistress Kerttu had fed me earlier. Liisa didn't arrive for it. Nor did she come in while I finished the minerals book after supper, or when Kata and I went to bed.

Sometime in the early morning hours I felt her crawl into bed next to us. She was cold, and her hair was damp. I wrapped my arms around her, rolled her across me as she giggled, and put her in the middle. She sighed contentedly as Kata and I snuggled up to her from either side.

Morning came, and Liisa explained over breakfast that the delivery had been long, and exhausting for the mother, but ultimately the only excitement involved had been the arrival into the world, safe and sound, of twin girls, finally born only minutes apart.   Mother and daughters were in perfect health, and the new father as proud as any could be. Liisa had gotten caught in the rain on her way back, which explained why she had arrived home as chilled as she was.

With breakfast over, it was time for another step on the inward journey to put me in touch with my core. It was easier this time to find my way into the center of myself, and of course the eyewall was still there. I determined that I would not make the mistake again of trying to fight it. Instead I tried to *feel* it, gain a sense of how it flowed and learn the rhythms of the gyre within it. It would take me in, and whirl me around, and deposit me outside again, but not actually do anything to me, and sometimes I caught a glimpse of brightness, a whisper of heat.

"You are beginning to glimpse your core," Kata told me, when I described what I had sensed. "You are close. Soon, you will touch it. Soon."

I remembered to take my staff with me when I went to staff training. We were working entirely on the intermediate techniques now. Eero taught me how to spin the staff into a strike that turned the energy of the rebound into a counterspin the other direction, and several more types of diversion block/strike and parry/strike. I was starting to notice the staff felt even firmer than it had, and told Eero about it.

"Listen to me, Járnhandr," he said seriously. "Like it or not, you are an Adept. You may not feel it yet, but you cannot keep denying it. You are shaping the staff to you. You do not intend to, I am sure; it just *happens*. You can no sooner *not* do it than you can stop breathing. That is why the staff feels different than it did. I told you: It is not just *a* staff now. It is *your* staff. It would be awkward, perhaps even feel unbalanced, in my hands. But it is becoming ever more perfect for yours.

"You should learn to accept this. I think you will not be able to avoid it for very much longer."

I thought deeply about what he had told me as I ascended the stairs up the tower. Instead of putting the staff in our rooms, I took it with me and carried it as I ran. I told myself that I wanted the practice; but partly, I also wanted to add a distraction so that I did not slip into contemplation again. I strictly limited myself to five laps of the wall. Then I put the staff away and went to the bathhouse, remembering to take clean clothes with me.

After my bath, I found my feet taking me to Matti's forge.

"Járnhandr!" he greeted me, when I got there. "This steel that you sent to me is tough to work. I hear its song, but it resists. How did your people forge it?"

"Large... uh..." I tried to find a way to express mechanical presses and machine tools. "Large, complex... shaping engines driven by various kinds of power," I managed eventually. "I perhaps should have warned you. It is well known to be difficult to work with. Almost as much so as..."

I realized I did not know a word in Saamen for titanium, either. There were a lot of terms related to technology, for which the words simply didn't exist.

"As much as?" Matti prompted me.

"There is a metal that I do not know a name for. Its... the salt of burning it makes a brilliant white, non-yellowing pigment that is very good for making paint. It is light, tough, resilient, and remains strong even at extreme temperatures." I thought. Come on, I'd just read a book about minerals. Did it mention any titanium-bearing minerals I knew? "It is found in rutile... and in..."

Try as I might, I could not find a word for ilmenite.

"There are other minerals, but most of them are rare, and I do not know the words for them, and I have no idea how to extract the metal from them anyway. And it is *legendarily* hard to work."

The forge kept drawing my attention. I wasn't sure why. I just put it down to distraction.

"Well, I will keep on with it," Matti said. "Its song is interesting. I hear the songs within it. I can hear how to make it, if I can figure out how to work it. Thank you for sending it to me. That was thoughtful."

"I'm glad it is of interest," I replied. "I hoped it would be. Until later, Smith Matti."

He gave me a friendly wave, and turned back to his anvil.

I wandered off to see what I could find to be useful at before I went back to my studies. I found a carpentry team putting up a gate who seemed a little shorthanded, so I lent my hands to the task, simply holding pieces in place for them as an extra set of hands, chatting idly with the two until the posts and crossbar were properly set and they knocked off for a break. It felt good.

"I'm Pertti," said one, "and this is Riku."

"I'm Alrekr," I replied.

Riku looked at me oddly.

"Ha!" he exclaimed. "I *KNEW* I'd seen you before! You are the new Adept! The one who married two Healers!"

Pertti laughed.

"Well, this is the first time I have ever been helped to erect a gate by an Adept," he said, grinning. "Come back any time you want. Sing strength into our work."

"I'd be glad to," I replied. "When I learn how."

I went back to the rooms, found a book on the trees of the region and the properties of their woods, and started reading that.

I had read about a quarter of the book by the time Liisa got home. She immediately came and sat down beside me, and snuggled against me. I put an arm around her and kept reading. She looked at the book.

"That is a good choice," she commented. "Lehtinen is highly regarded. What led you to choose that book in particular?"

"I figured it was probably a non-specialist book that I wouldn't have to learn any new dialect or script to read. And I spent much of the afternoon helping a pair of carpenters erect a gate. And I wanted to know more about what wood my staff is made of. Eero says I am shaping it to me."

Liisa looked at me, then at the staff, then got up and went to pick it up. She held it in her hands as though weighing it.

"He is right," she pronounced after a little. "I can feel it is tied to you. Are you beginning to believe yet that there is power within you, Alrekr?"

"Yes," I admitted. "Yes, I am."

"Good," she said. "Hold onto that belief." Then she set the staff back where I had stood it and came to sit next to me again. I pulled her against me, and she rested her head on my shoulder. I reflected again on how amazingly fortunate I was. This really *was* a second chance at life.

The more I read, the faster it came together. I was halfway through by the time Kata got home, supper minutes behind her. I had learned by then that my staff was cut from a wood called *rautakoivu*, iron birch. It was relatively uncommon, and required patience to work, but it was fine-grained, exceedingly tough, and resisted both water and fire well. According to Lehtinen, it *also* took bindings well. I began to understand that I had been uncommonly lucky to find it there among the staves. I began to wonder if it had been waiting there for me to find it.

We talked about the events of our days over supper, which featured the yellowish tubers, the wild-rice-like grain, whole roasted small birds, and a sizeable portion of spiced roasted meat. After supper I set the book aside, saving the rest for tomorrow; instead we all curled up on the couch next to each other and relaxed, while Kata and Liisa idly quizzed me on its content.

"You are doing very well, Alrekr," Kata told me at last. "We shall have to try you on some more difficult material. What you can read may give us insights into the nature of your Talent.

"But not tonight."

I agreed. Tonight, it was bedtime with my lovely ladies.

12: The Heart In The Eye

Over the following weeks, I kept up my reading, and kept working with my lovers—my chosen life partners, really—every morning on reaching my core. I had to abandon Lehtinen after the second book. Halfway through the first chapter of his third, I was running into words my mind would not grasp. It was frustrating.

The eyewall, as I had come to think of it, continued to balk me as well. I could not find a way to pass within it or to dissipate it. The harder I tried to break through it, the more firmly it tossed me out.

And then one night, as I lay awake strangely restless for the third night in a row, the realization came to me that perhaps that was the *problem*. I was going about this all wrong. I was making a fight of it, but what if I truly *was* fighting against *myself*?

I must have made some sound, because Liisa stirred where she was cuddled up by my side, lifted her head slightly, made a muffled questioning sound at me without opening her eyes. She snuggled closer, then began nuzzling my neck. I stroked her hip, ran my hand up her side. My thumb found her breast. And then, well, we both found all of each other. Finally I relaxed, and both lost and found myself within her, and her within me.

Finally, spent and soothed, we drifted off to sleep, intertwined. The last thing I remember was Kata rolling over and snuggling more tightly against my back.

Breakfast was soft poached eggs and strong black bread, then it was back to the tower top for more meditation and inward search. Once again, I quickly found my way to the eyewall, as I had begun to think of it. I felt more at home with it now, scarcely buffeted by it until I tried to push my way in. I knew its flows, its eddies.

And why *shouldn't* I know it, I realized?

The insight that had struck me last night came together and gelled at last. This was *not* a barrier against *me*, to be overcome. This was *my* barrier. I—*my* strength—had built this. I saw that now. What I had been struggling against was my unwillingness to believe, to *accept*, that this power was mine, that what everyone was patiently telling me was true. I had been hiding from *myself*. My core was not keeping me out. *I* was. *I* had been keeping myself out. Literally fighting myself. Kata had *told* me so, I remembered now, in plain words. I just hadn't been ready to internalize it yet.

But this was me. I finally *understood* that now. Everything else had changed; and so had I. It was my self-doubt that had been holding me back. And with that realization, finally I stopped doubting. This was *who I was now*. This was ME as I had always been *meant* to be. This barrier wasn't here to keep *me* out of my core. It was to keep *unwanted others* out. It would let in anyone I wanted it to; but first I had to let *myself* in.

And the key to that was realizing that in truth, the very center of me had been inside all along. In truth, I had *always been* inside. All I had to do was accept it.

The eyewall... *cleared*. The wall of ethereal cloud swirled and faded, and became as transparent as water. Then I was inside it. In front of me was... something. Something big. A shape that was not a shape. Round, yet not a sphere. More than a sphere. Hypersphere, my mind suggested. Again, I *felt* it more than I *saw* it. A pale light-that-was-not-light lit the place-that-was-not-a-place.

Of course I was curious—fascinated, even. So I reached out, not with my hand but with my *self*, and I touched it, as though I mentally laid my hand upon it. It seemed the obvious thing to do. But there was no surface there to touch. Instead, my—spiritual hand?—passed *into* it.

It blazed, raged, searing blue-white all around me.

I drew back from it reflexively, but I *felt* that blazing light flood into me, *through* me, without burning me. It didn't hurt; I *knew* it had done me no harm. But suddenly I felt more aware, more *alive*, than I'd ever felt before. So I put my imagined hand back.

The light suffused me, and spread to fill *everything*.

After a timeless interval I noticed that there was a stain amid the clear light, a dark, bloody streak that didn't belong there. It was wrong. It should not be there. It *offended* me. It was not of me.

Be whole, I thought, and brushed it away. Now all was as it should be. All was clean and clear. A distant, deep ache was suddenly gone. I smoothed the place where it had been.

I became aware after a while that a voice was calling me. Kata's, I thought. I turned my attention back outward... and I was sitting on the rooftop, Liisa's and Kata's hands in mine. I could see joy in their faces. And... something else.

"I found my way in, Kata," I said. "Or rather, realized I was already inside. I reached it... *touched* it."

"We know," Liisa told me, smiling happily. "Every strong Talented within a dozen leagues probably felt it. And I just watched you... simply *erase* the last remnants of your wounds from the sielunjuoja."

"Is it... usual for others to feel when a Talented first... opens? awakens?... their core?" I asked. But I suspected I already knew the answer.

"In the same room? Yes," Kata answered. "Within the same hall, yes. Anyone with Talent would feel it, even if they did not know what they felt. A strong Talent, on the way to Adept? Talented throughout Highwatch would know something had happened.

"This? This was *something else*. Something outside of my experience.

"I told you not long after you woke up, Alrekr, that I was sure you were at least an Adept, and probably more. You are *more*. There is no longer any possible question. There is power within you beyond any usual Adept. Now you must learn to use it and control it, and find where your Talents lie."

"Hello up there!" a voice came. It sounded like Master Timo. "May I come up?"

"Of course, Master Timo," Kata replied. Moments later, Timo's head came into sight up the stairs, followed by the rest of him. He walked over to us and stood behind Liisa.

"Adept Járnhandr now, in truth," he declared. "From the gatehouse, I felt your awakening. I would have to have been half-deaf not to.

"Are you ready *now* to believe what you are?"

"Yes, Master Timo," I replied respectfully. I bowed my head to him. "I have no further doubts." And it was true.

"Good," he said. "You have awoken from a long slumber."

"All my life," I agreed. "But now I understand. *That* was the insight that opened my core to me. That *this* is what I was always meant to be. Until I came *here*... I was not truly me. I was just... filling

201

the space that I occupied."

He nodded, as I climbed to my feet. Liisa and Kata stood along with me. I even *FELT* lighter.

"Good," Timo said. "This is very good. I have been wondering when you would break through.

"Be prepared to have many visitors over the next little while, Alrekr Járnhandr." I could already hear another set of footsteps on the outside stair. "An awakening such as yours has not been felt in Highwatch in... perhaps in living memory. Exactly what *will* you become, I wonder...?"

"Alrekr! It *WAS* you!" Varpu had just appeared at the top of the steps. She hurried over, started to reach out to me, then hesitated. I opened my arms and she gladly stepped into the hug. I was always ready for a Varpu hug. She was just so huggable.

"I *thought* it felt like you! But... such *strength!*"

Behind her, Raimo appeared at the top of the stairs. Vallaïnen was only a few steps behind, and Apprentice Vilja behind him.

I laughed.

"All right," I chuckled, "it looks as though we have a tower party. Did anyone bring the mead?" Master Timo chuckled merrily back, and Raimo shot me an approving grin.

Vallaïnen looked me up and down thoughtfully.

"Well, well," he told me. "Now I truly wonder whether you will indeed sing new things into being. I think you may have the strength for it. But we must train you. And it is possible that not all of the training you will need will be possible here at Highwatch."

Master Timo nodded agreement.

"It will depend on where your talents turn out to lie," he agreed. "And it may be that they will include healing... but... I do not think so. You do not *feel* like a healer, Alrekr. More and more, I believe your hypothesis: The world itself *told you* what to sing. And that has more than one implication.

"Soon now, I think, we will begin to learn where your talents lie."

"I, too, say this," Raimo declared. There was something odd in his tone. "I see you fully now, Alrekr Járnhandr. You are no longer hidden. And you are well and truly named. This name was yours, in truth, even before you claimed it. You do not fully understand the whole of your name yet. But in time, now, you will grow fully into it. I see this. It will be."

I looked at Raimo. That tone caught my attention, again.

"Your words sound... as though you are a seer," I said carefully. "It is not the first time I have noticed it."

Raimo nodded.

"It is a gift that comes with my Huldre blood," he agreed. "I do not see all. But what I do see, cannot be hidden from me. I have never been wrong.

"But... I still cannot *fully* see what you will become. That is *interesting.*"

"That is a great talent," I replied. I bowed my head to him. It just seemed the thing to do. I realized that I still had my arms full of Varpu, and that it was very nice, but that I should probably let go of her, so I did. Slowly.

At some point, someone sent for mead, and Senja brought it. And then Marketta and Esko showed up, and then Piia who walked straight over to me and hugged me tightly, and Paavo, and then Saana, and Knight-Commander Jaako, and two other Rangers whom I didn't know, and another older man who was introduced to me as Master Mason Perttunen, an Adept stonemason, and then Master Falconer Tuokkola. I had to suppress a chuckle at how much he resembled a hawk himself, with bright, darting eyes and a blade-like nose.

So it pretty much did end up a party, after all. I sent Senja for more mead, and told her to make sure she stayed after she brought it.

"*Now* will you let me call you Adept Járnhandr?" she asked, smiling happily. I grinned and agreed. I was done denying myself.

"As long as you still remember to call me Alrekr sometimes, Senja. Please." Senja agreed to that with a grin of her own.

Eventually, the impromptu gathering broke up. I found myself receiving kisses from Varpu, Senja, and unexpectedly Piia, as well as of course my lovely Kata and Liisa, and a bone-crushing hug from Raimo and a somewhat less forceful one from Vallaïnen. I kept finding my eyes oddly moist. Jaako settled for a firm arm-clasp.

"Thank you for finding me and bringing me home," I told Piia as I held her. She was tall and darkly pretty, but I could feel the strength in her, both physical and of her spirit. "It wasn't really until now that I realized how truly this—all of this—*IS* my home. The one I *should have* been born into." I gestured across all of Highwatch, and beyond. "If not for you and your team, I would have died out there."

"I am glad too that we found you, Adept Járnhandr," she replied. "I believe I was right to think it important. The Masters are saying that you may be the strongest Adept of this generation. Highwatch is fortunate to have you. Do you know yet where your talent lies?"

"Not yet, no."

"Well, you will find out," she assured me. "Who knows. Perhaps you will spend some of your time working with us in the Rangers. I think I would like that."

After everyone left, I took my staff and went to find Eero, but it was later in the day than I realized, and staff training was done for the day. My feet carried me instead to Matti's forge. He was working, or trying to work, the stainless again.

"Stubborn stuff," he muttered. "But I will master it." Then he turned to me.

"So I understand you reached your Awakening today, *Adept* Járnhandr," he told me, stressing the Adept. I held up my hands in mock surrender.

"I swear I am done trying to resist or deny it," I said.

"Good," he replied. "About time. You might have awakened sooner had you not worked so hard at not believing who you are."

"I know that *now*," I admitted. "Honestly. I... came from a place where it was hard to be *anything*. I had learned so deeply the idea that I did not matter, that I would never be anything of consequence. But now I finally understand that this is where, and who, I was always meant to be. It just... took time for me to be *ready* to accept that."

He looked at me with a measuring eye.

"Good," he said. "Now don't forget it." He looked at my staff.

"Did you bring that here to be shod?"

"Well," I replied, "Eero did tell me that I should get it shod, at some point, when I knew what it should be shod *with*. But I wasn't planning on it today."

"Hm," said Matti. "Well, I think *I* know what to shoe it with. If we can work the stuff. It is already tied to you. Hand me your staff."

I passed it to him absently. I didn't even see him pick up the piece of surgical stainless steel I had sent him, or really notice him lay the staff in a long soaking trough. My attention was entirely drawn to his forge. I found myself *listening to* it. It seemed... I could almost...

Matti gave me a long look.

"What is it?" he asked quietly. "Something about my forge has your attention."

"I... don't quite know," I said hesitantly. "I... think it wants me to *sing* to it."

"Well what are you waiting for, then?" Matti asked. "If it wants you to sing to it... then *sing*."

I looked at the forge. I listened to it. The hiss, the crackle, the roar. The muted thumping of the water-driven bellows. There was... it was almost... somewhere between a rhythm, and a melody. Not truly either, but a little of both, the way the wind sometimes sounds like a wordless voice crying out, or even actual words. I closed my eyes and listened to it.

Then, without conscious volition, I found myself almost whispering, a quiet chant that fit into the sounds of the forge. Words I did not *know*, again. Words new to me. But this time I had a feeling of what they *meant*. This time, I *learned* the words as I sang them. They came to me not as sounds alone, but with meanings. It was almost more that the *meanings* came to me, from within, from out of my own core this time, and I knew what they should *sound* like, how to speak them.

The forge's glow began to brighten, the fire at its core glowing whiter. Its roar grew stronger, and I raised my chant with it. I *FELT* the fire. I knew, somehow, that it would do my bidding. So long as I asked it politely, and in the right words.

With the right song.

Matti thrust the piece of stainless steel into the heart of the forge. I raised my voice a little more, and I sang the heart of the fire into the steel.

When it glowed white, Matti drew it out of the forge, laid it on his anvil, and quickly hammered it together into a solid billet. I could feel it starting to cool, and I found myself changing and strengthening my song. The steel and the forge were both right next to me. I... asked them both to *pretend* that the steel was still inside the forge.

205

The steel brightened again. Matti shot me an approving look, then hammer-welded the billet, worked it into a cylinder, drew it out, cut it into two pieces. He hammered them out into nearly-flat discs, thicker in the middle, then socketed a cylindrical platen into his anvil and hammered them smoothly into flat-bottomed, straight-sided cups. I held the forge's white heat in them as he worked.

He pulled my staff from the water and measured the ends against the cups, then put it back in, almost delicately hammered them a little smaller, rolled them on the face of the anvil, smoothing their sides, rounding the bottom edges slightly, peening the very edge just fractionally inward, forming a very slight inside lip. He slipped each one back onto the platen, one at a time; took a broad chisel and tapped a deep cross-hatch into the bottom faces, then worked a shallower diagonal knurling into the sides, delicately tapping the chisel with his hammer. He inspected them one more time, then laid them open end up on the anvil.

"Enough," he declared. I finished out the stanza and let my song drop, allowing the steel to start cooling. He retrieved my staff from the soaking trough and stood it against the wall, letting the surface water run off.

"So, Járnhandr," he said. "You are a firesinger. And probably more than that, as well. I almost dropped my hammer this morning, your awakening was so loud."

"I'm sorry," I said, reflexively. He laughed it off, a happy belly-laugh.

"Nothing to be sorry for!" he chuckled. "Nothing at all. I am glad you have finally fully joined us." I saw that he was watching the cups as they cooled. They were shading from yellow to orange now. "I am glad you have begun to realize your potential."

He eyed me sharply.

"All that has happened was meant to be, Járnhandr. Do not doubt that."

The orange was starting to shade toward red at the edges. He took my staff from the trough and drove one end into one of the cups. Steam and smoke poured from the ring of contact, and he leaned on it, pushing the wood down into the cup until it was fully seated. Then he lifted the staff, picking the cup up on the end, and in the same motion, plunged the capped end into the quench trough. There was a burst of steam bubbles as the water boiled around the new cap on the end of the staff. He held it for a count of five, then flipped it out and capped the other end the same way.

He let this end quench longer, about a fifteen count, then flipped the staff and gave the first cup another ten seconds. Then he dried off the staff with a rag and handed it to me for inspection. It was still slightly damp from its soak, but hardly any water had penetrated into the shaft. I realized he had soaked it so that the ends would not char and burn when he seated the caps.

"Does this suit?" he asked me.

Now that the hot steel had contracted, the tapered edges of the end caps were just barely proud of the wood of the shaft, the metal oxidized a deep blue and protruding beyond the wood no more than the thickness of my thumbnail. And he'd done all that *by eye*. I could feel that the staff had become a little more than a half-inch longer, and its weight distribution had shifted ever so slightly towards the ends. I spun it experimentally. It felt... *good*.

"It's wonderful," I told him. "I don't think I've ever seen such precise smithwork. You are truly a master smith, I can see that. What do I owe you?"

"Pshaw," he said, good-humoredly. "You sent me the metal, and helped me learn how to work it—and I think I know enough of it to make more, now, if I can find ores for all of the ingredients. I'm *honored* to do some work for you in return.

"I'll be glad, though, if you'll come back and sing my forge again when I need you to. Especially if I need to work more of this stubborn stuff. And perhaps... even this stuff, too."

He rummaged in a bin and pulled out a cluster of dark-orange crystals in a gray stone matrix, and dropped it into my hand. I almost dropped it. It was much heavier than I expected it to be. Scheelite, I realized after a moment. It had to be scheelite. Crystalline calcium tungsten tetroxide. This heavy, and that translucent fiery orange? It couldn't be anything else.

"This is called trollstone by some," he told me. "Fire crystal by others, for its color. I've managed to extract a little metal from a piece of it, a very dense metal, but I can't even *soften* it in my forge. It shrugs off the heat."

"I'm not surprised," I mused. "I think I know of this metal. I... if Saamen has a word for it, I don't know it."

"Not to my knowledge," he replied. I thought hard.

"I know two words for it," I said slowly. "One actually refers to this mineral itself, and basically just means 'heavy stone'. The other word is from a different language, and refers to its other well-known ore, and means 'wolf soot'. So perhaps we might call it... wolf metal? *Susimetalli?*"

"HAH!" Matti exclaimed delightedly (and emphatically). "A fine name. I declare it so! Wolf metal it is!"

"Its melting point is higher than anything else known to, uh, my past world. Which raises obvious problems trying to find something to melt it in. Like the old joke about the universal solvent."

"Hmm? What is that?" Matti asked curiously.

"It is a joking story about a man, a... an *alkemisti*, who devised a universal solvent, a liquid that would dissolve *anything*," I explained. Matti nodded. "And then he spent the rest of his life trying in vain to devise something to keep it in."

Matti laughed wholeheartedly, a deep, booming laugh.

"So how did yo... those smiths use it, then?" he asked.

I held up the chunk of scheelite.

"Actually," I replied, "the simplest way *I know of* is to crush this mineral and add it directly to the molten steel. Then let the, uh... the *kalsiumia* burn to quicklime and take it off with the slag."

"That is something I had not thought to try," he admitted. "Once it is extracted, on its own, I can do nothing with it.

"And what else do you know about our wolf-metal?"

"I know that it can be used to make steel either exceedingly hard," I replied, "or exceedingly tough. And I know that when correctly combined with lamp-black, it can be made into an extremely dense material, twice as dense as steel, somewhat brittle but so hard that you can whittle steel with it. But I don't know the secret of making that material."

"Indeed," he mused thoughtfully. "Well, if you feel like trying yourself against it some time, let me know."

He stuck out a hand, and I took it and shook. It was like shaking an iron bar.

"Good working with you, Firesinger Járnhandr. Enjoy the rest of your day. And don't forget that we have a sword to forge for you, some time when we are both ready."

A little later, just idly wandering, I stumbled across Raimo. He was working, on the spot, on a guard who had lost his footing coming down a stair off the wall and sprained an ankle. He had the guard's ankle in his hands, the boot lying nearby, chanting softly over it. I could see that it was slightly swollen, but I could also see that the swelling was fading; and I could, not with my eyes but somehow *inside*, see the *voima* that he was feeding into the injury as he healed it.

It wasn't very long before the ankle was sound again. The guard reached for his boot, but Raimo got it first. He turned it over and inspected it.

"I need to go and report in!" the guard protested. "I'm already late!"

"Then tell the Knight-Commander that I delayed you," Raimo replied. "And you can tell him also that I *ordered* you to take these boots to the cobbler. You *will* get these heels fixed. *Today.* Because I do not wish to have to heal you again tomorrow. Is that understood, Teppo?"

"Yes, Healer. Thank you, Healer." The guard looked sheepish. Raimo gave him his boot back, and he put it back on and hurried off toward the barracks.

Raimo turned and looked at me.

"Welcome, Alrekr," he said. "I see you have been to see Smith Matti." His glance flicked to the top of my staff, and back to me. Then he looked at the staff again. His eyes narrowed intently.

"Interesting, indeed," he mused. He looked at me with a raised eyebrow.

"... Yeeesss. Those end caps are tied to you. No doubt you would happen to know why?"

"Well," I told him, "they are made from one of the pieces of metal that came out of my knees."

Raimo nodded with a thoughtful expression.

"But there is more," he said. "Another bond. There is your hand in this, I think. Did you by chance...?"

"Smith Matti says I am a firesinger," I said.

"Aaaaaaah. And you sang to his forge?"

"Yes. It... it seemed it *wanted* me to. I—his forge has... caught and held my attention before. But I did not know then what it meant."

Raimo nodded knowingly.

"Matti told me that he could not work this metal without," I continued. "He said it is too stubborn. I know from past knowledge—and personal experience—that it is extremely difficult to work."

"Well, then," Raimo declared. "It seems you have landed already running. Be careful. Do not overstrain yourself."

"I will be careful," I nodded. "But this was... almost effortless."

"Really." Raimo's look was appraising.

"He has another metal that he wishes to try to experiment with. I know of no word for it in Saamen, and neither did Matti."

"A metal that Smith Matti does not know a word for?" Raimo's eyebrows rose in obvious surprise. "I thought there was no such thing."

"Indeed. But it is one that I know of. I recognized the ore by its weight and its appearance. From my past. It is distinctive." Raimo nodded again. "So we decided on a name for it based upon the names that I know for it. It is now wolf-metal—*susimetalli*."

"And you know the properties of this wolf-metal, no doubt?"

I nodded. "Most of them. It is very dense, it enables making very hard and very tough steels, and it withstands tremendous heat. Which is why Matti has not been able to work it so far. He does not have enough heat." I thought for a moment. "On a scale of temperature at which water freezes to ice at zero and boils to steam at a hundred, Matti's forge probably reaches somewhere above a thousand and a half. Perhaps a thousand and seven hundred. But wolf-metal does not melt until somewhat more than twice that."

Raimo's eyes widened.

"Twice hotter than Matti's forge. That is... a fierce heat indeed. Do you think that you can do it?"

"I do not know yet," I admitted. "And I do not believe his forge would survive it in any case. Fortunately, I do not think we will have to. I know of a way to make use of it at lower temperatures."

"Well, you continue to be filled with surprises, *Adept* Járnhandr," Raimo told me pointedly. I grinned sheepishly and just nodded. Then he grinned back, and clapped me on the shoulder.

"You should expect to be spending some of your time each day working with Smith Matti going forward, I imagine," he told me. "It will help him, it will thus help Highwatch, and it will help *you* to develop that skill. But... there is more, I think. I see there is more within you. But I do not yet know what."

Raimo bade me farewell and headed off to some other errand. I walked through the bailey, and then headed back to the rooms I shared with my lovers. I had a book to finish.

I finished my current reading book before either of my ladies came home, and was looking for another when Liisa came in.

"Hello, my love," she greeted me as she came in. She walked right over to me and kissed me. "Hmm. I smell the forge on you. You have been with Matti?"

"Yes. It appears I am a firesinger."

She clapped her hands in excitement.

"That is wonderful! We have not had a firesinger here in many years." She looked at my staff, leaning against the table, and examined the caps as Raimo had. Then she looked at me. "These new caps...?"

I nodded.

"Yes," I said. "One of the pieces from my knees."

"So that is why they are tied to you." She looked thoughtful. "Tell me then, what kind of a book were you looking for? I see you have finished with Lehtinen already. At least, his basic works."

"Well," I said, "I have read one on minerals, and two now on trees and woods. And had to abandon the third when I began running into words I could not grasp. I thought to perhaps look for one more specifically about metals."

Liisa looked at me and tapped a finger to her lips, thinking, then shook her head.

"... No, I don't think so," she mused thoughtfully. "Not for you. Not except for simple curiosity. You have been to Matti's forge several times, and now you have been there after your awakening, and you used your newly found Talent there. If metalworking was within your Talents, you would probably have reacted to the metals themselves in some way by now. So you are most likely *not* a metalworker.

"But we *do* know, now, that you *are* a firesinger. *So...*"

She reached to a different section of shelves entirely, and pulled down a larger, thicker book.

"Try this, instead. Vehviläinen's first volume on fire working. Let us see how much of it you can read."

I took it. It was heavy, and looked old.

"I am curious about something," I said. "You and Kata are both Healers. Why *do* you have so many books that are not about healing? Do you just like to study? Or does every Adept have a library like this?"

Liisa smiled.

"Not every Adept, Alrekr. Though many do. You will find, in time, that there are Adepts with skills that cannot be easily written down, nor learned by reading about them."

I took an educated guess.

"Raimo?"

"Exactly. Raimo is one such." She nodded again. "But we are not only Healers. We are also teachers." I understood immediately. "When we judge Vilja is ready to move on to her next stage of studies, when she advances to Journeyman, she will be coming here, now, to study. You don't object to that, I trust?"

"Not at all," I said. "She seems nice, and she has skill and thinks on her feet. And she helped, after..." My voice caught in my throat. "I owe her a debt."

Liisa nodded understanding.

"If we receive any further new apprentices here for training, in healing or any of several other disciplines that we are able to teach, then they too will come here for their first lessons. We of necessity also know something of medicinal herbs and plants, and of poisons, and venoms, and somewhat of brewing, and compounding, and distilling and purification. And of course, we teach reading, and writing."

I nodded.

"And I imagine other things as well, beyond those you listed?"

"Yes. And so we two have many more books, especially between the two of us, than most Adepts collect—although Master Timo's collection, for example, surpasses ours together. And I am told there are tens of thousands of books in the Collegium library.

"We pass on all of the knowledge that we can. Knowledge is to be shared freely. Always. This benefits all. If you are selfish with knowledge, and you hoard it, and it dies with you, then everyone is poorer for it."

"There was a similar sentiment expressed where I came from," I remarked. "But they got it slightly wrong."

Liisa gave me a curious look, so I explained.

"They said, 'Information wants to be free.' But no. That is wrong. Not information. *Information* is sometimes private, personal, not to be shared without consent, nobody's business but the person whom it is about. *Information* often wants to be private. But *knowledge*...? Yes. *Knowledge* wants to be free."

I sat down in front of the fire and started into the Vehviläinen book.

Vehviläinen rapidly became slow going. It was not the writing, as such; it was that some of it was written in a subtly different script, and I had to puzzle it out from context as I went. At first the new script seemed to writhe on the page as I tried to focus on it, but as I read more, it became clearer. I found myself repeatedly going back to be sure I had correctly understood something, and often discovered when I went back to it that there was in fact some nuance I had missed, or a subtlety of meaning that I had not grasped.

Three days into it, in fact, by which time I had struggled through most of the first five chapters, skimming past parts I did not understand, I went back to the beginning and started over. *Now* I understood much that had been unclear to me on my first start. From that point on, I was able to make steady progress.

I maintained my staff lessons, of course, and my daily runs. Eero asked to examine my staff, looking closely at the caps. He looked at me and nodded, but did not comment, instead handing the staff back without a word. I was starting to get the hang of many of the intermediate techniques. Not to worry; there were more. There were always more. I went by the forge nearly every day, getting used to the sound of the forge, learning the feel of it. I'd spend time there each day balancing out the heat through the forge, occasionally focusing it into an area where Matti wanted it, occasionally holding heat in something he was working on, sometimes holding it tightly within one area, sometimes keeping it even throughout.

Five days after I restarted Vehviläinen, Smith Matti sent a page mid-afternoon to fetch me. I put the book down, a bookmark in place, and went to see what he needed.

"Járnhandr!" he said, when I arrived. "Good. I would like you to try helping me with an experiment, please, if you can spare the time."

"Certainly," I said. "What do you have in mind?"

"I have a broken sword here to reforge." He held up a longsword, jaggedly snapped off about a third of its length from the point, its hilt removed. "And I wish to experiment with differentially tempering it, as you described. And I hoped you would be interested to help, and refine your firesinging skill."

"Interested?" I replied. "I would be *fascinated*."

Matti grinned approvingly.

"Well then," he said, "let's get started!"

"What's the plan?" I asked.

"An excellent question. You'll notice I fetched some nice sticky river clay." I hadn't, but I did now that he pointed it out.

"We will heat the blade to welding temperature, and I want you to see if you can concentrate the heat into the area of the break. I will sing it together as I forge it. I will also have to draw out the tang, just a little, enough to re-peen it. Once I am convinced the weld is sound, we will heat it and quench it, to harden it. Then I will apply the clay as you described to me.

"Then I will guide you as to the correct temperatures for tempering, and I want you to hold the heat as evenly throughout the blade as you can until the steel is ready, and then we will quench it... and see what we have.

"What do you say, Járnhandr?"

"I say, let's be at it. Let's see what we can do with it."

He grinned again.

"I hoped—and *expected*—you'd say that."

He thrust both pieces into the forge, and I chanted to the forge, falling easily back into the same rhythm as before. By now I was used to the feel of moving the heat around in the steel to where I wanted it— where *Matti* wanted it—to go. It wasn't long until I had it nearly as he wanted it.

"A little hotter, Járnhandr," Matti told me. I sang a little more heat into it, and in a few more minutes he nodded. He drew both pieces out of the fire and laid them on the anvil. The anvil wanted to draw the heat out of the steel, but I held it in the blade, drawing more from the forge as it was needed. Then Matti began to sing as well, as he began to weld the steel.

Matti's song was different from mine, and his tone deep and sonorous, but somehow... the two harmonized. I could see the two pieces of steel flowing together, guided by the hammer and the song. He drove the metal into the break, sparking as he struck it, sang the pieces together. There was a bright line where the break had been, then it was just a bright spot near one edge, and then... I could feel it was whole, the flow of the heat even and uninterrupted across the joint.

Matti turned it over one last time, examined the weld line closely, then rested his hammer.

"Back into the forge now," he said. "I want an even orange, like that spot there." He pointed into the forge bed, then laid the entire blade in. "We heat it evenly now, and quench. *Then* we temper."

I spread heat into the blade, end to end, until it reached the color he had asked for, pushing the heat into the core and out to the edges, into the point and the tang evenly. The blade looked oddly flat, as though it was not real. Then Matti picked it up with his tongs, pivoted, and dropped the entire sword into the quenching trough. He let the water boil furiously around it for a count of five, then picked it back out again.

"The tang will be too hard now," he explained. "We must soften just the very end."

He held the sword reversed, inserting just the last inch of the tang among the coals, until the tip of the tang was dull orange. Then he drew it gradually out and let it air-cool.

"There," he said. "Now the tip of the tang will be soft, so that it can be peened. And now, we temper. I want it an even light straw color. Do you know what I mean by that?"

"No," I said honestly. "But tell me when it's the color you want, and I'll hold it there."

"All right. I want to put the clay on before it goes back in. If only the edges are exposed, can you keep the heat constant throughout, even in the parts you can't see?"

I thought about it.

"Pretty certain I can, yes."

"All right, then."

Matti stirred the thick, wet clay he'd shown me earlier, then pulled out a large dollop and spread it out along the sword. He covered the entire tang and blade, then took a small wooden wedge and worked his

215

way down both edges, flicking the wet clay off about half a finger's width along the whole edge. I noticed he was doing it in a sawtooth pattern. Or maybe... *wolf* tooth?

He finished clearing both edges, poked the clay to be sure it was set enough to stay in place, then carefully turned the sword over and repeated the process on the other side. He wrapped the last inch of the tang in a double layer of clay.

Finally he looked up and straight at me.

"Well, here we go," he declared. "I hope I got this right."

He laid the sword gently, carefully back into the forge.

"Keep the end of the tang a little cooler, if you please. Not past dull red."

I sang to the forge and drew its heat into the steel. I could actually feel the clay slowing the transfer of heat, as it baked off. In a few minutes, the steel was already rising back towards red again. I sang softly to it and the forge, keeping the heat even throughout the blade, but pulling it away from the last few inches of the tang. I could see the edges and the point, but I realized I could *feel* the balance of the heat even where I couldn't see the metal. I *knew* it was even.

"A little more," Matti told me. "A little hotter." A pause. "Just a little more again." Then, "That's it. Can you hold it there for a little while?"

I nodded, and kept singing to it, feeling the flow of the heat, circulating it, balancing it, holding it even and steady, no part of the blade warmer or cooler than any other except for the cooler tip of the tang. I guided the heat away from that. Matti sang to it as well—but where I was singing to the heat, the fire, *he* was singing to the metal. I could not for the life of me tell what his song was doing.

Finally he nodded, picked the sword up with his tongs, and held it over the quenching trough, still singing to it. With his other hand, he gestured as though playing rock-paper-scissors—four fingers, three, two, one. Then a closed fist.

We stopped on the same note, and he dropped the sword into the water.

This time, he left it in there until the bubbling and steaming subsided entirely. He reached in with his hand and drew it out of the water, then laid it on his anvil and just barely tapped his way along it with his hammer, breaking away what remaining clay had not flaked off in the trough. The last flecks, he chased away with a wire brush. He took it by the tang, raised it, and sighted along it, first both flats, then the edges.

"It's true," he judged, satisfaction in his voice. "I was afraid it might warp in the quenching." He examined the weld location closely, running his fingernail along it. "Just a little repolishing and resharpening, and it'll be as good as new. No—BETTER than new. I can already feel it in the steel. This... it is nice. Listen."

He dangled the blade between his fingers by the very tip of the tang, and gently tapped it mid-way along its length with his hammer. The blade rang, a clear, pure note that took a long time to fade.

"Touch the tang," he told me. I reached out a fingertip and touched it lightly. Even after I could no longer hear it, I could feel the faint vibration. Like a tuning fork.

"We have done good work this day, Járnhandr. I'll have this finished up tomorrow. There's just a little finish work and re-polishing to do before I reassemble it. Be sure to come and look at it before I return it to its owner."

I nodded, and turned around. We had an audience.

I bade Matti farewell, and left. I had studies to get back to. I realized, looking at the sky, that we had been at it several hours.

"Isn't that Kauko's sword they just mended, together?" I heard someone ask as I was leaving.

"I think so," someone else agreed. "I admit, I teased him about it when he broke it. But now I think I am actually envious."

Kata was already home when I got back, sitting at the table with a tall mug of something. I could smell spices. Mulled wine? I stepped up behind her, bent over, and kissed the side of her neck. She giggled.

"Hello, beloved," I said, and sat down next to her.

"Alrekr," she said. "I heard you working with Matti today. How did it go?"

"Very well, I think," I replied. "We reforged a broken sword. Someone mentioned a name—Kauko, I think?"

"Ah, yes," she agreed, nodding. "The Ranger who was thrown from his horse. Perhaps the sword was cracked that day."

"Well, anyway," I told her, "Matti tried out a few new things today. I think Kauko is going to get his sword back better than new."

"And you?" she asked me. "What did you learn today?"

"How to work together with a master smith on a weapon," I said. "And how to spread the heat completely evenly through a sword blade and hold it there steady."

"That is a worthy day's work," Kata said. Then she leaned over and kissed me back. I pulled her into my lap and we sat and kissed a few times more.

"Fetch yourself a mug," she told me then. "The wine is next to the fireplace keeping warm." So I got myself a mug of wine, and then found my book, sat back down next to her, and went back to my studies.

"Vehviläinen, I see," Kata remarked. "Liisa picked that out for you?"

"Yes," I replied.

"A good choice. How is it going?"

"Fairly well. Now that I have learned how to read it. I went back to the start and began again."

Kata looked at me. It was her serious, thoughtful look.

"How far have you gotten, Alrekr?"

"The fifth chapter, before I returned to the beginning. But I am not quite back to it yet since starting over. It is only after restarting, that I realized how much in those first chapters I did not understand the first time."

"Do you recall, Alrekr, we told you that there are dialects used by different Talents?"

"I remember, yes. And I reached a point where I could progress no further with Lehtinen's third book."

"Alrekr, I cannot read beyond the third chapter of the book you are holding. I simply cannot make out the words. Up to part way through the third, I can follow it... mostly. But from the fourth chapter on, many of the words themselves escape me. I *cannot* read them."

I didn't understand that. That is, it matched my experience with Lehtinen—but I didn't understand *why*.

"How does that work? How can you—or I—read one thing but not another, when both are in Saamen?"

"They are in Saamen, yes. But the Saamen we are speaking now is not the Saamen that we use when we sing a healing—or that *you* sang to Matti's fire.   Think back to the seven-part healing we did on you. Can you remember a single word of what you sang?"

I thought back to the healing. Tried to recall the song.

"No," I confessed after a few moments. "I can't. I remember the *sound* of the song was... one of the most enthralling, stirring things I had ever heard. It was glorious. Beautiful. I could *feel* the whole room almost thrumming with the power. But I cannot recall one word of the song. Only the sound of it."

"You could feel the power because you are an Adept, Alrekr. But you could not, and cannot, understand the *words* of that power, the way we *used* that power to heal you, because you are not a Healer. You cannot feel or understand the ways that *voima* is used in healing. And because those aspects of *voima* are closed to you, so, too, is any way of describing or controlling them, or of writing them down. It is as though part of each *letter* were written using ink that you cannot see, in directions where you see no parchment to write on."

I thought about that.

"Then how did I heal the last of the sielunjuoja wound?" I asked, curious. "From what you say, I should not have been able to."

"That was a special case, Alrekr," Kata explained. "First, there was no *physical* injury left to heal. What remained was a psychic wound. A wound to your soul.

"And you did not... *heal* it, exactly. Not in the way that we heal. It was as though you simply *erased* it. I do not know, or *understand*, how. Neither does Liisa. Yes, we were watching as you did it. We *saw*. Yet we do not understand precisely *what* you did, or how."

I pondered that, too, then decided that was more than I wanted to get tangled up in right now.

"So," I said, changing the subject, "you're telling me that most of this book is written in... the language of fire-working?"

"The dialect of fire, yes.   Vehviläinen's opening chapters are written mostly in standard common Saamen. But by the fourth chapter, he is writing almost entirely in the dialect of fire. And... it is not simply that I do not understand it. I *cannot* learn it. I can *never* understand it. Unless somehow I can awaken some fire talent in myself, *as well as* Healing and Command. Which I doubt. If I could, I think it would have appeared by now."

"I think I see," I mused. "So Talents in this world are capable of amazing, almost unbelievable things... but you can *never* learn, or even try to study, a talent for which you do not already have the innate aptitude."

Kata nodded.

"Now you understand," she said.

"It seems... a mixed blessing. Such amazing abilities—but one cannot simply *decide* to study and learn one. You must have the gift."

"Exactly," Kata agreed. "And sometimes it is difficult, when no-one in a particular area has a certain skill. Sometimes an Adept must be fetched from far away to help out for a time."

"How often is that a Healer?"

"Healing, fortunately, is one of the more widespread Talents," she said. "But there is in particular more to the dialect of fire. There are said to be... *similarities* between the dialect of fire, and the language of dragons, Alrekr. Some of our oldest oral traditions tell us that the first fire mages in this land learned *from* the dragons how to sing fire."

I thought about that more, and longer.

"Are you telling me... that *I* might be able to speak to dragons?"

She thought for a moment, then nodded.

"It is... possible. Perhaps we will find out, some day."

That was a lot to think about.

"So how did *your* day go?" I asked. Kata laughed softly.

"Much less exciting than yours," she said. "An infected toenail on a mason who dropped a half-cut stone on his toe, a greenstick fracture in the right arm of a boy who fell out of a tree, and a woman who over-indulged on kylloberries."

"What are the results of kylloberry overindulgence, then?" I asked.

"Well, it is very uncomfortable," she replied, smiling slightly. "But on the bright side, they clean out the digestive tract."

"Ah," I said, chuckling. "I see. I imagine she won't do that again."

"You would think so, wouldn't you?" Kata agreed. "But this is the third time I have treated her for the same over-indulgence."

"Huh. She must really, really like kylloberries. Perhaps she should try eating half as many, twice as often?"

Kata laughed out loud.

"That's *exactly* what I suggested to her," she replied. And then I had to laugh as well.

Liisa came in just then. I went and met her halfway to the door, kissed her, and then got another mug and poured the last of the mulled wine into it for her. We all sat at the table sipping at our wine.

"How are your studies going, Alrekr?" Liisa asked.

"Going well, I think. I... understand the language of Vehviläinen's book, now."

"That is good. And? What of you? What are you learning? Is your skill developing?"

I thought. Closed my eyes.

"If I listen for it," I said slowly, "I can *hear*—or *feel*—Matti's forge from here." I raised an arm and pointed, down and across the bailey. "And... there... the kitchens, I think. The ovens. And something else..." I pointed again. "Over that way. I don't know what it is."

"The great fireplace in the Rangerhall," Kata said.

"And do you feel *this* fireplace, as well?" Liisa asked.

"I do," I agreed. "Now that I'm home here. But I have to be closer to it. No more than a little way outside the tower. It feels like... barely a spark."

I stopped and thought about my own answer for a moment, and realized that it led to a question.

"I know that Matti says his metals and ores sing to him. What do *you* feel? What can you sense?"

"We can feel when someone near us is sick or injured," Kata replied. "And we know what the injury is. We know when someone is dying, and will die no matter what we do. When someone dies suddenly or violently in the vicinity... we know."

"And the more people die in a single event," I took a guess, "the further away you can feel it, and the harder it hits. Am I right?"

"Yes, Alrekr," Liisa said. "You understand it well." Kata nodded agreement.

I decided not to ask any further questions in that vein. I didn't want to stir up possibly-painful memories—again.

We decided that evening to go and get our supper in the main hall instead of having it sent to our rooms. Not that it wasn't *nice* to eat supper in the privacy of our rooms, with my ladies all to myself; but I was long past any difficulty walking around Highwatch, and Liisa gently suggested that it would be good to socialize more.

We quickly found a spot at table with Esko, Marketta and Mistress Sirkka, and two others I did not know who turned out to be a seamstress and a brewer. A few minutes later Smith Matti walked in and took one of the two open spots.

"Ho, Járnhandr," he greeted me as he sat down. "That sword is polishing up nicely. You will like it, I think, when it is done." He scanned the table, with a nod to Mistress Sirkka. "A good evening to one and all."

Mistress Sirkka gracefully acknowledged the nod with her own, and the two of them made small talk the rest of the way through dinner. I listened to the shop-talk among the healers at table.

"So," Esko remarked to me after a while, "a firesinger, so I hear."

"And a good one," Matti interjected.

"I'm just starting to learn, really," I demurred. "Liisa has me reading Vehviläinen."

Matti snorted in good-natured disagreement.

"Just starting to learn, he says. Come to my forge tomorrow. Or perhaps better, overmorrow. Let me show you Kauko's sword that he helped me to mend and re-temper today."

"That was far more your work than mine," I protested. "All I did was balance the heat."

"Balance the heat better and more evenly than I can, and in *ways* that I cannot," Matti retorted. "I have been over a hundred years a smith. But I am no firesinger, and I cannot do what you did today. I can come close, with my forge and bellows; but I cannot *match* it. And I like that technique with the clay, too. I will be using that again, I can assure you."

"I can't take any credit for that except to tell you about it," I said. "That technique is usually credited to a smith more than twelve centuries dead named Amakuni Yasutsuna."

"That is true, Járnhandr," Matti agreed. "You have mentioned that name before. But still, I credit you for knowing about the technique and telling it to me. Would this be *common* knowledge, whence you came?"

"Well, no," I admitted. "Far from it, really. Many of my interests were unusual."

"Well there we are, then," Matti said. "We are doubly fortunate. To have you, *and* your knowledge. Undoubtedly you will have more to share."

"Kata and I certainly both count ourselves fortunate," Liisa remarked, smiling.

"*You* count yourselves fortunate?" I asked. I caught up her hand for a moment and kissed her fingers while I struggled to find adequate words.

"I was somehow plucked, by means or powers I do not understand, from a life I could endure no longer," I finally began. "I was found by your Rangers before I froze to death, I was brought here and healed of injuries that should have killed me; against any expectation I have ever had, I am deeply in love with *and married to* two of the most beautiful and wonderful women I have ever known; I am in a world full of wonders surrounded by friends among whom for possibly the first time in my life I *do not* feel an out-of-place stranger; and now I am discovering talents I could only ever dream of having, working alongside the finest smith I have ever met, and discovering that for possibly the first time, there is meaning to my life."

I reached to my other side and took Kata's hand as well.

"My friends, *fortunate* does not seem like a remotely adequate word. This world has saved my life and my soul."

"I told you, Járnhandr," Matti said gruffly. "All of this was meant to be."

Indeed, two days later, when I went to Matti's forge after my staff lesson, he had finished polishing out the blade and reassembled the hilt, and was in fact just finish-filing the freshly peened tang when I arrived. I saw bright metal on the ends of the pin through the hilt, as well.

"Járnhandr," he said. "A moment." He ran a few more light strokes, felt his work, and put the file down. "Come look at this in the daylight," he told me, and led the way outside, picking up a rag on the way. He handed me the rag first, then the sword.

I looked first at where I knew he had hammer-welded the broken blade. The joint was seamless. I could not tell where the break had been. The metal was polished to a uniform light, satiny gloss.

Then I looked at the edge. The temper line stood out clearly. Indeed, it was almost jagged, like the teeth of a wolf or some other ferocious beast. I noticed a few slightly uneven spots, but it was strong and clear, and the same width from end to end of the blade. The edge was sharp, but as befitted the type, a strong edge that would not chip on a shield rim, not the razor edge of a *katana*.

"Wolf's tooth *gunome*," I declared. "A new pattern. The first in the Sunlit Land."

I handed the sword back respectfully.

"This is magnificent work. I admit my practical experience is limited, but this is a good, strong *hamon*."

"Soon, I think we should talk about your sword," Matti replied. "I have some ideas."

Esko showed up as we were talking, with Raimo in tow. Esko too expressed great approval of the repaired sword. Raimo looked closely at the edge.

"What forms the pattern?" he asked.

"It is a line of demarcation between harder and softer steels," Matti explained. "Here, the crystals are smaller, finer. On this side, a little larger, differently shaped. The steel is harder at the edge, but a crack or chip will not spread. And the heart of the blade... pulls inward on the rest. The core of the blade is trying to make the sword shorter and narrower. That compresses the metal of the edge and makes it even stronger."

Raimo nodded silently.

"And this you learned from Járnhandr?" he asked.

"Smith Matti has added to and built upon the little I was able to tell him," I said. "He has added new dimensions to the technique, I think."

Just then, Matti looked past Raimo.

"Ranger Kauko!" he called. "It is done. Come."

Kauko, a lean, fair-haired man with a no-nonsense attitude and a wry smile, strode up to the forge a moment later. Matti handed him the sword, hilt first.

"It is better than new," Matti told Kauko. "Firesinger Járnhandr here helped me ereyesterday with the heat-treating."

Kauko was examining the blade closely.

"What is this patterning along the edge?" he asked.

"It is the mark of a new kind of differential tempering that Adept Járnhandr told me about," Matti told him. "It both makes the sword stronger, and enables it to hold a sharper edge for longer."

Kauko tried the edge with his thumb—properly, I noticed—and his eyebrows rose.

"Indeed, that is a bitter edge," he agreed approvingly. "And it will keep this edge?"

"For longer than it kept its original edge," Matti replied. "You should seldom need to stone it, and only lightly. Do not put it on a wheel. By hand, only. I will give you a suitable stone.

"I will be surprised if you manage to break this. But if somehow you should, come back and tell me exactly what happened. This is an untried technique, for me."

Kauko stepped back a little and tried a few practice swings, working up to whistling cuts and near-blurring snap cuts.

"It is good," he pronounced at last. "Better than new, indeed. I would swear it feels almost alive. My thanks to you both."

Matti had fetched the scabbard from out of the back of his forge by then. He passed it to Kauko, and Kauko sheathed the sword and strapped it on. Then he pulled out a leather pouch and tossed it to Matti.

"My thanks, Smith Matti," he said. Matti caught the pouch and reflexively weighed it in his hand. He raised an eyebrow questioningly.

"The agreed repair fee was forty silvers," he told Kauko. "This feels nearer twice that."

Kauko bowed.

"And cheap at the price, I think, Smith Matti," he declared. "You quoted me forty silvers to mend a broken sword, not to re-forge it better than new. I thank you again." He threw Matti a loose salute, nodded to me, then turned and left.

Matti looked at me, then opened the pouch. He counted out the coins, then put half back into the pouch and handed it to me.

"This is your share, Járnhandr," he said. "And I don't want to hear any argument."

I hesitated a moment, then nodded thanks. Kata had given me a little coin for incidental expenses, shirts and such, but I was running low. This would help that a lot.

I excused myself, and headed back to continue my reading.

13: The Gauru

Matti sent for my help twice more, above and beyond my near-daily visits, before I finished the first Vehviläinen volume and went on to the second of three. In one of those visits, we experimented with melting scheelite into a small batch of steel, which Matti then worked and experimented with as we heated it and let it cool, heated and quenched it, heated and cooled it again. It took more heat than the usual runs of steels, perhaps even more than the stainless steel, to work it.

Finally he took the small bar and worked it into a chisel, and then we heat-treated it. When I left, he was sharpening the new chisel, using plenty of water on the grindstone.

Vehviläinen's second book was more difficult material again, and I was starting to slow down. Four days into that second volume, I ran across something I wanted to try, right away.

I looked around the room. There was not a weapon to hand, but there was a poker among the tools next to the fireplace. It was heavy wrought iron. It would work.

I looked at the fire, and I chanted the fire a little hotter, a little brighter. I added another two logs, because I needed it to last, and spread the fire into the new logs as well, enough to get it well alight. Then I picked up the poker.

Singing softly to the fire, I extended my senses toward the poker. Not feeling the poker itself as a thing, but rather as a container, a space in which something could be. A place that could hold fire. I let my song wrap around it, define its shape, following the way Vehviläinen had described.

Rod, I told the poker. *I name you Rod.* The name was a label, and Vehviläinen said that such a label was necessary in order for this to work its best. And then I drew the fire into the poker, into the space defined by the poker's shape, twisted it around itself, knotted it there. The idea of fire. The heat of fire. The capacity for fire. I looped it circling forever inside the space that the poker defined, singing both to the fire and to the poker now, and to what I was crafting within the poker. And then I tied it off, and let my song end.

The fire returned to normal, though the logs were significantly diminished. The poker... *looked* normal. But every few seconds, a shadow of red-orange would flicker through it like a flame inside the iron.

I stepped outside into the hallway, well away from the fireplace. I held the poker high, upright in front of me.

"*Rod*," I said. And flame burst forth from the poker. YES!!! It had worked!

I *told* the fire to rest, and the flames died, and it was a normal poker again. "*Rod.*" Flames burst out.

I laughed despite myself. I had made an everlasting firelighter.

I willed the fire down again, and carefully touched the poker. It was barely warm. It simply *contained* the fire without being touched by it. And that made something else of Vehviläinen's explanation make sense.

I took the poker back inside the room and put it back by the fireplace. If I could bind fire into a poker, I ought to be able to bind it into anything else that was adequately solid. My staff, for instance. And it would hold a lot more fire than the poker would. But I wasn't ready to do that *just* yet. I wanted to be sure I wouldn't damage the staff, I'd need to come up with a good name for it... and you never know, I might well find something even *more* interesting. And truth to be told, I wasn't sure yet that binding fire into a staff was even going to be useful. Binding it into the poker was pretty much just a parlor trick, beyond what I had learned from doing it.

I poured myself more fruit juice, and went back to my studies.

I'd nearly finished Vehviläinen's second volume before the day came when Matti asked me if I could be there first thing in the morning the next couple of days.

"I'm ready to try forging your sword," he told me. "But first, we must prepare the steel for it."

The next morning I was there bright and early, right after breakfast. Matti had fresh iron ore, and crucibles, and stone ingot-casting molds, and several piles of mineral samples. I recognized scheelite, and what I thought was the orange-shot deep-red crystals of vanadinite, and black nodules that looked like meteoric iron, as well as others I had no idea about.   He had divided them into three piles containing different mixtures in each.

In the end, we worked on it most of the day.   We started each batch with a mixture of brown iron ore and the meteoric nodules, and I poured heat into them while Matti encouraged them to melt, until we had a puddle of nickel-iron in the crucible.   Then he would add in additional minerals, and he would sing the metal he wanted out of it, and let the rest join the slag.   When everything was molten and the crucible glowed white, both of us singing over the roar of the forge, he would sweep the slag off the top, and pour the clean molten metal into one of the stone molds.   We took a water break each time while the new ingot cooled somewhat, then he would tack a sprue onto the ingot, and then while I held the heat steady, he hammered it out, brushed it with lampblack, folded it, hammered it out again, brushed it, folded it, until he liked its song.   Then he would set that billet aside, and we would fill the crucible again, and start over.

At the end of our working day, we had a sizable audience, and three billets of steel.   Matti had marked each lightly with his new tungsten-steel chisel.   Aside from that, I could tell no difference between them at this point.   One might have been a little brighter, one a little darker.   I wasn't sure.   I didn't know the metals well enough to tell.

I ran into Liisa and Kata walking together shortly after I left the forge.   I was well aware I was filthy, but we were all three of us headed for the tower, so we went and collected fresh clothes, and then all three of us went to the sauna and the baths, to get the hot-metal smell of the forge off of me.

I was more aware of the heat in the stones in the sauna this time. Liisa noticed me gazing intently at them, and asked what had my attention.

"The stones," I explained.   "I can... *feel*... Tumarïnen's link in them.   I can see where it goes.   Follow it down."

Kata gave me a long look.

"You can see Tumarïnen's work?"

"It seems I can, now."

"Do you think you could... copy it?"

I thought about that for a while.

"Not yet, at least.   I don't think I can reach that far down.   Yet.

229

And I don't think I know yet how to bind the link so that they remain linked."

Without really thinking about it, I reached out and put my hand on one of the hot stones, feeling the patterns within it. I absently heard a sharply indrawn breath, but wasn't paying enough attention to tell whose it was. My attention was on the stone.

"I think... perhaps... yes, I see *part* of how he bound it," I said slowly. "Did Tumarïnen by chance happen to write a book?"

"He did, I believe," Kata replied. "I will send to the Collegium, and see if we can borrow a copy for you to read."

"Thank you, Kata," I said, as I sat back. "That would be greatly appreciated."

Liisa caught my hand and looked at it closely.

"Not a mark," she told Kata. "Not even reddened."

"How—*interesting*," Kata replied thoughtfully.

The next morning I returned to the forge, and we resumed where we had left off. Matti put all three ingots into the forge and had me channel heat into them until they reached working temperature, then hold them there.

He began by drawing all three ingots out to about twice their length. He took two, worked them into square sections, then hammered and sang them together seamlessly along their entire length. The third he split in two lengthwise, then worked both halves out until they were slabs a quarter their original thickness, slightly narrower than the block he had so far. Then he joined those to the wide faces of the block, the same way as he had joined the first two ingots.

"We must make sure there are absolutely no internal voids, Járnhandr," he told me as he examined the resulting billet. "Any void, any flaw, will weaken the blade."

He kept at it until, as he said, the song of the metal was pure, and without harshness or discordance. Only then did he begin drawing the combined billet out into a blade. I held the heat in it as evenly as I could, but we both had to pause from time to time to drink, as our throats grew hoarse.

"This would take enormously longer without a firesinger working with me," Matti remarked during one such break. "I would have to keep reheating it, and working it some more, and reheating, and reworking. With you holding the fire in it, I can work it as long as my throat holds out. We have done days of normal work already this day. Even with *this* tough steel."

As the hours passed by, Matti patiently drew the original ingot out into a ribbon of steel only about as wide as two fingers held together, tapering slightly toward the tip. It was slightly wedge-shaped in section, but he did not forge it all the way down to an edge, leaving some excess metal there. He shaped a rounded tang and the point, then rested his hammer at last.

"Let it cool now," he said. "Based on what you have told me, I have several days to a week of filing and grinding work before we are ready to do the final temper. And then we shall see whether we end with a sword blade, or a handful of shards."

"There's one other thing that will need to be done," I told him, "but I'm pretty sure it can wait for after tempering. Besides having fittings and a scabbard made, of course."

"What is that?" Matti asked.

"You will need to take a chisel and sign the tang. It's traditional."

Matti chuckled.

"I think I can accomplish that without angering Ilmarinen," he said. "And I have your sketches of the fitting parts, and my notes on your explanations. The—*habaki*, the *tsuba*, the...?" He stumbled over the unfamiliar words. "So many fittings."

"There are actually many others, on more elaborately mounted swords," I replied. "Though only these first six are really *necessary*. I still don't know what I'm going to use in place of *samé*. This does not seem like a place where sharkskin or rayskin can easily be found."

"Why don't you go talk to the Rangers?" Matti suggested. "One of them may be able to suggest something."

That wasn't a bad idea, actually. So the next day, I went to the Rangerhall.

The Rangerhall was in a part of the keep I had not been to before. But I realized that I could find my way to it by following the heat of what Kata had described as the great fireplace. Indeed, it was an impressively large fireplace, with several sets of fire irons and roasting spits around it. Evidently they did a fair bit of their own cooking.

Piia spotted me almost as soon as I entered the hall.

"Alrekr!" she called. "Over here!"

I followed where she beckoned me, and as soon as I was within reach she wrapped me in a hug, which I happily returned. I was becoming a huge fan of how unrestrained the people here were about hugging. Every hug felt as though it washed away a tiny little piece of the emptiness of my former life.

I recognized Ari, Simo and Paavo, and Piia quickly introduced me to the other members of her team. Ari pressed a tankard of mead into my hand. There were Ragne and Eino, archers, and Karel, their tracker. Simo, I knew now, was a divination mage, mostly, as I understood it. He *found* things. Paths. Lost things. Hidden things. Rifts. And, as it had turned out, me.

"So it was you, I understand, who detected the... rift... I apparently came through, right?" I asked. It was the first real opportunity I had gotten to talk to him about it.

"Yes," he said. "It was brief, but very strong. We had time to reach it before the echoes faded. Its smell still hung in the air. And there we found you, and—"

He cut off, but I finished for him.

"The sielunjuoja."

"... Yes. Perhaps it would have been better if we had not found her."

"*Do not* think that," I told him. "She had the choice... perhaps... *not* to embrace what she became. Had you not searched further and found her, perhaps she would have died in the night. Or perhaps, she would have crawled away and be preying on people even now.

"And..." I swallowed. "And I have closure, now. Smith Matti told me, 'All that has happened was meant to be.'"

Simo nodded.

"Matti is wise beyond what he may seem to those who do not know him," he told me.

"So," Piia asked, "what brings you here? Did you just come to see us and drink with us? Or did you need something in particular?"

"Actually," I replied, "Matti suggested that I should come. Though ... perhaps I should have come sooner.

"We are working on a sword, of a type you have not seen before, from my past world. My past life. And for the hilt, I need to find a… a material. To give a firm grip that will not slip even when wet with blood.

"In my past world, the traditional material was something called *samé*, the skin of a shark or ray, with the points of the denticles polished down—or it would rip the skin from your palms. And of course, being fish skin, it did not soften or deteriorate when it got wet.

"Matti suggested that you might perhaps have some ideas."

"Hmmm." Karel looked at me, musing. "A gar pike…? No, probably too smooth and flat. And the scales on a redbelly would be too fine.

"The under-arm scales on a gauru, perhaps?"

"It'd have to be a big gauru," Paavo remarked. "Fortunately, I think I know where to find one. I've been thinking we should deal with it at some point. I think it's the cause behind some missing sheep and goats. And one of those farms that lost livestock has small children."

He looked at me.

"What do you say? Want to go on a gauru hunt?"

"Sure," I agreed. "Why not?"

And that is how I came to be riding on horseback in the middle of a line of seven Rangers as we wound our way into the lower crags of the Spine of the World, a few leagues east of Highwatch, early in the afternoon. I was more than willing to accept these mounts in place of horses, I decided. Their gaits were both springier and smoother than an Earth horse, with an easy, pacing lope that was smooth as silk, and they could leap as though rocket-powered. The first such leap actually unhorsed me, to general laughter as soon as it was clear I was unhurt. The second time, I was ready, and it was thrilling.

Karel sniffed the air.

"Gauru territory scent marker," he declared. I smelled nothing. "From here, we go on foot."

We all dismounted. I was slightly sore, not having been on a horse in many years. Simo stayed with the horses, stating that he would be little help in a gauru hunt and it was best to keep the horses well away until it was dealt with. We went onward on foot, I with my staff at the ready.

A gauru, Karel had explained to me, was a reptile that dwelled in many regions of the Sunlit Land. The variant that lived in these crags ran anywhere from four to eighteen feet in length, including the powerful tail. They were fast, strong, aggressive, cunning, and venomous. Piia had instructed me that if the gauru were to get near to me, I was only to defend myself, not try to attack, and I should try not to get bitten.

"Of course," Ari joked, deadpan, "if you *should* get bitten, you are married to one of the best venom healers in Highwatch. So perhaps you should taunt it to bite you instead of one of us."

I couldn't help but laugh.

We wound our way into the high forests, moving slowly and quietly. After an hour or so, Karel held up a hand.

"We are close," he cautioned. He pointed at scattered cracked bones. "The lair should be somewhere near here."

"Somewhere up there," Paavo pointed, "if that's its trail. And I *think* it is."

We moved upslope, the direction he had indicated. I did my best to emulate the silence of the Rangers, testing each step with my toes as I saw them do. Nothing moved. Eventually the ground leveled slightly and we found ourselves looking at the mouth of a small cave from a distance of between thirty and forty yards. The short cliff curved around a broad clearing that fell away to the west. To the east, a low ridge protruded, and an area of low brush, not tall enough to conceal anything large.

Still, there was no movement.

Ari picked up a fist-size rock, and with a powerful side-arm throw, snapped it into the mouth of the cave. We heard it clatter inside... then nothing.

Karel slowly advanced on the cave mouth, studying the ground. He nodded to himself periodically. Paavo stayed three paces behind him, while Ragne and Eino covered them from fifteen yards back. Piia covered them in turn, another five yards behind them, and Ari watched over Piia and me.

Karel reached the cave mouth. Sniffed the air. Shook his head. Ducked inside the cave.

He came out about ten seconds later.

"Not here," he said. "It has been here recently, but... not now. We will have to find its trail."

Everyone came back, and we regrouped. Ari and Paavo took places downslope, Eino and Ragne covering them. Piia was near me, as Karel started to work his way around the edge of the open area, looking for fresh tracks, as I watched. I was looking downslope, Karel off to my right.

There was a crack of a snapping twig, or perhaps a displaced stone. Then the gauru exploded out of the brush on my left, and charged straight at me. It was a mass of gray and green, yellow wattles under its chin, a blood red crest on the top and back of its head. Now that I saw it, it was something like a large monitor lizard, similar to a Komodo dragon. Red eyes focused on me as Piia shouted an urgent warning.

I could use a tiger spear right now, I thought. And the thought triggered action. I slammed the butt of my staff into the ground, stamped my right heel down on it hard, and aimed the other end straight into the oncoming gauru's open mouth. Pike tactics. Except you're supposed to use them with a pike fifteen to eighteen feet long, not a six-and-a-half foot quarterstaff.

The staff shot into the gauru's mouth and drove into the back of its throat. Its own rush pushed the staff up and back, levering the gauru's forequarters off the ground. My left hand was actually inside its mouth, but it couldn't close its mouth with the staff in its throat. It couldn't get any closer, it couldn't get free as long as I could keep the staff up, it couldn't get traction to try to back away unless it could get the staff down, and its claws just barely couldn't reach me. I was face-to-face with the gauru from under two feet away, and the charnel stench of its breath almost made me gag. It was a standoff for the moment, but it had size and mass on me, and the standoff wouldn't last. It let out an enraged hissing shriek like a steam whistle.

I saw Piia step past me on my left, her sword raised, just as a white streak from downslope stabbed into the gauru's head. Ragne had just put an arrow through the gauru's left eye. A moment later, Piia's whirling two-handed swing opened its throat.

The gauru sagged, dark blood gouting from its gashed throat, but the fight was already leaving it. Ragne's arrow had gone straight into its brain. It toppled sideways, twitching, and after I was sure it wasn't moving with any independent volition any more, I pulled my staff out of its throat.

"That has to be the most unusual way I have ever seen anyone fight a gauru," Paavo commented dryly. "*Damn*, it's a big one."

"Don't knock it," Piia replied. "It worked."

"More by luck than by good judgment," I declared ruefully. "Thanks for that shot, Ragne." Ragne nodded acknowledgment.

"Don't sell yourself short," Piia told me. "You reacted as fast as any Ranger. I want you to teach me that move. Or all of us."

"It wasn't meant to be done with a staff," I said. "It was devised for use with the Swiss pike, to stop cavalry. A heavy spear fifteen to eighteen feet long."

"Well," Ari remarked calmly, "either way, it stopped the gauru and held it, long enough for Ragne and Piia to kill it quickly. It was well done, whether planned that way or not."

He turned downslope and gave a long, piercing whistle that echoed from the crags.

"Let's get this thing skinned," he said.

It took Ari, Paavo and Karel an hour to skin the gauru. By that time, Simo had rejoined us with the horses. Piia, Eino and I scouted the area the gauru had attacked from, and found that there was a gully nearly five feet deep hidden under the brush. It had completely concealed the gauru, which Karel paced out at almost twenty feet. He showed me the skin at the top of the inner arm and armpit. It was flexible, tough, and covered with small, hard pyramidal scales, about twelve or fourteen to the inch.

"Will this work for your sword hilt?" he asked.

"Karel," I replied, "I think this will make excellent samé. This was a good call. Though I'd prefer not to be that close to a gauru this size again in future."

He clapped me on the shoulder.

"The gauru outwitted all of us," he said. "It was well concealed, and downwind, and it waited until there was someone within range of its charge and nobody was looking its way. It must have been watching us the entire time. But you handled yourself well."

"Will you take any of the meat from the gauru?" I asked.

"No," Karel replied, shaking his head. "Gauru meat would only make you sick. It is poisonous. Only the hide is any use. And maybe the claws, for decoration. We'll leave the rest here. The lammergeiers will find it first, but there are other things that will eat gauru too. Many of them, you'd probably prefer not to meet." He looked up and scanned the sky, then pointed.

"See, they're already circling," he told me. I looked up to see a bird that must have had a wingspan over fifteen feet circling lazily about a thousand feet above us. "That one will be down as soon as we leave."

Karel cut out all four inner joint patches from the hide and gave them to me. "Wash them well in salt and wood ash," he told me. "Then you can cure or tan them."

The rest of the hide, from the neck down, they rolled up and packed on one of the horses. The horse was skittish, unsettled by the scent of gauru. Ari cut the crest off the gauru's head.

Then we returned to Highwatch.

It was early evening by the time we got back. Ari showed the crest around, telling the story of how the gauru had ambushed us, insisting on crediting Piia, Ragne and myself with the kill.

"Where did you run into one that big?" was a question I heard several times.

"Paavo got wind of it," was Ari's reply, "and Karel tracked it into the crags. And then Alrekr here held it at bay with his staff, while Piia and Ragne killed it."

After a little while, and one obligatory—though welcome—tankard of mead, I made my excuses and left to go beg some salt and a large bowl from the kitchen. When I got back to the tower, Liisa and Kata were already there. I dug some wood ash out of the fireplace, mixed it into my bowl of salt water, and put the pieces of gauru hide in to soak. Then after I washed my hands thoroughly, we went off to the main hall to get some supper, and I told them the story of how we had been ambushed by the gauru.

When I spoke of my hand being actually inside the gauru's mouth, Liisa took my left hand, raised it, and looked at it. Then she gave me an accusing look, rotated my arm so that I could see where she was looking, and pointed out a deep tear on the outside of my left wrist. It wasn't bleeding, but angry red threads were spreading from it.

Apparently the gauru's sharp teeth had still left their mark even though it couldn't close its mouth.

"You should be more careful around gauru," she told me.

"I didn't even feel it," I protested.

"You wouldn't have," she explained. "Gauru venom numbs the wound. So that you do not realize you have been bitten, if the bite is small. 'Just a scratch,' you think. And then the gauru just follows you until you fall over.

"Did nobody tell you that?"

"Uh, no," I said. "Nobody mentioned that to me. Or I would have checked myself more carefully."

Liisa sighed.

"The things that nobody mentions because 'everyone' knows them," she said. She laid her fingers on my wrist and chanted it clean, softly sang the gash closed. It tingled.

"Wear gloves next time you fight a gauru with a staff, my love," she cautioned me, when she was done.

"Next time I fight a twenty-foot gauru," I said, "I'll try not to do it with just a staff." She laughed and kissed me.

After my pieces of gauru-hide were well soaked and washed, I took them out and dried them off, then found a leatherworker who was willing to tell me how to cure them so that they would end up suitable for what I needed. It would take them about a week and a half to cure, he told me, and then offered to do it for me. I gladly agreed.

In the meantime, Matti was working—in between everything else he had to get done each day—on my sword; filing, and grinding, and coarse polishing, and forming the edge (but he had left it thick enough that it would not burn in the final tempering). He showed me his progress. It tapered smoothly and evenly, the *shinogi* even and straight, the *yokote* subtle but clearly defined.

The *steel*... The steel was a flat, deep, almost charcoal gray that seemed to have a visible depth to it—almost as though I could see dimly *into* it. It looked, I realized, almost as much like obsidian as like steel. I looked at it, and wondered what that meant.

He had made a *tsuba,* a guard, in a design of two opposed wolf heads within an outer ring, the *tsuba* pierced around their muzzles and open snarling jaws. The wolf heads had copper alloyed into the iron, giving them a brownish hue.

He had also made a *kashira*, a *kojiri*, a *fuchi*, a bronze *seppa*, and a plain white wooden *shiratsuka*, a 'white hilt', for handling the blade before it was finished, and he showed me the *habaki* in progress. He told me he had made arrangements with one of the master woodworkers, one Tauno, to make a proper *saya* and *tsuka* after the blade was finished, but asked that I talk to the woodworker myself to go over the construction of the *saya* and *tsuka* because he wanted to be certain that they were correct. I reminded him that several parts, notably the *koiguchi* and *kurikata*, were traditionally made from buffalo horn, but that I had no idea what a suitable substitute here would be.

"I thought about that myself," he replied. "About the least dangerous thing around here with a solid horn or claw big enough for that *koiguchi* is a dragonet, and it doesn't seem a good idea to anger the dragons." That was an opinion with which I immediately agreed. "So I asked Tauno whether he had any ideas, and he suggested using ironwood. I think it is a very good idea. It does not grow around here, but he has a few spare pieces and declared himself willing to donate one to the cause."

So I went to find Tauno, and we talked about *saya* and *tsuka*. I told him that I had some underarm gauru-hide curing to substitute for *samé* on the *tsuka*, and he agreed that it seemed it would be a suitable material once cured.

"How should the *saya* be finished?" Tauno asked me. "I'll use just a light oil on the, ah... *shirasaya*." He pronounced the word carefully. "But the proper *saya*?"

I considered how best to answer that.

"Well," I began, after some thought. "'Should' is a word with many meanings. The *traditional* finish is a lacquer called *urushi*. It is made from the sap of a tree that became named after the lacquer. The sap is poisonous to the touch—even inhaling its vapors can be dangerous—and it takes years to process it into a lacquer that can be safely handled. Even then, someone sensitive to it may break out in a rash simply from walking into a room where it is being applied. Once the actively poisonous ingredient in the sap was isolated, that too was named after the lacquer—*urushiol*. It is a clear yellow oil that soaks into the skin and burns it from within."

Tauno winced.

239

"That does not sound pleasant," he said. I agreed wholeheartedly.

"I will tell you now, I have no idea how to process the stuff or how to handle it safely. I am told that it took thousands of years to bring the art to its ultimate refinement.

"But I'm sure we don't need the traditional finish. Some of that stuff was pure conspicuous consumption—being seen to carry a sword whose *fittings* alone had to have taken years to make. *Incredibly beautiful* things. Sword fittings that were works of art in themselves. Dragons with detailed scales worked into the lacquer in powdered gold. Clouds drawn in mother-of-pearl. *Tsuba* inlaid with gold and *shakudo*.

"We don't need that. What *I* care about is that the finish protects the *saya* and the sword within it from the elements and minor knocks and scrapes. That's the important thing.

"Of the two of us, *you*, not I, are the expert woodworker. You know how best to accomplish that. I leave it entirely to your judgment."

Tauno looked thoughtful.

"Entirely?" he repeated.

"Entirely," I confirmed.

And then, it was time to wait, again. But I could wait. I had new reading material. A courier from the Collegium had brought a copy of Tumarïnen's book. I was struggling to grasp the new meanings in it, but it was *fascinating*. I was already finding things I thought I could apply.

14: Sekai No Kattā

After four more days, Matti pronounced the blade ready for its final tempering. So that afternoon, we took the blade, already coated in clay, and we heated the forge, and we prepared to temper it.

Matti placed the blade gently into the forge, so as not to crack the clay, and I sang the forge to an even bed of heat as Matti instructed me, holding the heat where he told me to in the blade, and then we waited. I sang to the forge, and Matti sang to the sword, and then I found myself singing to the sword as well as to the forge—though I wasn't entirely sure all of what I was singing into it. Part of it, I knew, was a binding. But I wasn't certain exactly what I was binding to it. I don't know whether Matti noticed that I was singing to more than just the forge. Whatever it was, I didn't think I should stop part-way, so I just continued, letting the song itself guide me.

Finally Matti held up a hand and we finished our songs. He waited for a few seconds, then picked up the sword with his tongs, turned around, and held it over the quenching trough.

"Ilmarinen favor this work," he muttered. Then he dropped it into the trough. There was an explosion of steam, but nothing else came out of the water. He left it until the bubbling stopped, then about thirty seconds more, before he reached into the trough and felt for the tang. He drew it out, still mostly covered in now-cracked clay. He let out a deep breath I did not realize he had been holding.

"It is intact," he announced. I could see the graceful curve. "All thanks, Ilmarinen."

He turned and laid it on his bench.

"We are done for today, Járnhandr," he told me. "Forgive me a little vanity, but I wish to clean and sharpen it, and give it its final polish, before you see it. Indulge me."

"Of course, Master Smith," I agreed. "How could I not?"

"Tell me one thing," he said, though, "before you go for the day. I *felt* you singing *something* into the blade, I think, beyond the heat of the forge. Yet we both know you are not a metalworker. What exactly were you doing?"

I looked at him and spread my hands.

"In perfect honesty," I said, "I don't entirely know. I did not even realize I was doing it until I had already begun... and then, I thought, I probably should not stop."

"Probably wise," Matti agreed. "No idea at all?"

"Part of it, I think, was a binding," I ventured. "But binding what, I do not know yet."

"Well, *this* promises to be interesting," Matti declared.

It ended up being nearly another week before he was willing to let me see it.

"Tauno is still working on your proper mountings," he said. "And he pointed out that from your notes, I had forgotten to make *menuki*. So I will make those, and I will deliver them to him in the next day or two. I shall make running wolves, I think. He asked that you show him exactly where the *menuki* should go.

"But he has delivered a... *shirasaya?*... for the sword, now that he knows its final shape. And I am done polishing it and sharpening it. So now I can properly show it to you."

He turned around and went to his bench, and retrieved a long curved shape wrapped in a clean cloth.

"I didn't want it to get dirty," he said as he unwrapped it. "Here." He handed me the sword in its white mountings.

The *shirasaya* and *shiratsuka* had been given a light oil finish, I saw. They were left slightly angular as I had described the Japanese tradition, the edges just very slightly softened. It was... a little heavier than I expected. I stepped fully into the daylight, eased it out a half inch or so with my thumb, then drew the first inch or two.

My *gods*. It was...

I drew it slowly the rest of the way. My jaw dropped. It was **a shard of midnight**. The blade was an impossibly deep charcoal-black that seemed to go deeper than the thickness of the blade. The *yakiba* was a silvery ghost like noctilucent cloud. I was not the least surprised to see Matti's wolf's-tooth *gunome*. The *kissaki* was long and elegant, perfectly proportioned.

I sighted along the blade and found it true. It felt light in my hands, perfectly balanced. It felt responsive. A little longer than some, just as I

242

preferred it. It felt like part of me. It felt... *deadly*. And yet somehow... just a slight touch unreal. Even ethereal, perhaps. And yet... still, it felt like *part* of me.

"It came up like that when I polished it out fully," Matti said from right behind me. I had not heard him step closer. "I have never seen anything like it before. It is no artifice of mine."

"What have we *made?*" I breathed.

"I do not know," Matti replied slowly. "But... something extraordinary, I think."

I tucked the *saya* through my belt to free my left hand, and gently touched the blade. A shock ran through me, jolted me, and what looked like lightning or a streak of blue fire raced away up and down the blade from where I had touched it. I felt a pulse of power ripple outward. A few people looked around. The sensitive ones, I thought. The Talented.

I *knew* that blue-white fire.

"I think I know what I bound it to," I said slowly, my voice hushed through no intention of mine. Something in me was reluctant to speak fully aloud.

"What, then?" Matti asked quietly. But I think he already knew the answer.

"Myself," I said. "I think I bound it to my own core."

"I think you should talk to some of the other masters about this," Matti said, after a long moment.

"Yes," I agreed. "So do I. But Kata and Liisa first. They should know. I don't know yet what this means."

"Neither do I," Matti agreed. He looked at the sword again.

"A weapon such as this is should be named."

I nodded slowly.

"Do you know what you will call it?"

I nodded again.

"I do," I replied. "Or rather, I know its name." And I did. With a bone-deep certainty. "It has already *told me.*"

Matti's eyebrows rose.

I closed my eyes, took a deep breath, and raised the sword

skyward. Then I opened my eyes and called out to the sky. I put my diaphragm into it.

"**SEKAI NO KATTĀ!**"

The blade flared blue-white. I felt it deep within me. I *felt* the bond between myself and the sword complete. The pulse of power jolted through me again, much stronger, but this time it was smooth. It flowed through me like a conduit. Like a river.

"More new words," Matti chuckled. "What does that mean?"

"Cutter of Worlds," I replied.

Matti nodded slowly. I could not read his expression.

"I should have expected it was you," Master-at-Arms Toivo said. Pre-occupied with the new sword, I had not noticed him approaching. "I am beginning to learn the feel of your Talent."

He looked at Sekai.

"This must be the curved sword that you told me about some time ago."

I lowered Sekai, pulled the *saya* from my belt, held it in a roughly proper position, and sheathed my new sword. I... did not have to think about it. I *knew exactly* where the point was without looking. I would swear the point *sought* the mouth of the *saya* and guided itself home. That was a new experience to me.

"It is," I agreed. "But... it is a great deal beyond what I was expecting. I am not certain yet what we have wrought."

Toivo looked at me with a measuring gaze.

"May I see it?" he asked.

"Of course."

I passed him Sekai. He took the sheathed sword, weighed it in his hand, then began to draw it. He stopped suddenly when he got a good look at the blade.

"What... *is* it?" he asked, with what sounded like awe in his voice.

"A shard of wolf-metal and night, bound to the core of my soul," I said slowly. "I cannot answer the question better than that. I do not fully understand it myself yet—neither what I did, nor how." Behind him, I saw several of the other masters approaching, as well as Kata, Raimo and Vallaïnen. And others. That pulse of power as I named my new sword seemed to have drawn a crowd.

"I do not think that I should draw this," he told me. "I already feel the power within it, and I fear it is beyond me."

"It will be alright," I assured him. "Nothing will happen."

He looked at me, then nodded and cautiously completed the draw. He tested its balance, shifted his grip.

"It is very different. Lighter than my own—yet heavy for such a narrow blade. I feel it does not have the spring of the blades I am used to. This is a very *different* weapon, I can tell—and used in very different ways, I do not doubt. It is meant for two hands, is it not?"

"Yes," I agreed. "These are actually storage mountings for now. Tauno is still working on its proper fittings, and Matti has two pieces left to complete as well. I will assemble it properly when all of the pieces are done. I will be needing some cords, as well. For the hilt and the *sageo*. They would—traditionally be silk, but I am sure kuurii fiber will work just as well."

"The what?" Toivo asked. "I do not know that word."

Matti laughed.

"Do not feel bad," he said, with a grin. "Since Járnhandr began teaching me to make this kind of sword, I think I have learned at least fifty new words in that language. There is a word for the hard dust-grained steel along the edge, and a word for the softer pearl-grained steel behind it, and a word for the line where they meet, and a word for the *pattern* in the line, and a word for the speckles of dust-grain just beyond that line, and a word for the faint line dividing the beveled face of the edge from the point, and... so many words. I do not think there is a single detail of this sword that does not have its own word."

I nodded agreement, and pointed at the *hamon* by way of example.

"This line is called *hamon*," I said. "It is the grain boundary where the hard edge, the *yakiba*, meets the *ji,* the tougher steel of the blade core. You see that the line has a pattern?" Toivo nodded. "Those patterns are called *gunome*, and even they have a reason for being. This particular pattern, we have named wolf's tooth *gunome*. It is Matti's invention."

"You said the—the *gunome*—has a *purpose*?" Toivo asked. "It is more than just a decorative pattern?"

"It does," I explained. "It prevents any crack in the edge from propagating far into the body of the blade or along the edge. Though... I do not know everything that Matti put into this metal, and I do not know *entirely* what happened to it during the final tempering. I am certain that the, uh... *metallurgi* of my past world would have classified it as a super-steel, but during the final temper..."

I ran down, not sure how to continue.

"He sang things into it that he himself does not fully understand yet," Matti finished for me. "Nor how that interacted with what I sang into the metal myself."

"Yes," I agreed. "That. And... I no longer know what it has become. I don't know if anything *could* crack it now."

"So," Toivo asked, "what is the... sag..."

"*Sageo*," I supplied. "It is a cord that is wrapped around the *saya*, the scabbard, and used to tie it to the *obi*—the sash—worn around the waist of a *Samurai*, a highly trained noble warrior of a land called, uh, *Nihon*, to keep the *saya* from pulling loose as the sword is drawn."

"It is not carried on a belt?"

"No," I said. "I have no belt in the right place to show you. I am going to have to start wearing an *obi*. Permit me..." I held out my hand. He sheathed Sekai and handed it back. I took it and held it against my side roughly where it would sit in a sash.

"Edge upward?" Toivo asked.

"Yes," I agreed.

"Interesting. And how do you draw it, then?"

"Like this," I said.

I took two steps back away from the accumulated audience, for safety distance, held the *saya* in place with my left hand, and rested my right on the hilt. I took a breath, and let it out. Then I stepped forward with my right foot, bending at the knees and dropping to a half-kneel, as I ripped Sekai out of the scabbard, sweeping slightly upward and to the right before stopping at full extension, the dark blade straight out in front of me just below head height. It seemed to me to happen almost in slow motion.

Or... no. No, not that, I realized after another moment. It felt as though *I* was moving at a normal, even relaxed, speed, but *the rest of the world* went into slow motion.

The world returned to normal as I finished the step, straightening up as I brought my left foot forward in turn, snapping Sekai's blade in a tight arc—'shaking the blood from the blade'—and finishing the motion by sheathing her.

"Name of Väinämöinen," Toivo exclaimed softly. "I do not believe I have ever seen anyone move that fast before."

"I'm... not quite sure what happened there myself," I said. "Everything seemed to slow down."

"You were almost a *blur*," Kata told me, stepping out of the audience. "I could not follow the movement."

"Nor could I," agreed Piia. I hadn't seen her arrive. "Do you think you can teach that?"

"I don't know, Piia," I replied. "Well, that is, yes, *and*... probably no. If Matti makes another of these, that I am careful NOT to sing any of myself into..." I paused, thought for a moment, and tried to explain.

"There is an art called *iaidō* or *iaijutsu* that is focused purely upon drawing the sword and striking in a single motion. That is what the name means: The art of drawing the sword. And I am not an expert in it, I do not know all of its—formal exercises; but I know a *little*, and could try to teach what I know of it and of *kenjutsu*. But those arts were developed for swords like this one, not swords like yours.

"But... I cannot explain what happened then. It felt almost as though Sekai altered *time*.

"I wonder if I can tell her not to... One moment."

I stepped back again, then drew again the same way. But this time I... I *told* Sekai that it was alright, there was no hurry, we were just demonstrating a technique.

And this time nothing happened. I drew and cut, with the world in normal time, finished the step, 'shook the blood', and sheathed the sword as I stepped through.

Toivo and Piia nodded appraisingly.

"I could see what you did that time," Piia told me. "A draw and a strike in one motion."

"That much," I said, "I think I can teach, yes." I stepped closer to my friends and beckoned them in. So many new friends. It was so wonderful. It made my heart sing.

"But... I do not know yet all that this sword can do. I am certain though that some of it I cannot teach you, because..."

247

I paused and looked around. Kata, Piia, Vallaïnen, Raimo, Master Timo... Toivo and Matti of course... good. Almost all of the people I wanted to talk to about this.

"Something... *happened* during the final tempering," I began to explain. "I found myself singing not just to Matti's forge, but to the sword as well, as we were tempering it. Not in the language of fire. Something... *else*. All that I recognized was that there was binding in it. But I was not sure what I was binding.

"Today I held the finished sword—finished except for its proper mountings—in my hands for the first time, and realized what I did. Kata, I am all but certain I bound the blade to my own core. And it—she—can do... *things*.

"She told me her name: *Sekai no Kattā*—Cutter of Worlds. It seems as though she can alter—manipulate—*time*. In limited ways. I am uncertain she is even completely physical any more. And... I think she is... *awake*. In a way that I do not know how to explain."

"May I see, please?" Raimo asked.

"Of course. Just one moment first, though. Kata... if you would? Just put your hand on the sword for a moment." I held Sekai out to her, and she put her hand on the hilt.

"Sekai and I are bonded, joined, and *you* and I are joined. Can you *feel* her?"

"... Yes," Kata replied after a moment. "Yes, I can."

"Good," I said.

"It... *she*, you say... feels like you... and yet also not-you."

Sekai, this is Kata. She is part of me. You are not to harm her. Ever.

I thought I got a sense of... *understanding* back. Understanding, and assent.

"I'm slightly afraid that I think that worked," I said, half to myself. Then I handed Sekai to Raimo.

"What worked?" Kata asked.

"I told Sekai that you are a part of me, and that she is never to harm you. And... I would swear I *felt* that she both understood, and assented."

Kata gave me a long, level look.

"What have you and Matti *made*, Alrekr?" she asked.

248

"I don't entirely know," I answered honestly, though I was fairly sure the question was rhetorical.

I looked at Raimo. He was holding Sekai in his hands, sheathed, and gazing off into the middle distance. After a minute, his eyes focused again. He looked at me.

"Alrekr," he declared. "You came here, in part, to forge this sword. Not necessarily in this *form*... but this *weapon*. I see this. You have taken another step along your Path. There is more, but it is hidden from me. Yet."

I bowed my head to him, and he handed Sekai back to me.

I turned to Matti.

"Matti, I lack as yet the understanding to be able to say how much I owe you," I told him. "And it is for you to say, in any case."

"You have paid for it a dozen times over with what I have learned from you already," he said, "and I do not doubt there will be more. Say nothing of it."

"As you will," I replied. My thoughts were too much in a whirl to try to argue.

"I think I wish to return to our rooms for now. If anyone has any questions to ask and wishes to accompany us, you are more than welcome."

That turned out to be Raimo, Vallaïnen, Master Timo, and Piia. Matti declared himself interested, but begged that he had work to do. So off we went. We passed Tommi in the hall, and I flagged him down and sent him on an errand to bring us some more mead.

We sat around the large table with our mead, and we talked. About katanas, and about how I had bound Sekai to myself, and other things. We were agreed that none of us knew quite what that meant. But I felt rather less uneasy about it for Raimo's assurance that I had somehow been *meant* to do it.

"Can you tell me any more about that?" I asked him.

"No," he said. "Not yet. It is hidden from me at this time. Only this much: That you were meant to come here. That you were meant to forge this sword—not necessarily this *form*, but... these *properties*— with Matti's help, and to bind it to yourself. And... I have a sense that you have a doom to fulfill using this sword. But what it might be is hidden from me.

"And... and... a voice out of time will guide you." His tone was suddenly strange and distant.

"What does that mean?" I asked.

Raimo looked at me.

"I... don't know," he said, his voice normal again. "But perhaps you will know when the time comes. That knowledge may help you decide what to do."

"That is the thing with prophecy," Master Timo said slowly. "Sometimes, by the time you know what a prophecy means, it is upon you. But perhaps when you encounter your—voice out of time—and realize that that is what it is, you will know that it is there to help."

"So what does it mean that—no... let me reword that. What are the implications of me having bound this sword to my own core? And what does it mean that it—*she*—seems to be... awake?"

"I wish I knew the answer to that myself," Timo mused. "I have never before heard of such a thing."

"I heard you tell Kata that you had told the sword that Kata was part of you," Vallaïnen said.

"Yes," I agreed.

"And that it was not to harm her, ever. And that you had the feeling that the sword understood and gave assent."

"Yes," I agreed, again. "And that really kind of freaks me out." And yet my hand was straying closer to Sekai. "I don't know if I'm imagining it."

"May I suggest an experiment?" Vallaïnen asked.

"Um. Sure."

"Please pass me your sword."

"Of course." I lifted Sekai, now somehow under my hand, and passed her across the table. Vallaïnen took hold of the scabbard.

"Thank you. Now: I wish you to deny me permission to use it."

"Um... All right. One moment."

Vallaïnen is not permitted to draw you, I thought to Sekai.

I felt Sekai acknowledge.

"It is done."

"So let me see, then, what happens if... uh. Huh." He struggled to draw Sekai. "It's... stuck? I can't even draw it." He tried again. "No. I cannot move it. Permit me..."

He passed Sekai to Piia. Piia took the saya and put one hand on the hilt. She looked at me, a questioning look. I nodded. She pulled gently, and eight inches of black blade slid free of the saya.

"Well," she said, in a deeply intrigued tone.

"Well," Vallaïnen agreed. "I wondered. What was your exact... instruction?"

"That you are not to be permitted to draw Sekai," I answered.

"Interesting. I suspected that might be the case, but of course I could not be sure."

He steepled his hands and pressed them against his lips for a moment.

"It does not answer the question of whether—Sekai—is awake and aware, as such. It still could be just you talking to yourself, so to speak. But it seems one consequence of your binding is that you can deny someone the use of your sword."

"That might be useful," I mused.

The restriction on Vallaïnen drawing you is removed, I thought.

"I just removed the restriction, by the way."

"Let's try something else," he suggested. "This, too, may or may not work—probably not, I would honestly guess—but I am curious to know whether it might. Hold out your hand and... see if you can call the sword to you. Visualize it in your hand."

"All right," I assented. I held up a hand as though gripping Sekai's hilt, and thought, *To my hand, now.*

I didn't stop to notice that Piia still had her hand on Sekai's hilt. It wouldn't have mattered had Sekai been in proper fittings. The tsuba would have pushed her hand out of harm's way. But I didn't have her proper fittings yet, just the shirasaya. There was no tsuba—no guard.

Sekai flashed out of the saya and slapped into my hand. Piia gasped in pain. She had not moved her hand in time, and the blade had sliced the fingers of her right hand to the bone as Sekai flew from the scabbard.

"Piia!" I blurted, aghast. "I'm *sorry*! ... Kata!" I mentally cursed myself for not checking. Her *RIGHT* hand, of all the places to injure her...! I could hardly have done worse.

But Kata was already there. She took Piia's hand, chanted for a measure, her voice rising, then switched directly into song. I could see the bleeding stop almost immediately, and the flesh began to knit together.

"Piia," I said, "I'm so sorry, I wasn't expecting anything like that to happen, it didn't occur to me to verify that your hand was out of the way."

"It's alright, Alrekr," Piia reassured me. "I've been injured before, and there's no better time to do it than with four Healers in the room."

"I wonder what would have happened," Raimo mused, "had you told... Sekai not to harm Piia, as you did Kata?" From Piia's other side, he reached over, put a hand on Piia's shoulder, and added a background chant to Kata's song.

"I don't know," I said, "but I'm not willing to risk repeating that to try the experiment. I don't *like* hurting those I care about. Even by accident." Piia shot me a smile.

Sekai, Piia is not to be harmed, I thought. Again, I felt assent.

"I'll be right back," I said, and went to find a rag to clean up the blood.

By the time I returned with a damp washcloth from upstairs, Kata and Raimo were done, Piia was working her hand in fingering exercises, and Liisa had arrived home.

"See," Piia showed me. "No lasting harm done." I could see a silk-fine, ruler-straight white scar across her fingers.

"It still should not have happened," I apologized, as I wiped up the blood from the table. I was relieved, but I still felt terrible. I saw blood on her left hand, so I washed her hands as well. "It was stupidly careless of me. I am truly sorry."

Piia shrugged.

"When warriors train with weapons," she told me, "accidents happen. It is inevitable. You said yourself, you were not expecting it to actually *work*. Neither was Vallaïnen." I nodded, but I still felt guilty. She looked at me again, reading my face.

"Alrekr," she said, "you must learn to accept that sometimes accidents happen that were not part of anyone's plan. Or you will become afraid to try anything new. And then, you will stop learning things."

I sighed, after a moment. She was right, of course.

"Nevertheless," I repeated, "I will try to be more careful." Piia reached out and put her hand on my shoulder, and I gathered her into a quick hug.

"I think I will not perform any further experiments with people close by, until I know more myself about what Sekai is capable of."

Then a thought occurred to me.

Piia looked at me and grinned.

"But you just had an idea you want to try, though, didn't you?"

"Well, yes," I admitted. "And I did just tell Sekai that you are not to be harmed." I took a deep breath.

"All right," I said, "just one more experiment."

I picked up Sekai and walked across the room, making sure no-one was even close to being in between myself and Piia, then turned to face Piia, Sekai's hilt toward her.

"Would you hold out your hand, please, Piia?"

She read my intention. With a smile of anticipation, she stepped away from the table and held out her hand as though loosely grasping a sword hilt.

To Piia, now, I thought to Sekai. A moment later, Sekai leapt from the scabbard, flew across the room, and shot directly into Piia's waiting hand. Liisa gasped in surprise, having arrived too recently to see the earlier experiment. Piia grinned, and whipped the dark blade through a fast figure-eight.

"... Oooooh," she said, then, looking intently at Sekai. "Very NICE." She looked at me.

"Tell Smith Matti I want the next one of these, please. Tell him I will insist if I must." She brought Sekai back and handed her to me, and I took her back and sheathed her.

"You realize," I said, "the next one of these will not be quite like Sekai." Then a thought hit me like a thunderbolt.

"Unless... I can figure out how to bind it to you?"

Piia's eyes widened for a moment, before she found words.

"... That would be amazing," she breathed.

"I… am pretty certain I would need to know your core," I said. I turned to Kata.

"And for that, I'll need your help and Liisa's, to learn how to reach another person's core than my own. I… feel… you and Liisa should be the first I learn to touch."

"Tomorrow," Liisa told me. "We will begin tomorrow."

"I think it is safe to say," Timo declared, "that you have discovered a new facet of your Talent. A new ability that I do not think I have ever even heard of before. So you are a firesinger, and… I suggest we call this new ability of yours soulbinding. Firesinger, then, and Soulbinder.

"You will write a book, of course." He didn't even make a question of it.

It got late, so I rang for a page and sent Senja to bring dinner for everyone. We continued talking over dinner, but we did not try any further experiments… yet. Liisa said she was pretty sure she knew where to get some flat-woven kuurii fiber cord to use for *ito* and for my *sageo*, and Kata was only too happy to direct me to a tailor who would make me some *obi* to my specifications. I introduced Liisa to *Sekai no Kattā*—and vice versa—and told Sekai that Liisa, too, was part of me and not to be harmed under any circumstances. Liisa, too, could feel Sekai; and she, too, said that Sekai felt *like* me, but also *not* like me.

"Eventually," Master Timo told me, "you will need to travel to the Collegium, Járnhandr. To tell them about this new Talent that you have discovered. Once you have mastered it. And you should probably start writing down what you know. As you learn it, I suggest, so that you do not inadvertently leave anything out."

He was right, I acknowledged. He promised he would arrange to have a supply of parchment delivered. And so, I began to ponder how I would write my book.

"I'm not sure I know how to put any of it into words yet," I said. "And… how will anyone else read it? I imagine I will find myself writing, beyond a certain point, in a dialect that others cannot read."

"And then," Timo pointed out, "one day, someone will come along and discover that they can read it. Probably one of the Sages, first."

Eventually, we chased everyone out and went to bed. We actually started a little that night on teaching me how to find and touch Kata and Liisa's cores.

"It will be easier," Liisa told me, "because we are already so closely joined. And we know of ways to *enhance* that joining..."

Yes, indeed we did.

First thing in the morning, I paid a visit to the leatherworker who was curing my gauru hide for me. I collected the by-now fully cured hide patches, and dropped them off with Tauno. Then I returned to my ladies, and we went back to meditation exercises.

This time, though, instead of Kata and Liisa entering my mind to guide me to finding my own core, Kata began to guide me into Liisa's. I was not shocked to find her soul a place of light. There were shifting shadows, but it seemed they only made the light brighter by contrast. I could not find which way to go, but Kata showed me how to feel my way, how to let Liisa herself take me by the spiritual hand and lead me in.

It took three sessions before I found my way, with their help, deep enough into Liisa's spirit to glimpse her core. It was golden and radiant, seeming more a column with no real defined edge than the hypersphere of blue fire I had found within myself. It was warm and comforting, and soothing to be near. I found I didn't want to move away.

After a while, Kata called me back out. I blinked, shook my head, and looked around me. And then I looked at Liisa, and I could not do anything but pull her to me and hold her close.

"I love you so much," I told her. She smiled, and kissed me, and I kissed her back.

"Would you know my core, now?" she asked.

"Anywhere," I replied.

"And do you think you could bind something to her?" Kata asked.

"I... *think* so," I said.

The next day, we switched roles. This time it was Liisa who led me into Kata's soul. It took only two sessions this time. Kata's soul was a place of peaceful green, like an alpine meadow, restful but never still, quiet yet never silent, as refreshing as a mountain stream. And her core, to me, was a limpid pool of light as green as her beautiful eyes, yet I could sense the strength and resolve within, the fierceness at the center of her spirit. I remembered her fury when the sielunjuoja attacked me. I saw now where that strength came from.

Kata was already in my arms when I opened my eyes. I didn't know which of us had pulled the other in, but it didn't matter. I held onto her, the third part that made up me, and I kissed her.

"I love you, Kata," I murmured.

"I love you too, Alrekr," she replied softly. She reached out and pulled Lisa to us as well, and all was well with our world.

"There is one thing that troubles me," I said later.

"Let me see if I can guess," Kata said. "You have seen our cores now, and you compare to yours, and it troubles you that yours is so much more powerful."

"That is it exactly," I agreed. "I do not know whether I am seeing truly, whether everyone's core looks looks different from the inside, or whether it really is... and... it seems *unfair*. If that makes any sense."

"You see truly, Alrekr," Kata told me. "It is not *unfair* in any meaningful way, any more than it is unfair that Liisa is taller than I am. It simply *is*. Your core is that much... stronger, deeper, than ours because you have so much more *power*. I confess I still do not understand quite how, or why, that is.

"We are both Adepts. Piia is not, not quite, although she is almost that strong—even though she has not yet manifested a Talent. You will *probably* find her core seems smaller than ours, when you touch it. But... she is not any the less for it.

"Yours... I do not even *know* truly what you are. Your firesinging *alone* is an adept-level Talent. And your... soulbinding? I simply do not know. And I am not certain that we have seen all, even yet."

That was a sobering thought.

Then another thought occurred to me.

"Kata, I came to with you in my arms," I said. "With no conscious volition on my part. What if... Piia...?"

Kata just smiled.

"Then it happens," she said. "She is a good person. She has kissed you before, when you broke through. So has Varpu. Did either do any harm then?"

"Well... no," I had to reply.

"And neither will it now. Do not let shadows of your past haunt you, Alrekr. You came from a place that was deeply broken, where you did not belong, and it deeply hurt you."

And then it was Piia's turn.

At her request, instead of the tower, we went outside Highwatch and a little way into the woods, a sunlit clearing.

"The top of your tower is a restful place for the three of you," she told us, "because it is where you live, a place of love to you. But this..." She gestured around at the trees, the foliage, the double sunlight in the clearing, brushed the soft moss on the flat rock we sat on.

"This is *my* place. This is where I feel at peace. This is where my spirit lives."

I understood at once.

"I can see that," I agreed. "You belong here. You *fit* here." She nodded.

We sat in a circle. Sort of. Perhaps more an ellipse. Piia and I knelt facing each other on the thick moss, holding hands, and then Liisa and Kata sat to either side, their hands on ours.

We all relaxed, and I closed my eyes, and I felt for Piia.

I could immediately feel both Kata and Liisa. They were familiar now. I knew them more deeply than I had ever known any other person. Perhaps more deeply than I knew myself.

But across from me was... nothing, at first. Then I realized that the 'nothing' was *itself* something. Quiet. Peace. Calm. It was not that there was nothing there. It was that she *utterly, perfectly* belonged here.

I carefully reached out and 'stepped' into the quiet.

Yes, this truly was Piia's place. Kata's soul was the bright, airy, sunlit green of an alpine meadow swept by mountain winds. Piia's was the deep, still green of an ancient forest. It was like stepping into a cathedral, and finding yourself speaking in whispers because you don't want to disturb the silence. Yet this was not the sepulchral silence of a cathedral. It was alive. It was just... at rest. At peace.

I very carefully, respectfully, felt for which way to go. It was as if there was... a breeze perhaps. Or the sound of a stream. So I followed it.

I found myself, eventually, looking at... It was not a tree. But it *felt* like a tree. Or an entire grove. A sense of deep, still, greenness. I found myself reaching out to touch it. It was... calming. This was Piia, I realized.

Liisa was right, or... *sort of* right. Piia's core *was* perhaps a little smaller than Liisa's or Kata's, did not show the obviously present Talent that theirs did. Although... I would swear I felt that there was something there. She was *close*, I thought, and surely needed only a little to nudge her over the edge. Perhaps there was already a Talent there waiting, and all she needed was to *discover* what it was.

And yet... good gods, the *strength* in her. This, I *knew* now, was a woman who would not give up, would not yield. *Ever.* She would succeed at what she set out to do, or she would die trying—and she would die trying, to the very last, to rip her foe's throat out with her bare teeth if she had to.

I think I opened my eyes at the same moment Piia opened hers. They were very close in front of mine, very brown, and *now* I saw both the deep wells of peace within them, and the strength that lay behind it. This woman was absolutely secure in herself. The thought came to me that in a very real sense, she had the soul of a samurai. Not to suggest in any way that there was somehow a Japanese warrior within her; but she was everything, in her heart, that a samurai strives to be. Calm, completely at peace with herself, and utterly without fear. But not, in any way, without feelings or compassion.

"I know you, Piia," I told her softly. "I *know* you now."

Piia nodded.

"I know," she replied. "And I know *you*, Alrekr." Her voice was quietly certain.

I let myself lean forward just a tiny bit more so that my forehead rested against hers, and we just sat like that for a little while. I felt her soul delicately touch against mine. Then almost at the same time, we both took deep breaths, raised our heads and sat up straight.

"So?" Kata asked, after a moment. "Can you bind a sword to her

258

now?"

"Yes," I replied, with absolute certainty. "It would be an honor."
And I meant it.

We walked back to Highwatch together in the late afternoon light.
Nobody said a word. There didn't seem to be a need. A little of Piia's
inner peace had spread to all of us, I think.

When we got back, Piia took hold of my hand a moment and
squeezed it, then still without a word, set off in the direction of the
Rangerhall. Kata and Liisa went to check in and see if they were
needed.

And I? I went to talk to Matti.

Matti had a bundle for me.

"All of your fittings are done," he told me. "Tauno dropped them
off yesterday. Perhaps you would do me the favor of showing me how
to assemble it all?"

"I would be honored," I said. So I went back to our rooms and
fetched Sekai in her *shirasaya*. Then I went back to the forge.

I began with the *tsuka*, the hilt. I recognized it as iron birch again.
Tauno had cut and neatly glued two pieces of the gauru-hide *samé*-
substitute in place already, I saw, and sanded or ground away a little of
the tips of the pyramidal scales to leave the surface grippy, yet not
actually sharp. Perfect.

I found the *fuchi*, and the *kashira*, and there was a roll of thick,
deep green woven *kuurii*-fiber tape. That would be ideal *ito*. Tauno
had included several *mekugi* in slightly different diameters, all slightly
tapered, also of iron birch.

That just left the *menuki*. And of course the hilt needed to be
drilled. Tauno had not had Sekai with him for reference.

"Ah, yes!" Matti said. "Here." And he handed me the *menuki* he
had made. They were running wolves, indeed, in bronze that matched
the *habaki*, the *fuchi* and the *kashira*. They were amazingly detailed.

"I need to dry-fit this before I wrap it," I said, holding the *tsuka*. "It
should be drilled for the *mekugi* before I begin wrapping."

"Of course," Matti agreed. "I will send for Tauno." He stepped
outside and called for a page.

I laid Sekai on Matti's bench and drew her out a few inches, then asked the loan of a tack hammer and a small punch from Matti. With those, I tapped the *mekugi* free, then tapped the *shiratsuka* loose. I looked at the tang, seeing Matti's signature for the first time. It was clear and bright. I nodded approval.

I slipped the *habaki*, the *seppa*, and the *tsuba* into place, then laid the tang on top of the *tsuka*, pushing all of the stacked parts firmly into position. I begged the loan of a piece of charcoal from Matti, then carefully marked the position of the *mekugi-ana*, just a fraction short so that driving the *mekugi* in would pull everything tightly together, compressing the leather *seppa* slightly. By the time I was done, Tauno had arrived, bringing with him a small hand drill. He very carefully bored a hole through the *tsuka* at my mark, after checking the position himself and nodding approval, turning it over and finishing from the other side as soon as the tip of the drill broke through. Meanwhile, I set the *tsuba* and the other fittings aside.

"Now," Tauno said, "let me see how this is done." Matti pulled up a barrel and offered Tauno a stool, and they both sat down to watch.

I held the menuki in place one at a time, adjusting them until I was certain I had the right positions, and then marking their positions with the charcoal.

"You see how the *menuki* guide the hands to the correct grip," I said as I adjusted the placement. Tauno nodded.

I sat down and unravelled the roll of *ito*, found the middle, lapped it around the open end of the *tsuka*, and began to wind it. I just went with a simple wrap, folding the tape as I went, twisting and crossing the tape at the meeting points, working carefully and pulling every twist tight, inserting the *menuki* when I reached my marks.

"This wrapping pattern is called *hineri maki*," I explained as I went. "There are more complex ones, such as *tsumami maki*, but I'm not an expert at this. It's the first time I've done it just from memory with nothing to refer to. So I'm not going to attempt anything fancy, just something basic that I'm reasonably confident I know how to do."

It still took me three tries to get it wrapped to my satisfaction. I threaded the ends through the *kashira* and tied them off tightly, leaving just a couple of inches free.

The *tsuka* was done. Now I could at last assemble Sekai properly into her mountings.

The *habaki* went on first, followed by a brass *seppa*, then a thin leather one, then the *tsuba*. I held the *tsuba* up to the light and admired it again before I slipped it into place, then the second brass *seppa*, and finally slipped on the finished *tsuka*. I picked up Sekai, held her vertically, and slapped the *kashira* twice into the palm of my hand to let the weight of the blade itself seat the tang fully into the *tsuka*.

The *mekugi-ana* lined up almost perfectly. The *mekugi* would pull the *tsuka* in just the tiniest fraction more when it went fully home. I took the one from the *shiratsuka* and checked it for fit. It seemed perfect. Three light taps with the tack hammer drove it flush.

I let out breath I didn't realize I'd been holding, stepped away from the bench into the fading daylight, and swung Sekai through a couple of cuts and blocks, first slowly, then at full speed. The hilt was tight and secure, and the grip felt good.

That left just the *saya*. I laid Sekai down, picked up the *saya*, and unwrapped the soft cloth it was wrapped in.

My breath caught. It was *gorgeous*. I was expecting it to be fully assembled of course, but more than that, Tauno had already threaded the *sageo* through the *kurikata* and wrapped it as I had described to him. The *kurikata* and *koiguchi*... felt like wood, but it was a wood so dark and dense I could barely even see the grain except when the light caught it right.

And the *finish*. I didn't know what kind of lacquer it was, but Tauno had finished it in a deep green lacquer with a hint of almost golden yellow to it, and... were those fish scales laid into the lacquer? There was just the barest hint of texture through the surface layers of lacquer. I looked at it for a long time before I came back to myself again. The thought came to me that it was almost the green of Piia's soul.

"This is utterly magnificent," I breathed at last. Tauno grinned.

"I truly do not how how to adequately thank you," I told him. "This is amazing work. *Is* that fish scales? It's as though the scales *grew* there."

"The lowly carp, believe it or not," Tauno explained. "It was the only local fish I could find with large enough scales for the effect I wanted. I laid each one separately into place to get that look."

"Tauno," I protested, "you did not have to go to this much trouble. Honestly. This is far beyond anything I was expecting."

"You *said* 'entirely to my discretion,'" Tauno reminded me, still grinning. "'Entirely.' And you confirmed it.

"*This* is my discretion. And it is an honor to do it. This sword that you and Matti forged together will become a legend, I think. It should have fittings worthy of it. This is iron birch, too, like the hilt, and I have sung strength enough into it that it should be all but unbreakable."

"I hold myself in your debt," I told him.

"And I hold that debt paid by what I have learned, Adept—or Master—Járnhandr," Tauno replied.

"Master? I—" was all I got out.

"Do not say it, Járnhandr!" Matti told me warningly. "You told me that you were done denying what you are. The word is all over Highwatch already that you have discovered an entire new discipline of Talent. If that is not a Master accomplishment, then I do not know what is."

I could not help but laugh.

"You win, Matti," I chuckled. "But it's a low trick using my own words against me." He grinned back.

"Do you want to see something else that we discovered Sekai can do?"

"All right," he nodded.

I checked that the way was clear, then held the beautiful new *saya* against my side with my left hand, and held out my right.

Sekai, to my hand.

Sekai flew from where she lay on Matti's bench directly into my hand. I caught her, snapped her through shaking-the-blood, and sheathed her, almost in a single motion. She snicked home perfectly.

Matti clapped his hands thunderously. Tauno stared, amazed.

"Is that a part of the binding?" Matti asked.

"Yes," I agreed. "So it seems. We have learned that I can also send her to someone else's hand, or tell her that someone is not to be harmed, or is forbidden to draw or wield her. We don't know what else she can do. Yet."

"Astounding, Járnhandr," Matti said, nodding.

"And by the way... this has somewhat distracted me from my

original purpose in coming by today, which was to relay to you that you already have an order for a second sword like Sekai. For Piia. And I am going to bind it to her as Sekai is bound to me."

"Well, well, well," Matti said, grinning.

"I think I need to decide what I am going to charge for a set of these fittings," Tauno said. "Since it's clear we're going to be making more. I have a decent supply of iron birch, and it is not terribly difficult to get; and enough ironwood for at least a dozen or so. And right now, Matti and I are the only two wrights in the Sunlit Land who know how to make these."

"And Járnhandr is the best firesinger around, and the only Soulbinder," Matti observed. "You mark my words, once the word spreads, people will be traveling here from the far ends of the Land in the hope of buying a Highwatch sword."

"Better practice signing your name, Matti," I said, with a grin of my own now.

"Will you bind them, Járnhandr?" Matti asked.

I hesitated.

"Only in special cases, I think," I replied. "I... will gladly do it for Piia. I would do it for you. For Piia's team, I would be willing, or perhaps for Master Toivo or Knight-Commander Jaako, I think. But to soul-bind a sword to someone, I must first know them well enough to know the feel of... to know their core. And I do not know how many people I am willing—or ready—to have that deep of a bond with."

"Understandable," Matti said, nodding. "But you can sing the fire for the forging and the final temper without binding the sword, yes?"

"Yes, now that I understand what I even did," I agreed. "I know enough now, I think, to do it only when I choose to.

"Anyway, I should be going. It's getting late."

Matti nodded.

"Say hello to your lovely ladies from me," he said, handing me the shirasaya, wrapped up in the cloth Tauno had delivered the saya in. "I will make you a small hammer for that hilt pin."

"I will," I promised. "Thank you."

I turned to Tauno.

"And thank you again, Master Tauno, for your magnificent work."

"It's an honor," Tauno said. "But I am not a Master."

I held up Sekai in her beautiful new fittings.

"If this is not a masterwork," I said, deliberately almost exactly quoting Matti's words from earlier, "then I truly do not know what is. Smith Matti, do you concur?" Matti nodded solemnly.

"And I will call as many other Masters here as it takes to convince you," he told Tauno.

"... Fair enough," Tauno conceded at last, with a grin. "Come to me again any time you need fine woodwork, Master Járnhandr."

"I will definitely be coming back to you for a proper stand for Sekai, for starters," I said. "But that's a discussion for another day." He nodded.

I made my farewells, and back home I went.

Unsurprisingly, Kata and Liisa had gotten back well before I had, and supper was already on the table waiting for me. It was kalakeitto, very similar to the lohikeitto, but I thought there were at least two different kinds of fish in it. I apologized for my lateness, and we made up for it with kisses, but then I made myself wait until we had eaten before I showed off Tauno's beautiful work on Sekai's fittings.

"This is *beautiful*," Kata declared, as she ran her fingers over the *saya*. "It even *feels* like a fish... except that it is not wet." I could not help but agree. They both examined the detail on the *tsuba*, the *menuki*, even the *kashira*, which I now noticed Matti had worked a wolf's-paw detail into. He really had gone all out with that wolf motif.

"There is... something," I began, awkwardly. I wasn't sure how to say it, but I knew I had to. "The... this afternoon. Piia." Kata began to smile. "I feel—it forged a bond..."

Liisa laughed gently, and I trailed off, bewildered. I didn't know what to think. But there was nothing unkind in her laughter. Not that I would ever believe at this point that there was an unkind thought hidden anywhere in Liisa's soul.

"Of *course* it did, Alrekr," she agreed, smiling. "Or rather, it *strengthened* a bond that was already there. Did you somehow believe that it would not?"

"I think," I replied slowly, "that I didn't think it through because I have still not fully internalized the idea that such a thing is even *possible."*

Kata nodded understandingly. She, too, was smiling.

"We knew before we began that it would be so," she reassured me. "You touched her soul, and she felt the touch of yours. How could it *not* strengthen your bond? The bond was already there. It was her team that brought you out of the mountains, she who first examined you as you lay where you had fallen, she who chose to try to bring you home, she who thought to send one of her best Rangers to have us meet you part-way so that we could begin healing you sooner. That single thought of hers might have made the difference.

"Piia saved your life, Alrekr, even if she has never outwardly told you so."

"She didn't need to," I replied. "I already know. And I have thanked her for it more than once. So she knows that I know."

Kata nodded.

"The two of you already had a bond. What harm if the bond grows stronger? She is a good person. We entirely approve. Had we felt there was anything wrong in her, we would have warned you as soon as you voiced what would be necessary."

"When I... surfaced, afterward," I said, "I noticed that the two of you no longer had your hands on ours. I was concerned..."

"That you had offended us, Alrekr?" Liisa asked. I nodded mutely.

"*No*, Alrekr," she continued. "It was simply obvious that you no longer needed our guidance to do this, and so there was no need for us to intrude."

"I was concerned that you might... feel that our relationship was threatened," I admitted.

Kata shook her head with a happy laugh.

"Alrekr, we have seen into your soul as you have seen into ours," she told me. "We both *know* the depth of your love for us. How could strengthening a bond to a friend threaten that?"

"Love is not something that you are granted a fixed amount of," Liisa said, "to ration out sparingly or hoard. Love expands to fill the space you allow it to. *Whatever* the cruel lessons of your past mis-taught you."

I sighed in relief.

"I will tell you this," I replied. "Now that I truly know her soul, I cannot think of a single person in Highwatch whom I would judge more fitting to bear a sword like Sekai. She is everything that a *samurai* aspires to be. Just... by being herself. It is simply who she is."

Liisa looked levelly at me, then stepped closer and put her arms around me. She looked me in the eyes.

"This is ghosts of your past whispering doubts and fears into your ear again, Alrekr," she told me. "Do not let them make you afraid to love. Do not let them make you doubt yourself. We trust you, and we *know* it is not within you to betray our trust, so long as we do not betray yours badly enough to hurt you again as you have been hurt before. And we will not betray you."

"I know you won't, Liisa," I said. And then *of course* I kissed her. I couldn't reach Kata from where Liisa and I were standing, but I held an arm out to her, and she happily joined in the hug, and then I could kiss her too.

15: Wind In The Forest

Later that week, I helped Matti to smelt the ingots for Piia's sword. He used slightly different proportions of additives in the steel this time.

"I think I may have used more of the wolf-metal in yours than I really needed to," he explained. "I have no concern about yours, not with what you have made it into. I am not certain anything could break it, now, while you live. But I am using less wolf-metal this time, lest I make the steel brittle. For that first moment in the water, the steel almost screamed. I was afraid that it was going to shatter in the quench."

Aside from the slightly different composition, forming Piia's steel ingots went no differently from mine. Hers were a little lighter gray. It went a little more quickly this time, with the experience gained from the first—and perhaps the lower tungsten content was a factor, too. I held the heat in the steel while Matti folded it, and dusted it, and folded it again, and again, and again, and again.

When the ingots were at last done, Matti and I decided we would forge the blade the next day, so I walked over to the Rangerhall to let Piia know. I figured she would want to see it happen, and I wanted her nearby when it happened so that I could start... for lack of any better word, *tuning* the blade to her.

I could feel as soon as I reached the Hall that she wasn't there. The *feel* of her was missing. Evidently her team was out on patrol. I left a message that I had been there looking for her, and went back to our rooms to work on my notes for my book.

It turned out Liisa was back early that day without too much of anything to do.

"You smell of the forge, love," she told me. So I scribbled a quick note for Kata, grabbed a set of clean clothes, took her by the hand, and led her—with a marked lack of protest—to the bath-house. Then we stripped off, and washed each other, and then went and sat in the sauna for a while.

"So have you found out any more about what Sekai can do?" she asked after a little while, leaning back against the wall with her eyes closed.

"Not yet," I said slowly, relaxing in the steam myself. "But to be honest, I haven't been trying *too* terribly hard. I cannot shake a feeling that the things we have discovered so far are almost parlor tricks. There is... a great deal more to Sekai, I think. But then, Sekai is bound to my core, and..." I trailed off.

"And there is more to yourself that remains unfound yet, I think," she finished, opening those lovely brown eyes and turning them on me.

I nodded.

"Sometimes I get... tantalizing glimpses," I said. "But I don't know what they are. But... I think Raimo was right. I *had* to make Sekai. I just don't know what for, yet."

Liisa leaned her head on my shoulder. Leaned up against me, like a cat.

"You know," she said, almost drowsily, "a while back when we were here, a few weeks I think, you said that you could see Tumarïnen's bindings on the hot stones."

"Mmmm," I answered, very relaxed myself, especially with Liisa against me now. "Yes, I did." I put my arm around her.

"You said that you couldn't follow them all the way down, then. Can you now?"

I thought about it. I reached out to the stones. I didn't need to touch them, now. I felt for the bindings. Followed them down, into the ground, into the rock, down and down, to where there were traces of fire in the rock, heat rising up from below. I felt the heat, followed it down, down to where the rocks were burning hot, to where they were hot enough to glow on their own if there were anyone to see them, any open space not already rock. And deeper yet, down to where the rocks themselves would melt, if only the pressure let them...

"... Alrekr? Alrekr, are you awake?" Liisa was shaking me gently.

"Liisa. My love. My beloved... Yes. Yes, I *can*. I can, now. And... I can reach deeper yet. *Much* deeper. Down into the inner fires of the world."

She pulled my head gently around toward her and kissed me.

"You didn't answer, for a little. I was starting to worry."

268

"I'm fine, love. I was just following the binding, and the heat, down."

"Do you think you could bind them as Tumarïnen did?"

"Perhaps not the same *way*. But I think I could do it, now. But I would not bind them that deep, or the stones would melt."

I kissed her back, caressed her body.

"But for now I think we are both as drowsy as warm cats, and I think we should go and take a dip in the cold pool before we fall asleep in here."

"Mmmm. In a minute," she said. "Or two."

So I slipped my other arm under her thighs and picked her up. She laughed softly and put her arms around my neck. I stood up, carried her to the deepest part of the cold pool, and jumped in, still carrying her. She let out a squeal as we hit the cold water, then we were briefly below the surface. A moment later we both popped up, and I gathered her to me again, gasping. She laughed again, and then kissed me fiercely.

We swam across the pool to a shallower edge, helped each other out, then settled into the warm pool to soak and cuddle for a bit. Kata came in a little later, stripped off and washed quickly, and joined us. So then the three of us soaked and cuddled together for a while. Matti came in while we were there, washed off himself, and gave us a friendly wave as he headed for the sauna.

After a little while longer, we climbed out, dried off and got dressed, then went to get supper. Truth to tell, I don't even remember clearly what we had. There was sliced meat, and a spiced sauce, and something like wild rice. We ate, and we talked with Esko and Marketta, and Saana, and Ranger Kauko ended up at our table too. I asked after Piia, and he told me that her team was out following up on a report. A couple of outlying farms had seemingly gone quiet and not been heard from.

A shiver ran down my spine.

"This is going to be bad," I heard myself say. Kauko gave me a sharp look.

"You know something?" he asked.

"No," I said. "Just... a sudden feeling."

"Is Piia's team in danger?" His tone was urgent.

"I don't know. Just..." I tried to put the feeling into words. "Something is on the move. 'Something wicked this way comes.'"

Kauko ate quickly, then left in a hurry. I took my ladies home, and tried to write, but my mind was not in it. So we took an early night, went to bed and curled up around each other. There was nothing on this world that was as wonderful as just lying in bed with Kata and Liisa in my arms.

But still, it took me hours to fall asleep.

The next morning, right after breakfast, I went over to the Rangerhall. Piia's team had not checked in. I asked to be informed as soon as there was any news. Then I went to Matti's foundry, advised him we would not be forging Piia's sword today, and busied myself managing the heat of the forge. I didn't really pay very much attention to what specific work Matti was doing; I just followed his instructions and put the heat where he wanted it.

Piia's team did not come in that day. My appetite was off at supper, and I did not finish eating. I was worried.

"I know you are concerned for Piia, Alrekr," Kata reassured me after supper. "Her team is the best in Highwatch, I think. I am sure they will be alright."

"It's... not just Piia," I said. Something still nagged in the back of my mind. "I know how strong Piia is. I think... part of what is worrying me is... what if they *have* run into something they couldn't handle? What is *out* there, Kata?"

There was a long silence.

"What if something has wandered across from beyond the Spine?" Liisa asked quietly.

Kata did not immediately answer.

"I think this is something I now need to know," I said. "Tell me about the Spine."

Kata nodded slowly.

"There is a reason Highwatch sits here," she began, her tone somber. "Why it watches these two passes. There are seven other main passes through the Spine. Each is guarded by a fortress, although Highwatch is the largest of them because it must guard two.

"We do not cross the Spine of the World. It is not just what lives *in* the Spine—though some of those are bad enough. It is what lies *beyond* it.

"A part of the agreement that was reached with the dragons, more than six centuries ago, was that we do not venture deeply into the Spine. It is where they lair, and where they raise their young. They will not permit men to approach their lairs. Early on, there were... incidents. The dragons did not take kindly to what happened.

"What is less well known is the dragons' part of that agreement. They guard the Spine. They seek to keep anything from coming through from the broken lands beyond.

"In the Spine are dragons, and trolls, and basilisks, and gaunts, and other monstrous things. But beyond the Spine, rumors and legend say there are true horrors, Alrekr.

"They are why Highwatch is here. We all live with this knowledge. Because some day, something might evade the dragons, and come through."

Kata's face looked tired, drawn. I got up, and went to her, and held her. Liisa joined a moment later. We went early to bed again, and we held each other tight. And the holding turned to touching, and the touching turned to kissing and nibbling, and the kissing turned into urgent lovemaking as we tried to banish the lurking uncertainty that whispered in the darkness.

After a while, we succeeded. Mostly. We fell asleep clinging tightly to each other.

Piia and her team came in shortly after noon the next day. I heard the commotion at the gate as I was on my way back to the forge, and hurried that way instead. I think I saw Piia at about the same time she saw me. She altered course slightly to head directly towards me. Neither of us ran, but she walked swiftly, and threw her arms around me as soon as we were in reach. I wrapped my arms around her, feeling the tension and the exhaustion in her. Her team caught up after a moment. I looked from face to face. They all looked tired... and grim.

I waited until I felt Piia relax just a little.

"Piia. What happened?"

She eased her hold enough to look straight at me.

"It was *bad*, Alrekr. Come. Please. I need to report in."

I walked with them and we headed for the Rangerhall. But we didn't get there before Knight-Commander Jaako met us.

"I am glad to see your safe return," he declared, first of all. "All of you." He reached out to take Piia's hands, then moved among the team, taking a hand here, squeezing a shoulder there.

"Come. I will hear your reports."

Piia took my hand and pulled me along. Jaako gave me a questioning look, but Piia just nodded firmly.

We went into the Hall, and Jaako clapped his hands once, then pointed to four other team leaders. They followed as he led us all into a side room off the main Hall. Everyone took seats around the table. Piia pulled me into the seat next to her.

"All right, Piia," Jaako said. "Whenever you are ready. In your own time."

Piia took a deep breath.

"We went to the Särkkä valley based on a report that members of the Halme family had not shown up for an expected and long-planned meeting," she began. There was a tightness in her voice.

"There was concern that beasts or brigands might have waylaid them on the road. But we did not find them on the road, nor signs of a fight. So we followed the road all the way to the valley, in quest of them.

"We went first to the Erkkilä farm at the mouth of the valley, who had also not been heard from. Then we went on from there to the Halme homestead, and the Salonen farm, and up to the Niinistö farm at the head of the valley."

Her hand tightened on mine as she spoke. I could hear the tension in her voice.

"They're all dead. Every last one. Nearly forty people. Even the children. Ripped apart. Some of them partly *eaten*. Every farm animal killed as well. Doors and walls smashed in. But nothing of value obviously taken. Food still on the tables.

"Some of them tried to stand and fight. It appeared Tuokki Erkkilä and his sons tried to make a stand across the road out, to let their womenfolk and children escape behind them. None of them made it out of the valley. The Erkkilä women and children were the first dead we found, all of them slaughtered while fleeing. Every living thing in the valley larger than a fox, dead.

"We found a trail out of the valley leading back towards the Spine. We tracked and pursued. We followed the trail through the forest, up into the crags, and on into the edge of the Spine.

"And then we lost the trail."

"There were faint echoes that might have been a rift," Simo said.

Jaako turned and looked at me.

"A rift like the one Adept Járnhandr here was found by?" he asked.

Simo waggled a hand uncertainly.

"I do not know for sure," he replied. "We were much closer when Járnhandr's opened. I *felt* it open. This was—perhaps a week old, I think. Maybe more.

"I would judge... it was not the *same*. Not quite. But there were similarities."

"This is why you wanted me to hear your report, Piia," I said. She nodded.

"In part," she agreed. Then she turned back to Jaako.

"Brigands would not have... eaten them. Beasts would not have broken in the walls like that. And it is not the work of a troll, nor of a gaunt.

"Something terrible came out of the Spine, I think."

There was silence for a long moment.

"What is your advice?" Jaako asked quietly.

Piia took a deep breath and let it out.

"I think," she said slowly, "we should warn the families in all of the valleys that are close to this region of the Spine, and tell them that they should evacuate. Take with them all that they can that is of value to them, but leave. We cannot guard every valley.

"And we should send word up and down the line to the other *linnavouret* of what happened in Särkkä."

273

Jaako looked around the table, at Piia's team and the other team leaders.

"Tell me every detail you think important," he said.

"We found... black blood, I think, on the trail," Karel added. "They managed to hurt something before they died. Whatever it was, it can be hurt."

"If it can be hurt, it can be killed," Piia stated flatly. The intensity in her voice came as no surprise to me. I heard the words she did not speak aloud: 'I will kill it.'

Jaako nodded. He looked around the table. Nobody else had anything to add. Then he looked at me again.

"Have you any insights, Adept Járnhandr?"

I shook my head slowly.

"I wish I did," I answered. "But... I have a feeling that somehow—I do not know how—this is all connected."

"You think that perhaps... this thing, whatever it was, came here because... you came here?" Jaako asked.

"No," I said. "I do not think so. I... suspect that if anything, it is the other way around. That somehow I am here because... it is here. Was going to be here. Because something is on the move. I do not know what. Nor how that can be."

Jaako nodded slowly. He looked around the table.

"Send riders up and down the line," he ordered. "And have them relay to the next. Tell the families of the outlying farms to pull back to the towns until we can guarantee their safety.

"Write down everything you can remember, Piia. Karel. Simo. Anyone else. I will send the report on. And I will request that reinforcements be sent, if any are available. Double our patrols. We will not be caught napping a second time. No more dead families."

Piia nodded grimly.

The meeting broke up and we drifted out. I saw a couple of the other team leads gathering their teams and briefing them. I walked with Piia. She held onto my hand. I could feel the weariness and the tightness within her.

"Alrekr," she told me, "it was not just because of the rift that I wanted you there when I gave my report. Nor just that I... felt you needed to know what had happened." She turned her head to look at me for a moment as we walked. "This *shook* me, Alrekr. The merciless, wanton slaughter for no reason other than to kill."

"I know," I replied. "I can feel that within you."

She stopped and looked straight at me.

"I do not know how this started, Alrekr." There was determination in her voice. Not that I had expected otherwise. "But something in me says that you will have a hand in ending it.

"I want to be there beside you, Alrekr, when that happens. I will have *vengeance* for this... massacre. There will be an accounting."

"There will," I agreed. She stepped forward and into a tight hug again.

"Come," I said, after a little. "You need to unwind." I led the way to the bath-house.

She looked me up and down as we sat together in the sauna, hand in hand. I could see and feel her starting to relax. I cannot deny I was looking at her, too. She was tightly muscled, like a lioness, yet not lean. She had a hard, fierce beauty of her own, very different from Kata or Liisa, but no less.

"You have grown strong since we pulled you out of that ravine, Alrekr."

I thought back over time. Time and space. To the half-remembered moments in the ravine, and before. So long broken.

Piia squeezed my hand, pulling my attention back.

"Did I say something wrong, Alrekr?"

I let my breath out.

"No, Piia. Sorry. Just... memories." I tried to gather my thoughts, unsure of how much I should say.

"Before I came here, Piia, I had not been physically whole for more than twenty years. In pain, for most of it. Ask Liisa and Kata sometime for their opinion of the healers of my former world. It got to the point where it was hard to think of myself other than... as crippled." My hand tightened without my volition. I had to make a conscious effort to relax it. "It took me so long to—not *accept*... I never *accepted* it. But to come to grips with all the things I could no longer do. I missed *so much* just being able to run, Piia." She was looking steadily at me, just letting me speak at my own speed. She slid closer and slipped her arm around me. It felt good to have her next to me, and I felt her tension easing as we talked. Perhaps it was taking her mind off what she had seen.

"For many of those years I could not *walk* without my foot breaking open and bleeding." I raised my left foot. "But now it is whole again. Something I never dared hope to see. There were times when I could not walk at all. I had to learn three times how to walk again, Piia. You have seen the end caps on my staff?" She nodded. "Matti made those out of metal that Kata and Liisa took out of my knees. That's almost like a little victory in itself."

"I heard about that," she agreed quietly. "They say you sang part of your own healing. Although you are not a Healer."

I nodded.

"Our best guess at an explanation is that the world told me what to sing," I recounted. "It hurt so much, making everything whole. But I have no adequate words to describe how it felt to *be* whole again after so long." I paused and turned my head so that I could look into her dark eyes.

"I have been *reborn* here, Piia. A second chance at life has been given to me. Except that this time... I feel my life *means* something. That it *matters* that I even exist."

"It matters to *me* that you exist, Alrekr," Piia said. And then she leaned closer, put her arm around my neck, and kissed me. For a moment, I froze, startled. But then I put my arms around her and held her close to me.

We broke the kiss, after a little. But we still held onto each other.

"You were *so badly* broken when we found you," she told me. "I was afraid you would die before we could get you to the healers. I have never seen anyone hurt worse than you were, who yet lived—and no few less hurt, who died. And... I remember feeling, even then, that it was terribly important that you should live. And now I believe that even more.

"But the scars of your body, I think, are nearly nothing compared to the scars of your soul. I see the signs in you of pain that still lies within you. One day, you will be free of it. I can see the strength you have won back. I can see how much Kata and Liisa have done to heal your inner pain. And I will help with that, as well, where I can. If I can."

We sat in the steam of the sauna, and we held each other tightly. I could feel the tension slowly leaving her body, her breathing slowing, calming. There was more kissing. I think both of us wanted to go further... but it was neither the time nor the place, and I was not going to do anything that might risk what I had with Kata and Liisa.

After a while, she took a deep breath, and let it out. Exactly the way I often did, I reflected. And just like that, her calm was back.

"Do you feel better?" I asked, after a little while.

"Yes," she replied. "Yes, I do. But... We should go. I don't really want to, but we should. Before I am too much tempted."

We dipped and dried off, then got dressed and walked back.

"Thank you for suggesting the sauna, Alrekr," Piia said to me as we walked. "You were right. I really *needed* that."

We stopped at the forge on the way back to the Hall.

"I am glad to see you returned," Matti told Piia. "Did Járnhandr mention we made the steel ingots for your sword?"

"We... had other things on our minds," I said. "I intended to. But events pushed it from my mind."

"What happened?" Matti asked.

I looked at Piia, unsure whether I should say anything, or how much.

"Something unknown came out of the Spine," she said levelly, "and slaughtered every family in Särkkä valley. Every last one of them, down to babes in arms. There will be a reckoning." The sauna really had helped. There was much less tension in her voice now. She was still angry—no, *furious*; but the horror of it was no longer eating at her.

Matti nodded solemnly.

"I think we should forge your sword," he declared. "Soon. Tomorrow?" He looked at me.

"I want you here when we forge it," I told Piia. "And at the final tempering. I will bind it to you then. But... I want you here for the forging as well. To start... *preparing* it for you. Tuning it to you. If that makes sense."

"Alrekr," Piia said, "you are the master at your craft. Even if it did not make the sense to me that it does, I would be here, if you say I should. And I should like to watch you at work, in any case."

"Tomorrow morning, then," I said. "Let us get an early start." Matti nodded.

Piia went to write her reports and compare notes with her team, and I went back to the tower room. But before I did anything else, I went up onto the roof with Sekai, and practiced what little I could remember of the first couple of sword *kata*. I had the feeling it was going to be very important.

When I came down off the roof, Kata and Liisa were home. I told them what Piia had told me.

"I don't know what it was, yet," I said. "Neither does Piia, or her team. None of them saw it. Black blood along the trail, Karel said. But one way or another, we are going to find it. And then we are going to kill it."

They looked at each other, faces pale.

"Be careful, beloved," Kata told me. "We almost lost you once. Twice."

"I will be careful, my love," I assured her. "I swear."

I spent a while then working on notes for my book on binding, both Tumarïnen's book and the last volume of Vehviläinen's set open on the table in front of me. We sent out to the kitchen to have supper brought, so that I would not have to interrupt my work. By the time we packed up for the night I had a rough outline drafted for at least the first part of my own book.

The three of us made love again that night, with less urgency than the night before, but that meant more time for passion. I had been a little afraid, I think, that somehow, in some way, it would not be as good after sitting there in the sauna for so long with Piia in my arms. Afraid that I would find myself thinking of Piia instead of Kata and Liisa.

But I was wrong. It was *better*.

The next morning, Piia was already waiting at the forge when I got there. Matti had set out a stool for her where she would be able to see everything, but not be in the way or at any risk of burns.

I started by singing the fire in the forge up to an even heat, putting a pool of heat right in front of Matti. I could feel the cool green presence of Piia off to my left and a little behind me. That was good.

Matti put the folded steel ingots into the fire, and I sang the fire into them, bringing them up to an even temperature throughout. Then he began drawing them out and shaping them, laminating them together into a billet for the blade, singing the metal together, joining the pieces into a perfect, flawless piece of metal, just as he had for Sekai. Then he began drawing it out into a blade.

As the first time, it took most of the day. As the shape of the blade began to take form, I reached out to Piia, and I began to lay a little of the green of her soul into the blade. Not too much, yet, just a little, just a hint, keying it to her, preparing it to receive the binding. I became used to her presence, the well of calm next to me. I think her being there actually helped me. Plus, this time, I knew what I was doing, and I was doing it consciously and deliberately.

Finally, we were done. The blade lay cooling on the anvil.

"It isn't curved," Piia said, as she looked at it.

"Not yet," Matti replied. "That happens as we quench it in its final tempering. It is both exhilarating, and terrifying." He grinned. "Now, I must file, and grind, and shape, and smooth the steel, the first light polish. And then we will temper it. And then the final polishing and sharpening, and the fittings."

"And in that tempering," I added, "is when I will bind it fully to you."

"For Járnhandr's fittings," Matti said, "I used wolves everywhere. I sense something of the wolf in him, perhaps. Or perhaps the eagle. But you... you are not a wolf person. What theme should I use for yours?"

"The forest," Piia answered instantly. I knew she was going to say it before she spoke.

She looked at me, smiling. I guess it must have showed on my face.

"You knew I was going to say that, didn't you?"

"Yes," I agreed, with a grin.

"So when do we temper it?"

"It will take me about four to five days to have it ready for tempering," Matti said. "About two hours all told to temper it. And then, if it comes out of the quench intact, about another seven to ten days while I polish it out and make the metal fittings, and Tauno makes and finishes the wooden parts. Around two weeks, in all."

Piia nodded.

"Is there anything I can do to help either of you prepare?"

Matti shook his head.

"It is just time and careful work," he said. "And not rushing it."

She turned to me.

"Alrekr?"

"We already did the preparation I needed to do," I said. "But there is something else you could help with."

"And that is?" Piia asked. But I had a feeling she already knew.

"I have done some sword-based martial arts," I said. "But I've never really trained to *fight* with a sword. Would you please train me properly?"

Piia smiled.

"Of course I will," she replied. "But... I don't know how much time we will have. I'll teach you as much as I can. But I can't make any promises about how good I can make you."

I nodded.

"I was expecting no differently," I said. "But I'll take whatever I can get."

For the next few days, we used what time Piia could spare to assess my skill—or lack. She drilled me with blunt training swords and padded jacks.

"You're pulling your blows when you strike at me," she said.

"I... don't want to hurt you," I admitted.

"You won't," she told me. "So don't do that."

We tried again.

"Harder," she kept telling me. "Strike harder. You need to stop being afraid of hitting me."

I knew absolutely that she was a lot better than I was. But gradually I convinced myself that she was *enough* better than me that I wasn't going to hit her unless she let me, and finally I stopped pulling my blows and started putting my full strength into my strikes. Of

280

course, she still parried me with little effort.

"There!" she declared. "That's much better. *Now* we can actually start working on your technique."

And so we worked, and drilled, and practiced, and she told me that while I had some bad habits to fix, and some techniques to hone, and some reflexes to form, I actually had a pretty firm grip on the basics. In particular, she said my snap-cuts were very good. I just needed a lot more real-world practice, particularly at blocking and parrying. She told me I needed to think more about guarding and defense, instead of being all attack. And I needed to stop overthinking it.

On the fourth day after Piia's team returned from Särkkä, we—which is to say, five full Highwatch Ranger teams, including Piia's, plus myself—went back to Särkkä Valley. Some of the people from the nearest town, those who had known and loved people in Särkkä, came with us as well. It ended up being a good hundred people, including thirty-five Rangers.

The Rangers scouted several leagues into the edge of the forest around the head of the valley to make sure nothing was lurking there, before we let anyone else enter the valley. I rode with Piia's team. Then we tore down the half-smashed buildings, and we built all of the wood into a single great pyre in the center of the valley. We swept through the entire valley from end to end, and we collected up every last tragic torn body, every body part, every stripped bone, every scrap of shredded clothing, the weapons of the fallen, and we laid them gently atop the pyre, their weapons in hand when we could, family members next to each other as much as we could manage, dead children in the arms of their dead parents. Sometimes it was... not easy to figure out which parts went together. *None* of it was easy.

Then we lit the pyre, and we stood around it and sang. Not songs of power. Songs of loss and grief and mourning. Songs of vengeance and resolve. Songs to *remember* the people who had lived and died here. There would be a *reckoning*.

Except for me. There was another task for my voice. I sang the fire to white heat, until nothing remained and the ground itself turned glassy. It was all I could do, now, for those who had died here.

It was a quiet and somber return to Highwatch.

And then it was time to temper Piia's sword.

Again, Matti had already prepared the clay coat and let it partly dry. I could see that he had done something different with the *gunome*, but I didn't peek too closely. Piia arrived a little after I did.

"Are we ready?" Matti asked.

I nodded. So did Piia.

"Sit where you did last time," he told her.

"Alrekr, what do you need from me?" she asked.

"Just be within my reach, right there," I replied. "That is all I need... for this tempering."

She met my eyes, and I met hers.

"Let us begin, then," Matti said.

I let myself sink into the fire in the forge, and I sang it to even heat, and Matti laid the clay-covered blade into the pool I created.

"You remember light straw," he said to me. Not a question. I nodded anyway. I sang the heat into the blade, circulating it, rolling it through the metal, balancing it just as we had the first time. And then I reached out for Piia. For the feel of her. The unshakable green calm of her core. I sang to the fire, and I sang to the sword, and I sang to Piia.

The feel of her suddenly became stronger, and I realized that she had stood and taken my hand. That was good. That was *very* good. I drank in the calm of her, and gently, I urged the heart of the sword to her soul, and tenderly wrapped the essence of her soul around the heart of the sword.

Then Matti said that it was time, and I tied off the binding, and let the fire rest. The blade began to cool. Matti picked it up with two pairs of tongs and held it over his quenching trough.

"Ready?" he said. Then he dropped it in.

There was the expected explosion of steam and spray of boiling water. Piia let out a gasp. But I could feel the core of the sword was intact. It had survived the tempering.

Matti waited until the water was still, then reached in and lifted the sword out. It seemed a fraction more deeply curved than Sekai, and an inch or so shorter. He held it up and sighted along the edge.

"It is true," he pronounced. "And it is sound." He turned and put it on his bench.

"Give me ten days," he said.

I still had Piia's hand, so I turned and led her out.

"I don't get to see it yet?" she asked, smiling.

"The man is an artist," I said, still well within Matti's hearing. "Let him have his great reveal."

"If I must," she agreed. I heard Matti snort in amusement behind us.

For the next nine days, I continued to train with Piia—and sometimes Paavo or Ari, when she was busy—in the early afternoons, except when her team was out on patrol, and practiced *kata* in the late afternoons, and worked on the beginnings of my book on soulbinding in the evenings. Three times Piia came and ate supper with us. Kata in particular pressed her about my progress.

"He is coming along very well," Piia replied. "Now that he has stopped pulling his blows when we spar, and is guarding himself properly. I have had second-year trainees who he would cut into dog-meat without breaking stride."

My eyebrows shot up in surprise.

"It's true, Alrekr," she assured me. "I didn't want you to feel overconfident. That is the only reason I had not said so before. But your instincts are good, your hand-eye coordination is good, your reflexes are fast when you don't over-think it, and there is an efficiency in your movements that some swordsmen never learn. You save the energy still left in one stroke, and feed it into the next, or you flow straight from a parry into a strike. And we are not even practicing with your preferred sword yet.

"We do need to work more on your defense, though. You are very strong in your attacks, but you need to always remember to defend as well. Sometimes you forget that."

I thought about what she had said, and she paused in thought as well.

"When my sword is ready," she mused, "I think we will both be training each other. I have no doubt you will have things to teach me."

The day came around that her sword was ready. Matti told me, when I arrived in the morning, that Tauno had told him the night before that all was complete, and he would be there shortly.

I went back to pick up a spare obi, then went to get Piia. I was already wearing Sekai. And of course since Ari and Paavo and Ragne were there when I found Piia, I told them as well, and Ragne called into the next room for Karel, and Karel brought Simo in tow, and then Kauko spotted us and wanted to know what the excitement was. And so in the end a good fifteen Rangers ended up following us to the forge.

Tauno was there by the time we got back, holding a white cloth-wrapped bundle. Matti stood to one side beaming like a proud father. We walked up to the forge and stopped, then Tauno stepped forward, bowed his head for a moment to Piia, and then presented the bundle to her with both hands.

Piia glanced sideways at me, then mirrored the slight bow, and held out her hands. Tauno laid the wrapped sword into her hands, then stepped back.

She unwrapped the cloth, revealing an arc of deep green. I heard her breath draw in. I reached out and offered a hand for the cloth to leave her both hands free. The *saya* was the deep green of ancient forest, and the *tsuba*, I could see, bore the billowing crown of an oak tree. What they called oak in the Sunlit Land was not *exactly* an oak, any more than the birches were exactly birch, or the horses exactly horses; but it was close enough. The wrapped *sageo* was red-brown, and so was the *ito* on the hilt. Tauno had wrapped it beautifully. His wrapping, in fact, was better than mine, I thought. I shot him a quick half-bow of respect.

She put her right hand on the hilt, and I felt it pulse softly. She slowly drew the blade. It was a ribbon of silver-gray steel, the *hamon* bright and clear. I looked at it, and recognized the pattern after a moment as trees. Matti had put trees in the *hamon*.

"Oak tree *gunome*," I declared.

The blade came free of the *saya*, and I knew without asking that she wanted to put both hands on her new sword. I silently offered a hand again, and she glanced my way, nodded thanks, and put the *saya* into my hand. I took a moment to sneak a closer look at the finish. There were red-brown flakes in the lacquer. Bark perhaps.

Piia put both hands on the hilt and held the sword out in front of her. I watched her close her eyes, breathe out and open them again. She dropped her left hand for a moment, took two fast steps clear of me, and whipped the sword through a blurring figure-eight. Then she put both hands on it again.

"What do I do?" she asked, quietly. "It feels as though it's... waiting for something."

"You should name it at some point, to complete the binding," I told her. "If you listen, it might be telling you a name already. Sekai did."

Piia held the sword raised in front of her and closed her eyes. I saw her take a deep breath, then slowly let it out. For a long moment, there was silence. Then her eyes flew open and she raised her head.

She raised the sword a little higher. Her voice rang out clearly.

"*Tuuli metsässä*." Wind in the Forest.

A ripple of deep green surged along Tuuli's blade, and a silent pulse swept out. It felt like Piia. A cheer rose from behind us. I had almost forgotten about our Ranger audience.

Piia turned and looked at me. Her eyes were bright, her cheeks flushed. She kept looking back and forth between me and Tuuli's blade.

"Congratulations, Piia," I said.

"This is... more than I dreamed," she told me, her voice scarcely above a whisper. I nodded. She lowered her hands and looked more closely at the sword again. She let her breath out, and I saw her feel for a scabbard.

"Here," I said. I stepped forward, put the *saya* into her left hand, showed her where it should ride just above her hip, adjusted the position of her hand slightly.

"Now bring Tuuli around to your left, edge up... yes, like that. Lay the back of the blade, that's called the *mune*, next to your thumb. So now you know exactly where the blade is relative to the *saya*. Then draw her forward... and let the point drop just a little... and in. And I think you will find that if you listen to her, she will not only tell you when you are aligned, she will actually guide herself into the *saya*, once you get used to how it feels. Like Sekai does."

She snapped Tuuli smoothlyhome into the *saya*.

"*Thank you*, Alrekr," she said, with feeling. Then she turned to Tauno. "And thank you, Master Tauno; and you, Smith Matti. She is beautiful."

"Like her owner," Matti replied. Piia smiled brilliantly.

"Tell me how much I owe you both."

"I am declaring this one to be a favor to Master Járnhandr," Matti announced. "And I'll brook no argument on it." Then he raised his voice to carry. "But the next one is five hundred silvers! *Three* hundred and fifty, to Highwatch Rangers and Guards. And you'll have to promise to get Master Járnhandr to teach you how to use it properly."

"Thank you, Matti," Piia replied. I thought I caught something glistening in the corner of her eye. Then she stepped over to Matti and hugged him.

"And Master Tauno? What do I owe you for the... beautiful scabbard?"

"I will follow Matti's lead," Tauno declared. "This one is a gift." Then he, too, raised his voice. "Orders, starting at sixty silver for a plain scabbard and wrapping, a hundred and fifty for one like this."

"May I see Tuuli more closely?" I asked.

"Of *course*," Piia agreed at once. She passed me Tuuli. I examined the detail of the tree that formed the *tsuba*, looked at the *kashira* and *kojiri* and the wood grain engraved into them. The *menuki* looked like windblown pines. Once again Matti had excelled himself. I was just now beginning to understand what an artist the man truly was.

I understood also, now, what my lovers had meant. Bound to Piia and in my hand, Tuuli *felt* like Piia, or like her soul... and yet also *not* like her.

I handed Tuuli back to her, only to have Paavo ask to look. With a smile, Piia handed Tuuli over and let her team, her friends, *our* friends, examine her new sword.

"The green pulse we felt from the blade at the naming," Ari asked. "What is that?"

"Tuuli is soulbound to Piia," I answered. "That was a flash of her soul. The mark of finalizing the binding. Let us call it the binding flash."

"So that is why it felt so familiar," he nodded. "What can it do?"

"We don't *completely* know yet," I hedged. "And I do not know whether Tuuli can do the same things Sekai can. I can tell Sekai that someone is not to be harmed... or is not allowed to wield her. I can call her to my hand, or send her to Piia's. And... I think she can alter time, a little. I do not know for certain whether she speeds me up, or slows everything around me down."

"Speeds you up?" Ari repeated. "Can you do this for *anyone?*"

"I *won't*, for just *anyone*," I answered him. "I have to be able to recognize the core of your soul, and that is a bond I am not willing to form lightly. But for you... I will. Or Paavo. Or any of your team. You are my *friends*. And also, I owe all of you my life."

"We would have done the same for anyone," Ari said gruffly.

"Nevertheless," I said. "'Anyone' would be as grateful as I am."

Ari grinned.

Matti was standing to one side, watching and smiling. I took a moment to step over to him.

"I meant what I said about you being an artist," I told him. "I am only now beginning to understand how *good* of an artist."

Matti's smile broadened.

"I do love the opportunity to create something of beauty," he replied. "It comes along so seldom."

"Perhaps you should *make* yourself time to create more things of beauty, then," I suggested.

Matto looked at me and scratched his chin.

"Perhaps you are right," he agreed, after a moment. "Thank you."

I took Piia aside a moment.

"I brought a gift for you," I told her. "A small one." I pulled out the obi from inside my tunic. It was a dark brown. She immediately looked at the blue one around my own waist, and smiled.

"Thank you, Alrekr," she said. "Show me how to tie it?" So I wrapped it around her waist and showed her how to tie it, then how to tuck Tuuli's *saya* through it—though actually, the upper part of her sword harness was already in the right place to use. Still, she would not always be wearing that harness.

"Now," she told me, "you will begin to train me as well. I will continue to train you in the sword, and you will train me in properly using *this* sword."

"It's a deal," I agreed, without hesitation.

16: See One, Do One, Teach One

It ended up being three days before we got any more training in, because Piia's team was sent out on a wide sweep along the crag line. It was uneventful, gladly; though Karel insisted, when they got back, that something was wrong. The sounds and scents of the forest were not what they should be. There were too few deer, too few birds. Too few of everything.

Nothing he said was individually alarming. But together? Yes. Even I could see there was a picture there. I didn't know what it painted... but I didn't like it.

"I have an idea," Piia said, before we began our next training session. "You told Sekai I am not to be harmed."

"I did," I agreed.

"Would you draw her, please?"

Wondering what she had in mind, I drew Sekai and held her out in front of me.

Piia nodded. Then before I could react, she darted out her left hand, wrapped it around Sekai's blade, and slid it down a good six inches. I gasped, but before I could do more, she looked at her open hand, then displayed it to me. I could see the pressure crease, but there was not a drop of blood.

"Well, that works," she declared.

"Piia, don't DO that to me," I said, my heart pounding. I'd half expected to see blood pouring from a lacerated hand.

"You *did* tell her not to harm me," Piia pointed out. "I thought before we went any further, we should test it and be sure."

"I... well, yes," I agreed. "But I would have preferred a less drastic test." My heart rate started to come back down. Piia looked at me closely. "I've seen—and *felt*—the wounds swords like these can leave," I continued. "I'm not sure you have really grasped yet how much damage they can do."

"I'm sorry, Alrekr," Piia said contritely. "I... didn't mean to alarm you so badly."

"It's alright," I replied. "Just try to warn me next time?"

"I promise," she agreed. Then she drew Tuuli. I saw her concentrate for a moment.

"Your turn," she told me.

Well, I thought, *in for a penny, in for a pound*. I took a deep breath, and slapped my open left palm hard against Tuuli's edge, as though I were trying to slap the blade away and had gotten it terribly wrong. It stung a little. That was all. I looked at my palm. Not a mark.

"Well," I observed. "Tested and proven."

"So here's my suggestion," Piia said. "From now on, we put away the training swords, and we train with these. Now that we know that our swords will not let us hurt each other."

I nodded. I could see the sense in it. Then I started to laugh.

"What is it?" Piia asked.

"It's—it would have been—such a completely and utterly mad idea, in my past world. And yet here and now, it actually makes sense."

After a moment, she began to laugh too.

"All right," I agreed. "Let's roll with it."

So we put away the training gear, and switched to training with Sekai and Tuuli.

For my part, I began by first teaching her to draw. The pressure with the thumb to loosen the *habaki* in the *koiguchi*, the nearly-straight draw pushing the *saya* backward as her right hand almost threw the sword forward, the snap of the wrist out to full extension. It didn't take her too long to get the hang of it.

For safety's sake, I reminded her to tell Tuuli that we were just practicing. We didn't know yet whether Tuuli could... *accelerate* her the way Sekai accelerated me, but it was better to play safe to start with. Form first, then speed. Slow is smooth; smooth is fast.

"You're used to making blocks and parries with the flat of the blade," I told her. "But with an edge as hard as this, you don't want to risk a blow striking the edge if you can avoid it. So twist your wrists just a little further, to block with the back of the blade, when you can."

We sparred, circling each other then closing for rapid exchanges of strikes. I could block or dodge her a little more than half the time, now, and occasionally get past her guard. We quickly learned that our mutual protection did not entirely extend to our clothes. And as one session followed another, we began to draw an audience.

She was striking with Tuuli as though with her other sword, though. Not that there was anything in any way bad or weak about her strikes, but she wasn't getting the full advantage that she *could* be.

"Remember that this is a different kind of sword designed for a different style of fighting," I advised. "The sword is designed for draw cuts. You're used to putting your back and shoulders into straight cuts while keeping your feet planted.

"Let your feet pivot. Put your *hips* into it. You are used to striking like this."

I took a stance as though holding a shield in my left hand, and cut overhand and down, shifting my weight forward on the strike as she had taught me, the sword a straight extension of my arm. She nodded critically, ever appraising my form. I knew the look.

"Now look again."

I raised Sekai into a vertical guard position, my hands almost back against my chest, and made a full-priest's-robe cut in slow motion, letting her see how I dropped slightly into my knees, how my feet pivoted slightly as my hips rotated, pulling my upper body around with them, the sword trailing slightly behind my wrists, my entire upper body pulling the blade around and down through the cut, recovering into a low guard.

She nodded slowly, thoughtfully.

"You're committing yourself more to the strike," she observed. "But I see how it develops the power." I nodded.

"And here's what it looks like at full speed."

I did it again, letting it flow this time. She nodded again.

"One more time at half speed, please?" she asked. I complied. She repeated it after me. Adjusted her stance slightly, and did it again. I watched her, nodding my approval. Then three times more, speeding up each time towards full speed. She had it.

"Much better," I said. "Let me teach you first *kata*. *Kata* are formal exercises for practicing form in different techniques." And so we started doing *kata* together, as part of our mutual cross-training.

On the third day of *kata*, Kauko came over to us after we finished.

"Can this exercise be done with a straight sword?" he asked me. "Or is it specific to the curved sword you carry?"

It was a good question. Behind him I saw Paavo scratching his chin, and a couple of regular Highwatch guards looked thoughtful too.

"It is an exercise specific to the fighting styles that were developed to best use this type of sword," I said finally, after some thought. "But I see no harm in learning it with a straight sword that has enough hilt to get two hands on. Especially if you ever have any plans to order a *katana* from Matti."

"Ka-ta-na?" he repeated carefully.

"That is the name for this type of sword in the land it comes from," I explained. "Another word is *Nihontō*, but that is a more general word that really just means 'sword from Nihon' anyway. In the same way, the historians of my past life would probably have called your sword an arming sword." I noticed it was becoming easier, and less painful, to talk about my past life, particularly in that way. I really was not the same person any more. More and more, it felt as though... what had happened before the rift, had happened to some other person.

Kauko nodded. And so for the next *kata* session, there were three of us. Then four, then six. Paavo joined us after Kauko, then Ari and Ilona, another Ranger from Kauko's team, small but fiery. It just... happened. It slowed us a little, because I had to bring the new— students, I realized—up to speed, and occasionally stop to correct a detail of stance or adjust someone's grip. Occasionally Master Toivo or Knight-Commander Jaako would stop by and watch our training for a little while.

"Alrekr," Piia asked me one day, "is there a good way to practice cutting in this style of fighting? I've tried it on the pells, but they are really meant for a different kind of combat. Good for training against brigands. But less so, I think, for what we hunt."

"You're... probably right," I agreed. I thought for a long moment. "What do we have around by way of straw? Not just randomly baled, like hay for horses. But unbroken straw in bundles, like thatch. Better yet, woven straw matting. It could be old and worn, I think that would be alright."

"There are thatchers around," Kauko volunteered. "I'm sure we could get some from them, or ask where they get their thatch. Why do you need straw? Or straw mats?"

"*Tameshigiri*," I explained. "Cutting practice. I could use some myself, I'm certain." I couldn't escape the thought that things were starting to get a little out of hand. All because I had mentioned Japanese swords to Master Toivo, months before.

But then I realized, if I had not said that to Toivo, Toivo would never have gotten curious and sent me to Matti. And had I never gone to Matti, I would not have learned about my firesinging Talent. And had I not known I was a firesinger, then I would not have been working with Matti at the forge, even if I had asked him to make me a sword, and I would not have discovered my soulbinding ability, and I would never have touched Piia's beautiful soul, and we would never have made Tuuli, and I would not be teaching this class now. And perhaps I would still be aimlessly reading, trying to figure out what my life was *for*.

"Alrekr? Alrekr?"

Piia was gently shaking my arm. I dragged my thoughts back to the present.

"Alrekr, is everything alright?"

"I'm fine, Piia. I... I just realized how interconnected all of this is. We are standing here today, training, we have Sekai and Tuuli, and... and I know *you*, know the depths of your soul, because... I've lost track even of the time. Four months ago? Five? Six? I was bored and frustrated, and looking for something to do to give me purpose, and decided to ask Master Toivo for some quarterstaff training."

Piia looked steadily into my eyes. She was almost as tall as I, and scarcely even had to look up.

"I believe you mentioned," she reminded me, "that Smith Matti told you once that all that has happened was meant to be."

I nodded.

"He did," I agreed. "It was not until this moment that the full weight of those words fell on me. It... is taking some mental adjustment."

She looked at me for a long moment, then turned to Kauko and the rest of our students.

"Class is over for today," she announced. "Come back tomorrow."

Then she took me by the hand.

"Come along, Alrekr," she told me. "This time it is you who needs a little peace in the sauna."

Who should we meet along the way, as it turned out, but my lovely ladies. They were coming the other way, talking over a healing case. Liisa spotted me about the same time I spotted them, and her face lit up. She altered course, pulling Kata with her, and I tugged at Piia's hand. We met in the middle and immediately glomped together into a four-way hug. I kissed my lovers, of course, which is why Piia got the first words in.

"We were headed to the sauna," Piia said. "Do the two of you have time to join us?"

Kata agreed enthusiastically, Liisa a moment behind. So on we went, together, and very shortly we were all sitting in the sauna together. Sekai and Tuuli we left outside with our clothes, of course. Nobody would touch them, without our permission. Not here.

I had Kata on my left, Piia on my right, and then Liisa was on the other side of Piia, all of us nestled snugly into a corner. I leaned my head back against the wall, holding Piia's and Kata's hands, and relaxed. Liisa, I saw, had Piia's other hand.

"So what is on your mind, Alrekr?" Piia asked after a while. Then she glanced at Kata and Liisa.

"He went gazing off into who knows where during our training session," she explained. "I thought... he needed some peace and rest to let his thoughts settle."

I squeezed her hand appreciatively.

"You heard what Raimo said," I began slowly, my words meant mostly for Kata and Liisa at that moment. "That I was meant to come here. *Meant* to forge Sekai."

"I remember," Kata agreed.

"It actually started with a question Piia asked. About practice with using Tuuli. There is something specifically called *tameshigiri*, cutting practice, or cutting testing. It uses... well, in—modern times, traditionally used soaked rice-straw matting, tightly tied into bundles and placed on a pole of green... uh. Something called *bamboo*. A kind of giant grass."

"That is why you asked about straw," Piia remarked, making the

294

connection.

"Yes. Historically, they *used* to use condemned criminals.

"And then we were talking about how to get straw, and our *kata* sessions have grown from the two of us to six, and suddenly I, who have never actually been in real close-quarters battle, am teaching sword arts. To people with far more real experience than I. And I found myself thinking that it was all getting out of hand."

Kata squeezed my hand.

"And then I started *really* thinking about it," I continued. "Liisa, you remember the day when we went walking around the keep, for exercise and because I needed to find something to do with my time? And you introduced me to Master Toivo?"

"I remember," Liisa replied. "That was when you started staff training."

"Yes," I agreed. "And do you remember him asking me what style of sword I prefer?" She nodded again.

"Had he not asked that, I would not have mentioned Japanese swords. And had I not mentioned Japanese swords, he would not have sent me to talk to Matti about whether one could be made, to satisfy his curiosity. I would never have told Senja to have one of the pieces of... non-rusting steel from my knees sent to Matti. And so I would not have been visiting the forge after I finally learned enough from the two of you to reach and awaken my core. Which would never have happened, I think, without your support and your guidance. And your love."

I could feel tears in the corners of my eyes.

"Had I not been visiting the forge, I think I would not have discovered my firesinging. And had I not sent Matti the rustless steel, likely he and I would never have talked about wolf-metal. And perhaps Sekai would not have been made at all, or at the least I would have been far less involved in the forging. And because I would not have been singing the forge-heat into Sekai's blade as Matti forged her, if she was forged at all, I would not have discovered my soulbinding.

"Had I not discovered soulbinding, I would not have Sekai, and Piia would not have asked if I could bind a sword to her." I squeezed Piia's hand again, and she squeezed back. "I would have had no reason to learn how to touch *your* souls, and I would not know you to the depths I do, I would not understand the whole of you both as I do now."

I admit, tears were running down my face by now. On my left,

Kata snuggled closer to me, switched hands, and put her right arm around me instead.

"I would never have touched Piia's soul, and seen the pillar of strength that she is, and we would not have forged Tuuli, and Piia would not have asked me to train her in how to use Tuuli properly, and I would not now be learning from her how to *really fight* with Sekai, and I would not be leading a class of five through what I can remember of *kenjutsu* and contemplating setting up a *tameshigiri* class.

"And all this comes back to... to feeling one day like a... a fifth shoe on a horse, and needing to find something useful to *do*."

I stopped for a moment, trying to marshal my thoughts and steady my breathing.

"Smith Matti told me one day, 'All that has happened was meant to be.' This day, the full weight of those words finally landed upon me. What if Liisa and I had gone on that walk one day later? Would everything still have happened the same way? What if Master Toivo had not asked me my preference in swords?"

I squeezed Kata's hand, and with my other, tried to reach for Liisa's without letting go of Piia's. It was a little awkward, but because we were in the corner, it worked.

"I would be poorer, but not know it, if I had not touched your souls. *Any* of the three of you," I realized as I said it. "You are *all* precious to me. Without any one of you, I would not be here. I would have died in the crags, or on the way down." Piia freed her left hand, leaving me holding her right and Liisa's left, and slipped her left arm in around me as well.

"This world has given me so much," I continued. "A new life. This place. You three. My talents. Sekai. Matti and Paavo and Vallaïnen and Raimo, and Senja and Mistress Kerttu and Master Timo and... more friends, *true* friends, than I can easily count. I—I simply cannot find words to say how much it all means.

"And yet we all know that something dread is stirring in the Spine of the World. Or beyond them. Already we have seen... a massacre. Entire families wiped from the world. All of their living generations, gone in a single day.

"What if part of what is *meant to happen* takes all of this away from us?"

I ran out of words.

Kata spoke first.

"Do not fear for what may never come," she told me. "I know, you have endured so much. That does not mean that loss is inevitable."

"You cannot know what the future brings," Piia said. "So live with no regrets. Live each day as though it were your last." I started to laugh, but it came out as almost a sob.

"Alrekr?" Liisa asked.

I fought my emotions back under control.

"Piia," I managed to get out after a few moments, "I told Kata and Liisa some weeks ago, after we touched souls, that you have the soul of a Samurai. What you just said is the most Samurai thing I think I have ever heard anyone say." She laughed at that, and her laughter helped calm me.

"You should probably tell me about these—*samurai*, then," she replied. "But perhaps not right now."

"I will," I promised.

"Raimo said he saw that you came here in part to forge Sekai," Liisa said. "I do not remember all that he said. We know—we *believe* we know—that the world itself told you what to sing to help in your own Healing." She looked at me, her face serious.

"I choose to believe that if these things were all meant to happen, then the world chose to bring you here, and it brought you here for a reason, and it *chose you* for a reason. And I think it is no coincidence that now is when something is stirring in, or beyond, the Spine.

"I choose to believe that the world brought you here purposefully to deal with whatever is on the move beyond the Spine, Alrekr. And I refuse to believe that the world is so cruel as to bring you here to do such a deed, and give you what you need to accomplish it, and then take everything back from you. Or to take you from us. You are ours. It *cannot have* you."

Then, very much to my surprise, she reached around with her other hand to touch Piia's cheek.

"And it cannot have you, either," Liisa told Piia. "If you are Alrekr's, then you are ours too."

I saw a sudden brightness in the corners of Piia's eyes. Liisa let go of our hands and put her arm around Piia instead, and then there was a general shuffling and rearrangement as we all tried to get arms as much

297

around each other as we could.

"All will end as it will end, Alrekr," Kata declared, as we sat there, all holding each other. "But I believe that Liisa has the right of it. This world, I think, does not try to betray those who serve and protect it honestly. It helped you to heal yourself... for a reason. It *chose you*... for a reason."

"Well then," I said, a little shakily, "I had best just hope it chose wisely."

"It did, Alrekr," Piia replied fiercely. "It chose very well. I could not be more certain of it."

We sat and steamed, all happy in each others' presence, while the tension drained away from me. I found myself gazing at the hot sauna stones.

"What are you thinking, Alrekr?" Liisa asked.

"I'm thinking," I mused, "that if I sort of copy Tumarinen's trick, I could make a demand water heater for that big stone bathtub in our rooms. We could drain the used water out through the garderobe. But I just can't figure out how to get the water *to* it."

"You will think of something, sooner or later," Kata told me, her head on my shoulder. I turned my head and kissed her forehead.

After a while we declared ourselves done, and slipped out for a quick cold dip and then a towel off. There were half a dozen people sitting soaking in the heated pool, but we paid them little mind.

"I have a suggestion," I said. "Supper for four sent to our rooms."

"I agree," Kata said at once. "You can come, Piia?"

"*Gladly* I will," Piia agreed. "And Alrekr can tell us all about— *samurai*."

So we sent a polite request to Mistress Kerttu for supper for four, and we walked to the tower. Piia observed that one of the weapon racks on the wall, near to the door, looked to have been designed for axes or perhaps maces, but that Tuuli sat in it very nicely.

"Huh," I mused. "Why hadn't I noticed that?" So I put Sekai on the same rack.

"Perhaps," Liisa suggested, "you were too focused on having the *exact* correct stand?"

"You could be right, at that," I agreed. "You even racked Tuuli the traditionally correct way, Piia."

She shot me a questioning look. "There's a right and a wrong way?"

"The tradition for horizontal display is exactly as you did it—edge up, and hilt to the right. There is symbology to do with honor involved."

Piia chuckled.

"Can I pretend I knew that, instead of getting lucky on an even chance?"

"I won't tell," I replied, grinning. Piia and Kata both laughed.

We sat around the table while we waited for supper to arrive, and I related what I could remember of the feudal period of Japanese history and the Shōgunate wars of unification, the Sengoku period and the dawn of the Edo period. Of Takeda Shingen, the Long Snake, and the Three Great Uniters, Oda Nobunaga, Toyotomi Hideyoshi, and Tokugawa Ieyasu, and the beginning of the Tokugawa Shōgunate.

Then supper arrived, another delight from Mistress Kerttu's kitchen, smallish birds about the size of game hens, stuffed and roasted whole and served with a tangy sauce, with imp fingers and yellow yams on the side. Conversation slowed to a trickle while we all took at least the edges off our appetites. Kata and Liisa had not been sparring and training, as Piia and I had; but a healer burns through a lot of energy. Even I knew that, and I'd only ever done it once.

With the historical background in place, I talked about Samurai and the code of *bushidō*, the Way of the Warrior, and about how at least in the ideal, honor and duty were everything to samurai. I spoke of Miyamoto Musashi and his Book of Five Rings, and the Hagakure that was the other major influence in *bushidō*—and Musashi's final *Dokkōdō*, the Path of Aloneness.

"That seems a very strict code," Piia mused. "But I find I agree with much of it."

"So do I," I said. "But I think Musashi was mistaken in saying not to be guided by love. I think love has guided some of the best decisions I have made in the Sunlit Land."

"What about being indifferent to where you live?" Liisa asked.

"Again, no," I hedged. "Though... it is subject to interpretation, I will admit. The wording is ambiguous. It could be taken several different ways."

"But your thought?" Liisa pressed me.

"*Treasure* the place where you live," I replied. "And if it is not a place worthy of being treasured, then *make* it one, if you can. I could *never* be indifferent to the Sunlit Land. I am still finding new wonders here."

When we were done eating, we all moved to the couch. There was just enough room to fit all four of us at once, if we didn't mind snuggling tightly together. And we didn't. I was in between Liisa and Piia this time. I was worn from the emotional roller-coaster earlier, and so I just sat back with my arms around them both, my fingers resting on Kata's shoulder, relaxed as much as I could, and enjoyed the moment.

"Alrekr," Kata asked after a little while, "what else would you change, if you were writing down your own version of Musashi's code? Beyond treasuring the place were you live, and allowing yourself to be guided by love?"

"Never be afraid to love," I said first, without hesitation. "You told me that yourself, Liisa." She nodded agreement. "Never bury the sadness or grief of yourself or others. Never just accept the way it is, when it is wrong."

I had to think a little, beyond those first three. "Be guided by what you desire, but not ruled by it, and do not mistake willful self-denial for virtue, nor forget the needs of others." I thought a little longer. "Never forget that true strength lies in mercy."

"The Way of Járnhandr," Piia stated quietly.

"Perhaps you should write it down," Liisa suggested from my other side.

"You should," Kata agreed.

"I..." I hesitated. "It feels... vain. As though I'd be writing it under false pretenses. I've made *so many* mistakes."

"But did you *learn* from them?" Kata asked.

"Some of them," I agreed, with a sigh. "Eventually. I hope it was enough."

"You don't have to start now," Piia said. "But when you feel ready... I think you should consider it. I think it would be important."

I nodded.

"I will think about it," I agreed. "But not tonight."

Piia eventually had to beg off.

"My team leaves on a sweep patrol tomorrow morning," she told us. "I need to go over it with everyone before we sleep, so that we can get an early start. We'll be sweeping up past the Särkkä valley again to see if there are any fresh trails that match what Karel tracked after..." She trailed off.

I nodded understanding. She got up and went to pick up Tuuli from the rack next to the door. I followed.

"Wish your team a safe sweep from me," I told her. "Good fortune go with you."

She nodded, and slipped Tuuli into her sash. Then she grabbed hold of me and kissed me, hard. I kissed back.

"I will be back, Alrekr," she reassured me. "Have no fear."

We tidied up from supper and called for a page to return the dishes to the kitchen, and then the three of us went to bed and cuddled up together.

"You took me by surprise today, Liisa," I said after we had snuggled and nuzzled for a while, and just come up for air from a kiss. "Piia too, I think."

Liisa smiled softly at me.

"You love her, do you not?"

"... Yes," I admitted. As much to myself, as anyone else.

"If you have seen into her soul, and you love her," Liisa told me, "then she must be worthy of your love. And we have both seen into *your* soul, and if she is worthy of your love, then we know she is worthy of ours. And I *like* her. A lot."

"Liisa told you before, beloved," Kata added, "love expands to fill the space you allow it to. The love you feel for her does not diminish your love for us. We see your soul, and we *know* that."

She nibbled my ear. I turned my head and kissed her as well. And from there, that led where it usually does.

17: The Eleventh Hour

While Piia's team was out on patrol, I used the time we would have spent training together to work more on the beginning of my book —except for sword *kata* class. With Piia, Ari and Paavo out on patrol, I was able to give some focused attention to Kauko and Ilona, to help them catch up. I also gained another student, Päivi, from a different team again, so she got a double dose of personal focus to get her started. I decided against trying to get everything in place for *tameshigiri* now. There would be time later.

Matti told me he was anticipating several more orders soon, so we spent two days of forge time making four sets of ingots of the same steel he had used to forge Tuuli.

"I'm pretty certain this mix will come through the quench intact without being bound," he told me, "but I won't try that high wolf-metal blend we used on yours again unless I know for certain it will be soulbound. I don't feel like pushing my luck on that."

"So who has expressed interest? If I might ask?"

"Ari and Paavo, from Piia's team. Usko, another Ranger whom I don't think you know yet. Master-at-Arms Toivo. And Knight-Commander Jaako. So far. But none have committed yet. I think they are waiting to see."

"Waiting to see what?"

"How the new swords do in battle, I expect."

I thought for a moment.

"Is it fair of me to hope we don't find that out too soon?"

Matti laughed heartily.

"Not unfair at all, and not unreasonable either. Those are the words of a man with more sense than bravado, a man who prefers peace to war. Which is as it should be."

Piia and her team came back in on the morning of the third day. I didn't see them come in, but Piia found me at the forge. Matti and I were making axe heads. She waited until we were done; but I had felt her approach, and knew she was there before she said anything.

"Hello, Alrekr," she said, a few breaths after I let the heat go and the last axe-head went into the quench.

"Hello, Piia, love," I replied as I turned. I took three steps forward, gathered her into my arms and held her tight. She hugged me back, then kissed me quickly.

"I take it all went smoothly."

"You could tell?"

"You seem happy and relaxed. You aren't a knot of wound-up fury like you were last time you came back from Särkkä."

"That is fair," she admitted, laughing. "And you?"

"We made four new sets of ingots for katanas," I said, "and we have a new student in the sword-*kata* class. Päivi."

"Oh, good," Piia replied. "I know Päivi. She is good. She is in Markku's team."

"How many Ranger teams *are* there at Highwatch, in all?" I asked. It hadn't occurred to me to ask before.

"Eight," she told me. "The other leads are Arja, Jouko, Kirsi—Kauko and Ilona are on Kirsi's team—Markku, Raili, Torsti, and Usko."

"Eight teams, seven per team?" She nodded. "Plus Knight-Commander Jaako." She nodded again. "Doesn't seem a lot."

"Eight Ranger teams can cover a lot of ground, Alrekr," she said. I nodded, certain she was right. "Fifty-six Rangers, used poorly, are the equal of a hundred to a hundred and fifty or more regular soldiers. Used properly? Perhaps twice, even three times that."

"Somehow that does not surprise me," I said. "All the teams are the same? Well, except for yours, that is?"

She waved a hand in partial agreement.

"There are variations," she explained. "The normal team of seven is four swords, two bows, one tracker. But we have Simo in place of our fourth sword. Usko's has three swords and three bows. And Torsti has an axewoman in place of a fourth sword—Kaija. She is *scarily* good with an axe. I have seen her quarter an apple in mid-air with her axes.

"But... mostly the same, yes."

I nodded understanding. She looked around at what we had been working on.

"How are your axe heads, Matti?" she asked.

"Judge for yourself," he replied. He picked up the last one we'd done, held it a foot above the anvil, and dropped it. It made a hard, but dull, CLANG. Then he picked it up again and dropped it a second time, edge down. This time it rang much more clearly. Piia's attention perked up immediately.

"Harder on the edge side," she said immediately. I grinned.

"And done in a single heating, forging and quenching," I said. "Matti had me shift the heat towards the edge before quenching it."

"I cannot do it that way by myself," Matti explained. "The iron conducts heat too well. But Járnhandr here just moves the heat around inside the metal to where we want it. Now they just need some final cleanup with a file and a quick introduction to the wheel. It speeds up the work of making them a lot. It is a single forging, now, with no separate temper step."

I took Piia's hand.

"Come with me, let's go and get something to eat. Perhaps we'll get lucky and find Kata or Liisa. Or both."

Actually, we found both, along with Raimo and Master Timo, and Vilja, and Esko and Marketta.

"Alrekr!" Kata greeted me. "Come join us! Today Vilja advances to Journeyman."

"Vilja!" I said. "Congratulations! Today is a good day all around."

I stepped around the table to Vilja and hugged her, then there was some shuffling around to free up two adjacent seats next to Kata for Piia and I. Liisa was across the table from us.

"So how went your patrol, Piia?" Liisa asked.

"We didn't find a thing," Piia replied. "But... the forest was too quiet. Too still. The beasts are afraid."

"Afraid of what?" Vilja asked.

"We don't know, exactly," Piia hedged. "But probably the thing that... eluded us in Särkkä valley last month. Whatever it was.

"But please, let us not speak of that here, now. We are supposed to be celebrating your advancement."

I reached for Piia's hand under the table and squeezed it. I hadn't missed that quick change of wording. I knew what she had been about to say. She held my hand tightly. Liisa didn't miss anything, either, and I am sure Master Timo caught the exchange.

We ate our luncheon, and drank mead—but not too much—and celebrated Vilja's advancement. Then it was time for sword training.

We went out to the spot in the bailey we'd taken over for our afternoon training. Everyone else was already there, so we did *kata* first as a warm-up, then Piia and I moved on to our own one-on-one training.

"You are getting much better, Alrekr," Piia said between breaths as we sparred. "It is getting much harder to get through your guard. And much harder to keep you from getting through mine."

"That is a good thing," I grunted in reply.

"What do you say we take the gloves off?"

I blinked for a moment and took a step back.

"You mean... drop the protections?"

"No, Alrekr," Piia said. "I would not take that risk. You say Sekai can speed you up. Let us find out whether Tuuli can do the same for me."

I thought... but not for long. I wanted to know too.

"All right," I agreed. "When I first discovered it, it was by accident. And I asked Sekai to stop by... telling her... that I was just practicing, and there was no hurry.

"So perhaps if we tell them that... there is no urgency, but speed us by half? And see what happens?"

Piia nodded.

"Let us try it," she said. I saw her gaze go distant for just a moment, and knew that she was speaking to Tuuli, so I told Sekai the same thing.

Then we tried it. Carefully.

It felt a little different... but only a little. Our clothes seemed to move slightly differently. Sekai felt the tiniest bit... heavier? No. Not heavier. It just took a little more effort to start her moving.

We began with practicing a few draws, at first. Piia had definitely gotten the hang of the *iai* draw, and if anything she was smoother than I was. I could tell that everything in the outside world looked just a bit slower. When I had the feel of it, I did a few more, drawing with full force, and Piia matched me. It felt smooth and fast, but I could not tell how much faster.

When we had the feel of it, we began sparring, a few gentle passages at first, then ramping it up towards what felt normal. After what I would guess at perhaps fifteen minutes, I had stopped noticing any difference in the feeling. It just felt... normal.

"I think they are well matched," I said. My voice didn't sound quite right to me.

"I think so," Piia agreed. "Let us stay at this for the rest of this practice. For today."

I nodded agreement. I noticed our clothes were paying a little more of a price when a strike got through, but our swords were still honoring the instruction to do no harm to us. This was really a hell of a way to train, I thought. Incredibly effective, yet also a little terrifying.

We called a halt when we began to tire. We were both sweating, so we went off to the sauna again. We peeled off our now slightly tattered clothes, and picked up washcloths from the basket... and then Piia looked at me. And instead of washing herself off, she began to wash me down instead.

I looked into her eyes. They were very steady. So I began to wash her down with the one I held. It was the first time I had explored her body this way. I enjoyed touching her.

When we were both clean, we put our washcloths in the soiled-laundry basket and went into the sauna. We sat holding hands... I for one thinking of nothing much of anything, really, beyond just Piia beside me. We worked well together. We were beginning to anticipate each other's moves almost as soon as they began.

"Full speed tomorrow?" Piia suggested, next to me.

I nodded slowly.

"It will be interesting," I said.

Piia moved a little closer and leaned against me. I let go her hand, and put my arm around her instead. A moment later, she did the same, then reached across with her right hand. I took it in my left, closed my eyes, and relaxed.

"I'm glad it was clear," I said.

"Mmm," she replied. "Peaceful. But too quiet."

"Something out of place."

"Not right, yet."

"We will set it to rights."

"We will. *My* forest. *Mine.*"

After a while, two other people came in, hand in hand, a young couple evidently, whom I didn't know. They gave us a friendly wave and took seats over the other side. There was a lot more giggling going on over that side of the sauna. I grinned, and looked at Piia. She smiled back, then leaned in and kissed me, and I kissed back. Then we kissed a bit more.

"We should probably go," she said softly.

"I know," I agreed. "Though I don't really want to."

"There will be other days," she told me.

We disentangled, stood up, and went outside to dip, dry off and dress. I went to work on my book, while Piia needed to plan her team's next patrol sweep, planned for the day after next. They would start from the eastern pass and sweep west and south, this time.

Neither Kata nor Liisa showed up by supper time. Concerned, I went to find them. I headed for the infirmary first. The odds were high that their absence meant something bad had happened.

I was right. I could hear their voices—and others—raised in healing song before I even entered the infirmary. I recognized Raimo's voice as well.

When I entered the infirmary I saw there were two teams at work. Kata, Liisa, and Raimo were working on a young woman, while Esko, Marketta and Marja worked on a young man. Both were clearly in bad shape. Varpu was sitting nearby. She looked tired.

I went and sat down next to her.

"What happened?" I asked.

"A runaway stone-cart," she told me, exhaustedly. "Taisto saw it coming and tried to push Ingrid out of its path, but there simply was not enough time, and it hit them together and half-crushed them. Vallaïnen had to go already, to lie down and rest. We sent a messenger to find Timo and Jaana, but they have not come yet. I fear we are losing them both."

I could hear the grief in her voice, but there was nothing I could do to help. I was not a Healer. I took her hand and squeezed it, and she squeezed back weakly. She even *felt* tired, faded. I felt for her soul, finding it somehow... wan.

"You have expended a lot of energy, haven't you?" I asked.

Varpu nodded.

"I am completely spent," she agreed. "I can do no more." I felt her sadness, and it hurt.

Thoughts ran through my head. I could not help the two injured. I was not a Healer. But... could I help the *Healers*? I had a lot of power, I knew now. Surely I could find a way to share some of it?

I was a Soulbinder. Perhaps the *only* Soulbinder. What else could I do with that? I thought back to my first days awake, and the feeling of Kata and Liisa feeding energy into me. And again, the torrents they poured into me after the attack, when my soul was ripped asunder. *Could I* do that?

I thought back carefully to what it had felt like. I could not remember the low words they had chanted. They were words of Healing, and my mind would not hold them. I would just have to devise my own.

I still had Varpu's hand. In my mind, I felt again for her soul, and I touched it with my own, and willed energy to move from one to the other. Words that I knew were soul-working formed in my mind. *From my soul, to yours. Accept this gift of strength.*

I began to chant softly the words that I somehow *knew* meant what I wanted, and I *pushed*.

Varpu looked up after a moment. She looked puzzled for a second, then she turned to me.

"Alrekr...? How?"

I nodded, and pushed harder. I could feel it was working. The trickle turned into a stream, as my confidence grew. I could *do* this. The stream turned into a torrent.

Varpu raised her head. There was hope in her face. I kept pushing.

For at least ten minutes I poured energy into her, as color returned to her cheeks. Then she put her other hand over mine.

"Enough, Alrekr," she told me. "*Thank* you. Please, help the others, if you can." There was a lot more strength in her voice, and her soul no longer looked as faded.

I stopped my chant and released her hand. She leaned in and quickly kissed me, then stood and walked over to stand next to Esko at the second table. She put her hands on... Taisto, I thought she had said?—and joined her voice to the song. It rang strong and clear, revitalized.

I got up and walked over to the other table. I took a spot between Kata and Liisa, just behind them, as Raimo across the table gave me a questioning look. Then he glanced at Varpu, then back at me.

I nodded, and put a hand on each of their shoulders. Kata turned her head for a moment, enough to see me from the corner of her eye. Gods, she looked—and *sounded*—tired. I felt for their souls, and began my own chant again, and pushed everything I could spare to them. Across the table, Raimo nodded his head slowly, understanding. After a few minutes, I heard their voices begin to strengthen, saw Liisa stand a little straighter. When they seemed mostly recovered, I switched tables and boosted Esko and Marketta as much as I could. Marja was the only one who seemed not to be flagging. She really did have amazing reserves of energy, as Kata had once told me.

I intended to give my last boost to Raimo, but after only two steps toward him I realized I was light-headed and swaying. Raimo looked at me, shook his head firmly, and looked pointedly toward the chairs instead. I nodded, waited a moment for my head to clear, then carefully walked over and sat down, perhaps a little more quickly than I had intended.

About twenty minutes later, Master Timo and Mistress Jaana came hurrying in. Timo took a place next to Raimo, while Jaana went straight to the other table. A moment later their voices were added to the healing song as well.

After another hour and a half or so, Kata let her song drop and stepped back from the table.

"Enough for now," she declared. "She is out of danger. We have more work to do, but all else will wait until the morrow." The team at the other table continued working a little longer, though Marketta gratefully stepped back and let Master Timo take her place. Kata came and sat next to me. She hung her head wearily for a minute or two, and I put my arm across her shoulders. A moment later Liisa came and sat on the other side of me, and I put my other arm around her.

Kata looked up after a little, and turned to look at me.

"You saved two lives today, Alrekr," she told me. "We were losing both of them."

"I know you were," I replied. "Varpu told me. I couldn't help *them*... but it occurred to me that just maybe, I could help all of *you* to help them. So I tried, with Varpu, to see if I could feed energy to her as I remembered you feeding it to me. And it worked."

About this time, the second team wound down as well. They checked over their patient, Taisto, one more time, and then I found myself surrounded by Healers.

"You continue to find surprising new depths, Master Járnhandr," Timo told me. "What I hear is that Highwatch owes you two lives this day. I am curious how you managed it."

"I am not a Healer, as you all well know," I began. "But... neither am I a stoneworker. Yet in the sauna, I realized that I could see a way to use firebinding to accomplish much of what Tumarïnen did with stoneworking and fireworking together.

"So it occurred to me that even though I cannot Heal, perhaps I could use my Soulbinding to push energy to another's soul the way Kata and Liisa—and Varpu—have used Healing to feed energy to my body. And to my great relief, it worked."

Timo nodded thoughtfully.

"A fresh way of looking at the problem," he mused. "Yours is, as far as is known to me, a new Talent never seen before. I am glad to see you learning more about what you can do with it."

"I may have an advantage you might not have thought of," I suggested.

"Oh?" Timo replied, interested. "And what is that?"

"I don't know what I *can't* do," I said, deadpan.

Timo thought about that for a moment, then he started to chuckle. Then the chuckle turned into a full-blown laugh, and then Esko started laughing as well.

"And so you find a way to do it *anyway*," Esko said, through his laughter. "I should try that myself some time." And then everyone was laughing.

"You make a good point," Timo remarked after a minute. "We become so used to the things that everyone knows cannot be done. But... sometimes perhaps they can, by looking at the problem in a different way."

I got up and walked over myself to look at the two patients. I was feeling a little better now. The girl—Ingrid?—was pale, but her breathing was steady. I put two fingers to the side of her neck and felt for her pulse, and it was regular and stable, if a little weak. Then I reached a little further and *just so very lightly* touched her soul. I could *feel* she was stable. Her soul was the cool blue of a clear mountain sky.

I checked on Taisto as well. There was a massive bruise up his chest and the side of his face, but his breathing, too, was smooth and steady, and his pulse strong. His soul was a stony gray, but there was an inner glow of warmth to it.

"Is he a mason?" I asked.

"Yes," Timo replied. He sounded surprised. "How did you know?"

"I guessed, from the color of his soul," I said. "But he has a warm heart, I think."

Varpu nodded.

"That describes him well," she agreed.

"Has anyone here eaten supper?" I asked. There were slow head-shakes all around the room, as I expected. "Then I suggest we all go and get something to eat, now."

That idea met with general agreement.

"Journeyman Vilja is about, I think," Timo said. "I shall have her keep a watchful eye on them."

Indeed, we found Vilja without too much difficulty. She came hurrying into the infirmary just as we were all headed out, as a group. She looked at us, worn and weary as we all were, and paled slightly.

"I just got back and got word of the accident," she said anxiously.

"Is it—are they...?"

"They will be fine, Vilja," Mistress Jaana said. Vilja sagged for a moment in relief. "But if you would, please take the overnight watch on them."

"Of course, Mistress," Vilja replied. She strode into the infirmary, and we headed on to the main hall.

While the rest of the group sorted out tables, I slipped away into the kitchen.

"Master Járnhandr," said Mistress Kerttu. "What can I do for you?"

"Not so much for me, Mistress," I told her. "You have nine weary healers newly arrived in the hall. What can you do to help restore them?"

Kerttu looked at me. I saw her brace herself.

"I heard about the accident," she said. "What of the... patients?"

"They are stable and well, Mistress," I reassured her. "They will be fine."

What might be the biggest smile I had ever seen from her lit up her face.

"You go back out to the hall and find a seat, Master Járnhandr, and we will bring out some food for you all very shortly. You are clearly exhausted yourself."

Indeed, only a few minutes after I went back out and sat down— Kata and Liisa had saved a space for me between them—a few of the serving girls brought out two large baskets of bread rolls, fresh from the oven, with large rolls of butter on a board, and jars of honey. A few minutes more and flagons of mead and kuurii juice were brought out, followed shortly by two large tureens of thick soup heavy with meat, imp fingers and yellow yams. Mistress Kerttu brought one of them out herself.

"I am so very glad to hear that your healing this night was successful," she said, to our two tables in general. "I heard about the accident. I know Taisto well, he is such a nice boy."

"It was a close thing," Esko remarked. "Two at once with such severe injuries? We had two Healers down from exhaustion, the rest of us except for Marja were close, and Timo and Jaana had not arrived yet.

And then Járnhandr here walked in, saw what was happening, and somehow revived five Healers, by himself."

"And almost completely spent himself doing it," Raimo added reprovingly.

"I'll be fine by tomorrow," I said.

"No, Alrekr, you will *not*," Kata told me. "Tomorrow you will take the day to rest. That is Healer's orders. In the morning, I think you will realize how much you overspent yourself this day."

"But Ingrid and Taisto are alive," I said. "So it was worth it."

"They are," Master Timo agreed. "Thanks in large part to you."

"It was all of you who did the hard work of healing them," I pointed out. "I could only buy you some extra time."

"That time was precious," Marketta replied. "You bought us time for Timo and Jaana to return."

We finished all of the soup and bread between us, and Esko asked if there was perhaps a little more? There was no more of the soup, as it turned out, but he declared the large plate of honeycakes that arrived instead a satisfactory substitute. I had three or four myself. They were very good, filled with chopped nuts, strongly reminiscent of baklava.

When we had eaten our fill, we all still sat there, tired, knowing we needed to move, but putting it off.

"What further treatment will they need?" I asked.

"We must work more on them," Marja said. "Taisto's cheekbone is still broken, and he has a lot of severe bruising that needs attention. And his ribs need a little more work."

"Ingrid lost a lot of blood," Liisa added. "We will need to finish restoring it, and finish healing the bones in her foot. But they are both safe for the night. And in the morning, we will be rested enough to continue. A benefit of the Healing talent is that we Healers recuperate energy quickly."

She looked sternly at me.

"You do not have that benefit, Alrekr." Then her expression softened. "But still, I am glad that you came when you did."

"I was concerned when neither of you were home by supper time," I explained. "I *knew* that something bad must have happened."

"For tonight," Timo declared, "we should all rest now. I will leave instruction for Vilja to summon myself, Jaana or Mistress Sirkka if there is need during the night, but I do not expect any relapse."

I for one was more than ready to agree. We all labored to our feet, and I took my two loves by the hand and we headed off to our quarters. We went straight upstairs, helped each other to undress, and fell into bed together.

I'm not sure I even remember my head hitting the pillow.

18: Light A Fire

Kata's prediction was entirely correct. I dragged myself out of bed the next morning feeling utterly wrung out.   Kata and Liisa seemed fairly well recovered, though I could see that they were both still more tired than normal. We took the lazy option and sent a page to have breakfast brought to us, and took our time working through the large pile of bacon and mushrooms and the pot of honeyed oatmeal. Or whatever passed for oats here, I supposed. If I thought about it, it was... slightly sweeter, slightly nuttier than what I had grown up with, but now it was my 'normal'. My idea of normal had shifted.

After we finished breakfast, Kata and Liisa headed back to the infirmary, and I sat and looked at my book notes. I felt too tired to write very much, but I did make a point of pushing myself to write down some notes on the boosting technique I had discovered the night before. That was important.

After I finished those notes, I sat there for a while trying to add more, but no thoughts would come. I was too weary. I put the pen and paper away, and went to the bath-house. I sat in the sauna for a while, one of four occupants this morning, then I went to the cold pool and swam a dozen or so laps.

I emerged feeling considerably refreshed. I dried off, dressed again, and went for a walk.

It was no surprise my feet took me to the forge.

"Ho, Járnhandr," Matti called as I approached. "Are you ready to sing some fire?"

"Not today, Matti, please," I apologized. "I am sorry. I am too weary today."

He gave me a long look.

"Yes, I see that now," he replied. "I heard something about you saving a healing yesterday. How is it that you, who are not a healer, can help healers? I am curious."

"Healers' souls are the same as anyone else's," I replied. "I cannot heal alongside them, but it turns out I can boost their souls and give them energy."

"So you gave them yours," Matti said, nodding. "And that is why you are exhausted this day. It was well done, I think. We can forge Paavo's sword another day."

"Paavo has placed an order, then?" I asked.

"Yes. He is the first. I am not sure whether Ari or Jaako will be the second. We will see. And you should consider what you will charge for soulbinding."

"For Paavo and Ari, nothing," I said at once. "For any of Piia's team, nothing. For anyone else... I will have to think about it. Perhaps I can find a way to bind to a person's core without needing to go as deep as I did for Piia."

"Do you regret that, Járnhandr?" Matti asked.

"Not for a second," I replied. "I would be a poorer person if I did not know Piia as deeply as I do now."

Matti looked at me and nodded.

"If I may offer a little advice?" he offered.

"Of course. Always."

"If you can find a way to soulbind beyond those who you are close to, *without*... putting undue weight on yourself, ask no less than two hundred silvers for it. If not three hundred. And even that may be low."

I added numbers in my head.

"For orders from outside Highwatch, that will put the cost close to a thousand silvers for a soulbound sword," I said.

Matti nodded agreement.

"And they will pay it gladly," he declared. "Once the word spreads of what a Highwatch soulbound sword can do."

I realized I was feeling just a very little less tired than I had been. I closed my eyes and thought about it, trying to analyze whether I was doing something I was not aware of. It did not take me too long to realize that I was drawing into myself from the forge. Just a little.

"Interesting," I murmured.

"Hmm?"

"I am drawing from your forge. Drawing energy from it. And did not even realize I was doing it."

"Well then by all means, sit here and draw from it."

"No, Matti," I replied. "If I am drawing heat off your forge, you cannot work. There are other fires I can draw from. I will see you later. Tomorrow perhaps."

A thought occurred to me.

"Oh... Piia's team leaves tomorrow for a patrol sweep west and south. We will be unable to forge Paavo's sword until they return, if he wants it soulbound—which I assume he will."

Matti nodded.

"Go find a fire, Járnhandr," he told me. "Refresh yourself."

The obvious place was the Rangerhall. I could feel *that* fireplace from across Highwatch. So that is where I went.

Paavo greeted me moments after I entered the Hall. He looked at me critically.

"You look weary," he said.

"I am," I agreed. "And so I came to sit in front of the fireplace here. I learned this day that I can draw energy from a large fire to refresh myself."

Paavo nodded.

"Useful," he observed. Then he turned and called for more wood to be added to the fire. I gratefully sank down on the closest bench to the fire.

"I am afraid training is off for today," I told him. "One should not train with swords when tired."

Paavo nodded agreement.

"Wise," he agreed. "I have ordered a sword like yours from Matti. Would you... consider soulbinding it for me?"

"Paavo," I replied, "you are a part of Piia's team. You are the closest I have in this land to brothers and sisters. Of *course* I will."

"Thank you, Master Járnhandr," he said.

"No," I corrected him. "Alrekr. To any of your team I am Alrekr." I reached and clasped his hand. "I said brothers and sisters, and I meant it."

Paavo nodded.

"Brothers in arms it is, then," he agreed. "I saw the last time you and Piia sparred. I would not willingly go up against you with a sword. Except sparring. You have become very much better than when you

319

began. You are every bit the equal of Ari or myself now."

"A lot of that, I think, is Piia's training, and Sekai," I told him. "When you have your own, you will understand."

"Then I have a lot to look forward to," he said. "Rest and recuperate, Alrekr. Word has spread about the two whose healing you saved last night. It was well done."

"You're the second person who has said that to me this day," I replied. "Though my ladies chided me for expending so much energy."

"Of course they did, Alrekr," Paavo told me. "All of Highwatch knows how deeply they love you, and how you love them.

"Now rest. We have a patrol sweep tomorrow, and I have duties to attend to." And he went off to see to them.

A little later, Piia came in, and walked over and sat down next to me without a word. None were needed. I put an arm around her, and sat and drew energy from the fire.

"Paavo has ordered a sword from Matti," I mentioned after a little while.

"I know," she said.

"I'm going to soulbind it for him."

She turned and kissed me.

"Thank you, Alrekr. Ari is thinking about it, too."

"I know. Matti mentioned it. And Commander Jaako, I understand."

"He has been watching us train, Alrekr. He is impressed."

"Well," I said, "I hope I don't disappoint him."

After a couple of hours sitting in front of the fire soaking up energy from it, I felt much refreshed. Liisa had noticed in the past that I was drawing from the sauna stones, I recalled. But I could draw a lot more from the fire than I could from the stones, and draw it faster and more easily. It *did* come at the cost of additional wood to maintain the fire.

"How do you feel about a late sparring session? I think I'm recovered enough, if we take it fairly easily."

Piia looked at me.

"I admit I had other ideas for you, Alrekr. But that would also be good. Not a good day to try it at full speed, though, as we planned to."

"I agree. But half boost, again, I think I can do. Perhaps just for a little while."

"Being careful," she nodded. "Good. Yes, let us do that. We can use one of the sparring rings outside."

And that is what we did. We took it easy, indeed, using a little boost from our swords, but focusing more on our form than on anything else. For the first time, I felt that I was perhaps getting close to being on par with Piia. It felt wonderful.

We sparred for about an hour before we called it enough for the day, and then went back to sit in front of the fire again. I soaked up energy from the fire for another hour or so before I got up from the bench.

"I have an urge to go and see how things are in the infirmary," I told Piia. "How long do you expect to be out on your sweep tomorrow?"

"Two days," Piia replied. "We will work our way around to the southwest, and then return by the direct route. One big loop."

"May it be uneventful," I wished. Then we kissed, and I went on my way.

At the infirmary, I found my lovers just preparing to leave for the day. Ingrid and Taisto were out of treatment and in a recovery room, and expected to make a full recovery.

"They insisted on the same room, Alrekr," Liisa told me. "So we had a second bed moved into one room. And *then* they insisted the beds be placed close enough together that they could hold hands." She had a huge smile.

"That sounds very much as though romance is in the air," I said, with a grin. Liisa nodded happily.

"Indeed, I think we will see a betrothal before long," Kata agreed.

"Shall we go and get some supper?" I suggested. Both agreed immediately, so off we went.

"You seem much... restored," Kata observed, on the way. I nodded.

"Today I learned that I can draw off energy from a large fire," I explained.

Liisa nodded thoughtfully.

"I remember you were drawing from the stones in the sauna one day," she remarked.

"Yes. But now I know that I can draw more from a fire, and with less effort."

"Well, let us find a place near to the fireplace in the feast-hall, then," Kata said. "You still seem tired." And that was what we did.

The main offering for supper was karjalanpaisti, which had become a favorite of mine. Funny about that. Mistress Kerttu sent out kuurii juice for the three of us along with the mead, and we were all grateful to take it.

"Paavo has placed an order with Matti for a sword," I said. Kata nodded.

"Will you soulbind it?" she asked.

"Yes," I replied. "I told him that as far as I am concerned, their team are the closest I have to brothers and sisters."

"And Piia?" Liisa asked. It was not a casual question, I knew. But I could not quite decode her tone and expression.

"No," I said slowly. "Piia is... more." Liisa nodded approvingly.

"Piia is not a part of our troth-bond," she mused. "But I think... she has become part of us, nevertheless." I nodded, glad that she agreed, and saw Kata nod agreement as well.

"How goes your training with her, Alrekr?" Kata asked.

"It is going very well," I said. "Paavo commented today on how much my swordwork has come along. Though I do not truly know how much of it is me, and how much I owe to Sekai. I *know* I owe a great deal to Piia's coaching. She has brought me a long way in a short time."

"She could not have done so had you not already had much of the groundwork, and the reflexes," came a voice I knew from behind us.

I turned. It was Knight-Commander Jaako, as I thought.

"Forgive my interruption," he apologized. "May I join you?"

"Of course," I said. "Be welcome."

He sat himself down in the one open chair at our table.

"You continue to build a reputation, Master Járnhandr," he said. "If not one thing, then another. These swords that you and Master Smith Matti have created are unheard of in this land.

"I am on the edge of deciding to order one for myself. If I were to do so... would you be willing to consider soulbinding it to me? I know that it is no small thing to ask."

I thought for a moment.

"Matti had mentioned that you were one of his order prospects," I replied. "And so I was already considering the question. I have already told Paavo that I will bind his. It is in my mind to see whether I can find a way to touch someone enough to bind a sword to them, without having to forge as deep a bond as I have with Piia." Jaako nodded, at that. "There is only so far I can spread myself. I am thinking I will make Paavo my first try at this."

"That is a good thought," Jaako agreed. Then he looked at me very directly.

"Piia adores you, you know."

"I am aware," I agreed. "And I love her also."

"And so do I," Liisa interjected.

"And I," Kata agreed. "She is ours. She has become a part of us. Not by anyone's plan or design, but... we are happy that it happened."

Jaako looked back and forth between us, surprise in his expression at first. Then he nodded slowly, and a broad smile split his face.

"I am glad to hear that," he said. "I was concerned that it might all end in tears. And she is my best team leader. Her well-being is my responsibility.

"But now I see that I was worried over nothing."

"Not nothing," I said. "You had a legitimate concern. I... was worried myself at first. I did not intend to forge such a strong bond. I feared that I had acted with insufficient thought for, and understanding of, the consequences. But my, my..." I hesitated. I found myself not wanting to say 'wives'. There was so much pain still tied to that word. "My life-partners convinced me that I had not made the mis-step I feared I might have."

I reached out and took their hands.

"I would not willingly or knowingly do anything that would hurt

323

Liisa or Kata. And neither would I willingly or knowingly hurt Piia. She has become precious to me. Her soul... fits... against mine in a different way than theirs."

"She adds strength to us," Liisa added.

Jaako nodded, his smile deeper, if anything.

"Watching the two of you spar is... eye-opening," he declared. "And Piia mentioned that your swords have the capability to, to... speed you even further than that." I nodded. "The two of you move as though you are one."

"We have not tried at full... boost yet," I replied. "We planned to today. But I spent myself completely last night and thought we should not risk it."

"I must say, you look quite unspent now," Jaako commented.

"It is no accident that we chose this table," I explained. "The entire time that we have been sitting here, I have been drawing energy from that fire. I learned today how to do that. But I thought Matti would not appreciate it were I to drain the heat from his forge."

Jaako chuckled.

"I imagine he would not, at that," he said. Then he cocked an eye at me. "However, I think that in your case, he would not have made too great an objection, under the circumstances."

"He did in fact encourage me to sit where I was," I agreed. "But there are other large, hot fires in Highwatch."

"And that is why you spent half the afternoon sitting in our Hall," Jaako said, nodding.

"Exactly," I confirmed. "Regaining energy I spent last night."

Kata was giving me a curious look. I raised a questioning eyebrow in her direction.

"I have been thinking about this," she said slowly. "I freely grant I am no firesinger, but this is not something I have ever heard of a firesinger being able to do."

I pondered. I had read Vehviläinen's first three books. We did not have copies of the other two. And I had encountered no such thing in Tumarïnen's book, either.

"You... do raise a question," I mused. "Can we borrow copies of Vehviläinen's other two books? I would like to see whether he says anything of it."

"I will see what I can do," Kata replied.

"You know, we... um. Hmm. Never mind."

"What, Alrekr?" Kata asked. I thought for a moment.

"I... can find no Saamen word," I said. "But Saamen and, uh, *Suomi* are very similar. Would you know what I meant if I spoke of a *painakone*?"

Kata frowned.

"I have never heard that word," she said. "What does it mean?"

I nodded to myself. Here, for once, was a case where the Talents of the Sunlit Land fell short of technology. A technology which I was increasingly learning to live without, and, I realized, seldom missing very much of it. But some of it would be handy now.

"All right, then." I thought about Saamen word roots I could use. "How about... perhaps we could call it a *kirjoituskone*?" No, wait, I realized. That was an actual Finnish word that meant a typewriter. It was close, but not quite right.

I tried again. "How about... *kirjoitekone*? A writing engine?"

She shook her head.

"I have not heard of such a thing. What is it?"

"It is a... a device for quickly making copies of books and other written things," I said. "Many copies in a comparatively short time. Page by page. You would have to..." There was no word for 'print,' of course. "You would have to individually prepare it for each page of a book, but then once prepared, you could make a hundred copies of that page in an hour."

Kata gasped.

"That would be *amazing!*" she exclaimed. "It would make it so easy to copy books!"

"Yes," I agreed. "But there is a problem. I think... that to copy—for instance—one of Vehviläinen's books, the... engine would have to understand the dialect of firesinging, and I think that means the engine itself would have to be able to access fire *voima*. And think as I might, I am utterly at a loss to even guess at how such a thing could be accomplished." Kata nodded thoughtfully.

"The only *other* way I can think of," I continued, "would be if every Adept who wished to have a book copied had to personally make the... plates to... copy each individual page. And even then I cannot say for sure whether that would work."

325

Kata nodded.

"But what about books written entirely in common Saamen?" she asked.

"Hmm. Yes," I agreed. "For those, it should present no problem."

"Can you write up a description and explanation that we could send to the Collegium?" Kata asked me.

"I... think so," I said. "It might take a little thought to figure out how to communicate some of the ideas in Saamen for which it has no words... yet."

"Take your time, Alrekr," Kata told me. "It is not urgent."

Jaako had been following along with considerable interest this whole time, but now he stood and excused himself.

"I am sorry to walk away from such an interesting discussion," he said, "but I have to be going." I was struck again as he stood by how *big* Jaako was. From a distance he didn't look overly large, because he was so perfectly normal in proportions, but when he stood I was reminded that he had a good five inches on me, perhaps six. I looked him up and down, thinking. He paused.

"Is there something, Járnhandr?"

"I was just thinking," I said. I tapped Sekai's hilt lightly. "An idea. Sekai is a *katana*. Or to use the more proper form of the word, an *uchigatana*. But for you, with your height and reach... I wonder whether we should be thinking in terms of a *tachi*. I think you would be terrifying with a *tachi*."

"What is that?" he asked curiously.

"Imagine a sword like Sekai, but more deeply curved, and as long as Liisa is tall," I said. His eyebrows rose. "I think I would be badly wrong if I did not guess you have the strength to wield one well."

A thoughtful look crossed his face.

"That... sounds intriguing," he admitted. "I have never seen a sword that length. But before you came to Highwatch, I had never seen a curved sword, either."

"It is of course more difficult to draw," I pointed out. "Simply because the blade is so long. Let me speak about it with Matti tomorrow, and see what he thinks about whether we can forge one."

He nodded, and half-bowed.

"I thank you again," he said. "Now I truly must go. Good night to

326

you all."

We got up, too, and headed back to our tower, hand in hand. When we got there, Kata looked thoughtfully at the fireplace.

"Can you regain energy from *this* fire, Alrekr?" she asked.

I looked at it, felt for it.

"I don't see why not, in principle," I said. "But it is a small fire. There is little energy in it to draw in the first place."

"Would you try?" she said. "I saw no... well, *little* change in the fire in the hall. But I am curious to see whether a fire this small dims or weakens when you draw from it. And to see how much you can draw."

"All right," I agreed. "As you wish, my love."

I reached for the fire and drew on it as hard as I could. I got a brief surge of energy from it. Then the fire did not simply dim. It went out, leaving the room lit only by the glowstones.

"Huh," I said. I hadn't expected that.

"Interesting indeed," Kata said slowly.

"That... might be a useful trick to know sometime," I mused. "A way to *put out* an unwanted fire."

I went to the fireplace, picked up Rod, invoked it, and went to relight the fire.

"Huh," I said, again. I tried harder. But the wood simply would not relight. It looked... pitted. It crumbled to powder when I poked hard at it. Kata watched intently. Eventually I had to empty the entire fireplace into the ash bucket and lay a new fire with fresh wood. *That* lit merrily at the first touch of Rod.

"How *very* interesting," I remarked.

"Indeed," Kata agreed. "As though you drained even the *capacity* for fire from the wood. I am certain now that I have heard of no firesinger ever doing *that* before."

Liisa, too, was paying close attention.

"Could there be some greater talent that lies beyond firesinging?" she asked.

Kata looked thoughtful.

"Alrekr is to my knowledge the first ever Soulbinder," she said, mostly to Liisa. "Why not this as well? We *both* know the power of his core."

She turned to me and put her hands upon me, then reconsidered, put her arms around me and held me close. I felt her reaching for my core. The way she did it, it felt like being kissed on the inside. I shivered deliciously, and held her tightly.

"... And he has grown even *stronger* now," she said. She drew her head back slightly to look at me.

"Exactly what *are* you, Alrekr Járnhandr?" Her tone was musing, curious.

"A man who loves you both very much," I said, "and counts himself incredibly fortunate to be here." She laughed, and kissed me. Exactly the outcome I had hoped for. "And what else, I do not know," I continued, less light-heartedly. "But it's been a hell of a ride finding out, so far."

"It does worry me a little," Liisa observed. "If, as we have wondered, the world brought you here for some specific purpose... then what purpose? You do not send for a cart horse to carry a single book."

She made a good point. I could not pretend it wasn't a thought that hadn't crossed my own mind. But then Piia came into my mind.

"That is not a problem for today," I said. "Let us not dwell on it. It is time for us to go to bed, I think."

That idea met with unanimous approval. And this night, unlike the last, we had the energy for lovemaking. We didn't let it go to waste.

19: Something Wicked

I went back to the forge after breakfast the next morning, returning to my normal routine. As I had promised Commander Jaako, I raised the subject of a *tachi* with Matti.

"An even greater forging challenge," he mused thoughtfully. "It will take half again as much steel, perhaps more. And that final quench will be terrifying. I'll need a longer—and wider—quench trough for it."

"Hmm," I observed. "You said 'will', not 'would'."

Matti looked at me, grinning broadly.

"You just put a new challenge in front of me, Járnhandr," he said. "Did you think for a second I wouldn't take it?"

I laughed out loud.

"I wouldn't have, had I given it a thought," I replied, answering his grin with my own.

"So why did this come up?" he asked. "What spurred the thought?"

"You have a probable order coming from Knight-Commander Jaako," I said. Matti nodded. "Have you looked at the *size* of the man?"

Matti paused.

"You make a good point," he agreed. "Did you happen to mention this—*tachi*—to him?"

"That is precisely why I brought it up," I said. Matti grinned again.

We had a couple of days' backlog to catch up on, so we didn't get to take any further steps down that path on that day. But we got most of the way through the pending work, and Matti sorted out ores for smelting a set of larger steel ingots for when we were caught up.

After we packed up for the day, I went to lead *kata* for Kauko, Ilona and Päivi. With only the three students again, I rotated through them letting each in turn take Sekai and try the movements of the *kata* with Sekai, to feel how different they felt with the *katana* instead of the longsword. Päivi, in particular, got it nearly immediately. I saw the

329

light go on and a smile spread across her face as understanding dawned, and I grinned.

That evening, we sent out for dinner again, and I sat down and clarified my notes on the soulbinding method of boosting. I didn't know whether anyone else would ever be able to use it. But it was worth writing it down, all the same.

"Kata," I asked, out of curiosity, "how much of this can you read?" I handed her a page of my notes. She pored over it, and I could see her lips move as she tried to parse words that would not stand still for her to read them. Finally she gave up.

"Perhaps half," she replied. I wrapped an arm around her.

"I'm sorry," I said. "I was... curious. I wondered how much of what I had written was in common Saamen, and how much not—and how much of what was *not*, you could puzzle out. Given that you already know how to do much the same using Healing."

Kata leaned over and kissed me.

"No apology needed, love," she told me. "I was curious as well. I know you would fare no better reading detailed notes on Healing were I to write them down."

"*Have* you written a book on Healing?" I asked. If she had, I wanted to see how far I could get through it.

"No," she said. "Better healers than I have written books. There are many books on healing, and I have read all I could obtain copies of. There is nothing I can add to any of them. Or I would have."

"Not even on head injuries?" I asked. "Everyone I have talked to has led me to believe that you are a miracle worker with head injuries."

I looked at Liisa for confirmation, and she nodded.

"When Kauko was thrown and smashed his head on a rock," I pointed out, "it was you—you, *specifically*, by name, and no other—whom Raimo sent for."

Kata hesitated, then thought for a while.

"There may be something in what you say," she mused. "I will give the matter thought, I promise." Then she kissed me again. I never tired of that.

The next day, Matti and I cleared the rest of the backlog, then smelted and folded a set of larger ingots for a *tachi*. Jaako had not yet confirmed his order, so we went no further than that, just in case. Matti told me, though, that he had ordered a second, larger quenching trough from the carpenters. One way or another, we would be forging a *tachi* before too long.

At *kata* class, I repeated what I had done yesterday, letting each student in turn go through the *kata* with Sekai, coaching and critiquing form in each individual technique. Kauko expressed a desire to stick with his reforged sword for now, though Ilona began to show more interest and was clearly beginning to get the feel of the different balance and heft. I was eager to spar, but... Piia would not be back until tomorrow, and as I thought upon what Jaako and Paavo had said, I had the feeling that it might be unfair to spar against these students with Sekai and the skills Piia had drilled into me, experienced Rangers though they all were.

Instead, I went back early to our rooms, and I spent the rest of the afternoon carefully writing down everything I could remember about printing presses and movable type, trying as far as I could to describe everything in terms that I hoped would let anyone with the necessary skills design and build a printing press based upon the description I had written.

When Liisa came in, I called her over.

"Liisa, my love, would you do something for me?"

"In just one moment," she replied. She walked over to me, threw her arms around my neck, and kissed me. Of course, I kissed her back and hugged her to me. The writing would wait.

"There, that is better," she declared, a few minutes later. I grinned. "Now, what did you wish to ask of me?"

I handed her the description I had just written out.

"I wrote this description today of what a—a *kirjoitekone* is, how it works, every detail I could remember," I explained. "I *hope* it is enough information to build one. Would you please read this and tell me whether you understand what I have written?"

She took the sheets, glanced over them quickly, then kissed me again and sat down to read them.

"If you find anything that is unclear or unreadable," I said, "please

331

tell me, and we will mark it, and we will go back over it later together and see how I can make it clearer."

She nodded and began to read.

"Well," she declared, when she was done, "first, there are no words that I could not read."

"That's a good start," I said.

"Beyond that... I think I understood *most* of it. There were parts I did not clearly follow; but it is less, I think, that I do not understand your explanations, and more that I do not understand the thing that you are describing and explaining. I think that you should show them to Smith Matti, or—no, better yet, to Mill-Master Kustaa. I think of all the people I know in Highwatch, he is the one most likely to understand what you are describing."

"That sounds like an excellent suggestion," I agreed. "I shall have to track him down and ask him to read them."

Not long after that, Kata arrived home. I asked her to read through my description as well, and she agreed that it was clearly written and fully in common Saamen, aside from the few Finnish words I had offered for printing, but needed someone with the skills of an artificer to fully understand what I was explaining. We strolled casually down to the great hall to get supper, finding a number of the other Healers and Matti, and ate supper there before coming back to spend a couple of hours snuggling in front of the fire with a bottle of honeywine, doing nothing in particular. Then after we finished the bottle, we decided we might as well continue our snuggling in bed.

So we got an early night, and did just that.

We had a leisurely breakfast the next morning in the hall, and then went about our days. Kata had no specific duties assigned her that day, while Liisa, it turned out, was to attend a confinement and delivery at a farm some three hours' travel to the south-east. I was glad that it was in the opposite direction to any anticipated danger.

For me, it was straight to the forge, only to find out that there was little work to do. Piia's team was due in today, I knew, but I was not sure when she would be coming in. So I asked for directions to the mill.

It was of course outside the wall, on the river that rushed down out of the mountains. It didn't take me long to find. Mill-Master Kustaa, however, was not there. I quickly realized that I had asked the wrong question.

I took the opportunity to take a look around the mill, though, escorted by one of the mill-hands to keep me out of trouble, an enthusiastic young man named Taivi who was only too glad to point out mechanical details to me. I took particular interest in such things as wooden and bronze gearing, power shafts running in plain bearings greased with tallow, wrought-iron fittings, pulleys carrying leather drive belts. By the time I completed my exploration, I had good confidence that if the Sunlit Land had the level of technology—no, *artifice*—needed to build and maintain this mill, it was sufficient to build a basic hand-powered printing press. And that, over time, ought to increase the supply of non-specialist general-knowledge books enough to open up much earlier literacy to nearly everyone.

I went back to Highwatch, and with the aid of a few pages, I was able to track down Mill-Master Kustaa. He listened to what I had to say, and told me that he would be only too happy to read my description and see whether he understood it well enough to assess whether he thought it could be built. We made an arrangement to meet the next day, and I would give him a copy of my notes to evaluate.

By then it was around noon, so I met Kata for luncheon, along with Raimo, Master Timo, and Vallaïnen. We ended up talking about the *kirjoitekone*, and I said that I had arranged to give a copy of my description to Mill-Master Kustaa, which of course meant that I needed to write up a second copy that evening. We sat for some time talking about what it might facilitate.

"I am pretty certain it won't work for any specialist books," I explained, "because I can't come up with any way to bind the *voima* aspects into the plates. But even if I could, the truth is I don't believe that the... engine could print them. We know from long experience that someone who cannot grasp the aspects of *voima* in the script of a book cannot even read the words, much less understand them—we tried it again just yesterday. I wrote out notes explaining how to use Soulbinding to transfer energy to another, and Kata—who, I remind you, can do that very same thing using Healing talent—could read barely half of it. So I don't think I can come up with a *kirjoitekone* that can copy a book written by an Adept without the Adept actually making the plates—and even then I am skeptical that it would work.

333

"But if we could make a *kirjoitekone* that could copy books in common Saamen—Kata, you and Liisa both teach as well as healing. How much more quickly and easily do you think children could be taught to read, if every child could be given their own reading primer?"

Kata's eyes widened. Timo and Vallaïnen both looked very thoughtful.

"That could be a wonder," Timo said. "Though possibly the scribes would complain that it threatened their livelihood if they were no longer needed every time someone must send a letter.

"If such an objection were to be raised," I replied, "I would point out that not everyone will be able to learn to read and write all at once, and there would be a great many more letters being written that those who could not write for themselves yet needed a scribe to answer for them."

"Not an unfair point," Vallaïnen chuckled.

"Kata and Liisa and I talked about this once. About how knowledge wants to be free, and how sharing knowledge as widely as possible makes everyone better off over the long run. I would hope that scribes would see the wisdom in this also."

"Sad to say," Raimo replied, "it would be far from the first time that selfishness and greed have led men to act against their own long-term best interest."

I sighed sadly.

"Indeed," I agreed. "That was an absolute plague in my past life. It ruined so much—because so many people could not stand to see another have the same things they had."

I thought for a moment further, then dragged myself out of it and shook my head. I wasn't falling into that trap again.

"But that is the past," I said. "It is out of my hands. Let it be done with."

We finished our luncheon, and went about our day. I ran—well, really, it had become more than merely *kata* practice; I ran my *kenjutsu* class, taking extra time over it that I would otherwise have spent sparring with Piia, and then I went and ran a little on the walls, and went for a quick sauna and dip.

I was walking back toward the main gate and keep after the bath-house when Piia's team came in. I saw them come in through the gate, looking calm and relaxed, and went to meet them.

"How was it?" I called, as soon as I was close enough.

"Clear," Ari called back to me as he dismounted. "Though still, the forest is quieter than it should be. Too many animals are fled or in hiding."

Piia dismounted and handed her reins to an ostler, then walked straight up to me, threw her arms around me and kissed me, and I kissed her back. Behind her, the rest of the team was dismounting as well. The ostlers were beginning to lead the horses away.

"Uneventful?" I said.

"Uneventful," she confirmed.

We all turned and began to walk in the direction of the Rangerhall. Then suddenly Simo froze. I felt something in the air that I did not know how to describe.

I looked at Simo. He was staring fixedly to the northwest.

"Simo?" Piia asked. "What?"

There was a pause.

"Rift," Simo said distantly. "A big one."

Piia hesitated for only a moment.

"MOUNT UP!" she called. "We're going back out!" She turned briefly to me as she headed back to her horse. "I'm sorry, Alrekr."

I turned to the nearest free ostler.

"Find me a horse," I told him. "Now. *Hurry.*" He ran into the stables.

I turned again to find Piia looking at me. I nodded to her. She hesitated... then a moment later, she nodded back.

A few minutes later, I was mounted on a red roan, and we were headed back out of Highwatch and arcing around it to the northwest. Simo led, and we followed.

"You really aren't dressed for this, Alrekr," Piia called to me as we rode.

"It can't be helped," I replied. "I have nothing better."

"Then we shall see about that when we get back," she told me.

An hour and a half saw us in the foothills above Highwatch, the forest starting to thin ahead of us.

"How far, Simo?" Piia asked.

"Can't... say," he replied, slowly. "Not close. But not far. Still ahead. Not in the pass. Nearer than that. That way." He pointed.

We slowed, and fanned out a little from the narrow column we'd ridden in so far. I thought I caught a whiff of something sour on the wind. Karel looked uneasy.

"What is that sour scent?" I asked.

"I don't know," he replied. Then, "Hold!"

Everyone stopped. He listened.

"Thought I heard... something," he said. Then his head snapped to the left. In that direction, I thought I heard a faint squeal.

"Boar," he said. "Running south. Fleeing... something."

The wind shifted a little more directly from the north. Karel's nostrils flared. One of the horses whinnied. I got a faint whiff of something thick, sour, rancid.

"*Troll*," Karel declared flatly.

"Simo, the horses," Piia said, dismounting as she spoke. "Everyone else, with me. Karel, lead. Avi, Ragne, left flank. Paavo, Eino, right. Alrekr, stay close to me."

I handed my reins to Simo and moved up onto Piia's right, about three paces away. Karel led, about five paces in front of us.

"A little to the west," he said quietly. We all adjusted, following his lead.

After a few minutes, I began to hear an irregular, fairly rapid thumping, but I did not know what it was.

"Coming right at us," Karel said. "And quickly."

I began to hear crashing ahead, then we reached the edge of a small clearing. A moment after, something came out of the trees on the other side. It was big, and it was blue-gray, and it smashed a tree aside as it broke out through the tree-line. It had to be over twenty feet tall.

"Flankers spread out," Piia ordered. "Here it comes."

It saw us, I think, and charged. Whether it saw us or not, it was coming straight at us. Its movements seemed slow, but it covered a lot of ground with each step. I felt each footfall through the ground.

"*Keep moving* when fighting a troll, Alrekr," Piia called to me. "Don't stand still. If it gets one good hit on you, it's over." She was circling left of its charge, I saw, so I drew Sekai and circled to the right.

"Full boost!" I called to Piia. She looked at me for a second, then nodded.

Full speed, I told Sekai. The world slowed.

All except Piia.

Karel was running back and forth in an evasive pattern, trying to draw the troll's attention, falling back between Piia and myself. Beyond Piia I could see Ari and, behind him, Ragne circling around. Eino and Paavo were doing the same behind me, I was sure. Ragne had already loosed an arrow. The arrow seemed to be moving almost lazily.

My tunic was much more conspicuous than the Rangers' leathers, I realized, which was why the troll wasn't following Karel's bait. It was looking directly at me, its left hand swinging my way in a low, flailing swipe.

But I had Sekai, and Sekai was boosting me. I backstepped and spun, dodging the blow, turning the momentum into a spinning draw-cut that slashed across the hand as it passed me. I felt the blade tug for a moment, and two fingers the size of summer sausages flew loose as I danced clear.

It bellowed. Okay, it was mad now. Or hurt. Probably both. It turned and glared at me as I dodged away sidewise. I looked up at it, at just the right moment to watch Eino's arrow smack into its face just at the inner corner of its left eye.

That drew an even louder bellow, still in slow motion. I saw its gaze start to shift away from me as it looked for what had just stung it in the face. I was alright with that. I glanced back that way and spotted Paavo, about halfway between the troll and Eino. Eino was just fitting another arrow.

I looked to see where Piia was. She was almost directly behind the troll, Ari closing on her. Behind them both, Ragne had just loosed a second arrow. I was back on the troll's side by now, the troll looking toward Paavo and Eino.

An idea flashed into my mind. The troll was distracted.

"ANKLES!" I shouted to Piia. "TAKE RIGHT!" Then I charged in.

Piia got it immediately. She sprinted for the troll's right leg, and I went for the left. I got there a second—subjective—before Piia did. I

337

pulled Sekai back over my right shoulder, then slashed with all my force across the back of its calf, letting my momentum carry me past and to its rear as I spun.

I heard the Achilles tendon go. Dark purple blood sprayed. Then I was past and heading away, in a perfect position to watch Piia do almost the same to its right leg. She spun and danced out to the side, heading outside the arc of its arm. The troll staggered, then in slow-motion, its knees buckled under it. I saw Ragne's third arrow smack into the back of its neck next to her second, then it went to its knees with a heavy thud that I felt through the ground. There were... suppurating wounds across its back. Something black oozed from them.

The troll flailed and managed to keep from falling forward, but began to topple backward instead as I dodged clear. It landed flat on its back with an even heavier *crash*, and a bass WHOOF! of sour exhaled air. I saw it start to roll my way, perhaps trying to get back to its feet. As it rolled, it looked directly at me.

The troll didn't bellow. It whimpered. I don't know how much humanity a troll has, but I would swear I saw fear in its eyes. Fear, and terrible pain.

The troll's left arm, the one with the maimed hand, started to rise. It looked as though its right arm wouldn't move. It lifted its head slightly. It seemed to be having difficulty breathing.

I took two quick paces forward, Sekai low at my left side, cut upward, and slashed through the troll's throat. I dodged most of the gush of dark blood as I ducked back.

The troll let its head and its arm drop, still looking at me. It sighed, a last bubbling breath that sprayed blood. Then its eyes slowly lost focus, and it died.

I released Sekai's boost.

"That was a very strange troll-fight," Ari said slowly from behind me. I looked at Piia. She nodded.

"Did you see its wounds?" I asked. "And its breathing sounded... labored."

"I did," she agreed. Then she sheathed Tuuli, took hold of the troll's right arm, and started dragging it out away from the body. Karel stepped in to help. The troll's upper arm was laid open to the bone on the inside, next to a matching gash that exposed several ribs. The wounds were black and seeping, and they *stank*.

"That's the foul smell I caught on the wind," I said. "The wounds." Karel nodded agreement.

Now that we knew to look, we saw other wounds, both slashes and deep punctures with black around them. Almost like gangrene, I thought.

"This troll was not set on attacking us," Karel said slowly. "We were just in its way. It was terrified, and running for its life."

"I think you are right," I agreed. "I... feel a little guilty. But perhaps the question is what it was running *from*."

Karel and Piia both nodded.

"There is little a troll runs from," Piia replied, "except perhaps a dragon. And I do not believe that these wounds were made by dragon-fire. Or dragon's talons."

She looked around.

"Nobody hurt?"

Everyone declared themselves good to go. On an impulse, I walked back to the troll's head and closed the huge eyes with my hand. Karel, watching, nodded approval.

Paavo whistled for Simo, and a few minutes later he caught up to us.

"The rift?" Piia asked.

"Still open," Simo nodded. "That way." The direction the troll had come from.

"We go on," Piia declared.

We mounted up again and headed onward. My horse was a little skittish at first at the smell of all the troll blood on me, and I could hardly blame it. There was a pungent note under the blood smell, too.

We rode on for another twenty minutes, leaving the upper fringes of the forest behind us, before Karel called a halt again.

"Movement ahead, I think," he advised. We were approaching the mouth of a deep ravine no more than twenty or thirty yards wide at the bottom.

"On foot from here," Piia ordered.

She left Simo in charge of the horses again. We spread out in a skirmish line, Piia in the center, Karel to her left, Ari and Paavo on the flanks, the two archers in the rear, and slowly advanced into the ravine.

"Does Simo always stay with the horses?" I asked Piia, keeping my voice low.

"I prefer not to risk him in battle if I can avoid it," Piia replied. "He is a, a finder, a seeker, a diviner, not a fighter. We are lucky to have him, and I will not chance him if I do not have to. Though he is not without means to fight, if he must."

I nodded.

"How many teams have... seekers?"

"Only mine. Which makes it doubly important to preserve him."

"Something ahead," Karel stated quietly. I listened, but heard nothing at first. Then... what *could* have been stone on stone came faintly down the ravine.

The ravine bent to the right, some distance ahead. We could not see beyond the bend, particularly since it was getting late in the afternoon—early evening, really—and the shadows were deepening in the steep-sided ravine. We were halfway to the bend when a knot of dark, misshapen figures came boiling around the corner. I saw what looked like spiked clubs, and barbed spears, and hacking... cleavers was the best word that fit. They yammered in a shrill and completely incomprehensible gabble as they ran at us.

"Cut them down!" Piia called. We drew, and charged to meet them. A barbed spear flew my way, passing just over my head. I batted it aside with Sekai and kept going.

The creatures were short, oddly proportioned, but they were fast, and they came onward without hesitation. I half-boosted and cut into them, staying far enough from Piia that we were not in each other's way, close enough that they could not force their way between us. To my right, Paavo centered himself in the remaining gap. One might have been able to slip past between him and the wall, or between him and me, but they did not try—they came directly for the five of us. We carved our way into the pack, severing limbs and heads, opening bodies, parrying everything that came our way. Then I glimpsed something fly by high overhead.

"WARE BEHIND!" I shouted, trying to look past the mob in front of us to see where it had come from. I saw them right away, half a dozen slingers and as many spearmen, up by the bend.

340

"Piia," I called. "Slingers." She glanced my way, I pointed with Sekai. I saw two more whatever-they-were go overhead, then one of the slingers went down with an arrow in its throat. A moment later, a second followed. Eino and Ragne had spotted them and were taking care of business.

"Never mind," I amended. Piia grinned.

"Speed?" she called to me. "Split them."

I nodded. We went to full boost and waded into the middle of the pack, cutting a path up the center. It was butchery. Behind us, Karel, Ari and Paavo denied any exit. After only a minute or so, we broke out through the back of the pack. I parried another thrown spear. Three spearers were left at the corner, and the last slinger went down as I looked. Piia and I turned around, trusting Eino and Ragne to take care of the last three spearers, and we smashed what remained of the pack between the five of us, then I released the boost.

"These did not inflict the wounds on that troll," I began to say, in the pause after I cut my last opponent down.

Then I saw Karel's eyes widen. I spun around, and so did Piia.

Something had just come around the bend. It was big, easily fifteen feet tall, almost black, a horror of spines and claws and too many legs, and a head on a jointed neck, with bulbous eyes and shearing jaws. It came toward us with a skittering sound. It looked like some unholy fusion of... perhaps spider crab and praying mantis? And yet neither of these. And WRONG. Horribly wrong.

"I'd wager THAT is what the troll was fleeing," Karel declared.

Piia and I looked at each other and nodded. Then before we could act, the thing leaped. It landed behind Ari and Paavo, between them and the two archers, and it went straight for the archers.

"TOGETHER!" I shouted, and at almost the same moment Piia shouted "REGROUP!" It looked too strong for any one of us. We couldn't let it separate us and kill us one by one.

The five of us behind it charged forward, and Eino and Ragne dodged and ran toward us either side of it. Eino made it by, but I saw a claw flash out towards Ragne. She screamed in pain, but managed to half-dive past it as it was turning around, and collapsed on the ground behind Ari. He fended off a flurry of claw strikes, Paavo and Karel running in to support him.

I told Sekai full speed again, and charged. Dodging and parrying

341

the claw that stabbed at me too slowly, I got beside—whatever it was—and struck at the spiked legs, aiming for the joints. I was aware of Piia running in behind me, then she dived and rolled under it, slashing at its underside as she rolled. Some semi-liquid glop that stank acridly gushed from beneath the... thing. I heard a grunt of pain from one of the others. Piia regained her feet inside the arc of its legs on the other side, then she slashed at the base of a leg and severed it completely. I heard her gasp in pain, but couldn't see the cause. I hacked through the top joint of the upper limb nearest to me, severing the leg, then stepped into the gap and cut at the next leg. I missed the joint, but Sekai's night-black blade flashed blue-white and sheared through the armor. The dark ichor that spurted smelled acrid, acidic. That leg failed as well, and the creature listed drunkenly towards me, the remaining legs on this side unable to hold it up, trying to bring its claws to bear but unable to turn far enough. On its other side, I saw Piia dart in and cut at it again, then spin away. It let out a hissing screech, the first sound it had made.

It craned its head over at Piia on that jointed neck, and I saw my opening. I jumped up onto the front-most leg, braced my foot against the spiny back for balance, ignoring a ripping sound, and thrust at full extension into the joint where its head met its neck, upward into the head. Sekai punched through the tough covering of the joint with only slight resistance. Then again, a second thrust, at a slightly different angle. I twisted Sekai's blade around inside its head.

It spasmed violently, and I jumped—or, just as much, was tossed—clear. I stumbled as I landed, rolling to regain my feet. The two legs left on this side folded under it, and it rolled over onto its side. Piia ducked in a third time and sliced it deeply open where the two main parts of its body met.

It gave one last screech, and went limp. Or as limp as an armored monstrosity can. It twitched for a long time, but it was only random twitches.

We checked quickly on our comrades. Karel was down. So was Ragne. Paavo's arm was gashed bone-deep, and he looked pale.

"I'll watch them," Eino told us. "You three go on!" We sprinted for the bend.

Nothing else lay beyond the bend, except for a rippling tear of blackness that hung in the air a few hundred yards on.

"The rift," Piia said.

"We need to close it," I said. "Before anything else comes through."

"How?" Ari demanded, as we approached.

"I'm not sure yet," I admitted. "But... I *think* we have this, Ari. Help the others."

Ari nodded, and headed back to our fallen comrades at a run.

"I can tell you one thing," Piia declared grimly. "I am all but certain this—or another creature like it—is what attacked Särkkä Valley."

I walked carefully forward and studied the rift, not getting too close. I felt it pulling.

"Do not step into it!" Piia warned me urgently. "You do not know where it leads!"

"I wasn't planning to," I replied. It looked much the same from all sides. Dark filaments spread from it. I had a strong feeling I should avoid them. It seemed to have a... *depth* to it, that went *into* it from all directions. Or *away from* all directions. It was hard to say. The air seemed curdled, twisted, around it. It didn't look *big* enough for that horror to have come through. But... I had the feeling that was deceptive.

And what if it hadn't? What if the mantis-crab-thing had *opened* it, from here? To call that pack through?

I stepped closer.

"Be careful, Alrekr," Piia said, behind me. "*Please.*"

I nodded, trying to figure out what I was seeing. I felt that Sekai wanted me to do... *something*. But I wasn't sure what. I... needed to *understand* this rift. I stepped closer.

"*Alrekr!*" Piia's tone was anxious, worried. But I... I could *feel* the rift. It was a knot... no, a twist... a tear. A twist and a tear that went... into *itself*, and somewhere else as well. It didn't actually take up any space *here*. It had pushed 'here' aside, and within, it ran to... somewhere else. A tunnel *outside* the real world.

Suddenly I knew what I had to do. And I knew why my sword's name was what it was.

"Sekai no Kattā," I said aloud, musing. Cutter of Worlds. Then I stepped forward almost to the edge of the rift, and focused my attention on the rift as I reached into it with Sekai's blade. I heard Piia gasp behind me, then I swept Sekai in a circle at my full reach just barely inside the rift. There was a feeling of cutting… *something*, a heavy resistance, a drag. Then it was done, and I took two, three quick steps backward.

In front of me, the rift was rippling, twisting. There was a sizzling hiss for a few seconds, then it collapsed with a dull, heavy **thump**, and was gone. Where it had been, the air was clear again, no longer curdled. The filaments seemed to slowly evaporate—and so, I noticed, did dark traces they had left on the walls of the ravine, though they left scars behind in the stone.

I sheathed Sekai and turned around, suddenly tired. Relief was replacing anxiety on Piia's face. She took three running strides towards me and threw her arms around me. I caught her and held her.

"You worried me, Alrekr," she said.

"I'm sorry, Piia," I replied. "I *had* to get that close to it to understand it enough to close it."

She let go of me after a moment, and we turned and hurried back to check on the others. Karel was on the ground, unconscious, face bloodied, bleeding from a messy head wound and a nasty gash on his left shoulder. The bleeding actually relieved me, because it was almost the only sign he was still alive. I checked the pulse in his neck. It was faint and thready.

Ragne's right thigh had been ripped open. Eino had taken his jack off and bound her wound as best he could with his shirt, but she wasn't going anywhere under her own power any time soon, and I could see blood pulsing alarmingly quickly through the improvised dressing. Paavo was sitting on the ground, pale, his eyes closed, wincing as Ari bound his arm.

"Can you ride?" Piia asked Paavo, kneeling next to him.

"No," he said. His voice was slurred. "I'm not sure I can even stand. My head is spinning. It's a little better if I keep my eyes closed."

"All three of them need healers, and soon," Ari stated. "But I'm not sure how we're going to move all three of them quickly when none can walk, or sit a horse. And I don't think Ragne will make it. She's losing too much blood." I could hear the tightness in his voice.

I looked down the ravine. Simo was not in sight. We'd come at least a quarter mile up.

"I... Wait a moment," I said hesitantly. I stepped out into the middle of the ravine and drew Sekai again, thinking hard about the feel of the rift. If I could *close* a rift, could I *open* one? With Sekai in hand, I focused on what the twisted tear had felt like. *Wrong* overpowered almost everything else. But... underneath that...

"Ari," I said, probably slightly distractedly. "Can you carry Karel?"

"Yes," he replied, with no hesitation.

"I can carry Ragne. Eino, can you and Simo get the horses back to Highwatch between you?"

"Yes," he replied, "but..."

"All right," I said. "I *think* I can do this."

This *HAD* to work. If it didn't, Ragne would die. No pressure.

I closed my eyes and raised Sekai, thought as hard, as clearly as I could, about the Highwatch infirmary, trying to recall every detail of the entry hall, focusing until I had the image perfect in my mind. I mentally muttered a brief apology to the world. And then I reached *past* everything around me, *past* the air in front of me, just like the rift I'd just closed, and cut smoothly downward, praying that it would work.

There was a whispering hiss as the air split open. I opened my eyes. The distortion in the air looked much like that around the rift I had just closed not long before, but there was no black knot, no dark filaments, no twisting, and the air did not look... curdled, as it had around the other. I was looking into the infirmary hallway. Not far in front, Vilja was staring my way, her eyes wide.

"Ari," I said, "take Karel. Piia, help Paavo. Eino, go, find Simo, take the horses back."

I held the rift open in my mind as I sheathed Sekai, took two steps over to Ragne, and carefully picked her up. She let out a gasping half-shriek of pain. Piia was already helping Paavo up, I saw.

"I'm *sorry*, Ragne," I told her. "It'll just be a moment."

Ari picked up Karel, took a deep breath, stepped into my rift, and vanished from sight. Piia had Paavo on his feet and was half-carrying him toward the rift. I let her take Paavo through before me, then stepped in carrying Ragne in my arms. I stumbled slightly as I landed on the far side, the floor several inches lower than I had expected, and she cried out again.

"*Sorry*, Ragne, sorry," I said. "You're safe now."

When I came through, Vilja had just directed Piia and Paavo into a room.

"Karel will need Kata," I told her. "Urgently."

Vilja nodded. "I have already sent for her," she agreed. She looked at Ragne's leg, and pointed. "That room for her. She and Karel are the most urgent. I will start on her right away. We have to stop that bleeding, or she will die."

I hesitated, then... I had the feeling I didn't need to actually *touch* my own rift. I had been gentle opening it. I just... *told* it that it could close now. It narrowed and vanished silently. I carried Ragne into the room Vilja indicated, and laid her as gently as I could on the table. As I let go of her, she clutched at my hand, and squeezed it tightly. I bent and kissed her forehead, stroked her fiery red hair. She looked pale.

"We've got you, Ragne," I told her. "You're going to be alright. I promise."

Vilja laid her hands on Ragne's leg, chanted one opening measure, and began to sing in a strong, clear voice. A moment later, Marketta came into the room, took her place opposite Vilja with a quick nod of approval, and joined her voice to Vilja's. She glanced my way, then down at Ragne, back to me, and nodded emphatically. I understood the wordless message. *It's alright now. We've got her.*

I left the room just in time to see Kata hurrying into the first room. Varpu and Raimo were already in the second. Liisa was just coming into the entry. She looked at me and froze.

"I'm alright," I reassured her quickly. "None of this is mine." But far too much of it was Ragne's.

I turned into the second room. Piia was still in there, with Paavo.

"There is venom in the wound," Varpu was saying. "That is why he cannot stand. Raimo, his arm, please; I will purge the venom from him." She glanced my way. "Alrekr, I could use one more here, please."

"Vilja and Marketta have Ragne," I told Piia, then turned to check on the first room. Kata, Vallaïnen, Marja and Liisa were all in there, Ari standing out of their way.

"Ragne's in good hands, she'll pull through," I said to Ari. He nodded gratefully. Kata was examining Karel's head wound. Her eyes flicked to me for a moment, then back to her work. She was focused on her patient. I didn't interrupt. They had Karel covered.

"Varpu could use another voice," I told Liisa. She nodded and hurried into the middle room, joining Raimo to work on Paavo's arm as Varpu cleared the venom from his body. I followed her in, and looked at Piia. I remembered her gasping in pain. There was a spreading red mark on her cheek, and the skin was blistered. It was terrifyingly close to her eye.

"Piia, you need a Healer as well," I told her.

"So do you, Alrekr," she replied.

I stopped, and looked down at myself. I hadn't noticed until she pointed it out, but my tunic was rent in a dozen places, and I had a number of shallow wounds I had been too busy to pay any attention to. Some of the blood *was* mine, after all.

I looked a lot worse than I felt, I realized. No wonder Liisa had been alarmed.

"All right," I agreed, "but you first. Whatever... burned your face, I don't want it getting into your eye."

Master Timo came in just in time to hear that last.

"Both of you sit down," he told us. "I will take care of both of you. But I agree with Alrekr—you first, Piia, before that gets into your eye. Where are the rest of your team?"

"Eino and Simo should be on their way back with the horses," Piia said. "They are unhurt, as is Ari."

"Ari, I know," Timo nodded. "I saw him as I came in."

He took a clean cloth from a pile, folded it into a pad, wetted it with something clear he poured from a stoneware bottle, and placed it against Piia's cheek, then began a low, quiet song I had not heard before. He sat and patiently sang for about a quarter hour before he lifted the pad and checked under it. The redness was much reduced, but there was a greenish stain on the cloth. He sniffed at it, wrinkled his face in distaste, then threw the cloth into the waste pile and went to get another.

"Some kind of vitriol," he declared, as he folded the new cloth and wetted it. "It is not hard to sing it out, just slow. But had it gotten into your eye, it would have burned your eye." He put the new pad in place and began again.

Paavo was starting to look a lot more alert now, but was still obviously groggy. Raimo and Liisa had gotten his jack and his shirt off of him, and were working on his arm. There was a lot of blood on his shirt. Varpu was still singing venom out of him.

After the second pass, Timo pronounced himself satisfied.

"All of the vitriol is out," he said, "and I have treated the burning. It will be a little swollen for a day or two, I expect." Piia nodded appreciatively.

"It feels a lot better," she said.

Master Timo turned to me.

"And now for you, Járnhandr," he told me. "Start by taking off that tunic and shirt, please. What remains of them." He looked me up and down. "And get that boot off, too."

I pulled Sekai from my sash, set her down, and did as he told me. After a good look at the tunic and shirt, I tossed them into the same waste pile Timo had used. My boot had a large gash up the side. So did my ankle and calf. I sighed, and ripped the already-torn leg of the breeches open to give Timo clear access.

Timo got another wet cloth and began cleaning me up.

"These are mostly superficial," he declared as he cleaned my wounds. "And I do not detect anything unclean in them—though some would still trouble you for a while if we don't heal them. Most of them you would not have if you had been... better dressed for the occasion."

"I told him that as we left," Piia remarked. "But there was no time to do anything about it. And had he not been with us... it is likely none of us would have made it back."

"You ran into something *that* bad?" Timo asked, frowning.

"A troll, first," Piia replied. "But that was the *least* of it."

"*Worse* than a troll?"

"I don't know what in Hel it was," I interjected. "But the troll was *running* from it."

With the blood cleaned off me, Timo looked me over.

"I am going to go and take Vilja's place, and send her to treat these," he said. "Ragne needs me more than you do right now. But if you're going to go fighting... things worse than trolls, please wear some better protection next time."

"I'll take care of that," Piia declared. "I'm going to see to it that he has proper Ranger gear."

Timo nodded approval, got up, and left. A minute later I heard his voice pick up in the next room, and a minute after that, Vilja came in, sat down next to me, and started closing my minor wounds. I relaxed and let her work on me. She had gentle hands. I hadn't really been aware of any of the gashes and scrapes individually—there had been higher priorities on my mind—but as she healed them, I came to realize that they added up to a significant background of aching and stinging. I felt quite a bit better by the time she was done.

"Thank you, *Journeyman* Vilja," I said, when she declared me fit to go. She gave me a big smile. "And thank you especially for so efficiently getting the care of my friends organized." She smiled again and hurried off, likely to see what else needed to be done. I put my torn boot back on, picked up Sekai, and Piia and I went to check on Karel and Ragne.

Kata was still working on Karel. It was the first time I had seen her work a head injury. I could see the delicacy of the care in her touch, and I would swear there was something different in *how* she was singing. After a moment she noticed our presence. She looked up for a moment, caught my eye, and nodded deeply, then went back to her work. Vallaïnen seemed to be working the gash in Karel's shoulder, while Marja cleaned up his facial injuries.

"Come," I said to Piia. "All is well in hand. He's in the best hands he could be."

We went to look in on Ragne. Marketta and Timo had the bleeding stopped and were working on closing the wound. It looked terrifying. That claw had laid her thigh open almost to the bone.

Piia walked over to Ragne and laid a hand on her shoulder for a moment. Ragne opened her eyes, smiled weakly up at Piia, and then closed them again. The smile stayed. Piia looked relieved.

I walked over and put an arm around Piia.

"Nobody is dying today," I told her.

"We'd better go report in," she replied.

20: Rangers Lead The Way

We collected Ari on our way out, planning to head straight to the Rangerhall, but the word had evidently gotten out. We hadn't even left the infirmary before we met Knight-Commander Jaako coming in.

"Piia," he said, as soon as he saw us. "How are your team?" He looked around, concerned. "I don't see nearly enough of you."

"Eino and Simo are bringing the horses back," Piia replied. "Karel, Paavo and Ragne were wounded, but are being treated and will recover. Though if Alrekr had not learned to open and close rifts this day, Ragne would have bled out before we got her a quarter of the way home. And had he not been with us, I think none of us would have come back."

"That bad." Jaako's face was grim. "And what happened to *you*, Járnhandr?"

"Superficial wounds," I said with a shrug. "Truth to tell, I was too busy to really notice them until we got back."

"By which," Piia interjected, "he means his tunic was hanging off him in shreds by the time the fight was over."

Jaako went into each treatment room in turn, checking on the injured team members.

"He will recover?" I heard him ask, in Karel's room. I assume he got only another nod in reply, as I heard no reply and no break in the healing songs.

After checking on each of the three, he came back out.

"Come," he told us. "I want a full report."

"That's exactly what we were on our way to do when you walked in," I said. He nodded acknowledgment.

"And I want to make him a Ranger," Piia added as the four of us walked. "Attached to my team."

"The last is no surprise," Jaako replied, smiling. "Nor the first, really, I suppose." He glanced my way. "What say you, Járnhandr? Are you willing to join us?"

«*We few, we happy few, we band of brothers,*» I quoted.

"What?" Jaako gave me a puzzled look. I realized that, quoting, I had spoken in English. I quickly translated.

"It is a line from a stage play," I explained. "By a poet and playwright from... almost five centuries before my time. Knight-Commander, I would be greatly honored."

Jaako nodded.

"And the stage-play? What is it about?"

"There is a lot to it," I answered. "But that particular scene invokes the bond of brotherhood among veterans of a particularly notable battle."

"I see," Jaako mused. "And thus why it came to you."

I nodded agreement.

When we walked into the Rangerhall, Jaako walked straight up to a group around a table.

"Pertti," he said.

"Commander?"

"This is Járnhandr. Take a good look at him, go to stores, pull two full sets of gear for him, bring it to my study." Then he hesitated for a moment. "No... bring it *here*. I think *everyone* should hear this report."

"Pertti has a very good eye for this," Piia explained. Pertti stood and looked at me critically, up and down, front and side.

"Hmm," I mused. "I met a carpenter named Pertti. Does that ever cause confusion?"

"Why would it cause confusion?" Pertti replied distractedly, as he measured me up. He held his hands out and gauged the width of my shoulders and hips. "He is Woodworker Pertti. I am Ranger Pertti. No confusion."

Lastly he asked me to lift one leg, and examined my foot closely, feeling the shape of it. Then, after a minute, he nodded and left.

Jaako walked to the front of the Hall, gesturing to the three of us to follow, which we did. He stepped up onto a bench.

"ALL ATTEND!" he bellowed. All conversation stopped suddenly, and everyone in the hall turned to look.

"Gather forward," he said. "This is the report of Piia's team."

352

There was a mass movement forward in the hall, people taking what seats there were or standing between the tables. A woman I did not know raised a hand. Jaako pointed at her.

"Raili," he called out.

"Piia," Raili said. "Before you start. *Please*—tell me this is *not* all that remains of your team."

"Eino and Simo are on their way back with the horses," Piia reassured her. "They are unhurt. Paavo, Karel and Ragne are in the infirmary, all three badly hurt, but all expected to make full recovery."

Raili let out a huge sigh of relief, and a small cheer went up. Two more hands went up.

"All else I will come to in time," Piia said. Then she began her report.

"Two days past, my team went out and traveled straight North to the foot of the crags. We swept west and south just below the tree-line, past both passes, and saw nothing, but that the forest was abnormally quiet. As is usual of late." There were dark mutters of agreement at that.

"We continued on south to the second watch tower, then out to the flatland and back to Highwatch by the most direct route.

"Scarcely after we arrived back in Highwatch, before our horses had even been stabled, Simo detected the opening of a rift. A big one, he said, somewhere in the crags, somewhere below and a little west of the western pass. We remounted and went straight back out. Alrekr went with us." She waved a hand at me. "Some of you already know him." There were a few chuckles.

"Where the forest begins to thin, Karel picked up something. We dismounted and went forward on foot. Shortly afterward, Karel scented a troll. And something else foul on the wind.

"A half mile further, we encountered the troll as we entered a clearing. It came straight at us. We killed it."

"By which she means," Ari interjected dryly, "that mostly she and Alrekr killed it." That spurred a low murmur of comments.

"We found that it had existing wounds," Piia went on. "Wounds that were sick, oozing, poisoned. The smell of the wounds matched what Karel and Alrekr scented.

"We suspect it did not *seek* to attack. We were simply in its way as

353

it was fleeing from something else." The murmuring grew louder at that, and Jaako held up a hand for quiet.

"We remounted and continued on upward past the tree-line. Simo guided us towards where he felt the rift. The trail led to a ravine. We dismounted there and went on foot again.

"A quarter mile into the ravine we encountered enemies. Between thirty and forty creatures, manlike, short, stunted, deformed to our eyes. Fairly crude weapons. Spears, spiked clubs, pole-axes, large slings. They came around a bend in the ravine at a run, and attacked us on sight. Eino and Ragne killed their slingers. I never got a chance to investigate what the slingers were throwing. Perhaps Eino can tell us when he returns.

"We split them left and right, then pincered them between us. We took only minor injuries. We three, Karel, Paavo were bunched together as we finished them between us. Eino and Ragne were between thirty and forty yards back."

She took a deep breath.

"As we finished the last of them... *something* came around the bend in the ravine. I have never seen its like before. Not of this world, I am almost certain. Many limbs, armored nearly all over, spiked, dark, almost black. Large eyes and massive jaws in a head on a jointed neck. More than twice the height of a tall man, and nearly as long.

"The very first thing it did was to leap over the five of us, landing between us and Eino and Ragne. I am certain it intended to kill them quickly first, then turn on us.

"I called a regroup. It struck at Ragne as she ran past it, and ripped her leg open. Ari stood over her where she fell, and defended her. Karel and Paavo supported him, while Alrekr and I attacked it. The joints are vulnerable. So is the underbelly. We got on either side of it while it was focused on the others, and went for its legs. We took several limbs off it, and it fell to its side, towards Alrekr. That exposed its belly, and I struck at it there. Then...? I did not quite see."

She looked at me.

"When it tried to crane over to reach Piia," I said, "it exposed the back of its neck. The joint where the head meets the neck is vulnerable, when extended. I attacked there, and between us, we killed it. It took a long time to finish dying."

"In that time," Piia continued, "Karel was down and Paavo disabled. Were it not for Alrekr and the soulbound swords, I think it would have killed us all. I am nearly certain that it was a creature like this that slaughtered the families in Särkkä Valley.

"Eino stayed to guard and treat the wounded. We three continued up the ravine. A little further, we found the rift. Alrekr, somehow, managed to close it."

"Permanently?" someone called out.

"I don't know yet," I answered. I looked back at Piia.

Right around this time, Pertti returned, his arms full of leather and cloth. Jaako directed him straight to me. I gladly took one of the shirts, for the moment, and slipped it on over my head—after a quick check of the upper part of my breeches for blood, troll or otherwise. I didn't want to get blood on a new, clean shirt.

"We returned for our wounded," Piia continued. "Karel was still unconscious. Paavo could no longer stand. Eino had dressed Ragne's wound, but she was bleeding out. Simo was not in sight.

"Alrekr was able to open a rift of his own, directly into the infirmary in the keep. We sent Eino to find Simo and bring the horses home. Ari carried Karel through, I helped Paavo, and last, Alrekr carried Ragne. His rift closed behind us."

There were many questions, relatively few that we had answers to. Why Paavo was envenomed, but Ragne was not. Where the thing had come from, and what connection there was between it and the mob that had preceded it.

"We *presume* that they both came out of the dark rift," I said. "But we did not see it happen. So it is only a guess. It could be wrong."

"We have heard it said that you came here through a rift yourself," someone else asked me. "And you closed one today, and opened another."

"Yes," I replied. "I... learned how to *open* one, I think, mainly by figuring out how to *close* one. The first—the one we believe I came through—was entirely beyond my control. I remember almost nothing about it except a twisting tunnel of darkness in the air. I had never actually had the chance to look closely at one before today."

"Can you tell us anything about what is the same, and what different, between the one you opened, and the one you closed, and the one you came here through?"

That was a pretty good question. Piia beat me to an answer while I was still thinking about it, though.

"For today's," Piia said, "I can tell you that Alrekr's was much... cleaner. No twisting blackness within it. No streamers of darkness. No monsters." There was some grim laughter at that. "But for the rest, the only person who *might* be able to tell you is Simo. And he is not back yet. Perhaps as soon as another hour."

After a little while longer, the questions began to tail off.

"Enough," Jaako called. "It is time to let these people rest. They had a hellishly hard fight this day, and they still have comrades in the infirmary.

"But one more thing. Please stand, Alrekr Járnhandr."

I looked at Jaako, then did as he asked. He took two steps to stand next to me.

"This day Alrekr Járnhandr joins us as a Ranger of Highwatch," he declared. "He will be attached to Piia's team." There was a brief moment of silence, then the assembled Rangers broke into a rousing cheer. Jaako picked up one of the leather Ranger jacks from the pile Pertti had brought, and draped it across my shoulders.

"Welcome, Ranger Járnhandr. You are one of us now. And already blooded in battle."

"A word! A word of joining!" a voice called from amid the Rangers.

Jaako chuckled.

"Do you have a word to offer us, Járnhandr?" he asked.

I thought a moment, then nodded.

"The world of my past life had Rangers also," I began. "Uh..." Saamen didn't have a word for 'State', as such. It took me a moment to come up with a close equivalent. "United, uh, Provinces Army Rangers. I was *not* one of them, honesty binds me to say. I will not steal their valor. But I know their motto."

I paused, then raised my voice.

"Rangers lead the way!" The cheering broke out anew, then someone echoed it from the back. "Rangers lead the way!" And another, and a fourth.

Jaako grinned.

"These Army Rangers," he said. "Were they good men, good fighters?"

I knew a deliberate cue line when I heard one. I knew how this worked.

"They were the *BEST*," I replied, to another cheer.

Ari stood and clapped his hands sharply. The voices stilled for a moment.

"There is one thing that both Piia and Alrekr have glossed over, as though it were in a normal day's work," he began. "Something that you should bear in mind when they say simply, 'We killed it.'

"The troll we encountered was already sick and wounded, it is true. But it went down faster than I have ever seen anyone take down a troll. And then... there was the other... *thing*. Whatever it was.

"Some of you have seen Piia and Alrekr sparring with their curved swords. A lucky few have seen them spar *fast*. Some of you may not know their soulbound swords can somehow... make them *faster*. Speed them up.

"I saw them both fight at full speed this day. Piia already mentioned this, and I will repeat it: Were it not for Alrekr and Piia and their soulbound swords, likely *none* of us would have come home this day. Between them, they killed a foul horror that likely slaughtered every living thing in Särkkä Valley. I do not know for sure, but I *hope* it was the same one."

There was another grim cheer at that. Everyone knew what had happened in Särkkä Valley, even the teams that had not come with us to clean up and give last rites to the dead. *Too many* dead.

"I am ordering a sword from Smith Matti tomorrow. Consider it."

Jaako pursed his lips for a moment in thought. Then he held up a hand, and the room quieted again.

"If any Ranger of Highwatch wishes to order one of these swords," he declared, "starting with Ari—and, I believe, Paavo—the Ranger treasury will cover half the cost." And that, too, brought a cheer.

I held up a hand myself and waited for the voices to quiet.

"There is something I should make clear," I said. "I... *cannot* give enough of myself to soulbind every sword as I did Piia's. Be aware of that. There is not enough of me to go around. I can only be pulled just so many ways. But I am *trying* to find a way that will let me do it more easily, without spreading myself so thin.

"If I can find a way to do that, I will bind as many as I can, for

357

Highwatch Rangers.

"But if you will excuse us now," I went on, "I for one am *hungry*, and also I wish to check on our brothers and sister in the infirmary again this night." I saw Piia nodding agreement, from the corner of my eye. "So if anyone wants to ask us anything further, please follow us to the dining hall and ask there."

I put Sekai down for a moment and put the Ranger jack on properly. My *obi*, I remembered, was sitting in a blood-soaked pile in the infirmary along with my ruined tunic and shirt, but I saw there was a broad leather sword harness in the pile of gear, very like Piia's, so I pulled that out, buckled it on, and tucked Sekai through the upper part of it. Then I offered Piia my hand, and we went back to the infirmary.

I heard Kata's voice as we approached, still singing. That wasn't a good sign. We went to that room first. Karel was still unconscious, but his shoulder wound was closed, and his face looked much better. Vallaïnen was assisting Kata now, singing a low counterpoint to her contralto. Marja and Paavo were sitting to the side. Kata looked at me, moving just her eyes. I didn't want to interrupt, but I walked over to her and rested my hand on her shoulder for a moment. She turned her head just enough to brush her cheek against my hand. I felt her energy level while I had the contact. She still had plenty left. Good.

I leaned close and whispered "I love you" next to her ear, then followed Piia over to Paavo.

"How are you doing?" Piia asked him.

"Better," he replied. "A little nauseous still. From the venom. Varpu says it should pass by tomorrow. Gods *DAMN*, that thing hit hard."

"Good to see you back on your feet," I told him. He nodded.

"I won't be doing any fighting for a few days, I think."

"I think that will be alright," Piia assured him. "We've earned a little rest. We are going for dinner. Join us in the hall if you feel up to it."

"I will think on it," he agreed.

We went to check on Ragne.

Ragne was asleep, Vilja standing by and keeping an eye on her. She seemed to have a lot more color.

"How is she, Vilja?" I asked. Vilja turned and gave me a quick hug, then hugged Piia as well.

"She will be fine," she told us. "We repaired her leg and replaced most of the blood she lost. It may be a little stiff for a few days, but she will make a full recovery. She needs rest now. We will move her to a recovery room in a few hours."

"Thank you, Vilja," Piia said sincerely. She hugged Vilja again.

Piia gently touched Ragne's hand, then we turned and left the room. As we passed by the first room, Paavo called out to us.

"Wait. I will walk with you."

He stood, and we waited for him to catch up. Then we left the infirmary, and almost walked straight into Eino and Simo coming in.

"Paavo!" Eino exclaimed. "You look a lot better than when I last saw you."

"I don't see Karel or Ragne," Simo said, concern on his face.

"Karel is still unconscious," Piia replied, pointing to the room Paavo had just left. "The healers are still at work." She pointed to Ragne's room. "Ragne is sleeping. She will be fine in a few days, but she needs to rest. Let her sleep."

Simo nodded, but went to look into both rooms anyway. Eino glanced at the Ranger jack I was wearing, grinned, and clapped me on the shoulder. Then we all five headed for the dining hall.

When we got there, a dozen other Rangers were ahead of us and had grabbed two of the long tables. Fortunately there were plenty of spaces left. I saw Liisa and Raimo sitting at another table, and went straight there. Liisa saw me coming and stood to meet me, and I gladly stepped into her hug and held her tightly.

"I'm *so* glad you're alright," she said fervently, after a few moments. "I'd only just gotten back, and I walked into the infirmary, and the first thing I saw was you covered in blood."

"Very *little* of it was mine," I told her. "But far too much of it was Ragne's. We nearly lost her." She squeezed me tighter.

"How did the confinement go?"

"The mother is in fine health," Liisa said, "But she will not deliver tonight. Perhaps late tomorrow, perhaps the next day. I will go back tomorrow. I expect all to be well."

After a minute or so, we loosened our grip. She took a half step back and looked me up and down.

"It looks good on you," she said. "But those breeches look rather silly now."

I laughed. Then I glanced at the other table.

"Come," I said, to her and to Raimo. "Come sit with us." She smiled and picked up her bowl, and Raimo nodded and picked up his. We went over to the tables the Rangers had claimed. I sat down next to Piia, Liisa sat on my other side, and Raimo next to her. Space had been made for Simo and Eino on the other side of the table. Piia was already bringing everyone up to date on Ragne's and Karel's status. Someone handed me a bowl of soup and a large bread roll.

"Healer," a female Ranger I did not know asked, "can you give us anything further about Karel?"

"Kata is still working on him, Helle," Liisa replied. "He took a very hard blow to the head. His skull was fractured, and there was a lot of bleeding inside his head. He may lose some of his recent memories. But he will be alright."

"Thank you, Healer," Helle replied.

"Simo," I said, "someone asked a good question after we made our report. I think you are the best to answer it." Simo looked questioningly at me, and waited.

"Four rifts. One that dropped me here. One above Särkkä Valley. One today in the crags. One that I opened between there and the infirmary. The first two, I never saw and know nothing about.

"What is similar between the four, and what is different? Can you say?"

Simo frowned and thought.

"Difficult to compare," he mused, at last. "The echoes at Särkkä, and the echoes of the one that brought you: similar. But not the same. Särkkä was... stronger, louder, though it was older, yet... less intense? And... also had a different feel. Dirtier. Fouler.

"Särkkä compared to today's. An echo, and an open rift. Today's, very strong, very loud. Very *wrong*. Hard to compare the actual rift to an echo of one. But very similar feel. The echo left after you closed it, from a distance, to the older echo at Särkkä... very much alike. I could easily believe Särkkä's echo was left by a rift very like today's."

He looked at me.

"Those three... they felt like brute force. Yours... almost *gentle*. I barely felt it open and close. Totally different. I might not have recognized it as a rift, had Eino not told me that is what you did."

"Interesting." I thought about that. "Is this, I wonder, another case where I am using a different path to achieve the same end?"

"If I may ask," Raimo inquired, "how did you open your rift?"

I had to think about that for a little, but doing so firmed the process in my mind.

"I focused my mind upon the infirmary entry hall," I replied. "Visualized every detail of it. Until I could *see* it in my mind's eye. And then..." I had to think about how to put it into words. "I... *asked* the space in between to open, and guided the placement of the opening with Sekai. As though I used Sekai to part a curtain—or *find* a part in it —without cutting it. Guiding it open."

"The rift today... it felt more as though someone—or something— simply smashed or ripped a hole," Simo said.

"And the one I came through?" I asked, through the last mouthful of my bread roll. I reached for another roll.

"Difficult to recall," he said, after a little thought. "Not as violent, certainly. But... noisier than yours. Not as clean. Stronger. A sense that it came from very far away."

I realized I'd finished my soup, and passed my bowl back for a refill. Everyone wanted more details about fighting the... mantis-crab-thing, whatever it was, and we told all we could. We mostly advised focusing on the joints in the armor, and those large eyes were possibly vulnerable as well. If one could get to them. We emphasized staying together in groups, not leaving single outliers that it could pick off first.

Gradually the conversation tailed off, and people began leaving.

"Don't forget," Piia reminded me, "you have gear to pick up at the Rangerhall."

I nodded tiredly. I wanted to go straight home. But I also wanted a little more time with Piia. And I wanted my new gear.

"I will be home very soon, Liisa," I promised. Then we all got up, and I went with Piia to collect my new gear.

I did an inventory when we got to the hall. There was a second jack like the one I had on, of tough but flexible leather with a few strategically-placed patches of brigandine-like armor, and two pairs of breeches the same. The leather felt like elk-hide or something similar. There were three more shirts, of a heavy cloth that had nearly the smoothness of kuurii fiber but was clearly tougher and stronger, and two pairs of boots.

"The boots are likely not an exact fit," Piia told me, "but they should serve until the cobblers can make you some properly fitted ones." They were significantly heavier than my boots, and I could feel there were thin armor splints on the shin, between the layers of leather. One of my boots had a large rip in the side after the fight today, so I put on the better fitting of the two pairs.

"Come," Piia said, picking up about half the pile. "I'll walk you back and help you carry them."

It was full dark now, and I looked up at the stars as we walked. I wondered whether any of them was the one I had come from—though I doubted it. Surely telescopes would have spotted this world if it were that close. And I wondered whether one of them was where the monster we had killed in the ravine had come from.

Liisa was of course already there when we got to the tower. Piia went to put down her share of the new gear and go, but Liisa caught her by the hand and drew her into a tight hug.

"Please stay," Liisa asked. "At least for a little while."

Piia said she could stay. So we carried all of my new gear upstairs, and then we came back downstairs and all cuddled tightly up on the couch together while Liisa questioned Piia about all that had happened. I had an arm around each of them, and Liisa clung tightly to me as Piia described the fight in the ravine.

"And then," Liisa said, "you somehow opened a—a rift—*right into the infirmary* and brought them home."

"It was the only way Ragne was going to live," I replied. "She was bleeding out. Quickly. It *had* to work."

"How did you know how to do it?" she asked.

"I..." I had to think about it. "I don't really know," I admitted after a moment. "But I'd just figured out how to *close* one, once I actually saw one in front of me. And I... kind of saw how it worked. Partly.

362

How it went *between* everything, *past* everything. I had to understand at least that much about it, to be able to close it.

"I thought that if Sekai could *close* a rift, maybe she could *open* one, if I could just figure out how to do it. And knowing that Ragne would die if I didn't was a hell of an incentive."

"I'm just glad it worked," Piia declared, with feeling.

"Well," Liisa observed after a moment, "it seems Kata and I were right, there *was* another talent hiding away in there. Firesinger, Soulbinder... and now Riftmaker. We were almost sure that what you had already shown... wasn't *enough* for what we saw within you."

"What I still don't understand," I mused slowly, "is why me? I was... pretty much a nobody. I mean ... I was not *without* skills. Even if few of them are of any use or even relevance here. But... this? It is still hard to take in. Why *me*? Where did it all *come* from?"

Liisa hesitated for a long time before she replied.

"That might be something Raimo can answer better than I can," she said at last. "But... let me try to see if I can put what *I* think, into words that make sense.

"Raimo thinks the world brought you here for a purpose. That it brought you here because it needed *what you would become* after it brought you here. How it... *knew*... that, I cannot even guess at. Unless the world *did* that, as well.

"That does not necessarily have a single thing to do with who and what you were in your... past life. Even if you already had all these talents latent within you there, they could do you no good. You have told us that there was no *voima* there, no Talent. So how do you know that the world did not choose you because you had those latent Talents already?"

That was true, I realized. If I somehow already had them, there would have been no possible way for me to know.

"You make a good point," I replied. "Whether I did or not, I *couldn't* possibly have known."

"Let me give you another thought, then, Alrekr," Liisa continued. "One just as likely or as unlikely to be true." She scooted around a little so that she could face me more directly.

"Consider that perhaps the world *did not care* what abilities you had or did not, because it could *give* you what it needed you to have."

She looked into my eyes and put her left hand over my heart.

"Perhaps, Alrekr, it chose you not because of *what* you are, but *who* you are.

"When you first woke up after arriving here, when you saw how healing you tired us, you were concerned for *us*, not yourself. You have given every piece of knowledge you have that could be helpful, as soon as you realized it could be helpful. When Ingrid and Taisto were crushed by the stone cart—you did not know who they were, but you spent your own energy to the point of exhaustion to help heal them anyway. Today you learned on the spot how to open a rift, because it was the only way you could think of to save Ragne from dying."

"You felt sadness for the troll," Piia added.

"And did you not, then?" I asked Piia.

"I... regret that we had to kill it," she agreed, quietly.

I looked back at Liisa. Something I never tired of.

"I like to think," Liisa told me, "that the world brought you here because in your heart, to the bottom of your soul, you are a good person. You are the person the world needed." And she leaned in and kissed me.

Then she turned to Piia.

"And you, Piia," she added. "You are a very good person too."

And then she leaned over and kissed Piia as well. Piia's eyes widened in surprise for a moment, but then she just relaxed into it, raised her left hand gently to Liisa's shoulder, pulling her into the kiss. It was beautiful and heartwarming to see. I won't deny it made my heart beat faster.

When they separated, Piia looked at me. I could see the hunger in her eyes, and I had no hesitation about kissing her as well. And then the three of us spent a couple of minutes all kissing each other as opportunity presented itself.

"If I am dreaming, then let this dream never end," I gasped when we broke off for breath. Piia laughed happily.

"Alrekr," Liisa asked, "I thought you already decided, back on the recovery room balcony, that you were not dreaming?"

I nodded.

"I'm just covering all possibilities," I declared, and Liisa laughed too.

"This is wonderful and amazing," Piia said after a minute, "and... But I should go. For now. I want to check on Ragne and Karel once more before I sleep."

"I'll come with you," I agreed. "I want to be sure Kata is holding up. And see how Karel is doing."

"Then let us all go," Liisa said.

So we all went back to the infirmary, where we found Karel still unconscious, and Kata resting. I went straight to Kata, and as she stood up, I caught her into a tight hug.

"How is he?" Piia asked, beating me to the question.

"It is slow work," Kata replied. "But he will recover. I expect he will lose some of his recent memory. As best I can reconstruct, he was hit in the face and shoulder, *hard*, which threw him back and his head hit a hard surface. It jarred his brain forward, then backward in his skull." I winced, and Kata caught it.

"Alrekr?" she asked. I hesitated for a moment.

"In my past life," I started to explain, "we called this a..."

"There is no Saamen word?" Kata said, guessing from experience.

I nodded. "Enough to say it was never good news. But here, I have seen you work miracles. You have worked miracles *on me*. Things I would not have believed possible. So I will try to put my fears aside.

"How are you doing? Are you tired?"

"I am fine, Alrekr. This work is difficult because it is precise, not difficult because it is exhausting. I will be fine. I sent to the kitchen for some juice already.

"I want to know all that happened to you... and how you brought them home. But you can tell me later. I see you are in the best of hands." I nodded, and kissed her.

"Do you think you will be home this night?" I asked.

"A few more hours' work before I feel confident leaving him to recuperate," Kata replied. "Ragne is fine. She is still sleeping. We will move her to a recovery room soon. She will need a few days." She looked at Piia.

"Piia, what happened to your face?" she asked. Piia's cheek was still reddened.

"I caught a spray of body fluids when I cut a leg off the thing that attacked us," Piia replied. "The fluids burn. Master Timo dealt with it. He says the remaining redness will fade in a day or so."

"That is good," Kata agreed. "As long as it was dealt with." She stretched and yawned. "Have no fear, Piia. We will take care of Karel."

"I will leave you to it," I said. "Goodnight, beloved." I kissed her again, then a third time for good measure. We went and looked in on Ragne, but did not risk disturbing her. She had regained more color in her cheeks, and was starting to look like her normal self.

We left the infirmary, and stopped outside for a last hug. Piia kissed both of us, then bade us goodnight and headed for the outside on her way back to the Rangerhall. Liisa and I set off back to our tower, where we went straight to bed and curled up around each other.

Kata came in some time in the early morning. I half remember rolling over and wrapping my arms around her.

We got up in the morning in a leisurely kind of way, and rang for a page to bring breakfast while we got dressed. I looked at the breeches I had worn the day before, and decided that they were a write-off as well. Something that had sprayed on them had eaten into the fabric overnight, and it tore like tissue. Doubtless the same ichor that had burned Piia's face. Or perhaps it was venom in the troll's blood.

Well, I'd been planning to wear the Ranger leathers anyway. I tried on everything. All of the clothing was a good fit—not perfect, true, but good *enough*. Pertti's eye was, indeed, good. One pair of boots wasn't *bad*, the other a little loose. I could wear the first pair for now, but in the long run I'd need both replaced. I made a mental note that I must see the cobblers today. I also needed to remember I was supposed to meet with Mill-Master Kustaa and give him a copy of my printing press notes. Which meant I needed to *write* that second copy.

We finished our breakfast, exchanged kisses, and Liisa and Kata left for the infirmary. Liisa, of course, had a confinement outside Highwatch to return to.

And I? I got out pen, ink, parchment and sand, and began to write

366

out a second copy of my printing press description.

I was done in an hour or so. Just in good time to go and find Kustaa, so off I went. I collected the ripped boot as well; it would be fine for wear around Highwatch, with some repairs.

I didn't have any difficulty finding Kustaa. He was already waiting just inside the keep, where we had agreed to meet. I suggested we find somewhere we could sit down, so we walked to the dining hall and set ourselves down in a quiet corner under a glowstone lantern. I gave him the copy I had just made.

Kustaa read it through once quickly, then went back to the beginning and started again, reading more slowly. This time he had questions as he went along. It was clear he was thinking about this as any good engineer of my now-impossibly-distant former acquaintance would have. I tried to remember his questions so that I would remember what I needed to clarify. Finally he set the sheets down.

"I see no foundational reason why such a thing as this describes could not be built," he said. "There will be a lot of iron parts that will all need to be carefully made and hand fitted. I am sure they are within Smith Matti's ability. Much of the unstressed framing, I think, can be hardwood.

"I would like to keep these for a few weeks, if I might, while I think about the details, and see if I can draft a design. Would that be acceptable?"

"That... is more than I expected," I admitted. "I sought only to have you tell me whether the explanation and description were sufficiently clear."

"So I understood from you," he agreed. "But... this is an interesting challenge. In some ways, not so different from the artificery that drives the mills, but in other ways, quite different. It must be much more precise. The millwork is much more tolerant of slip and play than this will be. But it does not need to carry nearly as much force.

"I... think it might be interesting to try to build one. I imagine it would be at the least a project of many months. Might I consult back with you when I have a design worked out with Smith Matti, and confirm that it is what you envision?"

"Master Kustaa," I replied, bowing my head, "that is far more than I dreamed we would do at this point. In my past world, the, uh, *kirjoitekone* was invented by a man named Gutenberg. In this world, in the Sunlit Land, I have a feeling history will talk about Kustaa's engine."

Kustaa raised an eyebrow.

"The idea is yours," he pointed out.

"No," I replied. "All I have done is to describe in general terms my best understanding of how something that I have already seen, that I did not invent, works. You are the one who is now planning to turn that general description into an actual working creation. Yours is the creativity that sees a way to build what I have described. Your name should go on it. Not mine."

He paused, then nodded his head, smiling.

"As you wish, Master Járnhandr," he agreed. "I will speak of this with Smith Matti when I have the picture a little clearer in my head. I thank you for bringing this to me. It will be *interesting*."

He excused himself, took the pages, and left. I headed for the cobblers, and fairly quickly found Olavi, the cobbler who had made my last pair of boots.

"Adept—no, *Master* Járnhandr, now," he greeted me. "What can I do for you?"

"I have two tasks for you, if you would," I replied. "First, I managed to badly rip this boot yesterday and would like it repaired, if you can."

I handed him the boot, and he examined it with a critical eye.

"Not difficult," he judged. "I will have to put a patch over it, of course. How did you come to rip it this way?"

"It happened during a fight, up in the crags," I told him.

"Ah," he nodded. "Yes. I heard something about that. Three Rangers badly injured. How are they?"

"Doing well," I replied. "All three should make a full recovery, though it was a chancy thing."

"That is good," he said. "I see that you are in Ranger leathers now. Have you joined the Rangers, then?"

"I have, yes," I agreed. "Which brings us to the second matter. I have some boots from Ranger stores, but one pair fits me... tolerably, the other poorly. I need two pairs of such boots made on my last. Can you do that?"

"That is not a problem," he declared. "There is a stock of the armor splints for that purpose, and I have all else I need. Three silvers for the repair, twenty-five each pair for the new boots. I will have the repair done by tomorrow, then about a week for each pair of boots."

I had enough, barely, to cover the repair and one pair of boots. I'd need to find a way to cover the second pair, though I was pretty sure it wouldn't be a major problem.

"That would be wonderful," I said. "Thank you, Olavi."

He took the damaged boot and bade me a good day. I headed for the forge, to see what the day's workload was like. Today was probably a good day to forge Paavo's sword, if Paavo felt up to it.

I didn't get there.

21: Moonshadow

As I walked across the bailey towards the forge, I first noticed shouts from the guards atop the wall. Then there came a heavy beating sound and a strong downward gust of wind from above. I and probably nearly everyone else in the bailey looked up. There was a great dark shape hanging in the sky over the bailey, wings beating, holding it in place.

It was a dragon. Holy *crap*, it was an actual *dragon*. People scattered. The dragon dropped lower, then raised its wings and dropped the last twenty feet or so with an earth-shaking THUD. It was difficult to estimate how big it was. It was a great dark-gray shape, the deep, solid gray of charcoal and basalt, but slightly lustrous, and its eyes were opalescent pools of fiery orange.

It cast its lambent gaze around the bailey, and after a few moments, its eyes settled on me. And then it spoke.

The voice was a rumble like tumbling rocks mixed with distant thunder, the words it said long and rolling. At first I could not understand it, but then meaning gradually formed within my mind.

«GATE-CLOSER. I,» then something long that I couldn't quite parse, «GREET YOU.»

«Uh,» I said, very intelligently. «Did you just call me 'Gate-closer'?» The words felt somehow strange coming out.

«YES. YOUR ACTION ON THE DAY JUST PASSED WAS FELT. YOUR... SCENT WAS UPON IT. I FOLLOWED THE SCENT HERE.»

«Is... that a problem?»

«NO. FAR FROM IT. IT IS WHAT WAS NECESSARY. IT WAS WELL DONE.»

The dragon looked around.

«MY PRESENCE IS OBSTRUCTING ACTIVITY. IS THERE A PREFERRED PLACE NEARBY WHERE WE COULD CONVERSE? A PLACE EASIER TO LAND, PERHAPS?»

I thought for a moment.

«I live in that tower.» I pointed. «Is that large enough for you to land on?»

The dragon craned its head around and looked where I was pointing.

«IT WILL SERVE. KINDLY JOIN ME THERE AT YOUR CONVENIENCE. I WILL

The dragon raised its head and its wings, leapt skyward, and then down-beat, *hard*. A massive blast of wind buffeted the bailey. Two strokes took it clear of the outer wall, gaining altitude, then it circled around and came in for a neat landing atop the tower.

I stood there for a moment, my mind spinning. A dragon—a *DRAGON*—had just spoken to me. And I had *understood* it, after the first few moments.

"Járnhandr!" Matti's voice. I looked around. He was standing a dozen yards away. "Did you just speak with a DRAGON?"

"It, uh... it certainly *seems* that way," I agreed, still a little dazed by it myself.

"And you *understood* it?"

"Yes. Um. Almost all. Did you?"

"Not a word," he said, shaking his head. "The dragon's, *or* yours."

"Wait," I said slowly. "You're telling me *I was speaking dragon?*"

Matti looked at me, then he began to chuckle, then to laugh.

"Why *NOT?*" he replied, in between whoops of laughter. "Just don't bring one home as a pet, Járnhandr." He got his breath back a bit. "Unless of course it can work the forge."

"Ranger Járnhandr," came another voice from behind me. Jaako's, I recognized. I turned around. Jaako was walking rapidly toward me from the direction of the Rangerhall, along with Piia, Ari, and half a dozen other Rangers, all looking both surprised and wary. "Is there something I *urgently* need to know? Beyond what is already obvious to all?"

Looking around, I saw Master Timo, Knight-Commander Mikkinen, and several more I did not know emerging from the keep.

"It's alright," I said. "I don't think there is anything wrong. Anything new, anyway. But if you'll excuse me, I believe I, uh, need to go and speak with a dragon.

"Uh... Piia. Would you like to meet a dragon? I think this involves you as well."

Piia swallowed.

"Um. Yes," she replied, after a moment, as a smile grew. "Yes, I think I would."

"Might I perhaps come along?" Jaako asked. "No dragon has spoken to a human in living memory, to my knowledge, and I confess to being greatly curious."

"I don't see a problem," I agreed. "I will make sure when we get atop the tower."

So the three of us walked across the bailey and into the base of the tower, and eventually emerged atop the wall, then climbed the outside stairs to the roof. The dragon looked around at us.

«GREETINGS ONCE AGAIN, GATE-CLOSER. THESE ARE FRIENDS OF YOURS?»

«They are,» I said. I held out a hand to Piia, and she stepped forward hesitantly and took my hand. I led her a little further around the tower to where the dragon did not need to wind its neck around quite so far. Jaako followed a few paces behind.

I gestured to Jaako.

«This is Jaako, who commands the... uh, wide-ranging warriors of this fortress.» I found I had to be careful about my wording, both to prevent stumbling and to find suitable words. It took a moment of fumbling to find a way to express 'rangers'. I assumed this meant I was speaking dragon again. But now was not the time to... well, maybe it was. In a moment.

«And this warrior is my friend Piia. She was with me yesterday.»

The dragon nodded its head towards first Piia, then Jaako.

«WARRIOR JAAKO, WARRIOR PIIA, I AM—» and again, that long, rolling... name, I realized. «I GREET YOU BOTH.»

I had to think about the name. Dragon speech was more different from the Saamen fire dialect than I had been led to believe—although the similarities were apparent. I thought I could begin to see how the dialect of fire could have arisen as an effort to cast the sounds and meanings of dragon speech into Saamen. I didn't know how I was understanding it, let alone *speaking* it. But this seemed subtly different again, in a way I couldn't put my finger on.

Finally I sorted it out in my head, and repeated back what I thought I had heard.

«Your pardon, please,» I said. «I wish to be sure I understood that correctly. 'The shadow cast by the third moon as it rises'?»

«YES,» the dragon replied. «THAT IS EXACTLY WHAT I SAID.»

«Good,» I replied. «I wanted to be sure I had it right.»

«THE POLITENESS IS APPRECIATED.»

"I just introduced you both," I said, to Piia and Jaako. "The dragon's name seems to be 'The Shadow Cast By The Third Moon As It Rises,' and... he, I think...? greets you." Jaako nodded his head in return.

"Welcome to Highwatch," he said.

«Jaako bids you welcome to this fortress,» I translated.

«POLITE,» said the dragon. «POLITENESS IS GOOD.» Then it (he?) looked directly at me again. «HOWEVER, IT IS YOU TO WHOM I WISH TO SPEAK.»

«Pardon me,» I said, «but... I do not understand how it is that I am able to speak to you and understand you.»

The dragon gave me what I would swear was a quizzical look.

«YOU DO NOT KNOW?» it asked.

«Um. Know what?»

«YOU UNDERSTAND ME BECAUSE YOU ARE FIREBORN.»

«I am sorry,» I had to say. «But what does that mean?»

The dragon tilted its head. Then it seemed to almost sigh.

«YOU CAN WIELD FIRE,» it stated, and paused, looking at me. «YES?»

I nodded agreement.

«THIS IS NOT BY CHANCE. IT IS BECAUSE OF WHAT YOU ARE. IT IS IMMEDIATELY OBVIOUS, TO ANOTHER DRAGON.»

«Wait,» I said, «*another* dragon?» But the dragon was not done. It continued after a moment.

«TO PUT IT IN THE SIMPLEST WAY I CAN, THERE IS A PIECE OF DRAGON SOUL WITHIN YOU. YOU ARE OF THE QUICK FOLK, ON THE OUTSIDE, BUT ON THE INSIDE, A PART OF YOUR SOUL IS DRAGON. THIS IS WHY YOU CAN WIELD FIRE. YOU CAN SPEAK AND UNDERSTAND THE TONGUE OF DRAGONKIND BECAUSE WITHIN, YOU ARE PARTLY A DRAGON, IN THE OUTER FORM OF A QUICK ONE.»

It was a long speech, which gave me time to absorb the meaning as the rolling words rumbled on. I heard more footsteps on the outside stairs, and risked a quick glance that way. I saw Raimo cautiously appear, then my lovely Kata, then an older man to whom I had not yet been introduced. I wasn't quite sure whether he looked more like a scholar or an administrator.

But that could be resolved later. I thought about what the dragon had told me.

«I find that difficult to accept,» I admitted. «I was born farther from here than I can fully comprehend, in a world where there are no dragons. How can I possibly be part dragon?»

«NEVERTHELESS, IT IS SO. YOU DOUBT?» The dragon paused. «HOLD UP YOUR HAND. YOUR MATE SHOULD STEP AWAY. SHE IS NOT FIREBORN... SHE IS YOUR MATE, YES?»

«Uh, that is complicated,» I said. «I seem to... somehow... have several.»

«OF COURSE YOU DO,» it said. «YOU ARE FIREBORN. I MYSELF HAVE FIVE MATES. FIERCE AND MAGNIFICENT, EVERY ONE. HOLD UP YOUR HAND.»

"Piia," I said, releasing her hand, "he says you should step back for a moment." She took two or three quick, but slightly hesitant, steps back and away.

"Alrekr, what are you doing?" she asked.

"I think it's alright," I told her. Then I held up my hand, as the dragon had told me.

The dragon nodded, then opened its mouth just slightly and spat a brief, narrow jet of searing golden flame at my hand, as thick as my thigh. Behind me I heard Kata give a short, horrified half-scream. Then the jet of flame hit my hand... and *splashed* like a spray of water. I felt the *force* of it, which was not inconsiderable, jolt back up my arm, but... it felt just pleasantly warm. There were other exclamations, as well, and I heard the sound of Tuuli half-leaving her scabbard.

For a long moment everyone froze. Then Piia stepped rapidly back to my side again, her right hand still on Tuuli's hilt, as I heard running footsteps from the stairs. I turned that way just in time to catch Kata as she threw herself at me, her face pale.

"It's alright, Kata, it's all right," I reassured her, holding her tight. She was shaking. "He was... illustrating something to me. Proving a point. Piia, it's alright."

«THIS IS ANOTHER OF YOUR MATES?» the dragon rumbled, behind me. «PLEASE CONVEY MY SINCERE APOLOGIES FOR FRIGHTENING HER.»

"He apologizes sincerely for frightening you, Kata," I relayed. "His name is The Shadow Cast By The Third Moon As It Rises."

I turned back to the dragon, keeping an arm around Kata.

«This is the High Healer Katariina,» I told—him. I was fairly sure now 'him' was correct. «You are correct, yes, she is another of my... mates. One of, uh, the first two.»

The dragon nodded its head.

«I GREET YOU, HIGH HEALER KATARIINA,» he said. «I APOLOGIZE AGAIN.» He turned his head and looked at Piia. «THIS ONE, PIIA, IS BRAVE. IT TAKES COURAGE TO DRAW A SWORD AGAINST A DRAGON.» Then he looked a little more directly at me.

«NOW DO YOU BELIEVE?»

«Since I arrived here,» I replied, «I have become used to believing things I once thought impossible. So what is one more? I have no other explanation I prefer.»

The dragon's vast chest heaved, rumbling echoingly. After a moment, I realized that he was laughing.

«Permit me a moment to explain to my friends,» I asked. I bent to kiss Kata. She kissed back fiercely, then grabbed a fistful of the collar of my jack and pulled back slightly. She looked into my eyes.

"Alrekr Járnhandr, my love and light," she told me, "as I live and breathe, please do not ever, *ever*, *EVER* do anything like that again without warning me first."

"I promise, beloved," I said. "I did not know what he was going to do. I suspect that his not warning me may have been deliberate."

I raised my voice to carry a little further.

"For those of you not yet introduced," I said, "this dragon is named The Shadow Cast By The Third Moon As It Rises." That name was a mouthful. "He has just... demonstrated a truth to me that I was having difficulty believing.

"He says that I am fireborn. And as best I understand, that means that my soul is part dragon."

"That... might explain a great deal," said the man I did not know. "We can speak of this—and make introductions—later."

I looked down at Kata. She was no longer shaking, but still clearly shaken. But now, curiosity was starting to replace that shock of fear.

"That must be why your core is so *bright*," she said. "Why you are so strong. Your Talents."

"What else does this mean?" Piia asked. She had re-sheathed Tuuli at some point, I noticed.

"It is why I can understand dragon speech," I replied, "and why I can speak it. And it is why the dragonfire did not hurt me."

I turned back to the dragon.

«Firesinging was the first Talent I discovered after I arrived here,» I asked. «Is that the same thing as being fireborn?» The dragon laughed softly again. For a dragon, that is. «I'm sorry if that is a foolish question,» I added.

«NO, YOU SEEK TO UNDERSTAND,» he replied. «NO QUESTION ASKED IN HONEST QUEST FOR UNDERSTANDING IS FOOLISH. WHAT YOU CALL FIRESINGING IS CLOSER TO A SHADOW OF BEING FIREBORN. YOU CAN SING FIRE *BECAUSE* YOU ARE FIREBORN. FIRE IS IN YOUR NATURE. THAT IS THE DRAGON PART OF YOU.

«IF YOU KNOW NOTHING OF THIS… THEN I MUST TEACH YOU.

«BUT THAT IS NOT WHY I SOUGHT YOU OUT. I SOUGHT YOU OUT BECAUSE YOU ARE THE CLOSER OF GATES.»

«Gates? Is that—» I began to ask if that was the same thing as a rift, and then realized that in dragonspeech, it was the same word. «Ah. I see. Yes. I learned only yesterday how to do this.»

«THE GATE YOU CLOSED YESTERDAY WAS SMALL. THE GATE YOU OPENED… ELEGANT. SUBTLE. WORTHY OF A DRAGON. BUT THEN, IT WOULD BE.

«THERE IS A MUCH GREATER GATE. IT IS A GREAT THREAT. IT HAS BEEN GROWING. WE CANNOT APPROACH IT. IT MUST BE CLOSED.»

«We… do not know of such a thing.»

«IT LIES BEYOND THESE MOUNTAINS. I WILL SHOW YOU. BUT NOT THIS DAY. I SHOULD GIVE YOU TIME TO ADJUST TO THIS KNOWLEDGE.

«I WILL RETURN, LATER. IS THIS A GOOD PLACE?»

«This is an ideal spot, I think. It is convenient to both of us.»

«GOOD. FAREWELL FOR NOW, THEN—AH.» The dragon paused. «FORGIVE ME. I HAVE GIVEN YOU MY NAME, BUT I NEGLECTED TO ASK YOURS.»

«My name is Alrekr… uh… I think Alrekr of the Iron Hand would come close.»

The dragon looked at me.

«CURIOUS. YOUR HANDS ARE OF FLESH AND BONE, NOT OF IRON… METAPHORICAL, THEN. ALREKR, WHOSE HANDS HOLD THE STRENGTH OF IRON. YES. THAT IS GOOD. THAT IS A PROPER DRAGON'S NAME FOR A FIREBORN. THAT WILL BE YOUR NAME AMONG DRAGONS. I SHALL TELL OF IT. ALREKR, WHOSE HANDS HOLD THE STRENGTH OF IRON, CLOSER OF GATES.»

«That's... quite a mouthful, for a... quick-folk name.» I realized that dragon speech lacked any single word that expressed 'human'.

«YOU MIGHT HAVE NOTICED WE DRAGONS HAVE LARGE MOUTHS.» Then he made that rumbling laugh again. I realized he had just made a joke, and I laughed too. Then I realized it gave me an opening.

«You might have noticed that ours are smaller,» I said. «If it does not offend, might I politely ask an indulgence? A *small* indulgence?»

The dragon chuckled again.

«AND WHAT INDULGENCE MIGHT THAT BE?»

«Dragon names are unwieldy in—uh, our mouths,» I said.

«AH. YES. THE SHORT SPEECH OF QUICK FOLK. THEY DO NOT SPEAK AS WE DO.»

«Would you be offended if, for—quick folk—purposes, I were to... shorten, summarize, the most significant parts of your name and refer to you as Moonshadow?»

The dragon paused, pondering.

«THAT IS AN ACCEPTABLE SHORT FORM,» he replied. «I TAKE NO OFFENSE BY IT. I ACCEPT THIS AS A NAME FOR USE AMONG QUICK FOLK. AND I WILL TRY TO REMEMBER TO USE A QUICK NAME WHEN I SPEAK WITH YOU.»

«That is considerate of you,» I said.

«WE DRAGONS ARE A CONSIDERATE PEOPLE,» he replied. «EXCEPT WHEN WE ARE ANGRY. THE GREAT GATE ANGERS US. BEING UNABLE TO DEAL WITH IT ANGERS US MORE.

«FAREWELL FOR THE MOMENT, ALREKR, GATE-CLOSER.»

«Farewell for now, Shadow Cast By The Third Moon As It Rises,» I replied.

Moonshadow spread his wings, launched himself into the air, then downstroked hard and climbed away. There was much less backblast this time, I noticed, with the height advantage of the tower.

"Would someone please explain to me all that just happened?" Raimo asked, with his usual unshakable calm.

"Let's go inside and send for some mead," I replied. "And then I will tell all of you everything I can."

My left arm was still around Kata. With my right, I reached for

Piia's hand, and then I led the way downstairs and into our tower. Dust had fallen from the ceiling beams on the upper floor, I noticed. Quite a bit of it. That would need to be cleaned up.

We went down to the main floor, where I found Master Timo, Vallaïnen, and Knight-Commander Mikkinen seated at the table.

"Your pardon, Master Alrekr," Mikkinen said. "We thought it better to wait here and not further crowd the top of the tower."

"Not a problem," I replied. I went to the front door and rang for a page, leaving the door open. Everyone had come down the stairs by that time.

I claimed a seat at the table with Kata on one side of me and Piia on the other. Jaako took a seat next to Piia, opposite Mikkinen, with Timo at that end. Raimo took the other end seat, while the stranger sat opposite me, one seat up from Vallaïnen. No sooner had I sat down, though, than the page arrived and knocked at the open door.

I looked over that way. It was Rami. He was practically bouncing with excitement. I waved him in.

"Master Járnhandr," he exclaimed, "we all saw the dragon! Is it true that you SPOKE with it?"

"With him," I corrected. "Yes, Rami. His name—his *short* name, for human tongues—is Moonshadow. Now if you would, kindly bring mead for everyone, please. Bring extra hands if you need. And later, I would like the upstairs rooms thoroughly dusted. Quite a bit of dust was shaken loose from the ceiling when the dragon landed."

"At once, Master Járnhandr!" he replied. Then he remembered his manners—always the polite one, Rami—and bowed to the table at large. "Masters, Honored," he said, "Knight-Commanders. It will only be a few minutes." He bowed a second time and left.

"An introduction first," Master Timo began. "Alrekr, this is Sage Nyysönen. He travelled here from the Collegium at my invitation and request. We hoped to find answers to some of the questions you have posed, both directly and by your arrival here.

"Sage Nyysönen, this is Master Alrekr Járnhandr, who, as you have seen, continues to surprise."

"Master Járnhandr," Nyysönen said, "I am honored to finally meet you. I apologize for not introducing myself before; I have been here

379

about a month now, but I wished to observe from a distance, in order to avoid—as much as I might—exerting any influence upon events." He was gray-haired and weathered, and looked almost ascetic, but his voice was deep and resonant.

"I understand that well," I replied.

"However, the arrival of a dragon—and that it SPOKE with you—rather changes matters," he continued. "That has not happened in living memory. So I decided it best to reveal myself."

"Commander Jaako mentioned the same thing," I remarked, with a nod toward Jaako, two seats over.

"Before I ask any information of you," he continued, "let me offer some of mine, regarding your seven-part healing of which much has been spoken. I understand the speculation came from you that despite having no Healing Talent, you were nevertheless able to take part in—and in some respects, steer—your own Healing, because the world itself accepted your self-image and told you in some way exactly what to sing to achieve it." I nodded.

"My fellows at the Collegium and I have discussed this matter at some length, and our consensus is that your speculation is substantially correct. We can come up with no other explanation that does not blatantly violate some major part or another of our understanding of the workings of Talent and *voima,* that have been established and refined over the course of more than a thousand years. So the exact details are still being argued over, but on the whole, the Collegium has accepted your hypothesis as our best understanding of the truth."

I nodded appreciatively.

"I thank you for telling me this," I replied. "To be honest, I have had far more wonders sprung upon me since that day and... really, I long since stopped thinking about it, and just accepted it as one more wonder in a land of boundless wonders.

"I think it's my turn. Let me start from the beginning and tell you as much as I can of what I just learned.

"The dragon's full name is The Shadow Cast By The Third Moon As It Rises. He has graciously consented to let us shorten that to Moonshadow.

"He came here specifically seeking me, because of the gate—er, rift—that I closed yesterday. He addressed me first as Gate-Closer. Gate and rift are the same word in dragon speech—they are both, uh, *jankankavoroullakko.*

"Anyway, he said that my... scent was on the gate-closing, and that he followed it here seeking me out. He told me that I am fireborn, and that this means—as best I understand it—that my soul is part dragon."

Several sets of eyebrows rose at that. But just then, Rami returned, with Tommi in tow, each of them bearing four tankards of mead. They distributed their burdens around the table, bowed again, and left. But I noticed they didn't go far. I shot them a grin through the open door.

"I understand your skepticism," I went on. "I had a little difficulty accepting it at first, as well. So, for those of you who were not on the roof with us, Moonshadow demonstrated something to me. He had me hold up my bare hand, and he spat dragon-fire into it." Kata's hand clenched for a moment on mine. I squeezed gently back.

I held up my open hand.

"As you can see, it did not burn me. It splashed from my hand like water. I felt the *force* of it push me back, but the dragon-fire itself was just... warm."

"The sauna!" Kata exclaimed. "This is why you did not burn yourself when you put your hand on Tumarïnen's heated rocks to feel the binding in them."

"I... imagine so, yes," I agreed. "It is also why I am a Firesinger. Moonshadow said that what we call the Firesinger talent is like a *shadow* of being fireborn. I think... what he meant by that is that at least in my case, being a Firesinger is a side effect of my being fireborn. He said that fire is in my nature."

"And *that's* why you can draw energy from fires to revitalize yourself," Piia mused, her face thoughtful.

"And a great deal more, I imagine I am about to learn," I said. "By the way, Piia, Moonshadow saw you part-draw Tuuli, and he said that you are very brave to draw a sword against a dragon. I heartily agree about your courage." Piia smiled happily.

"A warning would have been appreciated, though," she remarked, echoing Kata.

"I can understand that," I said. "But I can understand, in hindsight, why he did not. Anyone here, tell me: What would *you* do, if a dragon the size of a large house told you to hold up your hand because he was going to spit dragonfire into it?"

There was silence for a moment, then Raimo and Sage Nyysönen

381

simultaneously began to laugh. A moment later, half the rest of the table joined in. Even Piia couldn't repress a grin.

"All right, Alrekr," Kata conceded, smiling, "you make a good point. I will forgive him. This time. As long as you warn me next time."

"I promise, Kata," I replied.

"So," Nyysönen said after he stopped laughing, "what did you speak of after that?"

"Well, anyway, Moonshadow said that if I did not know I was fireborn, nor what it meant, then he would teach me.

"He said, though, that this is not why he sought me out. He came here seeking me because I closed the gate in the crags. He said that there is a much greater gate, beyond the Spine of the World, that it is growing, and that it is dangerous, and that they—the dragons—are unable to approach it. And it angers them."

Raimo had a thoughtful expression.

"I think I understand now why what lies in your future was hidden from me," he mused. "I was told by those who raised and taught me—my Huldre mother, in particular—that it is said something about dragons hides them and events around them from our sight of the future.

"I can see what you *are* when it is revealed to me, Alrekr. But if you are truly somehow part dragon... then that explains much of why your *future* has been a closed book to me."

"Is there anything more, Master Járnhandr?" Sage Nyysönen asked. "It seemed you spoke for quite some time."

"Um, well, dragon speech is quite... verbose," I said. "Much of the rest after that was a discussion of names. But he said that he will return to speak more of the great gate, that he will show it to me—but not today; and that he will teach me what it means to be Fireborn. But that first, he would give me a little time to adjust to this revelation. I have a feeling I am going to be learning some new things."

"A discussion of names, you say." Sage Nyysönen looked interested.

"Yes. Part of that was agreement that for convenience of us quick folk—that is the dragons' term for us, by the way; there is no single word in dragon tongue that means 'human' as such—Moonshadow was an acceptable short form, or summary, of his full name."

"I see," Nyysönen nodded. "And the other part? Or were there more? Pardon my curiosity. Everything to do with the dragons fascinates me."

"I'll tell you what," I offered, "the next time he comes, I will introduce you, if you like."

That really got the Sage's attention.

"I would consider myself *greatly* in your debt," he said.

"Anyway, the other part of the discussion was about my name. You see—uh..." I took a breath and glanced around the table, feeling slightly awkward.

"I think Moonshadow does not actually consider me to be a human. When speaking of me being Fireborn, he said it was 'immediately obvious to another dragon.' If I understand correctly what he meant by all that he said... I believe he considers me a dragon who happens to be confined in a human form."

Jaako started chuckling at that, then it turned to open laughter. Knight-Commander Mikkinen had been listening silently until now, but now he began to chuckle too.

"All right, Jaako," he said, through laughter, "you win, I concede. I cannot possibly top this."

"I don't understand," I said, grinning, "but there is clearly a private joke involved here."

"There is, shall we say, a certain rivalry between the two Knight-Commanders," Master Timo explained, chuckling himself. "As to which commands the more effective force. The Guard is much larger than the Ranger company, but the Rangers much more highly trained, and a Ranger team well commanded is much more effective than the same number of regular guards."

Mikkinen was nodding along with the explanation.

"But now Jaako has himself a DRAGON!" he declared through his laughter. "I am done. I yield."

I couldn't help it, I had to laugh too. And that started Piia and Kata off. I hugged them both to me happily.

After the laughter died down, Sage Nyysönen tried to steer the conversation back on course.

"So," he prompted me, "you were saying that the dragon

383

Moonshadow considers *you* to be a dragon, at least in spirit."

"Yes," I said. "And that means it is necessary, or proper, for me to have a proper draconic name. Or to put my name into a formal draconic form."

"And what is that?" Kata asked, curiously.

"Alrekr *kaitakijuokkatakuolikellettetuso saisakappellatakattumuo-vokataksassativentu nepentettiketsuomovokuuroukapalassattakima pentekkitsuuma sukuuvatutelimassassako jankankavoroullakkolletsissi nainavuutokoukitatepemmisteetva*," I said. It took almost a minute to say it. Kata blinked several times as it rolled on. Nyysönen listened intently.

"What, *exactly*, does all of that mean, in Saamen?" he asked, after I stopped speaking.

"To summarize it briefly: Alrekr, whose hands hold the strength of iron, Closer of Gates," I said. "But... it is more complex than that. That is a bare summary of it. Dragon speech contains a lot of... uh, meaning *about* meaning." No Saamen word for metadata or semantics. "It is verbose, but very rich, very detailed. 'Hands,' in this context, doesn't exactly mean just 'hands.' *Pentekkitsuuma* means more than *literal* iron. And *sukuuvatutelimassassako* carries contexts beyond simply 'hold.' It also conveys meanings of 'bear', 'embody', and 'contain.' And 'closer' conveys more than simply closing as in a door—there is also a meaning in there of ending, of bringing to a close, and other nuances. It is... complex."

"And yet, you understand it."

"Somehow, yes. Or I am beginning to. Though I am not sure I fully understand yet *how* I understand it."

"*Fascinating*," he declared. I started warming to this enigmatic man. He was clearly a true scholar.

"Anyway," I concluded, "now you all know about as much as I do at this moment."

Nyysönen nodded.

"I will admit," he stated, "I came here to study the phenomenon of the Adept out of nowhere who fell from a rift of unknown origin, who sang in his own Healing although not possessed of any discernable Healing talent. I still have unanswered questions—the *Collegium* has unanswered questions—about how that even *worked*. I doubt you fully understand how deeply this event shook our confidence in our understanding.

"But now it seems we have a greater and more urgent concern. And that must take precedence."

He bowed his head in my direction.

"I am at your disposal, Mas... *Fireborn* Járnhandr. If you have any questions I may be able to answer, ask, and I will answer as best I can."

I nodded acknowledgment back.

"I... greatly appreciate that, Sage Nyysönen. There is a slight chicken-and-egg problem, though." He raised a questioning eyebrow. "Uh—an idiom from my past. 'Which came first—the chicken, or the egg?'" I saw understanding dawn.

"Aaah, yes," he said, nodding. "Without a chicken, there can be no egg; but without an egg, there can be no chicken."

"Exactly," I agreed. "In order to know what questions you can answer, I must know what you know, and then I would not need to ask the question."

"I see the problem, yes," he replied, with a chuckle. "So ask me anything that you think it possible I *may* know the answer to. The worst case is that I do not."

"I will not hesitate to ask if I find myself facing any new questions," I said. "Thank you." A thought occurred to me.

"If I might ask—what *is* your particular Talent?" I could tell he was Adept level, at least.

"What else?" he replied, with a broad smile. "Study." Then I think he realized that the answer was incomplete, to me. "I can *see and observe* many kinds of things," he clarified, "many kinds of *voima*, but actually *do* little. That is the primary Talent of all Sages. It is what makes us Sages."

"Ah, I see," I said, as understanding dawned. He had broad access, but it was read-only. "You can *read* many kinds of *voima*, but for the most part *only* read them."

"Yes," he agreed. "That would be another good way to put it."

"Books, as well?"

"Yes. I can read books in many disciplines. And write or copy them, also. Much of the work of the Collegium is in making copies of the most important books."

I nodded. It made sense. This is what had made him a sage.

"Indulge me for a moment, if you would," I said. My notes on the soul-boosting technique were still on the table. I picked them up and passed them across to him.

"Can you read this?"

He took the notes and studied them. I saw his brow wrinkle in concentration, saw his lips move as he sounded words out to himself. It was clearly going slowly.

"Yes," he replied, after a few minutes. "*Most* of it. This... describes a technique for transferring soul-energy from one person to another, does it not?"

I nodded.

"That's it precisely," I replied. "Using the Soulbinding talent. Kata could not read it. I wondered whether perhaps you could. It is good to know that at least one other person besides myself can understand it."

"It will take me some study to get it all, I think," Nyysönen said. "But in broad strokes, yes, I am able to understand what you have written here. Whether I, or anyone else, can *put it into practice*, is another question."

"Anyway," I said, "I don't think there is very much we can usefully do for now until Moonshadow returns and tells me more. Though it already seems clear he wants me to close the... the great gate."

Raimo nodded.

"I cannot see what you *will* do," he declared, only the second time in this meeting he had spoken. "But I am sure now that yes, this is what the world brought you here *to* do."

"I did have a question," I said, pondering aloud. "Several, really. About how I could possibly have Talent when I came from a world with none. About why the... the world chose me. How I could be Fireborn when I came from a world with no dragons. Moonshadow did not answer that. Yet, at least.

"Liisa told me last night that she chooses to believe that the world brought me here not because of what I am, but because of who I am inside. That it *gave* me my Talents because they were what I would need." Pieces clicked together in my head. "Raimo, you told me that the world brought me here in part to forge Sekai. In some form." Raimo nodded.

"Could it be that the world *gave me* the Talents that I would need to forge and wield her?"

Both Raimo and Nyysönen looked thoughtful.

"The question treads upon unknown territory," Nyysönen replied. "Some of our oldest surviving records—such fragments as we have— suggest that the first to reach this land, those who survived the journey —a journey about which we know almost nothing—had no Talent and knew nothing of *voima,* and that the Talents arose later. There are records which suggest that the first Firesingers in the Sunlit Lands *learned* to sing fire from dragons. That the dragons helped us, early on. Before things grew strained between us."

"Kata has mentioned that," I agreed, nodding.

"So," he continued, "there is precedent for people arriving in this land from other... places where Talent and *voima* are unknown. And yet, Talent arose here. We have, as I mentioned, accepted as most likely correct your hypothesis that the world told you what to sing to complete your healing.

"It does not seem too great a stretch from there, if Raimo's Huldre sight tells him that the world brought you here to accomplish a purpose, that it also equipped you with the tools you would need to accomplish it.

"Why it chose you in particular, I can only speculate. Or why it went so far afield to bring you here. Your inner nature? Because you are somehow Fireborn despite all? Some other reason that we do not suspect?

"On that subject, I am told that you explained something of how far you believe yourself to have traveled to come here. But what reached my ears was fragmented and incomplete. I would consider it a great favor if you would repeat the explanation."

"All right," I gladly agreed. "I will try. Let me start with a question —two, actually, one of which I am already fairly sure of. It is clearly understood, I think, that the stars in the sky are suns like ours, correct?"

"Yes," Nyysönen replied. "We understand this well, that the stars are other suns that perhaps have worlds around them. We have studied the sky, and we have learned how to tell the bodies that circle with us around our suns as our moons circle around this world, from bodies immeasurably further away."

"All right, good," I said. "I might be able to describe to you ways to measure some of those distances, by the way." Nyysönen sat bolt upright at that. "And is it understood that the light of the suns—and of everything else that gives light—travels at a fixed speed?"

"We did not know it to be *fixed,*" he qualified, "but we know it to be exceedingly high."

"It is a complicated subject," I said. "I will try to share what I know of it, another time. Suffice it for now to say that if this world is roughly the same size as the one I came from, then light could travel all the way around it about seven times in a heartbeat."

Nyysönen thought for a moment.

"That sounds... plausibly close to some of our attempts to measure it," he agreed.

"The—sages of my past world also studied the sky," I said. "They used instruments made from glass—and other kinds—to magnify distant objects, and look far into the skies. By my time, they had advanced the art sufficiently to glimpse worlds around other suns and determine what types of worlds they were." Nyysönen nodded, clearly following along.

"The sages created a unit of distance called a light-year," I continued, "which is quite simply the distance that light travels in a year. That is a very great distance, as I am sure you must understand. We had scanned every star within hundreds of light-years of my world, perhaps thousands, looking for other habitable planets."

Nyysönen put it together before I got there.

"And, unless I miss my guess," he ventured, "you are about to tell me that your sages never once saw a world such as this one circling two suns."

"Yes," I agreed. "Exactly. So either this world is not in the same... space... at all as the world I came from, or it is at the least thousands of light-years away."

"A distance that light takes thousands of years to cross," he mused. "That is a truly *immense* distance. It is difficult to imagine, indeed. I confess I find myself unable to truly grasp it. I see now why what explanation reached us at the Collegium was unclear."

"I do have another question," I said hesitantly. I... strongly didn't want to ask it, in some ways. And yet I *needed* to. There was still an unresolved ache in my soul. "Something that I... *need* to know. Though... I am almost afraid to ask. It pertains to gates... rifts."

Nyysönen nodded.

"Ask, if you will," he said. "I will do my best to answer it."

I took a deep breath, and let it out slowly. Kata sensed something, and squeezed my hand.

"Is it known," I said, trying to best frame the question, "how much time it takes to travel through a rift?"

"Ah," he replied, nodding slowly. "I believe I see the relevance. Your arrival here.

"We have indeed studied that question. A scholar studying rifts, some two hundred years ago, contrived an ingenious way to test it. There is an artifice that we call a heartbeat crystal. It is similar to a glowstone, but rather than giving off a steady light, it emits regular beats of light at a constant rate, come what may. They can be created in pairs that beat at the *exact* same rate. Place such a pair side by side and watch them each day, or move them weeks' travel apart and then bring them back together a year later, and they will still be beating in exact time with each other, as closely as we can measure, never varying.

"This scholar took such a set of paired crystals, and he had a Riftmaker Adept create a rift as far away as he could, almost from the farthest north to the farthest south of the land, and then he sent an assistant to travel back and forth through the rift with one of the paired crystals as many times as he could while the adept held the rift open. The assistant was able to make seventeen return trips before the adept could hold the rift no longer.

"When the assistant returned from the final trip, the two crystals were almost a quarter beat out of step. Knowing the distance between the ends of the rift, the scholar was able to calculate that each trip through the rift took roughly the time that light was estimated to take to cover the same distance. But for the assistant and the crystal he was carrying, no time passed on the journey.

"Does that answer your question, Fireborn?"

I put the pieces together almost mechanically.

No measurable time passed while traveling through a rift.

Rift travel took place at or close to light speed.

This world was not within thousands of light-years of Earth.

Thousands of years had to have passed between when I entered that black twisted knot in the air, and when I found myself sprawled in the ravine amid twisted metal and broken glass.

Everything and everyone I had known before had been dead and gone for thousands of years before I ever landed in the ravine.

Including my son and daughter.

"I hope they had good lives," I managed to choke out. Then I broke down.

"I think we should go now," I heard Vallaïnen say softly, after a moment. "This is not the first such burden he has had to shed. Let us leave him with those who love him."

Our guests got up and filed quietly out, closing the door behind them. Then Kata and Piia helped me to my feet, guided me to the couch in front of the fireplace, and sat there with me and held me while I wept out every last bit of grief that still remained within me.

Rather later, I finally ran dry and found some semblance of calm again.

"Are you alright, Alrekr?" Kata asked, on my left.

"I will be, now, I think," I replied. I felt drained, but... somehow at peace, at last. "I finally *know*. Now I can let them go."

Kata nodded silently.

"I can feel that there is more peace within you," she told me. "As if a distant voice weeping in the background has gone away."

On my right, Piia nodded.

"I feel it also," she agreed. "You are... at rest now. As though you have accepted something."

"That is it exactly," I agreed, slowly. "I have finally accepted that a burden that I did not know how to carry... was never *in* my hands, even before you found me in that ravine.

"I know now that I can never know what happened to my son and daughter. But I hope that they found, or made, good lives. I will *believe* that they would have made me proud. Because I want to remember them that way."

Piia touched my cheek and turned my face a little more toward her.

"If they were anything like you, Alrekr," she told me, "then I do not see how they could have made you anything but proud."

"Thank you, Piia," I said. Then I pulled both of them close.

22: Fireborn

It was too late in the day, now, to even consider beginning Paavo's sword. But we had some time left before supper.

"I would like to walk, I think," I decided. "To let this new knowledge settle. So let us go and see if Karel is awake."

Piia heartily approved of this idea, so the three of us set out for the infirmary. It transpired that he and Ragne had been moved this morning to recovery rooms, so Kata asked which rooms they were in, and led us there instead. It was, as best I could recall, in the opposite direction mine had been.

When we got to Karel's room, the door was open, so we knocked to announce ourselves and went in. Karel was sitting up in bed. He looked tired, but he was awake. He looked up as we entered the room.

"Piia," he said, at once. "How much have I missed?"

Piia went straight to him and hugged him tightly, then sat on the edge of the bed. Kata and I pulled chairs over.

"How much do you *remember*?" she asked.

"I have been over it in my mind many times, trying to remember more," he replied. "Simo said there was a rift. We went to seek it." He glanced at me. "Járn..." He broke off. "Those are Ranger leathers."

"In good time, Karel," Piia said. "Simo and the rift. And then?"

"Járnhandr came with us," he continued. "We encountered a troll. Sick, wounded, perhaps diseased. We—mostly you and he—killed it. We examined its wounds, and then went onward into a ravine. I heard movement ahead, then..." He paused, then shook his head in frustration.

"Then *nothing* after that. Until I woke in this room."

Piia nodded.

"So that is where your memory ends," she said, squeezing his hand. "I will tell you that which you do not remember.

"We approached a bend in the ravine. A group of creatures came around the bend at a run—I don't know what they were, human-like, short, misproportioned, perhaps once human, perhaps something *like* human, perhaps some kind of *piru*—between thirty and forty of them, we did not have the time to count closely. They attacked as soon as they saw us. We killed them all, took no injuries to speak of.

"Then some demonic cursed thing came around the bend behind them. It leapt right into the middle of us, it ripped Ragne's leg and Paavo's arm open, Kata thinks it slammed you into a rock. Alrekr and I killed it, while Ari stood over Ragne and defended her.

"We left Eino to bind Ragne's wound and watch over the three of you while the remaining three of us went on. Past the bend we found the rift, and no further foes. I sent Ari back to help. Alrekr managed to close the rift. We returned.

"You were down unconscious, Paavo was poisoned and could no longer stand, Ragne was bleeding out. Alrekr somehow *opened* a rift directly to the infirmary. We sent Eino to help Simo get the horses back, Ari carried you through Alrekr's rift, I half-carried Paavo, Alrekr carried Ragne."

"How are they?" Karel broke in. *"Please."*

"Everyone is fine, now," Piia reassured him. "Paavo is up and walking, Ragne is recovering."

"She is in the room next to yours," Kata interjected.

Karel sighed in evident relief.

"Simo and Eino got back safely with the horses a few hours later. Jaako came to the infirmary to check on you all as soon as word reached him, then I reported all that had happened. Jaako inducted Alrekr into the Rangers. We are a team of eight now."

Karel grinned.

"That is why the leathers. I welcome you gladly, brother Alrekr. So all ends with good news. That is wonderful."

"Oh, I did not say that was the end of it," Piia said, grinning hugely. "This morning, a dragon stopped by to talk to Alrekr."

"Talk to—wait—a DRAGON?" Karel's jaw dropped.

"A dragon," Piia repeated. Kata nodded confirmation.

"And *NOBODY WOKE ME?*"

Piia burst out laughing, and Kata and I joined in a moment later.

"I *thought* I knew those voices," said a familiar voice from the doorway. I turned.

"Ragne!" I was closest, only three steps away, and I got there first. I swept her off her feet and hugged her tightly, then gently set her back down. She smiled happily at me.

"It is *so very* good to see you back on your feet, Ragne," I told her. Then Piia hugged her, and then Ragne walked over to Karel's bed, limping slightly, and hugged him in turn, then sat down on the edge of his bed where Piia had been.

"How are you feeling, Ragne?" Piia asked.

"Tired and a little stiff," Ragne admitted. "But I'll be back fit for duty before long."

"The stiffness should fade in another few days," Kata said. "It is good that you are up and around. That will help loosen it up. But do not overtire yourself."

Ragne nodded.

"I promise, Healer. Thank you."

"Thank Alrekr," Kata said. "If he had not brought you all straight back here through a rift, you would have bled to death."

"Is *that* how we got back?" Ragne asked. I nodded, and she looked at me.

"I think I remember you picking me up," she told me. "And what is this I hear about a dragon?"

"His name, shortened for humans, is Moonshadow," I recounted. "He sought me out here because I closed the rift we found, and he followed the... 'scent', he said."

"His name, 'for humans'?" Karel asked.

"His name among dragons, translated into Saamen, is The Shadow Cast By The Third Moon As It Rises," I said.

"That... is quite poetic," Ragne mused.

"The part Alrekr hasn't told you yet," Piia said, with a mischievous grin at me, "is that the reason he knows this is because Moonshadow considers him to be a dragon stuck in human form. They spent half the late morning and early part of the afternoon atop Járnhandr's Tower, conversing in dragon speech."

"Wait," I broke in, "what's this about Járnhandr's Tower?"

"You didn't know?" Piia replied. "That's what people have begun calling it." I blinked. Then my humor kicked in.

"Well that's not fair," I joked. "What about Kata and Liisa?"

"Oh," Piia replied, even more puckishly, "*everyone* knows *they* are yours."

"That's not what I meant!" I protested. But then everyone was laughing again, even my lovely Kata, and I couldn't help but join in.

"So tell me, new brother," Karel asked. "How is it that you are able to speak dragon speech?"

"Ah," I said. "Well, that's where it gets complicated. And yet, at the same time, it is where we at last begin getting answers. Moonshadow told me that I am Fireborn. That it is something another dragon sees immediately, he said. It means that my soul, *somehow*, is part human, part dragon. And yes, as Piia said, he considers me to be a dragon in human form. My firesinging Talent is... actually a *side effect* of this. And it is why I can understand and speak dragon."

"If the dragon considers you to be a dragon," Ragne asked thoughtfully, "and he has a name for use among humans, does that mean that you have a name for use among dragons?"

I had to admit, it was a pretty shrewd question.

"Yes," I replied. "I do, now." And I told Ragne and Karel my full name in dragon speech.

"*All* of that is your name?" Ragne asked, after a long moment.

"All of it," I confirmed. "It sounds verbose, but what it actually is, is incredibly detailed. It has an enormous depth of meaning."

"What is it in Saamen, then?" Ragne asked, looking curious now.

"Alrekr, whose hands hold the strength of iron, closer of gates," I said. "But I am coming to realize that that is only a shadow of the full meaning of the name in dragon speech. The name in dragon language carries so much more meaning that... I don't even know if I *can* translate it all. Yet."

"You are learning little by little what this new revelation means to you, are you not, Alrekr?" Kata asked quietly.

"I am, beloved," I agreed. "Piece by piece, like pebbles dropping into a pool."

I felt suddenly as though the room were closing in.

"Kata, love," I asked, "should Karel be alright to walk?"

Kata stood, walked over to Karel, cupped her hands around his head, concentrating. After a minute she nodded and lowered her hands.

"How do you feel, Karel?" she asked him. "Any headache? Dizziness? Double or blurred vision? Nausea?"

"I feel fine," he replied. "Just a little tired. And the missing memories trouble me."

"You should be fine, then," she said, "as long as someone is nearby to steady you in case you feel light-headed."

"Well, then," I suggested. "Who feels up to going to get an early supper? I, for one, missed luncheon."

Karel and Ragne both agreed that it would be good to get a walk, so the five of us set off for the hall, Piia walking next to Ragne, Kata and I on either side of Karel. Just before we reached the dining hall, we ran into Master Timo and Sage Nyysönen.

"Fireborn Járnhandr," Nyysönen greeted me, inclining his head. "I apologize sincerely. I did not know that my answer would bring you such grief."

"No, Sage Nyysönen," I replied. "Not at all. You misunderstand. It was not grief. It was catharsis. The *release* of a burden of grief and guilt that I had been holding onto because I did not know how to set it down."

"How so, Járnhandr?" Timo asked. "If that is not an overly personal question."

I took a deep breath, held it for a moment, and then let it out.

"In the world I came from," I began, "my past life, I had children. A son and a daughter. I... did not know how they fared. I did not know if they were alright, if there was something I *could*, or *should*, be doing to try to bring them here."

Nyysönen nodded slowly.

"I think I begin to understand," he said.

"Thanks to your answer," I told him, "I now know, once and for all, without any further doubt, that they were beyond any possible reach of mine long before I ever reached this land. That they, and their children, and their children's children, lived out their lives and died, perhaps as much as thousands of years before I fell out of that rift.

"There will have been... wergild, for lack of a better word. And an

395

inheritance. They will have been provided for. It should have been enough to set them well on their feet. I must trust that they made good use of it. I choose to believe that they lived their lives in a way to make me proud. I choose to remember them that way.

"Thank you, Sage Nyysönen, for your answer. From the bottom of my heart. Now, at last, I am fully at peace with my past."

Nyysönen half-bowed to me.

"In that case," he declared, "I am glad that my answer was able to bring you a release that it seems you very badly needed."

"Anyway," I continued, "we were on our way down to the hall to get something to eat. And give our two recently-wounded comrades here a chance to stretch their legs. Would you care to join us?"

"Your pardon," Nyysönen replied, "but I ate a late luncheon already after we left you. Another time, perhaps."

"As you will," I said. "And thank you again."

He nodded his head in acknowledgment, and then he and Timo walked on. We continued down to the dining hall. It was almost empty, in between mealtimes and cooked meals, but Mistress Kerttu directed one of her staff to put out a platter of bread rolls and fresh fruit for us, just a snack to tide us all over until supper. We sat and talked as we ate, keeping it light for now, before walking Karel and Ragne back to their rooms.

"Did the walk help?" I asked Ragne.

"Yes," she replied. "It perhaps aches a little more, but it helped loosen the stiffness. And it was good to have some company."

"And now you know that you and Karel are only a wall apart," I remarked. She smiled and nodded.

We left them there, and then Kata, Piia and I went to walk atop the wall. Today had been a day of revelations, and it was taking me a little time to come to grips with them. I did not know yet what being fireborn meant to me, how it would impact my future. As soon as I got used to one new thing, this world threw me another. Not that most of the surprises were not *good*—but it stretched me, kept me on my toes.

And *that* was good, too, I realized.

"A copper for your thoughts, Alrekr," Piia said, as we walked.

"I was just wondering when this world is going to stop throwing me new revelations about my life and what I am," I replied. "Learning that I could close—and open—gates... *almost* made a kind of sense. Kata, you had already said you suspected there were additional Talents I had not yet discovered." She nodded.

"But now to suddenly discover that I can speak the language of dragons, and be *told* by one that I am somehow part dragon myself... it is a lot to accept."

Piia nodded.

"I can understand that," she agreed. "But the dragon has said that he will teach you what you need to know. That must be a help."

"It is," I said. "Or I hope it will be. I had invaluable help coming to grips with what has changed in my life already." I pulled Kata a little tighter to me. "I don't know how I would have gotten through it without Kata—" I paused a moment, and bent to kiss her forehead —"and Liisa. And now, Piia, you help me to grow in different ways, as well." Piia smiled.

"In my past life I often used to wonder what was the point of my even *being* there. I felt meaningless, without purpose. Like a space waiting to be filled. But here... I actually *feel good* about being myself."

An afterthought came to me a moment later.

"I just wish that what 'myself' means would stand still for a little bit and let me catch up," I added, with a rueful chuckle. Both Kata and Piia laughed.

"From my perspective," Kata said, "none of the ways in which Liisa and I have seen you grow have been anything but good. We saw your nature in you in the first weeks—no, the first *days*—after you woke, and you have only become more 'you' as time has passed. More the man we love."

"Thank you, Kata," I replied. "Sincerely. That means an enormous amount to me.

"And I suppose I could have no better teacher about what it means to be part dragon, than a dragon. So there is that."

"I am confident that you will rise to this," Piia told me. "I have already seen how fast you learn and adapt when you have to. Ragne owes her life to it."

I nodded. That had been a terrifying moment. 'If this doesn't work, Ragne will die.'

I shivered for a moment, and pulled Piia a little closer as well. She didn't pull away.

We found ourselves back at the outside door into the tower. I was unsure what I should do next. I felt a bit at a loose end. Going to train or spar might have helped, but I knew my head wasn't really in it at the moment. I couldn't keep Piia or Kata from their duties indefinitely. And I wasn't sure I had the focus right now to work on the book I was trying to write.

"Would you like to just sit for a while, Alrekr?" Kata asked. "Until supper?" It was as though she had read my thoughts.

"I do not have to be anywhere," Piia said. "My team is on rest until we are back to full strength."

I looked back and forth between them. How did I somehow get to be so fortunate?

"I like this idea," I agreed. "Let us sit. And then we can send for supper for three." I looked at Piia. "If that's alright?"

Piia smiled.

"That would be very good," she agreed.

Kata led the way in and downstairs, and we sat together in front of the fire while I gazed into the flames and let my thoughts settle out.

"So was there anything else Moonshadow told you?" Piia asked after a while.

"Told me?" I pondered. "Well, no. Not exactly."

"Not exactly?" Kata asked.

"All right," I said, after a moment. "It *does* concern the two of you, after all."

Piia looked curiously at me.

"You recall," I began, "just before Moonshadow spat fire into my hand,"—I felt Kata's arm around me tighten for just a moment—"I said that he suggested you should step back for a moment."

"I remember," Piia nodded.

"What he *actually* said, as exactly as I can translate it into Saamen, was 'Your mate should step away. She is not fireborn. She *is* your mate, yes?'"

I thought Kata stifled a laugh, next to me. I wasn't quite sure exactly what Piia's expression meant. But she was smiling.

"What did you tell him, Alrekr?" Piia asked.

"I told him that it was complicated, and that I seemed to have several." Kata was definitely trying to hide a grin now. And I felt a smile spreading over my face as I recalled Moonshadow's response.

"And then...?" Piia said, the corners of her mouth twitching.

"He replied, 'Of *course* you do. You are Fireborn. I myself have five mates, fierce and magnificent, every one.'"

That did it. Kata and Piia both burst out in happy laughter, and I couldn't help but laugh with them.

After a while, we got ourselves back under control again.

"I don't feel very fierce," Kata said, after a pause for thought.

I looked at her.

"I recall a day on which you were, indeed, fierce and magnificent," I told her. "The second time you saved my life." She opened her mouth to speak, but then stopped, and closed it again, and thought.

"All right," she conceded, "I will grant that one. But fierce is not my normal way of being."

I pulled her tighter.

"Kata," I told her, "there are different kinds of fierce. Some fight fiercely to defend against a foe or a wild beast. You fight just as fiercely to save your patients. I have *seen* you. You do not give up, Kata. You will not yield. You do whatever it takes to save your patient. Until you drop from exhaustion. You and Liisa both fought for hours to save Ingrid's life."

Piia nodded.

"He is right, Kata," she agreed. "You are fierce in your own way."

"And *you*, Piia," Kata said. "*You* are fierce and magnificent."

"Oh gods, yes," I agreed instantly, thinking of Piia slicing that... creature's belly open as she dove and rolled *underneath* it. Piia smiled.

I almost thought she seemed about to ask some other question, but then she did not. Instead, she got up and rang for a page, and we sent for supper.

We ate supper together, and then Piia excused herself. I sat down and started trying to write down some more notes on soulbinding, while Kata did some study in a book that she told me was about memory loss resulting from head injuries, but she found nothing of new value in it. After a while I realized that I had drifted into a discussion of all of the weight of meanings in the draconic word for 'bind'. So I packed it up, and Kata and I went to bed. I lay with my arms around her, feeling the gentle rise and fall of her chest with her breathing, while nuances of the language of dragons slowly unfolded in my head.

Early the next day, I went straight to the forge and asked Matti if he was ready to forge a sword. He readily agreed, so I sent a runner for Paavo.

"You had better be prepared to do another tomorrow," Matti told me. "Ari came yesterday and gave me half down on a sword. Of course, there will still be most of a week's further work before the first is ready for tempering."

"Ari said the night before last that he was going to," I replied. "You should be ready for more orders. Commander Jaako has declared that the Ranger treasury will cover half the cost for any Highwatch Ranger who wishes to order a Highwatch *katana*."

"And what of the binding?" Matti asked. "Did you decide how you will handle that?"

"Truth be told," I said, "I have had little time to think much about it. But I know I must first find a way to soulbind without binding myself as well."

"Thinking instead about dragons and dragonish things, I'll wager," Matti guessed.

"You're more right than you know, Matti," I told him. And then I told him about Moonshadow telling me that I was Fireborn, and giving me proof. On a whim, I reached into the forge and pulled out a handful of glowing charcoal, and held it in my open hand for a moment in front of him. It just felt warm. Then I placed it back where I'd gotten it, and showed him my hand.

Matti examined my hand minutely, then gave me a very long look.

"That is impressive and strange, Járnhandr," he said. "So... what you are telling me, is that the dragon told you that you are somehow part dragon?"

400

I nodded.

"Specifically," I explained, "he told me that there is a piece of dragon in my soul." I paused, as secondary meanings unfolded in my mind yet again. "But the word that means 'piece' can also mean 'aspect', and... much more. Things that I do not know how to translate into Saamen yet."

Matti nodded thoughtfully, his eyebrows raised. Paavo arrived at that moment.

"Well," Matti declared, "never let it be said that you are not full of surprises, Járnhandr.

"Anyway, everyone is here. Are we all ready to forge a sword?"

"I think so," I replied.

"Tell me exactly what you need from me, Alrekr," Paavo said.

"Just sit over... there, within reach," I told him. I paused, trying to figure out what had just poked delicately at my attention and interrupted my thought. Something was different.

I looked at Matti. And again, back at Paavo. I was seeing a difference.

"Járnhandr?" Matti asked. "Is something wrong?"

I was still looking back and forth.

"No," I replied, after a long moment. "But I think perhaps something is *right*. Another thing... jarred loose."

I looked at Matti. Focused my attention on him. Concentrated.

Black, shot through with the hot red of embers.

I looked back at Paavo. Focused my attention on him the same way. Deep blue with shifting waves of green.

"You were born near the ocean," I heard myself say.

"...Yes," Paavo agreed. "But... how did you know?"

I stood lost in thought.

"Járnhandr?" Matti asked again.

"Matti," I said slowly. "I can see the colors of your soul now, without touching you. The black of iron, the red of the fire."

I turned to Paavo.

"Ocean waves and sea-grass."

His jaw dropped. "The beach next to the fishing pier," he said.

"How?"

"Járnhandr," Matti asked, more insistently, "did you know that there are glints of fire in your eyes when you do that?"

I took a deep breath.

"I need to ask Moonshadow about this when he next returns."

Paavo nodded thoughtfully.

"Piia told us all about your talk with the dragon," he said. "After she returned to the hall last night. This is some dragon thing?"

"I think so," I agreed. "It may perhaps lead to an answer to my soulbinding problem."

I hesitated, then shook my head to clear my thoughts.

"Let's forge a sword," I said.

"You did not finish saying what you need from me," Paavo reminded me.

"I just need you to be nearby," I told him. "Close enough that I can feel your soul to begin tuning the blade to you as we forge it. Then by the time it is ready for final temper, I will need to *know* your core so that I can bind your sword to it. I am hoping by then to have devised a way to do it that... does not forge the same depth of bond that I now have with Piia."

"What is wrong, brother Alrekr?" Paavo asked with a grin. "Don't you like me or something?"

I laughed.

"Not that way," I replied, grinning myself. Paavo laughed as well.

"To be serious, though, I can only bind myself that deeply to just so many people, I think. I can stretch myself only just so far."

Paavo nodded seriously.

"I understand, I think," he agreed. "But I am glad that you have such a bond with Piia."

"So am I," I said. And I meant it.

We forged Paavo's sword blade without incident. It seemed easier to keep his soul within my focus, easier to bring the blade into tune with it. Easier to hold the heat where Matti wanted it. And the work went more quickly. I don't know whether it was because I was gaining experience, because Matti was... or both. Probably both.

When the blade was done, Matti gave it a quick inspection and pronounced it good.

"There is not time to begin another today," Matti said. "But I would like to fit in one more set of ingots, if we might."

I nodded understanding. So we made another set of ingots.

I both heard and felt Moonshadow's arrival around halfway through the second ingot. It was alright. I knew somehow that he would not mind waiting a little longer.

We completed the ingots, and Matti put them away to finish cooling.

"I think I heard your new friend arrive," he said.

"Yes," I agreed. "I felt his arrival."

"You'd best be going, then."

I nodded, picked up my jack, and left. I wanted to make a stop along the way. I went to the infirmary.

I first encountered Marketta, moments after I entered the infirmary.

"Master Járnhandr," she greeted me. "Did you need something?"

"I was looking for Kata," I replied, "if she is not busy."

She told me Kata had just not long ago finished with a patient, and directed me to a room. I thanked her, and walked that way. When I walked in, I found not only Kata, but Liisa, Raimo and Vallaïnen. I walked straight up to them and tapped Liisa on the shoulder. She turned around, her face lit up, and I grabbed her, hugged her tight and kissed her.

"Welcome back, love," I said, after we broke the kiss. "Did all go well?"

"It did," she agreed. "A beautiful boy. Mother and son are doing well, and the father is proud and happy."

"All as it should be," I replied. Still holding her, I turned to the others.

"Moonshadow has returned," I said. "I am going to speak with him."

"We were just talking about your dragon acquaintance," Vallaïnen

403

said. "I imagine you do not have time to answer questions at this moment."

"Indeed," I agreed. "I should not keep him waiting too long. It would be impolite."

I turned to Kata.

"However, if you are not currently busy, I would like you to come with me."

"Of course," she said.

"Might I come too?" Liisa asked.

"Of course, beloved," I said. "I was about to ask you. But we should go now."

So the three of us went off, arm in arm, and we climbed to the top of the tower. Sage Nyysönen, it turned out, got there before we did. He was patiently waiting at the bottom of the outside stair.

"May I please join you, Fireborn?" he asked.

"Of course," I replied. And so up we went.

«FIREBORN ALREKR. I GREET YOU AGAIN,» Moonshadow said to me.

«Greetings and welcome to you, Shadow Cast By The Third Moon As It Rises,» I said. «Permit me to introduce, first, the Sage Nyysönen of the Collegium. You saw him yesterday but were not introduced. I myself was introduced to him for the first time only after you left yesterday.» I switched languages.

"Sage Nyysönen," I said, "the dragon Shadow Cast By The Third Moon As It Rises."

Nyysönen took a step forward and bowed to Moonshadow, and Moonshadow nodded his head in return.

«I WELCOME YOU, SAGE NYYSÖNEN OF THE COLLEGIUM. LEARNING IS ALWAYS TO BE RESPECTED.»

I relayed the greeting, and then Nyysönen's thanks in return. Then Moonshadow's head turned toward Liisa.

«I INFER THAT THIS IS ANOTHER OF YOUR MATES,» he told me.

«Indeed,» I agreed. «This is my other mate, Healer Liisa. She was not here yesterday as she was absent delivering a child.»

«A BRINGER FORTH OF LIFE,» Moonshadow said, bowing his head. «MY RESPECT, O HEALER. I GREET AND WELCOME YOU. YOU CHOOSE YOUR MATES WELL, FIREBORN ALREKR.»

"Moonshadow bids you respectful greetings and welcome," I told Liisa. "He seems to greatly respect you for bringing life into the world."

Liisa smiled, slightly nervously, and half-whispered thanks.

«She thanks you for your welcome,» I translated. «My mate Healer Katariina, you already met yesterday.»

«YES. I REMEMBER.»

«I am learning that I have many questions to ask about being Fireborn,» I said.

«THAT IS VERY GOOD,» Moonshadow replied. «SINCE MY GOAL THIS DAY IS TO BEGIN ANSWERING SUCH QUESTIONS.»

«In part this is why I asked Kata to come here this day. I have a favor to ask to satisfy my own curiosity, in the light of something discovered this morning. Would you permit her to examine your eyes?»

«OF COURSE.» Moonshadow lowered his head.

"Kata my love," I asked, "would you be so kind as to examine Moonshadow's eye?"

"Um," she began hesitantly. "Is something wrong? I have never seen a dragon's eye before. I have never seen a *dragon* before yesterday. What am I looking for?"

"I don't want to say yet," I told her, "because I don't want to prejudice your expectations. I would like you to look and tell me what you see."

She took a deep breath.

"All right," she agreed. She walked up close to Moonshadow's head, then closer yet. It did not escape me that his head was—his *jaws alone* were—larger than her entire body. She tentatively reached out a hand and lightly rested it on his head.

"He is very warm to the touch," she remarked. "Almost hot."

"Somehow that does not come as a surprise," I replied.

She stepped closer still, and began to examine Moonshadow's eye.

After a time, she stepped back.

"Thank you, Moonshadow," she said. I relayed it.

«YOU ARE WELCOME, HEALER KATARIINA,» said Moonshadow.

"Alrekr," she began, as she walked back to me. "Do you remember when I examined the eyes of Saana's hawk Kii, and I said that the new structure within your eye was similar to that in the eye of a

405

hawk, but modified to fit within a human eye?"

"I remember," I replied. Liisa too nodded agreement.

"I was wrong," Kata declared. "It is *EXACTLY* like the comparable structure in a *dragon's* eye, simply *scaled down* to the size of a human eye." She peered into my eyes, casting light into one again, and nodded to herself after a brief moment.

"But there is more. *Outwardly*, your eyes are human. But *within*, now that I have an example to compare to, they are the eyes of a dragon." She looked at me thoughtfully.

"This is why you wished me to look at Moonshadow without first telling me what you suspected, is it not?" Nyysönen was hanging on every word.

"Yes, Kata," I agreed. "Exactly. I suspected you might find something like this."

«Thank you, Moonshadow,» I said.

«DID SHE FIND WHAT YOU SOUGHT TO KNOW?»

«Yes. The internal structure of your eyes and mine are identical except in scale. As I rather expected.»

«OF COURSE. YOU ARE FIREBORN.

«NOW LET ME GUESS IN TURN AT WHY YOU WISHED TO KNOW THIS. WITH YOUR NEW KNOWLEDGE AND AWARENESS, YOUR DRAGON SIGHT IS AWAKENING. YES?»

«That... would seem to be the case, yes. I learned today that by concentrating in the right way, I can see the colors of people's souls simply by looking at them.»

«YES. THIS IS YOUR DRAGON SIGHT AWAKENING. GOOD. THIS COMES PLEASANTLY SOON.»

This might be my solution, I thought.

«How... far does this extend? Will it... enable, help, me to see people's soul-cores and know them well enough to forge soulbindings for them, without also forging the deep soul bonds I have with Kata, and Liisa, and Piia?»

«SOULBINDING. SO THAT IS WHY YOUR MATE PIIA'S SWORD FELT AS IT DID WHEN SHE PARTLY DREW IT YESTERDAY. YOURS FEELS SIMILAR, I SEE... BUT EVEN STRONGER. MIGHT I SEE IT BETTER, PLEASE? WOULD YOU DRAW IT AND LET ME EXAMINE IT?»

«Of course.»

"Excuse me one moment, please," I said to Kata and Liisa. "Moonshadow wishes to examine Sekai."

I took a step forward and drew Sekai, then held her out for examination, resting the flat of her blade on top of my left wrist, edge towards me. Moonshadow edged his head a little closer, inclining it to bring one eye near.

«HMM. AH. YES. I SEE. THE BINDING IS WELL AND CLEVERLY DONE. AND VERY STRONG. THERE... IS GREAT SKILL IN THE FORGING OF THIS BLADE. AND ARTISTRY UNKNOWN TO ME.»

«It was forged by Master Smith Matti, at the forge in the bailey below, with my assistance. He is indeed an artist, of surpassing skill. He is a metalsinger.»

«OF COURSE HE IS. YOU SAID HE IS A MASTER SMITH. HE SANG THE METAL, AND YOU SANG THE FLAME, AND BETWEEN YOU BOTH, THIS BLADE WAS BORN, YES? DID HE INVENT THIS CONSTRUCTION?»

«I brought knowledge of it with me from my past world. He took that knowledge and made metal reality of it.»

«INDEED. A TRUE MASTER.» He withdrew his head. «THIS IS THE INSTRUMENT BY WHICH YOU CLOSED THE GATE, AND OPENED YOUR OWN. THE HILT OF THE SWORD AND THE HAND ARE AS ONE.»

«Yes. I... cut the gate free of this world.»

«IT WAS WELL DONE, INDEED. BUT NOW WE SHOULD SPEAK OF YOUR ABILITIES, AND TEACH YOU HOW TO USE THEM. I MUST TEACH YOU WHAT YOU TRULY ARE, IF YOU ARE TO SUCCEED. THIS MAY TAKE SOME TIME. DO YOUR MATES AND YOUR GUEST WISH TO REMAIN? THERE SHOULD BE NO RISK TODAY. I INTEND NO FURTHER DEMONSTRATIONS SUCH AS YESTERDAY'S.»

«One moment. I will ask.»

I sheathed Sekai and stepped back. Both Kata and Liisa immediately took hold of me. Far be it from me to complain; I put my arms happily around them as well.

"I'm sorry to keep you all waiting," I said, pitching my voice to carry to Nyysönen as well, where he stood by the stairs.

"Let me bring you all up to date.

"Kata, the reason I wanted you to examine Moonshadow's eye is because I suspected exactly what you found. I noticed while helping Matti forge the blade of Paavo's sword today that I am... seeing more. Now all I need do is look at someone and focus my attention in a certain way, and I can see the colors of their soul, without needing to touch them.

"Moonshadow says that this is my dragon sight awakening. It was expected, although perhaps not this soon, and necessary. He was impressed by the skill that went into forging Sekai, and declared the binding to be well done. I haven't yet asked any further questions about that ability.

"He intends next to teach me about the Fireborn abilities I should have that I do not yet know about, and how to use them. He warns that it may take some time, but that there should be no risk and he intends no further demonstrations today like yesterday's, and asks if you wish to remain."

I turned slightly to Nyysönen.

"Sage Nyysönen, my guess is that you will wish to remain and see what you can learn."

The Sage nodded immediate agreement.

"Out of curiosity," he asked, "what colors do you see in *my* soul, Fireborn?"

I focused my attention on him. Liisa made a small startled noise.

"A light, warm gray shot through with... a dozen colors, twenty? Thirty? It is hard to say."

He nodded thoughtfully.

"I would like to stay, but would appreciate a chair, I think."

"I too will stay," Kata declared. "The chair is a good idea though. We will fetch some in a moment."

"And I," Liisa agreed. "Alrekr—did you know that for just a moment, there was fire in your eyes?"

"Smith Matti said the same thing," I replied. "I imagine Moonshadow will tell me that it is expected."

"We will fetch the chairs from the morning room, Alrekr," Kata said, before she and Liisa headed for the stairs. "They should serve."

I turned back to Moonshadow. A minute or two later, my loves reappeared, carrying the four wooden chairs from the morning room. We set them out and sat, we three in a group, Nyysönen just a little apart.

Over the next several hours, Moonshadow told me of things I

408

should expect. Drawing energy from fires was one thing I already knew. I also already knew, since yesterday, that no ordinary fire could hurt me any more—and that even dragon-fire shouldn't be able to do more than scorch me. He told me, too, that I should be able to see bindings on things so crafted. He seemed pleased when I told him I had already discovered that as well.

«What about my soul-binding ability?» I asked. «Is that, too, expected?»

«NO,» he said. «THAT WAS NOT EXPECTED AT ALL. IT IS NOT UNKNOWN FOR DRAGONS TO PERFORM SUCH COMPLEX BINDINGS. FOR A QUICK ONE, EVEN FIREBORN, TO ACCOMPLISH IT IS UNPRECEDENTED. AND YOU HAVE DONE IT AT LEAST TWICE THAT I KNOW OF.»

«I was hoping to do more,» I said. «Though I was also hoping to do it in a way that did not require me to bind myself so tightly to the one I am doing the binding for.»

«YOU... REGRET THE BINDING TO YOUR MATE?» That was strongly questioning.

«No! Not for a second! But... I do not wish to be bound that closely to every fellow Ranger, even on Piia's own team, for whom I bind a sword.»

«YOUR APPETITE FOR MATES HAS ITS LIMITS, THEN.» I blinked and started to frame a retort, but then realized Moonshadow was laughing. I couldn't help but chuckle myself.

«It's not that,» I replied, tongue-in-cheek. «It's that Commander Jaako and most of the other Rangers aren't my type.» Moonshadow's laughter, not quiet to start with, grew louder.

"Are you going to let us in on the joke, Alrekr?" Kata asked, smiling.

"I'll explain later," I said, chuckling. "I promise."

«WELL,» Moonshadow went on, «TO CONTINUE WITH OUR SUBJECT, YOUR SOULBINDING ABILITY IS AN UNEXPECTED DEVELOPMENT, YES. BUT IT IS A GOOD ONE. LACKING THE NATURAL ARMAMENTS OF A FULL-BLOODED DRAGON, IT IS VERY GOOD THAT YOU HAVE A WAY TO CREATE MORE EFFECTIVE WEAPONS TO ARM YOURSELF AND YOUR MATES. THOUGH TO DO SO FOR OTHERS THAN YOURSELF IS UNUSUAL. BUT WE LIVE IN UNUSUAL TIMES.

«I CAN INDEED TEACH YOU HOW TO ONLY LIGHTLY TOUCH THE SOUL-CORES OF OTHERS, ENOUGH TO PERFORM BINDINGS TO THEM—AND ENOUGH TO KNOW WHETHER YOU *SHOULD*. SO LET US SPEND THE REST OF

OUR TIME THIS DAY UPON THAT. PERHAPS YOUR SAGE WOULD VOLUNTEER TO BE A SUBJECT?»

«I rather imagine he would. But allow me instead to suggest using my brother Ranger for whom the next sword is destined. I have already begun attuning it lightly to him.»

«HMMMMM. YES. THAT SEEMS A WISE IDEA.»

"Liisa," I asked, "would you send for a page to fetch Paavo?"

"I'm not certain that will be necessary, Fireborn," Sage Nyysönen interjected. "The angle would prevent you seeing from where you are, but there is quite an audience gathering on the wall."

«Excuse me for one moment,» I said, and walked over to the stairs. I did not see Paavo, nor any other member of our team. Still, it had been a good thought—and I did see Senja and Rami there.

"Senja," I called down, "would you please find Paavo or Ari for me, or better yet both, and bring them here? And come up yourself, when you return, if you wish." She nodded vigorous assent. Then another thought occurred to me. "And Rami, please fetch us something to drink."

"It will be done, Master Járnhandr," Senja said, and she was off. Rami managed to bow deeply without taking his eyes off Moonshadow, then raced off toward the kitchens.

"You have some experiment in mind, Fireborn?" Nyysönen asked, interestedly.

"Um... less of an experiment, and more practice subjects," I said. "Moonshadow intends to teach me how to touch a soul-core lightly, for binding, without forging a tight bond to that person as I did to Piia. I can only carry just so many soul-bonds of that depth."

Nyysönen nodded in immediate understanding.

"Indeed," he said. "Even knowing nothing of soulbinding, it is obvious that it must be very demanding. Forgive my probing, but has he been able to tell you anything of interest about the ability?"

"Somewhat," I said. "It is certainly not unknown among dragons, though he says they seldom perform bindings of that level of complexity. He said though that it is... his exact word was unprecedented, for a quick— er, for a human to do so."

"A quick what?" Nyysönen asked.

"Uh. There is no single word in the language of dragons that means 'human,'" I answered. "The term Moonshadow uses is 'quick ones'. But I should expand upon that. In context, the freighting of meanings is not to suggest quick in the sense of speed, but instead conveys primary contexts of being both hasty, and short-lived."

"Hmmm." Nyysönen chuckled. "Well, from what I imagine a dragon's perspective must be, it is perhaps difficult to argue against either of those."

I heard footsteps on the stairs, and Rami appeared, carrying a large crock of fruit juice, with another page I did not know hot on his heels carrying a tray of wooden mugs. Still a third appeared, carrying a folding wooden table. She set down her table and unfolded it, then the boy with the tray of mugs set it down and pushed the mugs a bit to one side, then Rami set down his jug of juice.

"Mistress Kerttu sends her regards, Master Járnhandr," Rami announced. Then he and his companions stood and gazed in awe at Moonshadow. Liisa and Kata poured juice, and Liisa handed one to me. I took it gratefully.

«ARE THESE YOUNG OF YOURS?» Moonshadow asked. «I SEE NOTHING OF YOU IN THEM.»

«No,» I replied, «they are simply pages of this fortress carrying out an errand I asked of this one,» indicating Rami. «They are fine youths one and all, tireless and never shirking a task asked of them. I do not know who any of their parents are. But one thing is sure, you seem to be attracting an appreciative audience.»

Moonshadow chuckled again. The girl took an uncertain step backward, but I held up my hand.

"Don't be afraid," I told her. "He is just laughing."

"That is what it sounds like when a dragon laughs?" she asked.

"When this dragon laughs, at any rate," I agreed. She smiled.

"What is your name?" I asked her.

"Irja," she replied. "And this is Osmo, and this, Rami."

"Rami, I know already," I said. "This is the dragon Moonshadow, whose full name, translated into Saamen, is The Shadow Cast By The Third Moon As It Rises." Then I turned.

«These are Irja, and Rami, and Osmo,» I told Moonshadow, pointing to each in turn. Moonshadow inclined his head.

«I GREET YOU ALL,» he said, and I relayed the greeting, to huge grins from all three.

Just about this time, Senja arrived with Ari and Paavo in tow.

«And this is Senja, another most excellent page,» I said, «and my comrades Ari and Paavo of the Rangers. I have promised bound swords to both.»

«AH, AND THUS YOU SENT FOR BOTH. YES.» He nodded his head again. «MY GREETINGS TO YOU ALSO, PAGE SENJA.»

I relayed the greeting, and Senja made an excited bounce on her toes and clapped her hands. Then she remembered herself, and bowed politely in return.

"But now," I said, "I'm afraid this rooftop has become a little crowded, and I need to ask those who do not need to be here to go down."

"Thank you for the introduction, Master Járnhandr," Irja replied. "But now we *all* have duties to attend to." She particularly eyed Rami, who flushed a little.

"Thank you!" Rami said, and waved to Moonshadow. Then all four of them left down the outside stair.

«ARE YOU READY TO CONTINUE?» Moonshadow asked.

«Yes,» I said. «My apologies for the delay.»

«NO MATTER,» he replied. «IT WAS SHORT. NOW, ATTEND.»

First he taught me how to mask my own soul. It took a while for me to get it, but with repeated trial and error with Kata and Liisa helping, I was able to learn in a couple of hours to partially conceal my own soul, to the point that they—even with our close bond—saw it as dimmed and fogged, and could barely glimpse my core short of us going into the meditation exercise.

Moonshadow had me try next with Sage Nyysönen, with whom I had no such bond. He declared that when he tried to gauge my soul as I held the mask, it looked dim and ordinary to him, as though I had barely any Talent at all.

Moonshadow declared this a success.

«NOW,» he instructed me, «HOLDING IN PLACE ABOUT YOU THIS MASK THAT YOU HAVE LEARNED, TOUCH ONE OF YOUR COMRADES, SKIN TO SKIN, AND FOCUS YOUR DRAGON SIGHT AS WE DISCUSSED EARLIER. TO TAKE HIS

I held out my hand to Paavo.

"We are ready for the next step," I said. "Please take my hand." He stepped forward and took my hand with a firm grip. I focused my sight as Moonshadow had told me. Paavo's eyes widened for a moment.

«YOU SEE THE COLORS OF HIS SOUL,» Moonshadow said. It was just confirmation, not a question.

«Yes,» I said. «This much I have seen before.»

«GOOD. NOW FOCUS MORE DEEPLY. LOOK BEYOND THE SKIN, THE FLESH. FOCUS YOUR SIGHT AND LOOK THROUGH THE COLORS OF THE SOUL. LOOK BEYOND IT. BUT HOLD THE MASK. YOU ARE NOT THERE. YOU LOOK FROM AFAR. FOCUS YOUR SIGHT. FOCUS. TIGHTER. LOOK FARTHER. YOU ARE A DRAGON. *SEE* AS A DRAGON.»

I did as he told me, as he coached me along. I was somehow aware of my viewpoint... zooming in. Piercing through the layers of Paavo's soul. The more I focused, the more I could feel it, and the easier it became to recognize the feeling and... do it more.

I saw Paavo's core. It churned like the ocean, a ceaseless, yet peaceful gyre. Of blue and green. There was strength and power there, the power of the waves that wears rocks down to sand. And yet, along with it, a youthful playfulness that I knew would never grow old. This, I saw at once, was the source of his dry humor.

It worked. I let myself defocus back out, holding the mask.

"Did it work?" Paavo asked. "I felt... something. But I'm not sure what. Your... eyes... became very bright."

I glanced at my lovers. Kata nodded.

"In your core lies the strength of the ocean, my brother," I told him. "Ceaseless, ever in motion, yet ever at rest; unchanging, yet always new." I released his hand.

«YOU SUCCEEDED.» It wasn't a question. «DO YOU FEEL ANY DIFFERENT?»

I thought about it.

«No,» I said. «I know the strength at his core, now. But our bond of friendship... feels no stronger. Or at most a little.»

«CAN YOU BIND TO THIS?»

I thought again.

«Yes.»

«GOOD. NOW, THE OTHER. CALLING FOR TWO WAS A GOOD IDEA.»

"I can bind your sword now, Paavo," I told him. "Do you feel any different?"

"No," he said. "There was barely a touch. Like the feeling you sometimes get when something is watching you. Did it give you what you need?"

"It did," I confirmed. I offered my hand to Ari.

"Ari, you are next, if you would."

Ari took my hand, and again, I focused. He blinked.

"That is... startling," he said. "Your eyes."

"It is part of being Fireborn," I explained. "When you see that, I am focusing my dragon sight."

Then I focused in tightly.

It went quicker this time. His soul was... not the green of a forest, but the green of grass, endless grass. And then... tundra?

I kept pushing in, and I saw. Ice. Snow and ice. But always with fresh life beneath the snow. That was Ari.

I let go and let myself come out.

"You were born in the north," I declared, "on the plains, in the land of the ice and snow, and your core is the relentless strength of ice and snow that cracks rocks, but protects life under its cold blanket." Ari blinked, and nodded slowly. I suddenly recalled him standing defiantly over Ragne, in front of that... *thing*.

"I was indeed," he agreed.

«YOU SAW.»

«Yes.»

«AND YOU ARE YET UNBONDED.»

I... felt myself.

«Yes.»

«AND YOU CAN BIND TO HIM?»

«Yes. I am sure.»

«THIS IS GOOD. YOU HAVE LEARNED WELL. TOMORROW, WE WILL STUDY MORE. THERE IS MUCH MORE YET FOR YOU TO LEARN.»

I bowed.

«I am in your debt, Shadow Cast By The Third Moon As It Rises.»

«ALREKR, CLOSER OF GATES, IT IS IN ME TO THINK THAT YOU WILL REPAY ANY POSSIBLE DEBT IF YOU CAN CLOSE THE GREAT GATE. AND IF YOU CANNOT, THEN IT IS POSSIBLE THAT NO DEBTS WILL MATTER.»

That was a disquieting thought.

«NOW IT IS WELL DARK. I SHALL LEAVE YOU FOR THIS DAY. WE SHALL CONTINUE YOUR EDUCATION TOMORROW.»

«Fair winds, Moonshadow.»

He tensed himself and leapt into the air, then with a thunderous downstroke of vast black wings, he was soaring into the sky.

"Wow," I said. "That was a lesson and a half." I took a deep breath, held it for a five-count, and then let it out slowly.

"Your eyes were like twin pools of flame," Liisa told me. "Nearly as bright as Moonshadow's."

"If I might," Nyysönen asked, "would you mind telling me what you learned today?"

"I'd like to hear that myself," Paavo agreed, a moment ahead of Kata.

"Most certainly," I agreed. "But how about we tidy up first, then discuss it over supper?"

The suggestion met with no objections. So we tidied the tower top quickly and took everything back to the morning room, including the folding table, and set off to the dining hall. There, to my joy, we met up with Piia and Ragne. Piia drew me into a tight hug and kissed me, and I kissed her back.

"No Karel?" I asked.

"He was tired," Piia explained. "We saw you up on the tower for half the afternoon, but there was already a large crowd and I thought we should not crowd things further." I nodded understanding.

"Ragne," I said, "you're looking a lot better." She hugged me too.

"I'm *feeling* better, as well," she agreed. "The stiffness is fading, but I think it'll be with me a little while yet."

With eight of us now, we took a long table, Kata and Liisa on either side of me, and called for some food. Piia and Ragne were across the

415

table from me, Ari and the sage on either side of them, Paavo on the end of the table next to Ari. The main menu item of the day was *lihapullat*, meatballs in a creamy spiced sauce. It came with a basket of rolls of black bread, and of course there was mead.

"So how did things go today, Alrekr?" Piia asked, once we were settled.

"It was a very good day," I declared. "Before Moonshadow arrived, Matti and I got Paavo's sword blade forged, and another set of sword steel ingots made. Then I went to talk to Moonshadow, after picking up these two lovely ladies from the infirmary. We... noticed some new things while we worked on Paavo's sword, and there was something I wanted Kata to find out for me." I nodded to Kata.

"Shortly after we finished Healing Alrekr's body," Kata began, "he remarked that his vision was sharper than it had ever been before. I examined his eyes, and found several changes from what is normal for a human, including a new structure that I described to him. He said that it sounded like a structure in the eye of a hawk—I do not recall the term...?"

"*Pecten oculi*," I supplied. Nyysönen was listening intently.

"Yes. So I sent for a falconer and examined the eyes of her hawk. The structure was indeed similar, a... an internal wall heavily lined with blood vessels, though in Alrekr's eye the wall is circular instead of straight. I believed it to be an adaptation of the hawk's structure to a human eye. We considered the question resolved and thought no more of it, except to wonder at it.

"Today the dragon—Moonshadow—allowed me to examine his eye, and we learned that I was wrong. The structure is *similar* to the structure in the eye of a hawk, yes. But it—and the altered back of his eye—*all* of the back of his eye—is all but *identical* in structure to a dragon's eye. We saw it—but we did not know, before, what we were looking at."

"Is there a way that I might... see this for myself?" Nyysönen asked.

"You are welcome to look, if you can find a way," I offered.

"Whether you will be able to see it without a Healer's vision, I do not know," Kata told him. "But at the least, if I cannot find a way to show it to you, I will try to draw it for you."

Nyysönen nodded.

"That would be greatly appreciated," he replied. He turned to me.

"Can you describe to me what is different about your vision?"

"One moment," I said. "Kata. something just occurred to me. You told me that Healing cannot make someone into something they are not."

"Yes...?" Kata said.

"I *thought about* the vision of a hawk. But the world could not do that, because I am not a hawk. But it *could* give me the eyes of a dragon, because...?"

Kata's eyes widened for a moment, then narrowed in thought. So did Nyysönen's.

"You... may be right," he mused. Kata nodded agreement.

"But what *of* your... dragon vision, Fireborn?"

"My vision is sharper than ever before, by far," I replied. "I can discern objects sharply at great distances. There is no blind spot in my field of vision. My peripheral vision does seem to be slightly reduced, though. And by focusing my vision, I can see the colors of souls, I can see bindings placed upon things. I can see the details of Tumarïnen's work, clearly enough that I know how to replicate it—or at least, achieve the same result—without having seen it done or knowing any stoneworking."

Nyysönen nodded, fascinated. Several of those at the table to whom some or all of this was new were nodding along.

"After this examination," I continued, "Moonshadow instructed me in things that my dragon sight should enable me to do. Most, I had already discovered, though I had not realized that it should extend to all types of bindings. Since I had noticed only my own bindings and Tumarïnen's fire bindings, I had assumed that it was a consequence of my Firesinging that I could see fire bindings created by others. I did not realize that I could now see *all* kinds of bindings, as Moonshadow tells me I should be able to.

"I asked Moonshadow whether there was any way that I could see others' soul-cores enough to perform bindings, without also soul-bonding with them myself, as there are only so many such bonds I think I can hold. In response, he taught me first how to mask my own soul against being perceived by others."

"That was... strange and unsettling," Liisa interjected. "It *felt* as though you were somehow at a great distance, when I knew you were right in front of me." I squeezed her hand, and she squeezed back.

"That took me several hours to properly master," I went on. "And then once I had that, he taught me how to focus my dragon sight, without lowering the mask, to be able to see another's soul-core *without* forming a new bond to my own."

Ari nodded thoughtfully, and so did Piia.

"Enough to be able to bind swords?" Piia asked.

I nodded.

"This solves your dilemma about crafting soulbound swords, then."

"It does," I agreed. "To my great relief."

Piia looked at me, hesitating for a moment.

"Do you regret the bond you have formed to me, Alrekr?" she asked quietly.

"*No!*" I said, at once. "Not for an instant." She smiled happily. "Moonshadow asked me the same question. His tone implied... strong disapproval, I think, if I had."

"I think I would disapprove, too," Piia replied, still smiling. In fact, I think everyone at the table smiled at that. It made me glad.

"And that is where we left off for today," I finished.

"Fireborn, might I ask a favor?" Sage Nyysönen asked.

"What is the favor?" I asked in return.

"I have looked at your soul, masked from me," he said. "Would you permit me to see, unmasked? I have never seen the soul of a Fireborn. I promise to make no attempt to touch your core."

I thought briefly.

"I see no harm in it," I agreed. I reached my hand across the table. He grasped my hand, closed his eyes, took a deep breath and let it out. I could *feel* his mind probing at me, and I realized I could *choose* now to shut him out, or let him see. So I let him see.

His eyes flew open and he jerked upright. After a moment, he blinked, and released my hand.

"*Thank* you, Fireborn," he said. "Remarkable. You have... *tremendous* power. I can tell that much, even without seeing to your core. So *that* is what the soul of a Fireborn looks like. Your—masking, also, is effective indeed."

Kata took my hand, and I felt her contact immediately and welcomed her in.

"You continue to grow stronger, beloved," she said thoughtfully.

"The change is small, day to day. But when I think back... yes." From my other side Liisa, too, extended herself into me. I never tired of how wonderful this felt. I felt my pulse speed up.

"Yes," she agreed after a moment. "It is easy to miss the gradual change when we touch every day." She looked at me, her eyes coolly appraising. "Whatever you are becoming, I think that you are not done yet."

"Does that... trouble you?" I had to ask.

"*No,*" she said emphatically. "Wherever you go, we will go with you. Wherever this journey takes you. You are *ours.* We will not be parted from you." Kata nodded fervent agreement. Across the table, I noticed Piia's smile was beatific as she looked at us.

We took our time over supper. I basked in the presence of my lovers and my comrades, and allowed myself to carefully draw a little from the fire. Nyysönen had more questions, and so did Piia, who had not been there this day. I answered those I could.

Later, in our chambers, I realized there was something I did not know.

"Liisa," I asked, "what *does* my soul look like, from the outside?"

"It has changed much," she said. "When first we found you, it was dark, soiled, clouded with pain and loss. Thick with scars and wounds. And yet... with an inner fire beneath it all. Something at the very heart that would not give up, that clung to hope.

"Now, the clouds, the smoke, the wounds, have cleared and the fire shows clearly, rolling waves of fire, fierceness, determination... but behind the flames, a calmness, a strength, a place of peace and safety. I feel safe when I touch you."

"I, too," Kata agreed. "From doubt and uncertainty, from not believing in yourself, from being filled with pain and thinking only the worst of yourself, you have become a tower of strength. And you give freely of that strength. You *believe* in yourself, now."

"The two of you taught me that," I said.

Kata looked me seriously in the eyes.

"And Piia as well, I think." There was no reproach in her tone, only appreciation.

She was not wrong, and I said so. She smiled sweetly.

"So... what *was* the joke?"

I had to think for a moment.

"Ah!   Upon the tower top."   She nodded.   "I mentioned to Moonshadow that I sought to find a way to bind swords that would not bind *me* to them as tightly as to Piia.   He too asked if I regretted that binding, and I told him, no, not for a moment.   But that there were only so many people I was willing to be bound to that way."

"All right," she said, following along.   "And...?"

"Well, then," I said, "he asked, in jest, if that meant there was a limit to my appetite for mates."   Liisa giggled and covered her mouth with her hand.

"And you told him?" Kata asked, laughing softly.

"I told him that it wasn't that, but that Jaako and most of the other Rangers weren't my type."

Kata and Liisa both burst into peals of laughter, and I laughed with them.

"But Piia *is*," Kata said, after we stopped laughing.   Again, there was no reproach in it.   She was simply stating something we all knew.

"Yes," I agreed, after a moment.   "Piia is."

"That is good," she said.   "She is mine, too, I think.   She is much like you.   I am glad."

I pulled her close and kissed her.   It was much better than words.

23: Hold On Tightly

The next day, Matti was hard at work on Paavo's sword, so I called an early *kenjutsu* class in the Ranger training circles. Kauko was not with us, as Markku's team was out on a patrol sweep, but Kirsi's team was in, and both Ilona and Päivi joined us—as, this time, did Kirsi herself. I split the class and had Piia lead the others through *kata* while I worked one-on-one with Kirsi to bring her up to speed. She picked it up quickly. I let her use Sekai for part of it, so that she could learn how a *katana* felt different and balanced differently from a straight sword, and I showed her how to parry with the flat or the back to protect the hardened edge from damage.

I felt and heard Moonshadow arrive, shortly before we finished up our class. I got Kirsi through her first unbroken run of first *kata*, then had her do it again. I only had to correct a few minor errors of form. Then I called a halt to class.

"You'll have to forgive me," I announced. "Now *my* teacher is here."

"May I come along, Alrekr?" Piia asked.

"Of course," I agreed instantly. I gave her my hand, and we headed for the tower top.

«Shadow Cast By The Third Moon As It Rises, I greet you,» I said, as we reached the top of the tower. «You are early today.»

«INDEED, CLOSER OF GATES,» he replied. «I PLAN NO LESSON TODAY. TOMORROW WE WILL STUDY. BUT TODAY I WISH YOU TO SEE SOMETHING. YOU MUST KNOW WHAT YOU FACE. I WILL CARRY YOU THERE.»

«Carry me...?»

«IT IS SOME DISTANCE. YOU MUST RIDE.»

He shifted position, carefully placing a foreleg. I looked, and saw that if I were to climb up onto his foreleg, then up the leg, I could reach his shoulder, and from there, the wing root, and from there to his back, between his shoulders. But I saw nothing to hold on to.

«I think I see what you intend. But I do not see how I will stay on.»

«LOOK FIRST,» he replied. «AND THEN WE SHALL SEE.»

421

"He wants me to climb onto his back," I explained to Piia. "There is something he wishes me to see."

Piia looked levelly back at me.

"If you should see it, Alrekr, then I think perhaps I should as well. Can he—*will* he—carry us both?"

"I will ask," I replied. "I agree, and I would not leave you behind. But first, we need to figure out how to stay on."

I climbed up where Moonshadow indicated. It was easier than it looked. My boots found good purchase on his rough scales. When I reached his back, the large plates that armored his spine were smoother, and not uncomfortable to sit on. Moonshadow's body heat was like sitting astride a heating furnace. His back was not burning hot, but there was an abundance of warmth there. The edges of the large scales were almost... I wasn't sure whether the correct word was eroded, or filigreed. The holes were too small to provide handholds, though.

«Your scales. The edges look eroded. What did that?»

«AH, THAT,» he replied. «YES. IT IS A THING THAT COMES NATURALLY TO A DRAGON WITH AGE, AS THE SCALES GROW AND WEAR. THERE IS NO HARM IN IT, IT DOES NOT WEAKEN THE SCALE.»

Hmm. I pondered.

«May I try something?» I asked.

«OF COURSE.»

«Do you feel this?»

I took hold of the edge of one of the scales, using a couple of the holes, and tugged hard. It didn't move.

«BARELY,» he replied. «HAVE YOU A THOUGHT?»

«I do,» I agreed. «If I were to loop strong leather straps through these holes...»

«THEN YOU COULD HOLD TIGHTLY TO THE STRAPS TO KEEP YOURSELF IN PLACE,» Moonshadow finished for me. «A GOOD SOLUTION. I BELIEVE IT SHOULD WORK. I SHALL TRY TO AVOID DOING ANYTHING TOO SUDDEN.»

I looked to make sure there was room for two, and was confident there was.

«There is another question,» I began, as I started to climb down.

«YOUR MATE,» Moonshadow stated, before I could. «SHE WISHES TO COME ALSO, IF I JUDGE CORRECTLY.»

«You do,» I replied. «It was that obvious?»

«SHE IS YOUR MATE, ALREKR WHOSE HANDS HOLD THE STRENGTH OF IRON. SHOULD I HAVE BEEN SURPRISED?»

«I suppose not,» I replied, laughing. «Wait, please, if you would. I believe I know where I can quickly get some suitable strong straps.»

«OF COURSE,» he replied.

"Moonshadow is happy to carry both of us," I told Piia when I got down. "Almost before I raised the question, he had already guessed it, and seemed almost surprised that I even felt the need to ask. He said, 'She is your mate. Should I have been surprised?'"

Piia smiled happily and hugged me tightly. Then she pulled back just enough to look at me.

"We're going to have to talk about this mate business, you know," she said, seriously. I nodded.

"I know," I agreed. "I... admit I've been putting it off. And I probably shouldn't have. But... I don't know *how* to..."

She hugged me tightly again.

"We will work it out," she replied, and kissed me. "Probably not today. But we will work it out."

"For now," I said, "we need to find some long leather straps, if we are to stay on Moonshadow's back. I'm thinking there should be something suitable at the stables."

She nodded.

"A good thought," she declared. "So let us go."

Nearly an hour later, we were back with eight straps of latigo leather, seven or eight feet long, about an inch and a quarter wide, enough to get a good grip upon, each individually tested for strength by the stablemaster once we explained what we needed and why.

"I will tell you freely," he had told me, "you would not get me up there. But, were I a younger man... there was a time I would have." And I understood what he meant. *"We are only immortal for a limited time,"* I thought to myself.

Now, we climbed up on Moonshadow's back, and selected the best spots to thread the doubled straps through the age filigree in his back plates and pass them through their own loops, giving each of us a bundle of four ends to grasp in each hand to hold ourselves onto his back. We took our places, Piia behind me close against my back, and wound the straps around our hands.

«ARE YOU READY?» Moonshadow asked. «ONCE WE ARE IN FLIGHT I WILL BE UNABLE TO TURN MY HEAD AROUND THIS FAR TO YOU. YOU WILL HAVE TO SHOUT FOR ME TO HEAR YOU.»

«I understand,» I replied. «We are as ready as we will be without much more elaborate preparations.»

«THEN HOLD ON TIGHTLY. WE FLY.»

And with that, he leapt into the air.

The jolt of the initial launch was hard, but then he took a slow, gentle circle around Highwatch.

«ARE YOU BOTH ALRIGHT?» he called.

«We're fine so far,» I shouted back.

«GOOD,» he replied. «I HEAR YOU.»

He turned northwest and began to steadily climb.

A half hour later, we were crossing into the edge of the true Spine of the World. This was totally different than flying in an airliner. I felt... *elated*. This was truly flying. The air was cold up here, and Moonshadow's body heat was very welcome. The mountain range below us was incredibly, savagely rugged, and from this altitude I could see why it was called the Spine of the World. It did, indeed, look like a twisted spine.

«DOWN THERE,» he called, pointing with his head, «LIES MY NEST, AND MY MATES, AND MY YOUNG. SOME DAY SOON, WHEN TIME PERMITS US, I HOPE TO TAKE YOU THERE AND SHOW YOU, INTRODUCE YOU.»

Looking down, I could not tell exactly where he was trying to point, but I could see other dragons in flight here and there. I could not tell whether they were headed any place in particular, patrolling, or even hunting. But it was magnificent to see them. Then I realized that Piia probably couldn't, at this distance.

One, however, was climbing rapidly towards us. His (?) scales glinted in the double sunlight like polished bronze. Shortly afterward, he pulled up level with us, some hundred feet away.

"He is beautiful," Piia called over my shoulder.

«THIS IS THE CLOSER OF GATES?» the new dragon's voice came.

«INDEED,» Moonshadow replied. «THESE ARE FIREBORN ALREKR, WHOSE HANDS HOLD THE STRENGTH OF IRON, CLOSER OF GATES, AND ONE OF HIS MATES, RANGER PIIA, WHOSE HEART WILL NEVER QUAIL EVEN IN THE DARKEST DEPTHS.» Then he called back to us.

«THIS IS A NEPHEW OF MINE, THE GLINT OF FIRST SUNLIGHT OFF MOUNTAINTOP ICE IN THE MORNING.»

"He just introduced us," I told Piia. "This is a nephew of his, The Glint Of First Sunlight Off Mountaintop Ice In The Morning. He names you as Piia, Whose Heart Will Never Quail Even In The Darkest Depths." She laughed joyfully. Then I turned towards the other dragon.

«I am honored to make your acquaintance, Glint Of First Sunlight Off Mountaintop Ice In The Morning,» I shouted back, as loudly as I could.

«HIS MATE DOES NOT SPEAK THE DRAGON TONGUE,» Moonshadow added.

«YOU TAKE HIM TO SEE THE GREAT GATE, I DO NOT DOUBT?»

«EVEN SO,» Moonshadow replied.

«I SHALL FLY WITH YOU, THEN, AND GUARD.»

«THAT IS WELL,» Moonshadow agreed.

We crossed the entire mountain range, then began to descend into a vast bowl on the other side. It was rocky, broken and jumbled.

«ENEMIES BELOW,» First Sunlight called. Then he peeled off into a wing-over and dropped. Moonshadow followed, rather less precipitately, spiraling down in a steep bank.

«DO YOU SEE, GATE-CLOSER?» Moonshadow called to me. «IN THE CANYON THERE.» I wasn't sure which canyon he meant, but I looked for a canyon ahead of First Sunlight's track. I quickly found one, a dark column within it on the ground. First Sunlight swept over it perhaps half a mile up, before starting to turn around and drop further.

By now we were low enough that I could easily make out the column, though I was not sure whether Piia could or not. I could now recognize the larger shape in the middle as another of the mantis-crab things. Moonshadow circled steadily, giving us a good view into the canyon.

I pointed them out to Piia.

"Can you see?" I called.

"Barely," she replied. "Something larger in the middle?"

"One of the things we killed," I said.

"Then those others... are larger than what we fought."

"Yes."

Then First Sunlight came back in on his reverse track, more slowly, barely above the canyon walls this time. Worlds may change, but some things translate across any gulf. That column was about to have a very bad day.

"Attack run!" I barely had time for two words to Piia. Then First Sunlight let loose a searing stream of golden fire. He tracked up the entire length of the column from behind, and laid down a wave of flame that filled the canyon from side to side. When he had passed, no more than a half dozen of the dark creatures in the column still stood, and they staggered around at random, blazing like torches, toppling one by one. Piia cheered loudly from behind me, and Moonshadow bellowed too.

The mantis-crab stood untouched in the middle of the charred corpses, but First Sunlight was not done. He pulled up in a half-loop, folded his wings, and dropped like a rock. At the last instant I think the mantis-crab tried to leap aside, but it was too slow. First Sunlight dropped feet-first upon it and smashed it flat. He raised his head and bellowed, then launched himself back into the air. Side by side, we followed the canyon towards the center of the bowl. I was beginning to see things in the air far ahead.

Only a minute or two further down the canyon, we came upon another column.

«MINE!» Moonshadow bellowed, this time. He lined up along the canyon and, as First Sunlight had done, dropped to barely above the walls, braking.

«HOLD ON!» Then he began to inhale. And inhale, and inhale. I felt myself inhaling as well. Creatures started to break off from the front of the column, trying to flee, but it was too late. Moonshadow opened his maw, and searing fire filled the canyon to fifteen or twenty feet up the walls. An intense surge of exultation filled me, and I threw my head back and let loose a wordless roar of triumph into the sky as Moonshadow pulled up and away. Behind me I heard Piia join her voice to mine.

«THAT IS THE DRAGON SPIRIT WITHIN YOU, GATE-CLOSER!» Moonshadow bellowed.

I could see as Moonshadow began to turn and circle around that the mantis-crab had turned around to track us, which is why it had no warning at all when First Sunlight dropped on it like a bolt from the blue and crushed it as flat as the first.

We pulled up to what I estimated as about two thousand feet, and flew onward. The distant shapes resolved themselves to twisting, writhing filaments in the air. They thrashed like swarming eels. At their center lay a dark knot.

Perhaps a half mile out, Moonshadow and First Sunlight turned away and began to circle it, First Sunlight slightly above and behind us.

«THE GREAT GATE, GATE-CLOSER,» Moonshadow called. «WE DARE NOT APPROACH CLOSER. THESE RIBBONS OF FOULNESS WILL CLAW US FROM THE AIR. FIVE DRAGONS WERE LOST BEFORE WE LEARNED. THEIR NAMES HAVE JOINED OUR GREAT SONG OF PASSING. CAN YOU SEE IT CLEARLY?»

I could. I didn't know how much Piia could see.

«It looks the size of a... large dwelling,» I called back.

«YES,» Moonshadow replied. «IT GROWS STILL. SLOWLY, BUT IT GROWS STEADILY.»

"Piia, can you see?" I asked.

"I see something dark," she replied. "Much bigger than the one in the crags. And... those streamers in the air. Much larger, also. They look dangerous."

We circled it, keeping a safe distance, and I studied what I could see. There were columns and clots of creatures scattered throughout the bowl, especially below the shelter of the filaments in the sky.

«HAVE YOU SEEN ENOUGH FOR THIS DAY, CLOSER?» Moonshadow asked, after a time. «IT IS DANGEROUS TO REMAIN HERE, CLOSE TO THE GATE.» Some of the nearer ribbons seemed more active, as though they were reaching toward us.

«I have seen enough, I think. Let us leave this place.»

Moonshadow wheeled around and we began our flight back to Highwatch. First Sunlight followed us part of the way, then wished us hearty winds and peeled off.

It was late in the day when we landed, Moonshadow back-winging to a smooth rest. We unthreaded the straps before we dismounted.

«KEEP THOSE NEARBY, GATE-CLOSER,» Moonshadow said. «YOU WILL NEED THEM AGAIN. NOT THIS DAY, BUT SOON.»

As soon as we were both on the ground, Piia threw herself at me and clung tightly to me.

"That was *incredible*," she told me excitedly. "I have never felt such a feeling. Even without your sight... the mountains are incredible from above. The sunlight off the peaks. The wind, cold, yet so clear. *Dragons*. That... *fire*."

I heard Moonshadow chuckle.

«YOUR MATE SEEMS PLEASED,» he said.

«She enjoyed her first flight very much,» I replied. «And... we both found your fire... stirring. Thank you, from both of us. I only wish it were not in dire circumstances.»

«INDEED,» he replied. «THE GATE BEGAN SMALL. AT FIRST ONLY SMALL CREATURES CAME THROUGH, FRANTIC CREATURES SMALLER THAN QUICK FOLK, WITH CRUDE WEAPONS. BUT THEN IT BEGAN TO SLOWLY GROW. WHEN IT GREW LARGE ENOUGH, THE LARGER MARCHERS YOU SAW THIS DAY BEGAN COMING THROUGH. SO FAR WE HAVE KEPT THEM FROM PASSING BEYOND THE GREAT BOWL.

«BUT THE GATE CONTINUED TO GROW, AND AFTER A TIME THE FLAME-PROOF STALKERS BEGAN TO COME THROUGH. THOSE TOO, AS YOU SAW, WE CAN STOP WITH LITTLE DIFFICULTY, AS LONG AS THEY REMAIN ISOLATED. IN SUFFICIENT NUMBERS, THEY MIGHT BE A THREAT TO US.

«BUT THE GATE HAS NEARLY TRIPLED IN SIZE SINCE THEY BEGAN TO COME THROUGH. WE ARE GROWING ALARMED AT WHAT MIGHT COME THROUGH NEXT. AND AS YOU NOW KNOW, IT HAS BEGUN TO SPIN OUT SMALLER GATES, WIDELY SPREAD. SO FAR THEY HAVE LASTED LITTLE TIME, BUT WE SUSPECT IT WILL NOT REMAIN SO.

«BUT THEN WE BECAME AWARE OF YOU. AND HERE WE ARE.»

There were footsteps on the outside stairs as he spoke, and shortly after, the Sage appeared at the top of the stairs, followed in short order by Commander Jaako, Master Timo, Kata, and Ari.

"Welcome back, Fireborn Alrekr, Ranger Piia," Jaako greeted us. "You seem to have had quite the adventure. First dragons and Fireborn, then dragon-borne Rangers. What will it be next?"

I determinedly resisted the urge to break into 'I want to live a life of danger!' I think Piia caught it, though. She gave me a questioning look, a subtle smile playing about her lips.

"Later," I told her quietly.

«SAGE, KNIGHT-COMMANDER, HEALER KATARIINA, MATE OF ALREKR, RANGER ARI, FRIEND OF ALREKR, I GREET YOU,» Moonshadow declared. I relayed the greetings, in my unofficial capacity as Only Available Translator. And that whimsical thought spurred another.

«You know,» I began, «I have a question. Things were mentioned to me about a peace settlement arrived at some centuries ago. Not to get into all of the details right now of what happened, but I'm curious how it was actually resolved—how it was negotiated. How you spoke to each other.»

«HMM. YES,» Moonshadow mused. «IT WAS A DIFFICULT TIME. THERE HAD BEEN... MISUNDERSTANDINGS, AND SOME OF THE QUICK PEOPLE BEHAVED BADLY FOR A TIME. SO DID SOME DRAGONS. THERE WAS STRIFE. WE ARE NOT WELL EQUIPPED TO SPEAK YOUR TONGUE. BUT SOME OF THE QUICK FOLK WHO KEPT THEMSELVES APART FROM THE STRIFE TOOK THE TIME TO LEARN OURS. AND ONCE WE COULD SPEAK TOGETHER, FROM THEN IT WAS ONLY A MATTER OF TIME UNTIL ALL WAS RESOLVED.

«I REMEMBER IT WELL.»

«You *remember* it?» I asked. Moonshadow nodded.

«OF COURSE. I WAS THERE, AND DRAGON MEMORIES ARE LONG. BUT FOR NOW, I SHOULD DEPART. AND YOU NOW HAVE MUCH TO SPEAK OF, I IMAGINE. FAREWELL, ALREKR, GATE-CLOSER. WE SHALL SPEAK MORE TOMORROW, AND I SHALL TEACH YOU MORE OF WHAT YOU MUST KNOW.»

«Farewell for now, Moonshadow. Hearty winds to you.»

Moonshadow chuckled, and launched himself into the air.

I looked around the tower top.

"Huh," I said, as something clicked in my head. "Moonshadow was *at* the settlement talks six hundred plus years ago. Implying he himself is much older than that. 'A voice out of time will guide you.'"

"Raimo's prophecy," Kata said slowly, as understanding dawned. I nodded agreement.

"Anyway," I declared, "I don't know about any of the rest of you, but I'm hungry. Neither I nor Piia have eaten. Kata, where is Liisa?"

"Healing a crushed hand with Esko," Kata replied. "A stoneworker again. The same one who broke his foot. And may have had some involvement with the runaway cart. And there was a past incident with a chisel. He seems accident-prone."

"Perhaps he should be found some safer duties until he learns to be more careful?" I ventured to suggest.

"Odd that you should suggest that," Kata agreed, smiling. "That is exactly what I recommended—strongly—to Master Mason Perttunen when I sought him out after I left the infirmary."

I chuckled, and I wasn't the only one.

"Well anyway," I said, "let's get some food."

We headed off to the dining hall, and over supper, talked about the events of the day. What we had learned about the Great Gate, as Moonshadow called it, including that the dragons dared not approach within very much less than a half mile of it, because of the streamers of writhing darkness that radiated into the sky from it.

"The short version is, they have had little trouble so far in keeping all that has come through it mostly contained within that great bowl," I summarized, "But they are greatly concerned what might come through next. It has to be closed. And apparently that means me."

"Do you believe that you can do it, Fireborn?" Sage Nyysönen asked.

"I... don't know, yet," I admitted. "I have only closed one so far. And it was much smaller, and the way I closed that one will most likely not work on this one. It is simply too big. Not to mention much stronger.

"But... I think there is urgency. I will *have* to be ready, soon. Somehow. I think for a while, my studies with Moonshadow will have to be my first priority, whenever he is here. And perhaps practice when he is not."

Kata put her hand upon my left hand.

"Alrekr," she told me. "Calm. All will be all right." I realized I was on the edge of hyperventilating. I nodded, put my other hand on

430

Piia's, and then took several deep breaths and let them out slowly.

"To change the subject," I continued, "Commander Jaako, you may or may not have heard that with Moonshadow's help, I have a way now to read soul-cores well enough to bind swords to them, without bonding myself as well. This removes that limit upon how many such I can craft."

Jaako nodded.

"Thank you for telling me," he replied. "I believe I will talk to the Master Smith shortly about an order for a... *tachi*, I believe you said?"

"Yes," I agreed. "That would make yours the first *tachi* we forge. I... imagine it may be more difficult. I know that Smith Matti already commissioned a larger quenching trough to enable us to forge and temper one. I have no doubt it will also take more time."

"I can be patient," Jaako stated.

"I should warn you also that I myself have never used a *tachi*. You will need to adapt what I can teach you to it."

Jaako nodded. "That should be an interesting challenge, then," he replied. "Better and better."

There came a time when we could pretend no longer that we were not done eating. We stood and abandoned our table. As people began to drift away, Piia hugged me tightly first, and then Kata. As they broke apart, Kata stretched up and lightly kissed Piia's cheek. I could not read the look that passed between them.

"Oh!" Almost at the last moment, Piia turned to me. "Alrekr, you started to laugh at something, up on the tower. And you told me only, 'Later'. This is later. May I ask?"

I grinned.

"Of course," I replied. "It was spurred by Commander Jaako's comment about dragon-borne Rangers." Piia looked at me oddly, and after a moment, so did Kata.

"Why is that funny?" Kata asked.

"Well," I began. "Piia, I am sure you remember that I spoke of there being Rangers in the world of my past life?"

"Yes. 'Rangers Lead the Way'," she quoted.

"Exactly," I agreed. "There actually were... hmm. Actually this will take a fair bit of explaining. Will you walk with us?"

"Of course," she said with a happy smile. So off the three of us went, hand in hand. We went up one floor and stopped quickly by the infirmary first, to check upon Liisa's Healing. She smiled when we walked into the room, and still looked fresh. She paused for a moment.

"Esko is doing most of this," she told us. "It is exacting and patient work, not terribly tiring. I will be home in an hour or two."

Kata nodded.

"I... had words with Master Mason Perttunen," she said to Liisa. Liisa and Esko both nodded. I thought the young man they were working on paled slightly. "We will see you when you get home."

Esko paused as well, for just a moment.

"Go, Liisa," he said. "I have the rest of this. Vilja can help me finish it." Then he resumed his song. Liisa came with us.

"So," Piia asked. "Why is the idea of dragon-borne Rangers funny?"

"Well," I began again. "It is a small step from 'dragon-borne' to 'air-borne'. That term has particular meaning. Keep it in mind." Piia nodded.

"There were no dragons in the world of my past life, as you all know. But there were many... complex artifices made first of wood and cloth, then later of metal, that were capable of flying. Some were huge, and could carry many people within them.

"Some of them were made for fighting each other, and sometimes they would be... struck out of the air, but their... navigator still alive. And sometimes they simply failed, broke, fell. So artifices of bundled, folded fine cloth were invented to save the navigators, to trap the air so that they fell slowly enough to survive the fall.

"After a time, some fighting forces were developed that would fly to the battlefield quickly from far away in these artifices of metal, these air-craft, then leap from it in masses using these folded cloths to descend quickly to the area of battle. These came to be called airborne divisions."

I saw Piia start to get a calculating look. A smile started to grow. I was really coming to like her smile.

"One in particular, a Ranger, uh, force known as the 82nd Airborne, had a particular nickname, and a specific song that they took as their own, that invoked that nickname. The rhyming of the song does not work in Saamen, but the part I can remember of the song goes like this:

"'I want to be an Airborne Ranger, I want to live a life of danger...'"

Piia burst out laughing.

"And so when Commander Jaako said dragon-borne Rangers...?" Kata began.

"Yes," I agreed. "My mind went straight to that song." Then I paused, as Liisa began to laugh as well.

"It's funny," I mused. "It all feels so long ago now. As though it all happened to somebody else."

"It did, Alrekr," Liisa told me. "It is good that the past brings you amusement now, not pain and grief. One day it will not matter to you at all."

I looked at her, and could not help but smile.

"That day is already here," I told her. "I have let it go." I held my hands up, turned around, gesturing to the three of them and everything around us.

"*This* is real now. *This* is what matters. You three. Highwatch. This land. Dragons. *These* things matter."

Then we were at the door to our rooms. Piia drew all three of us into a hug.

"I should go now," she said. "Goodnight." Then she kissed each of us, and left.

We went inside, and went to bed early.

Later, as we lay together, I found myself gazing in a casual kind of way at the souls of my two lovers. Was it really *just* my awakening dragon vision? Or did they seem... a little *brighter*? A little stronger than before?

24: The Fire Inside

Moonshadow arrived early again the next day, while my lovers and I were still eating breakfast. I finished up quickly and went up atop the tower.

«GREETINGS ONCE MORE, ALREKR, GATE-CLOSER,» he declared. «IT IS TIME WE DISCUSSED YOUR FIRE.»

«My... fire,» I managed, very intelligently. «My fire? You mean... like dragon fire?»

Moonshadow laughed.

«NOT *LIKE* DRAGON FIRE,» he replied. «*YOUR* DRAGON FIRE. WITHIN YOU IS THE SOUL OF A DRAGON, AND THUS FIRE. YOU *MUST* LEARN TO REACH IT AND BRING IT FORTH.»

«Uh... all right,» I said hesitantly. «How do we do that?»

«TO BEGIN WITH,» he told me, «SINCE WE WILL BE WORKING WITH DRAGONFIRE, YOU SHOULD WARN YOUR FRIENDS TO STAY CLEAR.»

«That seems an eminently sensible suggestion,» I agreed. «Excuse me a moment, please, while I make arrangements.»

I went back down the stair and inside, where my lovely ladies were just finishing up breakfast.

"So what is the lesson plan for today, Alrekr?" Kata asked me.

"Fire," I replied. "Moonshadow just informed me that we are going to be working on... teaching me to 'reach and bring forth,' he said, my inner fire."

"Inner fire? You mean... dragon fire? Just how dragonlike are you going to become, Alrekr?" Liisa asked me, laughing. "I'm not so sure about finding scales in our bed." At that, I laughed too.

"I have good confidence that I am not going to start growing scales," I assured her. "But Moonshadow did caution me that it would be wise to see that people keep their distance while I am working. So I am thinking that I will station a page at the bottom of the outside stair to warn people not to come up, without calling up first to be sure it is safe. I don't want anyone to suddenly appear and catch an unexpected splash of dragonfire."

"I... think that wise," Kata agreed. "Enjoy your lessons, beloved. We will see you later." Then she kissed me, and I kissed Liisa, and they both headed off to the infirmary. I rang for a page, and Tommi showed up within minutes.

"Tommi," I told him, "I have a special duty for you this day."

"Does it involve the dragon?" he asked brightly. I laughed.

"In a manner of speaking, yes," I agreed. I closed the door and led him upstairs and out.

"Today Moonshadow and I will be working with dragonfire," I explained on the way. "What I need you to do is to stand guard at the foot of this stair and see that nobody—*and that includes you*—comes up the stair, to the tower top, without first calling up to announce themselves **and waiting for a response**. Is that clear? Nobody comes up this stair without either me, or someone else who would know, first saying that it is safe."

Tommi nodded solemnly.

"No-one shall pass me, Mas—... Fireborn," he said. It was spreading. I grinned and let it go. There would be no stopping it, and I was done doubting myself. I went back up to the tower top.

«ARE YOU READY NOW TO BEGIN?» Moonshadow asked.

«I am,» I replied. «I have appointed a page to guard the stairs. He will allow none to come up without warning.»

«THEN LET US BEGIN WITH THE FEELING OF DRAGONFIRE,» he said. «LET US TRY THIS. FIRST MASK YOUR SOUL AS I TAUGHT YOU, AND THEN TOUCH MY CORE.»

Masking was straightforward, by now. Then I felt for Moonshadow's core as he had told me.

His soul was rolling fire, yet somehow all in order, as though every flame was under control. I looked deeper. There was a *lot* of 'deeper' to go. This was my first look into a dragon's soul, and it gave me a new perspective. But... I could see and understand, *now*, that there was a similarity in my own. That made me think hard.

Eventually, I found his core. It was a vast furnace. And yet... within the furnace... wisdom, ancient knowledge. I had the feeling that answers to questions of the ages lay here, if I took the time to seek them —and knew what questions to ask. Once again, I remembered Raimo's words: "A voice out of time will guide you."

But I had not been invited to do that. I made sure I knew the feel of his core, and then I withdrew.

«GOOD,» he declared. «I FELT YOUR TOUCH.

«NOW RAISE YOUR HANDS, AND I WILL DIRECT FIRE INTO THEM. THIS TIME, FOCUS ON THE FEEL OF THE FIRE, ITS ESSENCE. I WISH YOU TO SEEK WITHIN IT ECHOES OF MY CORE. SEEK THAT WHICH IS SIMILAR BETWEEN MY CORE, AND MY FIRE.»

I nodded, raised my hands in front of me, and Moonshadow released a stream of fire into my hands. I was expecting it this time. It splashed from my hands as before, and I leaned into it a little.

As Moonshadow had instructed me, I opened myself to the fire and tried to sense its essence. It was different from a normal fire or even Matti's forge—more intense, more *alive*. I closed my eyes to better focus on it. There was something cleaner, purer, more *elemental* about it.

After a while, I thought I was getting it. But...

«Could you... a little more?» I asked. «A little stronger?»

Moonshadow laughed.

«I HAVE BEEN GRADUALLY INCREASING THE STRENGTH ALREADY, GATE-CLOSER,» he told me. «HAD YOU NOT NOTICED? YOU ARE DOING WELL. I SHALL INCREASE IT FURTHER.»

I felt the difference in the next blast, longer and more intense, and I realized I was gaining energy from it. With this... yes, I started to feel there was perhaps something there that specifically *felt* like Moonshadow.

«More,» I heard myself say. The next was stronger again. I had to lean strongly into it, but I could take it. I was starting to grasp it. Another, stronger still, then another, and...

Yes. I had it now, I thought. I could *feel* the connection, *feel* what... signed, what *fingerprinted* this as specifically Moonshadow's flame. I cast my mind back to the dragon airstrikes in the canyons beyond the Spine, and somehow knew that First Sunlight's fire would... *feel* different. And I even thought I might have an inkling, perhaps, of how.

«I have it,» I declared. «I think.» I opened my eyes.

«DO YOU WISH TO *SEE* WHAT YOU LAST ACCEPTED?» Moonshadow asked. He sounded amused.

«Why not?» I replied. My hands were still raised in a guard position, and I was still braced.

Moonshadow inhaled briefly and let out a massive gout of flame. It paled next to the massive waves of fire he and First Sunlight had unleashed in the canyon, but the column of fire was thicker than my body, and it streamed out beyond the walls of the tower when it splashed away from my hands. I felt the *shove* of force as it struck, and I also clearly felt this time the surge of energy I absorbed from it. I felt full almost to bursting, I realized. I noticed there were layers of blackened scorch-marks on the stones that roofed and walled the tower.

I don't know why it was funny, but I found myself laughing. No... not *funny*. *Exhilarating*. That was the right word.

«SO,» Moonshadow said after a little. «NEXT, I WISH YOU TO FEEL WITHIN YOURSELF. YOU KNOW NOW THE SIMILARITY BETWEEN MY FLAME AND MY CORE. SEEK FOR THAT SAME, WITHIN YOUR OWN CORE. REST, SEEK, AND FIND YOUR FLAME WITHIN YOURSELF.»

I nodded, thinking. Then I sat down on the roof and began to delve into myself.

When I came to myself again, it was dark. Moonshadow was a great black shadow against the night.

"I think perhaps I have it," I said.

"Good," Piia replied, from right beside me. I startled, and she laughed.

"We decided it was safe to venture up when the fountains of fire had stopped half an hour before," she told me. "Tommi guarded you faithfully until then. I have been watching over you since."

I reached and hugged her, and I tried again, in dragontongue this time.

«I think I have it.»

«GOOD. IT HAS BECOME LATE. YOUR MATE HAS BEEN WATCHING OVER YOU SINCE BEFORE THE SUN SET.»

«I did not realize it had been so long.»

«NO MATTER. WE WOULD HAVE WATCHED OVER YOU ALL THE NIGHT,

IF NEED BE.»

«Thank you sincerely, Shadow Cast By The Third Moon As It Rises.»

«WE SHALL RESUME ON THE MORROW. FOR NOW, I DEPART. YOUR MATE DOUBTLESS WISHES YOUR ATTENTION. UNTIL THE MORROW, GATE-CLOSER.»

A moment later, he was airborne and circling away.

"Thank you for watching over me, Piia," I said. She simply smiled.

"Come," she told me. "You must be hungry by now."

Liisa met us at the outside door.

"Good," she said, "I thought I heard you on the stairs." She hugged me tightly, then turned around and led us inside and downstairs. Kata was at the table, studying a book, until she heard footsteps on the stairs; then she looked up and smiled. She got up and came to meet us, and we all gathered into a big hug.

"So what was the lesson today?" Kata asked.

"Fire," I said, perhaps a little obviously. Liisa snorted in amusement. "Is that lihakeitto I smell?"

"It is," Liisa agreed. "We waited for you." The pot had been placed on the floor in front of the fireplace, I saw, to keep it warm, so I walked over, picked it up, and carried it to the table. Liisa handed out bowls and we sat down to eat.

"Now, really," Liisa said, "what was today's lesson all about? There was a lot of fire flying, but we really couldn't tell what was going on."

With the edge off my hunger, I tried to give a more informative and less self-evident answer.

"Today," I explained, in between mouthfuls, "we started out first with me learning the feel of Moonshadow's soul-core, enough to recognize him by it. Then we advanced from there to me learning the feel of his flame, until I could recognize what about his flame was distinctly his, what about it uniquely identified *him*. And, I think, simply getting *used to* being hit with that much flame at one time."

"So that is what all of the fire was about," Kata nodded. "It was quite a spectacular display. Does it tire you to block his fire?"

"No," I replied. "Exactly the opposite, in fact. After a while, I noticed I was gaining energy from it. Absorbing some of it. I have never felt so full of energy before."

"Interesting," Piia mused thoughtfully. "And perhaps useful to know."

"And believe me," I added, "if you think anything that happened on the tower today was spectacular, you should have seen what Moonshadow and First Sunlight—uh, The Glint Of First Sunlight Off Mountaintop Ice In The Morning—let loose yesterday."

Piia nodded emphatically.

"A canyon thirty yards wide filled from one side to the other with a sea of fire, to twice the height of this ceiling," she said.

"So then," I continued, "once I saw what there was of Moonshadow in his fire, what made it uniquely his, *then* we began on what I think was the hardest part so far: Seeking that same... *flavor* within myself. Something within me that... feels... it's hard to explain. Something that bears the same relationship to my core, as Moonshadow's fire does to his."

"And... did you find it?" Liisa asked.

"I think so," I replied cautiously. "But I am *absolutely not* trying to experiment with it in here." That made all three laugh.

"Is there a lesson plan for tomorrow?" Kata asked.

"I imagine," I said tentatively, "that Moonshadow is going to want to find a way to... 'bring forth' my fire, as he told me. But I'm really not sure quite how he expects me to accomplish that. I'm... pretty certain I'm not physiologically equipped to breathe fire."

"Indeed," Kata agreed, "I am fairly sure we would have noticed that when we last examined you."

"Though we could always examine you again," Liisa suggested, with a grin. And we all laughed at that, too.

"What's the answer to that, Alrekr?" Piia asked, after a little.

"I don't know," I admitted honestly. "Maybe... if I can *block* dragonfire with my hands, maybe I can throw it somehow as well?" Then I shook my head a moment later. "That makes no sense, does it?"

"Who knows?" Kata remarked. "This is new to all of us."

I nodded. "I hope Moonshadow has answers," I said.

"We are all here to help you, however you need us," Piia reminded me.

Liisa got up, took my hand, and led me over to the couch in front of the fireplace. She sat down and pulled me down next to her, and I slipped my arm around her. Piia and Kata followed. Kata brought her book, I noticed, and sat down in the chair, half facing us, the book in her lap. Piia sat down on my other side.

"Kata, what are you reading?" I asked. "It looks... old."

"Pekkala's first book on dragons," she explained. "It is a long shot, I know... but I thought it might tell us something useful. Something that might help you."

"I hope so," I agreed. "Have you found anything that seems of use yet?"

"No," she replied. "In fact, I have been coming to a growing suspicion that this book is... less than..."

She paused, then started over.

"Well, all right, I will be honest. From what we have seen so far of Moonshadow—I suspect a lot of this book is simply *wrong*. It was written over seven hundred years ago, during the period of dragon troubles, and I am coming to think that may have unduly colored Pekkala's viewpoint.

"At that, it is only by the sheerest chance that we even have a copy. It was a gift to me more than fifteen years ago from someone who thought I might find it interesting. I am starting to seriously doubt whether it will be of any use to us. But I don't know what other resources we have."

She pulled her chair a little closer, turning it to more directly face us, and spread the book in her lap.

"Look," she said, and pointed at a passage next to a drawing. "Here, Pekkala says that a dragon's scales will tear a man's flesh, its internal fires burn he who touches it. But just yesterday you and Piia *rode* upon Moonshadow's back. You were gone for hours."

"And we spent every minute of our absence upon his back in the air," Piia agreed.

"Even so, yes. And neither of you is any the worse for wear."

"Well, I for one was a little stiff upon dismounting," I admitted, with a grin. "But oh, it was... exhilarating. Especially when Moonshadow made his attack run down the canyon. I wanted to roar fire into the sky myself." Piia put her arm around me and hugged fiercely, and looked at me.

"I felt the same," she told me. "But I think... I felt it from *you*, Alrekr, at least as much as from myself."

"... Through our soul bond," I thought aloud, looking at her. "And I... was getting—uh... was feeling it in part from Moonshadow through the dragon soul part, I think perhaps now. His fierceness, his exultation at a foe destroyed. Perhaps that is why it felt so... stirring."

"Who would have known," Liisa mused, her hand draped upon my shoulder, "when you were first brought to us on that day. When we first saw you upon a stretcher between two horses, pale, bloodied and broken. So much has happened, so much has changed."

I hugged her closer, and turned my head and kissed her.

"Do you feel a kinship with Moonshadow specifically," Kata asked, "or with dragonkind in general?"

"I... don't know," I mused, pondering the question. "I have only been introduced to one other dragon, and that one a nephew of his, so he said. And at a hundred feet distance."

"First Sunlight," Piia added. "He is beautiful. All gleaming burnished bronze, bright as the sun, where Moonshadow is black as iron and dark as night."

"They are both magnificent," I agreed. "First Sunlight is a sight to see, certainly."

We sat there for a while discussing dragons and Pekkala's book, as it grew late. Finally Piia stood.

"I should be going," she declared. "You need to sleep. And I... need to think."

I got up and walked her to the door. At the door she turned and put her arms around me, and hugged me fiercely. I hugged her back.

"It is half in my mind to ask you to walk me back to the Hall, Alrekr," she told me. "But I... might... I... should not. Not now. There will be time. After we all talk about... what we—"

She stopped herself and took a deep breath. Then she kissed me quickly.

"Goodnight, Alrekr," she said. And then she turned and left.

I closed the door and returned slowly to the fireplace. Liisa wrapped her arm around me again.

"You *know* she loves you," she told me. I nodded.

"And we love her," Kata added. "All three of us."

"And unless I badly misread," I replied, "she has come to love both of you as well."

Kata nodded.

"So why are you *holding back*, my love?" she asked.

I blinked.

"We have told you, more than once," Liisa said. "Love expands to fill the space you allow it."

"But... we three... we are married," I began. "And somehow... I was never good at relationships, but this, somehow, even with *three* of us, has been stable so far, and healthy, and *GOOD*."

"So if three of us, then why not four of us?" Kata asked quietly, seriously.

The question, right out in the open like that, hit me between the eyes.

"I..." I hesitated, then stopped. Then I tried again.

"I had enough difficulty accepting that three people in a committed relationship was not looked at questioningly here," I got out at last. "Let alone that I could *manage* such a thing without... making mistakes and hurting all of us. I am torn between the desire to make it four, even knowing now that—that it seems all four of us *want* this... and the *fear* that it might break what we have. It would be too high a price to pay. And..."

I didn't really want to voice it, but I had to.

"It feels as though this is all coming to a head," I admitted. "Everything I... sense, feel... about dragons, everything I get from Moonshadow, convinces me that they are not hasty—people. But Moonshadow has been here each day without fail. I think there is *urgency* here. I don't know how much *time* we have. It would be so terribly unfair, if..."

"If you did not come back from whatever is coming, Alrekr?" Liisa asked.

I nodded miserably.

"Do you not trust Piia to make that decision for herself?"

I stopped and thought about that deeply. When she put it like that... the answer was suddenly incredibly obvious. I felt like an idiot.

"If not Piia," I replied at last, "then who?"

I turned and kissed Liisa.

"You are right, Liisa, of course. It is not my place to make such a decision for anyone else."

Kata set her book aside, then pulled me to my feet.

"Come," she told us. "Let us all go to bed and get some rest. But soon, we must all talk. *All four* of us."

I nodded agreement, and followed her, pulling Liisa behind me.

Moonshadow was not quite so early the next morning. We actually had time to finish breakfast and start our days. I went to the forge to check on the progress on Paavo's sword.

"One more day before we are ready to temper, Fireborn," Matti told me.

I looked at him.

"You too?" I asked, with a grin.

"You *know* it has a ring to it," he replied, grinning right back at me. I laughed, and so did he. I realized no longer felt self-conscious about it. It simply was.

"Do you have a design in mind for the fittings?"

"I overheard you saying when we forged it, that he was born by the sea," Matti replied. "So I thought some great sea creature."

I nodded.

"I think that would suit Paavo," I agreed.

It was there at the forge that Piia found me a few minutes later.

"Alrekr," she said, before she threw her arms around me and kissed me. "Paavo, Karel and Ragne are all officially fit for duty again, *light* duty at least, and we are taking a short patrol just out to the feet of the two passes and back. We do not *anticipate* any trouble. But if there *should* be something...? Will you be able to...?"

I knew what she was hesitating to ask.

"I felt something in the air when the rift in the crags opened," I told her, "though I did not know what it was. If I could feel it, I am certain that Moonshadow would feel it and know it. If there is a rift, we will come to your aid, have no doubt. And I am *certain* that nothing less will give you any trouble."

She smiled brilliantly.

"Good," she said. "That was my thinking too. But I am glad that you agree. I... did not want us to go out without you knowing where we were, without a word. I would not do that to you. We will probably be back late. After sunset. Perhaps after moonrise, even."

I nodded.

"And when you come back, Piia, or tomorrow if that is late in the night, we will talk. *All* of us. I *promise*."

She smiled, more deeply this time, and kissed me again.

"May your lesson go well today, Alrekr," she told me, and pointed to the sky. "Your teacher is on the way." I looked where she pointed, and sure enough, Moonshadow was visible in the sky already, no more than minutes out.

"Safe patrol to the team," I wished her. "Until later, Piia. And, Piia — I love you."

"I love you too, Alrekr," she assured me, with a beautiful, brilliant smile. She kissed me one more time, long and slowly. Then she turned for the stables, and I ran for the tower.

Moonshadow landed while I was still on the stair.

«GATE-CLOSER,» he greeted me, as I reached the tower top.

«Moonshadow,» I replied, nodding.

«TIME GROWS SHORT. WE MUST COMPLETE YOUR TRAINING SOON. THERE ARE... CHANGES IN THE GREAT GATE. THE LAST TIME WE SAW SUCH CHANGES WAS SHORTLY BEFORE THE STALKERS FIRST APPEARED.»

«And you do not know exactly what this change heralds,» I guessed. «But it is likely not good news.»

«PRECISELY,» he replied. «SO LET US BEGIN. I BELIEVE YOU SAID THAT YOU FOUND THE HEART OF YOUR INNER FIRE.»

«Uh,» I hedged. «I found *something*. I do not know for certain that it is what you bade me seek.»

«THEN LET US TRY TO BRING IT FORTH,» he told me. «OF COURSE THIS PRESENTS CERTAIN... DIFFICULTIES, SINCE YOU DO NOT HAVE THE PHYSICAL FORM OF A DRAGON, AND YOU CANNOT BREATHE FIRE AS A DRAGON DOES.»

«My... mates and I spoke of exactly this problem last night,» I agreed.

«THEN LET US SEE WHAT WE CAN DEVISE. YOU KNOW NOW THAT YOU NEED HAVE NO FEAR OF FIRE. YOU KNOW THAT YOU CAN PUSH FIRE ASIDE. LET US SEE IF YOU CAN HOLD FIRE IN YOUR HAND, AS A FIRST STEP. MINE FIRST, THEN YOURS.»

«A caution before we begin. Piia asked that we should be on alert should a gate appear near the passes where she is going on patrol today. If a gate opens... she may need our assistance. If there is a... a stalker, I believe you called them.»

«REST ASSURED I WILL INFORM YOU IMMEDIATELY SHOULD A GATE FORM, GATE-CLOSER. WE WILL SUPPORT YOUR MATE TOGETHER, SHOULD SHE NEED IT.»

«Thank you, Moonshadow.»

So we worked with fire. Again and again I tried to catch and hold a little of Moonshadow's fire. And finally, I managed it. A ball of golden fire burning in my hand. I held it up, wondering at it, then after a little while, I let it go.

«AGAIN,» Moonshadow told me. After a few more tries, I managed it a second time. And then a third, and a fourth, and a fifth, one after the other.

«GOOD. NOW, LET US TRY WITH YOURS. YOU *KNOW* IN YOUR HEART THAT YOU CAN DO IT. *I* KNOW THAT YOU CAN DO IT.»

I tried, and tried again, and again, and yet again, reaching within myself according to Moonshadow's guidance. Moonshadow was relentlessly insistent, allowing me only brief rests.

«YOU *MUST* LEARN THIS, GATE-CLOSER,» he told me.

And then it happened. A clear blue flame burning hotly in my hand that had not been there a moment before. I began to laugh, mingled joy and relief. I could actually do this.

«AGAIN,» Moonshadow said. I let it go and tried again... and after a few more tries, I got it again. A third time, and a fourth.

«BOTH HANDS,» Moonshadow instructed me. I tried that. Now that I knew how to do it, calling flame from within myself into my left hand was no harder than my right.

«MORE,» he told me. «BRING FORTH MORE. BOTH HANDS AT ONCE.»

Calling forth *more* fire was not more difficult than calling forth a little; it just took more energy. It took noticeable effort as I started drawing larger amounts.

«NOW,» Moonshadow said, «TRY THROWING IT OUT FROM YOUR HAND.»

At first I tried throwing it like a ball. That... didn't go well. All I did was break my ball of flame and scatter it. It was like trying to throw a handful of water.

«NOT *WITH* YOUR HAND,» Moonshadow corrected me. «DO NOT SEEK TO THROW IT *WITH* YOUR HAND. CAST IT FORTH *FROM* YOUR HAND.»

At first, I couldn't grasp the idea. Or rather, I thought I knew what he meant, I just couldn't figure out how to put it into practice.

Then, late in the afternoon, I managed a thin stream of fire, instead of a ball.

«GOOD!» Moonshadow declared. «AGAIN! PUSH *HARDER*.»

I pushed harder, called more flame. After a few more tries, I managed a stream of flame as thick as my wrist that extended out a dozen yards.

«YES!» Moonshadow roared. «KEEP AT IT, GATE-CLOSER. YOU ARE GETTING IT. BUT YOU WILL NEED MORE. THIS IS STILL NOT ENOUGH.»

I tried harder, drew more of myself, the fire I now knew how to reach. I shot a column of blue-white fire as thick as my thigh fifty yards into the sky. I found myself laughing wildly.

«AGAIN,» Moonshadow told me. «CAST IT FORTH AT ME. LET ME FEEL YOUR POWER.»

I did as he said, the lance of fire striking squarely on his chest and splashing to either side.

«MARVELLOUS, GATE-CLOSER!» Moonshadow declared, laughing. «I FEEL YOUR STRENGTH INDEED. YOU ARE GETTING THIS! AND YOUR FIRE BURNS HOT. HOTTER EVEN THAN MY OWN. I AM *IMPRESSED*.»

«I am also getting *tired*,» I observed. «This is draining my energy, quickly.»

«LET ME GIVE YOU SOME BACK, THEN,» Moonshadow replied. I held up my hands and he poured fire into them, and I gratefully absorbed as much as I could. After a half dozen of his fire-blasts I felt somewhat recovered, enough for another try. But it was clear that this was going to have limits.

«I do not know how much I can usefully do with this, Moonshadow,» I told him. «It drains me too fast. I have to put too much energy into each blast. Half a dozen good blasts will leave me exhausted.»

«HMMM,» Moonshadow pondered. «YES. YOU DO NOT HAVE THE ENERGY RESERVES OF A DRAGON BODY. YOUR INNER FIRE IS INTENSE AND PURE, BUT IT IS SMALL. THIS IS A PROBLEM. COME, REST AGAINST ME AND RECOVER YOUR ENERGY WHILE I CONSIDER.»

He mused in thought, while I rested and drew energy from his inner fires.

«I THINK WE MUST USE YOUR SWORD,» he told me at last. «I THINK THAT PERHAPS IT IS WHAT THE SWORD YOU CRAFTED IS TRULY *FOR*. THIS PERHAPS IS *WHY* THE ABILITY TO SOUL-BIND WEAPONS TO YOU LIES WITHIN YOU. BINDING THEM TO OTHERS, I THINK, MAY BE MERELY A SIDE EFFECT, AS YOUR FIRESINGING ABILITY IS A SIDE-EFFECT OF BEING FIREBORN.»

«Do you mean... I must draw from Sekai?» I asked.

«NO. THAT IS THE SAME AS DRAWING FROM YOURSELF. REMEMBER: THE HILT OF THE SWORD AND THE HAND ARE AS ONE. YOU MUST LEARN TO CHANNEL YOUR FIRE *THROUGH* YOUR SWORD, I THINK. BUT I DO NOT KNOW HOW TO TELL YOU TO DO IT. YOU MUST LEARN IT YOURSELF. I WILL HELP AS MUCH AS I CAN. LEARN *QUICKLY*, GATE-CLOSER.»

«I will try,» I agreed. And try I did. For the rest of the day, and into the night. But I could not get it. Something was eluding me.

Finally I had to beg off.

«Please, Moonshadow,» I said. «I am exhausted. I need to rest. I can do no more today.»

«THEN REST FOR NOW, AND WE SHALL TRY AGAIN ON THE MORROW,» Moonshadow replied. «BUT FIRST LET ME GIVE YOU BACK SOME OF THE ENERGY THAT YOU HAVE SPENT IN YOUR EFFORTS. WE HAVE MADE GREAT PROGRESS TODAY. I AM SURE THAT YOU ARE CLOSE. YOU WILL BREAK THROUGH SOON, I HAVE NO DOUBT.»

For the next half an hour, Moonshadow belched gouts of fire at me and I absorbed all I could.

«Enough for now,» I told him after a while, somewhat recovered. «I will be restored by morning, I think.»

«THEN REST WELL UNTIL MY RETURN, GATE-CLOSER,» Moonshadow said. And with that, he leapt from the tower and flew away towards the mountains.

I walked tiredly down the stairs and inside. Downstairs, Kata, Liisa and Sage Nyysönen were waiting for me.

"I am hungry," I declared. "Let us all go and get some food."

"You are also *tired*, Alrekr," Liisa told me. "It shows in your very step. We will send for food. Sit with us and rest until it arrives."

"If we go to the hall," I said, "then I can recover myself somewhat from the fire. It is not a long walk."

Liisa agreed that made better sense, so off we all went to the dining hall and picked a table close to the fire, where a large pot of lohikeitto was brought to us shortly. I pulled both of my lovers as close and tight to me as I could. I wasn't certain how many more chances I was going to have.

"There has been an impressive display of fire from the tower top this day," Nyysönen said, as we set about the soup. "Could I trouble you please to tell me what transpired? The dragon's fire I recognize by now—brilliant and golden. But the... spears of brilliant blue flame—those are new. Was that...?"

"Yes," I agreed. "That is my own fire, thrown from my hands."

"That... was *you*?" Liisa asked. She sounded amazed.

"Yes," I confirmed. "But it drains me quickly. I do not have the vast energy reserves of a dragon. Moonshadow says we need to do something about that, at some point. It takes all I can recover from three or four bolts of Moonshadow's fire to regain what I spend on one."

"You can actually regain energy from absorbing the dragon's fire?" Nyysönen asked, for confirmation.

"Yes," I confirmed. "It is a particularly intense source of heat, exceptionally pure and elemental, and I can gain a lot of energy from it in a short time. I can also recover somewhat simply by resting against him, drawing from his internal fires. I cannot draw enough that way for him to more than notice. My capacity is too small."

"Can you... describe the process of any of these to me?" he asked.

"Please," I begged. "Not now. I need food and rest. Ask me later." I hesitated. "Either there will be plenty of time later... or it will not matter."

He nodded somber understanding. Kata snuggled a little tighter.

"I should leave the three of you to yourselves, I think," Nyysönen said politely. "Rest well, Fireborn."

449

"Thank you, Sage Nyysönen," I replied. We sat and finished our soup, then a little longer while I drew on the fire a bit more, and then we returned to our tower.

"If you have learned to throw your fire," Kata asked as we sat by the fire, "does that mean that you are done with lessons for now?"

"Well, for tonight, at any rate," I qualified my answer. "We must resume tomorrow. There is, we think, at least one thing more that I need to master, and that, Moonshadow thinks, is how to channel my fire through Sekai. But he can give me little help with it, because dragons do not use weapons. Their talons, their breath, their wings are their weapons."

"More than that troubles you, does it not, Alrekr?" Kata said, looking levelly at me.

"Yes," I admitted. "Moonshadow said... there are changes in the Great Gate. Changes that they last saw before what they call the Stalkers came through. They are... *dangerously difficult* for us to kill. Easy for the dragons.

"But what if something new comes through that is as hard for the dragons to kill, as the stalkers are for us?" I paused.

"I don't know how much time we have, Kata. And I am terrified of losing the two of you. Piia. Everything that I have here."

"You do not *know* that things will go badly, Alrekr," Liisa reminded me.

"No," I agreed. "But neither do I *know* that they will go well."

"Then let us make the best of what time we may have," Kata told me. She got up from the couch, took my hand, and she and Liisa led me upstairs.

25: The Hilt Of The Sword

We were woken by a heavy THUD upon the roof of the tower, but even had that not woken us, the bellow that followed it would have.

«**GATE-CLOSER**,» I heard from where we lay entwined. «**COME NOW.**»

All three of us were suddenly awake. Liisa and Kata both looked at me, serious, uncertain. It was not light yet.

"This is a bad sign, I think," Kata said. I scrambled out of bed and dressed quickly. Then I grabbed hold of my two lovers and hugged them fiercely, kissed them both, putting everything I felt into it.

"Come back to us, my love," Liisa said unsteadily.

"If I possibly can," I told her. "I swear it."

Then I picked up Sekai and the riding straps, and went outside and up to the tower top.

«GATE-CLOSER,» Moonshadow told me, as soon as I arrived. «THERE IS NO MORE TIME. WE MUST GO NOW. SOMETHING COMES. WE SEE THE SIGNS IN THE GATE. WHAT YOU HAVE LEARNED... WILL HAVE TO BE ENOUGH.

«I SENSE THAT YOU ARE CLOSE TO THE FINAL INSIGHT, GATE-CLOSER. CONTINUE TO SEEK IT ANY WAY YOU CAN. YOU MUST CLOSE THE GATE.»

I climbed to his shoulder and began to thread the riding straps.

«I THINK YOUR MATE COMES. SOMEONE APPROACHES AT A RUN.»

Moments later, I heard running footsteps on the stairs. Then Piia appeared at the top of the stairs, a little out of breath.

"Alrekr!" she called up to me. "Alrekr Járnhandr, you *WILL* tell me that you have both sets of straps ready."

"Piia," I called back. "Look on the ground next to your feet. Throw them up to me."

She looked down, picked up the second set of straps, and tossed them up to me. I began to thread one as she climbed up, then she took and secured the next.

"Moonshadow says something is coming," I told her. "We are out of time. We have to go and close the gate *now*. But... I don't know if I

451

can close it. Yet."

She looked at me, her face utterly serious.

"You will have a better chance with Tuuli at your back," she told me.

"I... know," I agreed. "But... I know you of all people need no protecting or sheltering, Piia, but still I hate to risk you."

"Risk me," she replied, "or risk everything."

I didn't like it, but I could not deny the truth in it.

The straps were done. Kata and Liisa, dressed now, appeared at the top of the stairs as we settled ourselves into place.

"Come back to us!" Kata called out. "BOTH of you!"

I nodded, my throat tight.

«ARE YOU READY, GATE-CLOSER?» Moonshadow asked.

«As ready as we will ever be,» I replied. «Fly, my friend.»

Moonshadow raised his head and bellowed a wordless, bugling battle cry. Then he launched us all into the air, and we turned northwest.

The sky began to lighten behind us as we crossed into the mountains. By the time we reached the far side, both suns were climbing in the east, though the immediate foot of the mountains still lay in shadow. I let myself absorb as much energy as I could hold from Moonshadow as we flew. Far ahead of us, I could see dragons circling over the bowl, the morning sun glinting off their scales. I saw more as we drew closer. Fifteen, seventeen... eighteen? Perhaps more.

«WE WILL CLEAR A WAY FOR YOU BOTH,» Moonshadow declared. «BUT AS LONG AS THE GATE STANDS, WE DARE APPROACH NO CLOSER THAN THE OUTER FRINGE OF THE FILAMENTS. FROM THAT POINT ON, ALL IS UP TO YOU.»

As we approached, he bellowed a call. After a few moments, a dragon that might, I think, have been First Sunlight took position to our right, and two more that I did not know joined us shortly after. I could see now there were at least thirty dragons in the air, perhaps more that I could not see on the far side of the Great Gate. We began to descend, choosing a path, an approach.

«THERE, I THINK,» Moonshadow stated. «WE WILL CLEAR THE WAY.»

452

We began to descend rapidly toward where a canyon opened out into a broad fan of rubble and rock outcrops. In front and below us, the lead dragon dropped down into the canyon and unleashed a scorching wave of fire. Another picked it up down the next stretch. I saw a dragon plummet, wings suddenly furled, and knew a stalker was about to meet its end. Then the lead dragons peeled away to either side, and Moonshadow was braking, descending. He back-winged to almost a hover, dropping the last few feet to the ground.

«THIS IS AS CLOSE AS I DARE CARRY YOU,» he told us. «LEAVE THE STRAPS IN PLACE. THEY WILL NOT TROUBLE ME, AND YOU MAY NEED TO USE THEM AGAIN QUICKLY. MAY FORTUNE FAVOR YOU, GATE-CLOSER ALREKR, RANGER PIIA OF THE UNQUENCHABLE SPIRIT. MAY YOUR HANDS HAVE THE STRENGTH OF IRON, AND YOUR HEARTS TOGETHER NEVER QUAIL.»

We climbed down quickly.

«We will see you again soon, Moonshadow,» I replied. «I hope.»

«FOES APPROACHING,» he warned. I followed his gaze. A column was coming into sight around the right side of the canyon-mouth ahead. I estimated the mid-size creatures between eight and nine feet in height, gauging by the stalker among them.

«I WILL BURN THE SMALLER ONES,» Moonshadow declared.

«The stalker is ours, then,» I said. He nodded. I pointed to an outcrop from the side of what remained of the canyon wall.

"Cover, there. Quickly." Piia and I sprinted to the cover of the rocks, out of sight of the column.

As the column approached, the creatures broke into a run. Great, shaggy, almost ursine beasts, three-eyed, with claws that looked a foot long. One sweep of those, I was sure, would disembowel a man. They began to hoot and scream as they charged.

Moonshadow let them get within fifty yards before he let loose his fire. It washed over them, and the hoots turned to agonized howls that were quickly stilled. Moonshadow spun away and launched himself into the air, directly away from the gate, out from under the filaments that were already reaching toward him. The stalker leapt after him, but after one great leap, stopped, staring futilely after him, claws raised.

I drew Sekai and pointed 'Right' to Piia. She nodded and drew Tuuli.

"Full speed," she whispered. I nodded agreement.

We boosted, burst from our cover, and sprinted for the stalker. Its head began to turn, then we were upon it, our swords whirling. We hacked the two hindmost pairs of legs off it before it could react, then the next as it tried to turn. I parried a claw that struck at me, lopping it off at the joint, as Piia leapt up onto its back and drove Tuuli into the joint where the armored neck met the body. Tuuli flashed green as she struck. The stalker let out a brief screech, then she made a draw-cut from within it, ripping Tuuli out through the joint, and it collapsed like a puppet with its strings cut.

"One," she announced. "For the Erkkila family."

We returned to cover and planned our path, looking for a route that concealed us as much as possible. We had nearly half a mile to go. The gate, I could see from here, was larger than when we had first seen it, several days before.

In a few minutes, we decided upon our route and set out along it, moving quickly between one patch of cover and the next. At one point we had to stop and wait while another patrolling column passed in front of us. It was very clear this was no random horde milling about without direction, but an organized, intelligently-directed invasion, of which what we had seen so far was perhaps just the advance guard, a bridgehead. Further out in the bowl, away from the gate, the dragons were going after anything that moved. And for all I knew, laying down fire on empty ground just to draw attention. Either way, it seemed to be working. The light dimmed as we moved further under the writhing clot of filaments.

We heard a roar from behind us as we crossed a hundred-yard gap between two patches of cover, and spun around to see a group of four of the giant bear-things charging at us. Piia drew Tuuli, but I hesitated for a second—then instead of Sekai, I thrust out my right hand, reached into my core, and *pushed*. A column of my soul-fire shot out. The first two bear-things, struck directly, simply exploded in a spray of blood and scraps. The other two went up like blazing torches, their roars and snarls turning into agonized screams. They staggered randomly for a few seconds, fell to all fours, then toppled and lay still. We sprinted for the next cover, in case we had drawn attention.

Piia looked at me as she sheathed Tuuli.

"That is an impressive new trick, love," she remarked. "You learned that yesterday?"

"I did," I agreed. "Let's keep moving."

Finally we were in the last cover, about a hundred and fifty yards from the gate. It was a great, black, yawning void in the air that had to be forty feet wide now. The ground below it was broken rubble. For thirty yards or more out from the actual gate, the air was curdled, twisted, opaque.

Outside the rubble, stalkers circled. At least two.

We waited, to be sure.

No... there were *three*. They circled ceaselessly perhaps fifty or sixty yards out. At any given time, at least one was hidden behind the gate.

Piia pointed. About a third of the way around lay a spot where we could get closer, within sixty yards or so. I nodded, and we planned a route, then carefully back-tracked and began to work our way around to there.

We twice had to lie low while another column passed nearby, but finally we reached that closest point.

"We let the closest get just past us," Piia whispered. "The other two will be out of line of sight. We ambush that one and kill it quickly. That will leave us two. But the fight will probably draw the other two, unless we are lucky, and we will likely have to fight both of them together. If we're really lucky we might be able to make it back to cover before the next is in sight, but I am certain they will be alerted, and they may summon reinforcements. So perhaps that might work against us in any case."

I nodded.

"A good plan, I think," I agreed. "I'm not happy about the idea of fighting two of them at once. But I have good confidence we can kill one each, working together, and better two of them than three. And better two, than two plus who knows what reinforcements. So I have no better idea."

We set our ambush and waited for them to be in the right positions. Two, I noticed, were slightly closer together than the third, so we waited for those two to be on the far side. As we waited, I pulled Piia to me for a moment and kissed her.

"I love you, Piia," I told her, again. Then we were fiercely, desperately kissing each other.

After a minute or two, Piia pulled away.

"I love you too, Alrekr," she assured me. "But now it is time. Let us kill these things, and then close a gate."

We boosted and sprinted from behind our target. It was seemingly unaware. We killed it almost exactly as we had the first, right down to the screech, longer and louder this time, as Piia called out "For the Salonen farm!" And that screech tore it.

The remaining two came charging, leaping, around the Gate. They were on us in moments. We gave ourselves room between us to fight freely without blocking each other, and readied to take on one each.

They didn't follow our plan. They both went for Piia. I tried to fend one away from her, but it wasn't working. As soon as I tried to get past one and go for its legs, it would leap away, then back. They were coordinating their attack, and it was obvious their intent was to double-team us and kill us one at a time. And those leaps of theirs gave them the mobility advantage to balance out our boosted speed.

For long seconds, it was a stalemate. As I looked past them, I saw more forces headed our way from out of the broken terrain. They didn't even *have* to kill us themselves. All they had to do was delay us, hold us at bay, until their reinforcements arrived.

Piia saw them too. She looked quickly back and forth between the two stalkers. I saw an expression of calm come over her face, and in that instant I knew what she was going to do.

I started to open my mouth, but before I could get a word out, she turned fully towards the stalker nearer to me, turning her back on the other as she attacked furiously. For an instant its attention was focused solely on her and away from me. I rolled in and hewed off the two front legs on the near side, then Piia took a claw off it as I poured everything I had into a full-power blow at the joint where its armored neck met its body, *knowing* there was not going to be enough time.

Sekai, flaring blue, sheared through its carapace and bisected it, exactly at the moment that the third stalker's claw slammed into Piia from behind and impaled her. Her mouth opened wide in a silent gasp of agony.

"PIIA!!!" I screamed. She looked at me and managed a brief half-smile, as the claw lifted her towards the great shearing jaws.

Then with a scream of pain, she wrenched herself around on the claw, pulled Tuuli far back behind her right shoulder. She screamed again, a raw scream of pure fury this time, and Tuuli lit up, a blaze of green, as she unleashed a full-power two-handed stroke that struck its head and the topmost two feet of its armored neck off in a single blow.

The stalker collapsed like a broken toy and spilled her to the ground, Tuuli still in her hand. I was at her side in a second. Oh *gods*, there was *so much blood*.

She managed a weak smile at me.

"The way is clear, Alrekr," she gasped. "I love you. Go. Close... th..." Then her eyes closed.

I screamed in... rage? Grief? Pain? All of these things.

I wasn't going to lose her. *Couldn't* lose her. **Not now**.

I looked around at the foes approaching across the broken ground, under cover of the filaments above us. I had perhaps a minute. Two, at the most. I'd done it before, I could do it again. I pulled up the remembered mental image of the infirmary entrance hall, and I thought *Find Liisa, find Kata*, as I slit the air.

It was *difficult*, this close to the gate. The nearby presence of the great gate twisted everything. But *my* gate opened. A treatment room, I think. I had no time to spare to look around. Kata stood about ten feet away, talking to Raimo. I could hear no sound. She glanced our way and her eyes widened in surprise.

I *pulled* the edge of my gate under Piia, and she dropped through, still loosely holding Tuuli. The surprise on Kata's face turned to horror. She looked back up at me an instant before I let the gate go.

I had maybe ninety seconds. I took four, five fast steps closer, feeling the gate pulling at me.

Then I caught myself about to make a terrible mistake. If I tried to close this rift the way I had the first, I realized I would be drawn into it. And I suddenly *knew* that if I did that, I would come out the far end with all that was to happen here long over and done, and no way back. *Everything* I cared about would be lost.

I stepped back again and looked at the huge rift, asking Sekai to boost me as much as she possibly could, to buy time to *think*. I'd used a lot of boost this day, and could feel the drain of it. The oncoming creatures slowed. I thought as hard and as fast as I could, about what I would have to do, and how to do it. I *could not* enter the gate itself.

And then I suddenly knew the answer. That tunnel that I knew lay within the Gate... had to exist *somewhere*.

I raised Sekai... and I opened my own gate, *not* into the Great Gate, but into the space in which *the Gate itself existed*, outside of everything. Not *within* the Gate, but *beside* it. And I stepped in.

I stood... somewhere. Nowhere. Anywhere. I wasn't even sure what I was standing *on*, but it didn't seem to matter. The world itself, perhaps.

The gate was in front of me. In this perspective, it was a twisting tunnel that seemed to be made up of luminous spider webs, against featureless blackness shot through with shimmering threads, and threads, and more threads. I could see pulsations running along its length towards me. Each pulse left it just that tiny bit larger than before.

I cut into the gate with Sekai, and the glowing strands parted, cut pieces drifting away. When they brushed against my skin, they burned, stung. I cut more, further. But my cut began to close. I tried to cut faster, but still the cut closed behind me as I cut. And the larger I made my cut, the faster it drew closed.

This wasn't going to work. It was too big, too strong. I could not do it enough damage this way, fast enough. It was repairing, healing, itself faster than I could whittle away at it—and I felt the space was trying to spit me out. There had to be something else, some better way. Something I had not thought of. Even though I was not feeling any shortness of breath—or even a need to breathe—in this strange place, I was *certain* I couldn't remain here very long, and that meant I needed to find my answer quickly.

Raimo, Sage Nyysönen, Moonshadow, *everyone* agreed that the world had brought me here to do this. It didn't matter at the moment whether it had brought me here because I already possessed the tools to do it, or whether it had given them to me. What mattered was that I *had* the tools. I *had to* have the tools, or everything was lost. I just had to *figure out* what the right tool was, and how to use it.

And I was running out of time, I knew. Even aside from the question of how long I could endure here, or remain here, I could *feel* something in the fabric of the gate itself. Something was *coming*.

Something big enough that I felt it through the gate even here. If I didn't figure out a way to close this gate before it got here, things were going to get very, very bad.

Come on, I thought desperately to myself. You are the Closer of Gates. How are you going to do this? Raimo had told me that the world *brought* me here, in part, to forge Sekai. It *had* to be something to do with Sekai.

Then I thought the same thing in dragontongue. You are the Closer of Gates.

I stopped.

I thought, *really thought*, about those words, and let my mind follow the richness of meaning of the words in dragontongue, and I suddenly realized what I had been missing. All of the extra meanings of 'Close' expanded in my head. End. Sever. And more. And the meanings of 'Gate', and its contexts. Not just an opening, or a barrier. A joining of two places. A line of demarcation, a line of parting. A place where two places meet.

There is no swordsman, only the sword.

The hilt of the sword and the hand are as one.

The name of my sword. Sekai no Kattā.

I sever the place where two worlds meet.

I finally *understood*. *I* am the Cutter of Worlds.

I sheathed Sekai, closed my eyes. I dropped my knees slightly in the... nowhere. Standing on the world, perhaps. It didn't matter, I realized, precisely *where* I was standing. Distance here, wherever 'here' even *was*, seemed more of an *idea* than a rigid, measurable thing. I took a firm grip on Sekai's hilt.

There is no swordsman, only the sword. The hilt of the sword and the hand are as one.

Equal opposites. Symmetry. Yin and yang, combining into unity. I am the sword, and the sword is me.

I took a deep breath and held it for a moment, then opened my eyes.

I did not wield Sekai, exactly. Sekai was... my *instrument*, my *focus*. I wielded my core.

I wielded *myself*.

"IAI!!!" Sekai flashed out, draw and strike to full extension, in a single explosive motion. A shard of night, but lit now from within by a near-blinding blue-white glare. A searing sheet of flame leapt out, following her blade, extending her blade. *WAS* her blade. **My** blade, made of my own inner fire.

I put everything I had into it, and my strike severed the gate all at once in a single blazing cut. I saw the long tunnel snap away, fraying, dissipating, disintegrating as it went. The cobweb strands burned as they floated away. Anything within the long, long length of that tunnel, I knew somehow, would not be coming back. *Ever.* And neither would I, had I been *within* the gate.

My own gate unraveled behind me, torn apart by the backwash. For a moment I felt a prickling rush of fear, not knowing how I would escape. Then it was replaced by peace, and the knowledge that everything that mattered to me was safe.

... Except Piia. Oh *gods*, Piia.

Then as the near end of the Great Gate collapsed, it swirled, a vortex that dragged at me, yanked at me, spat me out.

I flew through the air—*air again!*—and landed with a crash that dazed me and drove the breath from my lungs. I tried to struggle up, regain my feet, but could only manage to roll over. What remained of the gate was a twisting, spinning knot in the air, a hundred yards away, that was sucking in the creatures closest to it. The wind buffeted and tore at me. Perhaps it was just as well not to be standing right now, I reflected.

My hand was empty.

Sekai, I thought, *to my hand, NOW.*

Sekai came whistling from somewhere nearby like a meteor, and slapped into my hand. A few seconds later, there came a rushing, tearing, ripping sound. It grew louder, swelled, rose to almost a scream, then what remained of the gate imploded with a thunderclap that echoed back off the cliffs where the canyons ended, nearly three quarters of a mile away. The blast slapped me back to the ground as it passed over me, and left my ears ringing. Pieces of... creatures... began to rain desultorily down. A stalker's head landed nearby, and bounced once. In the clearing sky above, the black filaments were dissipating, evaporating like morning mist.

I managed to roll over onto my knees first, then staggered to my feet. It appeared everything left alive in the bowl was converging on my general vicinity. I looked at what was coming my way, and knew there was no possible way I was going to kill them all on my own, especially not weary as I was. And I hadn't the energy left to open a gate to escape. I'd spent all I had, destroying the Great Gate.

The nearest group was a hundred yards in front of me and coming on fast. I raised Sekai and prepared myself to die, determined to take as many with me as I could. One or another of them would get through and kill me. But it would not be *that* one, I decided, nor would it be the one behind. I regretted that I wouldn't have the chance to say goodbye.

That is when the dragons arrived. I heard the rush of wind over dragon wings behind me, a moment before a searing double blast simply obliterated the closest group in front of me, leaving nothing but charred cinders. Two dragons swept over my head barely fifty feet up. Another inferno erupted to my left, as three dragons close together laid down a rolling lake of fire. I heard the CRUNCH-THUD as a dragon stomped a stalker flat.

Hot damn, the close air support was here. I might survive this after all. I took a moment to look around. The sky looked full of dragons, and they meant business. One might almost have thought they had a grudge to settle or something. And they were settling it as only dragons could.

Moonshadow landed nearby.

«I SALUTE YOUR VICTORY, GATE-CLOSER!» he bellowed. Then he looked around.

«GATE-CLOSER. WHERE IS YOUR *PIIA-MATE*?»

«She... Moonshadow, I need to get back to Highwatch as fast as you can get me there. I sent her back there through a Gate. She was dying. I *hope* she is still alive. But I don't *know*. And I am too exhausted to open another for myself.»

She has to be alive, I kept telling myself. She *has* to be alive.

«CAN YOU STAY ON MY BACK, GATE-CLOSER?»

461

«I... think so.»

«MOUNT, THEN. QUICKLY.»

I sheathed Sekai, climbed up as quickly as I could manage, and after a moment's consideration, did my best to tie myself in place with the riding straps.

«Go,» I said. Moonshadow hurled himself into the air and turned toward Highwatch. Behind us, the rest of the dragons were cleaning house with a vengeance. I leaned forward and laid on his back, absorbing energy from his internal fires. I rested, and felt consciousness slipping away.

26: We Are Family

I did not wake, until I was jarred awake by Moonshadow's landing. It was late afternoon, and I felt somewhat recovered after a couple of hours sprawled on Moonshadow's back, soaking up his inner heat. I was still tired, but I could function. I forced myself to slow down and untie myself from the straps where I had tied myself on, glad I had taken the time to do it.

«LEAVE THE STRAPS FOR NOW, GATE-CLOSER,» Moonshadow told me. «GO AND FIND YOUR MATE. I WILL WAIT AS LONG AS YOU NEED.»

I climbed down, and I ran, straight around the walls to the keep, and in on the upper floor, and down, and straight to the infirmary. Ari, Ragne, Simo, Eino and Paavo were huddled in a corner outside the infirmary. Ari held out a hand, his face pale, but I dodged past. I grabbed Marja, the first healer I saw.

"Where is Piia?" I asked her urgently.

"Fireborn Alrekr," she replied hesitantly, "she— we—"

"Marja," I repeated, desperately. "*Where. Is. She.*"

Marja pointed silently. The look on her face told me things I did not want to hear.

I ran for the treatment room she pointed out.

There was a sheet over Piia. It was pulled up over her face.

I went to her side and lifted the sheet, pulled it back. Her face was pale. Bloodless. She was... cold to the touch.

I threw back my head and howled my grief until my lungs were empty. Then I half-collapsed over her, sobbing. I put my arm under her shoulders, and I half lifted her, and held her to me. She was utterly limp. The tears poured from me. She couldn't be dead. Not *now*. Not Piia. It wasn't fair. We'd *WON*. It wouldn't have happened without her. She *couldn't* be dead.

I heard hesitant footsteps behind me. A hand upon my shoulder.

"I am *so sorry*, Alrekr," Kata said, brokenly. "She lost too much blood. We could not save her. She was losing blood faster than we could replace it. She bled out and died, before we could stop the bleeding and close her wounds."

I held Piia, and I wept my heart out. But... something was nagging at me.

She was... dead. Intellectually, I knew that, no matter how much I did not want to accept it. So why could I *still feel her presence*? Was it just wishful thinking?

I raised my head. I looked around the room, my vision blurred by tears. Her clothes, rent asunder and soaked with blood, were piled on a side table. Next to them lay Tuuli.

I laid her gently down, and kissed her cold lips.

"I *love you*, Piia," I told her through my tears, even though I knew she could not hear me.

I forced myself to straighten up, and turned to Kata. She put her arms around me just as Liisa came into the room, red-eyed. Liisa came straight to me, and the three of us held each other, sharing our mutual loss. None of us had words. In the doorway to the room, I dimly saw Ari, and Ragne, and I wasn't sure who else. Ari was holding the others back.

"It is his turn to grieve, now," I distantly heard Ari say. "Give him a little time."

But... something *nagged* still at my attention. Something that *insisted upon* being heard.

After a few more minutes, I let go for a moment, and I stepped over to the side table, following the... *something*. Whatever presence I was sensing. I didn't want to look at the ghastly rents in her jack.

Could it be Tuuli I was feeling?

I picked up Tuuli.

I froze. **How**...?

"Kata," I said, slowly. "How close did you come to healing her wounds?"

Kata's mouth opened, but no words came out. She just slowly shook her head, her eyes haunted.

"Not close *enough*, Alrekr," Liisa told me. "It was a *terrible* wound. She is—was—all torn apart inside." She was crying, too. "We ran out of time."

"Can you close them the rest of the way?" I asked. "Even now?"

Liisa looked at me, confusion and grief mingling on her face.

"We... *could*, Alrekr, but it is too late," she replied.

"I *know* you can replace lost blood," I told her. "You did it for Ragne. I *know* you can mend her body. Can you do it when she— she —"

I couldn't bring myself to say the word.

"*Alrekr*," Kata broke in. "*Listen to me*. Yes. We could. It would be *hard*, it would take a full six, but we could do it. But it would do no good." Tears were streaming down her cheeks. "It is *too late*, Alrekr. I am *so sorry*. She is dead. You must accept that."

"No, Kata," I protested. "She—"

"*Yes*, Alrekr," she repeated. "I *know* you love her. We *all* love her. I wish with all my heart it were otherwise. But *she is dead*."

I know Kata thought I was in denial. I desperately hoped I wasn't.

I took two steps back toward her, grabbed her hand, and put it on Tuuli's hilt, and *held* it there.

"*NO*, Kata," I told her. "She *ISN'T*."

Kata opened her mouth to speak, but then she stopped. Her eyes opened wide. She stared down at the sword for a long moment.

"*How—?*"

She looked back up at me. I saw hope kindle in her eyes. Then she whirled toward the entryway.

"*RAIMO! VALLAÏNEN! MARJA! ESKO!*" she shouted. "*I NEED YOU, NOW!*"

She spun back, looked at me, her eyes bright with new hope. Then as running feet sounded in the hallway, she stepped back to the table, drew the sheet down, and put one hand at Piia's shoulder, the other at her hip. There was still a hideous gash in Piia's side. I could see torn internal organs through it. Liisa blinked at me, unsure what was happening, then hurried unquestioningly to take her place opposite Kata.

I saw Ari clear the way into the room. Raimo was the first one in. He stopped, looking a question at Kata as Vallaïnen came in a second or two behind him.

"We must finish mending her body," Kata told him. "*Quickly.*"

"But she—" Raimo began.

"*She's in the sword,*" Kata said. "I don't begin to understand *how,* but she's in the sword. I didn't believe it at first, either. But Alrekr is right, it's *her.* I... *know* the feel of her soul."

Raimo looked at me. My throat was too tight to speak through, but I nodded, hard, and my expression must have told him all he needed to know. He and Vallaïnen took their places as Marja came in, followed by Esko.

Marja looked at Piia. Looked at Vallaïnen. He just nodded to her, once. Marja and Esko took their places, Kata chanted one quick lead measure, and then they all began to sing.

I slipped Tuuli into my belt, right next to Sekai, then stepped next to the head of the bed. I gently touched Piia's cheeks. She felt so cold. I spread my hands across her upper chest, my thumbs on her collarbones, my fingertips next to her heart.

"Tell me as soon as she is whole," I said. Then I reached for the fire, drew ever so lightly on it, and began, with ex*quisite* care, to whisper warmth back into her.

Over the next three, perhaps four hours, I watched as Piia's flesh knit together, saw the terrible wound in her side close, saw some semblance of color return to her skin as they sang new blood back into her body. But she lay there still and unmoving.

Finally Kata paused for a moment.

"She is as whole as we can make her, Alrekr. But I do not know how you think you will do this. We can hold her body from any... deterioration... for a little while. But whatever you intend to do, do it *quickly.*"

I nodded. I had inched Piia's body degree by tiny degree back up to normal body temperature. Now... we had to somehow get her back.

I took Tuuli from my belt and laid her upon Piia's chest. I folded her hands over the hilt. Then I focused my attention upon both her and Tuuli. I thought through the chants and songs I used for binding, the threads of the binding that held Piia and Tuuli together as one, and started a chant that I felt *SHOULD* be the right thing to call her back. I could *see her* there within the sword, the colors of her soul filling Tuuli.

I know you're in there, Piia, I thought. Sang. Both. *Come back to us,* I begged her. *Please. Tuuli, it is time to put her back. Her body is whole once more.* But nothing happened. I kept trying, kept singing.

Now, please, Tuuli.

Something was... blocking. Tuuli was not ready to let her go, yet. Something more had to happen.

Her heart, I realized. Her heart was not beating.

I paused my song for a moment.

"Liisa," I said, "change places with me, please. I need that space. I need to stand where you are."

Liisa stepped back and switched places with me, as I stepped around to Piia's side. I moved Tuuli down as far as I could, re-positioned Piia's hands upon the hilt.

"Someone hold her hands there, on the hilt, please." Marja put out a steadying hand.

I put my hands flat on Piia's chest, between her breasts, over her heart. I knew how to do this. Just compressions. Oxygenation would take care of itself as the compressions moved her chest. I started my chant again, and PUSH on the beat and PUSH and PUSH and PUSH and PUSH and PUSH, and I just kept it up, singing to her, singing to Tuuli, singing her back home, please, oh *please*, PUSH and PUSH and PUSH and PUSH, *please work*, and PUSH and PUSH and...

There was a tiny exhalation.

PUSH and PUSH and PUSH and PUSH and PUSH and— A faint cough.

I summoned all the energy I could spare, and with the next PUSH, I poured it into her, into her soul, *urged* her back.

Then all of a sudden I felt her soul slide from Tuuli back into her body.

Piia's eyes flew open wide. Her body arched, spasmed, dropped flat. There was a moment of terrifying silence, then she drew in a deep, shuddering breath. She let it out with a sound that was equal parts gasp and scream. But it was *her*. She was back.

Her eyes closed, flickered, then after a heart-stoppingly long moment, opened again. With my hands still on her chest, I could feel her heart beating, weakly at first and then more strongly, more steadily, on its own. She looked up and found me, and a faint smile crossed her face. Then it grew. Her eyes focused more, and she looked around her, just her eyes moving, then back to me.

"Hello, beloved," she said softly. They were the sweetest words I had ever heard. Her gaze shifted to Liisa, and her smile grew, and then to Kata, and it grew still more. I wrapped my arms around her, half-lifted her, pulled her to me, and held her close. She reached a hand out, clutched at Kata. Then the three of us were huddled together around her, Kata, Liisa and myself, and there were tears of relief and joy, and hugs and *cheering* from the other Healers, and we were kissing each other, all four of us, and we didn't care who saw.

After a little, we drew back to catch our breath. I reached for the sheet and pulled it up, and Piia wrapped it loosely around herself.

"What happened?" she asked. Her voice was a little weak, a little shaky, but I was more glad than I could express to be hearing it. "Did you close the Gate?"

"I did," I confirmed. "We won. Thanks to you. And the dragons are cleaning up all that remains, with great... fervor and ferocity. But you... you bled out before your wound could be healed. But Tuuli held onto you and *would not let you go.*"

Piia looked down at Tuuli, changed her grip, pulled the sword back onto herself.

"Thank you, Tuuli," she said fervently.

Kata, her cheeks still wet, looked at me, at Liisa—then straight at Piia. I think she knew she didn't need to ask out loud for our assent. It was a foregone conclusion at this point.

"Piia," she said, her voice unsteady. "Marry us?"

"Yes," said Piia, still weakly, but with a radiant smile. "Of *course* I will."

And that was it. That *was* the talk. It was all the talk any of us needed at this point. Nothing else seemed important. All the lesser details, we could work out later. And then there was a lot more kissing.

"Does she need any further healing?" I asked. "Anything at all?"

"Only rest," Raimo assured me. "Rest and recuperation. She will be fine, Alrekr. *Now.* Thanks to you and Tuuli. I foresee no complications." It was his seer voice. I found I was immensely glad to hear it.

"*Thank you*, Raimo," I replied, from the heart. Raimo smiled broadly.

"I will have a recovery room readied," Marja said.

"No," I declared firmly. I wrapped the sheet a little better around Piia, and then I picked her up in my arms, Tuuli held tightly in her hand. "She can recuperate with us. She will have care and attention—and our love—day and night."

Piia put her other arm around my neck, pulled my head down, and kissed me. Then I carried her through the hallways all the way to our tower, and set her down on the couch in front of the fire, our favorite place to sit. We all sat around her and held her tightly.

"I need to go take the riding straps off Moonshadow," I said after a while, "and tell him you're alright. He was worried about you. Almost the first thing he said after he landed was to ask where you were, when he looked around and did not see you." Piia smiled and nodded.

"Be sure to thank him from me for bringing you home," she told me. I nodded and got up, and Kata immediately slipped closer, into the spot where I'd been, and cuddled up tightly to Piia.

I went upstairs, outside, and started up the tower stairs.

Wait.

I came here with *one* dragon. Now there were *six*. One on the roof of the keep itself, and four more atop towers, besides Moonshadow. Guards on the walls, people in the bailey, all were pointing and gazing in amazement at the dragons. I was glad to see that everyone seemed to be past alarm at their presence.

I recognized First Sunlight. The other four were new to me.

I continued up to the roof.

«HOW IS YOUR PIIA-MATE, GATE-CLOSER?» Moonshadow asked as soon as I appeared at the top of the stair. «DOES SHE LIVE?»

«She lives, Moonshadow,» I confirmed. «It was a terribly close thing, but she lives.»

Moonshadow raised his head and let out a great roar of exultation.

469

«THE GATE-CLOSER'S MATE LIVES!»

The roar was echoed seconds later by the other five dragons. It might have been the loudest sound I had ever heard, except perhaps for the implosion of the Great Gate.

«We were worried,» Moonshadow said to me. He pointed with his head towards a large dragon the color of oiled bronze on the top of the next tower. «We have talked since you departed. The Sound Of Wind Blowing Across The Northern Ice—she is one of my mates— saw you both fighting, saw her struck down, saw her kill the stalker that struck her down, saw you open a Gate for her and send her through it. So as soon as all was scoured in the Great Bowl, she and these others followed us here. We have been waiting for word, and hoping.»

My throat felt tight.

«She *died*, Moonshadow,» I said, my voice cracking. «Her wound was so terrible that she bled out before the healers could stop the bleeding and close it. But Tuuli, the sword I made for her and bound to her, caught her soul and held onto it, *would not let* her slip away, until we could make her body whole again. And then, somehow, we managed to put her back.»

Moonshadow nodded solemnly.

«That is a mighty working indeed, then,» he replied, clearly impressed. «Truly worthy of the dragon you are within. Did you *know* that your binding would do that?»

«No,» I said. «But I cannot express how glad I am that it did. Neither in... quick tongue nor in dragon tongue.»

«You should go back to her now, friend Alrekr, Closer of Gates,» he said. «Your place now, as you surely well know, is at her side. But when there is time, I will come and fetch you both, and take you to my nest, where you can properly meet my mates and my young. All dragons will honor your name and hers after this day.»

«I should take those straps off you,» I said. «Let me do that a moment.» I started climbing up. «Do you know what the key was, to unlocking channelling my fire through Sekai?»

«No, but I will after you tell me,» Moonshadow rumbled.

I laughed, grateful for the levity.

«There were three key parts, really,» I began, as I unthreaded the straps. «Realizing all of the meanings packed within the words Closer

470

of Gates in dragontongue.   The name of my sword—Cutter of Worlds. And one precious thing that you said to me. 'The hilt of the sword and the hand are as one.'

«Had you not told me that, I would not have reached that moment of understanding, and I would have failed.»

«Hmph,» Moonshadow said. «I prefer to believe that you would have come to your insight anyway. The world knows who you are. It chose one who would accomplish that which needed to be done. And you still have not told me the actual insight.»

«Hah. You're right,» I chuckled, as I detached the last strap.

«The... title you call me by. And the name of my sword. One and the same meaning. 'I sever the place where two worlds meet.'»

«Aaaaaaaaaaahhhhh. Yes. I see. You are learning to think as the dragon you are, Gate-Closer. Very good.»

I climbed back down.

«Thank you for everything, Moonshadow. *Everything.*»

«You have done a greater service than I, friend Alrekr. Give my regards to your mates. All of them. We will meet again. Soon. And we will continue with your education. Do not lose those straps.»

He launched himself into the air, and the other dragons followed. They circled several times, climbing and calling back and forth, then streamed away to the northwest.

I went back downstairs, to all of my loves.

"Moonshadow sends his regards, beloved," I said, leaning over the back of the couch to kiss Piia. "And five other dragons came to sit vigil as well, First Sunlight and four more, until they knew how you fared."

Piia smiled beatifically.

"I feel that must be a rare honor," she said.

"I am half-starved," I declared. "Is anyone else ready to eat?"

As I expected, the idea met with no opposition. I opened the door and rang for a page. The echoes of the bell had not even faded before Senja came running around the corner from the stairs nearby. I laughed happily aloud.

"Admit it," I said, smiling, "you were waiting for the bell."

"I *gladly* admit it," she agreed. "I *hoped* one of you would call. Is it true?"

"Is what true?" I asked. "A lot has happened this day."

"Well, everyone knows that you flew off on a dragon with Ranger Piia early this morning," she began. "And then... we heard that... she *died.* But now people are whispering that you *brought her back* from the dead?"

"Piia?" I called. "Are you up for a visitor?" Piia looked over, smiled, and nodded.

"Come on in, Senja," I told her. I took her by the hand and led her in and over toward the fireplace and the couch.

"To our great joy, Piia is indeed, as you can see, alive and well. 'She was only *mostly* dead,'" I quoted, "''and *mostly* dead is a *little bit* alive.'"

"Tuuli saved me," Piia declared. "And Alrekr, and Kata, and Liisa, and I love them all."

Senja looked back and forth between the four of us, at the way Kata and Liisa and Piia were all cuddled so tightly together, Kata's head resting on Piia's shoulder, and her eyes grew wide. I saw the huge smile begin. Kata and Liisa and I exchanged glances and grins, remembering a very similar day.

"*Yes*, Senja," I confirmed.

Senja whooped and leapt in the air. Then she did a somersault. Then a back-flip. I almost thought I felt the air in the room moving with her. She came up with her face flushed and her eyes shining, bouncing on her toes with excitement. Then she leapt at me and hugged me. Then she leaned over the couch to hug Liisa, and Kata, and then, gently and very carefully, Piia.

She took a couple of deep breaths, her face slightly flushed.

"Forgive me, Honoreds. What did you need done?"

"We would like some food sent, please," I requested. "Supper for four. Something gentle on the stomach. Make certain it includes honeywine and kuurii juice, for recuperation. And please find every other member of Piia's Ranger team that you can, and Commander Jaako, and tell them that she is alive. Oh! And please ask... Ragne, probably, if she could bring some of Piia's clothes here. The gear she was wearing... will need major repairs, if it's savable at all. We left... uh, what remained... in the infirmary."

"At once," Senja declared, bowing to each of us. "Honored Healers. Ranger Piia. Fireborn Alrekr."

Then she was off.

I closed the door and came and sat back down in the open spot, slipping my arm around Kata's waist and kissing her pretty neck. Finally we could all relax. We knew what I had been brought here for, and it was *DONE*... and we had all, somehow, survived it, by the skin of our teeth. I found myself shaking with the reaction.

"We have a small crisis," I announced after a while. "I just realized I no longer have enough arms." My—*all three* of my loves laughed at that. I wasn't going to even try to understand *how* this had happened. It was a thing to just be gratefully accepted. I was going to have to work even harder not to let them down.

"We will surmount this crisis, one way or another," Liisa replied, her eyes twinkling. "We always do."

"I guess we do, don't we?" I agreed. That helped. I chuckled a bit.

"Truth is, after the gate imploded, I didn't think I was getting out of there. I *wouldn't* have, were it not for the dragons."

"The dragons are wonders," Piia declared. And then we just relaxed and basked in the presence of each other.

A while later there came a knock at the door. Probably our supper. I got up again, and went to answer the door.

Jaako was there. And Ari, and Paavo, and Ragne, and behind them Eino and Simo and Karel. The entire team was here. And Sage Nyysönen, and Master Timo and Mistress Jaana, and Vallaïnen, and Raimo. They were all carrying food, except for Ragne, who—as requested—had an armful of clothes for Piia. Senja was there grinning happily in the back.

"We have guests," I announced. "*Many* guests. And they brought food." I turned back to the door.

"You had better all come in. You know where the table is."

They all filed in one after another. Senja waved, and turned to go.

"No, come on, Senja," I told her, "you should come in as well. You're practically part of the family." She smiled happily, hugged me,

473

and came in.

There was a joyful reunion going on over by the couch, and a considerable amount of food was being set out on the table. Piia excused herself for a minute and disappeared upstairs with the clothes Ragne had brought her, wrapped in her sheet, then reappeared a few minutes later clad in a shirt and Ranger breeches. We all gathered around the table and set to on the food. Piia, I noticed, didn't take very much.

I stepped up next to her and slipped an arm around her.

"Not much appetite?" I asked. "Not that it isn't completely understandable under the circumstances."

She nodded and snuggled into me.

"I'm very glad to be in one piece," she told me, "but I feel as thin as parchment. I'm sure I will feel better in a few days." She turned her head toward me, and we kissed. We kissed several times, actually.

We had to bring down the chairs from the morning room to have enough, but we got everyone sorted out. My loves were clustered around me... or actually, it is truer to say that we were all clustered around Piia. Our triad was a tetrad, now.

"So," Jaako said, after giving everyone a while to eat uninterrupted. "This has been a day book-ended by bellowing dragons, morning and evening. Would the two of you, in your own time, please bring us up to date on at least the high points of what happened since Highwatch's abrupt and *loud* awakening this morning?"

"All right," I said. "I will begin. This is... my and Piia's report.

"Today was *supposed* to be another day of tutoring, building on yesterday. But we were awakened by Moonshadow's arrival, calling for me with great urgency. I suspected it meant that we had run out of time. I went to the tower top, where Moonshadow told me that the dragons believed something was imminently about to come through the gate, that they feared they might not be able to defeat."

"That is where and when I found him," Piia added, "fitting the riding straps. We mounted up, and Moonshadow took us back to the gate. He took us as close as he dared, other dragons clearing our landing area of enemies as we came in."

"We killed another stalker—that is what the dragons call the thing we killed up in the crags, near the pass—right after we landed," I continued, "right after Moonshadow incinerated the column of... beasts it was... controlling? Reinforcing? Leading? Great shaggy bear-like things, eight or nine feet tall, with three eyes and foot-long claws."

"We worked our way closer to the—Gate," Piia said, "finding it to be guarded by three more stalkers circling it." I saw Ragne flinch.

"*Three?*" Ari interjected grimly. "*One* was bad enough."

I nodded agreement. I reached out and took Piia's hand.

"Piia saw a spot from which we could ambush one of them on its own," I said, "out of sight of the other two. And we did that, and we killed it. But the other two were on us almost immediately, *and* they called reinforcements."

"They were working together, intelligently," Piia said. "They coordinated their attacks and evasion to keep us from effectively attacking either one. They sought to either kill us one at a time, or delay us until their reinforcements arrived and then overwhelm us."

"And both were focusing on Piia first," I added. "Which is why she distracted the one nearer to me with an all-out attack, *knowing* she was leaving her back exposed to the other. I was able to use that distraction to kill the second—uh, *third*, all told—but as I did so, the last impaled her." I'm not sure which of our hands clenched tighter. "Then as the... thing was lifting her to its jaws, she *wrenched herself around* on its claw and beheaded it."

"Which left Alrekr temporarily unopposed, and clear to destroy the Gate," Piia declared.

"It also left you *dying*, beloved," I said to her, before turning back to our audience. "I'd already learned how to open a gate to Highwatch infirmary, so I did it a second time."

"Ten feet in front of me," Kata confirmed quietly.

"I had time only to drop Piia through that gate," I went on. "I knew she was in the best hands possible. Then I needed to deal with the gate. Sekai's time alteration bought me the time I needed to devise a plan to attack the gate, by opening a gate of my own into... not the Gate itself, but the space in which it *existed*, right next to the Gate. I... I think I may have been actually standing upon *the world itself*. I don't know for sure.

"Once I was in there, nothing outside could touch me, and I had a breathing space in which to figure out how to destroy it. Its remnants spat me out as it collapsed, and threw me to the ground a hundred yards from what remained of the gate, with seemingly every enemy left alive in there heading for my vicinity. Fortunately, that was far enough not to be drawn back into it as it collapsed.

"I fully expected to die then. But moments after the remains of the gate imploded, as soon as the sky was clear enough, the dragons came in, and they saved me. Today I learned in earnest why ground troops love close air support.

"Moonshadow flew me back to Highwatch sprawled on his back, passed out from exhaustion most of the way, while the rest—there were more than thirty of them there that I saw—scoured that bowl of every living thing. Särkkä Valley has been well and truly avenged."

"Piia... bled out before we could close her wounds," Liisa choked out.

"We know," Ragne said gently. "And we *know* that you and the other Healers did all you could. You saved me, you saved Karel. But you cannot save everyone." Her voice cracked for a moment. "And yet — yet *somehow*— you *did*, after all...?"

"When Alrekr arrived back," Kata explained, "he realized that her soul was *still there*, held safe within her sword." That was a stunning revelation to nearly everyone in the room. The Sage actually dropped his spoon.

"So *that* is how you worked this miracle!" Ari exclaimed.

"And *that*," I declared, "is when half the healers in Highwatch came at a run to finish putting her body back together and refill her with blood, while I *very carefully* warmed her back to a living temperature.

"And then... somehow... we got her soul back into her body from Tuuli."

"Alrekr got her heart beating again," Kata commented. "A purely physical method I have never seen before."

"And here we all are," I finished.

"Except for one more wonderful thing," Liisa added, eyes still damp, but smiling again now.

"And what is that?" Master Timo asked. But his eyes were twinkling. I suspect he already knew.

"Piia agreed to marry us," I said, unable to keep the joy from my face.

There was a moment of silence as the world seemed to hold its breath.

"Come *on*, Ranger Járnhandr," Jaako laughed, grinning broadly, "leave *one or two* for the rest of us."

The room exploded into happy laughter. Then it was hugs all around, and more kisses, and congratulations, and more hugs. Ari just about squashed me flat.

"If I might beg a little clarification," Sage Nyysönen asked a while later, amid the hubbub of discussion after the celebration and congratulations had died down a little. "This—Great Gate—is closed now. For now, or for all time?"

"For all time," I confirmed, certain of it now. "I severed it from this world. It is *gone*. It can never be re-opened again between that world and this one."

"Can I ask how you *know* that?"

"You can most certainly *ask*," I replied, "but I don't know how well I can answer. When I stood... within the place where the Gate existed —call it Gate-space... I could see it as a great tunnel stretching off into a vast distance. A once-tiny thread, blown up and stretched to... a huge size. I saw other threads, *so many* of them, places where a Gate between worlds *could* be. Threads tying this world to others, where Gates could be opened, and closed, and opened again. But all of the gates between that world and this share that single thread. Separate strands of the one thread.

"I don't know how to explain to you *how* I know this. But somehow, I know—*now*—that only one thread, however many strands lie within it, joins any two worlds... and once completely severed, that thread can *never* be mended or re-attached. From that end, or this. And whatever was on the way is gone into the void, forever, and utterly destroyed. Unmade."

"And the small gate, in the crags?" Paavo asked.

"That... was forked off the larger gate, I now understand," I explained. "It too is gone forever. And the gate near Särkkä as well. *All* of the small gates that depended from that great gate are gone and cannot be re-opened, ever, now that it is severed."

"Could a new gate be opened in a different spot?" Ari asked.

"No. Not from that world. That other world, wherever it is, no longer connects to this one at all. Possibly they might travel to another world again, and from there, here... but I think that we need not worry about that bridge until we come to it. There are countless worlds out there, and the chances of them finding another path leading here is, I believe, one in... a million? A billion? More?

"And if they should, *now*, we can sever that thread as easily as any other."

"How *did* you sever it?" Jaako asked me.

"The short answer to that," I replied, choosing my words carefully, "is that I channeled my own inner fire through Sekai against it. I tried first simply cutting it with Sekai... but that was not working. It was healing itself faster than I cut it. I had to cut it all in a single stroke."

"It was that inner fire that you spent the previous day learning, was it not?" Nyysönen asked.

"It was," I confirmed.

"But you had more yet to learn?"

"Yes," I replied. "And I did not actually learn the last vital insight until I was within the gate space."

I saw Nyysönen begin to frame the question.

"Yes, I will tell you the insight," I said, with a smile. "I am getting there."

He chuckled sheepishly.

"It took repeating a few things to myself in dragon tongue, with its vast depth of secondary meanings, and thinking about and *understanding* those meanings, in the context of a Japanese saying and of something Moonshadow told me, and the name—*Sekai no Kattā*, Cutter of Worlds—that my sword told me when I first bound it to myself.

"I'm not going to try to teach you enough dragontongue—*here and now*—to understand those parts. Later, gladly. But I realized that when viewed in the right context, Closer of Gates and Cutter of Worlds... *overlap* in meaning. Both, with the right perspective, can be restated in a third way: 'I sever the place where two worlds meet.'

"Moonshadow told me, several times, 'The hilt of the sword and the hand are as one.' I didn't understand, when he said it, what he meant by that. But I realized that it is complementary to a... a saying in Japanese sword arts, 'There is no swordsman, only the sword.'

"I didn't realize until this day that when I named Sekai, she was not just telling me her name. She was... *recognizing* me by mine."

I could see the expressions on Nyysönen's face changing as he put the pieces together and figured it out.

"Are you saying," he ventured cautiously, "that... you and your sword are one and the same?"

I grinned and nodded. It was so much more fun—for both of us—to give him the pieces and let him work out the answer himself, than to just flat-out tell him.

"In a certain context, yes. I *can* wield Sekai simply as a sword. But I learned today I can also use her as a focus, a conduit, to wield *myself*, my soul-core. Because without knowing it, I made her into a part of me. In that certain context, I am the sword, and the sword is me."

"So you wielded your own soul-core, *through* your sword, that is part of you, as a weapon to sever the gate?" He had it.

"Yes," I confirmed. "And it is that same relationship between soul-bound sword and bearer that enabled us to save Piia. Her sword is *part* of her, as mine is part of me. Her soul *never left her*. It just... had to temporarily move into a *different part of her* while we repaired her body and got her heart beating again."

"*Amazing* and fascinating," he declared. "We *must* delve into this further."

I nodded.

"A *lot* of things had to come together for us all to be here together on this day," I said, "with the threat banished. And I am immensely thankful for every last one of them."

There were other discussions, other conversations, but eventually we chased all of our guests out and asked Senja, who had been listening attentively to every word, to arrange cleanup.

"You know," I told Kata, as I watched Senja organize three other pages to clear everything, "I think she will go far once she finds her calling."

Kata smiled back at me.

"I am sure she will," she agreed. "She has not manifested a Talent yet... but... I think she will. And it will probably be soon. Did you feel the *voima* circling her today?"

"I... did not notice," I confessed. "Though I would swear I felt the air moving with her." Kata looked thoughtful at that.

As soon as everything was cleared, we all went upstairs and to bed, the other three of us cuddled around Piia as much as we could.

"Piia?" I asked, as we lay there all in each other's arms, one big happy tangle. "Please promise me one thing."

"What is that, Alrekr?"

"Please, don't ever, *ever*, EVER do that again. That was *far* too close to losing you."

"I promise to *try*, Alrekr," she said, smiling softly. And that was good enough.

Unlike my memorable *first* wedding night in the Sunlit Land, this one was very low-key. Just lots of gentle, loving cuddling, as the other three of us were determined to be gentle and careful with our recuperating newest partner. I had one arm wrapped tightly around Piia, Kata was lying between us half atop Piia with her head nestled between Piia's breasts, my other arm across her back and my fingers resting on her hip, and Liisa had her arms around Piia and Kata from Piia's other side. Piia fell asleep after a while, her head against my cheek. I could feel her heart beating steadily, until I fell asleep as well.

All was right with the world, at least for now. The crisis was over, and all of the people who I loved the most were alive at the end of it, though it had been a *terrifyingly* close thing—and somehow, *all four* of us were now together. I was where I belonged, and finally I *knew* it. So much had been in the wind for so long—so many doubts, so many fears; but at last, I was starting to feel confident that this was all going to work out.

27: The Fire Still Burns

When I woke up the next morning, Piia had rolled over and had her arms around Liisa. Kata had snuggled up next to me. Liisa still had an arm over Piia (or again), her fingers resting on Piia's hip, so I twined mine with them and very gently nuzzled the back of Piia's neck. Eventually Liisa started to stir.

"Good morning, love," she murmured. "How's Piia?"

"Sleeping peacefully," I replied quietly. "I'm not going to disturb her until she wakes on her own. She had a rough day to end all rough days."

"Good idea," she agreed. So we touched and stroked each other for a while, across Piia, and waited for Kata and Piia to wake up. Liisa lightly checked Piia just to be certain, but when neither stirred after a while, we quietly got up, and I went to call a page to have breakfast for four sent.

When breakfast arrived, we set it out in the morning room, then we checked on our other two partners again. Piia had rolled onto her back, so I leaned over her and started gently kissing her here and there until she woke up. After a minute, she started to smile, her eyes still closed.

"Mmmmmm," she murmured happily. "Keep doing that." Then she opened her eyes and looked at me.

"Good morning, beloved," I said. "How are you feeling?"

She thought about that for a moment, as Kata yawned sleepily and stretched.

"Wrung out," she replied. "Tired. Aching. But alive. Alive is very good."

"It is," I agreed fervently. "Ready for breakfast?"

"Breakfast sounds good," Kata said sleepily, next to us, still yawning. I kissed her good-morning too, and then we all got up and had a leisurely breakfast.

"I know Raimo assured us there would be no complications," Kata told Piia after breakfast, "but I'm going to check you over anyway, just to be sure. I don't want to take any chances, after yesterday."

So Kata gave Piia a quick examination, and so did I. I wanted to be sure the soul restoration had fully taken. (Not that I was sure what I would do about it if it seemed it hadn't. I was *absolutely* figuring this out as I went along.) As far as I could see, it *had*, and everything looked stable as far as I could tell.

Her core looked a little wan, though, so I sat for a while with my arms around her and chanted energy from my core into hers. I knew I could spare it; I had a much better feel for how much energy I actually *had* now—and it was enough *more* that even I could feel the increase—and I couldn't think of a better cause. When I was done, her core looked brighter, and so did her eyes and her smile.

We all four took that first day as a day of rest, and spent a fair bit of it in the sauna and the baths. We all took luncheon at the Rangerhall, which gave all of the other Rangers a chance to catch up and see that Piia was well and recovering from her close brush with death. There were many, many congratulations to all four of us on Piia joining our marriage, and of course *EVERYONE* had to hear every detail of the fight to reach the gate. It was a bit tough to re-tell, but at the same time, it was a bonding experience for all of us—even if it was one I never wanted to repeat. A good half of the Rangers present asked to inspect Tuuli and Sekai, and by mass demand, I was persuaded into a demonstration of my dragon-fire, blowing a practice pell into flaming pieces from forty yards away.

I soul-boosted Piia twice more during the day, each time she started looking a little weary. I wanted to be absolutely certain she would be alright. She let me do it without objection, once I assured her that I could spare the energy without difficulty.

The last two things that we did that day were to arrange to temper Paavo's sword the next day, and to send word to the Sage so that he could observe, as I was certain he would want to. Then we all returned to our tower.

We had supper sent to our rooms again, just the four of us this time. And then that evening, that night, we slowly, carefully, patiently, gently, figured out how to make lovemaking work with four people, without leaving anyone out.

Of course, once we managed to get into that we/us state, we had a big advantage—it's much easier to know what feels good for everyone, when each person can feel what every other person is feeling. With *three* of us, it had been transcendent. With **four**... there were no adequate words. There was just one big 'us', until we all drifted off to sleep, all sprawled together. It didn't seem to make any difference that Piia had not discovered a Talent yet.

The next day, we had a leisurely breakfast again, then Kata and Liisa went off to the infirmary, while Piia and I went to meet Paavo and Sage Nyysönen at the forge. Paavo had not arrived yet when Piia and I got there, so we sat and chatted with Matti while I brought the forge to a nice even heat. I hardly had to focus now to do something that simple. I was able to carry on a conversation at the same time.

Matti didn't miss that, even though I didn't really notice at first.

"Járnhandr," he said, "are you doing that *without* singing to it, now?"

I paused, while I thought carefully about what I was doing.

"Not exactly," I replied, after a few moments. "It's... for something this simple, just balancing the forge, I... apparently don't need to sing aloud any more. Just having the song in my head seems to be enough. But as soon as we bring the blade to the heat, then I will need to sing to it."

Matti nodded.

"Your abilities are still growing, aren't they?"

"I don't know whether it's that," I hedged after another moment's thought, "or whether I'm just still learning what they are. And improving with practice."

"I imagine this will interest the Sage," Piia observed.

"Doubtless. And here he comes now," said Matti. I turned around, and sure enough, Sage Nyysönen was just approaching the forge. I waved a greeting, and he returned it.

"How are you, young lady?" he asked Piia, as soon as he entered the forge. "Are you recovering well?"

"Very well, thank you," Piia replied. "I have the very *best* caregivers in the world." Even the stoic Sage had to smile at that.

"Good, good," he agreed. "And Fireborn Járnhandr? All is well with you?"

"Now that I'm certain Piia is alright, yes," I told him. "So are you ready to see how a sword is bound today?"

"I look forward to it," he declared. "When will you begin

preparing?"

Aha, I thought to myself.

"I already have," I answered, with a slight smile. And I waited. I saw him begin to frame the question, and then I saw him stop. He looked intently around the forge, and specifically at the forge itself. He watched it for a minute or more, then looked at me, then back at the forge, with a growing smile.

"All right," he said after several minutes of close scrutiny, "I give up. I can see that you *are* maintaining the forge at an even heat. But how are you doing it?"

Matti chuckled.

"I wondered how long it would take you to catch on," I replied with a grin. "Not very long at all, just as I expected. I discovered only a few minutes before you arrived that for a simple task like leveling the heat in the forge, I no longer need to sing aloud, it is sufficient—*now*—to maintain the song in my head."

"Interesting," he mused, with a smile. "As you gain practice, do you think? Or as your abilities grow as your dragon nature awakens, and the task becomes easier for you?"

Piia, Matti and I all laughed.

"That is *exactly* the question we were pondering right before you arrived," Matti declared, grinning. Then Nyssönen laughed as well.

"Anyway, we're just waiting on Paavo now," I said. "I don't imagine he'll be long."

Indeed, Paavo showed up a few minutes later, and a few minutes after that, we got started. Matti already had the blade coated with clay and the clay partly dried. We arranged people where everyone could see and Paavo was within my reach, then I chanted the forge heat up. Matti laid the blade into the forge, and I began to sing the heat into it. This was the fourth time I had done this, and by this time I no longer needed to see the blade at all to know when the heat was correct.

When the heat was right, I masked my core as Moonshadow had taught me, reached out to Paavo, and began to sing a binding between the sword and his core. Singing him and the sword together, as I *now* understood that I was doing. So many of the things that the bound swords could do made obvious sense, once I understood that, though I still did not even *begin* to understand where the time-tampering ability of Sekai and Tuuli came from.

I realized after a time that my binding was done. It had been the quickest and easiest yet. I nodded to Matti, and he nodded in return, but kept singing to the steel for a little longer before he, too, was done. Again I maintained the heat until he was ready, and then we quenched the sword.

Once again, it came out of the quench bath intact. Matti knocked off the clay, sighted along it, and pronounced it true.

"We've yet to have a failure," I remarked. "I admit I'm curious. I don't know what the failure rate was, historically, but I do know it was not at all unknown for blades to shatter in the quench. Have we just been lucky so far? Is it that you are starting out with far superior steels? Is it that we have two Adepts singing *voima* into the sword as it is forged? Is it the soul-binding? Or a combination of all of these?"

Matti just shrugged.

"I do not know," he replied. "But I sing as much strength as I can into every blade I forge, simply as a matter of course."

"I would lean towards the 'All of these reasons' answer," Sage Nyysönen stated. It was no different from my own thoughts, and I nodded agreement.

"So that's it for today, is that right?" Paavo asked.

"Yes," Matti confirmed. "Now is the time to finish up the fittings, to do the grinding, the final sharpening, and polishing. I made your, ah, *tsuba* already. Here."

He picked up a *tsuba* from his bench and handed it to Paavo. Paavo looked at it, and his eyes widened.

"*Leviataan*," he breathed. "But—how did you know what they look like?"

"I cheated, lad," Matti replied, grinning. "I borrowed a book." That brought a round of general laughter. Paavo handed the *tsuba* back.

"Has anyone told you, Smith Matti," he said, "that you are an artist?"

Matti grinned again, and looked at Piia and at me.

"Perhaps," he chuckled. "Someone might have mentioned it. Anyway, a week to ten days and all will be finished."

Paavo nodded. Then he looked at Piia.

"Will it, uh..." He trailed off.

"Preserve your soul?" I finished for him. He nodded.

"In truth, I don't know," I replied. "I have a far tighter bond to Piia than I do to you. But the strength of the sword's bond to you... perhaps no less. I... still find it *terrifying* that we had to find out." Beside me, Piia took my hand and squeezed.

"If you ask me for a call? I would say, do not plan to rely on it. And I can't guarantee to be able to bring you back. Possibly, only Piia I am close enough to. And Kata and Liisa of course. And I do not *know* for certain that I could bring Piia back a second time."

I became aware that I was squeezing Piia's hand almost painfully tight, and loosened my grip a little.

"But in the worst of all cases... well, if all else is lost, the chance exists that it *might* work. And of course, we would *try*."

"Fair enough," Paavo nodded. "It is an amazing thing just to know that the chance is there."

"What of those who come to Highwatch from elsewhere for swords?" Matti asked.

"I... think that we should not speak of this ability outside of Highwatch," I concluded, after some thought. "So far as we know, only I can do this, and by the time I could travel anywhere it would surely be too late. Better not to raise false hopes."

Nyssönen nodded gravely.

"A wise decision, I think," he agreed. "And doubtless true. Experiments have been performed. The body breaks down after death. By a few days after death, it will no longer hold *voima* of any kind, at all. No matter how fast you pour it in, it pours straight back out."

"And if someone hears the story, and asks?" Piia pointed out.

"Then we tell them what we know to be true," I said, reluctantly. "That it has only been known to work once, for someone who was already in the hands of the Healers when her body failed, who was revived within only a few hours, and to whose soul I have a tighter, stronger bond than to any but my own. I do not want an idea to spread that we are selling a way to cheat death. That can probably end no way but badly."

Matti and the Sage both nodded agreement.

"Wise," Nyssönen declared again. "But eventually the word will spread. I doubt you can prevent that. And the Collegium should know."

I sighed, agreeing. It's always the ramifications that get you.

"I hope this doesn't end up causing a problem," I said. "There used to be a saying from my previous life that the road to—uh, *helvetti* is paved with good intentions." It didn't even hurt any more to say it, I realized.

Nyssönen nodded, pondering that.

"A good caution against acting unthinkingly," he agreed. "But I do not think that you can fairly apply it in this case. The future can, and must, be dealt with only as it comes. *All* actions have consequences, and we can never fully choose them because we cannot know the future. The best that we can do is choose as wisely as we can based upon what we are aware of, upon what seems evident, avoiding obvious harms that we can foresee. This principle has guided us for more than a thousand years.

"I cannot find any fault with your action in this. Any small difficulty growing out of this revelation about your soul-binding pales to insignificance, next to the consequences had something come through that gate that not even the dragons could stand against."

I considered his words. Indeed, perspective was everything.

"Let me ask you something, Fireborn," he continued. "Would you have decided differently in this, had you foreseen the complications that trouble you now?"

"No," I said instantly. I didn't even have to think about it. I stepped closer to Piia, put my arm around her, and pulled her tightly to me. "I would have given almost anything to have Piia back. Anything that did not require trading someone else." I could not keep a catch out of my voice. Piia hugged me back.

"You are right," I told the Sage, nodding. "The important thing, now, is that Piia is here. We will address the future as it comes." I took a deep breath and let it out. Piia leaned in and kissed my cheek, and then I turned my head so that we could kiss properly. She smiled serenely at me.

"Anyway," I said, "be that as it may. Were you able to see

anything of the binding?"

"Part of it," Nyysönen replied. "Not all. I should like to observe a few more times, if I may."

"Of course," I replied. "You are more than welcome. But for now, I imagine we should leave Matti to his work."

Paavo headed off back to the Hall. Piia looked at me.

"I have some gear to replace," she told me. "And I suppose I should be collecting my other things from my room in the Hall. There aren't many. Will you come with me?"

"Of course," I said at once. "Did you need to ask?"

"Not really," she replied, smiling. "But I like to hear you say yes."

I laughed, and followed her.

Indeed, Piia didn't have a great deal to be moved. Her room was small, with just a bed and a little space to store her clothes and her weapons.

"You recall the day when you were recharging yourself at the fire, Alrekr?" she asked me. "And I mentioned I had other ideas in mind for you?"

"I remember, yes," I agreed.

"That day, I really wanted to bring you here to my room, and share my bed with you. But I was unsure whether I should... and you needed to recover. And I think it has all worked out better in the end, anyway."

I nodded, understanding.

"You know," I mused, "this is probably our last chance to try out this bed together."

She smiled happily.

"I like the way you think," she said, and reached for me.

It turned out there was actually a little more to move than the two of us could carry in one trip. But that was alright, because it also turned out that Kirsi passed by as we were gathering Piia's things, and offered a hand. So we got it all in one trip after all.

"Ranger Járnhandr..." Kirsi began as we crossed the bailey.

"Alrekr," I corrected her. "To any Ranger of Highwatch, just Alrekr. You are my brothers and sisters."

Kirsi smiled.

"Alrekr, then," she said, "I have decided I am going to order a sword from Matti. Would you... be willing... to soulbind it for me? I know that you told us all that it demands a lot from you."

"Kirsi," I replied, "I would be glad to. With some instruction and guidance from Moonshadow, I have learned how to greatly ease what it needs from me. We tempered and bound Paavo's this morning and proved that it works. Of *course* I will bind yours for you."

Kirsi smiled at that, and so did Piia.

"Thank you, Alrekr," Kirsi said. "I will give him my order tomorrow."

The next day, we resumed the sword class. I could not help noticing that while we were still using *kata* as a way of teaching forms for properly using the new swords, what we were teaching was drifting further and further away from *kenjutsu*, as we combined it with the existing Ranger training techniques and what Piia and I had learned from fighting stalkers. It had begun as *kenjutsu* practice to develop form, yes. But it was clearly becoming something both more, and different.

We all talked about it over supper, as we sat in the main dinner hall that evening—the four of us, all of the rest of Piia's team, and Jaako, Kirsi and Matti, all thirteen of us at a long table together.

"If I might ask a question," Jaako ventured after a little. "You do not wish to continue calling it by the name of the art from your previous life, because you have added to what you remember of it and extended it beyond what it was? Combined what both of you know?"

"A good summary," I agreed, nodding. "And why make many people learn words of another language that they will use for no other purpose?"

"And you doubtless plan to continue incorporating all else that you learn from others here?" Jaako continued. I agreed again.

"Indeed," I said, "we are all learning. There is always more to learn."

"Is there some reason, then," he asked, "not to simply call it the Highwatch school of the sword?"

I looked at Piia. She flashed a smile. I glanced around the table.

"I see no reason under these suns," I declared. "And I can't think of a better name. Better to call a thing what it has become, than what it started out being. It avoids confusion."

And so that's what we did.

Late afternoon the next day, after Piia and I got back from teaching sword school, the four of us were sitting together in our favorite spot, the couch in front of the fireplace. I had just finished pushing another soul-boost into Piia, and still had my arms around her in my lap. Kata sat against me on our left, Piia's legs across her lap, studying a book she was resting atop Piia's knees. On my right, Liisa was snuggled up against me, her head on my shoulder, an arm around Piia's waist.

"How are you feeling, love?" I asked Piia. She stretched like a cat.

"Mmmmmm," she murmured. "I feel really good. I feel... whole again. *Better* than whole." She draped her left arm around my neck.

"Let me take a quick look at you," Liisa said. She put her free hand on Piia's shoulder as well. I could feel her focus.

"Huh," she mused slowly, after a few seconds. Then she paused, and focused again.

"Alrekr?" she asked.

"Is something wrong?"

"No. I'm sure not. But... how many *times* have you soul-boosted Piia since she came home with us?"

"Uh," I mumbled. "Um... I wasn't really counting. A dozen? Fourteen? Fifteen? I've been boosting her whenever she looked tired. I wanted to be as certain as possible that she recovered fully. What is it?"

Liisa didn't answer me right away.

"Kata?" she asked. "Check me, please. Both against when we first brought Piia home after healing her, and against the reading in the forest."

Kata shot Liisa a curious glance, then set her book down and reached for Piia's hand. Piia looked as puzzled as I was. I felt Kata focus on Piia, and... well, I already had my arms around her. I looked at her too. 'Against the reading in the forest,' Liisa had said. I cast my memory back to that day, when I had first seen the beauty of Piia's core, and I compared carefully to now.

490

I saw it at once.

I came out, and I looked at Kata. She nodded. And so did Liisa.

"I love you all very, very much," Piia said earnestly, "but would someone please tell me what is going on?"

"Your soul is stronger than it was," Kata told her.

"Your core is brighter," I agreed. "And I think it has grown larger as well."

"I wasn't certain whether I was imagining that," Liisa said, nodding agreement in turn.

I let go Piia's hand and took Kata's instead. The memory of that vision of Kata's core was burned into my memory as well, alongside the image of coming to with her in my arms. I compared carefully. It was unmistakable, now.

"So is yours, Kata," I said. And then I looked at Liisa's, as well.

"Yours too," I confirmed. "I *thought*... after we returned from the small gate in the crags, your two souls seemed a little brighter. But I wasn't sure I wasn't imagining it. That I wasn't just seeing it more clearly. *Now*... seeing Piia as well... now, I'm certain."

"What does it mean?" Piia asked.

"When Alrekr soul-boosts one of us?" Kata speculated. "I... I suspect a small part of it—is *permanent*."

"And I've done it for you fourteen or fifteen times in four days," I pointed out. "On top of when I helped your soul from Tuuli back into you. I gave you *every last drop I could spare* right then."

"You do not have a Talent, do you?" Kata asked Piia. Piia shook her head.

"Not that I have ever discovered," she confirmed.

"But if I look at your soul now," Kata continued, "if I pretend I knew nothing about you... I would guess you an Adept."

We were all silent for a minute or so.

"Should we ask the Sage about this?" Liisa asked.

"I think we should *tell* the Sage," I countered. "I think we need to *ask* Moonshadow."

Kata thought about that.

"Do you have any way to call to him?" Piia asked.

"Not that I know of," I said, shaking my head. "We'll just have to wait."

We told Sage Nyssönen what we had discovered the next day. But it ended up being four more days after that before Moonshadow next returned, by which time Kata and Jaako had agreed that Piia was fully fit for duty again. I kept soul-boosting Piia anyway, for the moment, but just once or twice a day now.

By coincidence, Moonshadow landed atop the tower just as Paavo was taking delivery of his new sword. Piia and I were there to see it, of course. He had elected a plain, utilitarian *saya*, but that had not stopped Tauno from tinting the lacquer a deep ocean blue. The *gunome* looked like breaking waves.

"Is there anything more—wait," Paavo said, answering his own question. "I need to give it its name now, don't I?"

"That wasn't really a question, was it?" I replied, smiling.

Paavo smiled back.

"I *know* its—*his*—name," he declared. He tucked the *saya* through his belt, took three steps back, and drew to full extension, then held it.

"*Nousuvesi*," he announced. High Water. The pulse of power that raced up the blade and swept out across the bailey was the blue of the ocean on a sunny day.

"Whose is next?" I asked Matti, as Paavo settled up payment with him and Tauno. "Ari's?"

"Yes," Matti agreed. "And then Jaako's, and then Kirsi's."

I nodded.

"Well, if you'll excuse me," I said, "we need to go talk to a dragon."

"Would it be an imposition if I were to come along?" Matti asked. "I would like to meet your dragon."

"He isn't my dragon," I corrected. "Nor any but his own. And his mates'. But I'm sure he would not mind. He has already complimented your forging skill."

So Piia and I took Matti to meet Moonshadow. I waylaid a page—Irja, if I was remembering her name correctly—on the way to send word to Kata and Liisa.

«ALREKR, GATE-CLOSER,» Moonshadow rumbled as soon as we reached the top of the tower. «AND PIIA, OF THE UNQUENCHABLE SPIRIT, MATE OF ALREKR. ARE YOU WELL, MATE PIIA?»

«She is fully recovered,» I told him. «And actually, we had a question about that.

«First, though, please let me confirm: All remaining danger from the Great Gate is gone and past, is that correct?»

«IT IS, GATE-CLOSER,» Moonshadow verified. «WE HUNTED DOWN AND DESTROYED A NUMBER OF STRAGGLERS OVER THE COURSE OF THE PAST TEN DAYS OR SO. ONE OR TWO MAY STILL ELUDE US, SOMEWHERE. BUT THE DANGER HAS PASSED, YES. THERE IS NO FURTHER THREAT.»

«That is the best news I have had since the day of the battle,» I declared.

I relayed the news and Moonshadow's good wishes. Then I introduced Matti.

«This is Master Smith Matti, whose hand forged Sekai, and Tuuli, and High Water, the sword of my sword-brother Ranger, Paavo.»

Moonshadow inspected Matti and nodded his head.

«I SEE YOUR STRENGTH WITHIN YOU,» he declared. «I GREET YOU, HMMM... YES, MATTI, WHOSE VOICE KNOWS THE SONGS OF ALL METALS, WORLDSBANE-FORGER. WELCOME.» He dipped his head again.

"Moonshadow greets you, Matti," I said. "He names you Matti Whose Voice Knows The Songs of All Metals, and titles you Worldsbane-Forger. I think he likes you."

"I'm not sure I entirely like the sound of world's bane," Matti said doubtfully.

"Don't worry about that," I reassured him. "Dragontongue is incredibly rich in subtle meaning. Worldsbane is still another alternate... *rendering* of Sekai's name, Cutter of Worlds. He is honoring you as the smith who forged the weapon that closed the Great Gate."

"Well," Matti replied, looking pleased. He bowed to Moonshadow. "I suppose that's a different thing, then."

About this time we heard familiar footsteps on the stairs. As I thought, it turned out to be Kata and Liisa. Moonshadow greeted them as well, and I relayed the greetings.

«YOU SAID THAT YOU HAD A QUESTION,» he reminded me.

«Yes,» I agreed. «We... no, let me start further back. Some weeks ago, there was an accident. Two people at one time were very severely

493

injured, and my mates Kata and Liisa—and all of the other available healers—were exhausted, with more yet to do to save them. I discovered that night that while I cannot myself help with the healing, I could give of my energy to them, push it into their souls, and enable them to continue.»

«Hmmmmm,» Moonshadow mused. «I BELIEVE I SENSE IN GENERAL WHERE YOUR QUESTION LEADS. CONTINUE.»

«After Piia was so terribly wounded, even after we healed her body and restored her to it, her soul looked... dim, wan. And so I gave her as much soul-energy as I could spare, three or four times a day at first, to help her recover.»

Moonshadow nodded his head.

«Some days ago we discovered that *all* of my mates' soul-cores—but *especially* Piia's—have become... brighter, stronger. Seemingly permanently.»

Moonshadow nodded again.

«GOOD,» he declared. «IT IS AS I THOUGHT. THIS IS A THING THAT I HAD BEEN GOING TO TEACH YOU ANYWAY, BUT YOU HAVE DISCOVERED IT YOURSELF. VERY GOOD. WE CALL IT THE BREATH OF THE SPIRIT. WE USE IT WHEN RAISING OUR YOUNG.

«YES, YOU ARE CORRECT, IT PERMANENTLY STRENGTHENS THE SPIRIT—IF THE SPIRIT HAS ROOM TO GROW. AND DRAGON SPIRITS HAVE A GREAT DEAL OF ROOM TO GROW, AS WE GROW TO MATURITY.» He chuckled. «HOWEVER, I DOUBT YOU CAN USE IT IN THE MANNER WE DO. SHOW ME HOW YOU DO IT, AND THEN I WILL SHOW YOU OUR WAY.»

I nodded, and brought my loves up to date.

"Moonshadow informs me that what I have been doing sounds like something that he calls spirit breath," I said. "He was already planning to teach it to me, but is pleased that I discovered it for myself. We are about to perform an exchange of demonstrations of our techniques." There were nods of acknowledgment all round. "I presume you have no objection, Piia...?"

"Of course not," she replied. "And I am starting to recognize your name, and mine, when he speaks them."

"That is good," I said, with a grin. So I took her hands, and for a few minutes, I chanted energy from myself into her soul. Moonshadow observed, and nodded his head.

«I SEE,» he pronounced. «YES, YOU HAVE INDEED DISCOVERED THE BREATH OF THE SPIRIT, THOUGH YOUR MEANS IS INEFFICIENT, PROBABLY BECAUSE YOU DID NOT FULLY UNDERSTAND WHAT YOU WERE DOING.»

«Indeed,» I replied, «I would have to agree I did not, or the question would likely not have arisen.»

«INDEED,» Moonshadow agreed. «OF COURSE, YOU CANNOT USE IT EXACTLY IN THE MANNER THAT A DRAGON IN PHYSICAL FORM DOES. BUT ATTEND CLOSELY NOW, AND SEE WHAT I DO WITHIN.»

Moonshadow inhaled slightly, then moved his head closer to me—and Piia, who was still standing right beside me. I focused my sight on Moonshadow, watching what he did, and I saw how he drew off a wisp, like a breath, of his soul-core. And then he exhaled over both of us. The blast was hot, but not burning hot, and to my vision it glowed slightly, like a luminous mist. But it *felt* incredible. Piia's hand found mine and clenched. I heard her draw a shuddering breath, and I am sure mine matched.

"That was..." she began after a moment, but then trailed off. I could only nod.

«YOU SAW?» Moonshadow asked.

«Yes, I believe I did,» I answered, after I caught my breath. «Thank you. I will see if I can use this to... refine my technique.»

«I WILL CAUTION YOU, ALREKR GATE-CLOSER,» Moonshadow told me. «USE IT CAREFULLY AND SPARINGLY. THOUGH YOU HAVE IN PART THE SOUL-CORE OF A DRAGON—AND THOUGH I SEE THAT YOUR STRENGTH, AND YOUR SPIRIT, CONTINUE TO GROW—YOU DO NOT HAVE THE DEPTH OF A DRAGON'S CORE. YOU COULD INJURE YOURSELF IF YOU USE THE BREATH OF THE SPIRIT TO EXCESS.»

«Thank you for the warning, Moonshadow,» I replied. «I will be careful.»

«DOES THIS RESOLVE YOUR QUESTION?»

«Yes, thank you,» I replied. «It does.»

«GOOD. ON, THEN, TO THE ACTUAL PURPOSE OF MY VISIT HERE TODAY. NOW THAT YOUR MATE PIIA IS FULLY RECOVERED, I WISH TO INVITE YOU AND ALL OF YOUR MATES TO VISIT MY NEST, TO MEET MINE. THERE IS AN OBLIGATION OF HOSPITALITY, BUT EVEN WERE THERE NOT, I WOULD EXTEND THE INVITATION ANYWAY FOR THE SAKE OF SIMPLE FRIENDSHIP.

«CAN YOU COME? IT WILL OF COURSE REQUIRE FLIGHT. OUR NESTS ARE INTENTIONALLY INACCESSIBLE FROM THE GROUND.»

«Let me ask,» I said. «Piia, I'm sure, will accept as eagerly as I, but I must ask Healer Kata and Healer Liisa.»

Moonshadow nodded, and I turned to my lovely ladies.

"So," I relayed, "Moonshadow came here today to invite us all to visit his nest and meet his family." I looked at Piia. "You, I'm sure, will not hesitate." She grinned eagerly. I turned back to Kata and Liisa.

"But how do the two of you feel about flying dragonback?"

At first, they both simply looked stunned. But then a smile began to spread across Liisa's face.

"To fly with a dragon," she breathed. Her excitement was obvious, and infectious. Kata started to smile as well, then made a half-bow to Moonshadow.

"Tell him that I would be deeply honored," she said.

So we made arrangements, and on the morning of the second day after, Moonshadow returned, with his mate Northern Wind—or, in full, The Sound Of Wind Blowing Across The Northern Ice. I made proper introductions all around, then we fitted riding straps—of which we had of course procured a second set, in the meantime. We had come up with one or two small improvements, as well. It was a little more difficult to attach the straps on Northern Wind, as her back-plates were not quite as deeply filigreed as Moonshadow's, but we managed. Moonshadow explained that Northern Wind was some centuries younger than he, and that as a dragon aged, the scales both darkened and grew more filigreed.

Then we mounted up. I took Liisa with me on Moonshadow, seating her in front of me where I could keep my arms around her for extra stability for her first flight, while Kata rode in front of Piia on Northern Wind's back. Liisa gasped at the take-off, and I could feel she was tense at first, but she soon settled down to enjoy the flight as Moonshadow and Northern Wind beat their way steadily into the jagged, snow-covered peaks of the Spine. After a while, she relaxed enough to twist around and kiss me, her eyes dancing with excitement.

"This view... it's *beautiful!*" she declared. I just nodded emphatically.

We landed after about two hours of flight at Moonshadow's nest, a great cavern high in the side of a mountain. Outside, the wind was biting, but within the cavern it was almost swelteringly warm. After we dismounted, Moonshadow introduced us to his other four mates, and to the two young of his family who still lived within the nest—The Light That Shimmers In The Northern Skies, a youth of a hundred years or so, brilliant as burnished brass, and a playful golden-scaled youngster only about eighteen feet long, whom Northern Wind proudly informed us had hatched only twelve years previously and had not yet chosen a name. Moonshadow explained to me how dragons drew the world's molten inner heat up from within to heat their nests, and showed me how it was done, though we both agreed that I lacked the strength to do it in such quantity and should not try. There were limits to a human body, and I needed to stay within them. Still, he was impressed at how far down into the roots of the world I could extend my sight; and I understood how it was done, having previously studied Tumarïnen's technique in some depth... so to speak.

We spent most of the day there, occasionally being introduced to other dragons who stopped by in response to Moonshadow's invitation to meet us. Shortly before the suns set, we mounted up again, and Moonshadow and Northern Wind took us home. Northern Light flew along with us on the return trip. We switched around this time, Kata riding with me on Moonshadow's back, and Liisa with Piia on Northern Wind. We got to see the suns set behind the Spine, from the air. It's difficult to hug a dragon larger than a house, but Kata settled for spreading her arms out along Moonshadow's side and resting her cheek for a moment against his scales as she dismounted.

"Thank you, Moonshadow," she said fervently.

«WE SHALL VISIT AGAIN SOON,» Moonshadow told me, as we unthreaded the straps. «IT IS TIME, I THINK, THAT DRAGONS AND QUICK FOLK SPOKE MORE OFTEN. WE SEE IN YOU HOW YOUR PEOPLE HAVE GROWN WISER. PERHAPS WE CAN BOTH LEARN FROM EACH OTHER, NOW.»

«That would be wonderful,» I replied. «We will look forward to it.»

Then Moonshadow, and Northern Wind, and Northern Light left, and the four of us went to get some supper and talk about our day.

Jaako sent Piia's team—*our* team—out on a patrol sweep the next day. We went southwest until we hit the lower edge of the crags, then worked our way up north through the forests toward the passes. The forest was no longer deathly still. It was still quiet, but life was returning. The birds were back, and we saw deer, and foxes, and *tanna*, a rotund and chattersome rodent the size of a large dog. We checked the ravine where we had tracked the first gate to, to within sight of the remains of the stalker, but could bring ourselves to approach no closer than a hundred and fifty yards or so. We could see from there that the flesh was rotting out of the carapace in black semi-liquid runnels. The *stench* was indescribable, stomach-turning even at that distance. We could scarcely leave the ravine soon enough.

We continued from there across the feet of both passes, and on through the forests eastward another half-day's travel toward Särkkä, before we turned and headed back toward Highwatch. We saw nothing amiss. Things were returning to normal, and we so reported when we returned. The people who had evacuated from the high farms and border villages would be able to return to their homes. Jaako sent out the word, to great relief and celebration.

28: Epilogue

Over the coming weeks, we made Ari's sword, and Jaako's *tachi*, and then a sword for Kirsi. Jaako went to older, half-forgotten Norse root-words to name his sword, declaring it *Fjandrhamár*—Foe-hammer. He began attending the sword school, and we began to adapt our teaching again as we learned together how to best fit our techniques to Jaako and *Fjandrhamár*. And that was just the beginning.

As the word spread, the demand for Highwatch swords spread with it, as Matti had predicted. Matti had to take on an apprentice to handle all of the routine forge tasks like horseshoes, hinges, ploughshares and nails, while he spent almost all of his time forging swords and their fittings. Almost everyone who came to Highwatch to buy a sword went through the sword school to learn how to use it properly. After a while, even some who did not buy Highwatch swords came to Highwatch just to attend the school.

Senja found her calling... literally. It turned out she was a storm-caller—a storm mage. It was a wonder to watch her dance along the edge of the wall or across a rooftop, as her winds gusted around her and carried her beautiful, clear voice, the rain not touching her unless she chose it. Her winds would not let her fall.

Piia, too, broke through one day. It came as no surprise that her Talent related to the forests she so loved. We discovered while idly playing in the forest one day that she could slip into the shadow of a tree, and emerge from another a moment later, hundreds of yards away.

I realized something, after a while.

"*Tuuli metsässä*," I said, thoughtfully. Wind in the Forest. Piia looked at me curiously. Then I repeated it, in dragon tongue. And then I chose a slightly different weighting of the many shades of meaning, and translated that back into Saamen.

"I move through the forest like wind."

Understanding dawned on her face.

"Like you and Sekai," she said, wonderingly.

"Yes," I agreed. "Like me and Sekai."

"*Nousuvesi*," she mused. "What do you suppose that Paavo might

499

discover in himself?"

"I don't know," I replied after a moment. "But it's an interesting question, isn't it?"

Later we learned that with the right song, she could travel leagues through the forest in just a few minutes, and even take a few others— the entire team, as she grew more comfortable with it—with her. Sage Nyssönen stated that he knew of no such Talent, and declared it another new discovery. No-one was sure what to call it, so I suggested Forestwalk; and that is what we settled on.

Mill-Master Kustaa's first press was not a success, but it showed him where he had made mistakes or omissions in his design, and he and Smith Matti were able to correct them in the second one—which worked well. Of course, Kustaa immediately set about designing a third model to correct the imperfections he saw in the second.

I ended up not writing my planned book on soulbinding. Instead, as it turned out, I worked with Sage Nyysönen, and we wrote together what ended up being a four-volume set on the nature of being Fireborn, soulbinding, and enough of the dragon tongue to properly understand all of the rest of it.

At the insistence of my loves, I also agreed to write *The Way of Járnhandr*—on the condition that Kata write her book on treating head injuries. It was not until the other Healers began reading and discussing her drafts, that she finally understood how much nuance and subtlety there was in what she did that was *not* common knowledge to all Healers.

But I refused to write *The Way of Járnhandr* alone. Piia and I wrote it together, and Liisa helped as well. It was not *my* work. It was *ours*. And that was how it *should* be. *Always*.

POST-IT NOTES

Where is the Sunlit Land?

I can't tell you. It's not really a meaningful question, and I don't know the answer anyway. It is... *somewhere else*. It's not even really a parallel world.

Try this thought experiment. Imagine that you have two yardsticks, and you throw them on the floor so that they land across each other. One is our world. One is the Sunlit Land. They don't necessarily cross at the same point on each—it might be, say, eleven inches on one yardstick and seventeen on the other.

Now imagine that they might cross more than once. And the crossing points might be different distances apart on each yardstick. And you can't *necessarily* travel across any given crossing in both directions.

Are you starting to get the idea?

Auringon Valaista Maata, as the people who live there call it, was originally settled by mostly the people who in our world became Finns, with a small admixture of Karelians and Sami, and a few Varangians—or Norse, the people you probably think of as Vikings. (But that isn't really correct. Viking isn't an ethnicity; it's a vocation, or an occupation. It's something you *do*, not something you *are*. Norse isn't really correct either, but it's closer than Viking. It at least identifies a culture, not an activity.)

They quickly assimilated the Varangians and Karelians into their culture, and incorporated pieces of Norse culture and Norse language into their own, but their language is still very close to Finnish. Their culture... has gone its own separate way, a blend of the three, that then grew in its own direction. The people of the Sunlit Land *are not Finns*; that is important. But they *used to be* the people who would *become* the modern Finns, and the roots of Finnish culture and myth are still the dominant ones in their oral history. They kept the creation myth of Ilmarinen, the smith-god who sang and hammered the sky itself into being, because it matches their experience in the Sunlit Land—because *that is how voima works* in their actual living experience. You sing. So **obviously** the story *must* be at least partly true.

Their cuisine has drifted a lot, not least due to having a different range of ingredients readily available—but despite ingredient substitutions, some Finnish classics such as *lohikeitto, kalakeitto* and *rieska* are still immediately recognizable. (The difference between *kalakeitto* and *lohikeitto* is really only that *lohikeitto* is made *specifically* with salmon, while *kalakeitto* is made with any fish to hand.)

How long have they been there? Also unanswerable. Time there, or time here? It's not so much that time does not flow at the same rate there as it does here, as that it is simply a different place with *different* time. Their recorded history in the Sunlit Land goes back more than a thousand years, but it is unclear how much time before that written history is recorded only in oral tradition—or whether a thousand years ago *there* is the same thousand years *here*.

How did they first get there? Nobody knows. Nobody was in a position to write it down at the time, and what little there was that could be understood of it was lost from their oral traditions by the time they started writing things down again, aside from a few disjointed phrases. Fire and destruction, a tunnel of night. But it scarcely mattered, because by then they had already begun learning new things. So very *many* new things. The first of them called themselves simply *elävät*—the living; those who lived—or *saapuneet*—those who arrived. The people who survived the journey.

The language they speak, Saamen, is a mixture of the languages they started out with, mostly Finnic at its roots but still retaining some Norse words. But it has evolved in interesting directions, because of *voima* and what they call Talent. There are multiple disciplines of Talent, and each has its own dialect of Saamen. Not because of any insularity or desire to keep secrets—far from it; the people of the Sunlit Land are by-and-large open-minded, open-hearted, and generous, and there is a common shared belief that all knowledge should be freely shared, because they realized early on that *everyone ends up better off* that way. Rather, it is a consequence of how *voima* and language work.

Voima has many aspects, and each major discipline uses and manipulates its own aspects of *voima*. *Nobody* understands *all* of the multiple aspects of *voima* (though some of the sages can at least glimpse many). Many people cannot sense or manipulate it at all, or only dimly, in small ways. For instance, almost anyone with any

Talent sensitivity at all can learn to cast a simple light. But the way most Talents use and manipulate *voima* is through song. Song puts the mind into the right framework to safely use *voima*, and helps to ensure that it is used in a controlled way. To sing a working into reality, or to write down what you did, you need to be able to describe the aspects of *voima* that you are using, and what you are doing with them. And that means that the language you use to talk about them has to be capable of describing them, expressing them.

But if you cannot sense or use that aspect, you cannot understand the words. It doesn't matter how much you study a passage written in the language of a different discipline—fire, or metalworking, or healing, or woodworking, or husbandry. If you cannot sense *that* aspect of *voima*, you cannot grasp the words. You will never understand them. You *cannot* understand them. Your mind cannot grasp the meaning of either the words, or the symbols, because that aspect of *voima* is forever beyond you.

More Books From Sean Fenian

The Stardock Trilogy

Humanity is not alone in the universe. We are far from even the only intelligent species in our *galaxy*. It was foolish, arrogant, and naïve of us to think we were.

The Chrrt'ktk't are one such intelligent species. But Sean Fenian's best-selling *Stardock Trilogy* is not about the Chrrt'ktk't. It's not even about humanity and the Chrrt'ktk't. It is about what happens to humanity, and how the future of humanity is changed, when the Chrrt'ktk't abandon a mobile shipyard with a burned-out hyperdrive core in the Solar System as a decoy to distract pursuit—and how it changes the life of a retired engineer who finds himself chosen, more or less by chance, as custodian of the Chrrt'ktk't shipyard, and all of the lives he changes in turn.

Praise for *The Stardock Trilogy*:

"These three books were a delightful, well written tale of a hopeful future, populated with a cast of characters that were easy to root for and interesting alien species."

"An excellent read and finally a well thought out plan forward that does not include a forever war!"

"This has been a wonderful trilogy to enjoy. Great character development and storyline."

"Happy because it is well written with solid scientific underpinnings and because it shows a side of humanity that I wish we would all strive for."

Agency (with Robert Auerbach)

Ciáran mac Cool is a *de-facto* operative for... he's not sure. He doesn't know where his orders come from, and he's in too deep to back out—even though at least one assignment almost got him killed. And yet, his assignments always seem to do some *good* in the world.

Then one day the Box tells him to reach a specific location, with no further explanation, giving him barely enough advance warning to get there.. Soon he will find himself working alongside a young law associate to unearth revelations that will shake the course of events in ways he never imagined.

BECOMING REAL

Michael Hagerty—*GhostRayder*, to his fans—reviewed video games and made game videos for a living. He was intimately familiar with virtual worlds. They were his everyday bread and butter. He was quite certain he understood very clearly the lines of demarcation between game and reality, between what was physical, and what was virtual. What was real, and what was not.

Then one day, not long after he reviewed a newly released VR open-world adventure game, a mystery source sent him a modified version of the game, and asked him to go back in and try it again.

Michael would soon find out, amid a high-stakes game of hide-and-seek with shady multinational corporations and shadowy government agencies, that the question of real or virtual, human or not, was far more nuanced and less clear-cut than he had ever believed possible.

Sean Fenian's Becoming Real is an exploration of the natures of humanity and reality.

Or perhaps it's a commentary on some of the blind spots of video game design.

Or perhaps it's an SF postmodern love story with a twist.

Or perhaps, it's all of these things... and more.

PRAISE FOR *BECOMING REAL*:

"This edges out [Frank] Herbert's Dragon in the Sea as the best sci fi book I ever read. [...] You really must read this."

"It makes you think about some big social issues that are quickly becoming more relevant and may turn vital much sooner than you'd expect."

"Without question some of the best books I have read in years. I compare them to books by David Weber, John Ringo, and Nathan Lowell."

GODTHIEF

The Prophecy of Tendarrion—or at least, one likely reading thereof—said that the time was coming for the goddess Jirilis to die.

Jirilis, understandably, was rather unhappy about this. Her plans for the future did not involve dying yet. But, a prophecy is a prophecy.

Prophecies, however, are notoriously fickle about exactly what precise interpretation of them turns out in the end to be correct. The possibly existed of finding an exploitable loophole. But Jirilis could not exploit it *herself*. That was, to greatly oversimplify the explanation, 'against the rules.' Prophecy and the powers of gods didn't work that way.

Jirilis needed a champion. Not one who could win battles for her, not one who could slay mighty enemies for her, not one who would spread her word or perform heroic deeds in her name.

No, Jirilis needed a champion who could *subvert a prophecy*. And she had an idea that she knew just who that might be. She had had her eye on him for some time, in fact.

Fortunately, he was already coming to *her*. Though he might need a little help.

That was alright. Jirilis had one of the most powerful incentives to help him that there could possibly be.

Sean Fenian's *Godthief* is a standalone fantasy novel set in an alternate world that might or might not be 'real'. It delves into the natures of gods and the mechanisms of prophecy, and what we really mean when we say the word 'Paladin', all against a background of the aftermath of a thousand-years-past, almost-world-shattering demon war.

PRAISE FOR *GODTHIEF*:

"Excellent and consistent world building. If you enjoy fantasy without the swords and magical combat, this is for you."

"Well paced, imaginative, exciting tale. Sean Fenian is a skilled world builder. I look forward to reading more adventures set here."

About Sean Fenian

Sean Fenian is a generalist and open-source evangelist, recently retired from several decades of working in the information technology sector. He is broadly knowledgeable in many subjects, with a long-standing informed layman's interest in physics and related science in particular. He has been an avid reader of SF and fantasy since his teens, and first became aware of, and began campaigning on, environmental issues in the late 1970s. He is proficient with weapons both ancient and modern, has trained in four different martial arts, and believes that understanding basic firearms safety is like knowing basic first aid, CPR, or how to use a fire extinguisher. He believes that it is a basic human duty and responsibility to treat all beings fairly and decently, and that the true measure of a person is how you treat others.

His past volunteer activities include educational historical re-enactment, marine mammal rescue, and handicapped riding therapy. He has been formally diagnosed on the autistic spectrum, but stubbornly persists in trying to understand people anyway.

He dreams many things. Occasionally, some of them become reality. But only occasionally.

Sean's books are read in fourteen countries, at last count, and his bestselling *Stardock Trilogy* is also available as audiobooks on the Audible platform, published by Podium Entertainment.

www.ingramcontent.com/pod-product-compliance
Lightning Source LLC
Chambersburg PA
CBHW072010020726
47501CB00006B/1756